Stranger in a Strange Land

Also by

ROBERT A. HEINLEIN

ROBERT A. HEINLEIN

Assignment in Eternity
The Best of Robert Heinlein
Between Planets
The Cat Who Walks Through Walls
Citizen of the Galaxy
Destination Moon
The Door into Summer
Double Star
Expanded Universe: More Worlds of
Robert A. Heinlein
Farmer in the Sky
Methuselah's Children
Friday
Glory Road
The Green Hills of Earth
Grumbles from the Grave
Have Space Suit—Will Travel
I Will Fear No Evil
Job: A Comedy of Justice
The Man Who Sold the Moon
The Menace From Earth
Methuselah's Children
The Moon Is a Harsh Mistress
The Notebooks of Lazarus Long
The Number of the Beast

Orphans of the Sky
The Past Through Tomorrow:
Future History Stories
Podkayne of Mars
The Puppet Masters
Red Planet
Revolt in 2100
Rocket Ship Galileo
The Rolling Stones
Sixth Column
Space Cadet
The Star Beast
Starman Jones
Starship Troopers
Three by Heinlein
Time Enough for Love
Time for the Stars
To Sail Beyond the Sunset
Tomorrow, the Stars (Ed.)
Tunnel in the Sky
The Unpleasant Profession of
Jonathan Hoag
Waldo & Magic, Inc.
The Worlds of Robert A. Heinlein

STRANGER IN A STRANGE LAND

Robert A. Heinlein

AN ACE/PUTNAM BOOK
Published by G. P. Putnam's Sons
New York

An Ace/Putnam Book
Published by G. P. Putnam's Sons
Publishers Since 1838
200 Madison Avenue
New York, New York 10016

ISBN 0-399-13586-3

Printed in the United States of America

FOR
ROBERT CORNOG
FREDRIC BROWN
PHILLIP JOSÉ FARMER

contents

preface

IF YOU THINK that this book appears to be thicker and contain more words than you found in the first published edition of *Stranger in a Strange Land,* your observation is correct. This edition is the original one—the way Robert Heinlein first conceived it, and put it down on paper.

The earlier edition contained a few words over 160,000, while this one runs around 220,000 words. Robert's manuscript copy usually contained about 250 to 300 words per page, depending on the amount of dialogue on the pages. So, taking an average of about 275 words, with the manuscript running 800 pages, we get a total of 220,000 words, perhaps a bit more.

This book was so different from what was being sold to the general public, or to the science fiction reading public in 1961 when it was published, that the editors required some cutting and removal of a few scenes that might then have been offensive to public taste.

The November 1948 issue of *Astounding Science Fiction* contained a letter to the editor suggesting titles for the issue of a year hence. Among the titles was to be a story by Robert A. Heinlein—"Gulf."

In a long conversation between that editor, John W. Campbell, Jr., and Robert, it was decided that there would be sufficient lead time to allow all the stories that the fan had titled to be written, and the magazine to come out in time for the November 1949 date. Robert promised to deliver a short story to go with the title. Most of the other authors also went along with the gag. This issue came to be known as the "Time Travel" issue.

Robert's problem, then, was to find a story to fit the title assigned to him.

So we held a "brainstorming" session. Among other unsuitable notions, I suggested a story about a human infant, raised by an alien race. The idea was just too big for a short story, Robert said, but he made a note about it. That night he went into his study, and wrote some lengthy notes, and set them aside.

For the title "Gulf" he wrote quite a different story.

The notes sat in a file for several years, at which time Robert began to write what was to be *Stranger in a Strange Land*. Somehow, the story didn't quite jell, and he set it aside. He returned to the manuscript a few times, but it was not finished until 1960: this was the version you now hold in your hands.

In the context of 1960, *Stranger in a Strange Land* was a book that his publishers feared—it was too far off the beaten path. So, in order to minimize possible losses, Robert was asked to cut the manuscript down to 150,000 words—a loss of about 70,000 words. Other changes were also requested, before the editor was willing to take a chance on publication.

To take out about a quarter of a long, complicated book was close to an impossible task. But, over the course of some months, Robert accomplished it. The final word count came out at 160,087 words. Robert was convinced that it was impossible to cut out any more, and the book was accepted at that length.

For 28 years it remained in print in that form.

In 1976, Congress passed a new Copyright Law, which said, in part, that in the event an author died, and the widow or widower renewed the copyright, all old contracts were cancelled. Robert died in 1988, and the following year the copyright for *Stranger in a Strange Land* came up for renewal.

Unlike many other authors, Robert had kept a copy of the original typescript, as submitted for publication, on file at the library of the University of California at Santa Cruz, his archivists. I asked for a copy of that manuscript, and read that and the published versions side by side. And I came to the conclusion that it had been a mistake to cut the book.

So I sent a copy of the typescript to Eleanor Wood, Robert's agent. Eleanor also read the two versions together, and agreed with my verdict. So, after the notification to the publisher, she presented them with a copy of the new/old version.

No one remembered the fact that such drastic cutting had been done on this book; over the course of years all the editors and senior officers at the publishing house had changed. So this version was a complete surprise to them.

They decided to publish the original version, agreeing that it was better than the cut one.

You now have in your hands the *original* version of *Stranger in a Strange Land,* as written by Robert Anson Heinlein.

The given names of the chief characters have great importance to the plot. They were carefully selected: Jubal means "the father of all," Michael stands for "Who is like God?" I leave it for the reader to find out what the other names mean.

—Virginia Heinlein
Carmel, California

part one

HIS MACULATE ORIGIN

i

ONCE UPON A TIME when the world was young there was a Martian named Smith.

Valentine Michael Smith was as real as taxes but he was a race of one.

The first human expedition from Terra to Mars was selected on the theory that the greatest danger to man in space was man himself. At that time, only eight Terran years after the founding of the first human colony on Luna, any interplanetary trip made by humans necessarily had to be made in weary free-fall orbits, doubly tangent semi-ellipses—from Terra to Mars, two hundred fifty-eight days, the same for the return journey, plus four hundred fifty-five days waiting at Mars while the two planets crawled slowly back into relative positions which would permit shaping the doubly-tangent orbit—a total of almost three Earth years.

Besides its wearing length, the trip was very chancy. Only by refueling at a space station, then tacking back almost into Earth's atmosphere, could this primitive flying coffin, the *Envoy,* make the trip at all. Once at Mars she might be able to return—if she did not crash in landing, if water could be found on Mars to fill her reaction-mass tanks, if some sort of food could be found on Mars, if a thousand other things did not go wrong.

But the physical danger was judged to be less important than the psychological stresses. Eight humans, crowded together like monkeys for almost three Terran years, had better get along much better than humans usually did. An all-male crew had been vetoed as unhealthy and socially unstable from lessons learned earlier. A ship's company of four married couples had been decided on as optimum, if the necessary specialties could be found in such a combination.

The University of Edinburgh, prime contractor, sub-contracted crew selection to the Institute for Social Studies. After discarding the chaff of volunteers useless through age, health, mentality, training, or temperament, the Institute still had over nine thousand candidates to work from, each sound in mind and body and having at least one of the necessary special skills. It was expected that the Institute would report several acceptable four-couple crews.

No such crew was found. The major skills needed were astrogator, medical doctor, cook, machinist, ship's commander, semantician, chemical engineer, electronics engineer, physicist, geologist, biochemist, biologist, atomics engineer, photographer, hydroponicist, rocket engineer. Each crew member would have to possess more than one skill, or be able to acquire extra skills in time. There were hundreds of possible combinations of eight people possessing these skills; there turned up three combinations of four married couples possessing them, plus health and intelligence—but in all three cases the group-dynamicists who evaluated the temperament factors for compatibility threw up their hands in horror.

The prime contractor suggested lowering the compatibility figure-of-merit; the Institute stiffly offered to return its one dollar fee. In the meantime a computer programmer whose name was not recorded had the machines hunt for three-couple rump crews. She found several dozen compatible combinations, each of which defined by its own characteristics the couple needed to complete it. In the meantime the machines continued to review the data changing through deaths, withdrawals, new volunteers, etc.

Captain Michael Brant, M.S., Cmdr. D. F. Reserve, pilot (unlimited license), and veteran at thirty of the Moon run, seems to have had an inside track at the Institute, someone who was willing to look up for him the names of single female volunteers who might (with him) complete a crew, and then pair his name with these to run trial problems through the machines to determine whether or not a possible combination would be acceptable. This would account for his action in jetting to Australia and proposing marriage to Doctor Winifred Coburn, a horse-faced spinster semantician nine years his senior. The Carlsbad Archives pictured her with an expression of quiet good humor but otherwise lacking in attractiveness.

Or Brant may have acted without inside information, solely through that trait of intuitive audacity necessary to command an exploration. In any case lights blinked, punched cards popped out, and a crew for the *Envoy* had been found:

Captain Michael Brant, commanding—pilot, astrogator, relief cook, relief photographer, rocketry engineer;

Dr. Winifred Coburn Brant, forty-one, semantician, practical nurse, stores officer, historian;

Mr. Francis X. Seeney, twenty-eight, executive officer, second pilot, astrogator, astrophysicist, photographer;

Dr. Olga Kovalic Seeney, twenty-nine, cook, biochemist, hydroponicist;

Dr. Ward Smith, forty-five, physician and surgeon, biologist;

Dr. Mary Jane Lyle Smith, twenty-six, atomics engineer, electronics and power technician;

Mr. Sergei Rimsky, thirty-five, electronics engineer, chemical engineer, practical machinist & instrumentation man, cryologist;

Mrs. Eleanora Alvarez Rimsky, thirty-two, geologist and selenologist, hydroponicist.

The crew had a well-rounded group of skills, although in some cases their secondary skills had been acquired by intensive coaching during the last weeks before blast-off. More important, they were mutually compatible in their temperaments.

Too compatible, perhaps.

The *Envoy* departed on schedule with no mishaps. During the early part of the voyage her daily reports were picked up with ease by private listeners. As she drew away and signals became fainter, they were picked up and rebroadcast by Earth's radio satellites. The crew seemed to be both healthy and happy. An epidemic of ringworm was the worst that Dr. Smith had to cope with—the crew adapted to free fall quickly and no anti-nausea drugs were used after the first week. If Captain Brant had any disciplinary problems, he did not choose to report them to Earth.

The *Envoy* achieved a parking orbit just inside the orbit of Phobos and spent two weeks in photographic survey. Then Captain Brant radioed: "We will attempt a landing at 1200 tomorrow GST just south of Lacus Soli." No further message was ever received.

IT WAS A QUARTER of an Earth century before Mars was again visited by humans. Six years after the *Envoy* was silent, the drone probe *Zombie,* sponsored jointly by the Geographic Society and La Société Astronautique Internationale, bridged the void and took up an orbit for the waiting period, then returned. The photographs taken by the robot vehicle showed a land unattractive by human standards; her recording instruments confirmed the thinness and unsuitability of the Area atmosphere to human life.

But the *Zombie*'s pictures showed clearly that the "canals" were engineering works of some sort and there were other details which could only be interpreted as ruins of cities. A manned expedition on a major scale and without delay surely would have been mounted had not World War III intervened.

But the war and the delay resulted eventually in a much stronger, safer expedition than that of the lost *Envoy*. The Federation Ship *Champion,* manned by an all-male crew of eighteen experienced spacemen and carrying more than that number of male pioneers, made the crossing under Lyle Drive in only nineteen days. The *Champion* landed just south of Lacus Soli, as Captain van Tromp intended to search for the *Envoy*. The second expedition reported to Earth by radio daily, but three despatches were of more than scientific interest. The first was:

"Rocket Ship *Envoy* located. No survivors."

The second worldshaker was: "Mars is inhabited."

The third was: "Correction to despatch 23-105: One survivor of *Envoy* located."

iii

CAPTAIN WILLEM VAN TROMP was a man of humanity and good sense. He radioed ahead: "My passenger must not, repeat, must not be subjected to the strain of a public reception. Provide low-gee shuttle, stretcher and ambulance service, and armed guard."

He sent his ship's surgeon Dr. Nelson along to make sure that Valentine Michael Smith was installed in a suite in Bethesda Medical Center, transferred gently into a hydraulic bed, and protected from outside contact by marine guards. Van Tromp himself went to an extraordinary session of the Federation High Council.

At the moment when Valentine Michael Smith was being lifted into bed, the High Minister for Science was saying testily, "Granted, Captain, that your authority as military commander of what was nevertheless primarily a scientific expedition gives you the right to order unusual medical service to protect a person temporarily in your charge, I do not see why you now presume to interfere with the proper functions of my department. Why, Smith is a veritable treasure trove of scientific information!"

"Yes. I suppose he is, sir."

"Then why—" The science minister broke off and turned to the High Minister for Peace and Military Security. "David? This matter is obviously now in my jurisdiction. Will you issue the necessary instructions to your people? After all, one can't keep persons of the caliber of Professor Kennedy and Doctor Okajima, to mention just two, cooling their heels indefinitely. They won't stand for it."

The peace minister did not answer but glanced inquiringly at Captain van Tromp. The captain shook his head. "No, sir."

"Why not?" demanded the science minister. "You have admitted that he isn't sick."

"Give the captain a chance to explain, Pierre," the peace minister advised. "Well, Captain?"

"Smith isn't sick, sir," Captain van Tromp said to the peace minister, "but he isn't well, either. He has never before been in a one-gravity field. He now weighs more than two and one half times what he is used to and his muscles aren't up to it. He's not used to Earth-normal air pressure.

He's not used to *anything* and the strain is likely to be too much for him. Hell's bells, gentlemen, I'm dog tired myself just from being at one-gee again—and I was born on this planet."

The science minister looked contemptuous. "If acceleration fatigue is all that is worrying you, let me assure you, my dear Captain, that we had anticipated that. His respiration and heart action will be watched carefully. We are not entirely without imagination and forethought. After all, I've been out myself. I know how it feels. This man Smith must—"

Captain van Tromp decided that it was time to throw a tantrum. He could excuse it by his own fatigue—very real fatigue, he felt as if he had just landed on Jupiter—and he was smugly aware that even a high councilor could not afford to take too stiff a line with the commander of the first successful Martian expedition.

So he interrupted with a snort of disgust. *"Hnh!* 'This man Smith—' This *'man!'* Can't you see that that is just what he is *not?"*

"Eh?"

"Smith . . . is . . . not . . . a . . . *man."*

"Huh? Explain yourself, Captain."

"Smith is not a *man.* He is an intelligent creature with the genes and ancestry of a man, but he is not a man. He's more a Martian than a man. Until we came along he had never laid eyes on a human being. He thinks like a Martian, he feels like a Martian. He's been brought up by a race which has nothing in common with us. Why, they don't even have sex. Smith has never laid eyes on a woman—still hasn't if my orders have been carried out. He's a man by ancestry, a Martian by environment. Now, if you want to drive him crazy and waste that 'treasure trove of scientific information,' call in your fat-headed professors and let them badger him. Don't give him a chance to get well and strong and used to this madhouse planet. Just go ahead and squeeze him like an orange. It's no skin off me; I've done my job!"

The ensuing silence was broken smoothly by Secretary General Douglas himself. "And a good job, too, Captain. Your advice will be weighed, and be assured that we will not do anything hastily. If this man, or man-Martian, Smith, needs a few days to get adjusted, I'm sure that science can wait—so take it easy, Pete. Let's table this part of the discussion, gentlemen, and get on to other matters. Captain van Tromp is tired."

"One thing won't wait," said the Minister for Public Information.

"Eh, Jock?"

"If we don't show the Man from Mars in the stereo tanks pretty shortly, you'll have riots on your hands, Mr. Secretary."

"Hmm— You exaggerate, Jock. Mars stuff in the news, of course. Me decorating the captain and his brave crew—tomorrow, that had better be. Captain van Tromp telling of his experiences—after a night's rest of course, Captain."

The minister shook his head.

"No good, Jock?"

"The public expected the expedition to bring back at least one real live Martian for them to gawk at. Since they didn't, we need Smith and need him badly."

" 'Live Martians?' " Secretary General Douglas turned to Captain van Tromp. "You have movies of Martians, haven't you?"

"Thousands of feet."

"There's your answer, Jock. When the live stuff gets thin, trot on the movies of Martians. The people will love it. Now, Captain, about this possibility of extraterritoriality: you say the Martians were not opposed to it?"

"Well, no, sir—but they were not for it, either."

"I don't follow you?"

Captain van Tromp chewed his lip. "Sir, I don't know just how to explain it. Talking with a Martian is something like talking with an echo. You don't get any argument but you don't get results either."

"Semantic difficulty? Perhaps you should have brought what's-his-name, your semantician, with you today. Or is he waiting outside?"

"Mahmoud, sir. No, Doctor Mahmoud is not well. A—a slight nervous breakdown, sir." Van Tromp reflected that being dead drunk was the moral equivalent thereof.

"Space happy?"

"A little, perhaps." These damned groundhogs!

"Well, fetch him around when he's feeling himself. I imagine this young man Smith should be of help as an interpreter."

"Perhaps," van Tromp said doubtfully.

This young man Smith was busy at that moment just staying alive. His body, unbearably compressed and weakened by the strange shape of space in this unbelievable place, was at last somewhat relieved by the softness of the nest in which these others had placed him. He dropped the effort of sustaining it, and turned his third level to his respiration and heart beat.

He saw at once that he was about to consume himself. His lungs were beating almost as hard as they did at home, his heart was racing to distribute the influx, all in an attempt to cope with the squeezing of space—

and this in a situation in which he was smothered by a poisonously rich and dangerously hot atmosphere. He took immediate steps.

When his heart rate was down to twenty per minute and his respiration almost imperceptible, he set them at that and watched himself long enough to assure himself that he would not inadvertently discorporate while his attention was elsewhere. When he was satisfied that they were running properly, he set a tiny portion of his second level on guard and withdrew the rest of himself. It was necessary to review the configurations of these many new events in order to fit them to himself, then cherish and praise them—lest they swallow him up.

Where should he start? When he had left home, enfolding these others who were now his own nestlings? Or simply at his arrival in this crushed space? He was suddenly assaulted by the lights and sounds of that arrival, feeling it again with mind-shaking pain. No, he was not yet ready to cherish and embrace that configuration—back! back! back beyond his first sight of these others who were now his own. Back even before the healing which had followed his first grokking of the fact that he was not as his nestling brothers . . . back to the nest itself.

None of his thinkings had been in Earth symbols. Simple English he had freshly learned to speak, but much less easily than a Hindu uses it to trade with a Turk. Smith used English as one might use a code book, with tedious and imperfect translation for each symbol. Now his thoughts, pure Martian abstractions from half a million years of wildly alien culture, traveled so far from any human experience as to be utterly untranslatable.

In the adjoining room an interne, Dr. "Tad" Thaddeus, was playing cribbage with Tom Meechum, Smith's special nurse. Thaddeus had one eye on his dials and meters and both eyes on his cards; nevertheless he noted every heart beat of his patient. When a flickering light changed from ninety-two pulsations per minute to less than twenty, he pushed the cards aside, jumped to his feet, and hurried into Smith's room with Meechum at his heels.

The patient floated in the flexible skin of the hydraulic bed. He appeared to be dead. Thaddeus swore briefly and snapped, "Get Doctor Nelson!"

Meechum said, "Yessir!" and added, "How about the shock gear, Doc? He's far gone."

"Get Doctor Nelson!"

The nurse rushed out. The interne examined the patient as closely as possible but refrained from touching him. He was still doing so when an older doctor came in, walking with the labored awkwardness of a man long in space and not yet adjusted to high gravity. "Well, Doctor?"

"Patient's respiration, temperature, and pulse dropped suddenly, uh, about two minutes ago, sir."

"What have you done for him, or to him?"

"Nothing, sir. Your instructions—"

"Good." Nelson looked Smith over briefly, then studied the instruments back of the bed, twins of those in the watch room. "Let me know if there is any change." He started to leave.

Thaddeus looked startled. "But, Doctor—" He broke off.

Nelson said grimly, "Go ahead, Doctor. What is your diagnosis?"

"Uh, I don't wish to sound off about your patient, sir."

"Never mind. I asked for your diagnosis."

"Very well, sir. Shock—atypical, perhaps," he hedged, "but shock, leading to termination."

Nelson nodded. "Reasonable enough. But this isn't a reasonable case. Relax, son. I've seen this patient in this condition half a dozen times during the trip back. It doesn't mean a thing. Watch." Nelson lifted the patient's right arm, let it go. It stayed where he had left it.

"Catalepsy?" asked Thaddeus.

"Call it that if you like. Calling a tail a leg doesn't make it one. Don't worry about it, Doctor. There is nothing typical about this case. Just keep him from being bothered and call me if there is any change." He replaced Smith's arm.

When Nelson had left, Thaddeus took one more look at the patient, shook his head and joined Meechum in the watch room. Meechum picked up his cards and said, "Crib?"

"No."

Meechum waited, then added, "Doc, if you ask me, that one in there is a case for the basket before morning."

"No one asked you."

"My mistake."

"Go out and have a cigarette with the guards. I want to think."

Meechum shrugged and left. Thaddeus opened a bottom drawer, took out a bottle and poured himself a dose intended to help his thinking. Meechum joined the guards in the corridor; they straightened up, then saw who it was and relaxed. The taller marine said, "Howdy, pal. What was the excitement just now?"

"Nothing much. The patient just had quintuplets and we were arguing about what to name them. Which one of you monkeys has got a butt? And a light?"

The other marine dug a pack of cigarettes out of a pocket. "How're you fixed for suction?" he asked bleakly.

"Just middlin'. Thanks." Meechum stuck the cigarette in his face and talked around it. "Honest to God, gentlemen, I don't know anything about this patient. I wish I did."

"What's the idea of these orders about 'Absolutely No Women'? Is he some kind of a sex maniac?"

"Not that I know of. All that I know is that they brought him in from the *Champion* and said that he was to have absolute quiet."

" 'The *Champion!*' " the first marine said. "Of course! That accounts for it."

"Accounts for what?"

"It stands to reason. He ain't had any, he ain't seen any, he ain't touched any—for months. And he's sick, see? If he was to lay hands on any, they're afraid he'd kill hisself." He blinked and blew out a deep breath. "I'll bet I would, under similar circumstances. No wonder they don't want no bims around him."

Smith had been aware of the visit by the doctors but he had grokked at once that their intentions were benign; it was not necessary for the major part of him to be jerked back from where he was.

At the hour in the morning when human nurses slap patient's faces with cold, wet cloths under the pretense of washing them, Smith returned from his journey. He speeded up his heart, increased his respiration, and again took note of his surroundings, viewing them with serenity. He looked the room over, noting without discrimination and with praise all its details, both important and unimportant. He was, in fact, seeing it for the first time, as he had been incapable of enfolding it when he had been brought there the day before. This commonplace room was not common-place to him; there was nothing remotely like it on all Mars, nor did it resemble the wedge-shaped, metal-walled compartments of the *Champion*. But, having relived the events linking his nest to this place, he was now prepared to accept it, commend it, and in some degree to cherish it.

He became aware that there was another living creature in the room with him. A granddaddy longlegs was making a futile journey down from the ceiling, spinning as it went. Smith watched it with delight and wondered if it were a nestling form of man.

Doctor Archer Frame, the interne who had relieved Thaddeus, walked in at that moment. "Good morning," he said. "How do you feel?"

Smith turned the question over in his mind. The first phrase he recognized as a formal sound, requiring no answer but which could be repeated —or might not be. The second phrase was listed in his mind with several possible translations. If Doctor Nelson used it, it meant one thing; if Captain van Tromp used it, it was a formal sound, needing no reply.

He felt that dismay which so often overtook him in trying to communicate with these creatures—a frightening sensation unknown to him before he met men. But he forced his body to remain calm and risked an answer. "Feel good."

"Good!" the creature echoed. "Doctor Nelson will be along in a minute. Feel like some breakfast?"

All four symbols in the query were in Smith's vocabulary but he had trouble believing that he had heard them rightly. He knew that he was food, but he did not "feel like" food. Nor had he had any warning that he might be selected for such an honor. He had not known that the food supply was such that it was necessary to reduce the corporate group. He was filled with mild regret, since there was still so much to grok of these new events, but no reluctance.

But he was excused from the effort of translating an answer by the entrance of Dr. Nelson. The ship's doctor had had little rest and less sleep; he wasted no time on speech but inspected Smith and the array of dials in silence.

Then he turned to Smith. "Bowels move?" he asked.

Smith understood this; Nelson always asked about it. "No, not yet."

"We'll take care of that. But first you eat. Orderly, fetch in that tray."

Nelson fed him two or three bites, then required him to hold the spoon and feed himself. It was tiring but gave him a feeling of gay triumph, for it was the first unassisted action he had taken since reaching this oddly distorted space. He cleaned out the bowl and remembered to ask, "Who is this?" so that he could praise his benefactor.

"What is this, you mean," Nelson answered. "It's a synthetic food jelly, based on amino acids—and now you know as much as you did before. Finished? All right, climb out of that bed."

"Beg pardon?" It was an attention symbol which he had learned was useful when communication failed.

"I said get out of there. Sit up. Stand up. Walk around. You can do it. Sure, you're weak as a kitten but you'll never put on muscle floating in that bed." Nelson opened a valve at the head of the bed; water drained out. Smith restrained a feeling of insecurity, knowing that Nelson cherished him. Shortly he lay on the floor of the bed with the watertight cover wrinkled around him. Nelson added, "Doctor Frame, take his other elbow. We'll have to help him and steady him."

With Dr. Nelson to encourage him and both of them to help him, Smith stood up and stumbled over the rim of the bed. "Steady. Now stand up on your own," Nelson directed. "Don't be afraid. We'll catch you if necessary."

He made the effort and stood alone—a slender young man with underdeveloped muscles and overdeveloped chest. His hair had been cut in the *Champion* and his whiskers removed and inhibited. His most marked feature was his bland, expressionless, almost babyish face—set with eyes which would have seemed more at home in a man of ninety.

He stood alone for a moment, trembling slightly, then tried to walk. He managed three shuffling steps and broke into a sunny, childlike smile. "Good boy!" Nelson applauded.

He tried another step, began to tremble violently and suddenly collapsed. They barely managed to break his fall. "Damn!" Nelson fumed. "He's gone into another one. Here, help me lift him into the bed. No—fill it first."

Frame did so, cutting off the flow when the cover skin floated six inches from the top. They lugged him into it, awkwardly because he had frozen into the foetal position. "Get a collar pillow under his neck," instructed Nelson, "and call me when he comes out of it. No—let me sleep, I need it. Unless something worries you. We'll walk him again this afternoon and tomorrow we'll start systematic exercise. In three months I'll have him swinging through the trees like a monkey. There's nothing really wrong with him."

"Yes, Doctor," Frame answered doubtfully.

"Oh, yes, when he comes out of it, teach him how to use the bathroom. Have the nurse help you; I don't want him to fall."

"Yes, sir. Uh, any particular method—I mean, how—"

"Eh? Show him, of course! Demonstrate. He probably won't understand much that you say to him, but he's bright as a whip. He'll be bathing himself by the end of the week."

Smith ate lunch without help. Presently a male orderly came in to remove his tray. The man glanced around, then came to the bed and leaned over him. "Listen," he said in a low voice, "I've got a fat proposition for you."

"Beg pardon?"

"A deal, a bargain, a way for you to make a lot of money fast and easy."

" 'Money?' What is 'money'?"

"Never mind the philosophy; everybody needs money. Now listen I'll have to talk fast because I can't stay in here long—and it's taken a lot of fixing to get me in here at all. I represent Peerless Features. We'll pay you sixty thousand for your exclusive story and it won't be a bit of trouble to you—we've got the best ghost writers in the business. You just talk and answer questions; they put it together." He whipped out a piece of paper. "Just read this and sign it. I've got the down payment with me."

Smith accepted the paper, stared thoughtfully at it, holding it upside down. The man looked at him and muffled an exclamation. "Lordy! Don't you read English?"

Smith understood this well enough to answer. "No."

"Well— Here, I'll read it to you, then you just put your thumb print in the square and I'll witness it. 'I, the undersigned, Valentine Michael Smith, sometimes known as the Man from Mars, do grant and assign to Peerless Features, Limited, all and exclusive rights in my true-fact story to be titled *I Was a Prisoner on Mars* in exchange for—'"

"Orderly!"

Dr. Frame was standing in the door of the watch room; the paper disappeared into the man's clothes. "Coming, sir. I was just getting this tray."

"What were you reading?"

"Nothing."

"I saw you. Never mind, come out of there quickly. This patient is not to be disturbed." The man obeyed; Dr. Frame closed the door behind them. Smith lay motionless for the next half hour, but try as he might he could not grok it at all.

iv

GILLIAN BOARDMAN WAS CONSIDERED professionally competent as a nurse; she was judged competent in wider fields by the bachelor internes and she was judged harshly by some other women. There was no harm in her and her hobby was men. When the grapevine carried the word that there was a patient in special suite K-12 who had never laid eyes on a woman in his life, she did not believe it. When detailed explanation convinced her, she resolved to remedy it. She went on duty that day as floor supervisor in the wing where Smith was housed. As soon as possible she went to pay a call on the strange patient.

She knew of the "No Female Visitors" rule and, while she did not consider herself to be a visitor of any sort, she sailed on past the marine guards without attempting to use the door they guarded—marines, she had found, had a stuffy habit of construing their orders literally. Instead she went into the adjacent watch room. Dr. "Tad" Thaddeus was on duty there alone.

He looked up. "Well, if it ain't 'Dimples!' Hi, honey, what brings you here?"

She sat on the corner of his desk and reached for his cigarettes. " 'Miss Dimples,' to you, chum; I'm on duty. This call is part of my rounds. What about your patient?"

"Don't worry your fuzzy head about him, honey chile; he's not your responsibility. See your order book."

"I read it. I want to have a look at him."

"In one word—no."

"Oh, Tad, don't go regulation on me. I know you."

He gazed thoughtfully at his nails. "Ever worked for Doctor Nelson?"

"No. Why?"

"If I let you put your little foot inside that door, I'd find myself in Antarctica early tomorrow, prescribing for penguins' chilblains. So switch your fanny out of here and go bother your own patients. I wouldn't want him even to catch you in this watch room."

She stood up. "Is Doctor Nelson likely to come popping in?"

"Not likely, unless I send for him. He's still sleeping off low-gee fatigue."

"So? Then what's the idea of being so duty struck?"

"That's all, Nurse."

"Very well, Doctor!" She added, "Stinker."

"Jill!"

"And a stuffed shirt, too."

He sighed. "Still okay for Saturday night?"

She shrugged. "I suppose so. A girl can't be fussy these days." She went back to her duty station, found that her services were not in immediate demand, picked up the pass key. She was balked but not beaten, as she recalled that suite K-12 had a door joining it to the room beyond it, a room sometimes used as a sitting room when the suite was occupied by a Very Important Person. The room was not then in use, either as part of the suite or separately. She let herself into it. The guards at the door beyond paid no attention, unaware that they had been flanked.

She hesitated at the inner door between the two rooms, feeling some of the sharp excitement she used to feel when sneaking out of student nurses' quarters. But, she told herself, Dr. Nelson was asleep and Tad wouldn't tell on her even if he caught her. She didn't blame him for keeping his finger on his number—but he wouldn't report her. She unlocked the door and looked in.

The patient was in bed, he looked at her as the door opened. Her first impression was that here was a patient too far gone to care. His lack of expression seemed to show the complete apathy of the desperately ill. Then she saw that his eyes were alive with interest; she wondered if his face were paralysed? No, she decided; the typical sags were lacking.

She assumed her professional manner. "Well, how are we today? Feeling better?"

Smith translated and examined the questions. The inclusion of herself in the first query was confusing, but he decided that it might symbolize a wish to cherish and grow close. The second part matched Nelson's speech forms. "Yes," he answered.

"Good!" Aside from his odd lack of expression she saw nothing strange about him—and if women were unknown to him, he was certainly managing to conceal it. "Is there anything I can do for you?" She glanced around, noted that there was no glass on the bedside shelf. "May I get you water?"

Smith had spotted at once that this creature was different from the others who had come to see him. Almost as quickly he compared what he was seeing with pictures Nelson had shown him on the trip from home to this place—pictures intended to explain a particularly difficult and puzzling configuration of this people group. This, then, was a "woman."

He felt both oddly excited and disappointed. He suppressed both in order that he might grok deeply, with such success that Dr. Thaddeus noticed no change in the dial readings in the next room.

But when he translated the last query he felt such a surge of emotion that he almost let his heartbeat increase. He caught it in time and chided himself for an undisciplined nestling. Then he checked his translation.

No, he was not mistaken. This woman creature had offered him the water ritual. It wished to grow closer.

With great effort, scrambling for adequate meanings in his pitifully poor list of human words, he attempted to answer with due ceremoniousness. "I thank you for water. May you always drink deep."

Nurse Boardman looked startled. "Why, how sweet!" She found a glass, filled it, and handed it to him.

He said, "You drink."

Wonder if he thinks I'm trying to poison him? she asked herself—but there was a compelling quality to his request. She took a sip, whereupon he took the glass from her and took one also, after which he seemed content to sink back into the bed, as if he had accomplished something important.

Jill told herself that, as an adventure, this was a fizzle. She said, "Well, if you don't need anything else, I must get on with my work."

She started for the door. He called out, "No!"

She stopped. "Eh? What do you want?"

"Don't go away."

"Well . . . I'll have to go, pretty quickly." But she came back to the bedside. "Is there anything you want?"

He looked her up and down. "You are . . . 'woman'?"

The question startled Jill Boardman. Her sex had not been in doubt to the most casual observer for many years. Her first impulse was to answer flippantly.

But Smith's grave face and oddly disturbing eyes checked her. She became aware emotionally that the impossible fact about this patient was true: he did not know what a woman was. She answered carefully, "Yes, I am a woman."

Smith continued to stare at her without expression. Jill began to be embarrassed by it. To be looked at appreciatively by a male she expected and sometimes enjoyed, but this was more like being examined under a microscope. She stirred restively. "Well? I look like a woman, don't I?"

"I do not know," Smith answered slowly. "How does woman look? What makes you woman?"

"Well, for pity's sake!" Jill realized confusedly that this conversation was further out of hand than any she had had with a male since about her twelfth birthday. "You don't expect me to take off my clothes and show you!"

Smith took time to examine these verbal symbols and try to translate them. The first group he could not grok at all. It might be one of those formal sound groups these people so often used . . . yet it had been spoken with surprising force, as if it might be a last communication before withdrawal. Perhaps he had so deeply mistaken right conduct in dealing with a woman creature that the creature might be ready to discorporate at once.

He knew vaguely that he did not want the nurse to die at that moment, even though it was certainly its right and possibly its obligation to do so. The abrupt change from the rapport of the water ritual to a situation in which a newly won water brother might possibly be considering withdrawal or discorporation would have thrown him into panic had he not been consciously suppressing such disturbance. But he decided that if

Jill died now he must die at once also—he could not grok it in any other wise, not after the giving of water.

The second half of the communication contained only symbols that he had encountered before. He grokked imperfectly the intention but there seemed to be an implied way out for him to avoid this crisis—by acceding to the suggested wish. Perhaps if the woman took its clothes off neither of them need discorporate. He smiled happily. "Please."

Jill opened her mouth, closed it hastily. She opened it again. "Huh? Well, I'll be darned!"

Smith could grok emotional violence and knew that somehow he had offered the wrong reply. He began to compose his mind for discorporation, savoring and cherishing all that he had been and seen, with especial attention to this woman creature. Then he became aware that the woman was bending over him and he knew somehow that it was not about to die. It looked into his face. "Correct me if I am wrong," it said, "but were you asking me to take my clothes off?"

The inversions and abstractions required careful translation but Smith managed it. "Yes," he answered, while hoping that it would not stir up a new crisis.

"That's what I thought you said. Brother, you aren't ill."

The word "brother" he considered first—the woman was reminding him that they had been joined in the water ritual. He asked the help of his nestlings that he might measure up to whatever this new brother wanted. "I am not ill," he agreed.

"Though I'm darned if I know how to cope with whatever is wrong with you. But I won't peel down. And I've got to get out of here." It straightened up and turned again toward the side door—then stopped and looked back with a quizzical smile. "You might ask me again, real prettily, under other circumstances. I'm curious to see what I might do."

The woman was gone. Smith relaxed into the water bed and let the room fade away from him. He felt sober triumph that he had somehow comforted himself so that it was not necessary for them to die . . . but there was much new to grok. The woman's last speech had contained many symbols new to him and those which were not new had been arranged in fashions not easily understood. But he was happy that the emotional flavor of them had been suitable for communication between water brothers—although touched with something else both disturbing and terrifyingly pleasant. He thought about his new brother, the woman creature, and felt odd tingles run through him. The feeling reminded him of the first time he had been allowed to be present at a discorporation and he felt happy without knowing why.

He wished that his brother Doctor Mahmoud were here. There was so much to grok, so little to grok from.

Jill Boardman spent the rest of her watch in a mild daze. She managed to avoid any mistakes in medication and she answered from reflex the usual verbal overtures made to her. But the face of the Man from Mars stayed in her mind and she mulled over the crazy things he had said. No, not "crazy," she corrected—she had done her stint in psychiatric wards and she felt certain that his remarks had not been psychotic.

She decided that "innocent" was the proper term—then she decided that the word was not adequate. His expression was innocent, but his eyes were not. What sort of creature had a face like that?

She had once worked in a Catholic hospital; she suddenly saw the face of the Man from Mars surrounded by the head dress of a nursing sister, a nun. The idea disturbed her, for there was nothing female about Smith's face.

She was changing into street clothes when another nurse stuck her head into the locker room. "Phone, Jill. For you." Jill accepted the call, sound without vision, while she continued to dress.

"Is this Florence Nightingale?" a baritone voice asked.

"Speaking. That you, Ben?"

"The stalwart upholder of the freedom of the press in person. Little one, are you busy?"

"What do you have in mind?"

"I have in mind taking you out, buying you a bloody steak, plying you with liquor, and asking you a question."

"The answer is still 'No.' "

"Not *that* question. Another one."

"Oh, do you know another one? If so, tell me."

"Later. I want you softened up by food and liquor first."

"Real steak? Not syntho?"

"Guaranteed. When you stick a fork into it, it will turn imploring eyes on you."

"You must be on an expense account, Ben."

"That's irrelevant and ignoble. How about it?"

"You've talked me into it."

"The roof of the medical center. Ten minutes."

She put the street suit she had changed into back into her locker and put on a dinner dress kept there for emergencies. It was a demure little number, barely translucent and with bustle and bust pads so subdued that they merely re-created the effect she would have produced had she been wearing nothing. The dress had cost her a month's pay and did not look it, its subtle power being concealed like knock-out drops in a drink. Jill looked at herself with satisfaction and took the bounce tube up to the roof.

There she pulled her cape around her against the wind and was looking for Ben Caxton when the roof orderly touched her arm. "There is a car over there paging you, Miss Boardman—that Talbot saloon."

"Thanks, Jack." She saw the taxi spotted for take-off, with its door open. She went to it, climbed in, and was about to hand Ben a backhanded compliment on gallantry when she saw that he was not inside. The taxi was on automatic; its door closed and it took to the air, swung out of the circle, and sliced across the Potomac. Jill sat back and waited.

The taxi stopped on a public landing flat over Alexandria and Ben Caxton got in; it took off again. Jill looked him over grimly. "My, aren't we getting important! Since when has your time become so valuable that you send a robot to pick up your women?"

He reached over, patted her knee, and said gently, "Reasons, little one, reasons—I can't afford to be seen picking you up—"

"Well!"

"—and you can't afford to be seen being picked up by me. So simmer down. I apologize. I bow in the dust. I kiss your little foot. But it was necessary."

"Hmm . . . which one of us has leprosy?"

"Both of us, in different ways. Jill, I'm a newspaperman."

"I was beginning to think you were something else."

"And you are a nurse at the hospital where they are holding the Man from Mars." He spread his hands and shrugged.

"Keep talking. Does that make me unfit to meet your mother?"

"Do you need a map, Jill? There are more than a thousand reporters in this area, not counting press agents, ax grinders, winchells, lippmanns, and the stampede that headed this way when the *Champion* landed. Every one of them has been trying to interview the Man from Mars, including me. So far as I know, none has succeeded. Do you think it would be smart for us to be seen leaving the hospital together?"

"Umm, maybe not. But I don't really see that it matters. I'm not the Man from Mars."

He looked her over. "You certainly aren't. But maybe you are going to help me see him—which is why I didn't want to be seen picking you up."

"Huh? Ben, you've been out in the sun without your hat. They've got a marine guard around him." She thought about the fact that she herself had not found the guard too hard to circumvent, decided not to mention it.

"So they have. So we talk it over."

"I don't see what there is to talk about."

"Later. I didn't intend to let the subject come up until I had softened you with animal proteins and ethanol. Let's eat first."

"Now you sound rational. Where? Would your expense account run to the New Mayflower? You *are* on an expense account, aren't you?"

Caxton frowned. "Jill, if we eat in a restaurant, I wouldn't want to risk one closer than Louisville. It would take this hack more than two hours to get us that far. How about dinner in my apartment?"

" '—Said the Spider to the Fly.' Ben, I remember the last time. I'm too tired to wrestle."

"Nobody asked you to. Strictly business. King's X, cross my heart and hope to die."

"I don't know as I like that much better. If I'm safe alone with you, I must be slipping. Well, all right, King's X."

Caxton leaned forward and punched buttons; the taxi, which had been circling under a "hold" instruction, woke up, looked around, and headed for the apartment hotel where Ben lived. He then dialed a phone number and said to Jill, "How much time do you want to get liquored up, sugar foot? I'll tell the kitchen when to have the steaks ready."

Jill considered it. "Ben, your mousetrap has a private kitchen."

"Of sorts. I can grill a steak, if that is what you mean."

"I'll grill the steak. Hand me the phone." She gave orders, stopping to make sure that Ben liked endive.

The taxi dropped them on the roof and they went down to his flat. It was unstylish and old-fashioned; its one luxury was a live grass lawn in the living room. Jill stopped in the entrance hall, slipped off her shoes, then stepped bare-footed into the living room and wiggled her toes among the cool green blades. She sighed. "My, that feels good. My feet have hurt ever since I entered training."

"Sit down."

"No, I want my feet to remember this tomorrow, when I'm on duty."

"Suit yourself." He went into his pantry and mixed drinks.

Presently she pattered after him and became domestic. The steak was waiting in the package lift; with it were pre-baked potatoes ready to be popped into short-wave. She tossed the salad, handed it to the refrigerator, then set up a combination on the stove to grill the steak and have the potatoes hot simultaneously, but did not start the cycle. "Ben, doesn't this stove have a remote control?"

"Of course."

"Well, I can't find it."

He studied the setup on the control panel, then flipped an unmarked switch. "Jill, what would you do if you had to cook over an open fire?"

"I'd do darn well. I was a Girl Scout and a good one. How about you, smarty?"

He ignored it, picked up a tray and went back to the living room; she followed and sat down at his feet, spreading her skirt to avoid grass stains. They applied themselves seriously to martinis. Opposite his chair was a stereovision tank disguised as an aquarium; he switched it on from his chair, guppies and tetras faded out and gave way to the face of a commentator, the well-known winchell Augustus Greaves.

"—it can be stated authoritatively," the stereo image was saying, "that the Man from Mars is being kept constantly under hypnotic drugs to keep him from disclosing these facts. The administration would find it extremely embarrassing if—"

Caxton flipped it off. "Gus old boy," he said pleasantly, "you don't know a durn thing more about it than I do." He frowned. "Though you might be right about the government keeping him under drugs."

"No, they aren't," Jill said suddenly.

"Eh? How's that, little one?"

"The Man from Mars isn't being kept under hypnotics." Having blurted more than she had meant to, she added carefully, "He's got a nurse and a doctor all to himself on continuous watch, but there aren't any orders for sedation."

"Are you sure? You aren't one of his nurses—or are you?"

"No. They're male nurses. Uh . . . matter of fact, there's an order to keep women away from him entirely and a couple of tough marines to make sure of it."

Caxton nodded. "I heard about that. Fact is, you don't know whether they are drugging him or not. Do you?"

Jill stared into her empty glass. She felt annoyed to have her word doubted but realized she would have to tell on herself to back up what she had said. "Ben? You wouldn't give me away? Would you?"

"Give you away? How?"

"Any way at all."

"Hmm . . . that covers a lot of ground, but I'll go along."

"All right. Pour me another one first." He did so, Jill went on. "I know they don't have the Man from Mars hopped up—because I talked with him."

Caxton gave a slow whistle. "I knew it. When I got up this morning I said to myself, 'Go see Jill. She's the ace up my sleeve.' Honey lamb, have another drink. Have six. Here, take the pitcher."

"Not so fast, thanks."

"Whatever you like. May I rub your poor tired feet? Lady, you are about to be interviewed. Your public waits with quivering impatience. Now let's begin at the beginning. How—"

"No, Ben! You promised—remember? You quote me just one little quote and I'll lose my job."

"Mmm . . . probably. How about 'from a usually reliable source'?"

"I'd be scared."

"Well? Are you going to tell Uncle Ben? Or are you going to let him die of frustration and then eat that steak by yourself?"

"Oh, I'll talk—now that I've talked this much. But you can't use it." Ben kept quiet and did not press his luck; Jill described how she had outflanked the guards.

He interrupted. "Say! Could you do that again?"

"Huh? I suppose so, but I won't. It's risky."

"Well, could you slip me in that way? Of course you could! Look, I'll dress up like an electrician—greasy coveralls, union badge, tool kit. You just slip me the pass key and—"

"No!"

"Huh? Look, baby girl, be reasonable. I'll bet you four to one that half the hospital staffers around him are ringers, stuck in there by one news service or another. This is the greatest human-interest story since Colombo conned Isabella into hocking her jewels. The only thing that worries me is that I may find another phony electrician—"

"The only thing that worries me is *me,*" Jill interrupted. "To you it's just a story; to me it's my career. They'd take away my cap, my pin, and ride me out of town on a rail. I'd be finished as a nurse."

"Mmm . . . there's that."

"There sure is that."

"Lady, you are about to be offered a bribe."

"How big a bribe? It'll take quite a chunk to keep me in style the rest of my life in Rio."

"Well . . . the story is worth money, of course, but you can't expect me to outbid Associated Press, or Reuters. How about a hundred?"

"What do you think I am?"

"We settled that, we're dickering over the price. A hundred and fifty?"

"Pour me another drink and look up the phone number of Associated Press for me, that's a lamb."

"It's Capitol 10-9000. Jill, will you marry me? That's as high as I can go."

She looked up at him, startled. "What did you say?"

"Will you marry me? Then, when they ride you out of town on a rail, I'll be waiting at the city line and take you away from your sordid existence. You'll come back here and cool your toes in my grass—*our* grass— and forget your ignominy. But you've durn well got to sneak me into that hospital room first."

"Ben, you almost sound serious. If I phone for a Fair Witness, will you repeat the offer?"

Caxton sighed. "Jill, you're a hard woman. Send for a Witness."

She stood up. "Ben," she said softly, "I won't hold you to it." She rumpled his hair and kissed him. "But don't ever joke about marriage to a spinster."

"I wasn't joking."

"I wonder. Wipe off the lipstick and I'll tell you everything I know, then we'll consider how you can use it without getting me ridden on that rail. Fair enough?"

"Fair enough."

She gave him a detailed account. "I'm sure he wasn't drugged. I'm equally sure that he was rational—although why I'm sure I don't know, for he talked in the oddest fashion and asked the darnedest questions. But I'm sure. He isn't psychotic."

"It would be odder still if he hadn't talked in an odd fashion."

"Huh?"

"Use your head, Jill. We don't know much about Mars but we do know that Mars is very unlike Earth and that Martians, whatever they are, certainly are not human. Suppose you were suddenly popped into a tribe so far back in the jungle that they had never laid eyes on a white woman. Would you know all the sophisticated small talk that comes from a lifetime in a culture? Or would your conversation sound odd? That's a very mild analogy; the truth in this case is at least forty million miles stranger."

Jill nodded. "I figured that out . . . and that is why I discounted his odd remarks. I'm not dumb."

"No, you're real bright, for a female."

"Would you like this martini poured in your thinning hair?"

"I apologize. Women are lots smarter than men; that is proved by our whole cultural setup. Gimme, I'll fill it."

She accepted the peace offerings and went on, "Ben, that order about not letting him see women, it's silly. He's no sex fiend."

"No doubt they don't want to hand him too many shocks at once."

"He wasn't shocked. He was just . . . interested. It wasn't like having a man look at me at all."

"If you had humored him on that request for a private viewing, you might have had your hands full. He probably has all the instincts and no inhibitions."

"Huh? I don't think so. I suppose they've told him about male and female; he just wanted to see how women are different."

" 'Vive la différence!' " Caxton answered enthusiastically.

"Don't be more vulgar than you have to be."

"Me? I wasn't being vulgar, I was being reverent. I was giving thanks to all the gods that I was born human and not Martian."

"Be serious."

"I was never more serious."

"Then be quiet. He wouldn't have given me any trouble. He would probably have thanked me gravely. You didn't see his face—I did."

"What about his face?"

Jill looked puzzled. "I don't know how to express it. Yes, I do!—Ben, have you ever seen an angel?"

"You, cherub. Otherwise not."

"Well, neither have I—but that is what he looked like. He had old, wise eyes in a completely placid face, a face of unearthly innocence." She shivered.

" 'Unearthly' is surely the right word," Ben answered slowly. "I'd like to see him."

"I wish you had. Ben, why are they making such a thing out of keeping him shut up? He wouldn't hurt a fly. I'm sure of it."

Caxton fitted his fingertips together. "Well, in the first place they want to protect him. He grew up in Mars gravity; he's probably weak as a cat."

"Yes, of course. You could see it, just looking at him. But muscular weakness isn't dangerous; myasthenia gravis is much worse and we manage all right with such cases."

"They would want to keep him from catching things, too. He's like those experimental animals at Notre Dame; he's never been exposed."

"Sure, sure—no antibodies. But from what I hear around the mess hall, Doctor Nelson—the surgeon in the *Champion,* I mean—Doctor Nelson took care of that on the trip back. Repeated mutual transfusion until he had replaced about half of his blood tissue."

"Really? Can I use that, Jill? That's news."

"All right, just don't quote me. They gave him shots for everything but housemaid's knee, too. But, Ben, even if they want to protect him from infection, that doesn't take armed guards outside his door."

"Mmmm . . . Jill, I've picked up a few tidbits you may not know. I haven't been able to use them because I've got to protect my sources, just as with you. But I'll tell you; you've earned it—just don't talk."

"Oh, I won't."

"It's a long story. Want a refill?"

"No, let's start the steak. Where's the button?"

"Right here."

"Well, push it."

"Me? You offered to cook dinner. Where's that Girl Scout spirit you were boasting about?"

"Ben Caxton, I will lie right here in the grass and starve before I will get up to push a button that is six inches from your right forefinger."

"As you wish." He pressed the button to tell the stove to carry out its pre-set orders. "But don't forget who cooked dinner. Now about Valentine Michael Smith. In the first place there is grave doubt as to his right to the name 'Smith.' "

"Repeat, please?"

"Honey, your pal appears to be the first interplanetary bastard of record. I mean 'love child.' "

"The hell you say!"

"Please be more ladylike in your speech. Do you remember anything about the crew of the *Envoy?* Never mind, I'll hit the high points. Eight people, four married couples. Two couples were Captain and Mrs. Brant, Doctor and Mrs. Smith. Your friend with the face of an angel appears to be the son of Mrs. Smith by Captain Brant."

"How do they know? And, anyhow, who cares?" Jill sat up and said indignantly, "It's a pretty snivelin' thing to dig up a scandal after all this time. They're all dead—let 'em alone, I say!"

"As to how they know, you can figure that out. Blood typing, Rh factor, hair and eye color, all those genetic things—you probably know more about them than I do. Anyhow it is a mathematical certainty that Mary Jane Lyle Smith was his mother and Captain Michael Brant was his father. All the factors are matters of record for the entire crew of the *Envoy;* there probably never were eight people more thoroughly measured and typed. Also it gives Valentine Michael Smith a wonderfully fine heredity; his father had an I.Q. of 163, his mother 170, and both were tops in their fields.

"As to who cares," Ben went on, "a lot of people care very much—and a lot more will care, once this picture shapes up. Ever heard of the Lyle Drive?"

"Of course. That's what the *Champion* used."

"And every other space ship, these days. Who invented it?"

"I don't—Wait a minute! You mean *she*—"

"Hand the little lady a cigar! Dr. Mary Jane Lyle Smith. She knew she had something important, even though development work remained to be done on it. So before she left on the expedition, she applied for a dozen-odd basic patents and placed it all in a corporate trust—*not* a non-profit corporation, mind you—then assigned control and interim income to the Science Foundation. So eventually the government got control of it—but your friend with the face of an angel owns it. No possible doubt. It's worth millions, maybe hundreds of millions; I couldn't guess."

They brought in dinner. Caxton used ceiling tables to protect his lawn; he lowered one down in front of his chair and another to Japanese height so that Jill could sit on the grass. "Tender?" he asked.

"Ongerful!" she answered with her mouth full.

"Thanks. Remember, I cooked it."

"Ben," she said after swallowing, "how about Smith being a—I mean, being illegitimate? Can he inherit?"

"He's not illegitimate. Doctor Mary Jane was at Berkeley, and California laws deny the concept of bastardy. Same for Captain Brant, as New Zealand also has civilized laws on the subject. While under the laws of the home state of Doctor Ward Smith, Mary Jane's husband, a child born in wedlock is legitimate, come hell or high water. We have here, Jill, a man who is the Simon-pure legitimate child of three different parents."

"Huh? Now wait a minute, Ben; he can't be it both ways. One or the other but not both. I'm not a lawyer but—"

"You sure ain't. Such legal fictions bother a lawyer not at all. Smith is legitimate different ways in different jurisdictions, all kosher and all breaking his way—even though he is probably a bastard in his physical ancestry. So he inherits. Besides that, while his mother was wealthy, both his fathers were at least well to do. Brant was a bachelor until just before the expedition; he had ploughed most of his scandalous salary as a pilot on the Moon run back into Lunar Enterprises, Limited. You know how that stuff has boomed—they just declared another three-way stock dividend. Brant had one vice, gambling—but the bloke won regularly and invested that, too. Ward Smith had family money; he was a medical man and scientist by choice. Smith is heir to both of them."

"Whew!"

"That ain't half, honey. Smith is heir to the entire crew."

"Huh?"

"All eight signed a 'Gentlemen Adventurers' contract, making them all mutually heirs to each other—all of them *and* their issue. They did it with great care, using as models similar contracts in the sixteenth and seventeenth centuries that had stood up against every effort to break them. Now these were all high-powered people; among them they had quite a lot. Happened to include considerable Lunar Enterprises stock, too, besides what Brant held. Smith might turn out to own a controlling interest, or at least a key bloc in a proxy fight."

Jill thought about the childlike creature who had made such a touching ceremony out of just a drink of water and felt sorry for him. But Caxton went on: "I wish I could sneak a look at the *Envoy's* log. I know they recovered it—but I doubt if they'll ever release it."

"Why not, Ben?"

"Because it's a nasty story. I got just enough to be sure before my informant sobered up and clammed up. Dr. Ward Smith delivered his wife of child by Caesarian section—and she died on the table. He seems to have worn his horns complacently until then. But what he did next shows that he knew the score; with the same scalpel he cut Captain Brant's throat—then cut his own. Sorry, hon."

Jill shivered. "I'm a nurse. I'm immune to such things."

"You're a liar and I love you for it. I was on police beat for three years, Jill; I never got hardened to it."

"What happened to the others?"

"I wish I knew. If we don't break the bureaucrats and high brass loose from that log, we'll never know—and I am enough of a starry-eyed newsboy to think we should know. Secrecy begets tyranny."

"Ben, he might be better off if they gypped him out of his inheritance. He's very . . . uh, unworldly."

"The exact word, I'm sure. Nor does he need all that money; the Man from Mars will never miss a meal. Any of the governments and any of a thousand-odd universities and scientific institutions would be delighted to have him as a permanent, privileged guest."

"He'd better sign it over and forget it."

"It's not that easy. Jill, you know about the famous case of General Atomics versus Larkin, et al.?"

"Uh, not really. You mean the Larkin Decision. I had to study it in school, same as everybody. But what's it got to do with Smith?"

"Think back. The Russians sent the first rocket to the Moon, it crashed. The United States and Canada combine to send another one; it gets back but leaves nobody on the Moon. So when the United States and the Commonwealth are getting set to send a colonizing one jointly under the nominal sponsorship of the Federation and Russia is mounting the same deal on their own, General Atomics steals a march by sending one of their own from an island leased from Ecuador—and their men are still there, sitting pretty and looking smug when the Federation vessel shows up . . . followed by the Russian one.

"You know what happened. General Atomics, a Swiss corporation American controlled, claimed the Moon. The Federation couldn't just brush them off; that would have been too raw and anyhow the Russians wouldn't have held still. So the High Court ruled that a corporate person, a mere legal fiction, could not own a planet; therefore the real owners were the flesh-and-blood men who had maintained the occupation—Larkin and associates. So they recognized them as a sovereign nation and took them into the Federation—with some melon slicing for those on the inside and fat concessions to General Atomics and its daughter corporation, Lunar Enterprises. This did not entirely suit anybody and the Federation High Court was not all powerful in those days—but it was a compromise everybody could swallow. It resulted in some tight rules for colonizing planets, all based on the Larkin Decision and intended to avoid bloodshed. Worked, too—it's a matter of history that World War Three did *not* result from conflict over space travel and such. So now the Larkin Decision is solidly a part of our planetary law and applies to Smith."

Jill shook her head. "I don't see the connection. Martinis—"

"Think, Jill. By our laws, Smith is a sovereign nation in himself—and sole owner of the planet Mars."

$$V$$

JILL LOOKED ROUND-EYED. "I've certainly had too many martinis Ben. I would swear that you said that that patient owns the planet Mars."

"He does. He maintained occupation of it, unassisted, for the required length of time. Smith *is* the planet Mars—King, President, sole civic body, what you will. If the skipper of the *Champion* had not left colonists behind, Smith's tenure might have failed. But he did, and that continues occupation even though Smith came to Earth. But Smith doesn't have to split with them; they are mere immigrants until he grants them Martian citizenship."

"Fantastic!"

"It surely is. Also it's legal. Honey, do you now see why so many people are interested in who Smith is and where he came from? And why

the administration is so damned anxious to keep him under a rug? What
they are doing isn't even vaguely legal. Smith is also a citizen of the United
States and of the Federation, by derivation—dual citizenship with no conflict. It's illegal to hold a citizen, even a convicted criminal, incommuni-
cado anywhere in the Federation; that's one of the things we settled in
World War Three. But I doubt if Smith knows his rights. Also, it has been
considered an unfriendly act all through history to lock up a visiting
friendly monarch—which is what he is—and not to let him see people,
especially the press, meaning *me*. You still won't sneak me in as a thumb-
fingered electrician?"

"Huh? You've got me worse scared than ever. Ben, if they had caught
me this morning, what do you think they would have done to me?"

"Mmm . . . nothing rough. Just locked you in a padded cell, with a
certificate signed by three doctors, and allowed you mail on alternate leap
years. They aren't mad at you. I'm wondering what they are going to do to
him."

"What *can* they do?"

"Well, he might just happen to die—from gee-fatigue, say. That
would be a fine out for the administration."

"You mean *murder* him?"

"Tut, tut! Don't use nasty words. I don't think they will. In the first
place he is a mine of information; even the public has some dim notion of
that. He might be worth more than Newton and Edison and Einstein and
six more like them all rolled into one. Or he may not be. I don't think they
would dare touch him until they were sure. In the second place, at the very
least, he is a bridge, an ambassador, a unique interpreter, between the
human race and the only other civilized race we have as yet encountered.
That is certainly important but there is no way to guess just how important. How are you on the classics? Ever read H. G. Wells' *The War of the
Worlds?*"

"A long time ago, in school."

"Consider the idea that the Martians might decide to make war on us
—and win. They might, you know, and we have no way of guessing how
big a club they can swing. Our boy Smith might be the go-between, the
peacemaker, who could make the First Interplanetary War unnecessary.
Even if this possibility is remote, the administration can't afford to ignore
it until they *know*. The discovery of intelligent life on Mars is something
that, politically, they haven't figured out yet."

"Then you think he is safe?"

"Probably, for the time being. The Secretary General has to guess and
guess right. As you know, his administration is shaky."

"I don't pay any attention to politics."

"You should. It's only barely less important than your own heartbeat."

"I don't pay any attention to that, either."

"Don't talk when I'm orating. The majority headed by the United States could slip apart overnight—Pakistan would bolt at a nervous cough. In which case there would be a vote of no confidence, a general election, and Mr. Secretary General Douglas would be out and back to being a cheap lawyer again. The Man from Mars can make or break him. Are you going to sneak me in?"

"I am not. I'm going to enter a nunnery. Is there more coffee?"

"I'll see."

They both stood up. Jill stretched and said, "Oh, my ancient bones! And, Lordy, look at the time! Never mind the coffee, Ben; I've got a hard day tomorrow, being polite to nasty patients and standing clear of internes. Run me home, will you? Or send me home, I guess that's safer. Call a cab, that's a lamb."

"Okay, though the evening is young." He went into his bedroom, came out carrying an object about the size and shape of a small cigarette lighter. "Sure you won't sneak me in?"

"Gee, Ben, I *want* to, but—"

"Never mind. I wouldn't let you. It really is dangerous—and not just to your career. I was just softening you up for this." He showed her the little object. "Will you put a bug on him?"

"Huh? What is it?"

"The greatest boon to divorce lawyers and spies since the Mickey Finn. A microminiaturized wire recorder. The wire is spring driven so that it can't be spotted by a snooper circuit. The insides are transistors and resistors and capacitors and stuff, all packed in plastic—you could drop it out of a cab and not hurt it. The power is about as much radioactivity as you would find in a watch dial, but shielded. The wire is good for twenty-four hours. Then you slide out a spool and stick in another one—the spring is part of the spool, already wound."

"Will it explode?" she asked nervously.

"You could bake it in a cake."

"But, Ben, you've got me scared to go back into his room now."

"Unnecessary. You can go into the room next door, can't you?"

"I suppose so."

"This thing has donkey's ears. Fasten the concave side flat against a wall—surgical tape will do nicely—and it picks up every word spoken in the room beyond. Is there a closet or something?"

She thought about it. "I'm bound to be noticed if I duck in and out of that adjoining room too much; it's really part of the suite he's in. Or they may start using it. Look, Ben, his room has a third wall in common with a room on another corridor. Will that do?"

"Perfect. Then you'll do it?"

"Umm . . . give it to me. I'll think it over and see how the land lies."

Caxton stopped to polish it with his handkerchief. "Put on your gloves."

"Why?"

"Possession of it is slightly illegal, good for a short vacation behind bars. Always use gloves on it and the spare spools—and don't get caught with it."

"You think of the nicest things!"

"Want to back out?"

Jill let out a long breath. "No. I've always wanted a life of crime. Will you teach me gangster lingo? I want to be a credit to you."

"Good girl!" A light blinked over the door, he glanced up. "That must be your cab. I rang for it when I went to get this."

"Oh. Find my shoes, will you? No, don't come up to the roof. The less I'm seen with you from here on the better."

"As you wish."

As he straightened up from putting her shoes on, she took his head in both hands and kissed him. "Dear Ben! No good can come of this and I hadn't realized you were a criminal type—but you're a good cook, as long as I set up the combination . . . and I just might marry you if I can trap you into proposing again."

"The offer remains open."

"Do gangsters marry their molls? Or is it 'frails'? We'll see." She left hurriedly.

Jill Boardman placed the bug without difficulty. The patient in the adjacent room in the next corridor was bedfast; Jill often stopped to gossip. She stuck it against the wall over a closet shelf while chattering about how the maids just *never* dusted high in the closets.

Removing the spool the next day and inserting a fresh one was just as easy; the patient was asleep. She woke while Jill was still perched on a chair and seemed surprised; Jill diverted her with a spicy and imaginary ward rumor.

Jill sent the exposed wire by mail, using the hospital's post office as the impersonal blindness of the postal system seemed safer than a cloak &

dagger ruse. But her attempt to insert a third fresh spool she muffed. She had waited for a time when the patient was asleep but had just mounted the chair when the patient woke up. "Oh! Hello, Miss Boardman."

Jill froze with one hand on the wire recorder. "Hello, Mrs. Fritschlie," she managed to answer. "Have a nice nap?"

"Fair," the woman answered peevishly. "My back aches."

"I'll rub it."

"Doesn't help much. Why are you always fiddling around in my closet? Is something wrong?"

Jill tried to reswallow her stomach. The woman wasn't *really* suspicious, she told herself. "Mice," she said vaguely.

" 'Mice?' Oh, I can't abide mice! I'll have to have another room, right away!"

Jill tore the little instrument off the closet wall and stuffed it into her pocket, jumped down from the chair and spoke to the patient. "Now, now, Mrs. Fritschlie—I was just looking to see if there were any mouse holes in that closet. There aren't."

"You're *sure?*"

"Quite sure. Now let's rub the back, shall we? Easy over."

Jill decided she could not plant the bug in that room again and concluded that she would risk attempting to place it in the empty room which was part of K-12, the suite of the Man from Mars. But it was almost time for her relief before she was free again. She got the pass key.

Only to find that she did not need it; the door was unlocked and held two more marines; the guard had been doubled. One of them glanced up as she opened the door. "Looking for someone?"

"No. Don't sit on the bed, boys," she said crisply. "If you need more chairs, we'll send for them." She kept her eye on the guard while he got reluctantly up; then she left, trying to conceal her trembling.

The bug was still burning a hole in her pocket when she went off duty; she decided to return it to Caxton at once. She changed clothes, shifted it to her bag, and went to the roof. Once in the air and headed toward Ben's apartment she began to breathe easier. She phoned him in flight.

"Caxton speaking."

"Jill, Ben. I want to see you. Are you alone?"

He answered slowly, "I don't think it's smart, kid. Not now."

"Ben, I've got to see you. I'm on my way over."

"Well, okay, if that's how it's got to be."

"Such enthusiasm!"

"Now look, hon, it isn't that I—"

" 'Bye!" She switched off, calmed down and decided not to take it out on poor Ben—fact was they both were playing out of their league. At least she was—she should have stuck to nursing and left politics alone.

She felt better when she saw Ben and better yet when she kissed him and snuggled into his arms. Ben was such a dear—maybe she really should marry him. But when she tried to speak he put a hand over her mouth, then whispered close against her ear, "Don't talk. No names and nothing but trivialities. I may be wired by now."

She nodded and he led her into the living room. Without speaking she got out the wire recorder and handed it to him. His eyebrows went up when he saw that she was returning not just a spool but the whole works but he made no comment. Instead he handed her a copy of the afternoon *Post.*

"Seen the paper?" he said in a natural voice. "You might like to glance at it while I wash up."

"Thanks." As she took it he pointed to a column; he then left, taking with him the recorder. Jill saw that the column was Ben's own syndicated outlet.

THE CROW'S NEST
by Ben Caxton

Everyone knows that jails and hospitals have one thing in common: they both can be very hard to get out of. In some ways a prisoner is less cut off than a patient; a prisoner can send for his lawyer, can demand a Fair Witness, he can invoke *habeas corpus* and require the jailor to show cause in open court.

But it takes only a simple NO VISITORS sign, ordered by one of the medicine men of our peculiar tribe, to consign a hospital patient to oblivion more thoroughly than ever was the Man in the Iron Mask.

To be sure, the patient's next of kin cannot be kept out by this device —but the Man from Mars seems to have no next of kin. The crew of the ill-fated *Envoy* had few ties on Earth; if the Man in the Iron Mask— pardon me; I mean the "Man from Mars"—has any relative who is guarding his interests, a few thousand inquisitive reporters (such as your present scrivener) have been unable to verify it.

Who speaks for the Man from Mars? Who ordered an armed guard placed around him? What is his dread disease that no one may catch a glimpse of him, nor ask him a question? I address *you*, Mr. Secretary General; the explanation about "physical weakness" and "gee-fatigue" won't wash; if that were the answer, a ninety-pound nurse would do as well as an armed guard.

Could this disease be financial in nature? Or (let's say it softly) is it political?

There was more, all in the same vein; Jill could see that Ben was deliberately baiting the administration, trying to force them to bring Smith out into the open. What that would accomplish she did not know, her own horizon not encompassing high politics and high finance. She felt, rather than knew, that Caxton was taking serious risk in challenging the established authorities, but she had no notion of the size of the danger, nor of what form it might take.

She thumbed through the rest of the paper. It was well loaded with follow-up stories on the return of the *Champion,* with pictures of Secretary General Douglas pinning medals on the crew, interviews with Captain van Tromp and other members of his brave company, pictures of Martians and Martian cities. There was very little about Smith, merely a medical bulletin that he was improving slowly but satisfactorily from the effects of his trip.

Ben came out and dropped some sheets of onion skin in her lap. "Here's another newspaper you might like to see," he remarked and left again.

Jill soon saw that the other "newspaper" was a transcription of what her first wire had picked up. As typed out, it was marked "First Voice," "Second Voice," and so on, but Ben had gone back and written in names wherever he had been able to make attributions later. He had written across the top: "All voices, identified or not, are masculine."

Most of the items were of no interest. They simply showed that Smith had been fed, or washed, or massaged, and that each morning and afternoon he had been required to get up and exercise under the supervision of a voice identified as "Doctor Nelson" and a second voice marked "second doctor." Jill decided that this must be Dr. Thaddeus.

But one longish passage had nothing to do with the physical care of the patient. Jill read it and reread it:

Doctor Nelson: How are you feeling, boy? Are you strong enough to talk for a while?

Smith: Yes.

Doctor Nelson: A man wants to talk to you.

Smith: (pause) Who? (Caxton had written in: All of Smith's speeches are preceded by long pauses, some longer than others.)

Nelson: This man is our great (untranscribable guttural word—Martian?). He is our oldest Old One. Will you talk with him?

Smith: (very long pause) I am great happy. The Old One will talk and I will listen and grow.

Nelson: No, no! He wants to ask you questions.

Smith: I cannot teach an Old One.

Nelson: The Old One wishes it. Will you let him ask you questions?

Smith: Yes.

(Background noises, short delay.)

Nelson: This way, sir. Uh, I have Doctor Mahmoud standing by, ready to translate for you.

Jill read "New Voice." Caxton had scratched this out and had written in: "Secretary General Douglas!!!"

Secretary General: I won't need him. You say Smith understands English.

Nelson: Well, yes and no, Your Excellency. He knows quite a number of words, but, as Mahmoud says, he doesn't have any cultural context to hang the words on. It can be rather confusing.

Secretary General: Oh, we'll get along all right, I'm sure. When I was a youngster I hitchhiked all through Brazil, without knowing a word of Portuguese when I started. Now, if you will just introduce us—then leave us alone.

Nelson: Sir? I think I had better stay with my patient.

Secretary General: Really, Doctor? I'm afraid I must insist. Sorry.

Nelson: And I am afraid that *I* must insist. Sorry, sir. Medical ethics—

Secretary General: (interrupting) As a lawyer, I know a little something of medical jurisprudence—so don't give me that "medical ethics" mumbo-jumbo, really. Did this patient select you?

Nelson: Not exactly, but—

Secretary General: Just as I thought. Has he had any opportunity to make a choice of physicians? I doubt it. His present status is that of ward of the state. I am acting as his next of kin, *de facto*—and, you will find, *de jure* as well. I wish to interview him alone.

Nelson: (long pause, then very stiffly) If you put it that way, Your Excellency, I withdraw from the case.

Secretary General: Don't take it that way, Doctor; I didn't mean to get your back hair up. I'm not questioning your treatment. But you wouldn't try to keep a mother from seeing her son alone, now would you? Are you afraid that I might hurt him?

Nelson: No, but—

Secretary General: Then what is your objection? Come now, introduce us and let's get on with it. This fussing may be upsetting your patient.

Nelson: Your Excellency, I will introduce you. Then you must select another doctor for your . . . ward.

Secretary General: I'm sorry, Doctor, I really am. I can't take that as final—we'll discuss it later. Now, if you please?

Nelson: Step over here, sir. Son, this is the man who wants to see you. Our great Old One.

Smith: (untranscribable)

Secretary General: What did he say?

Nelson: Sort of a respectful greeting. Mahmoud says it translates: "I am only an egg." More or less that, anyway. He used to use it on me. It's friendly. Son, talk man-talk.

Smith: Yes.

Nelson: And you had better use simple one-syllable words, if I may offer a last advice.

Secretary General: Oh, I will.

Nelson: Good-by, Your Excellency. Good-by, son.

Secretary General: Thanks, Doctor. See you later.

Secretary General: (continued) How do you feel?

Smith: Feel fine.

Secretary General: Good. Anything you want, just ask for it. We want you to be happy. Now I have something I want you to do for me. Can you write?

Smith: 'Write?' What is 'write?'

Secretary General: Well, your thumb print will do. I want to read a paper to you. This paper has a lot of lawyer talk, but stated simply it says that you agree that in leaving Mars you have abandoned—I mean, given up—any claims that you may have there. Understand me? You assign them in trust to the government.

Smith: (no answer)

Secretary General: Well, let's put it this way. You don't own Mars, do you?

Smith: (longish pause) I do not understand.

Secretary General: Mmm . . . let's try it this way. You want to stay here, don't you?

Smith: I do not know. I was sent by the Old Ones. (Long untranscribable speech, sounds like a bullfrog fighting a cat.)

Secretary General: Damn it, they should have taught him more English by now. See here, son, you don't have to worry about these things. Just let me have your thumb print here at the bottom of this page. Let me have your right hand. No, don't twist around that way. *Hold still!* I'm not going to hurt you . . . *Doctor!* Doctor Nelson!

Second Doctor: Yes, sir?

Secretary General: Get Doctor Nelson.

Second Doctor: Doctor Nelson? But he has left, sir. He said you took him off the case.

Secretary General: Nelson said that? *Damn* him! Well, *do* something. Give him artificial respiration. Give him a shot. Don't just stand there—can't you see the man is dying?

Second Doctor: I don't believe there is anything to be done, sir. Just let him alone until he comes out of it. That's what Doctor Nelson always did.

Secretary General: Blast Doctor Nelson!

The Secretary General's voice did not appear again, nor that of Doctor Nelson. Jill could guess, from gossip she had picked up around the hospital, that Smith had gone into one of his cataleptic withdrawals. There were only two more entries, neither of them attributed. One read: No need to whisper. He can't hear you. The other read: Take that tray away. We'll feed him when he comes out of it.

Jill was giving the transcription a third reading when Ben reappeared. He was carrying more onionskin sheets but he did not offer them to her; instead he said, "Hungry?"

She glanced inquiringly at the papers in his hand but answered, "Starved."

"Let's get out of here and shoot a cow."

He said nothing more while they went to the roof and took a taxi, and he still kept quiet during a flight to the Alexandria platform, where they switched to another cab. Ben selected one with a Baltimore serial number. Once in the air he set it for Hagerstown, Maryland, then settled back and relaxed. "Now we can talk."

"Ben, why all the mystery?"

"Sorry, pretty foots. Probably just nerves and my bad conscience. I don't *know* that there is a bug in my apartment—but if I can do it to them, they can do it to me . . . and I've been showing an unhealthy interest in things the administration wants kept doggo. Likewise, while it isn't likely that a cab signaled from my flat would have a recorder hidden in the cushions, still it might have; the Special Service squads are thorough. But this cab—" He patted its seat cushions. "They can't gimmick thousands of cabs. One picked at random should be safe."

Jill shivered. "Ben, you don't really think they would . . ." She let it trail off.

"Don't I, now! You saw my column. I filed that copy nine hours ago.

Do you think the administration will let me kick it in the stomach without doing something about it?"

"But you have always opposed this administration."

"That's okay. The duty of His Majesty's Loyal Opposition is to oppose. They expect that. But this is different; I have practically accused them of holding a political prisoner . . . one the public is very much interested in. Jill, a government is a living organism. Like every living thing its prime characteristic is a blind, unreasoned instinct to survive. You hit it, it will fight back. This time I've *really* hit it." He gave her a sidelong look. "I shouldn't have involved you in this."

"Me? I'm not afraid. At least not since I turned that gadget back over to you."

"You're associated with me. If things get rough, that could be enough."

Jill shut up. She had never in her life experienced the giant ruthlessness of giant power. Outside of her knowledge of nursing and of the joyous guerilla warfare between the sexes, Jill was almost as innocent as the Man from Mars. The notion that she, Jill Boardman, who had never experienced anything worse than a spanking as a child and an occasional harsh word as an adult, could be in physical danger was almost impossible for her to believe. As a nurse, she had seen the consequences of ruthlessness, violence, brutality—but it could not happen to *her*.

Their cab was circling for a landing in Hagerstown before she broke the moody silence. "Ben? Suppose this patient does die. What happens?"

"Huh?" He frowned. "That's a good question, a very good question. I'm glad you asked it; it shows you are taking an interest in the work. Now if there are no other questions, the class is dismissed."

"Don't try to be funny."

"Hmm . . . Jill, I've been awake nights when I should have been dreaming about you, trying to answer that one. It's a two-part question, political and financial—and here are the best answers I have now: If Smith dies, his odd legal claim to the planet Mars vanishes. Probably the pioneer group the *Champion* left behind on Mars starts a new claim—and almost certainly the administration worked out a deal with them before they left Earth. The *Champion* is a Federation ship but it is more than possible that the deal, if there was one, leaves all the strings in the hands of that redoubtable defender of human rights, Mr. Secretary General Douglas. Such a deal could keep him in power for a long time. On the other hand, it might mean nothing at all."

"Huh? Why?"

"The Larkin Decision might not apply. Luna was uninhabited, but

Mars *is* inhabited—by Martians. At the moment, Martians are a legal zero. But the High Court might take a look at the political situation, stare at its collective navel, and decide that human occupancy meant nothing on a planet already inhabited by non-human natives. Then rights on Mars, if any, would have to be secured from the Martians themselves."

"But, Ben, that would logically be the case anyhow. This notion of a single man *owning* a planet . . . it's fantastic!"

"Don't use that word to a lawyer; he won't understand you. Straining at gnats and swallowing camels is a required course in all law schools. Besides, there is a case in point. In the fifteenth century the Pope deeded the entire western hemisphere to Spain and Portugal and nobody paid the slightest attention to the fact that the real estate was already occupied by several million Indians with their own laws, customs, and notions of property rights. His grant deed was pretty effective, too. Take a look at a western hemisphere map sometime and notice where Spanish is spoken and where Portuguese is spoken—and see how much land the Indians have left."

"Yes, but— Ben, this isn't the fifteenth century."

"It is to a lawyer. They still cite Blackwell, Code Napoleon, or even the laws of Justinian. Mark it down, Jill; if the High Court rules that the Larkin Decision applies, Smith is in a position to grant or withhold concessions on Mars which may be worth millions, or more likely billions. If he assigns his claim to the present administration, then Secretary Douglas is the man who will hand out the plums. Which is just what Douglas is trying to rig. You saw that bug transcript."

"Ben, why should anybody want that sort of power?"

"Why does a moth fly toward a light? The drive for power is even less logical than the sex urge . . . and stronger. But I said this was a two-part question. Smith's financial holdings are almost as important as his special position as nominal king-emperor of Mars. Possibly more important, for a High Court decision could knock out his squatter's rights on Mars but I doubt if anything could shake his ownership of the Lyle Drive and a major chunk of Lunar Enterprises; the eight wills are a matter of public record— and in the three most important cases he inherits with or without a will. What happens if he dies? I don't know. A thousand alleged cousins would pop up, of course, but the Science Foundation has fought off a lot of such money-hungry vermin in the past twenty years. It seems possible that, if Smith dies without making a will, his enormous fortune will revert to the state."

" 'The state?' Do you mean the Federation or the United States?"

"Another very good question to which I do not know the answer. His natural parents come from two different member countries of the Federation and he was born outside all of them . . . and it is going to make a crucial difference to some people who votes those blocks of stock and who licenses those patents. It won't be Smith; he won't know a stock proxy from a traffic ticket. It is likely to be whoever can grab him and hang onto him. In the meantime I doubt if Lloyd's would write a policy on his life; he strikes me as a very poor risk."

"The poor baby! The poor, poor infant!"

vi

THE RESTAURANT IN HAGERSTOWN had "atmosphere" as well as good food, which meant that it had tables scattered not only over a lawn leading down to the edge of a little lake but also had tables in the boughs of three enormous old trees. Over all was a force field roof which kept the outdoors dining area perpetually summer even in rain and snow.

Jill wanted to eat up in the trees, but Ben ignored her and bribed the maître d'hôtel to set up a table near the water in a spot of his choice, then ordered a portable stereo tank placed by their table.

Jill was miffed. "Ben, why bother to come here and pay these prices if we can't eat in the trees and have to endure that horrible jitterbox?"

"Patience, little one. The tables up in the trees all have microphone circuits; they have to have them for service. This table is not gimmicked— I hope—as I saw the waiter take it from a stack of unused ones. As for the tank, not only is it unAmerican and probably subversive to eat without watching stereo but also the racket from it would interfere even with a directional mike aimed at us from a distance . . . assuming that Mr. Douglas's investigators are beginning to take an interest in us, which I misdoubt they are."

"Do you really think they might be shadowing us, Ben?" Jill shivered. "I don't think I'm cut out for a life of crime."

"Pish and likewise tush! When I was working on the General Synthetics bribery scandals I never slept twice in the same place and ate nothing but packaged food I had bought myself. After a while you get to like it— stimulates the metabolism."

"My metabolism doesn't need it, thank you. All I require is one elderly, wealthy private patient."

"Not going to marry me, Jill?"

"After my future husband kicks off, yes. Or maybe I'll be so rich I can afford to keep you as a pet."

"Best offer I've had in months. How about starting tonight?"

"*After* he kicks off."

During their cocktails the musical show plus lavish commercials which had been banging their eardrums from the stereo tank suddenly stopped. An announcer's head and shoulders filled the tank; he smiled sincerely and said, "NWNW, New World Networks and its sponsor of the hour, Wise Girl Malthusian Lozenges, is honored and privileged to surrender the next few minutes to a special, history-making broadcast by the Federation Government. Remember, friends, every wise girl uses Wise Girls. Easy to carry, pleasant to take, guaranteed no-fail, and approved for sale without prescription under Public Law 1312. Why take a chance on old-fashioned, unesthetic, harmful, unsure methods? Why risk losing his love and respect? Remember . . ." The lovely, lupine announcer glanced aside and hurried through the rest of his commercial: "I give you the Wise Girl, who in turn brings you the Secretary General—and the Man from Mars!"

The 3-D picture dissolved into that of a young woman, so sensuous, so unbelievably mammalian, so seductive, as to make every male who saw her unsatisfied with local talent. She stretched and wiggled and said in a bedroom voice, "*I* always use Wise Girl."

The picture dissolved and a full orchestra played the opening bars of *Hail to Sovereign Peace*. Ben said, "Do *you* use Wise Girl?"

"None o' your business!" She looked ruffled and added, "It's a quack nostrum. Anyhow, what makes you think I need it?"

Caxton did not answer; the tank had filled with the fatherly features of Mr. Secretary General Douglas. "Friends," he began, "fellow citizens of the Federation, I have tonight a unique honor and privilege. Since the triumphant return of our trail-blazing ship *Champion*—" He continued in a few thousand well-chosen words to congratulate the citizens of Earth on their successful contact with another planet, another civilized race. He managed to imply that the exploit of the *Champion* was the personal accomplishment of every citizen of the Federation, that any one of them could have led the expedition had he not been busy with other serious work—and that he, Secretary Douglas, had been chosen by them as their humble instrument to work their will. The flattering notions were never stated baldly, but implied; the underlying assumption being that the common man was the equal of anyone and better than most—and that good old Joe Douglas embodied the common man. Even his mussed cravat and cowlicked hair had a "just folks" quality.

Ben Caxton wondered who had written the speech. Jim Sanforth, probably—Jim had the most subtle touch of any member of Douglas' staff in selecting the proper loaded adjective to tickle and soothe an audience; he had written advertising commercials before he went into politics and had absolutely no compunctions. Yes, that bit about "the hand that rocks the cradle" was clearly Jim's work—Jim was the sort of jerk who would entice a young girl with candy and consider it a smart operation.

"Turn it off!" Jill said urgently.

"Huh? Shut up, pretty foots. I've got to hear this."

"—and so, friends, I have the honor to bring you now our fellow citizen Valentine Michael Smith, the Man from Mars! Mike, we all know you are tired and have not been well—but will you say a few words to your friends? They all want to see you."

The stereo scene in the tank dissolved to a semi-close-up of a man in a wheel chair. Hovering over him like a favorite uncle was Douglas and on the other side of the chair was a nurse, stiff, starched, and photogenic.

Jill gasped. Ben whispered fiercely, "Keep quiet! I don't want to miss a word of this."

The interview was not long. The smooth babyface of the man in the chair broke into a shy smile; he looked at the cameras and said, "Hello, folks. Excuse me for sitting down. I'm still weak." He seemed to speak with difficulty and once the nurse interrupted to take his pulse.

In answer to questions from Douglas he paid compliments to Captain van Tromp and the crew of the *Champion,* thanked everyone for his rescue, and said that everyone on Mars was terribly excited over contact with Earth and that he hoped to help in welding strong and friendly relations between the two planets. The nurse interrupted again, but Douglas said gently, "Mike, do you feel strong enough for just one more question?"

"Sure, Mr. Douglas—if I can answer it."

"Mike? What do you think of the girls here on Earth?"

"Gee!"

The baby face looked awestruck and ecstatic and turned pink. The scene dissolved again to the head and shoulders of the Secretary General. "Mike asked me to tell you," he went on in fatherly tones, "that he will be back to see you as soon as he can. He has to build up his muscles, you know. The gravity of Earth is as rough on him as the gravity of Jupiter would be to us. Possibly next week, if the doctors say he is strong enough." The scene shifted back to the exponents of Wise Girl lozenges and a quick one-act playlet made clear that a girl who did not use them was not only out of her mind but undoubtedly a syntho in the hay as well; men would cross the street to avoid her. Ben switched to another channel, then turned to Jill and said moodily, "Well, I can tear up tomorrow's column and look around for a new subject to plug. They not only made my today's squawk look silly but it appears that Douglas has him safely under his thumb."

"Ben!"

"Huh?"

"That's not the Man from Mars!"

"What? Baby, are you *sure?*"

"Sure I'm sure! Oh, it looked like him, it looked a great deal like him. Even the voice was similar. But it was *not* the patient I saw in that guarded room."

Ben tried to shake her conviction. He pointed out that several dozen other persons were known to have seen Smith—guards, internes, male nurses, the captain and crew members of the *Champion,* probably others. Quite a few of that list must have seen this newscast—or at least the administration would have to assume that some of them would see it and spot the substitution . . . if there had been a substitution. It did not make sense—too great a risk.

Jill did not offer logical rebuttal; she simply stuck out her lower lip and insisted that the person on stereo was not the patient she had met. Finally she said angrily, "All right, all right, have it your own way! I can't prove I'm right—so I must be wrong. Men!"

"Now, Jill . . ."

"Please take me home."

Ben silently went for a cab. He did not accept one from outside the restaurant even though he no longer thought that anyone would be taking interest in his movements; he selected one from the landing flat of a hotel across the way. Jill remained chilly on the flight back. Presently Ben got out the transcripts of the sounds picked up from Smith's hospital room and reread them. He read them still again, thought for a while, and said, "Jill?"

"Yes, Mr. Caxton?"

"I'll 'mister' you! Look, Jill, I'm sorry, I apologize. I was wrong."

"And what leads you to this momentous conclusion?"

He slapped the folded papers against his palm. "This. Smith could not possibly have been showing this behavior yesterday and the day before and then have given that interview tonight. He would have flipped his controls . . . gone into one of those trance things."

"I am gratified that you have finally seen the obvious."

"Jill, will you kindly kick me in the face a couple of times, then let up? This is serious. Do you know what this means?"

"It means they used an actor to fake an interview. I told you that an hour ago."

"Sure. An actor and a good one, carefully typed and coached. But it implies much more than that. As I see it, there are two possibilities. The first is that Smith is dead and—"

"Dead!" Jill suddenly was back in that curious water-drinking ceremony and felt the strange, warm, unworldly flavor of Smith's personality, felt it with unbearable sorrow.

"Maybe. In which case this ringer will be allowed to stay 'alive' for a week or ten days, until they have time to draw up whatever papers they want him to sign. Then the ringer will 'die' and they will ship him out of town, probably with a hypnotic injunction not to talk so strong that he would choke up with asthma if he tried to spill it—or maybe even a transorbital lobotomy if the boys are playing for keeps. But if Smith *is* dead, we can just forget it; we'll never be able to prove the truth. So let's assume that he is still alive."

"Oh, I do hope so!"

"What is Hecuba to you, or you to Hecuba?" Caxton misquoted. "If he is still alive, it could be that there is nothing especially sinister about it. After all, a lot of public figures use doubles for some of their appearances; it does not even annoy the public because every time a yokel thinks that he has spotted a double it makes him feel smart and in the know. So it may be that the administration has just yielded to public demand and given them that look at the Man from Mars we have all been yapping for. It could be that in two or three weeks our friend Smith will be in shape to stand the strain of public appearances, at which time they will trot him out. But I doubt it like hell!"

"Why?"

"Use your pretty curly head. The Honorable Joe Douglas has already made one attempt to squeeze out of Smith what he wants . . . and failed miserably. But Douglas can't afford to fail. So I think he will bury Smith deeper than ever . . . and that is the last we will ever see of the true Man from Mars."

"*Kill* him?" Jill said slowly.

"Why be rough about it? Lock him in a private nursing home and never let him learn anything. He may already have been removed from Bethesda Center."

"Oh, dear! Ben, what are we going to *do?*"

Caxton scowled and thought. "I don't have a good plan. They own both the bat and the ball and are making the rules. But what I am going to do is this: I'm going to walk into that hospital with a Fair Witness on one side and a tough lawyer on the other and demand to see Smith. Maybe I can force them to drag it out into the open."

"I'll be right behind you!"

"Like mischief you will. You stay out of this. As you pointed out, it would ruin you professionally."

"But you need me to identify him."

"Not so. I flatter myself that I can tell a man who was raised by non-humans from an actor pretending to be such a man in the course of a very short interview. But if anything goes wrong, you are my ace in the hole—a person who knows that they are pulling hanky-panky concerning the Man from Mars and who has access to the inside of Bethesda Center. Honey, if you don't hear from me, you are on your own."

"Ben, they wouldn't hurt *you?*"

"I'm fighting out of my weight, youngster. There is no telling."

"Uh . . . oh, Ben, I don't like this. Look, if you do get in to see him, what are you going to do?"

"I'm going to ask him if he wants to leave the hospital. If he says he does, I'm going to invite him to come along with me. In the presence of a Fair Witness they won't dare stop him. A hospital isn't a prison; they don't have any legal right to hold him."

"Uh . . . then what? He really does need medical attention, Ben; he's not able to take care of himself. I know."

Caxton scowled again. "I've been thinking of that. I can't nurse him. You could, of course, if you had the facilities. We could put him in my flat—"

"—and I could nurse him. We'll do it, Ben!"

"Slow down. I thought of that. Douglas would pull some legal rabbit out of his hat, a deputation in force would call, and Smith would go right back to pokey. And so would both of us, maybe." He wrinkled his brow. "But I know one man who could give him shelter and possibly get away with it."

"Who?"

"Ever heard of Jubal Harshaw?"

"Huh? Who hasn't?"

"That's one of his advantages; everybody knows who he is. It makes him hard to shove around. Being both a doctor of medicine and a lawyer he is three times as hard to shove around. But most important he is so rugged an individualist that he would fight the whole Federation Department of Security with just a potato knife if it suited his fancy—and *that* makes him eight times as hard to shove around. But the point is that I got well acquainted with him during the disaffection trials; he is a friend I can count on in a pinch. If I can get Smith out of Bethesda, I'll take him to Harshaw's place over in the Poconos—and then just let those jerks try to hide him under a rug again! Between my column and Harshaw's love for a fight we'll give 'em a bad time."

vii

DESPITE A LATE EVENING Jill was ready to relieve the night floor nurse ten minutes early the next morning. She intended to obey Ben's order to stay out of his proposed attempt to see the Man from Mars but she was determined to be close by when it happened . . . just in case. Ben might need reinforcements.

There were no longer marine guards in the corridor. Trays, medications, and two patients to be prepared for surgery kept her busy the first two hours; she had only time to check the knob of the door to suite K-12. It was locked, as was the door to the adjoining sitting room. The door to the watch room on its other side was closed. She considered sneaking in again to see Smith through the connecting sitting room, now that the guards were gone, but decided to postpone it; she was too busy. Nevertheless she managed to keep a close check on everyone who came onto her floor.

Ben did not show up and discreet questions asked of her assistant on the switchboard reassured her that neither Ben nor anyone else had gone in to see the Man from Mars while Jill was busy elsewhere. It puzzled her; while Ben had not set a time, she had had the impression that he had intended to storm the citadel as early in the day as possible.

Presently she felt that she just had to snoop a bit. During a lull she knocked at the door of the suite's watch room, then stuck her head in and pretended surprise. "Oh! Good morning, Doctor. I thought Doctor Frame was in here."

The physician at the watch desk was strange to Jill. He turned away from the displayed physio data, looked at her, then smiled as he looked her up and down. "I haven't seen Dr. Frame, Nurse. I'm Dr. Brush. Can I help?"

At the typical male reaction Jill relaxed. "Nothing special. To tell the truth I was curious. How is the Man from Mars?"

"Eh?"

She smiled and winked. "It's no secret to the staff, Doctor. Your patient—" She gestured at the inner door.

"Huh?" He looked startled. "Did they have *him* in this suite?"

"What? Isn't he here now?"

"Not by six decimal places. Mrs. Rose Bankerson—Dr. Garner's patient. We brought her in early this morning."

"Really? But what happened to the Man from Mars? Where did they put him?"

"I haven't the faintest. Say, did I really just miss seeing Valentine Smith?"

"He was here yesterday. That's all I know."

"And Dr. Frame was on his case? Some people have all the luck. Look what I'm stuck with." He switched on the Peeping Tom above his desk; Jill saw framed in it, as if she were looking down, a water bed; floating in it was a tiny old woman. She seemed to be asleep.

"What's her trouble?"

"Mmm . . . Nurse, if she didn't have more money than any person ought to have, you might be tempted to call it senile dementia. As it is, she is in for a rest and a check-up."

Jill made small talk for a few moments more, then pretended to see a call light. She went back to her desk, dug out the night log—yes, there it was: *V. M. Smith, K-12—transfer.* Below that entry was another: *Rose S. Bankerson (Mrs.)—red K-12 (diet kitchen instrd by Dr. Garner—no orders —flr nt respnbl).*

Having noted that the rich old gal was no responsibility of hers, Jill turned her mind back to Valentine Smith. Something about Mrs. Bankerson's case struck her as odd but she could not put her finger on it, so she put it out of her mind and thought about the matter that did interest her. Why had they moved Smith in the middle of the night? To avoid any possible contact with outsiders, probably. But where had they taken him? Ordinarily she would simply have called "Reception" and asked, but Ben's opinions plus the phony broadcast of the night before had made her jumpy about showing curiosity; she decided to wait until lunch and see what she could pick up on the gossip grapevine.

But first Jill went to the floor's public booth and called Ben. His office informed her that Mr. Caxton had just left town, to be gone a few days. She was startled almost speechless by this—then pulled herself together and left word for Ben to call her.

She then called his home. He was not there; she recorded the same message.

Ben Caxton had wasted no time in preparing his attempt to force his way into the presence of Valentine Michael Smith. He was lucky in being able to retain James Oliver Cavendish as his Fair Witness. While any Fair Witness would do, the prestige of Cavendish was such that a lawyer was hardly necessary—the old gentleman had testified many times before the High Court of the Federation and it was said that the wills locked up in his head represented not billions but trillions. Cavendish had received his training in total recall from the great Dr. Samuel Renshaw himself and his professional hypnotic instruction had been undergone as a fellow of the Rhine Foundation. His fee for a day or fraction thereof was more than Ben made in a week, but Ben expected to charge it off to the *Post* syndicate—in any case, the best was none too good for this job.

Caxton picked up the junior Frisby of Biddle, Frisby, Frisby, Biddle, & Reed as that law firm represented the *Post* syndicate, then the two younger men called for Witness Cavendish. The long, spare form of Mr. Cavendish, wrapped chin to ankle in the white cloak of his profession, reminded Ben of the Statue of Liberty . . . and was almost as conspicuous. Ben had already explained to Mark Frisby what he intended to try (and Frisby had already pointed out to him that he had no status and no rights) before they called for Cavendish; once in the Fair Witness's presence they conformed to protocol and did not discuss what he might be expected to see and hear.

The cab dropped them on top of Bethesda Center; they went down to the Director's office. Ben handed in his card and said that he wanted to see the Director.

An imperious female with a richly cultivated accent asked if he had an appointment. Ben admitted that he had none.

"Then I am afraid that your chance of seeing Dr. Broemer is very slight. Will you state your business?"

"Just tell him," Caxton said loudly, so that others waiting would hear, "that Caxton of the *Crow's Nest* is here with a lawyer and a Fair Witness to interview Valentine Michael Smith, the Man from Mars."

She was startled almost out of her professional hauteur. But she recovered and said frostily, "I shall inform him. Will you be seated, please?"

"Thanks, I'll wait right here."

They waited. Frisby broke out a cigar, Cavendish waited with the calm patience of one who has seen all manner of good and evil and now counts them both the same, Caxton jittered and tried to keep from biting his nails. At last the snow queen behind the desk announced, "Mr. Berquist will see you."

"Berquist? Gil Berquist?"

"I believe his name is Mr. Gilbert Berquist."

Caxton thought about it—Gil Berquist was one of Secretary Douglas's large squad of stooges, or "executive assistants." He specialized in chaperoning official visitors. "I don't want to see Berquist; I want the Director."

But Berquist was already coming out, hand shoved out before him, greeter's grin plastered on his face. "Benny Caxton! How are you, chum? Long time and so forth. Still peddling the same old line of hoke?" He glanced at the Fair Witness, but his expression admitted nothing.

Ben shook hands briefly. "Same old hoke, sure. What are you doing here, Gil?"

"If I ever manage to get out of public service I'm going to get me a column, too—nothing to do but phone in a thousand words of rumors each day and spend the rest of the day in debauchery. I envy you, Ben."

"I said, 'What are you doing here, Gil?' I want to see the Director, then get five minutes with the Man from Mars. I didn't come here for your high-level brush off."

"Now, Ben, don't take that attitude. I'm here because Dr. Broemer has been driven almost crazy by the press—so the Secretary General sent me over to take some of the load off his shoulders."

"Okay. I want to see Smith."

"Ben, old boy, don't you realize that every reporter, special correspondent, feature writer, commentator, free-lance, and sob sister wants the same thing? You winchells are just one squad in an army; if we let you all have your way, you would kill off the poor jerk in twenty-four hours. Polly Peepers was here not twenty minutes ago. She wanted to interview him on love life among the Martians." Berquist threw up both hands and looked helpless.

"I want to see Smith. Do I see him, or don't I?"

"Ben, let's find a quiet place where we can talk over a long, tall glass. You can ask me anything you want to."

"I don't want to ask you anything; I want to see Smith. By the way, this is my attorney, Mark Frisby—Biddle & Frisby." As was customary, Ben did not introduce the Fair Witness; they all pretended that he was not present.

"I've met Frisby," Berquist acknowledged. "How's your father, Mark? Sinuses still giving him fits?"

"About the same."

"This foul Washington climate. Well, come along, Ben. You, too, Mark."

"Hold it," said Caxton. "I don't want to interview you, Gil. I want to see Valentine Michael Smith. I'm here as a member of the press, directly representing the *Post* syndicate and indirectly representing over two hundred million readers. Do I see him? If I don't, say so out loud and state your legal authority for refusing me."

Berquist sighed. "Mark, will you tell this keyhole historian that he can't go busting into a sick man's bedroom just because he has a syndicated column? Valentine Smith made one public appearance just last night—against his physician's advice I might add. The man is entitled to peace and quiet and a chance to build up his strength and get oriented. That appearance last night was enough, more than enough."

"There are rumors," Caxton said carefully, "that the appearance last night was a fake."

Berquist stopped smiling. "Frisby," he said coldly, "do you want to advise your client on the law concerning slander?"

"Take it easy, Ben."

"I know the law on slander, Gil. In my business I have to. But whom am I slandering? The Man from Mars? Or somebody else? Name a name. I repeat," he went on, raising his voice, "that I have heard that the man interviewed on TV last night was not the Man from Mars. I want to see him myself and ask him."

The crowded reception hall was very quiet as everyone present bent an ear to the argument. Berquist glanced quickly at the Fair Witness, then got his expression under control and said smilingly to Caxton, "Ben, it's just possible that you talked yourself into the interview you wanted—as well as a lawsuit. Wait a moment."

He disappeared into the inner office, came back fairly soon. "I arranged it," he said wearily, "though God knows why. You don't deserve it, Ben. Come along. Just you—Mark, I'm sorry but we can't have a crowd of people; after all, Smith is a sick man."

"No," said Caxton.

"Huh?"

"All three of us, or none of us. Take your choice."

"Ben, don't be silly; you're receiving a very special privilege. Tell you what—Mark can come along and wait outside the door But you certainly don't need *him.*" Berquist glanced toward Cavendish; the Witness seemed not to hear.

"Maybe not. But I've paid his fee to have him along. My column will state tonight that the administration refused to permit a Fair Witness to see the Man from Mars."

Berquist shrugged. "Come along, then. Ben, I hope that slander suit really clobbers you."

They took the patients' elevator rather than the bounce tube out of deference to Cavendish's age, then rode a slide-away for a long distance past laboratories, therapy rooms, solaria, and ward after ward. They were stopped once by a guard who phoned ahead, then let them through; they were at last ushered into a physio-data display room used for watching critically ill patients. "This is Dr. Tanner," Berquist announced. "Doctor, this is Mr. Caxton and Mr. Frisby." He did not, of course, introduce Cavendish.

Tanner looked worried. "Gentlemen, I am doing this against my better judgment because the Director insists. I must warn you of one thing. Don't do or say *anything* that might excite my patient. He is in an extremely neurotic condition and falls very easily into a state of pathological withdrawal—a trance, if you choose to call it that."

"Epilepsy?" asked Ben.

"A layman might easily mistake it for that. It is more like catalepsy. But don't quote me; there is no clinical precedent for this case."

"Are you a specialist, Doctor? Psychiatry, maybe?"

Tanner glanced at Berquist. "Yes," he admitted.

"Where did you do your advanced work?"

Berquist said, "Look, Ben, let's see the patient and get it over with. You can quiz Dr. Tanner afterwards."

"Okay."

Tanner glanced over his dials and graphs, then flipped a switch and stared into a Peeping Tom. He left the desk, unlocked a door and led them into an adjoining bedroom, putting a finger to his lips as he did so. The other four followed him in. Caxton felt as if he were being taken to "view the remains" and suppressed a nervous need to laugh.

The room was quite gloomy. "We keep it semi-darkened because his eyes are not accustomed to our light levels," Tanner explained in a hushed voice. He turned to a hydraulic bed which filled the center of the room. "Mike, I've brought some friends to see you."

Caxton pressed closer. Floating therein, half concealed by the way his body sank into the plastic skin covering the liquid in the tank and farther concealed by a sheet up to his armpits, was a young man. He looked back at them but said nothing; his smooth, round face was expressionless.

So far as Ben could tell this was the man who had been on stereo the night before. He had a sudden sick feeling that little Jill, with the best of intentions, had tossed him a live grenade—a slander suit that might very well bankrupt him. "You are Valentine Michael Smith?"

"Yes."

"The Man from Mars?"

"Yes."

"You were on stereo last night?"

The man in the tank bed did not answer. Tanner said, "I don't think he knows the word. Let me try. Mike, you remember what you did with Mr. Douglas last night?"

The face looked petulant. "Bright lights. Hurt."

"Yes, the lights hurt your eyes. Mr. Douglas had you say hello to people."

The patient smiled slightly. "Long ride in chair."

"Okay," agreed Caxton. "I catch on. Mike, are they treating you all right here?"

"Yes."

"You don't have to stay here, you know. Can you walk?"

Tanner said hastily, "Now see here, Mr. Caxton—" Berquist put a hand on his arm and he shut up.

"I can walk . . . a little. Tired."

"I'll see that you have a wheel chair. Mike, if you don't want to stay here, I'll help you get out of bed and take you anywhere you want to go."

Tanner shook off Berquist's hand and said, "I can't have you interfering with my patient!"

"He's a free man, isn't he?" Caxton persisted. "Or is he a prisoner here?"

Berquist answered, "Of course he is a free man! Keep quiet, Doctor. Let the fool dig his own grave."

"Thanks, Gil. Thanks all to pieces. So he is free to leave if he wants to. You heard what he said, Mike. You don't have to stay here. You can go anywhere you like. I'll help you."

The patient glanced fearfully at Tanner. "No! No, no, no!"

"Okay, okay."

Tanner snapped, "Mr. Berquist, this has gone quite far enough! My patient will be upset the rest of the day."

"All right, Doctor. Ben, let's get the show on the road. You've had enough, surely."

"Uh . . . just one more question." Caxton thought hard, trying to think what he could squeeze out of it. Apparently Jill had been wrong—yet she had *not* been wrong!—or so it had seemed last night. But something did not quite fit although he could not tell what it was.

"One more question," Berquist begrudged.

"Thanks. Uh . . . Mike, last night Mr. Douglas asked you some questions." The patient watched him but made no comment. "Let's see, he asked you what you thought of the girls here on Earth, didn't he?"

The patient's face broke into a big smile. "Gee!"

"Yes. Mike . . . *when and where did you see these girls?*"

The smile vanished. The patient glanced at Tanner, then he stiffened, his eyes rolled up, and he drew himself into the foetal position, knees drawn up, head bent, and arms folded across his chest.

Tanner snapped, "Get them out of here!" He moved quickly to the tank bed and felt the patient's wrist.

Berquist said savagely, "That tears it! Caxton, will you get out? Or shall I call the guards and have you thrown out?"

"Oh, we're getting out all right," Caxton agreed. All but Tanner left the room and Berquist closed the door.

"Just one point, Gil," Caxton insisted. "You've got him boxed up in there . . . so just where *did* he see those girls?"

"Eh? Don't be silly. He's seen lots of girls. Nurses . . . laboratory technicians. You know."

"But I don't know. I understood he had nothing but male nurses and that female visitors had been rigidly excluded."

"Eh? Don't be any more preposterous than you have to be." Berquist looked annoyed, then suddenly grinned. "You saw a nurse with him on stereo just last night."

"Oh. So I did." Caxton shut up and let himself be led out.

They did not discuss it further until the three were in the air, headed for Cavendish's home. Then Frisby remarked, "Ben, I don't suppose the Secretary General will demean himself to sue you, since you did not print it. Still, if you really do have a source for that rumor you mentioned, we had better perpetuate the evidence. You don't have much of a leg to stand on, you know."

"Forget it Mark. He won't sue." Ben glowered at the floor of the cab. "How do we know that was the Man from Mars?"

"Eh? Come off it, Ben."

"How do we *know*? We saw a man about the right age in a hospital bed. We have Berquist's word for it—and Berquist got his start in politics issuing denials; his word means nothing. We saw a total stranger, supposed to be a psychiatrist . . . and when I tried to find out where he had studied psychiatry I got euchred out. How do we *know*? Mr. Cavendish, did you see or hear anything that convinced you that this bloke was the Man from Mars?"

Cavendish answered carefully, "It is not my function to form opinions. I see, I hear—that is all."

"Sorry."

"By the way, are you through with me in my professional capacity?"

"Huh? Oh, sure. Thanks, Mr. Cavendish."

"Thank *you,* sir. It was an interesting assignment." The old gentleman took off the cloak that set him apart from ordinary mortals, folded it carefully and laid it on the seat. He sighed, relaxed, and his features lost professional detachment, warmed and mellowed. He took out cigars, offered them to the others; Frisby took one and they shared a light. "I do not smoke," Cavendish remarked through a thick cloud, "while on duty. It interferes with optimum functioning of the senses."

"If I had been able to bring along a crew member of the *Champion,*" Caxton persisted, "I could have tied it down. But I thought surely I could tell."

"I must admit," remarked Cavendish, "that I was a little surprised at one thing you did not do."

"Huh? What did I miss?"

"Calluses."

"Calluses?"

"Surely. A man's life history can be told from his calluses. I once did a monograph on them, published in *The Witness Quarterly*— like Sherlock Holmes' famous monograph on tobacco ash. This young man from Mars . . . since he has never worn our sort of shoes and has lived in gravity about one third of ours, should display foot calluses consonant with his former environment. Even the time he recently spent in space should have left their traces. Very interesting."

"Damn! Good Lord, Mr. Cavendish, why didn't you suggest it to me?"

"Sir?" The old man drew himself up and his nostrils dilated. "It would not have been ethical. I am a Fair Witness, not a participant. My professional association would suspend me for much less. Surely you know that."

"Sorry. I forgot myself." Caxton frowned. "Let's wheel this buggy around and go back. We'll take a look at his feet—or I'll bust the place down with Berquist's fat head!"

"I'm afraid you will have to find another Witness . . . in view of my indiscretion in discussing it, even after the fact."

"Uh, yes, there's that." Caxton frowned.

"Better just calm down, Ben," advised Frisby. "You're in deep enough now. Personally, I'm convinced it was the Man from Mars. Occam's razor, least hypothesis, just plain horse sense."

Caxton dropped them, then set the cab to cruise while he thought. Presently he punched the combination to take him back to Bethesda Medical Center.

He was less than half way back to the Center when he realized that his trip was useless. What would happen? He would get as far as Berquist, no farther. He had been allowed in once—with a lawyer, with a Fair Witness. To demand to be allowed to see the Man from Mars a second time, all in one morning, was unreasonable and would be refused. Nor, since it was unreasonable, could he make anything effective out of it in his column.

But he had not acquired a widely syndicated column through being balked. He intended to get in.

How? Well, at least he now knew where the putative "Man from Mars" was being kept. Get in as an electrician? Or as a janitor? Too obvious; he would never get past the guard, not even as far as "Dr. Tanner."

Was "Tanner" actually a doctor? It seemed unlikely. Medical men, even the worst of them, tended to shy away from hanky-panky contrary to their professional code. Take that ship's surgeon, Nelson—he had quit, washed his hands of the case simply because—

Wait a minute! Dr. Nelson was one man who could tell offhand whether that young fellow was the Man from Mars, without checking calluses, using trick questions, or anything. Caxton reached for buttons, ordered his cab to ascend to parking level and hover, and immediately tried to phone Dr. Nelson, relaying through his office for the purpose since he neither knew where Dr. Nelson was, nor had with him the means to find out. Nor did his assistant Osbert Kilgallen know where he was, either, but he did have at hand resources to find out; it was not even necessary to draw on Caxton's large account of uncollected favors in the Enclave, as the *Post* syndicate's file on Important Persons placed him at once in the New Mayflower. A few minutes later Caxton was talking with him.

To no purpose—Dr. Nelson had not seen the broadcast. Yes, he had heard about it; no, he had no reason to think the broadcast had been faked. Did Dr. Nelson know that an attempt had been made to coerce Valentine Smith into surrendering his rights to Mars under the Larkin Decision? No, he did not know it, had no reason to believe so . . . and would not be interested if it were true; it was preposterous to talk about anyone "owning" Mars; Mars, belonged to the Martians. So? Let's propose a hypothetical question, Doctor; if someone were trying to—

But Dr. Nelson had switched off. When Caxton tried to reconnect, a recorded voice stated sweetly: "The subscriber has voluntarily suspended service temporarily. If you care to record—" Caxton switched off.

Caxton made a foolish statement concerning Dr. Nelson's parentage. But what he did next was much more foolish; he phoned the Executive Palace, demanded to speak to the Secretary General.

His action was more a reflex than a plan. In his years as a snooper, first as a reporter, then as a lippmann, he had learned that close-held secrets could often be cracked by going all the way to the top and there making himself unbearably unpleasant. He knew that such twisting of the tiger's tail was dangerous, for he understood the psychopathology of great power as thoroughly as Jill Boardman lacked knowledge of it—but he had habitually relied on his relative safety as a dealer in still another sort of power almost universally feared and appeased by the powerful.

What he forgot was, that in phoning the Palace from a taxicab, he was not doing so publicly.

Caxton was not put through to the Secretary General, nor had he expected to be. Instead he spoke with half a dozen underlings and became more aggressive with each one. He was so busy that he did not notice it when his cab ceased to hover and left the parking level.

When he did notice it, it was too late; the cab refused to obey the orders he at once punched into it. Caxton realized bitterly that he had let himself be trapped by a means no professional hoodlum would fall for: his call had been traced, his cab identified, its idiot robot pilot placed under orders of an over-riding police frequency—and the cab itself was being used to arrest him and fetch him in, all most privately and with no fuss.

He wished keenly that he had kept Fair Witness Cavendish with him. But he wasted no time on this futility but cleared the useless call from the radio and tried at once to call his lawyer, Mark Frisby.

He was still trying when the taxicab landed inside a courtyard landing flat and his signal was cut off by its walls. He then tried to leave the cab, found that the door would not open—and was hardly surprised to discover that he was becoming very light-headed and was fast losing consciousness—

viii

JILL TRIED TO TELL HERSELF that Ben had gone charging off on another scent and simply had forgotten (or had not taken time) to let her know. But she did not believe it. Ben, incredibly busy as he was, owed much of his success, both professional and social, to meticulous attention to human details. He remembered birthdays and would rather have welched on a poker debt than have forgotten to write a bread-and-butter note. No matter where he had gone, nor how urgent the errand, he could have—and *would* have!—at least taken two minutes while in the air to record a reassuring message to her at her home or at the Center. It was an unvarying characteristic of Ben, she reminded herself, the thing that made him a lovable beast in spite of his many faults.

He *must* have left word for her! She called his office again at her lunch break and spoke with Ben's researcher and office chief, Osbert Kilgallen. He assured her solemnly that Ben had left no message for her, nor had any come in since she had called earlier.

She could see past his head in the screen that there were other people in the office; she decided it was a poor time to mention the Man from Mars. "Did he say where he was going? Or when he would be back?"

"No. But that is not unusual. We always have a few spare columns on the hook to fill in when one of these things comes up."

"Well . . . where did he call you from? Or am I being too snoopy?"

"Not at all, Miss Boardman. He did not call; it was a statprint message, filed from Paoli Flat in Philadelphia as I recall."

Jill had to be satisfied with that. She lunched in the nurses' dining room and tried to interest herself in food. It wasn't, she told herself, as if anything were really wrong . . . or as if she were in love with the lunk or anything silly like that.

"Hey! Boardman! Snap out of the fog—I asked you a question."

Jill looked up to find Molly Wheelwright, the wing's dietician, looking at her. "Sorry. I was thinking about something else."

"I said, 'Since when does your floor put charity patients in luxury suites?' "

"I didn't know that we did."

"Isn't K-12 on your floor? Or have they moved you?"

"K-12? Certainly. But that's not a charity case; it's a rich old woman, so wealthy that she can pay to have a doctor watch every breath she draws."

"Humph! If she's wealthy, she must have come into money awfully suddenly. She's been in the N.P. ward of the geriatrics sanctuary for the past seventeen months."

"Must be some mistake."

"Not mine—I don't let mistakes happen in my diet kitchen. That tray is a tricky one and I check it myself—fat-free diet (she's had her gall bladder out) and a long list of sensitivities, plus concealed medication. Believe me, dear, a diet order can be as individual as a fingerprint." Miss Wheelwright stood up. "Gotta run, chicks. I wish they would let me run *this* kitchen for a while. Hogwallow Cafeteria!"

"What was Molly sounding off about?" one of the nurses asked.

"Nothing. She's just mixed up." But Jill continued to think about it. It occurred to her that she might locate the Man from Mars by making inquiries around the diet kitchens. She put the idea out of her mind; it would take a full day to visit all the diet kitchens in the acres of ground covered by the sprawling buildings. Bethesda Center had been founded as a naval hospital back in the days when wars were fought on oceans; it had been enormous even then. It had been transferred later to Health, Education, & Welfare and had expanded; now it belonged to the Federation and was still larger, a small city.

But there was something odd about Mrs. Bankerson's case. The hospital accepted all classes of patients, private, charity, and government; the floor Jill was working on usually had only government patients and its luxury suites were occupied by Federation Senators or other official guests able to command flossy service. It was unusual for a paying private patient to have a suite on her floor, or to be on her floor in any status.

Of course Mrs. Bankerson could be overflow, if the part of the Center open to the fee-paying public had no such suite available. Yes, probably that was it.

She was too rushed for a while after lunch to think about it, being busy with incoming patients. Shortly a situation came up in which she needed a powered bed. The routine action would be to phone for one to be sent up—but the storage room was in the basement a quarter of a mile away and Jill wanted the bed at once. She recalled that she had seen the powered bed which was normally in the bedroom of suite K-12 parked in the sitting room of that suite; she remembered telling one of those marine guards not to sit on it. Apparently it had simply been shoved in there to get it out of the way when the flotation bed had been installed for Smith.

Possibly it was still sitting there, gathering dust and still charged out to the floor. Powered beds were always in short supply and cost six times as much as an ordinary bed. While, strictly speaking, it was the wing superintendent's worry, Jill saw no reason to let overhead charges for her floor run up unnecessarily—and besides, if it was still there, she could get it at once. She decided to find out.

The sitting room door was still locked. She was startled to find that her pass key would not open it. Making a mental note to tell maintenance to repair the lock, she went on down the corridor to the watch room of the suite, intending to find out about the bed from the doctor watching over Mrs. Bankerson.

The physician on watch was the same one she had met before, Dr. Brush. He was not an interne nor a resident, but had been brought in for this patient, Jill had learned from him, by Dr. Garner. Brush looked up as she put her head in. "Miss Boardman! Just the person I want to see!"

"Why didn't you ring? How's your patient?"

"She's all right," he answered, glancing up at the Peeping Tom, "But I definitely am *not.*"

"Trouble?"

"Some trouble. About five minutes' worth. And my relief is not in the building. Nurse, could you spare me about that many minutes of your valuable time? And then keep your mouth shut afterwards?"

"I suppose so. I told my assistant floor supervisor I would be away for a few minutes. Let me use your phone and I'll tell her where to find me."

"No!" he said urgently. "Just lock that door after I leave and don't let anybody in until you hear me rap 'Shave and a Haircut' on it, that's a good girl."

"All right, sir," Jill said dubiously. "Am I to do anything for your patient?"

"No, no, just sit there at the desk and watch her in the screen. You won't have to do anything. Don't disturb her."

"Well, if anything does happen, where will you be? In the doctors' lounge?"

"I'm not going that far—just to the men's washroom down the corridor. Now shut up, please, and let me go—this is *urgent.*"

He left and Jill obeyed his order to lock the door after him. Then she looked at the patient through the viewer and ran her eye over the dials. The elderly woman was again asleep and the displays showed her pulse strong and her breathing even and normal; Jill wondered why Dr. Garner considered a "death watch" necessary?

Then she remembered why she had come in there in the first place and decided that she might as well find out if the bed was in the far room without bothering Dr. Brush about it. While it was not quite according to Dr. Brush's instructions, she would not be disturbing his patient—certainly she knew how to walk through a room without waking a sleeping patient!—and she had decided years ago that what doctors did not know rarely hurt them. She opened the door quietly and went in.

A quick glance assured her that Mrs. Bankerson was in the typical sleep of the senile. Walking noiselessly she went past her to the door to the sitting room. It was locked but her pass key let her in.

She was pleased to see that the powered bed was there. Then she saw that the room was occupied—sitting in an arm chair with a picture book in his lap was the Man from Mars.

Smith looked up and gave her the beaming smile of a delighted baby.

Jill felt dizzy, as if she had been jerked out of sleep. Jumbled ideas raced through her mind. Valentine Smith *here?* But he couldn't be; he had been transferred somewhere else; the log showed it. But he *was* here.

Then all the ugly implications and possibilities seemed to line themselves up . . . the fake "Man from Mars" on stereo . . . the old woman out there, ready to die, but in the meantime covering the fact that there was another patient in here . . . the door that would not open to her pass-key—and, lastly, a horrid vision of the "meat wagon" wheeling out of here some night, with a sheet concealing the fact that it carried not one cadaver, but two.

When this last nightmare rushed through her mind, it carried in its train a cold wind of fear, the realization that she herself was in peril through having stumbled onto this top-secret fact.

Smith got clumsily up from his chair, held out both hands while still smiling and said, "Water brother!"

"Hello. Uh . . . how are you?"

"I am well. I am happy." He added something in a strange, choking speech, then corrected himself and said carefully, "You are here, my brother. You were away. Now you are here. I drink deep of you."

Jill felt herself helplessly split between two emotions, one that crushed and melted her heart—and an icy fear of being caught here. Smith did not seem to notice. Instead he said, "See? I walk! I grow strong." He demonstrated by taking a few steps back and forth, then stopped, triumphant, breathless, and smiling in front of her.

She forced herself to smile. "We are making progress, aren't we? You keep growing stronger, that's the spirit! But I must go now—I just stopped in to say hello."

His expression changed instantly to distress. "Do not go!"

"Oh, but I must!"

He continued to look woebegone, then added with tragic certainty, "I have hurted you. I did not know."

"Hurt me? Oh, no, not at all! But I must go—and quickly!"

His face was without expression. He stated rather than asked, "Take me with you, my brother."

"What? Oh, I *can't.* And I *must* go, at once. Look, don't tell anyone that I was in here, please!"

"Not tell that my water brother was here?"

"Yes. Don't tell *anyone.* Uh . . . I'll try to come back, I really will. You be a good boy and wait and don't tell anyone."

Smith digested this, looked serene. "I will wait. I will not tell."

"Good!" Jill wondered how the devil she possibly could get back in to see him—she certainly couldn't depend on Dr. Brush having another convenient case of trots. She realized now that the "broken" lock had not been broken and her eye swept around to the corridor door—and she saw why she had not been able to get in. A hand bolt had been screwed to the surface of the door, making a pass key useless. As was always the case with hospitals, bathroom doors and other doors that could be bolted were so arranged as to open also by pass key, so that patients irresponsible or unruly could not lock themselves away from the nurses. But here the locked door kept Smith in . . . and the addition of a simple hand bolt of the sort not permitted in hospitals served to keep out even those with pass keys.

Jill walked over and opened the bolt. "You wait. I'll come back."

"I shall waiting."

When she got back to the watch room she heard already knocking the *Tock! Tock! Ti-tock, tock!* . . . Tock, tock! signal that Brush had said he would use; she hurried to let him in.

He burst in, saying savagely, "Where the hell were you, nurse? I knocked three times." He glanced suspiciously at the inner door.

"I saw your patient turn over in her sleep," she lied quickly. "I was in arranging her collar pillow."

"Damn it, I told you simply to sit at my desk!"

Jill knew suddenly that the man was even more frightened than she was—and with more reason. She counter-attacked. "Doctor, I did you a favor," she said coldly. "Your patient is not properly the responsibility of the floor supervisor in the first place. But since you entrusted her to me, I had to do what seemed necessary in your absence. Since you have questioned what I have done, let's get the wing superintendent and settle the matter."

"Huh? No, no—forget it."

"No, sir. I don't like to have my professional actions questioned without cause. As you know very well, a patient that old can smother in a water bed; I did what was necessary. Some nurses will take any blame from a doctor, but I am not one of them. So let's call the superintendent."

"What? Look, Miss Boardman, I'm sorry I said anything. I was upset and I popped off without thinking. I apologize."

"Very well, Doctor," Jill answered stiffly. "Is there anything more I can do for you?"

"Uh? No, thank you. Thanks for standing by for me. Just . . . well, be sure not to mention it, will you?"

"I won't mention it." You can bet your sweet life I won't mention it, Jill added silently. But what do I do now? Oh, I wish Ben were in town! She got back to her duty desk, nodded to her assistant, and pretended to look over some papers. Finally she remembered to phone for the powered bed she had been after in the first place. Then she sent her assistant to look at the patient who needed the bed (now temporarily resting in the ordinary type) and tried to think.

Where was Ben? If he were only in touch, she would take ten minutes relief, call him, and shift the worry onto his broad shoulders. But Ben, damn him, was off skyoodling somewhere and letting her carry the ball.

Or was he? A fretful suspicion that had been burrowing around in her subconscious all day finally surfaced and looked her in the eye, and this time she returned the stare: Ben Caxton would not have left town without letting her know the outcome of his attempt to see the Man from Mars. As a fellow conspirator it was her right to receive a report and Ben always played fair . . . always.

She could hear sounding in her head something he had said on the ride back from Hagerstown: *"—if anything goes wrong, you are my ace in the hole . . . honey, if you don't hear from me, you are on your own."*

She had not thought seriously about it at the time, as she had not really believed that anything could happen to Ben. Now she thought about it for a long time, while trying to continue her duties. There comes a time in the life of every human when he or she must decide to risk "his life, his fortune, and his sacred honor" on an outcome dubious. Those who fail the challenge are merely overgrown children, can never be anything else. Jill Boardman encountered her personal challenge—and accepted it—at 3:47 that afternoon while convincing a ward visitor that he simply could not bring a dog onto the floor even though he had managed to slip it past the receptionist and even if the sight of this dog was just what the patient needed.

The Man from Mars sat down again when Jill left. He did not pick up the picture book they had given him but simply waited in a fashion which may be described as "patient" only because human language does not embrace Martian emotions nor attitudes. He merely held still with quiet happiness because his brother had said that he would return. He was prepared to wait, without doing anything, without moving, for several years if necessary.

He had no clear idea how long it had been since he had first shared water with this brother; not only was this place curiously distorted in time and shape, with sequences of sights and sounds and experiences new to him and not yet grokked, but also the culture of his nest took a different grasp of time from that which is human. The difference lay not in their much longer lifetimes as counted in Earth years, but in a basically different attitude. The sentence, "It is later than you think," could not have been expressed in Martian—nor could "Haste makes waste," though for a different reason: the first notion was inconceivable while the latter was an unexpressed Martian basic, as unnecessary as telling a fish to bathe. But the quotation, "As it was in the Beginning, is now and ever shall be," was so Martian in mood that it could be translated more easily than "two plus two makes four"—which was not a truism on Mars.

Smith waited.

Brush came in and looked at him; Smith did not move and Brush went away.

When Smith heard a key in the outer door, he recalled that this sound had been one that he had heard somewhat before the last visit of his water brother, so he shifted his metabolism in preparation, in case the sequence occurred again. He was astonished when the door opened and Jill slipped in, as he had not been aware that the outer door was a door. But he grokked it at once and gave himself over to the joyful fullness which comes only in the presence of one's own nestlings, one's chosen water brothers, and (under certain circumstances) in the presence of the Old Ones.

His joy was somewhat sullied by immediate awareness that his brother did not fully share it . . . in truth, he seemed more distressed than was possible save in one about to discorporate because of some shameful lack or failure.

But Smith had already learned that these creatures, so much like himself in some ways, could endure emotions dreadful to contemplate and still not die. His Brother Mahmoud underwent a spiritual agony five times daily and not only did not die but had urged the agony on him as a needful thing. His Brother Captain van Tromp suffered terrifying spasms unpredictably, any one of which should have, by Smith's standards, produced immediate discorporation to end the conflict—yet that brother was still corporate so far as he knew.

So he ignored Jill's agitation.

Jill handed him a bundle. "Here, put these on. Hurry!"

Smith accepted the bundle and stood waiting. Jill looked at him and said, "Oh, dear! All right, get your clothes off. I'll help you."

She was forced to do more than help; she had to undress and dress him. He had been wearing a hospital gown, a bathrobe, and slippers, not because he wanted them but because he had been told to wear them. He could handle them himself by now, but not fast enough to suit Jill; she skinned him quickly. She being a nurse and he never having heard of the modesty taboo—nor would he have grasped an explanation—they were not slowed up by irrelevancies; the difficulties were purely mechanical. He was delighted and surprised by the long false skins Jill drew over his legs, but she gave him no time to cherish them, but taped the women's stockings to his thighs in lieu of a garter belt. The nurse's uniform she dressed him in was not her own, but one that she had borrowed from a larger woman on the excuse that a cousin of hers needed one for a masquerade party. Jill hooked a nurse's cape around his neck and reflected that its all-enclosing straight drape covered most of the primary and secondary sex characteristics—at least she hoped that it would. The shoes were more difficult, as they did not fit well and Smith still found standing and walking in this gravity field an effort even barefooted.

But at last she got him covered and pinned a nurse's cap on his head. "Your hair isn't very long," she said anxiously, "but it is practically as long as a lot of the girls wear it and it will have to do." Smith did not answer as he had not understood much of the remark. He tried to think his hair longer but realized that it would take time.

"Now," said Jill. "Listen carefully. No matter what happens, don't say a word. I'll do all the talking. Do you understand me?"

"Don't talk. I will not talk."

"Just come with me—I'll hold your hand. And don't say a word. But if you know any prayers, *pray!*"

"Pray?"

"Never mind. You just come along and don't talk." She opened the outer door, took a quick glance outside, then took his hand and led him out into the corridor.

No one seemed especially interested. Smith found the many strange configurations upsetting in the extreme; he was assaulted by images he could not bring into focus. He stumbled blindly along beside Jill, with his eyes and senses almost disconnected to protect himself against chaos.

She led him to the end of the corridor and stepped on a slide-away leading crosswise. He almost fell down and would have done so if Jill had not caught him. A chambermaid looked curiously at them and Jill cursed under her breath—then was very careful in helping him off. They took an elevator to the roof, Jill being quite sure that she could never pilot him up a bounce tube.

On the roof they encountered a major crisis, though Smith was not aware of it. He was undergoing the keen delight of seeing sky; he had not seen sky since the sky of Mars. This sky was bright and colorful and joyful —it being a typical overcast Washington grey day. In the meantime Jill was looking around helplessly for a taxi. The roof was almost deserted, something she had counted on, since most of the nurses who came off duty when she did were already headed home fifteen minutes ago and the afternoon visitors were gone. But the taxis were, of course, gone too. She did not dare risk an air bus, even though one which went her way would be along in a few minutes.

She was about to call a taxi when one headed in for a landing. She called to the roof attendant. "Jack! Is that cab taken? I need one."

"It's probably the one I called for Dr. Phipps."

"Oh, dear! Jack, see how quick you can get me another one, will you? This is my cousin Madge—she works over in South Wing—and she has a terrible laryngitis and I want to get her out of this wind."

The attendant looked dubiously toward the phone in his booth and scratched his head. "Well . . . seeing it's you, Miss Boardman, I'll let you take this one and call another one for Dr. Phipps. How's that?"

"Oh, Jack, you're a lamb! No, Madge, don't try to talk; I'll thank him. Her voice is gone completely; I'm going to take her home and bake it out with hot rum."

"That ought to do it. Old-fashioned remedies are always best, my mother used to say." He reached into the cab and punched the combination for Jill's home from memory, then helped them in. Jill managed to get in the way and thereby cover up Smith's unfamiliarity with this common ceremonial. "Thanks, Jack. Thanks loads."

The cab took off and Jill took her first deep breath. "You can talk now."

"What should I say?"

"Huh? Nothing. Anything. Whatever you like."

Smith thought this over. The scope of the invitation obviously called for a worthy answer, suitable to brothers. He thought of several, discarded them because he did not know how to translate them, then settled on one which he thought he could translate fairly well but which nevertheless conveyed even in this strange, flat speech some of the warm growing-closer brothers should enjoy. "Let our eggs share the same nest."

Jill looked startled. "Huh? What did you say?"

Smith felt distressed at the failure to respond in kind and interpreted it as failure on his own part. He realized miserably that, time after time, he had managed to bring agitation to these other creatures when his purpose had been to create oneness. He tried again, rearranging his sparse vocabulary to enfold the thought somewhat differently. "My nest is yours and your nest is mine."

This time Jill managed to smile. "Why, how sweet! My dear, I am not sure that I understand you, but if I do, that is the nicest offer I have had in a long time." She added, "But right now we are up to our ears in trouble— so let's wait a while, shall we?"

Smith had understood Jill hardly more than Jill had understood him, but he caught his water brother's pleased mood and understood the suggestion to wait. Waiting was something he did without effort, so he sat back, satisfied that all was well between himself and his brother, and enjoyed the scenery. It was the first time he had seen this place from the air and on every side there was a richness of new things to try to grok. It occurred to him that the apportation used at home did not permit this delightful viewing of what lay between. This thought almost led him to a comparison of Martian and human methods not favorable to the Old Ones, but his mind automatically shied away from heresy.

Jill kept quiet, too, and tried to get her thoughts straight. Suddenly she realized that the cab was heading down the final traffic leg toward the apartment house where she lived—and she realized just as quickly that home was the last place for her to go, it being the first place they would look once they figured out how Smith had escaped and who had helped him. She did not kid herself that she had covered her tracks. While she knew nothing of police methods, she supposed that she must have left fingerprints in Smith's room, not to mention the people who had seen them walk out. It was even possible (so she had heard) for a technician to read the tape in this cab's pilot and tell exactly what trips it had made that day and where and when.

She reached forward, slapped the order keys, and cleared the instruction to go to her apartment house. She did not know whether that would wipe the tape or not—but she was not going to head for a place where the police might already be waiting.

The cab checked its forward motion, rose out of the traffic lane and hovered. Where could she go? Where in all this swarming city could she hide a grown man who was half idiot and could not even dress himself?—a man who was the most sought-after person on the globe? Oh, if Ben were only here! Ben . . . *where are you?*

She reached forward again, picked up the phone and rather hopelessly punched Ben's number, expecting to hear the detached voice of an automation inviting her to record a message. Her spirits jumped when a man's voice answered . . . then slumped again when she realized that it was not Ben but his majordomo, Osbert Kilgallen. "Oh. Sorry, Mr. Kilgallen. This is Jill Boardman. I thought I had called Mr. Caxton's home."

"You did. But I always have his home calls relayed to the office when he is away more than twenty-four hours."

"Then he is still away?"

"I'm afraid so. Is there anything I can do for you?"

"Uh, no. Look, Mr. Kilgallen, isn't it strange that Ben should just drop out of sight? Aren't you worried about him?"

"Eh? Why should I be? His message said that he did not know how long he would be away."

"Isn't that rather odd in itself?"

"Not in Mr. Caxton's work, Miss Boardman."

"Well . . . I think there is something *very* odd about his being away this time! I think you ought to report it. You ought to spread it over every news service in the country—in the world!"

Even though the cab's phone had no vision circuit Jill felt Osbert Kilgallen draw himself up. "I'm afraid, Miss Boardman, that I will have to interpret my employer's instructions myself. Uh . . . if you don't mind my saying so, there is always some . . . 'good friend' phoning Mr. Caxton frantically every time he leaves town."

Some babe trying to get a hammer lock on him, Jill interpreted angrily—and this Osbert character thinks I'm the current one. It put out of her mind the half-formed thought of asking Kilgallen for help; she switched off as quickly as possible.

But where could she go? The obvious solution popped into her mind. If Ben was missing—and the authorities had a hand in it—the last place they would be likely to look for Valentine Smith would be Ben's apartment. Unless, she corrected, they connected her with Ben, which she did not think that they did.

They could dig a bite to eat out of Ben's buttery—she wouldn't risk ordering anything from the basement; they might know he was away. And she could borrow some of Ben's clothes for her idiot child. The last point settled it; she set the combination for Ben's apartment house. The cab picked out the new lane and dropped into it.

Once outside the door to Ben's flat Jill put her face to the hush box by the door and said emphatically, "Karthago delenda est!"

Nothing happened. Oh *damn* him! she said frantically to herself; he's changed the combo. She stood there for a moment, knees weak, and kept her face away from Smith. Then she again spoke into the hush box. It was a Raytheon lock, the same voice circuit actuated the door or announced callers. She announced herself on the forlorn chance that Ben might have returned. "Ben, this is Jill."

The door slid open.

They went inside and the door closed. Jill thought for an instant that Ben had let them in, then she realized that she had accidentally hit on his new door combination . . . intended, she guessed, as a gracious compliment combined with a wolf tactic. She felt that she could have dispensed with the compliment to have avoided the awful panic she had felt when the door had refused to open.

Smith stood quietly at the edge of the thick green lawn and looked at the room. It again was a place so new to him as not to be grokked at once, but he felt immediately pleased with it. It was less exciting than the moving place they had just been in, but in many ways more suited for enfolding together the self. He looked with interest at the view window at one end but did not recognize it as a window, mistaking it for a living picture like those he had been used to at home . . . the suite he had been in at Bethesda contained no windows, it being in one of the newer wings, and thus far he had never acquired the idea of "window."

He noticed with approval that the simulation of depth and movement in the "picture" was perfect—some very great artist among these people must have created it. Up until this time he had seen nothing to cause him to think that these people possessed art; his grokking of them was increased by this new experience and he felt warmed.

A movement caught his eye; he turned to find his brother removing the false skins as well as the slippers from its legs.

Jill sighed and wiggled her toes in the grass. "Gosh, how my feet do hurt!" She glanced up and saw Smith watching her with that curiously disturbing baby-faced stare. "Do it yourself if you want to. You'll love it."

He blinked. "How do?"

"I keep forgetting. Come here, I'll help you." She got his shoes off, untaped the stockings and peeled them off. "There, doesn't that feel good?"

Smith wiggled his toes in the cool grass, then said timidly, "But these live?"

"Sure, they're alive. It's real live grass. Ben paid a lot to have it that way. Why, the special lighting circuits alone cost more than I make in a month. So walk around and let your feet enjoy it."

Smith missed much of the speech but he did understand that the grass was made up of living beings and that he was being invited to walk on them. "Walk on living things?" he asked with incredulous horror.

"Huh? Why not? It doesn't hurt this grass; it was specially developed for house rugs."

Smith was forced to remind himself that a water brother could not lead him into wrongful action. Apprehensively he let himself be encouraged to walk around—and found that he did enjoy it and that the living creatures did not protest. He set his sensitivity for such things as high as possible; his brother was right, this was their proper being—to be walked on. He resolved to enfold it and praise it; the effort was much like that of a human trying to appreciate the merits of cannibalism—a custom which Smith found perfectly proper.

Jill let out a sigh. "Well, I had better stop playing. I don't know how long we will be safe here."

"Safe?"

"We can't stay here, not very long. They may be checking on every conveyance that left the Center this very minute." She frowned and thought. Her place would not do, this place would not do—and Ben had intended to take him to Jubal Harshaw. But she did not know Harshaw; she was not even sure where he lived—somewhere in the Poconos, Ben had said. Well, she would just have to try to find out where he lived and call him. It was Hobson's choice; she had nowhere else to turn.

"Why are you not happy, my brother?"

Jill snapped out of her mood and looked at Smith. Why, the poor infant didn't even know anything was wrong! She made a real effort to look at it from his point of view. She failed, but she did grasp that he had no notion that they were running away from . . . from what? The cops? The hospital authorities? She was not sure quite what she had done, or what laws she had broken; she simply knew that she had pitted her own puny self against the combined will of the Big People, the Bosses, the ones who made decisions.

But how could she tell the Man from Mars what they were up against when she did not understand it herself? Did they have policemen on Mars? Half the time she found talking to him like shouting down a rain barrel. Heavens, did they even have rain barrels on Mars? Or rain?

"Never you mind," she said soberly. "You just do what I tell you to do."

"Yes."

It was an unmodified, unlimited acceptance, an eternal yea. Jill suddenly had the feeling that Smith would unhesitatingly jump out the window if she told him to—in which belief she was correct; he would have jumped, enjoyed every scant second of the twenty-storey drop, and accepted without surprise or resentment the discorporation on impact. Nor would he have been unaware that such a fall would kill him; fear of death was an idea utterly beyond him. If a water brother selected for him such a strange discorporation, he would cherish it and try to grok.

"Well, we can't stand here pampering our feet. I've got to feed us, I've got to get you into different clothes, and we've got to leave. Take those off." She left to check Ben's wardrobe.

She selected for him an inconspicuous travel suit, a beret, shirt, underclothes, and shoes, then returned. Smith was as snarled as a kitten in knitting; he had tried to obey but now had one arm prisoned by the nurse's uniform and his face wrapped in the skirt. He had not even removed the cape before trying to take off the dress.

Jill said, "Oh, dear!" and ran to help him.

She got him loose from the clothes, looked at them, then decided to stuff them down the oubliette . . . she could pay Etta Schere for the loss of them later and she did not want cops finding them here—just in case. "But you are going to have to have a bath, my good man, before I dress you in Ben's clean clothes. They've been neglecting you. Come along." Being a nurse, she was inured to bad odors, but (being a nurse) she was fanatic about soap and water . . . and it seemed to her that no one had bothered to bathe this patient recently. While Smith did not exactly stink, he did remind her of a horse on a hot day. Soap suds were indicated.

He watched her fill the tub with delight. There had been a tub in the bathroom of the suite he had been in but Smith had not known it was used to hold water; bed baths were all that he had had and not many of those; his trancelike withdrawals had interfered.

Jill tested the water's temperature. "All right, climb in."

Smith did not move. Instead he looked puzzled.

"Hurry!" Jill said sharply. "Get in the water."

The words she used were firmly parts of his human vocabulary and Smith did as she ordered, emotion shaking him. This brother wanted him to place his whole body in the water of life. No such honor had ever come to him; to the best of his knowledge and belief no one had ever before been offered such a holy privilege. Yet he had begun to understand that these others did have greater acquaintance with the stuff of life . . . a fact not yet grokked but which he had to accept.

He placed one trembling foot in the water, then the other . . . and slipped slowly down into the tub until the water covered him completely.

"Hey!" yelled Jill, and reached in and dragged his head and shoulders above water—then was shocked to find that she seemed to be handling a corpse. Good Lord! he couldn't *drown,* not in that time. But it frightened her and she shook him. "Smith! Wake up! Snap out of it."

Smith heard his brother call from far away and returned. His eyes ceased to be glazed, his heart speeded up and he resumed breathing. "Are you all right?" Jill demanded.

"I am all right. I am very happy . . . my brother."

"You sure scared me. Look, don't get under the water again. Just sit up, the way you are now."

"Yes, my brother." Smith added several words in a curious croaking meaningless to Jill, cupped a handful of water as if it were precious jewels and raised it to his lips. His mouth touched it, then he offered the handful to Jill.

"Hey, don't drink your bath water! No, I don't want it, either."

"Not drink?"

His look of defenseless hurt was such that Jill again did not know what to do. She hesitated, then bent her head and barely touched her lips to the offering. "Thank you."

"May you never thirst!"

"I hope you are never thirsty, too. But that's enough. If you want a drink of water, I'll get you one. But don't drink any more of this water."

Smith seemed satisfied and sat quietly. By now Jill was convinced that he had never taken a tub bath before and did not know what was expected of him. She considered the problem. No doubt she could coach him . . . but they were already losing precious time. Maybe she should have let him go dirty.

Oh, well! It was not as bad as tending a disturbed patient in an N.P. ward. She had already got her blouse wet almost to the shoulders in dragging Smith off the bottom; she took it off and hung it up. She had been dressed for the street when she had crushed Smith out of the Center and was wearing a little, pleated pediskirt that floated around her knees. Her jacket she had dropped in the living room. She glanced down at the skirt.

Although the pleats were guaranteed permanized, it was silly to get it wet. She shrugged and zipped it off; it left her in brassiere and panties.

Jill looked at Smith. He was staring at her with the innocent, interested eyes of a baby. She found herself blushing, which surprised her, as she had not known that she could. She believed herself to be free of morbid modesty and had no objection to nudity at proper times and places—she recalled suddenly that she had gone on her first bareskin swimming party at fifteen. But this childlike stare from a grown man bothered her; she decided to put up with clammily wet underwear rather than do the obvious, logical thing.

She covered her discomposure with heartiness. "Let's get busy now and scrub the hide." She dropped to her knees beside the tub, sprayed soap on him, and started working it into a lather.

Presently Smith reached out and touched her right mammary gland. Jill drew back hastily, almost dropping the sprayer. "Hey! None of that stuff!"

He looked as if she had slapped him. "Not?" he said tragically.

" 'Not,' " she agreed firmly. She looked at his face and added softly. "It's all right. Just don't distract me with things like that when I'm busy."

He took no more inadvertent liberties and Jill cut the bath short, letting the water drain and having him stand up while she showered the soap off him. Then she dressed with a feeling of relief while the blast dried him. The warm air startled him at first and he began to tremble, but she told him not to be afraid and had him hold onto the grab rail back of the tub while he dried and she dressed.

She helped him out of the tub. "There, you smell a lot better and I'll bet you feel better."

"Feel fine."

"Good. Let's get some clothes on you." She led him into Ben's bedroom where she had left the clothes she had selected. But before she could even explain, demonstrate, or assist in getting shorts on him, she was shocked almost out of the shoes she had not yet put back on.

"OPEN UP IN THERE!"

Jill dropped the shorts. She was frightened nearly out of her senses, feeling the same panic she felt when a patient's respiration stopped and blood pressure dropped in the middle of surgery. But the discipline she had learned in operating theater came to her aid. Did they actually know anyone was inside? Yes, they must know—else they would never have come here. That damned robo-cab must have given her away.

Well, should she answer? Or play 'possum?

The shout over the announcing circuit was repeated. She whispered to

Smith, *"Stay here!"* then went into the living room. "Who is it?" she called out, striving to keep her voice normal.

"Open in the name of the law!"

"Open in the name of what law? Don't be silly. Tell me who you are and what you want before I call the police."

"We *are* the police. Are you Gillian Boardman?"

"Me? Of course not. I'm Phyllis O'Toole and I'm waiting for Mr. Caxton to come home. Now you had better go away, because I'm going to call the police and report an invasion of privacy."

"Miss Boardman, we have a warrant for your arrest. Open up at once or it will go hard with you."

"I'm not your 'Miss Boardman' and I'm calling the police!"

The voice did not answer. Jill waited, swallowing. Shortly she felt radiant heat against her face. A small area around the door's lock began to glow red, then white; something crunched and the door slid open. Two men were there; one of them stepped in, grinned at Jill and said, "That's the babe, all right. Johnson, look around and find him."

"Okay, Mr. Berquist."

Jill tried to make a road block of herself. The man called Johnson, twice her mass, put a hand on her shoulder, brushed her aside and went on back toward the bedroom. Jill said shrilly, "Where's your warrant? Let's see your credentials—this is an outrage!"

Berquist said soothingly, "Don't be difficult, sweetheart. We don't really want you; we just want *him.* Behave yourself and they might go easy on you."

She kicked at his shin. He stepped back nimbly, which was just as well, as Jill was still barefooted. "Naughty, naughty," he chided. "Johnson! You find him?"

"He's here, Mr. Berquist. And naked as an oyster. Three guesses what they were up to."

"Never mind that. Bring him here."

Johnson reappeared, shoving Smith ahead of him, controlling him by twisting one arm behind his back. "He didn't want to come."

"He'll come, he'll come!"

Jill ducked past Berquist, threw herself at Johnson. With his free hand he slapped her aside. "None of that, you little slut!"

Johnson should not have slapped her. He had not hit her hard, not even as hard as he used to hit his wife before she went home to her parents, and not nearly as hard as he had often hit prisoners who were reluctant to talk. Up to this time Smith had shown no expression at all and had said nothing; he had simply let himself be forced into the room with the passive, futile resistance of a puppy who does not want to be walked on a leash. But he had understood nothing of what was happening and had tried to do nothing at all.

When he saw his water brother struck by this other, he twisted and ducked, got free—and reached in an odd fashion for Johnson.

Johnson was not there any longer.

He was not anywhere. The room did not contain him. Only blades of grass, straightening up where his big feet had been, showed that he had ever been there. Jill stared through the space he had occupied and felt that she might faint.

Berquist closed his mouth, opened it again, said hoarsely, "What did you do with him?" He looked at Jill rather than Smith.

"Me? I didn't do *anything.*"

"Don't give me that. What's the trick? You got a trap door or something?"

"Where did he *go?*"

Berquist licked his lips. "I don't know." He took a gun from under his coat. "But don't try any of your tricks with me. You stay here—I'm taking him along."

Smith had relapsed into his attitude of passive waiting. Not understanding what it was all about, he had done only the minimum he had to do. But guns he had seen before, in the hands of men on Mars, and the expression on Jill's face at having one aimed at her he did not like. He grokked that this was one of the critical cusps in the growth of a being wherein contemplation must bring forth right action in order to permit further growth. He acted.

The Old Ones taught him well. He stepped toward Berquist; the gun swung to cover him. Nevertheless he reached out—and Berquist was no longer there. Smith turned to look at his brother.

Jill put a hand to her mouth and screamed.

Smith's face had been completely blank. Now it became tragically forlorn as he realized that he must have chosen wrong action at the cusp. He looked imploringly at Jill and began to tremble. His eyes rolled up; he slipped slowly down to the grass, pulled himself tightly into a foetal ball and was motionless.

Jill's own hysteria cut off as if she had thrown a switch. The change was an indoctrinated reflex: here was a patient who needed her; she had no time for her own emotions, no time even to worry or wonder about the two men who had disappeared. She dropped to her knees and examined Smith.

She could not detect respiration, nor could she find a pulse; she pressed an ear against his ribs. She thought at first that heart action had stopped completely, but, after a long time, she heard a lazy *lub-dub,* followed in four or five seconds by another.

The condition reminded her of schizoid withdrawal, but she had never seen a trance so deep, not even in class demonstrations of hypnoanesthesia. She had heard of such deathlike states among East Indian fakirs but she had never really believed the reports.

Ordinarily she would not have tried to rouse a patient in such a state but would have sent for a doctor at once. But these were not ordinary circumstances. Far from shaking her resolve, the events of the past few minutes had made her more determined than ever not to let Smith fall back into the hands of the authorities. But ten minutes of trying everything she knew convinced her that she could not rouse this patient with means at hand without injuring him—and perhaps not even then. Even the sensitive, exposed nerve in the elbow gave no response.

In Ben's bedroom she found a battered flight case, almost too big to be considered hand luggage, too small to be a trunk. She opened it, found it packed with voicewriter, toilet kit, a complete outfit of male clothing, and everything else that a busy reporter might need if called out of town suddenly—even to a licensed audio link to permit him to patch into phone service wherever he might be. Jill reflected that the presence of this packed bag alone tended strongly to prove that Ben's absence was not what Kilgallen thought it was, but she wasted no time thinking about it; she simply emptied the bag and dragged it into the living room.

Smith outweighed her, but muscles acquired handling patients twice her size enabled her to dump him into the big bag. Then she had to refold him somewhat to allow her to close it. His muscles resisted force, but under gentle pressure steadily applied he could be repositioned like putty. She padded the corners with some of Ben's clothes before she closed him up. She tried to punch some air holes but the bag was a glass laminate, tough as an absentee landlord's heart. She decided that he could not suffocate quickly with his respiration so minimal and his metabolic rate down as low as it must be.

She could barely lift the packed bag, straining as hard as she could with both hands, and she could not possibly carry it any distance. But the bag was equipped with "Red Cap" casters. They cut two ugly scars in Ben's grass rug before she got it to the smooth parquet of the little entrance way.

She did not go to the lobby on the roof, since another air cab was the last thing she wanted to risk, but went out instead by the service door in the basement. There was no one there but a young man who was checking an incoming kitchen delivery. He moved slowly aside and let her roll the bag out onto the pavement. "Hi, sister. What you got in the kiester?"

"A body," she snapped.

He shrugged. "Ask a jerky question, get a jerky answer. I should learn."

part two

HIS PREPOSTEROUS HERITAGE

ix

THE THIRD PLANET OUT from Sol was in its normal condition. It had on it 230,000 more human souls today than yesterday, but, among the five billion terrestrials such a minute increase was not noticeable. The Kingdom of South Africa, Federation associate member, had again been cited before the High Court for persecution of its white minority. The lords of women's fashions, gathered in solemn conclave in Rio, had decreed that hem lines would go down and that navels would again be covered. The three Federation defense stations swung silently in the sky, promising instant death to any who disturbed the planet's peace. Commercial space stations swung not so silently, disturbing the planet's peace with endless clamor of the virtues of endless trademarked trade goods. Half a million more mobile homes had set down on the shores of Hudson Bay than had migrated by the same date last year, the Chinese rice belt had been declared an emergency malnutrition area by the Federation Assembly, and Cynthia Duchess, known as the Richest Girl in the World, had dismissed and paid off her sixth husband. All was normal.

The Reverend Doctor Daniel Digby, Supreme Bishop of the Church of the New Revelation (Fosterite) had announced that he had nominated the Angel Azreel to guide Federation Senator Thomas Boone and that he expected Heavenly confirmation of his choice some time today; all the news services carried the announcement as straight news, the Fosterites having wrecked too many newspaper offices in the past. Mr. and Mrs. Harrison Campbell VI had a son and heir by host-mother at Cincinnati

Children's Hospital while the happy parents were vacationing in Peru. Dr. Horace Quackenbush, Professor of Leisure Arts at Yale Divinity School, issued a stirring call for a return to faith and a cultivation of spiritual values; there was a betting scandal involving half the permanent professionals of the West Point football squad and its line coach; three bacterial warfare chemists were suspended at Toronto for presumption of emotional instability—all three announced that they would carry their cases, if necessary, to the Federation High Court. The High Court upset a ruling of the Supreme Court of the United States in re eligibility to vote in primaries involving Federation Assemblymen in the case of *Reinsberg vs. the State of Missouri.*

His Excellency, the Most Honorable Joseph E. Douglas, Secretary General of the World Federation of Free States, picked at his breakfast omelet and wondered peevishly why a man could not get a decent cup of coffee these days. In front of him his morning newspaper, prepared by the night shift of his information staff, moved past his eyes at his optimum reading speed in a feedback executive scanner, custom-built by Sperry. The words would flow on as long as he looked in that direction; if he turned his head, the machine would note it and stop instantly.

He was looking that way now and the projected print moved along the screen, but he was not really reading but simply avoiding the eyes of his boss across the table. Mrs. Douglas did not read newspapers; she had other ways of finding out what she needed to know.

"Joseph—"

He looked up and the machine stopped. "Yes, my dear?"

"You have something on your mind."

"Eh? What makes you say that, my dear?"

"Joseph! I haven't watched you and coddled you and darned your socks and kept you out of trouble for thirty-five years for nothing. I know when there is something on your mind."

The hell of it is, he admitted to himself, she *does* know. He looked at her and wondered why he had ever let her bully him into no-termination contract. Originally she had been only his secretary, back in the days (he thought of them as "The Good Old Days") when he had been a state legislator, beating the bushes for individual votes. Their first contract had been a simple ninety-day cohabitation agreement, supposedly to economize scarce campaign funds by saving on hotel bills; both of them had agreed that it was merely a convenience, with "cohabitation" to be construed simply as living under one roof . . . and she hadn't darned his socks even then!

He tried to remember how and when the situation had changed. Mrs.

Douglas's official biography *Shadow of Greatness: One Woman's Story* stated that he had proposed to her during the counting of ballots in his first election to office—and that such was his romantic need that nothing would do but old-fashioned, death-do-us-part marriage.

Well, he didn't remember it that way—but there was no use arguing with the official version.

"Joseph! Answer me!"

"Eh? Nothing at all, my dear. I spent a restless night."

"I know you did. When they wake you up in the middle of the night, don't you think I know it?"

He reflected that her suite was a good fifty yards across the palace from his. "How do you know it, my dear?"

"Hunh? Woman's intuition, of course. What was the message Bradley brought you?"

"Please, my dear—I've got to finish the morning news before the Council meeting."

"Joseph Edgerton Douglas, don't try to evade me."

He sighed. "The fact is, we've lost sight of that beggar Smith."

"Smith? Do you mean the Man from Mars? What do you mean: '—lost sight of—?' That's ridiculous."

"Be that as it may, my dear, he's gone. He disappeared from his hospital room sometime late yesterday."

"Preposterous! How could he do that?"

"Disguised as a nurse, apparently. We aren't sure."

"But— Never mind. He's gone, that's the main thing. What muddle-headed scheme are you using to get him back?"

"Well, we have some of our own people searching for him. Trusted ones, of course. Berquist—"

"Berquist! *That* garbage head! When you should have every police officer from the FDS down to precinct truant officers searching for him you send Berquist!"

"But, my dear, you don't see the situation. We *can't*. Officially he isn't lost at all. You see there's—well, the *other* chap. The, uh, 'official' Man from Mars."

"*Oh . . .*" She drummed the table. "I told you that substitution scheme would get us in trouble."

"But, my dear, you suggested it yourself."

"I did not. And don't contradict me. Mmm . . . send for Berquist. I must talk to him at once."

"Uh, Berquist is out on his trail. He hasn't reported back yet."

"Uh? Berquist is probably half way to Zanzibar by now. He's sold us out. I never did trust that man. I told you when you hired him that—"

"When *I* hired him?"

"Don't interrupt. —that any man who would take money two ways would take it three ways just as quickly." She frowned. "Joseph, the Eastern Coalition is behind this. It's a logical certainty. You can expect a vote-of-confidence move in the Assembly before the day is out."

"Eh? I don't see why. Nobody knows about it."

"Oh, for Heaven's sake! Everyone will know about it; the Eastern Coalition will see to that. Now keep quiet and let me think."

Douglas shut up and went back to his newspaper. He read that the Los Angeles City-County Council had voted to petition the Federation for aid in their smog problem, on the grounds the Ministry of Health had failed to provide something or other, it did not matter what—but a sop must be thrown to them as Charlie was going to have a difficult time being re-elected with the Fosterites running their own candidate—he needed Charlie. Lunar Enterprises was off two points at closing, probably, he decided, because of—

"Joseph."

"Yes, my dear?"

"Our own 'Man from Mars' is the one and only; the one the Eastern Coalition will pop up with is a fake. That is how it must be."

"But, my dear, we can't make it stick."

"What do you mean, we can't? We're stuck with it, so we've *got* to make it stick."

"But we *can't*. Scientists would spot the substitution at once. I've had the devil's own time keeping them away from him this long."

"Scientists!"

"But they can, you know."

"I don't know anything of the sort. Scientists indeed! Half guess work and half sheer superstition. They ought to be locked up; they ought to be prohibited by law. Joseph, I've told you repeatedly, the only true science is astrology."

"Well, I don't know, my dear. Mind you, I'm not running down astrology—"

"You'd better not! After all it's done for *you.*"

"—but I am saying that some of these science professors are pretty sharp. One of them was telling me the other day that there is a star that weighs six thousand times as much as lead. Or was it sixty thousand? Let me see—"

"Bosh! How could they possibly know a thing like that? Keep quiet,

Joseph, while I finish this. We admit nothing. Their man is a fake. But in the meantime we make full use of our Special Service squads and grab him back, if possible, before the Eastern Coalition makes its disclosure. If it is necessary to use strong measures and this Smith person gets shot resisting arrest, or something like that, well, it's too bad, but I for one won't mourn very long. He's been a nuisance all along."

"Agnes! Do you know what you are suggesting?"

"I'm not suggesting anything. People get hurt every day. This matter must be cleared up, Joseph, for everybody. The greatest good of the greatest number, as you are so fond of quoting."

"But I don't want to see the lad hurt."

"Who said anything about hurting him? But you must take firm steps, Joseph; it's your duty. History will justify you. Which is more important? —to keep things running on an even keel for five billion people, or to go soft and sentimental about one man who isn't even properly a citizen?"

Douglas didn't answer. Mrs. Douglas stood up. "Well, I can't waste the rest of the morning arguing intangibles with you, Joseph; I've got to get hold of Madame Vesant at once and have a new horoscope cast for this emergency. But I can tell you this: I didn't give the best years of my life putting you where you are today just to have you throw it away through lack of backbone. Wipe the egg off your chin." She turned and left.

The chief executive of the planet remained at the table through two more cups of coffee before he felt up to going to the Council Chamber. Poor old Agnes! So ambitious. He guessed he had been quite a disappointment to her . . . and no doubt the change of life wasn't making things any easier for her. Well, at least she was loyal, right to her toes . . . and we all have our shortcomings; she was probably as sick of him as he—no point in that!

He straightened up. One damn sure thing!—he wasn't going to let them be rough with that Smith lad. He was a nuisance, granted, but he was a nice lad and rather appealing in a helpless, half-witted way. Agnes should have seen how easily he was frightened, then she wouldn't talk that way. Smith would appeal to the maternal in her.

But as a matter of strict fact, did Agnes have any "maternal" in her? When she set her mouth that way, it was hard to see it. Oh shucks, all women had maternal instincts; science had proved that. Well, hadn't they?

Anyhow, damn her guts, he wasn't going to let her push him around. She kept reminding him that she had put him into the top spot, but he knew better . . . and the responsibility was his and his alone. He got up, squared his shoulders, pulled in part of his middle, and went to the Council Chamber.

All during the long session he kept expecting someone to drop the other shoe. But no one did and no aide came in with any message for him. He was forced to conclude that the fact that Smith was missing actually was close held in his own personal staff, unlikely as that seemed.

The Secretary General wanted very badly to close his eyes and hope that the whole horrid mess would go away, but events would not let him. Nor would his wife let him.

Agnes Douglas' personal saint, by choice, was Evita Peron, whom she fancied she resembled. Her own *persona*, the mask that she held out to the world, was that of helper and satellite to the great man she was privileged to call husband. She even held this mask up to herself, for she had the Red Queen's convenient ability to believe anything she wished to believe. Nevertheless, her own political philosophy could have been stated baldly (which it never was) as a belief that men should rule the world and women should rule men.

That all of her beliefs and actions derived from a blind anger at a fate that had made her female never crossed her mind . . . still less could she have believed that there was any connection between her behavior and her father's wish for a son . . . or her own jealousy of her mother. Such evil thoughts never entered her head. She loved her parents and had fresh flowers put on their graves on all appropriate occasions; she loved her husband and often said so publicly; she was proud of her womanhood and said so publicly almost as often—she frequently joined the two assertions.

Agnes Douglas did not wait for her husband to act in the case of the missing Man from Mars. All of her husband's personal staff took orders as readily from her as from him . . . in some cases, even more readily. She sent for the chief executive assistant for civil information, as Mr. Douglas's press agent was called, then turned her attention to the most urgent emergency measure, that of getting a fresh horoscope cast. There was a private, scrambled link from her suite in the Palace to Madame Vesant's studio; the astrologer's plump, bland features and shrewd eyes came on the screen almost at once. "Agnes? What is it, dear? I have a client with me."

"Your circuit is hushed?"

"Of course."

"Get rid of the client at once. This is an emergency."

Madame Alexandra Vesant bit her lip, but her expression did not change otherwise and her voice showed no annoyance. "Certainly. Just a moment." Her features, faded out of the screen, were replaced by the "Hold" signal. A man entered the room, stood waiting by the side of Mrs. Douglas' desk; she turned and saw that it was James Sanforth, the press agent she had sent for.

"Have you heard from Berquist?" she demanded without preamble.

"Eh? I wasn't handling that; that's McCrary's pidgin."

She brushed the irrelevancy aside. "You've got to discredit him before he talks."

"Huh? You think Berquist has sold us out?"

"Don't be naive. You should have checked with me before you used him."

"But I didn't. It was McCrary's job."

"You are supposed to know what is going on. I—" Madame Vesant's face came back on the screen. "Sit down over there," Mrs. Douglas said to Sanforth. "Wait." She turned back to the screen. "Allie dear, I want fresh horoscopes for Joseph and myself, just as quickly as you possibly can cast them."

"Very well." The astrologer hesitated. "I can be of much greater assistance to you, dear, if you will tell me something of the nature of the emergency."

Mrs. Douglas drummed on the desk. "You don't actually have to know, do you?"

"Of course not. Anyone possessing the necessary rigorous training, mathematical skill, and knowledge of the stars could calculate a horoscope, knowing nothing more than the exact hour and place of birth of the subject. You know that, dear. You could learn to do it yourself . . . if you weren't so terribly busy. But remember: the stars incline but they do not compel. You enjoy free will. If I am to make the extremely detailed and difficult analysis necessary to advise you in a crisis, I must know in what sector to look. Are we most concerned with the influence of Venus? Or possibly with Mars? Or will the—"

Mrs. Douglas decided. "With Mars," she interrupted. "Allie, I want you to cast a third horoscope."

"Very well. Whose?"

"Uh . . . Allie, can I trust you?"

Madame Vesant looked hurt. "Agnes, if you do not trust me, it would be far better for you not to consult me. There are others who can give you scientific readings. I am not the only student of the ancient knowledge. I understand that Professor von Krausemeyer is well thought of, even though he is sometimes inclined to . . ." She let her voice trail off.

"Please, please! Of course I trust you! I wouldn't think of letting anyone else perform a calculation for me. Now listen carefully. No one can hear from your side?"

"Of course not, dear."

"I want you to cast a horoscope for Valentine Michael Smith."

" 'Valentine Mich—' The Man from Mars?"

"Yes, yes. Allie, he's been kidnapped. *We've got to find him.*"

Some two hours later Madame Alexandra Vesant pushed herself back from her work table and sighed. She had had her secretary cancel all appointments and she really had tried; several sheets of paper, covered with diagrams and figures, and a dog-eared nautical almanac were in front of her and testified to her efforts. Alexandra Vesant differed from some other practicing astrologers in that she really did attempt to calculate the "influences" of the heavenly bodies, using a paper-backed book titled *The Arcane Science of Judicial Astrology and Key to Solomon's Stone* which had been given to her by her late husband, Professor Simon Magus, the well-known mentalist, stage hypnotist and illusionist, and student of the secret arts.

She trusted the book as she had trusted him; there was no one who could cast a horoscope like Simon, when he was sober—half the time he had not even needed to refer to the book, he knew it so well. She knew that she would never have that degree of skill, so she always referred to the almanac and to the manual. Her calculations were sometimes a little fuzzy, for the same reason that her checkbook sometimes did not balance; Becky Vesey (as she had been known as a child) had never really mastered the multiplication tables and she was inclined to confuse sevens with nines.

Nevertheless her horoscopes were eminently satisfactory; Mrs. Douglas was not her only distinguished client.

But this time she had been a touch panicky when the wife of the Secretary General demanded that she cast a horoscope for the Man from Mars. She had felt the way she used to feel when some officious idiot from the audience committee had insisted on retying her blindfold just before the Professor was to ask her questions. But she had discovered 'way back then, as a mere child, that she had natural stage presence and inner talent for the right answer; she had suppressed her panic and gone on with the show.

Now she had demanded of Agnes the exact hour, date, and place of birth of the Man from Mars, being fairly sure that the data could not be supplied.

But the information had been supplied, and most precisely, after a short delay, from the log of the *Envoy*. By then she was no longer panicky, had simply accepted the information and promised to call back as soon as the horoscopes were ready.

But now, after two hours of painful arithmetic, although she had completed new findings for Mr. and Mrs. Douglas, she was no farther ahead with Smith than when she had started. The trouble was very simple —and insuperable. Smith had not been born on Earth.

Her astrological bible did not include the idea of human beings born anywhere else; its anonymous author had lived and died before even the first rocket to the Moon. She had tried very hard to find a logical way out of the dilemma, on the assumption that all the principles were included in her manual and that what she must do was to find a way to correct for the lateral displacement. But she found herself lost in a mass of unfamiliar relationships; when it came right down to it she was not even sure whether or not the signs of the Zodiac were the same when seen from Mars . . . and what could one possibly do without the signs of the Zodiac?

She could just as easily have tried to extract a cube root, that being the hurdle that had caused her to quit school.

She got out from a bottom desk drawer a tonic she kept at hand for such difficult occasions. She took one dose quickly, measured out a second, and thought about what Simon would have done. After a while she could hear his even, steady tones: "Confidence, kiddo, confidence! Have confidence in yourself and the yokels will have confidence in you. You owe it to them."

She felt much better now and started writing out the results of the two horoscopes for the Douglases. That done, it turned out to be easy to write one for Smith, and she found, as she always did, that the words on paper proved themselves—they were all so beautifully *true!* She was just finishing as Agnes Douglas called again. "Allie? Haven't you finished yet?"

"Just completed," Madame Vesant answered with brisk self-confidence. "You realize, of course, that young Smith's horoscope presented an unusual and very difficult problem in the Science. Born, as he was, on another planet, every aspect and attitude had to be recalculated. The influence of the Sun is lessened; the influence of Diana is missing almost completely. Jupiter is thrown into a novel, perhaps I should say 'unique,' aspect, as I am sure you will see. This required computation of—"

"Allie! Never mind that. Do you know the answers?"

"Naturally."

"Oh, thank goodness! I thought perhaps you were trying to tell me that it was too much for you."

Madame Vesant showed and sincerely felt injured dignity. "My dear, the Science never alters; only the configurations alter. The means that predicted the exact instant and place of the birth of Christ, that told Julius Caesar the moment and method of his death . . . how could it fail now? Truth is Truth, unchanging."

"Yes, of course."

"Are you ready for the readings?"

"Let me switch on 'recording'—go ahead."

"Very well. Agnes, this is a most critical period in your life; only twice before have the heavens gathered in such strong configuration. Above all, you must be calm, not hasty, and think things through. On the whole the portents are in your favor . . . provided you do not fight them and avoid ill-considered action. Do not let your mind be distressed by surface appearances—" She went on at length, giving good advice. Becky Vesey always gave good advice and she gave it with great conviction because she always believed it. She had learned from Simon that, even when the stars seemed darkest, there was always some way to soften the blow, some aspect which the client could use toward greater happiness . . . if she would only find it and point it out.

The tense face opposite her in the screen calmed and began nodding agreement as she made her points. "So you see," she concluded, "the mere temporary absence of young Smith at this time is not a bad thing, but a necessity, resulting from the joint influences of your three horoscopes. Do not worry and do not be afraid; he will be back—or you will hear from him—very shortly. The important thing is to take no drastic or irrevocable action until that time. Be calm."

"Yes, I see that."

"Just one more point. The aspect of Venus is most favorable and potentially dominant over that of Mars. In this case, Venus symbolizes yourself, of course, but Mars is both your husband and young Smith—as a result of the unique circumstance of his birth. This throws a double burden on you and you must rise to the challenge; you must demonstrate those qualities of calm wisdom and restraint which are peculiarly those of woman. You must sustain your husband, guide him through this crisis, and soothe him. You must supply the earth-mother's calm wells of wisdom. That is your special genius . . . and now is the time you must use it."

Mrs. Douglas sighed. "Allie, you are simply wonderful! I don't know how to thank you."

"Don't thank me. Thank the Ancient Masters whose humble student I am."

"I can't thank them so I'll thank you. This isn't covered by your retainer, Allie. There will be a present."

"Not necessary at all, Agnes. It is my privilege to serve."

"And it is my privilege to appreciate service. No, Allie, not another word!"

Madame Vesant let herself be coaxed, then switched off, feeling warmly content from having given a reading that she just *knew* was right. Poor Agnes! Such a good woman inside . . . and so twisted up with conflicting desires. It was a privilege to smooth her path a little, make her heavy burdens a little easier to carry. It made her feel good to help Agnes.

It made Madame Vesant feel good to be treated as an almost-equal by the wife of the Secretary General, too, although she did not think of it that way, not being snobbish at heart. But young Becky Vesey had been so insignificant that the precinct committeeman could never remember her name even though he noticed her bust measurement. Becky Vesey had not resented it; Becky liked people. She liked Agnes Douglas now.

Becky Vesey liked everybody.

She sat a while longer, enjoying the warm glow and the respite from pressure and just a nip more of the tonic, while her shrewd and able brain shuffled the bits and pieces she had picked up. Presently, without consciously making a decision, she called her stockbroker and instructed him to sell Lunar Enterprises short.

He snorted. "Allie, you're crazy. That reducing diet is weakening your mind."

"You listen to me, Ed. When it is down ten points, cover me, even if it is still slipping. Wait for it to turn. When it rallies three points, buy into it again . . . then sell when it gets back to today's closing."

There was a long silence while he looked at her. "Allie, you know something. Tell Uncle Ed."

"The stars tell me, Ed."

Ed made a suggestion astronomically impossible and added, "All right, if you won't, you won't. Mmm . . . I never did have sense enough to stay out of a crooked game. Mind if I ride along with you on it, Allie?"

"Not at all, Ed, as long as you don't go heavy enough to let it show. This is a delicate special situation, with Saturn just balanced between Virgo and Leo."

"As you say, Allie."

Mrs. Douglas got busy at once, happy that Allie had confirmed all her judgments. She gave orders about the campaign to destroy the reputation of the missing Berquist, after sending for his dossier and looking it over; she closeted herself with Commandant Twitchell of the Special Service squads for twenty minutes—he left her looking thoughtfully unhappy and immediately made life unbearable for his executive officer. She instructed Sanforth to release another of the "Man from Mars" stereocasts and to include with it a rumor "from a source close to the administration" that Smith was about to be transferred, or possibly had already been transferred, to a sanitarium high in the Andes, in order to provide him with a climate for convalescence as much like that of Mars as possible. Then she sat back and thought about how to nail down the Pakistan votes for Joseph.

Presently she got hold of him and urged him to support Pakistan's claim to the lion's share of the Kashmir thorium. Since he had been wanting to do so all along but had not, up to now, convinced her of the necessity, he was not hard to persuade, although a little nettled by her assumption that he had been opposing it. With that settled, she left to address the Daughters of the Second Revolution on *Motherhood in the New World*.

—
X
—

WHILE MRS. DOUGLAS WAS SPEAKING too freely on a subject she knew too little about, Jubal E. Harshaw, LL.B., M.D., Sc.D., bon vivant, gourmet, sybarite, popular author extraordinary, and neopessimist philosopher, was sitting by his swimming pool at his home in the Poconos, scratching the thick grey thatch on his chest, and watching his three secretaries splash in the pool. They were all three amazingly beautiful; they were also amazingly good secretaries. In Harshaw's opinion the principle of least action required that utility and beauty be combined.

Anne was blonde, Miriam was red-headed, and Dorcas was dark; in each case the coloration was authentic. They ranged, respectively, from pleasantly plump to deliciously slender. Their ages spread over fifteen years but it was hard to tell off hand which was the eldest. They undoubtedly had last names but Harshaw's household did not bother much with last names. One of them was rumored to be Harshaw's own granddaughter but opinions varied as to which one it was.

Harshaw was working as hard as he ever worked. Most of his mind was occupied with watching pretty girls do pretty things with sun and water; one small, shuttered, sound-proofed compartment was composing. He claimed that his method of literary composition was to hook his gonads in parallel with his thalamus and disconnect his cerebrum entirely; his habits lent some credibility to the theory.

A microphone on a table at his right hand was hooked to a voicewriter in his study but he used the voicewriter only for notes. When he was ready to write he used a human stenographer and watched her reactions. He was ready now. "Front!" he shouted.

"Anne is 'front,' " answered Dorcas. "But I'll take it. That splash was Anne."

"Dive in and get her. I can wait." The little brunette cut the water; a few moments later Anne climbed out, put on a towel robe, dried her hands on it, and sat down on the other side of the table. She said nothing, nor did she make any preparations; Anne had total recall, never bothered with recording devices.

Harshaw picked up a bucket of ice cubes over which brandy had been poured, took a deep swig. "Anne, I've got a really sick-making one. It's about a little kitten that wanders into a church on Christmas Eve to get warm. Besides being starved and frozen and lost, the kitten has—God knows why—an injured paw. All right; start: 'Snow had been falling since—' "

"What pen name?"

"Mmm . . . better use 'Molly Wadsworth' again. This one is pretty icky. And title it *The Other Manger.* Start again." He went on talking while watching her closely. When tears started to leak out of her closed eyes he smiled slightly and closed his own eyes. By the time he finished, tears were running down his cheeks as well as hers, both bathed in a catharsis of schmaltz.

"Thirty," he announced. "You can blow your nose. Send it off and for God's sake don't let me see it or I'll tear it up."

"Jubal, aren't you ever ashamed?"

"No."

"Someday I'm going to kick you right in your fat stomach for one of these."

"I know. But I can't pimp for my sisters; they'd be too old and I never had any. Get your fanny indoors and take care of it before I change my mind."

"Yes, boss."

She kissed his bald spot as she passed behind his chair. Harshaw yelled, "Front!" again and Miriam started toward him. But a loudspeaker mounted on the house behind him came to life:

"Boss!"

Harshaw uttered one word and Miriam clucked at him reprovingly. He added, "Yes, Larry?"

The speaker answered, "There's a dame down here at the gate who wants to see you—and she's got a *corpse* with her."

Harshaw considered this for a moment. "Is she pretty?" he said to the microphone.

"Uh . . . yes."

"Then why are you sucking your thumb? Let her in." Harshaw sat back. "Start," he said. "City montage dissolving into a medium two-shot, interior. A cop is seated in a straight chair, no cap, collar open, face covered with sweat. We see only the back of the other figure, which is depthed between us and the cop. The figure raises a hand, bringing it back and almost out of the tank. He slaps the cop with a heavy, meaty sound, dubbed." Harshaw glanced up and said, "We'll pick up from there." A ground car was rolling up the hill toward the house.

Jill was driving the car; a young man was seated beside her. As the car stopped near Harshaw the man jumped out at once, as if happy to divorce himself from car and contents. "There she is, Jubal."

"So I see. Good morning, little girl. Larry, where is this corpse?"

"In the back seat, Boss. Under a blanket."

"But it's *not* a corpse," Jill protested. "It's . . . Ben said that you . . . I mean—" She put her head down on the controls and started to cry.

"There, my dear," Harshaw said gently. "Very few corpses are worth it. Dorcas—Miriam—take care of her. Give her a drink . . . and wash her face."

He turned his attention to the back seat, started to lift the blanket. Jill shrugged off Miriam's proffered arm and said shrilly, "You've got to listen! He's not dead. At least I hope not. He's . . . oh dear!" She started to cry again. "I'm so dirty . . . and so scared!"

"Seems to be a corpse," Harshaw said meditatively. "Body temperature is down to air temperature, I should judge. The rigor is not typical. How long has he been dead?"

"But he's not dead! Can't we get him out of there? I had an *awful* time getting him in."

"Surely. Larry, give me a hand. And quit looking so green, Larry. If you puke, you'll clean it up." Between them they got Valentine Michael Smith out of the back seat and laid him on the grass by the pool; his body remained stiff, still huddled together. Without being told Dorcas had gone in and fetched Dr. Harshaw's stethoscope; she set it on the ground by Smith, switched it on and stepped up the gain.

Harshaw stuck the headpiece in his ears, started sounding for heart beat. "I'm afraid you're mistaken," he said gently to Jill. "This one is beyond my help. Who was he?"

Jill sighed. Her face was drained of expression and she answered in a flat voice, "He was the Man from Mars. I tried so hard."

"I'm sure you did—*the Man from Mars?*"

"Yes. Ben . . . Ben Caxton said you were the one to come to."

"Ben Caxton, eh? I appreciate the confid—*hush!*" Harshaw emphasized the demand for silence with a hand upheld while he continued to frown and listen. He looked puzzled, then surprise burst over his face. "Heart action! I'll be a babbling baboon. Dorcas—upstairs, the clinic—third drawer down in the locked part of the cooler; the code is 'sweet dreams.' Bring the whole drawer and pick up a 1 cc. hypo from the sterilizer."

"Right away!"

"Doctor, no stimulants!"

Harshaw turned to Jill. "Eh?"

"I'm sorry, sir. I'm just a nurse . . . but this case is different. I *know.*"

"Mmm . . . he's my patient now, nurse. But about forty years ago I found out I wasn't God, and about ten years thereafter I discovered I wasn't even Aesculapius. What do you want to try?"

"I just want to try to wake him up. If you do anything to him, he just goes deeper into it."

"Hmm . . . go ahead. Just as long as you don't use an ax. Then we'll try my methods."

"Yes, sir." Jill knelt beside him, started gently trying to straighten out his limbs. Harshaw's eyebrows went up when he saw that she had succeeded. Jill took Smith's head in her lap and cradled it gently in her hands. "Please wake up," she said softly. "This is Jill . . . your *water brother.*"

The body stirred. Very slowly the chest lifted. Then Smith let out a long bubbling sigh and his eyes opened. He looked up at Jill and smiled his baby smile. Jill smiled back. Then he looked around and the smile left him.

"It's all right," Jill said quickly. "These are all friends."

"All friends?"

"That's right. All of them are your friends. Don't worry—and don't go away again. Everything is all right."

He did not answer but lay still with his eyes open, staring at everything and everyone around him. He seemed as content as a cat in a lap.

Twenty-five minutes later Harshaw had both of his patients in bed. Jill had managed to tell him, before the pill he gave her took hold, enough of the situation to let him know that he had a bear by the tail. Ben Caxton was missing—he'd have to try to figure out something to do about that—and young Smith was as hot as a dry bearing . . . although he had been able to guess that when he heard who he was. Oh, well, life might be amusing for a while; it would keep back that grey boredom that lay always just around the corner.

He looked at the little utility car that Jill had arrived in. Lettered across its sides was: READING RENTALS—Permapowered Ground Equipment of All Sorts—"Deal with the Dutchman!"

"Larry, is the fence hot?"

"No."

"Switch it on. Then before it gets dark I want you to polish every possible fingerprint off that heap. As soon as it is dark, drive it over the other side of Reading—better go almost to Lancaster—and leave it in a ditch. Then go to Philadelphia, catch the shuttle for Scranton, come home from Scranton."

"Sure thing, Jubal. Say—is he *really* the Man from Mars?"

"You had better hope that he isn't, because if he is and they catch you before you dump that wagon and they associate you with him, they'll probably interrogate you with a blow torch. But I think he is."

"I scan it. Should I rob a few banks on the way back?"

"Probably the safest thing you can do."

"Okay, Boss." Larry hesitated. "Do you mind if I stay over night in Philly?"

"What in God's name can a man find to do at night in Philadelphia?"

"Plenty, if you know where to look."

"Suit yourself." Harshaw turned away. "Front!"

Jill slept until shortly before dinner, which in that household was a comfortable eight o'clock. She awoke refreshed and feeling alert, so much so that she sniffed the air incoming from the grille over her head and surmised correctly that the doctor had offset the hypnotic she had been given with a stimulant. While she was asleep someone had removed the dirty and torn street clothes she had been wearing and had left a simple, off-white dinner dress and sandals. The clothes fit her fairly well; Jill concluded that they must belong to the one the doctor had called Miriam. She bathed and painted her face and combed her hair and went down to the big living room feeling like a new woman.

Dorcas was curled in a big chair, doing needle point; she looked up, nodded in a friendly manner as if Jill were always part of the household, turned her attention back to her fancy work. Harshaw was standing and stirring gently a mixture in a tall and frosty pitcher. "Drink?" he said.

"Uh, yes, thank you."

He poured two large cocktail glasses to their brims, handed her one. "What is it?" she asked.

"My own recipe, a comet cocktail. One third vodka, one third muriatic acid, one third battery water—two pinches of salt and add a pickled beetle."

"Better have a highball," Dorcas advised. Jill noticed that the other girl had a tall glass at her elbow.

"Mind your own business," Harshaw advised without rancor. "The hydrochloric acid is good for the digestion; the beetle adds vitamins and protein." He raised his glass to Jill and said solemnly, "Here's to our noble selves! There are damned few of us left." He almost emptied his glass, replenished it before he set it down.

Jill took a cautious sip, then a much bigger one. Whatever the true ingredients, the drink seemed to be exactly what she needed; a warm feeling of well-being spread gently from her center of gravity toward her extremities. She drank about half of it, let Harshaw add a dividend. "Look in on our patient?" he asked.

"No, sir. I didn't know where he was."

"I checked him a few minutes ago. Sleeping like a baby—I think I'll rename him Lazarus. Do you think he would like to come down to dinner?"

Jill looked thoughtful. "Doctor, I really don't know."

"Well, if he wakes I'll know it. Then he can join us, or have a tray, as he wishes. This is Freedom Hall, my dear. Everyone does absolutely as he pleases . . . then if he does something I don't like, I just kick him the hell out. Which reminds me: I don't like to be called 'Doctor.' "

"Sir?"

"Oh, I'm not offended. But when they began handing out doctorates for comparative folk dancing and advanced fly-fishing, I became too stinkin' proud to use the title. I won't touch watered whiskey and I take no pride in watered-down degrees. Call me Jubal."

"Oh. But the degree in medicine hasn't been watered down, as you call it."

"No. But it is time they called it something else, so as not to have it mixed up with playground supervisors. Never mind. Little girl, just what is your interest in this patient?"

"Eh? I told you. Doct—Jubal."

"You told me what happened; you didn't tell me why. Jill, I saw the way you looked at him and spoke to him. Do you think you are in love with him?"

Jill was startled. She glanced at Dorcas; the other girl appeared not to be hearing the conversation. "Why, that's preposterous!"

"I don't see anything preposterous about it. You're a girl; he's a boy—that's usually a nice setup."

"But— No, Jubal, it's not that at all. I . . . well, I thought he was being held a prisoner and I thought—or Ben thought—that he might be in danger. I wanted to see him get his rights."

"Mmm . . . my dear, I'm always suspicious of a disinterested interest. You look as if you had a normal glandular balance, so it is my guess that it is either Ben, or this poor boy from Mars, or both. You had better take your motives out in private and have a look at them. Then you will be better able to judge which way you are going. In the meantime, what do you want *me* to do?"

The unqualified scope of the question made it difficult for Jill to answer. What did she want? What did she expect? From the time she had crossed her Rubicon she had thought of nothing but escape—and getting to Harshaw's home. She had no plans. "I don't know."

"I thought not. You had told me enough to let me know that you were A.W.O.L. from your hospital, so, on the assumption that you might wish to protect your license, I took the liberty, while you were asleep, of having a message sent from Montreal to your Chief of Nursing. You asked for two weeks emergency leave because of sudden illness in your family. Okay? You can back it up with details later."

Jill felt sudden and shaking relief. By temperament she had buried all worry about her own welfare once she had made her decision; nevertheless down inside her was a heavy lump caused by what she had done to an on-the-whole excellent professional standing. "Oh, Jubal, thank you!" She added, "I'm not really delinquent in watch standing yet; today was my day off."

"Good. Then you are covered like a tent. What do you want to do?"

"I haven't had time to think. Uh, I suppose I should get in touch with my bank and get some money—" She paused, trying to recall what her bank balance was. It was never large and sometimes she forgot to—

Jubal cut in on her thoughts. "If you get in touch with your bank, you will have cops pouring out of your ears. Hadn't you better stay here until things level off?"

"Uh, Jubal, I wouldn't want to impose on you."

"You already have imposed on me. Don't worry about it, child. There are always free-loaders around here, coming and going . . . one family stayed seventeen months. But nobody imposes on me against my will, so relax about it. If you turn out to be useful as well as ornamental, you can stay forever. Now about our patient: you said you wanted him to get his 'rights.' I suppose you expected my help in that?"

"Well, I . . . Ben said—Ben seemed to think that you would help."

"I like Ben but he does not speak for me. I am not in the slightest interested in whether or not this lad gets his so-called rights. I don't go for the 'True Prince' nonsense. His claim to Mars is lawyers' hogwash; as a lawyer myself I need not respect it. As for the wealth that is supposed to be coming to him, the situation results from other people's inflamed passions and our odd tribal customs; he has earned none of it. In my opinion he would be lucky if they bilked him out of it—but I would not bother to scan a newspaper to find out which outcome eventuated. If Ben expected me to fight for Smith's 'rights,' you have come to the wrong house."

"Oh." Jill felt suddenly forlorn. "I guess I had better make arrangements to move him."

"Oh, no! Not unless you wish, that is."

"But I thought you said—"

"I said I was not interested in a web of legal fictions. But a patient and guest under my roof is another matter. He can stay, if he likes. I just wanted to make it clear that I had no intention of meddling with politics to suit any romantic notions you or Ben Caxton may have. My dear, I used to think I was serving humanity . . . and I pleasured in the thought. Then I discovered that humanity does not want to be served; on the contrary it resents any attempt to serve it. So now I do what pleases Jubal Harshaw." He turned to Dorcas as if the subject were closed. "Time for dinner, isn't it, Dorcas? Is anyone doing anything about it?"

"Miriam." She put down her needlepoint and stood up.

"I've never been able to figure out just how these girls divide up the work."

"Boss, how would you know?—since you never do any." Dorcas patted him on the stomach. "But you never miss any meals."

A gong sounded and they went in to eat. If the redheaded Miriam had cooked dinner, she had apparently done so with all modern shortcuts; she was already seated at the foot of the table and looked cool and beautiful. In addition to the three secretaries, there was a young man slightly older than Larry who was addressed as "Duke" and who included Jill in the conversation as if she had always lived there. There was also a middle-aged couple who were not introduced at all, who ate as if they were in a restaurant and left the table as soon as they were finished without ever having spoken to the others.

But the table talk among the others was lively and irreverent. Service was by non-android serving machines, directed by controls at Miriam's end of the table. The food was excellent and, so far as Jill could tell, none of it was syntho.

But it did not seem to suit Harshaw. He complained that his knife was dull, or the meat was tough, or both; he accused Miriam of serving leftovers. No one seemed to hear him but Jill was becoming embarrassed on Miriam's account when Anne put down her knife and fork. "He mentioned his mother's cooking," she stated bleakly.

"He is beginning to think he is boss again," agreed Dorcas.

"How long has it been?"

"About ten days."

"Too long." Anne gathered up Dorcas and Miriam with her eyes; they all stood up. Duke went on eating.

Harshaw said hastily, "Now see here, girls, not at meals. Wait until—" They paid no attention to his protest but moved toward him; a serving machine scurried out of the way. Anne took his feet, each of the other two an arm; French doors slid out of the way and they carried him out, squawking.

A few seconds later the squawks were cut short by a splash.

The three women returned at once, not noticeably mussed. Miriam sat down and turned to Jill. "More salad, Jill?"

Harshaw returned a few minutes later, dressed in pajamas and robe instead of the evening jacket he had been wearing. One of the machines had covered his plate as soon as he was dragged away from the table; it now uncovered it for him and he went on eating. "As I was saying," he remarked, "a woman who can't cook is a waste of skin. If I don't start having some service around here I'm going to swap all of you for a dog and shoot the dog. What's the dessert, Miriam?"

"Strawberry shortcake."

"That's more like it. You are all reprieved till Wednesday."

Gillian found that it was not necessary to understand how Jubal Harshaw's household worked; she could do as she pleased and nobody cared. After dinner she went into the living room with the intention of viewing a stereocast of the evening news, being anxious to· find out if she herself played a part in it. But she could find no stereo receiver, nor was there anything which could have concealed a tank. Thinking about it, she could not recall having seen one anywhere in the house. Nor were there any newspapers, although there were plenty of books and magazines.

No one joined her. After a while she began to wonder what time it was. She had left her watch upstairs with her purse, so she looked around for a clock. She failed to find one, then searched her excellent memory and could not remember having seen either clock or calendar in any of the rooms she had been in.

But she decided that she might as well go to bed no matter what time it was. One whole wall was filled with books, both shelves and spindle racks. She found a spool of Kipling's *Just So Stories* and took it happily upstairs with her.

Here she found another small surprise. The bed in the room she had been given was as modern as next week, complete with automassage, coffee dispenser, weather control, reading machine, etc.—but the alarm circuit was missing, there being only a plain cover plate to show where it had been. Jill shrugged and decided that she would probably not oversleep anyway, crawled into bed, slid the spool into the reading machine, lay back and scanned the words streaming across the ceiling. Presently the speed control slipped out of her relaxed fingers, the lights went out, and she slept.

Jubal Harshaw did not get to sleep as easily; he was vexed with himself. His initial interest in the situation had cooled off and reaction had set in. Well over a half century earlier he had sworn a mighty oath, full of fireworks, never again to pick up a stray cat—and now, so help him, by the multiple paps of Venus Genetrix, he had managed to pick up two at once . . . no, three, if he counted Ben Caxton.

The fact that he had broken his oath more times than there were years intervening did not trouble him; his was not a small mind bothered by logic and consistency. Nor did the mere presence of two more pensioners sleeping under his roof and eating at his table bother him. Pinching pennies was not in him. In the course of nearly a century of gusty living he had been broke many times, had several times been wealthier than he now was; he regarded both conditions as he did shifts in the weather, and never counted his change.

But the silly foofooraw that he knew was bound to ensue when the busies caught up with these children disgruntled him in prospect. He considered it certain that catch up they would; a naive child like that Gillian infant would leave a trail behind her like a club-footed cow! Nothing else could be expected.

Whereupon people would come barging into his sanctuary, asking stupid questions and making stupid demands . . . and he, Jubal Harshaw, would have to make decisions and take action. Since he was philosophically convinced that all action was futile, the prospect irritated him.

He did not expect reasonable conduct from human beings; he considered most people fit candidates for protective restraint and wet packs. He simply wished heartily that they would leave him alone!—all but the few he chose for playmates. He was firmly convinced that, left to himself, he would have long since achieved nirvana . . . dived into his own belly button and disappeared from view, like those Hindu jokers. Why couldn't they leave a man *alone?*

Around midnight he wearily put out his twenty-seventh cigarette and sat up; the lights came on. "Front!" he shouted at the microphone beside his bed.

Shortly Dorcas came in, dressed in robe and slippers. She yawned widely and said, "Yes, Boss?"

"Dorcas, for the last twenty or thirty years I've been a worthless, useless, no-good parasite."

She nodded and yawned again. "Everybody knows that."

"Never mind the flattery. There comes a time in every man's life when he has to stop being sensible—a time to stand up and be counted—strike a blow for liberty—smite the wicked."

"Ummm . . ."

"So quit yawning, the time has come."

She glanced down at herself. "Maybe I had better get dressed."

"Yes. Get the other girls up, too; we're going to be busy. Throw a bucket of cold water over the Duke and tell him I said to dust off the babble machine and hook it up in my study. I want the news, all of it."

Dorcas looked startled and all over being sleepy. "You want Duke to hook up *stereovision?*"

"You heard me. Tell him I said that if it's out of order, he should pick a direction and start walking. Now get along with you; we've got a busy night ahead."

"All right," Dorcas agreed doubtfully, "but I think I ought to take your temperature first."

"Peace, woman!"

Duke had Jubal Harshaw's stereo receiver hooked up in time to let Jubal see a late rebroadcast of the second phony interview with the "Man from Mars." The commentary included the rumor about moving Smith to the Andes. Jubal put two and two together and got twenty-two, after which he was busy calling people until morning. At dawn Dorcas brought him his breakfast, six raw eggs beaten into brandy. He slurped them down while reflecting that one of the advantages of a long and busy life was that eventually a man got to know pretty near everybody of real importance—and could call on them in a pinch.

Harshaw had prepared a time bomb but did not propose to trigger it until the powers-that-be forced him to do so. He had realized at once that the government could haul Smith back into captivity on the grounds that he was incompetent to look out for himself . . . an opinion with which Harshaw agreed. His snap opinion was that Smith was both legally insane and medically psychopathic by all normal standards, the victim of a double-barreled situational psychosis of unique and monumental extent,

first from being raised by non-humans and second from having been translated suddenly into a society which was completely alien to him.

Nevertheless he regarded both the legal notion of sanity and the medical notion of psychosis as being irrelevant to this case. Here was a human
animal who had made a profound and apparently successful adjustment to
an alien society . . . but as a malleable infant. Could the same subject, as
an adult with formed habits and canalized thinking, make another adjustment just as radical, and much more difficult for an adult to make than for
an infant? Dr. Harshaw intended to find out; it was the first time in decades he had taken real interest in the practice of medicine.

Besides that, he was tickled at the notion of balking the powers-that-
be. He had more than his share of that streak of anarchy which was the
political birthright of every American; pitting himself against the planetary
government filled him with sharper zest for living than he had felt in a
generation.

xi

AROUND A MINOR G-TYPE STAR fairly far out toward one edge of a
medium-sized galaxy the planets of that star swung as usual, just as they
had for billions of years, under the influence of a slightly modified inverse
square law that shaped the space around them. Three of them were big
enough, as planets go, to be noticeable; the rest were mere pebbles, concealed in the fiery skirts of the primary or lost in the black outer reaches of
space. All of them, as is always the case, were infected with that oddity of
distorted entropy called life; in the cases of the third and fourth planets
their surface temperatures cycled around the freezing point of hydrogen
monoxide—in consequence they had developed life forms similar enough
to permit a degree of social contact.

On the fourth pebble out the ancient Martians were not in any important sense disturbed by the contact with Earth. The nymphs of the race
still bounced joyously around the surface of Mars, learning to live, and
eight out of nine of them dying in the process. The adult Martians, enormously different in body and mind from the nymphs, still huddled in or
under the faerie, graceful cities, and were as quiet in their behavior as the

nymphs were boisterous—yet were even busier than the nymphs, busy with a complex and rich life of the mind.

The lives of the adults were not entirely free of work in the human sense; they had still a planet to take care of and supervise, plants must be told when and where to grow, nymphs who had passed their 'prenticeships by surviving must be gathered in, cherished, fertilized, the resultant eggs must be cherished and contemplated to encourage them to ripen properly, the fulfilled nymphs must be persuaded to give up childish things and then metamorphosed into adults. All these things must be done—but they were no more the "life" of Mars than is walking the dog twice a day the "life" of a man who controls a planet-wide corporation in the hours between those pleasant walks . . . even though to a being from Arcturus III those daily walks might seem to be the tycoon's most significant activity—no doubt as a slave to the dog.

Martians and humans were both self-aware life forms but they had gone in vastly different directions. All human behavior, all human motivations, all man's hopes and fears, were heavily colored and largely controlled by mankind's tragic and oddly beautiful pattern of reproduction. The same was true of Mars, but in mirror corollary. Mars had the efficient bipolar pattern so common in that galaxy, but the Martians had it in a form so different from the Terran form that it would have been termed "sex" only by a biologist, and it emphatically would not have been "sex" to a human psychiatrist. Martian nymphs were female, all the adults were male.

But in each case in function only, not in psychology. The man-woman polarity which controlled all human lives could not exist on Mars. There was no possibility of "marriage." The adults were huge, reminding the first humans to see them of ice boats under sail; they were physically passive, mentally active. The nymphs were fat, furry spheres, full of bounce and mindless energy. There was no possible parallel between human and Martian psychological foundations. Human bipolarity was both the binding force and the driving energy for all human behavior, from sonnets to nuclear equations. If any being thinks that human psychologists exaggerate on this point, let it search Terran patent offices, libraries, and art galleries for creations of eunuchs.

Mars, being geared unlike Earth, paid little attention to the *Envoy* and the *Champion*. The two events had happened too recently to be of significance—if Martians had used newspapers, one edition a Terran century would have been ample. Contact with other races was nothing new to Martians; it had happened before, would happen again. When the new other race had been thoroughly grokked, then (in a Terran millennium or so) would be time for action, if needed.

On Mars the currently important event was of a different sort. The discorporate Old Ones had decided almost absent-mindedly to send the nestling human to grok what he could of the third planet, then turned attention back to serious matters. Shortly before, around the time of the Terran Caesar Augustus, a Martian artist had been engaged in composing a work of art. It could have been called with equal truth a poem, a musical opus, or a philosophical treatise; it was a series of emotions arranged in tragic, logical necessity. Since it could have been experienced by a human only in the sense in which a man blind from birth could have a sunset explained to him, it does not matter much to which category of human creativity it might be assigned. The important point was that the artist had accidentally discorporated before he finished his masterpiece.

Unexpected discorporation was always rare on Mars; Martian taste in such matters called for life to be a rounded whole, with physical death taking place at the appropriate and selected instant. This artist, however, had become so preoccupied with his work that he had forgotten to come in out of the cold; by the time his absence was noticed his body was hardly fit to eat. He himself had not noticed his own discorporation and had gone right on composing his sequence.

Martian art was divided sharply into two categories, that sort created by living adults, which was vigorous, often quite radical, and primitive, and that of the Old Ones, which was usually conservative, extremely complex, and was expected to show much higher standards of technique; the two sorts were judged separately.

By what standards should this opus be judged? It bridged from the corporate to the discorporate; its final form had been set throughout by an Old One—yet on the other hand the artist, with the detachment of all artists everywhere, had not even noticed the change in his status and had continued to work as if he were corporate. Was it possibly a new sort of art? Could more such pieces be produced by surprise discorporation of artists while they were working? The Old Ones had been discussing the exciting possibilities in ruminative rapport for centuries and all corporate Martians were eagerly awaiting their verdict.

The question was of greater interest because it had not been abstract art, but religious (in the Terran sense) and strongly emotional: it described the contact between the Martian Race and the people of the fifth planet, an event that had happened long ago but which was alive and important to Martians in the sense in which one death by crucifixion remained alive and important to humans after two Terran millennia. The Martian Race had encountered the people of the fifth planet, grokked them completely, and in due course had taken action; the asteroid ruins were all that remained, save that the Martians continued to cherish and praise the people they had destroyed. This new work of art was one of many attempts to grok all parts of the whole beautiful experience in all its complexity in one opus. But before it could be judged it was necessary to grok how to judge it.

It was a very pretty problem.

On the third planet Valentine Michael Smith was not concerned with the burning issue on Mars; he had never heard of it. His Martian keeper and his keeper's water brothers had not mocked him with things he could not grasp. Smith knew of the destruction of the fifth planet and its emotional importance, just as any human school boy learns of Troy and Plymouth Rock, but he had not been exposed to art that he could not grok. His education had been unique, enormously greater than that of his nestlings, enormously less than that of an adult; his keeper and his keeper's advisers among the Old Ones had taken a large passing interest in seeing just how much and of what sort this nestling alien could learn. The results had taught them more about the potentialities of the human race than that race had yet learned about itself, for Smith had grokked very readily things that no other human being had ever learned.

But just at present Smith was simply enjoying himself with a light-heartedness he had not experienced in many years. He had won a new water brother in Jubal, he had acquired many new friends, he was enjoying delightful new experiences in such kaleidoscopic quantity that he had no time to grok them; he could only file them away to be relived at leisure.

His brother Jubal had assured him that he would grok this strange and beautiful place more quickly if he would learn to read, so he had taken a full day off to learn to read really well and quickly, with Jill pointing to words and pronouncing them for him. It had meant staying out of the swimming pool all that day, which had been a great sacrifice, as swimming (once he got it through his head that it was actually *permitted)* was not merely an exuberant, sensuous delight but almost unbearable religious ecstasy. If Jill and Jubal had not told him to do otherwise, he would never have come out of the pool at all.

Since he was not permitted to swim at night he read all night long. He was zipping through the Encyclopedia Britannica and was sampling Jubal's medicine and law libraries as dessert. His brother Jubal had seen him leafing rapidly through one of the books, had stopped him and questioned him about what he had read. Smith had answered carefully, as it reminded him of the tests the Old Ones had occasionally given him. His brother had seemed a bit upset at his answers and Smith had found it necessary to go into an hour's contemplation on that account, for he had been quite sure that he had answered with the words written in the book even though he did not grok them all.

But he preferred the pool to the books, especially when Jill and Miriam and Larry and Anne and the rest were all splashing each other. He had not learned at once to swim as they did, but had discovered the first time that he could do something they could not. He had simply gone down to the bottom and lain there, immersed in quiet bliss—whereupon they had hauled him out with such excitement that he had almost been forced to withdraw himself, had it not been evident that they were concerned for his welfare.

Later that day he had demonstrated the matter to Jubal, remaining on the bottom for a delicious time, and he had tried to teach it to his brother Jill . . . but she had become disturbed and he had desisted. It was his first clear realization that there were things that he could do that these new friends could not. He thought about it a long time, trying to grok its fullness.

Smith was happy; Harshaw was not. He continued his usual routine of aimless loafing, varied only by casual and unplanned observation of his laboratory animal, the Man from Mars. He arranged no schedule for Smith, no programme of study, no regular physical examinations, but simply allowed Smith to do as he pleased, run wild, like a puppy growing up on a ranch. What supervision Smith received came from Gillian—more than enough, in Jubal's grumpy opinion, as he took a dim view of males being reared by females.

However, Gillian Boardman did little more than coach Valentine Smith in the rudiments of human social behavior—and he needed very little coaching. He ate at the table with the others now, dressed himself (at least Jubal thought he did; he made a mental note to ask Jill if she still had to assist him); he conformed acceptably to the household's very informal customs and appeared able to cope with most new experiences on a "monkey-see-monkey-do" basis. Smith started his first meal at the table using only a spoon and Jill cut up his meat for him. By the end of the meal he was attempting to eat as the others ate. At the next meal his table manners were a precise imitation of Jill's, including superfluous mannerisms.

Even the twin discovery that Smith had taught himself to read with the speed of electronic scanning and appeared to have total recall of all that he read did not tempt Jubal Harshaw to make a "project" of Smith, one with controls, measurements, and curves of progress. Harshaw had the arrogant humility of the man who has learned so much that he is aware of his own ignorance and he saw no point in "measurements" when he did not know what he was measuring. Instead he limited himself to notes made privately, without even any intention of publishing his observations.

But, while Harshaw enjoyed watching this unique animal develop into a mimicry copy of a human being, his pleasure afforded him no happiness. Like Secretary General Douglas, Harshaw was waiting for the other shoe to drop.

Waiting with increasing tenseness— Having found himself coerced into action by the expectation of action against him on the part of the government, it annoyed and exasperated him that nothing as yet had happened. Damn it, were the Federation cops so stupid that they couldn't track an unsophisticated girl dragging an unconscious man all across the countryside? Or (as seemed more likely) had they been on her heels the whole way?—and even now were keeping a stake-out on his place? The latter thought was infuriating; to Harshaw the notion that the government might be spying on his home, his castle, with anything from binoculars to radar, was as repulsive as the idea of having his mail opened.

And they might be doing that, too! he reminded himself morosely. Government! Three fourths parasitic and the other fourth stupid fumbling —oh, he conceded that man, a social animal, could not avoid having government, any more than an individual man could escape his lifelong bondage to his bowels. But Harshaw did not have to like it. Simply because an evil was inescapable was no reason to term it a "good." He wished that government would wander off and get lost!

But it was certainly possible, or even probable, that the administration knew exactly where the Man from Mars was hiding . . . and for reasons of their own preferred to leave it that way, while they prepared— what?

If so, how long would it go on? And how long could he keep his defensive "time bomb" armed and ready?

And where the devil was that reckless young idiot Ben Caxton?

Jill Boardman forced him out of his spiritual thumb-twiddling. "Jubal?"

"Eh? Oh, it's you, bright eyes. Sorry, I was preoccupied. Sit down. Have a drink?"

"Uh, no, thank you. Jubal, I'm worried."

"Normal. Who isn't? That was a mighty pretty swan dive you did. Let's see another one just like it."

Jill bit her lip and looked about twelve years old. "Jubal! *Please* listen! I'm terribly worried."

He sighed. "In that case, dry yourself off. The breeze is getting chilly."

"I'm warm enough. Uh, Jubal? Would it be all right if I left Mike here? Would you take care of him?"

Harshaw blinked. "Of course he can stay here. You know that. The girls will look out for him . . . and I'll keep an eye on him from time to time. He's no trouble. I take it you're leaving?"

She didn't meet his eye. "Yes."

"Mmm . . . you're welcome here. But you're welcome to leave, too, if that's what you want."

"Huh? But, Jubal—I don't *want* to leave!"

"Then don't."

"But I *must!*"

"Better play that back. I didn't scan it."

"Don't you *see,* Jubal? I like it here—you've been wonderful to us! But I can't stay any longer. Not with Ben missing. I've *got* to go look for him."

Harshaw said one word, emotive, earthy, and vulgar, then added, "How do you propose to look for him?"

She frowned. "I don't know. But I can't just lie around here any longer, loafing and swimming—with Ben missing."

"Gillian, as I pointed out to you before, Ben is a big boy now. You're not his mother—and you're not his wife. And I'm not his keeper. Neither of us is responsible for him . . . and you haven't any call to go looking for him. Have you?"

Jill looked down and twisted one toe in the grass. "No," she admitted. "I haven't any claim on Ben. I just know . . . that if *I* turned up missing . . . Ben would look for me—until he found me. So *I've* got to look for *him!*"

Jubal breathed a silent malediction against all elder gods in any way involved in contriving the follies of the human race, then said aloud, "All right, all right, if you must, then let's try to get some logic into it. Do you plan to hire professionals? Say a private detective firm that specializes in missing persons?"

She looked unhappy. "I suppose that's the way to go about it. Uh, I've never hired a detective. Are they expensive?"

"Quite."

Jill gulped. "Do you suppose they would let me arrange to pay, uh, in monthly installments? Or something?"

"Cash at the stairs is their usual way. Quit looking so grim, child; I brought that up to dispose of it. I've already hired the best in the business to try to find Ben—so there is no need for you to hock your future to hire the second best."

"You didn't tell me!"

"No need to tell you."

"But— Jubal, what did they find out?"

"Nothing," he said shortly. "Nothing worth reporting, so there was no need to put you any further down in the dumps by telling you." Jubal scowled. "When you showed up here, I thought you were unnecessarily nervy about Ben—I figured the same as his assistant, that fellow Kilgallen, that Ben had gone yiping off on some new trail . . . and would check in when he had the story wrapped up. Ben does that sort of stunt—it's his profession." He sighed. "But now I don't think so. That knothead Kilgallen—he really does have a statprint message on file, apparently from Ben, telling Kilgallen that Ben would be away a few days; my man not only saw it but sneaked a photograph and checked. No fake—the message was sent."

Jill looked puzzled. "I wonder why Ben didn't send me a statprint at the same time? It isn't like him—Ben's very thoughtful."

Jubal repressed a groan. "Use your head, Gillian. Just because a package says 'Cigarettes' on the outside does not prove that the package contains cigarettes. You got here last Friday; the code groups on that statprint message show that it was filed from Philadelphia—Paoli Station Landing Flat, to be exact—just after ten thirty the morning before—10.34 A.M. Thursday. It was transmitted a couple of minutes after it was filed and was received at once, because Ben's office has its own statprinter. All right, now *you* tell *me* why Ben sent a printed message to his own office—during working hours—instead of telephoning?"

"Why, I don't think he would, ordinarily. At least I wouldn't. The telephone is the normal—"

"But you aren't Ben. I can think of half a dozen reasons, for a man in Ben's business. To avoid garbles. To insure a printed record in the files of I.T.&T. for legal purposes. To send a delayed message. All sorts of reasons. Kilgallen saw nothing odd about it—and the simple fact that Ben, or the syndicate he sells to, goes to the expense of maintaining a private statprinter in his office shows that Ben uses it regularly.

"However," Jubal went on, "the snoops I hired are a suspicious lot; that message placed Ben at Paoli Flat at ten thirty-four on Thursday—so one of them went there. Jill, that message was not sent from there."

"But—"

"One moment. The message was filed from there but did not originate there. Messages are either handed over the counter or telephoned. If one is handed over the counter, the customer can have it typed or he can ask for facsimile transmission of his handwriting and signature . . . but if it is filed by telephone, it has to be typed by the filing office before it can be photographed."

"Yes, of course."

"Doesn't that suggest anything, Jill?"

"Uh . . . Jubal, I'm so worried that I'm not thinking straight. What should it suggest?"

"Quit the breast-beating; it wouldn't have suggested anything to me, either. But the pro who was working for me is a very sneaky character; he arrived at Paoli with a convincing statprint made from the photograph that was taken under Kilgallen's nose—and with business cards and credentials that made it appear that he himself was 'Osbert Kilgallen,' the addressee. Then, with his fatherly manner and sincere face, he hornswoggled a young lady employee of I.T.&T. into telling him things which, under the privacy amendment to the Constitution, she should have divulged only under court order—very sad. Anyhow, she did remember receiving that message for file and processing. Ordinarily she wouldn't remember one message out of hundreds—they go in her ears and out her fingertips and are gone, save for the filed microprint. But, luckily, this young lady is one of Ben's faithful fans; she reads his 'Crow's Nest' column every night—a hideous vice." Jubal blinked his eyes thoughtfully at the horizon. *"Front!"*

Anne appeared, dripping. "Remind me," Jubal said to her, "to write a popular article on the compulsive reading of news. The theme will be that most neuroses and some psychoses can be traced to the unnecessary and unhealthy habit of daily wallowing in the troubles and sins of five billion strangers. The title is 'Gossip Unlimited'—no, make that 'Gossip Gone Wild.' "

"Boss, you're getting morbid."

"Not me. But everybody else is. See that I write it some time next week. Now vanish; I'm busy." He turned back to Gillian. "She noticed Ben's name, so she remembered the message—quite thrilled about it, because it let her speak to one of her heroes . . . and was irked, I gather, because Ben hadn't paid for vision as well as voice. Oh, she remembers it . . . and she remembers, too, that the service was paid for by cash from a public booth—in Washington."

" 'In Washington'?" repeated Jill. "But why would Ben call from—"

"Of course, of course!" Jubal agreed pettishly. "If he's at a public phone booth anywhere in Washington, he can have both voice and vision direct to his office, face to face with his assistant, cheaper, easier, and quicker than he could phone a stat message to be sent *back* to Washington from a point nearly two hundred miles away. It doesn't make sense. Or, rather, it makes just one kind of sense. Hanky-panky. Ben is as used to hanky-panky as a bride is to kisses. He didn't get to be one of the best winchells in the business through playing his cards face up."

"Ben is not a winchell! He's a lippmann!"

"Sorry, I'm color-blind in that range. Keep quiet. He might have believed that his phone was tapped but his statprinter was not. Or he might have suspected that both were tapped—and I've no doubt they are, by now, if not then—and that he could use this round-about relay to convince whoever was tapping him that he really was away from Washington and would not be back for several days." Jubal frowned. "In the latter case we would be doing him no favor by finding him. We might be endangering his life."

"Jubal! No!"

"Jubal, yes," he answered wearily. "That boy skates close to the edge, he always has. He's utterly fearless and that's how he's made his reputation. But the rabbit is never more than two jumps ahead of the coyote . . . and this time maybe one jump. Or none. Jill, Ben has never tackled a more dangerous assignment than this. If he has disappeared voluntarily—and he may have—do you want to risk stirring things up by bumbling around in your amateur way, calling attention to the fact that he has dropped out of sight? Kilgallen still has him covered, as Ben's column has appeared every day. I don't ordinarily read it—but I've made it my business to know, this time."

"Canned columns! Mr. Kilgallen told me so."

"Of course. Some of Ben's perennial series on corrupt campaign funds. That's a subject as safe as being in favor of Christmas. Maybe they're kept on file for such emergencies—or perhaps Kilgallen is writing them. In any case, Ben Caxton, the ever-ready Advocate of the Peepul, is still officially on his usual soap box. Perhaps he planned it that way, my dear—because he found himself in such danger that he did not dare get in touch even with you. Well?"

Gillian glanced fearfully around her—at a scene almost unbearably peaceful, bucolic, and beautiful—then covered her face with her hands. "Jubal . . . I don't know *what* to do!"

"Snap out of it," he said gruffly. "Don't bawl over Ben—not in my presence. The worst that can possibly have happened to him is death . . . and that we are all in for—if not this morning, then in days, or weeks, or

years at most. Talk to your protégé Mike about it. He regards 'discorporation' as less to be feared than a scolding—and he may be right. Why, if I
told Mike we were going to roast him and serve him for dinner tonight, he
would thank me for the honor with his voice choked with gratitude."

"I know he would," Jill agreed in a small voice, "but I don't have his
philosophical attitude about such things."

"Nor do I," Harshaw agreed cheerfully, "but I'm beginning to grasp
it—and I must say that it is a consoling one to a man of my age. A
capacity for enjoying the inevitable—why, I've been cultivating that all my
life . . . but this infant from Mars, barely old enough to vote and too
unsophisticated to stand clear of the horse cars, has me convinced that I've
just reached the kindergarten class in this all-important subject. Jill, you
asked if Mike was welcome to stay on. Child, he's the most welcome guest
I've ever had. I want to keep that boy around until I've found out what it
is that he knows and I don't! This 'discorporation' thing in particular . . .
it's not the Freudian 'death-wish' cliché, I'm sure of that. It has nothing to
do with life being unbearable. None of that 'Even the weariest river' stuff
—it's more like Stevenson's 'Glad did I live and gladly die and I lay me
down with a will!' Only I've always suspected that Stevenson was either
whistling in the dark, or, more likely, enjoying the compensating euphoria
of consumption. But Mike has me halfway convinced that he really knows
what he is talking about."

"I don't know," Jill answered dully. "I'm just worried about Ben."

"So am I," agreed Jubal. "So let's discuss Mike another time. Jill, I
don't think that Ben is simply hiding any more than you do."

"But you said—"

"Sorry. I didn't finish. My hired men didn't limit themselves to Ben's
office and Paoli Flat. On Thursday morning Ben called at Bethesda Medical Center in company with the lawyer he uses and a Fair Witness—the
famous James Oliver Cavendish, in case you follow such things."

"I don't, I'm afraid."

"No matter. The fact that Ben retained Cavendish shows how seriously he took the matter; you don't hunt rabbits with an elephant gun. The
three were taken to see the 'Man from Mars'—"

Gillian gaped, then said explosively, "That's impossible! They
couldn't have come on that floor without my knowing it!"

"Take it easy, Jill. You're disputing a report by a Fair Witness . . .
and not just any Fair Witness. Cavendish himself. If he says it, it's gospel."

"I don't care if he's the Twelve Apostles! He wasn't on my floor last
Thursday morning!"

"You didn't listen closely. I didn't say that they were taken to see our friend Mike—I said they were taken to see 'The Man from Mars.' The phony one, obviously—that actor fellow they stereovised."

"Oh. Of course. And Ben caught them out!"

Jubal looked pained. "Little girl, count to ten thousand by twos while I finish this. Ben did not catch them out. In fact, even the Honorable Mr. Cavendish did not catch them out—at least he won't say so. You know how Fair Witnesses behave."

"Well . . . no, I don't. I've never had any dealings with Fair Witnesses."

"So? Perhaps you weren't aware of it. *Anne!*"

Anne was seated on the springboard; she turned her head. Jubal called out, "That new house on the far hilltop—can you see what color they've painted it?"

Anne looked in the direction in which Jubal was pointing and answered, "It's white on this side." She did not inquire why Jubal had asked, nor make any comment.

Jubal went on to Jill in normal tones, "You see? Anne is so thoroughly indoctrinated that it doesn't even occur to her to infer that the other side is probably white, too. All the King's horses and all the King's men couldn't force her to commit herself as to the far side . . . unless she herself went around to the other side and looked—and even then she wouldn't assume that it stayed whatever color it might be after she left . . . because they might repaint it as soon as she turned her back."

"*Anne* is a Fair Witness?"

"Graduate, unlimited license, and admitted to testify before the High Court. Sometime ask her why she decided to give up public practice. But don't plan on anything else that day—the wench will recite the truth, the whole truth, and nothing but the truth, and that takes time. Back to Mr. Cavendish— Ben retained him for open witnessing, full disclosure, without enjoining him to privacy. So when Cavendish was questioned, he answered, in full and boring detail. I've got a tape of it upstairs. But the interesting part of his report is what he does *not* say. He never states that the man they were taken to see was *not* the Man from Mars . . . but not one word can be construed as indicating that Cavendish accepted the exhibit he was called to view as being in fact the Man from Mars. If you knew Cavendish—and I do—this would be conclusive. If Cavendish had seen Mike, even for a few minutes, he would have reported what he had seen with such exactness that you and I, who know Mike, would know that he had seen him. For example, Cavendish reports in precise professional jargon the shape of this exhibit's ears . . . and it does not match Mike's ear shape at all. Q.E.D.; he didn't see Mike. Nor did Ben. They were shown a phony. Furthermore Cavendish knows it, even though he is professionally restrained from giving opinions or conclusions."

"But I told you so. They never came near my floor."

"Yes. But it tells us something more. This occurred hours before you pulled your jail break for Mike—about eight hours earlier, as Cavendish sets their arrival in the presence of the phony 'Man from Mars' at 9.14 Thursday morning. That is to say, the government still had Mike under their thumb at that moment. In the same building. They could have exhibited him. Yet they took the really grave risk of offering a phony for inspection by the most noted Fair Witness in Washington—in the country. Why?"

He waited. Jill answered slowly, "You're asking me? I don't know. Ben told me that he intended to ask Mike if he wanted to leave the hospital —and help him to do so if he said, 'Yes.' "

"Which Ben did try, with the phony."

"So? But, Jubal, they couldn't have known that Ben intended to do that . . . and, anyhow, Mike wouldn't have left with Ben."

"Why not? Later that day he left with you."

"Yes—but I was already his 'water brother,' just as you are now. He has this crazy Martian idea that he can trust utterly anyone with whom he has shared a drink of water. With a 'water brother' he is completely docile . . . and with anybody else he is stubborn as a mule. Ben couldn't have budged him." She added, "At least that is the way he was last week—he's changing awfully fast."

"So he is. Too fast, maybe. I've never seen muscle tissue develop so rapidly—I'm sorry I didn't weigh him the day you arrived. Never mind, back to Ben—Cavendish reports that Ben dropped him and the lawyer, a chap named Frisby, at nine thirty-one, and Ben kept the cab. We don't know where Ben went then. But an hour later he—or let's say somebody who said he was Ben—phoned that message to Paoli Flat."

"You don't think it was Ben?"

"I do not. Cavendish reported the license number of the cab and my scouts tried to get a look at the daily trip tape for that cab. If Ben used his credit card, rather than feeding coins into the cab's meter, his charge number should be printed on the tape—but even if he paid cash the tape should show where the cab had been and when."

"Well?"

Harshaw shrugged. "The records show that that cab was in for repairs and was never in use Thursday morning. That gives us two choices: either a Fair Witness misread or misremembered a cab's serial number . . . or somebody tampered with the record." He added grimly, "Maybe a jury would decide that even a Fair Witness could glance at a cab's serial number and misread it, especially if he had not been asked to remember it —but *I* don't believe it . . . not when the Witness is James Oliver Cavendish. Cavendish would either be certain of that serial number—or his report would never mention it."

Harshaw scowled and went on, "Jill, you're forcing me to rub my own nose in it—and I don't like it, I don't like it at all! Granted that Ben could have sent that message, it is most unlikely that he could have tampered with the daily record of that cab . . . and still less believable that he had any reason to. No, let's face it. Ben went somewhere in that cab— and somebody who could get at the records of a public carrier went to a lot of trouble to conceal where he went . . . and sent a phony message to keep anyone from realizing that he had disappeared."

" 'Disappeared!' Kidnapped, you mean!"

"Softly, Jill. 'Kidnapped' is a dirty word."

"It's the only word for it! Jubal, how can you sit there and do nothing when you ought to be shouting it from the—"

"Stop it, Jill! There's another word. Instead of kidnapped, he might be dead."

Gillian slumped. "Yes," she agreed dully. "That's what I'm really afraid of."

"So am I. But we'll assume he is not, until we have seen his bones. But it's one or the other—so we assume that he is kidnapped. Jill, what's the greatest danger about kidnapping? No, don't bother your pretty head; I'll tell you. The greatest danger to the victim is a hue-and-cry—because if a kidnapper is frightened, he will almost always kill his victim. Had you thought of that?"

Gillian looked woeful and did not answer. Harshaw went on gently, "I am forced to say that I think it is extremely likely that Ben is dead. He has been gone too long. But we've agreed to assume that he is alive—until we know otherwise. Now you intend to look for him. Gillian, can you tell me how you will go about this? Without increasing the risk that Ben will be done away with by the unknown party or parties who kidnapped him?"

"Uh— But we know who they are!"

"Do we?"

"Of course we do! The same people who were keeping Mike a prisoner—the government!"

Harshaw shook his head. "We don't know it. That's an assumption based on what Ben was doing when last seen. But it's not a certainty. Ben has made lots of enemies with his column and by no means all of them are in the government. I can think of several who would willingly kill him if they could get away with it. However—" Harshaw frowned. "Your assumption is all we have to go on. But not 'the government'—that's too sweeping a term. 'The government' is several million people, nearly a million in Washington alone. We have to ask ourselves: Whose toes were being stepped on? What person or persons? Not 'the government'—but what individuals?"

"Why, that's plain enough, Jubal. I told you, just as Ben told it to me. It's the Secretary General himself."

"No," Harshaw denied. "While that may be true, it's not useful to us. No matter who did what, if it is anything rough or illegal, it won't be the Secretary General who did it, even if he benefits by it. Nobody would ever be able to prove that he even knew about it. It is likely that he would *not* know about it—not the rough stuff. No, Jill, we need to find out which lieutenant in the Secretary General's large staff of stooges handled this operation. But that isn't as hopeless as it sounds—I think. When Ben was taken in to see that phony 'Man from Mars,' one of Mr. Douglas's executive assistants was with him—tried to talk him out of it, then went with him. It now appears that this same top-level stooge also dropped out of sight last Thursday . . . and I don't think it is a coincidence, not when he appears to have been in charge of the phony 'Man from Mars.' If we find him, we may find Ben. Gilbert Berquist is his name and I have reason—"

"Berquist?"

"That's the name. And I have reason to suspect that—Jill, what's the trouble? Stop it! Don't faint, or swelp me, I'll dunk you in the pool!"

"Jubal. This 'Berquist.' Is there more than one Berquist?"

"Eh? I suppose so . . . though from all I can find out he does seem to be a bit of a bastard; there might be only one. But I mean the one on the Executive staff. Why? Do you know him?"

"I don't know. But if it is the same one . . . I don't think there's any use looking for him."

"Mmm . . . talk, girl."

"Jubal . . . I'm sorry—I'm terribly sorry—but I didn't tell you quite everything."

"People rarely do. All right, out with it."

Stumbling, stuttering, and stammering, Gillian managed to tell about the two men who suddenly were not there. Jubal simply listened. "And that's all," she concluded sadly. "I screamed and scared Mike . . . and he went into that trance you saw him in—and then I had a simply *terrible* time getting here. But I told you about that."

"Mmm . . . yes, so you did. I wish that you had told me about this, too."

She turned red. "I didn't think anybody would believe me. And I was scared. Jubal, can they do anything to us?"

"Eh?" Jubal seemed surprised. "Do what?"

"Send us to jail, or something?"

"Oh. My dear, it has not yet been declared a crime to be present at a miracle. Nor to work one. But this matter has more aspects than a cat has hair. Keep quiet and let me think."

Jill kept quiet. Jubal held still about ten minutes. At last he opened his eyes and said, "I don't see your problem child. He's probably lying on the bottom of the pool again—"

"He is."

"—so dive in and get him. Dry him off and bring him up to my study. I want to find out if he can repeat this stunt at will . . . and I don't think we need an audience. No, we do need an audience. Tell Anne to put on her Witness robe and come along—tell her I want her in her official capacity. I want Duke, too."

"Yes, Boss."

"You're not privileged to call me 'Boss'; you're not tax deductible."

"Yes, Jubal."

"That's better. Mmm . . . I wish we had somebody here who never would be missed. Regrettably we are all friends. Do you suppose Mike can do this stunt with inanimate objects?"

"I don't know."

"We'll find out. Well, what are you standing there for? Haul that boy out of the water and wake him up." Jubal blinked thoughtfully. "What a way to dispose of—no, I mustn't be tempted. See you upstairs, girl."

xii

A FEW MINUTES LATER Jill reported to Jubal's study. Anne was there, seated and enveloped in the long white robe of her guild; she glanced at Jill, said nothing. Jill found a chair and kept quiet, as Jubal was at his desk and dictating to Dorcas; he did not appear to notice Jill's arrival and went on dictating:

"—from under the sprawled body, soaking one corner of the rug and seeping out beyond it in a spreading dark red pool on the tiled hearth, where it was attracting the attention of two unemployed flies. Miss Simpson clutched at her mouth. 'Dear me!' she said in a distressed small voice, 'Daddy's favorite rug! . . . and Daddy, too, I do believe.' End of chapter, Dorcas, and end of first installment. Mail it off. Git."

Dorcas stood up and left, taking along her shorthand machine, and nodding and smiling to Jill as she did so. Jubal said, "Where's Mike?"

"In his room," answered Gillian, "dressing. He'll be along soon."

" 'Dressing'?" Jubal repeated peevishly. "I didn't say the party was formal."

"But he has to get dressed."

"Why? It makes no never-mind to me whether you kids wear skin or fleece-lined overcoats—and it's a warm day. Chase him in here."

"Please, Jubal. He's got to learn how to behave. I'm trying so hard to train him."

"Hmmph! You're trying to force on him your own narrow-minded, middle class, Bible Belt morality. Don't think I haven't been watching."

"I have not! I haven't concerned myself with his morals; I've simply been teaching him necessary customs."

"Customs, morals—is there a difference? Woman, do you realize what you are doing? Here, by the grace of God and an inside straight, we have a personality untouched by the psychotic taboos of our tribe—and you want to turn him into a carbon copy of every fourth-rate conformist in this frightened land! Why don't you go whole hog? Get him a brief case and make him carry it wherever he goes—make him feel shame if he doesn't have it."

"I'm not doing anything of the sort! I'm just trying to keep him out of trouble. It's for his own good."

Jubal snorted. "That's the excuse they gave the tomcat just before his operation."

"Oh!" Jill stopped and appeared to be counting ten. Then she said formally and bleakly, "This is your house, Doctor Harshaw, and we are in your debt. If you will excuse me, I will fetch Michael at once." She got up to leave.

"Hold it, Jill."

"Sir?"

"Sit back down—and for God's sake quit trying to be as nasty as I am; you don't have my years of practice. Now let me get something straight: you are not in my debt. You can't be. Impossible—because I never do anything I don't want to do. Nor does anyone, but in my case I am always aware of it. So please don't invent a debt that does not exist, or before you know it you will be trying to feel gratitude—and that is the treacherous first step downward to complete moral degradation. You grok that? Or don't you?"

Jill bit her lip, then grinned. "I'm not sure I know what 'grok' means."

"Nor do I. But I intend to go on taking lessons from Mike until I do. But I was speaking dead seriously. 'Gratitude' is a euphemism for resentment. Resentment from most people I do not mind—but from pretty little girls it is distasteful to me."

"Why, Jubal, I don't resent you—that's silly."

"I hope you don't . . . but you certainly will if you don't root out of your mind this delusion that you are indebted to me. The Japanese have five different ways to say 'thank you'—and every one of them translates literally as resentment, in various degrees. Would that English had the same built-in honesty on this point! Instead, English is capable of defining sentiments that the human nervous system is quite incapable of experiencing. 'Gratitude,' for example."

"Jubal, you're a cynical old man. I do feel grateful to you and I shall go on feeling grateful."

"And you are a sentimental young girl. That makes us a perfect complementary pair. Hmm . . . let's run over to Atlantic City for a weekend of illicit debauchery, just us two."

"Why, Jubal!"

"You see how deep your gratitude goes when I attempt to draw on it?"

"Oh. I'm ready. How soon do we leave?"

"Hummph! We should have left forty years ago. Shut up. The second point I want to make is that you are right; the boy does indeed have to learn human customs. He must be taught to take off his shoes in a mosque and to wear his hat in a synagogue and to cover his nakedness when taboo requires it, or our tribal shamans will burn him for deviationism. But, child, by the myriad deceptive aspects of Ahriman, don't brainwash him in the process. Make sure he is cynical about each part of it."

"Uh, I'm not sure how to go about that. Jubal—well, Mike just doesn't seem to have any cynicism in him."

"So? Yes. Well, I'll take a hand in it. What's keeping him? Shouldn't he be dressed by now?"

"I'll go see."

"In a moment. Jill, I explained to you why I had not been anxious to accuse anyone of kidnapping Ben . . . and the reports I have had since serve to support the probability that that was a tactically correct decision. If Ben is being unlawfully detained (to put it at its sweetest), at least we have not crowded the opposition into getting rid of the evidence by getting rid of Ben. If he is alive he stands a chance of staying alive. But I took other steps the first night you were here. Do you know your Bible?"

"Uh, not very well."

"It merits study, it contains very practical advice for most emergencies. '—every one that doeth evil hateth the light—' John something or other, Jesus speaking to Nicodemus. I have been expecting at any moment an attempt to get Mike away from us, for it didn't seem likely that you had managed to cover your tracks perfectly. And if they do try? Well, this is a lonely place and we haven't any heavy artillery. But there is one weapon that might balk them. Light. The glaring spotlight of publicity. So I made some phone calls and arranged for any ruckus here to have publicity. Not just a little publicity that the administration might be able to hush up—but great gobs of publicity, worldwide and all at once. The details do not matter—where and how the cameras are mounted and what line-of-sight linkages have been rigged, I mean—but if a fight breaks out here, it will be picked up by three networks and, at the same time, a number of hold-for-release messages will be delivered to a wide spread of V.I.P.s—all of whom would like very much to catch our Honorable Secretary General with his pants down."

Harshaw frowned. "The weakness in this defense is that I can't maintain it indefinitely. Truthfully, when I set it up, my worry was to set up fast enough—I expected whatever popped, to pop inside of twenty-four hours. Now my worry is reversed and I think we are going to have to force some action quickly, while I can still keep a spotlight on us."

"What sort of action, Jubal?"

"I don't know. I've been fretting about it the past three days, to the point where I can't enjoy my food. But you gave me a glimmering of a new approach when you told me that remarkable story about what happened when they tried to grab you two in Ben's apartment."

"I'm sorry I didn't tell you sooner, Jubal. But I didn't think anybody would believe me—and I must say that it makes me feel good that you do believe me."

"I didn't say I believed you."

"What? But you—"

"I think you were telling the truth, Jill. But a dream is a true experience of a sort and so is a hypnotic delusion. But what happens in this room during the next half hour will be seen by a Fair Witness and by cameras which are—" He leaned forward and pressed a button. "—rolling right now. I don't think Anne can be hypnotized when she's on duty and I'll lay long odds that cameras can't be. We should be able to find out what kind of truth we're dealing with—after which we should be able to decide how to go about forcing the powers-that-be to drop the other shoe . . . and maybe figure a way that will help Ben at the same time. Go get Mike."

Mike's delay was not mysterious, merely worrisome to him. He had managed to tie his left shoestring to his right—then had stood up, tripped himself, fallen flat, and, in so doing, jerked the knots almost hopelessly tight. He had spent the rest of the time analysing his predicament, concluding correctly why he had failed, and slowly, slowly, slowly getting the snarl untied and the strings correctly tied, one bow to each shoe, unlinked. He had not been aware that his dressing had taken long; he had simply been troubled that he had failed to repeat correctly something which Jill had already taught him. He confessed his failure abjectly to her even though he had repaired it by the time she came to fetch him.

She soothed and reassured him, combed his hair, and herded him in to see Jubal. Harshaw looked up. "Hi, son. Sit down."

"Hi, Jubal," Valentine Michael Smith answered gravely, sat down—waited. Jill had to rid herself of the impression that Smith had bowed deeply, when in fact he had not even nodded.

Harshaw put aside a hush-mike and said, "Well, boy what have you learned today?"

Smith smiled happily, then answered—as always with a slight pause. "I have today learned to do a one-and-a-half gainer. That is a jumping, a dive, for entering our water by—"

"I know, I saw you doing it. But you splashed. Keep your toes pointed, your knees straight, and your feet together."

Smith looked unhappy. "I rightly did not it do?"

"You did it very rightly, for a first time. Watch how Dorcas does it. Hardly a ripple in the water."

Smith considered this slowly. "The water groks Dorcas. It cherishes him."

" 'Her.' Dorcas is a 'her,' not a 'him.' "

" 'Her,' " Smith corrected. "Then my speaking was false? I have read in Webster's New International Dictionary of the English Language, Third Edition, published in Springfield, Massachusetts, that the masculine gender includes the feminine gender in speaking. In Hagworth's Law of Contracts, Fifth Edition, Chicago, Illinois, 1978, on page 1012, it says—"

"Hold it," Harshaw said hastily. "The trouble is with the English language, not with you. Masculine speech forms do include the feminine, when you are speaking in general—but not when you are talking about a particular person. Dorcas is always 'she' or 'her'—never 'he' or 'him.' Remember it."

"I will remember it."

"You had better remember it—or you may provoke Dorcas into proving just how female she is." Harshaw blinked thoughtfully. "Jill, is the lad sleeping with you? Or with one of you?"

She barely hesitated, then answered flatly, "So far as I know, Mike doesn't sleep."

"You evaded my question."

"Then perhaps you had better assume that I intended to evade it. However, he is not sleeping with *me.*"

"Mmm . . . damn it, my interest is scientific. However, we'll pursue another line of inquiry. Mike, what else have you learned today?"

"I have learned two ways to tie my shoes. One way is only good for lying down. The other way is good for walking. And I have learned conjugations. 'I am, thou art, he is, we are, you are, they are, I was, thou wast—'"

"Okay, that's enough. What else?"

Mike smiled delightedly. "To yesterday I am learning to drive the tractor, brightly, brightly, and with beauty."

"Eh?" Jubal turned to Jill. "When did this happen?"

"Yesterday afternoon while you were napping, Jubal. It's all right—Duke was very careful not to let him get hurt."

"Umm . . . well, obviously he did not get hurt. Mike, have you been reading?"

"Yes, Jubal."

"What?"

"I have read," Mike recited carefully, "three more volumes of the Encyclopedia, Maryb to Mushe, Mushr to Ozon, P to Planti. You have told me not to read too much of the Encyclopedia at one reading, so I then stopped. I then read the *Tragedy of Romeo and Juliet* by Master William Shakespeare of London. I then read the *Memoirs of Jacques Casanova de Seingalt* as translated into English by Arthur Machen. I then read *The Art of Cross-Examination* by Francis Wellman. I then tried to grok what I had read until Jill told me that I must come to breakfast."

"And did you grok it?"

Smith looked troubled. "Jubal, I do not know."

"Is anything bothering you, Mike?"

"I do not grok all fullness of what I read. In the history written by Master William Shakespeare I found myself full of happiness at the death of Romeo. Then I read on and learned that he had discorporated too soon —or so I thought I grokked. Why?"

"He was a blithering young idiot."

"Beg pardon?"

"I don't know, Mike."

Smith considered this. Then he muttered something in Martian and added, "I am only an egg."

"Eh? You usually say that when you want to ask a favor, Mike. What is it this time? Speak up."

Smith hesitated. Then he blurted out, "Jubal my brother, would please you ask Romeo why he discorporated? I cannot ask him; I am only an egg. But you can—and then you could teach me the grokking of it."

For the next several minutes the conversation became very tangled. Jubal saw at once that Mike believed that Romeo of Montague had been a living, breathing person, and Jubal managed with no special shock to his own concepts to realize that Mike expected him to be able, somehow, to conjure up Romeo's ghost and demand of him explanations for his conduct when in the flesh.

But to get over to Mike the idea that none of the Capulets and Montagues had ever had any sort of corporate existence was another matter. The concept of fiction was nowhere in Mike's experience; there was nothing on which it could rest, and Jubal's attempts to explain the idea were so emotionally upsetting to Mike that Jill was afraid that he was about to roll up into a ball and withdraw himself.

But Mike himself saw how perilously close he was coming to that necessity and he had already learned that he must not resort to this refuge in the presence of his friends, because (with the exception of his brother Doctor Nelson) it always caused them emotional disturbance. So he made a mighty effort, slowed down his heart, calmed his emotions, and smiled. "I will waiting till a grokking comes of itself."

"That's better," agreed Jubal. "But hereafter, before you read anything, ask me or ask Jill, or somebody, whether or not it is fiction. I don't want you to get mixed up."

"I will ask, Jubal." Mike decided that, when he did grok this strange idea, that he must report the fullness to the Old Ones . . . and suddenly found himself wondering if the Old Ones knew about "fiction." The completely incredible idea that there might be something which was as strange to the Old Ones as it was to himself was so much more revolutionary (indeed heretically so) than the sufficiently weird concept of fiction that he hastily put it aside to cool, saved it for future deep contemplation.

"—but I didn't," his brother Jubal was saying, "call you in here to discuss literary forms. Mike, you remember the day that Jill took you away from the hospital?"

" 'Hospital'?" Mike repeated.

"I'm not sure, Jubal," Jill interrupted, "that Mike ever knew that it was a hospital—at least I never told him it was one. Let me try it."

"Go ahead."

"Mike, you remember the place where you were, where you lived alone in a room, before I dressed you and took you away."

"Yes, Jill."

"Then we went to another place and I undressed you and gave you a bath."

Smith smiled in pleased recollection. "Yes. It was a great happiness."

"Then I dried you off—and then two men came."

Smith's smile wiped away. He relived that critical cusp of decision and the horror of his discovery that, somehow, he had chosen wrong action and hurt his water brother. He began to tremble and huddle into himself.

Jill said loudly, "Mike! Stop it! Stop it at once! Don't you dare go away!"

Mike took control of his being and did what his water brother required of him. "Yes, Jill," he agreed.

"Listen to me, Mike. I want you to think about that time—but you mustn't get upset or go away. Just remember it. There were two men there. One of them pulled you out into the living room."

"The room with the joyful grasses on the floor," he agreed.

"That's right. He pulled you out into the room with the grass on the floor and I tried to stop him. He hit me. Then he was gone. You remember?"

"You are not angry?"

"What? No, no, not at all. But I was frightened. One man disappeared, then the other one pointed a gun at me—and then he was gone, too. I was very frightened—but I was not angry."

"You are not angry with me now?"

"Mike, dear—I have *never* been angry with you. But sometimes I have been frightened. I was frightened that time—but I am not afraid now. Jubal and I want to know what happened. Those two men were there, in that room with us. And then you did something . . . and they were gone. You did it twice. What was it you did? Can you tell us?"

"Yes, I will tell you. The man—the big man—hit you . . . and I was frightened, too. So I—" He croaked a phrase in Martian, then looked puzzled. "I do not know words."

Jubal said, "Mike, can you use a lot of words and explain it a little at a time?"

"I will try, Jubal. Something is there, in front of me. It is a wrong thing and it must not be there. It must go. So I reach out and—" He stopped again and looked perplexed. "It is such a simple thing, such an easy thing. Anyone can do it. Tying shoe laces is much more hard. But the words not are. I am very sorry. I will learn more words." He considered it. "Perhaps the words are in Plants to Raym, or Rayn to Sarr, or Sars to Sorc. I will read them tonight and tell you at breakfast."

"Maybe," Jubal admitted. "Just a minute, Mike." He got up from his desk, went to a corner and returned with a large carton which had lately contained twelve fifths of brandy. "Can you make this go away?"

"This is a wrong thing and it must not be here?"

"Well, assume that it is."

"But—Jubal, I must *know* that it is a wrong thing. This is a box. I do not grok that it exists wrongly."

"Mmm— I see. I think I see. Suppose I picked up this box and threw it at Jill's head? Threw it hard, so that it would hurt her?"

Smith said with gentle sadness, "Jubal, you would not do that to Jill."

"Uh . . . damn it, I guess I wouldn't. Jill, will you throw the box at me? Good and hard—a scalp wound at least, if Mike can't protect me."

"Jubal, I don't like the idea much better than you do."

"Oh, come on! In the interest of science . . . and Ben Caxton."

"But—" Jill jumped up suddenly, grabbed the box, threw it right at Jubal's head. Jubal intended to stand and take it—but instinct and habit won out; he ducked.

"Missed me," he said. "But where is it?" He looked around. "Confound it, I wasn't watching. I meant to keep my eyes right on it." He looked at Smith. "Mike, is that the way—what's the matter, boy?"

The Man from Mars was trembling and looking unhappy. Jill hurried to him and put her arms around his shoulders. "There, there, it's all right, dear! You did it beautifully—whatever it is. It never touched Jubal. It simply vanished."

"I guess it did," Jubal admitted, looking all around the room and chewing his thumb. "Anne, were you watching?"

"Yes."

"What did you see?"

"The box did not simply vanish. The process was not quite instantaneous but lasted some measurable fraction of a second. From where I am sitting it appeared to shrink very, very rapidly, as if it were disappearing into the far distance. But it did not go outside the room, for I could see it right up to the instant it disappeared."

"But where did it go?"

"That is all I can report."

"Mmm . . . we'll run off the films later—but I'm convinced. Mike—"

"Yes, Jubal?"

"Where is that box now?"

"The box is—" Smith paused. "Again I have not words. I am sorry."

"I'm not sorry, but I'm certainly confused. Look, son, can you reach in again and haul it out? Bring the box back here?"

"Beg pardon?"

"You made it go away; now make it come back."

"How can I do that? The box is *not.*"

Jubal looked very thoughtful. "If this method ever becomes popular, we'll have to revise the rules concerning corpus delecti. 'I've got a little list . . . they never will be missed.' Jill, let's find something else that will make a not-quite-lethal weapon; this time I'm going to keep my eyes open. Mike, how close do you have to be to do this trick?"

"Beg pardon?"

"What's your range? If you had been standing out there in the hall-way and I had been clear back by the window—oh, say thirty feet—could you have stopped that box from hitting me?"

Smith appeared mildly surprised. "Yes."

"Hmm . . . come over here by the window. Now look down there at the swimming pool. Suppose that Jill and I had been over on the far side of the pool and you had been standing right where you are. Could you have stopped the box from here?"

"Yes, Jubal."

"Well . . . suppose Jill and I were clear down the road there at the gate, a quarter of a mile away. Suppose we were standing just this side of those bushes that shield the gate, where you could see us clearly. Is that too far?"

Smith hesitated a long time, then spoke slowly. "Jubal, it is not the distance. It is not the seeing. It is the knowing."

"Hmm . . . let's see if I grok it. Or grok part of it. It doesn't matter how far or how close a thing is. You don't even have to see it happening. But if you know that a bad thing is happening, you can reach out and stop it. Right?"

Smith looked slightly troubled. "Almost it is right. But I am not long out of the nest. For knowing I must see. But an Old One does not need eyes to know. He knows. He groks. He acts. I am sorry."

"I don't know what you are sorry about, son," Jubal said gruffly. "The High Minister for Peace would have declared you Top Secret ten minutes ago."

"Beg pardon?"

"Never mind. What you do is quite good enough in this vicinity." Jubal returned to his desk, looked around thoughtfully and picked up a ponderous metal ash tray. "Jill, don't aim at my face this time; this thing has sharp corners. Okay, Mike, you stand clear out in the hallway."

"Jubal . . . my brother . . . *please* not!"

"What's the trouble, son? You did it beautifully a few minutes ago. I want one more demonstration—and this time I won't take my eyes off it."

"Jubal—"

"Yes, Jill?"

"I think I grok what is bothering Mike."

"Well, tell me then, for I don't."

"We set up an experiment where I was about to hurt you by hitting you with that box. But both of us are his water brothers—so it upset Mike that I even tried to hurt you. I think there is something very unMartian about such a situation. It puts Mike in a dilemma. Divided loyalty."

Harshaw frowned. "Maybe it should be investigated by the Committee on un-Martian Activities."

"I'm not joking, Jubal."

"Nor was I—for we may need such a committee all too soon. I wonder how Mrs. O'Leary's cow felt as she kicked the lantern? All right, Jill, you sit down and I'll re-rig the experiment." Harshaw handed the ash tray to Mike. "Feel how heavy it is, son, and see those sharp corners."

Smith examined it somewhat gingerly. Harshaw went on, "I'm going to throw it straight up in the air, clear to the ceiling—and let it hit me in the head as it comes down."

Mike stared at him. "My brother . . . you will now discorporate?"

"Eh? No, no! It won't kill me and I don't want to die. But it will cut me and hurt me—unless you stop it. Here we go!" Harshaw tossed it straight up within inches of the high ceiling, tracking it with his eyes like a soccer player waiting to pass the ball with his head. He concentrated on watching it, while one part of his mind was considering jerking his head aside at the last instant rather than take the nasty scalp wound the heavy, ugly thing was otherwise sure to give him—and another small piece of his mind reckoned cynically that he would never miss this chattel; he had never liked it—but it had been a gift.

The ash tray topped its trajectory, and stayed there.

Harshaw looked at it, with a feeling that he was stuck in one frame of a motion picture. Presently he remembered to breathe and found that he needed to, badly. Without taking his eyes off it he croaked, "Anne. What do you see?"

She answered in a flat voice, "That ash tray is five inches from the ceiling. I do not see anything holding it up." Then she added in tones less certain, "Jubal, I *think* that's what I'm seeing . . . but if the cameras don't show the same thing, I'm going to turn in my robe and tear up my license."

"Um. Jill?"

"It floats. It just floats."

Jubal sighed, went to his chair and sat down heavily, all without taking his eyes off the unruly ash tray. "Mike," he said, "what went wrong? Why didn't it disappear like the box?"

"But, Jubal," Mike said apologetically, "you said to stop it; you did not say to make it go away. When I made the box go away, you wanted it to *be* again. Have I done wrongly?"

"Oh. No, you have done exactly right. I keep forgetting that you always take things literally." Harshaw recalled certain colloquial insults common in his early years—and reminded himself forcefully never, *never* to use any of such to Michael Valentine Smith—for, if he told the boy to drop dead or to get lost, Harshaw now felt certain that the literal meaning of his words would at once ensue.

"I am glad," Smith answered soberly. "I am sorry I could not make the box be again. I am sorry twice that I wasted so much food. But I did not know how to help it. Then a necessity was. Or so I grokked."

"Eh? What food?"

Jill said hastily, "He's talking about those two men, Jubal. Berquist and the cop with him—if he was a cop. Johnson."

"Oh, yes." Harshaw reflected that he himself still retained unMartian notions of food, subconsciously at least. "Mike, I wouldn't worry about wasting that 'food.' They probably would have been tough and poor flavor. I doubt if a meat inspector would have passed them. In fact," he added, recalling the Federation convention about "long pig," "I am certain that they would have been condemned as unfit for food. So don't worry about it. Besides, as you say, it was a necessity. You grokked the fullness and acted rightly."

"I am much comforted," Mike answered with great relief in his voice. "Only an Old One can always be sure of right action at a cusp . . . and I have much learning to learn and much growing to grow before I may join the Old Ones. Jubal? May I move it? I am tiring."

"You want to make it go away now? Go ahead."

"But now I cannot."

"Eh? Why not?"

"Your head is no longer under it. I do not grok wrongness in its being, where it is."

"Oh. All right. Move it." Harshaw continued to watch it, expecting that it would float to the spot now over his head and thus regain a wrongness. Instead the ash tray moved downward at a slow, steady speed, moved sideways until it was close above his desk top, hovered for a moment, then slid to an empty spot and came in to an almost noiseless landing.

"Thank you, Jubal," said Smith.

"Eh? Thank *you,* son!" Jubal picked up the ash tray, examined it curiously. It was neither hot nor cold nor did it make his fingers tingle—it was as ugly, over-decorated, commonplace, and dirty as it had been five minutes earlier. "Yes, thank *you.* For the most amazing experience I've had since the day the hired girl took me up into the attic." He looked up. "Anne, you trained at Rhine."

"Yes."

"Have you seen levitation before?"

She hesitated slightly. "I've seen what was called telekinesis with dice —but I'm no mathematician and I could not testify that what I saw was telekinesis."

"Hell's bells, you wouldn't testify that the sun had risen if the day was cloudy."

"How could I? Somebody might be supplying artificial light from above the cloud layer. One of my classmates could apparently levitate objects about the mass of a paper clip—but he had to be just three drinks drunk and sometimes he couldn't do it at all. I was never able to examine the phenomenon closely enough to be competent to testify about it . . . partly because I usually had three drinks in me by then, too."

"Then you've never seen anything like this?"

"No."

"Mmm . . . I'm through with you professionally; I'm convinced. But if you want to stay and see what else happens, hang up your robe and drag up a chair."

"Thanks, I will—both. But, in view of the lecture you gave Jill about mosques and synagogues, I'll go to my room first. I wouldn't want to cause a hiatus in the indoctrination."

"Suit yourself. While you're out, wake up Duke and tell him I want the cameras serviced again."

"Yes, Boss. Don't let anything startling happen until I get back." Anne headed for the door.

"No promises. Mike, sit down here at my desk. You, too, Jill—gather 'round. Now, Mike, can you pick up that ash tray? Show me."

"Yes, Jubal." Smith reached out and took it in his hand.

"No, no!"

"I did wrongly?"

"No, it was my mistake. Mike, put it back down. I want to know if you can lift that ash tray *without* touching it?"

"Yes, Jubal."

"Well? Are you too tired?"

"No, Jubal. I am not too tired."

"Then what's the matter? Does it have to have a 'wrongness' about it?"

"No, Jubal."

"Jubal," Jill interrupted, "you haven't *told* him to do it—you've just asked him if he could."

"Oh." Jubal looked as sheepish as he was capable of looking, which was not much. "I should learn. Mike, will you please, without touching it with your hands, lift that ash tray a foot above the desk?"

"Yes, Jubal." The ash tray raised, floated steadily above the desk. "Will you measure, Jubal?" Mike said anxiously. "If I did wrongly, I will move it up or down."

"That's just fine! Can you hold it there? If you get tired, tell me."

"I can. I will tell."

"Can you lift something else at the same time? Say this pencil? If you can, then do it."

"Yes, Jubal." The pencil ranged itself neatly by the ash tray.

By request, Mike added other small articles from the desk to the layer of floating objects. Anne returned, pulled up a chair and watched the performance without speaking. Duke came in, carrying a step ladder, glanced at the group, then looked a second time, but said nothing and set the ladder in one corner. At last Mike said uncertainly, "I am not sure, Jubal. I—" He stopped and seemed to search for a word. "I am idiot in these things."

"Don't wear yourself out."

"I can think one more. I hope." A paper weight across the desk from Mike stirred, lifted—and all the dozen-odd floating objects fell down at once. Mike seemed about to weep although no tears formed. "Jubal, I am sorry. I am utmostly sorry."

Harshaw patted his shoulder. "You should be proud, not sorry. Son, you don't seem to realize it, but what you just did is—" Jubal searched for a comparison, rapidly discarded the many that sprang to his mind because he realized that they touched nothing in Mike's experience. "What you did is much harder than tying shoestrings, much more wonderful to us than doing a one-and-a-half gainer perfectly. You did it, uh, 'brightly, brightly, and with beauty.' You grok?"

Mike looked surprised. "I am not sure, Jubal. I should not feel shame?"

"You must not feel shame. You should feel proud."

"Yes, Jubal," he answered contentedly. "I feel proud."

"Good. Mike, I cannot lift even one ash tray without touching it."

Smith looked startled. "You cannot?"

"No. Can you teach me?"

"Yes, Jubal. You—" Smith stopped speaking, looked embarrassed. "I again have not words. I am sorry. But I will read and I will read and I will read, until I find the words. Then I will teach my brother."

"Don't set your heart on it."

"Beg pardon?"

"Mike, don't be disappointed if you do not find the right words. You may not find them in the English language."

Smith considered this quite a long time. "Then I will teach my brother the language of my nest."

"Maybe. I would like to try—but you may have arrived about fifty years too late."

"I have acted wrongly?"

"Not at all. I'm proud of you. You might start by trying to teach Jill your language."

"It hurts my throat," put in Jill.

"Try gargling with aspirin." Jubal looked at her. "That's a silly excuse, nurse—but it occurs to me that this gives me an excuse to put you on the payroll . . . for I doubt if they will ever take you back at Bethesda. All right, you're my staff research assistant for Martian linguistics . . . which includes such extra duties as may be necessary. Take that up with the girls. Anne, put her on the payroll—and be sure it gets entered in the tax records."

"She's been doing her share in the kitchen since the day after she got here. Shall I date it back?"

Jubal shrugged. "Don't bother me with details."

"But, Jubal," Jill protested shrilly, "I don't think I *can* learn Martian!"

"You can *try,* can't you? That's all Columbus did."

"But—"

"What was that idle chatter you were giving me about 'gratitude'? Do you take the job? Or don't you?"

Jill bit her lip. "I'll take it. Yes . . . Boss."

Smith timidly reached out and touched her hand. "Jill . . . I will teach."

Jill patted his. "Thanks, Mike." She looked at Harshaw. "And I'm going to learn it just to spite you!"

He grinned warmly at her. "That's a motive I grok perfectly—you'll learn it all right. Now back to business— Mike, what else can you do that we can't do? Besides making things go away—when they have a 'wrongness'—and lifting things without touching them."

Smith looked puzzled. "I do not know."

"How could he know," protested Jill, "when he doesn't really know what we can and can't do?"

"Mmm . . . yes. Anne, change that job title to 'staff research assistant for Martian linguistics, culture, and techniques.' Jill, in learning their language you are bound to stumble onto Martian things that are different, really different—and when you do, tell me. Everything and anything about a culture can be inferred from the shape of its language—and you're probably young enough to learn to think like a Martian . . . which I misdoubt I am not. And you, Mike, if you notice anything which you can do but we don't do, tell me."

"I will tell, Jubal. What things will be these?"

"I don't know. Things like you just did . . . and being able to stay on the bottom of the pool much longer than we can. Hmm . . . Duke!"

"Yes, Boss? I've got both hands full of film. Don't bother me."

"You can talk, can't you? I noticed the pool is pretty murky."

"Yeah. I'm going to add precipitant tonight and vacuum it in the morning."

"How's the count?"

"The count is okay, the water is safe enough to serve at the table. It just looks messy."

"Let it stay murky for the time being. Test it as usual. I'll let you know when I want it cleaned up."

"Hell, Boss, nobody likes to swim in a pool that looks like dishwater. I would have tidied it up long before this if there hadn't been so much hooraw around here this week."

"Anybody too fussy to swim in it can stay dry. Quit jawing about it, Duke; I'll explain later. Films ready?"

"Five minutes."

"Good. Mike, do you know what a gun is?"

"A gun," Smith answered carefully, "is a piece of ordnance for throwing projectiles by the force of some explosive, as gunpowder, consisting of a tube or barrel closed at one end, where the—"

"Okay, okay. Do you grok it?"

"I am not sure."

"Have you ever seen a gun?"

"I do not know."

"Why, certainly you have," Jill interrupted. "Mike, think back to that time we were talking about, in the room with the grass on the floor—but don't get upset now! The big man hit me, you remember."

"Yes."

"The other man pointed something at me. In his hand."

"Yes. He pointed a bad thing at you."

"That was a gun."

"I had thought that the word for that bad thing might be 'gun.' The Webster's New International Dictionary of the English Language, Third Edition, published in—"

"That's fine, son," Harshaw said hastily. "That was certainly a gun. Now listen to me carefully. If someone points a gun at Jill again, what will you do?"

Smith paused rather longer than usual. "You will not be angry if I waste food?"

"No, I would not be angry. Under those circumstances no one would be angry at you. But I am trying to find out something else. Could you make just the gun go away, without making the man who is pointing it go away?"

Smith considered it. "Save the food?"

"Uh, that isn't quite what I mean. Could you cause the gun to go away without hurting the man?"

"Jubal, he would not hurt at all. I would make the gun go away, but the man I would just stop. He would feel no pain. He would simply be discorporate. The food he leaves after him would not damage at all."

Harshaw sighed. "Yes, I'm sure that's the way it would be. But could you cause to go away just the gun? Not do anything else? Not 'stop' the man, not kill him, just let him go on living?"

Smith considered it. "That would be much easier than doing both at once. But, Jubal, if I left him still corporate, he might still hurt Jill. Or so I grok it."

Harshaw stopped long enough to remind himself that this baby innocent was neither babyish nor innocent—was in fact sophisticated in a culture which he was beginning to realize, however dimly, was far in advance of human culture in some very mysterious ways . . . and that these naive remarks came from a superman—or what would do in place of a "superman" for the time being. Then he answered Smith, choosing his words most carefully as he had in mind a dangerous experiment and did not want disaster to follow from semantic mishap.

"Mike . . . if you reach a—'cusp'—where you must do something in order to protect Jill, you do it."

"Yes, Jubal. I will."

"Don't worry about wasting food. Don't worry about anything else. Protect Jill "

"Always I will protect Jill."

"Good. But suppose a man pointed a gun at someone—or simply had it in his hand. Suppose you did not want or need to kill him . . . but you needed to make the gun go away. Could you do it?"

Mike paused only briefly. "I think I grok it. A gun is a wrong thing. But it might be needful for the man to remain corporate." He thought. "I can do it."

"Good. Mike, I am going to show you a gun. A gun is a wrong thing."

"A gun is a very wrong thing. I will make it go away."

"Don't make it go away as soon as you see it."

"Not?"

"Not. I will lift the gun and start to point it at you. Like this. Before I can get it pointed at you, make it go away. But don't stop me, don't hurt me, don't kill me, don't do *anything* to me. Just the gun. Don't waste me as food, either."

"Oh, I never would," Mike said earnestly. "When you discorporate, my brother Jubal, I hope to be allowed to eat of you myself, praising and cherishing you with every bite . . . until I grok you in fullness."

Harshaw controlled a seasick reflex he had not felt in decades and answered gravely, "Thank you, Mike."

"It is I who must thank you, my brother—and if it should come to be that I am selected before you, I hope that you will find me worthy of grokking. Sharing me with Jill. You would share me with Jill? Please?"

Harshaw glanced at Jill, saw that she had kept her face serene—reflected that she probably was a rock-steady scrub nurse. "I will share you with Jill," he said solemnly. "But, Mike, no one of us will be food today, nor any time soon. Right now I am going to show you this gun—and you wait until I say . . . and then you be very careful, because I have many things to do before I am ready to discorporate."

"I will be careful, my brother."

"All right." Harshaw leaned over, grunting slightly, and opened a lower drawer of his desk. "Look in here, Mike. See the gun? I'm going to pick it up. But don't do anything until I tell you to. Girls—get up and move away to the left; I don't want it pointed at you. Okay. Mike, not yet." Harshaw reached for the gun, a very elderly police special, took it out of the drawer. "Get ready, Mike. *Now!*"—and Harshaw did his very best to get the weapon aimed at the Man from Mars.

His hand was suddenly empty. No shock, no jar, no twisting—the gun was gone and that was all.

Jubal found that he was shaking, so he stopped it. "Perfect," he said to Mike. "You got it before I had it aimed at you. That's utterly perfect."

"I am happy."

"So am I. Duke, did that get in the camera?"

"Yup. I put in fresh film cartridges. You didn't say."

"Good." Harshaw sighed and found that he was very tired. "That's all today, kids. Run along. Go swimming. You, too, Anne."

Anne said, "Boss? You'll tell me what the films show?"

"Want to stay and see them?"

"Oh, no! I couldn't, not the parts I Witnessed. But I would like to know—later—whether or not they show that I've slipped my clutches."

"All right."

xiii

WHEN THEY HAD GONE, Harshaw started to give instructions to Duke—then instead said grumpily, "What are you looking sour about?"

"Boss, when are we going to get rid of that ghoul?"

" 'Ghoul'? Why, you provincial lout!"

"Okay, so I come from Kansas. You won't find any cases of cannibalism in Kansas—they were all farther west. I've got my own opinions about who is a lout and who isn't . . . but I'm eating in the kitchen until we get rid of him."

Harshaw said icily, "So? Don't put yourself out. Anne can have your closing check ready in five minutes . . . and it ought not to take you more than ten minutes to pack up your comic books and your other shirt."

Duke had been setting up a projector. He stopped and straightened up. "Oh, I didn't mean that I was quitting."

"It means exactly that to me, son."

"But— I mean, what the hell? I've eaten in the kitchen lots of times."

"So you have. For your own convenience, or to keep from making extra work for the girls. Or some such. You can have breakfast in bed, for all of me, if you can bribe the girls to serve it to you. But nobody who sleeps under my roof refuses to eat at my table because he doesn't want to eat with others who eat there. I happen to be of an almost extinct breed, an old-fashioned gentleman—which means I can be a real revolving son of bitch when it suits me. And it suits me right now . . . which is to say that no ignorant, superstitious, prejudiced bumpkin is permitted to tell me who is, or is not, fit to eat at my table. If I choose to dine with publicans and sinners, that is my business. But I do not choose to break bread with Pharisees."

Duke turned red and said slowly, "I ought to pop you one—and I would, if you were my age."

"Don't let that stop you, Duke. I may be tougher than you think . . . and if I'm not, the commotion will probably bring the others in. Do you think you can handle the Man from Mars?"

"*Him?* I could break him in two with one hand!"

"Probably . . . if you could lay a hand on him."

"Huh?"

"You saw me try to point a pistol at him. Duke—*where's that pistol?* Before you go flexing your biceps, stop and think—or whatever it is you do in place of thinking. Find that pistol. Then tell me whether or not you still think you can break Mike in two. But find the pistol first."

Duke wrinkled his forehead, then went ahead setting up the projector. "Some sort of sleight-of-hand. The films will show it."

Harshaw said, "Duke. Stop fiddling with that projector. Sit down. I'll take care of it after you've left and run off the films myself. But I want to talk to you a few moments first."

"Huh? Jubal, I don't want you touching this projector. Every time you do, you get it out of whack. It's a delicate piece of machinery."

"Sit down, I said."

"But—"

"It's my projector, Duke. I'll bust the damned thing if it suits me. Or I'll get Larry to run it for me. But I do not accept service from a man after he has resigned from my employ."

"Hell, I didn't resign! You got nasty and sounded off and fired me—for no reason."

"Sit down, Duke," Harshaw said quietly. "Either sit down . . . and let me try to save your life—or get off this place as fast as you can and let me send your clothes and wages after you. Don't stop to pack; it's too risky. You might not live that long."

"What the hell do you mean?"

"Exactly what I say. Duke, it's irrelevant whether you resigned or were fired; you terminated your employment here when you announced that you would no longer eat at my table. Nevertheless I would find it distasteful for you to be killed on my premises. So sit down and I will do my best to avoid it."

Duke looked startled, opened his mouth—closed it and sat down. Harshaw went on, "Are you Mike's water brother?"

"Huh? Of course not. Oh, I've heard such chatter—but it's nonsense, if you ask me."

"It is not nonsense and nobody asked you; you aren't competent to have an opinion about it." Harshaw frowned. "That's too bad. I can see that I am not only going to have to let you go—and, Duke, I don't want to fire you; you do a good job of keeping the gadgetry around here working properly and thereby save me from being annoyed by mechanical buffoonery I am totally uninterested in. But I must not only get you safely off the place but I must also find out at once who else around here is not a water brother to Mike . . . and either see to it that they become such—or get them off the place before anything happens to them." Jubal chewed his lip and stared at the ceiling. "Maybe it would be sufficient to exact a solemn promise from Mike not to hurt anyone without my specific permission. Mmmm . . . no, I can't risk it. Too much horse play around here—and there is always the chance that Mike might misinterpret something that was meant in fun. Say if you—or Larry, rather, since you won't be here—picked up Jill and tossed her into the pool, Larry might wind up where that pistol went, before I could explain to Mike that it was all in fun and Jill was not in danger. I wouldn't want Larry to die through my oversight. Larry is entitled to work out his own damn foolishness without having it cut short through my carelessness. Duke, I believe in everyone's working out his own damnation his own way . . . but nevertheless that is no excuse for an adult to give a dynamite cap to a baby as a toy."

Duke said slowly, "Boss, you sound like you've come unzipped. Mike wouldn't hurt anybody—shucks, this cannibalism talk makes me want to throw up but don't get me wrong; I know he's just a savage, he doesn't know any better. Hell, Boss, he's gentle as a lamb. He would never hurt anybody."

"You think so?"

"I'm sure of it."

"So. You've got two or three guns in your room. I say he's dangerous. It's open season on Martians, so pick a gun you trust, go down to the swimming pool, and kill him. Don't worry about the law; I'll be your attorney and I guarantee that you'll never be indicted. Go ahead, do it!"

"Jubal . . . you don't mean that."

"No. No, I don't really mean it. Because you *can't*. If you tried it, your gun would go where my pistol went—and if you hurried him you'd probably go with it. Duke, you don't know what you are fiddling with— and I don't either except that I know it's dangerous and you don't. Mike is not 'gentle as a lamb' and he is not a savage. I suspect *we* are the savages. Ever raise snakes?"

"Uh . . . no."

"I did, when I was a kid. Thought I was going to be a zoologist then. One winter, down in Florida, I caught what I thought was a scarlet snake. Know what they look like?"

"I don't like snakes."

"Prejudice again, rank prejudice. Most snakes are harmless, useful, and fun to raise. The scarlet snake is a beauty—red, and black and yellow —docile and makes a fine pet. I think this little fellow was fond of me, in its dim reptilian fashion. Of course I knew how to handle snakes, how not to alarm them and not give them a chance to bite, because the bite of even a non-poisonous snake is a nuisance. But I was fond of this baby; he was the prize of my collection. I used to take him out and show him to people, holding him back of his head and letting him wrap himself around my wrist.

"One day I got a chance to show my collection to the herpetologist of the Tampa zoo—and I showed him my prize first. He almost had hysterics. My pet was not a scarlet snake—it was a young coral snake. The American cobra . . . the most deadly snake in North America. Duke, do you see my point?"

"I see that raising snakes is dangerous. I could have told you."

"Oh, for Pete's sake! I already had rattlesnakes and water moccasins in my collection. A poisonous snake is not dangerous, not any more than a loaded gun is dangerous—in each case, if you handle it properly. The thing that made that coral snake dangerous was that I hadn't known what it was, what it could do. If, in my ignorance, I had handled it carelessly, it would have killed me as casually and as innocently as a kitten scratches. And that's what I'm trying to tell you about Mike. He seems as gentle as a lamb—and I'm convinced that he really is gentle and unreservedly friendly with anyone he trusts. But if he doesn't trust you—well, he's not what he seems to be. He seems like an ordinary young male human, rather under-developed, decidedly clumsy, and abysmally ignorant . . . but bright and very docile and eager to learn. All of which is true and not surprising, in view of his ancestry and his strange background. But, like my pet snake, Mike is more than he appears to be. If Mike does not trust you, blindly and all out, he can be instantly aggressive and much more deadly than that coral snake. Especially if he thinks you are harming one of his water brothers, such as Jill—or me."

Harshaw shook his head sadly. "Duke, if you had given way to your natural impulse to take a poke at me, a few minutes ago when I told you some homely truths about yourself, and if Mike had been standing in that doorway behind you . . . well, I'm convinced that you would have stood no chance at all. None. You would have been dead before you knew it, much too quickly for me to stop him. Mike would then have been sorrowfully apologetic over having 'wasted food'—namely your big, beefy carcass. Oh, he would feel guilty about that; you heard him a while ago. But he wouldn't feel guilty about killing you; that would just be a necessity you had forced on him . . . and not a matter of any great importance anyhow, even to you. You see, Mike believes that your soul is immortal."

"Huh? Well, hell, so do I. But—"

"Do you?" Jubal said bleakly. "I wonder."

"Why, certainly I do! Oh, I admit I don't go to church much, but I was brought up right. I'm no infidel. I've got faith."

"Good. Though I've never been able to understand 'faith' myself, nor to see how a just God could expect his creatures to pick the one true religion out of an infinitude of false ones—by faith alone. It strikes me as a sloppy way to run an organization, whether a universe or a smaller one. However, since you do have faith and it includes belief in your own immortality, we need not trouble further over the probability that your prejudices will result in your early demise. Do you want to be cremated or buried?"

"Huh? Oh, for cripe's sake, Jubal, quit trying to get my goat."

"Not at all. I can't guarantee to get you off my place safely as long as you persist in thinking that a coral snake is a harmless scarlet snake—any blunder you make may be your last. But I promise you I won't let Mike eat you."

Duke's mouth dropped open. At last he managed to answer, explosively, profanely, and quite incoherently. Harshaw listened, then said testily, "All right, all right, but pipe down. You can make any arrangements with Mike you like. I thought I was doing you a favor." Harshaw turned and bent over the projector. "I want to see these pictures. Stick around, if you want to, until I'm through. Prob'ly safer. Damn!" he added. "The pesky thing savaged me."

"You tried to force it. Here—" Duke completed the adjustment Harshaw had muffed, then went ahead and inserted the first film cartridge. Neither of them re-opened the question of whether Duke was, or was not, still working for Jubal. The cameras were Mitchell servos; the projector was a Yashinon tabletop tank, with an adapter to permit it to receive Land Solid-Sight-Sound 4 mm. film. Shortly they were listening to and watching the events leading up to the disappearance of the empty brandy case.

Jubal watched the box being thrown at his head, saw it wink out in midair. "That's enough," he said. "Anne will be pleased to know that the cameras back her up. Duke, let's repeat that last bit in slow motion."

"Okay." Duke spooled back, then announced, "This is ten-to-one."

The scene was the same but the slowed-down sound was useless; Duke switched it off. The box floated slowly from Jill's hands toward Jubal's head, then quite suddenly ceased to be. But it did not simply wink out; under slow-motion projection it could be seen shrinking, smaller and smaller until it was no longer there.

Jubal nodded thoughtfully. "Duke, can you slow it down still more?"

"Just a sec. Something is fouled up with the stereo."

"What?"

"Darned if I can figure it out. It looked all right on the fast run. But when I slowed it down, the depth effect was reversed. You saw it. That box went away from us fast, mighty fast—but it always looked closer than the wall. Swapped parallax, of course. But I never took that cartridge off the spindle. Gremlins."

"Oh. Hold it, Duke. Run the film from the other camera."

"Unh . . . oh, I see. That'll give us a ninety-degree cross on it and we'll see properly even if I did jimmy this film somehow." Duke changed cartridges. "Zip through the first part, okay? Then undercranked ten-to-one on the part that counts."

"Go ahead."

The scene was the same save for angle. When the image of Jill grabbed the box, Duke slowed down the show and again they watched the box go away.

Duke cursed. "Something was fouled up with the second camera, too."

"So?"

"Of course. It was looking at it around from the side so the box should have gone out of the frame to one side or the other. Instead it went straight away from us again. Well, didn't it? You saw it. Straight away from us."

"Yes," agreed Jubal. " 'Straight away from us.' "

"But it *can't*—not from both angles."

"What do you mean, it can't? It already did." Harshaw added, "If we had used doppler-radar in place of each of those cameras, I wonder what they would have shown?"

"How should I know? I'm going to take both these cameras apart."

"Don't bother."

"But—"

"Don't waste your time, Duke; the cameras are all right. What is exactly ninety degrees from everything else?"

"I'm no good at riddles."

"It's not a riddle and I meant it seriously. I could refer you to Mr. A. Square from Flatland, but I'll answer it myself. What is exactly at right angles to everything else? Answer: two dead bodies, one old pistol, and an empty liquor case."

"What the deuce do you mean, Boss?"

"I never spoke more plainly in my life. Try believing what the cameras see instead of insisting that the cameras must be at fault because what they saw was not what you expected. Let's see the other films."

Harshaw made no comment as they were shown; they added nothing to what he already knew but did confirm and substantiate. The ash tray when floating near the ceiling had been out of camera angle, but its leisurely descent and landing had been recorded. The pistol's image in the stereo tank was quite small but, so far as could be seen, the pistol had done just what the box appeared to have done: shrunk away into the far distance without moving. Since Harshaw had been gripping it tightly when it had shrunk out of his hand, he was satisfied—if "satisfied" was the right word, he added grumpily to himself. "Convinced" at least.

"Duke, when you get time, I want duplicate prints of all of those."

Duke hesitated. "You mean I'm still working here?"

"What? Oh, damn it! You can't eat in the kitchen, and that's flat. Duke, try to cut your local prejudices out of the circuit and just listen for a while. Try really hard."

"I'll listen."

"When Mike asked for the privilege of eating my stringy old carcass, he was doing me the greatest honor that he knew of—by the only rules he knows. What he had 'learned at his mother's knee,' so to speak. Do you savvy that? You heard his tone of voice, you saw his manner. He was paying me his highest compliment—and asking of me a boon. You see? Never mind what they think of such things in Kansas; Mike uses the values taught him on Mars."

"I think I'll take Kansas."

"Well," admitted Jubal, "so do I. But it is not a matter of free choice for me, nor for you—nor for Mike. All three of us are prisoners of our early indoctrinations, for it is hard, very nearly impossible, to shake off one's earliest training. Duke, can you get it through your skull that if *you* had been born on Mars and brought up by Martians, you yourself would have exactly the same attitude toward eating and being eaten that Mike has?"

Duke considered it, then shook his head. "I won't buy it, Jubal. Sure, about most things it's just Mike's hard luck that he wasn't brought up in civilization—and my good luck that I was. I'm willing to make allowances for him. But this is different, this is an instinct."

" 'Instinct,' *dreck!*"

"But it is. I didn't get any 'training at my mother's knee' not to be a cannibal. Hell, I didn't need it; I've always known it was a sin—a nasty one. Why, the mere thought of it makes my stomach do a flip-flop. It's a basic instinct."

Jubal groaned. "Duke, how could you learn so much about machinery and never learn anything about how you yourself tick? That nausea you feel—that's not an instinct; that's a conditioned reflex. Your mother didn't have to say to you, 'Mustn't eat your playmates, dear; that's not nice,' because you soaked it up from our whole culture—and so did I. Jokes about cannibals and missionaries, cartoons, fairy tales, horror stories, endless little things. But it has nothing to do with instinct. Shucks, son, it couldn't possibly be instinct . . . because cannibalism is historically one of the most widespread of human customs, extending through every branch of the human race. Your ancestors, my ancestors, everybody."

"*Your* ancestors, maybe. Don't bring mine into it."

"Um. Duke, didn't you tell me you had some Indian blood?"

"Huh? Yeah, an eighth. In the Army they used to call me 'Chief.' What of it? I'm not ashamed of it. I'm proud of it."

"No reason to be ashamed—nor proud, either, for that matter. But, while both of us certainly have cannibals in our family trees, chances are that you are a good many generations closer to cannibals than I am, because—"

"Why, you bald-headed old—"

"Simmer down! You were going to listen; remember? Ritual cannibalism was a widespread custom among aboriginal American cultures. But don't take my word for it; look it up. Besides that, both of us, simply as North Americans, stand a better than even chance of having a touch of the Congo in us without knowing it . . . and there you are again. But even if both of us were Simon-pure North European stock, certified by the American Kennel Club, (a silly notion, since the amount of casual bastardy among humans is far in excess of that ever admitted)—but even if we were, such ancestry would merely tell us *which* cannibals we are descended from . . . because every branch of the human race, without any exception, has practiced cannibalism in the course of its history. Duke, it's silly to talk about a practice being 'against instinct' when hundreds of millions of human beings have followed that practice."

"But— All right, all right, I should know better than to argue with you, Jubal; you can always twist things around your way. But suppose we all did come from savages who didn't know any better—I'm not admitting it but just supposing. Suppose we did. What of it? We're civilized now. Or at least *I* am."

Jubal grinned cheerfully. "Implying that I am not. Son, quite aside from my own conditioned reflex against munching a roast haunch of— well, you, for example—quite aside from that trained-in emotional prejudice, for coldly practical reasons I regard our taboo against cannibalism as an excellent idea . . . because we are *not* civilized."

"Huh?"

"Obvious. If we didn't have a tribal taboo about the matter so strong that you honestly believed it was an instinct, I can think of a long list of people I wouldn't trust with my back turned, not with the price of beef what it is today. Eh?"

Duke grudged a grin. "Maybe you've got something there. I wouldn't want to take a chance on my ex-mother-in-law. She hates my guts."

"You see? Or how about our charming neighbour on the south, who is so casual about other people's fences and live stock during the hunting season? I wouldn't want to bet that you and I wouldn't wind up in his freezer if we didn't have that taboo. But Mike I would trust utterly— because Mike *is* civilized."

"Huh?"

"Mike is utterly civilized, Martian style. Duke, I don't understand the Martian viewpoint and probably never shall. But I've talked enough with

Mike on this subject to know that the Martian practice isn't at all dog-eat-dog . . . or Martian-eat-Martian. Surely they eat their dead, instead of burying them, or burning them, or exposing them to vultures. But the custom is highly formalized and deeply religious. A Martian is never grabbed and butchered against his will. In fact, so far as I have been able to find out, the idea of murder isn't even a Martian concept. Instead, a Martian dies when he decides to die, having discussed it with and been advised by his friends and having received the consent of his ancestors' ghosts to join them. Having decided to die, he does so, as easily as you close your eyes—no violence, no lingering illness, not even an overdose of sleeping pills. One second he is alive and well, the next second he's a ghost, with a dead body left over. Then, or maybe later (Mike is always vague about time factors) his closest friends eat what he no longer has any use for, 'grokking' him, as Mike would say, and praising his virtues as they spread the mustard. The new ghost attends the feast himself, as it is sort of a bar mitzvah or confirmation service by which the ghost attains the status of 'Old One'—becomes an elder statesman, if I understand it."

Duke made a face of disgust. "God, what superstitious junk! Turns my stomach."

"Does it? To Mike it's a most solemn—but joyful—religious ceremony."

Duke snorted. "Jubal, you don't believe that stuff about ghosts, do you? Oh, I know you don't. It's just cannibalism combined with the rankest sort of superstition."

"Well, now, I wouldn't go that far. I admit that I find these Martian 'Old Ones' a little hard to swallow—but Mike speaks of them as matter-of-factly as we talk about last Wednesday. As for the rest—Duke, what church were you brought up in?" Duke told him; Jubal nodded and went on: "I thought it might be; in Kansas most belong to yours or to one enough like it that you would have to look at the sign out in front to tell the difference. Tell me . . . how did you feel when you took part in the symbolic cannibalism that plays so paramount a part in your church's rituals?"

Duke stared at him. "What the devil do you mean?"

Jubal blinked solemnly back. "Were you actually a church member? Or were you simply sent to Sunday School as a kid?"

"Huh? Why, certainly I was a church member. My whole family was. I still am . . . even though I don't go much."

"I thought perhaps you weren't entitled to receive it. But apparently you are, so you know what I'm talking about, if you stop to think." Jubal stood up suddenly. "But I don't belong to your church nor to Mike's, so I shan't attempt to argue the subtle differences between one form of ritual cannibalism and another. Duke, I've got urgent work to do; I can't spend any more time trying to shake you loose from your prejudices. Are you leaving? If you are, I think I had better chaperone you off the place, make sure you're safe. Or do you want to stay? Stay and behave yourself, I mean —eat at the table with the rest of us cannibals."

Duke frowned. "Reckon I'll stay."

"Suit yourself. Because from this moment forward I wash my hands of any responsibility for your safety. You saw those movies; if you're bright enough to hit the floor with your hat, you've figured out that this man-Martian we've got staying with us can be unpredictably dangerous."

Duke nodded. "I got the point. I'm not as stupid as you think I am, Jubal. But I'm not letting Mike run me off the place, either." He added, "You say he's dangerous . . . and I see how he could be, if he got stirred up. But I'm not going to stir him up. Shucks, Jubal, I like the little dope, most ways."

"Mmm . . . damn it, I still think you underestimate him, Duke. See here, if you really do feel friendly toward him, the best thing you can do is to offer him a glass of water. Share it with him. Understand me? Become his 'water brother.' "

"Uh . . . I'll think about it."

"But if you do, Duke, don't fake it. If Mike accepts your offer of water-brotherhood, he'll be dead serious about it. He'll trust you utterly, no matter what—so don't do it unless you are equally willing to trust him and stand by him, no matter how rough things get. Either all out—or don't do it."

"I understood that. That's why I said, 'I'll think about it.' "

"Okay. But don't take too long making up your mind . . . because I expect things to get very rough before long."

xiv

IN THE VOLANT LAND OF LAPUTA, according to the journal of Lemuel Gulliver recounting his *Travels into Several Remote Nations of the World*, no person of importance ever listened or spoke without the help of a servant, known as a "climenole" in Laputian—or "flapper" in rough English translation, as such a servant's only duty was to flap the mouth and ears of his master with a dried bladder whenever, *in the opinion of the servant,* it was desirable for his master to speak or listen.

Without the consent of his flapper it was impossible to gain the attention of any Laputian of the master class.

Gulliver's journal is usually regarded by Terrans as a pack of lies composed by a sour churchman. As may be, there can be no doubt that, at this time, the "flapper" system was widely used on the planet Earth and had been extended, refined, and multiplied until a Laputian would not have recognized it other than in spirit.

In an earlier, simpler day one prime duty of any Terran sovereign was to make himself publicly available on frequent occasions so that even the lowliest might come before him *without any intermediary of any sort* and demand judgment. Traces of this aspect of primitive sovereignty persisted on Earth long after kings became scarce and impotent. It continued to be the right of an Englishman to "Cry Harold!" although few knew it and none did it. Successful city political bosses held open court all through the twentieth century, leaving wide their office doors and listening to any gandy dancer or bindlestiff who came in.

The principle itself was never abolished, being embalmed in Articles I & IX of the Amendments to the Constitution of the United States of America—and therefore nominal law for many humans—even though the basic document had been almost superseded in actual practice by the Articles of World Federation.

But at the time the Federation Ship *Champion* returned to Terra from Mars, the "flapper system" had been expanding for more than a century and had reached a stage of great intricacy, with many persons employed solely in carrying out its rituals. The importance of a public personage could be estimated by the number of layers of flappers cutting him off from ready congress with the plebian mob. They were not called "flappers," but were known as executive assistants, private secretaries, secretaries to private secretaries, press secretaries, receptionists, appointment clerks, et cetera. In fact the titles could be anything—or (with some of the most puissant) no title at all, but they could all be identified as "flappers" by function: each one held arbitrary and concatenative veto over any attempted communication from the outside world to the Great Man who was the nominal superior of the flapper.

This web of intermediary officials surrounding every V.I.P. naturally caused to grow up a class of unofficials whose function it was to flap the ear of the Great Man without permission from the official flappers, doing so (usually) on social or pseudo-social occasions or (with the most successful) via back-door privileged access or unlisted telephone number. These unofficials usually had no formal titles but were called a variety of names: "golfing companion," "kitchen cabinet," "lobbyist," "elder statesman," "five-percenter," and so forth. They existed in benign symbiosis with the official barricade of flappers, since it was recognized almost universally that the tighter the system the more need for a safety valve.

The most successful of the unofficials often grew webs of flappers of their own, until they were almost as hard to reach as the Great Man whose unofficial contacts they were . . . in which case secondary unofficials sprang up to circumvent the flappers of the primary unofficial. With a personage of foremost importance, such as the Secretary General of the World Federation of Free States, the maze of by-passes through unofficials would be as formidable as were the official phalanges of flappers surrounding a person merely very important.

Some Terran students have suggested that the Laputians must have been, in fact, visiting Martians, citing not only their very unworldly obsession with the contemplative life but also two concrete matters: the Laputians were alleged to have known about Mars' two moons at least a century and half before they were observed by Terran astronomers, and, secondly, Laputa itself was described in size and shape and propulsion such that the only English term that fits is "flying saucer." But that theory will not wash, as the flapper system, basic to Laputian society, was unknown on Mars. The Martian Old Ones, not hampered by bodies subject to space-time, would have had as little use for flappers as a snake has for shoes. Martians still corporate conceivably could use flappers but did not; the very concept ran contrary to their way of living.

A Martian having need of a few minutes or years of contemplation simply took it. If another Martian wished to speak with him, this friend would simply wait, as long as necessary. With all eternity to draw on there could be no reason for hurrying—in fact "hurry" was not a concept that could be symbolized in the Martian language and therefore must be presumed to be unthinkable. Speed, velocity, simultaneity, acceleration, and other mathematical abstractions having to do with the pattern of eternity were part of Martian mathematics, but not of Martian emotion. Contrariwise, the unceasing rush and turmoil of human existence came not from mathematical necessities of time but from the frantic urgency implicit in human sexual bipolarity.

Dr. Jubal Harshaw, professional clown, amateur subversive, and parasite by choice, had long attempted to eliminate "hurry" and all related emotions from his pattern. Being aware that he had but a short time left to live and having neither Martian nor Kansan faith in his own immortality, it was his purpose to live each golden moment as if it were eternity—without fear, without hope, but with sybaritic gusto. To this end he found that he required something larger than Diogenes' tub but smaller than Kubla's pleasure dome and its twice five miles of fertile ground with walls and towers girdled round; his was a simple little place, a few acres kept private with an electrified fence, a house of fourteen rooms or so, with running secretaries laid on and all other modern conveniences. To support his austerely upholstered nest and its rabble staff he put forth minimum effort for maximum return simply because it was easier to be rich than to be poor—Harshaw merely wished to live exactly as he liked, doing whatever he thought was best for him.

In consequence he felt honestly aggrieved that circumstances had forced on him a necessity for hurry and would not admit that he was enjoying himself more than he had in years.

This morning he found it needful to speak to the third planet's chief executive. He was fully aware of the flapper system that made such contact with the head of government all but impossible for the ordinary citizen, even though Harshaw himself disdained to surround himself with buffers suitable to his own rank—Harshaw answered his telephone himself if he happened to be at hand when it signalled because each call offered good odds that he would be justified in being gratifyingly rude to some stranger for daring to invade his privacy without cause—"cause" by Harshaw's definition, not by the stranger's.

Jubal knew that he could not hope to find the same conditions obtaining at the Executive Palace; Mr. Secretary General would not answer his own phone. But Harshaw had many years of practice in the art of outwitting human customs; he tackled the matter cheerfully, right after breakfast.

Much later he was tired and very frustrated. His name alone had carried him past three layers of the official flapper defense, and he was sufficiently a narrow-gauge V.I.P. that he was never quite switched off. Instead he was referred from secretary to secretary and wound up speaking voice-&-vision to a personable, urbane young man who seemed willing to discuss the matter endlessly and without visible irritation no matter what Harshaw said—but would not agree to connect him with the Honorable Mr. Douglas.

Harshaw knew that he would get action if he mentioned the Man from Mars and that he certainly would get very quick action if he claimed to have the Man from Mars with him, but he was far from certain that the resultant action would be a face-to-face hookup with Douglas. On the contrary, he calculated that any mention of Smith would kill any chance of reaching Douglas but would at once produce violent reaction from subordinates—which was not what he wanted. He knew from a lifetime of experience that it was always easier to dicker with the top man. With Ben Caxton's life very possibly at stake Harshaw could not risk failure through a subordinate's lack of authority or excess of ambition.

But this soft brush-off was trying his patience. Finally he snarled, "Young man, if you have no authority yourself, let me speak to someone who has! Put me through to Mr. Berquist."

The face of the staff stooge suddenly lost its smile and Jubal thought gleefully that he had at last pinked him in the quick. So he pushed his advantage. "Well? Don't just sit there! Get Gil on your inside line and tell him you've been keeping Jubal Harshaw waiting. Tell him how *long* you've kept me waiting." Jubal reviewed in his own excellent memory all that Witness Cavendish had reported concerning the missing Berquist, plus the report on him from the detective service. Yup, he thought happily, this lad is at least three rungs down the ladder from where Berquist was—so let's shake him up a little . . . and climb a couple of rungs in the process.

The face said woodenly, "We have no Mr. Berquist here."

"I don't care where he is. Get him! If you don't know Gil Berquist personally, ask your boss. Mr. Gilbert Berquist, personal assistant to Mr. Douglas. If you've been around the Palace more than two weeks you've at least seen Mr. Berquist at a distance—thirty-five years old, about six feet and a hundred and eighty pounds, sandy hair a little thin on top, smiles a lot and has perfect teeth. You've seen him. If you don't dare disturb him yourself, dump it in your boss's lap. But quit biting your nails and do *something*. I'm getting annoyed."

Without expression the young man said, "Please hold on. I will enquire."

"I certainly will hold on. Get me Gil." The image in the phone was replaced by a moving abstract pattern; a pleasant female voice recorded, said, "Please wait while your call is completed. This delay is not being charged to your account. Please relax while—" Soothing music came up and covered the voice; Jubal sat back and looked around. Anne was waiting, reading, and safely out of the telephone's vision angle. On his other side the Man from Mars was also out of the telephone's sight pickup and was watching images in stereovision and listening via ear plugs.

Jubal reflected that he must remember to have that obscene babble box placed in the basement where it belonged, once this emergency was over. "What you got, son?" he asked, leaned over and turned on the speaker to low gain.

Mike answered, "I don't know, Jubal."

The sound confirmed what Jubal had suspected from his glance at the image: Smith was listening to a broadcast of a Fosterite service. The imaged Shepherd was not preaching but seemed to be reading church notices: "—junior Spirit-in-Action team will give a practice demonstration before the supper, so come early and see the fur fly! Our team coach, Brother Hornsby, has asked me to tell you boys on the team to fetch only your helmets, gloves, and sticks—we aren't going after sinners this time. However, the Little Cherubim will be on hand with their first-aid kits in case of excessive zeal." The Shepherd paused and smiled broadly, "And now wonderful news, My Children! A message from the Angel Ramzai for Brother Arthur Renwick and his good wife Dorothy. Your prayer has been approved and you will go to heaven at dawn Thursday morning! Stand up, Art! Stand up, Dottie! Take a bow!"

The camera angle made a reverse cut, showing the congregation and centering on Brother and Sister Renwick. To wild applause and shouts of *"Hallelujah!"* Brother Renwick was responding with a boxer's handshake over his head, while his wife blushed and smiled and dabbed at her eyes beside him.

The camera cut back as the Shepherd held up his hand for silence. He went on briskly, "The Bon Voyage party for the Renwicks will start promptly at midnight and the doors will be locked at that time—so get here early and let's make this the happiest revelry our flock has ever seen, for we're all proud of Art and Dottie. Funeral services will be held thirty minutes after dawn, with breakfast immediately following for the benefit of those who have to get to work early." The Shepherd suddenly looked very stern and the camera panned in until his head filled the tank. "After our last Bon Voyage, the sexton found an empty pint bottle in one of the Happiness rooms . . . of a brand distilled by sinners. That's past and done, as the brother who slipped has confessed and paid penance sevenfold, even refusing the usual cash discount—I'm sure *he* won't backslide. But stop and think, My Children— Is it worth risking eternal happiness to save a few pennies on an article of worldly merchandise? Always look for that happy, holy seal-of-approval with Bishop Digby's smiling face on it. Don't let a sinner palm off on you something 'just as good.' Our sponsors support us; they deserve your support. Brother Art, I'm sorry to have to bring up such a subject—"

"That's okay, Shepherd! Pour it on!"

"—at a time of such great happiness. But we must never forget that—" Jubal reached over and switched off the speaker circuit.

"Mike, that's not anything you need to see."

"Not?"

"Uh—" Jubal thought about it. Shucks, the boy was going to have to learn about such things sooner or later. "All right, go ahead. But come talk to me about it later."

"Yes, Jubal."

Harshaw was about to add some advice intended to offset Mike's tendency to take literally anything he saw or heard. But the telephone's soothing "hold" music suddenly went down and out, and the screen filled with an image—a man in his forties whom Jubal at once labeled in his mind as "cop."

Jubal said aggressively, "You aren't Gil Berquist."

The man said, "What is your interest in Gilbert Berquist?"

Jubal answered with pained patience, "I wish to speak to him. See here, my good man, are you a public employee?"

The man barely hesitated. "Yes. You must—"

"I 'must' nothing! I am a citizen in good standing and my taxes go to pay your wages. All morning I have been trying to make a simple phone call—and I have been passed from one butterfly-brained bovine to another, and every one of them feeding out of the public trough. I am sick of it and I do not intend to put up with it any longer. And now *you*. Give me your name, your job title, and your pay number. Then I'll speak to Mr. Berquist."

"You didn't answer my question."

"Come, come! I don't have to answer your questions; I am a private citizen. But you are not . . . and the question I asked you any citizen may demand of any public servant. O'Kelly versus State of California 1972. I demand that you identify yourself—name, job, number."

The man answered tonelessly, "You are Doctor Jubal Harshaw. You are calling from—"

"So that's what took so long? Stopping to have this call traced. That was stupid. I am at home and my address can be obtained from any public library, post office, or telephone information service. As to who I am, everyone knows who I am. Everyone who can read, that is. Can you read?"

The man went on, "Dr. Harshaw, I am a police officer and I require your cooperation. What is your reason—"

"Pooh to you, sir! I am a lawyer. A private citizen is required to cooperate with the police under certain specified conditions only. For example, during hot pursuit—in which case the police officer may still be required to show his credentials. Is this 'hot pursuit,' sir? Are you about to dive through this blasted instrument? Second, a private citizen may be required to cooperate within reasonable and lawful limits in the course of police investigation—"

"This is an investigation."

"Of what, sir? Before you may require my cooperation in an investigation, you must identify yourself, satisfy me as to your bona-fides, state your purpose, and—if I so require—cite the code and show that a 'reasonable necessity' exists. You have done none of these. I wish to speak to Mr. Berquist."

The man's jaw muscles were jumping but he answered quietly, "Dr. Harshaw, I am Captain Heinrich of the Federation S.S. Bureau. The fact that you reached me by calling the Executive Palace should be ample proof that I am who I say I am. However—" He took out a wallet, flipped it open, and held it close to his own vision pickup. The picture blurred, then quickly refocused. Harshaw glanced at the I.D. thus displayed; it looked authentic enough, he decided—especially as he did not care whether it was authentic or not.

"Very well, Captain," he growled. "Will you now explain to me why you are keeping me from speaking with Mr. Berquist?"

"Mr. Berquist is not available."

"Then why didn't you say so? In that case, transfer my call to someone of Berquist's rank. I mean one of the half-dozen people who work directly with the Secretary General, as Gil does. I don't propose again to be fobbed off on some junior assistant flunky with no authority to blow his own nose! If Gil isn't there and can't handle it, then for God's sake get me someone of equal rank who can!"

"You have been trying to telephone the Secretary General."

"Precisely."

"Very well, you may explain to me what business you have with the Secretary General."

"And I may not. Are you a confidential assistant to the Secretary General? Are you privy to his secrets?"

"That's beside the point."

"That's exactly the point. As a police officer, you should know better. I shall explain, to some person known to me to be cleared for sensitive material and in Mr. Douglas' confidence, just enough to make sure that the Secretary General speaks to me. Are you sure Mr. Berquist can't be reached?"

"Quite sure."

"That's too bad, he could have handled it quickly. Then it will have to be someone else—of his rank."

"If it's that secret, you shouldn't be calling over a public phone."

"My good Captain! I was not born yesterday—and neither were you. Since you had this call traced, I am sure you are aware that my personal phone is equipped to receive a maximum-security return call."

The Special Service officer made no direct reply. Instead he answered, "Doctor, I'll be blunt and save time. Until you explain your business, you aren't going to get anywhere. If you switch off and call the Palace again, your call will be routed to this office. Call a hundred times . . . or a month from now. Same thing. Until you decide to cooperate."

Jubal smiled happily. "It won't be necessary now, as you have let slip —unwittingly, or was it intentional?—the one datum needed before we act. If we do. I can hold them off the rest of the day . . . but the code word is no longer 'Berquist.' "

"What the devil do you mean?"

"My dear Captain, please! Not over an unscrambled circuit surely? But you know, or should know, that I am a senior philosophunculist on active duty."

"Repeat?"

"Haven't you studied amphigory? Gad, what they teach in schools these days! Go back to your pinochle game; I don't need you." Jubal switched off at once, set the phone for ten minutes refusal, said, "Come along, kids," and returned to his favorite loafing spot near the pool. There he cautioned Anne to keep her Witness robe at hand day and night until further notice, told Mike to stay in earshot, and gave Miriam instructions concerning the telephone. Then he relaxed.

He was not displeased with his efforts. He had not expected to be able to reach the Secretary General at once, through official channels. He felt that his morning's reconnaissance had developed at least one weak spot in the wall surrounding the Secretary and he expected—or hoped—that his stormy session with Captain Heinrich would bring a return call . . . from a higher level.

Or something.

If not, the exchange of compliments with the S.S. cop had been rewarding in itself and had left him in a warm glow of artistic post-fructification. Harshaw held that certain feet were made for stepping on, in order to improve the breed, promote the general welfare, and minimize the ancient insolence of office; he had seen at once that Heinrich had such feet.

But, if no action developed, Harshaw wondered how long he could afford to wait? In addition to the pending collapse of his "time bomb" and the fact that he had, in effect, promised Jill that he would take steps on behalf of Ben Caxton (why couldn't the child see that Ben probably could *not* be helped—indeed, was almost certainly beyond help—and that any

direct or hasty action minimized Mike's chance of keeping his freedom?)—
in addition to these two factors, something new was crowding him: Duke
was gone.

Gone for the day, gone for good (or gone for bad), Jubal did not
know. Duke had been present at dinner the night before, had not shown up
for breakfast. Neither event was noteworthy in Harshaw's loosely coupled
household and no one else appeared to have missed Duke. Jubal himself
would not ordinarily have noticed unless he had had occasion to yell for
Duke. But this morning Jubal had, of course, noticed . . . and he had
refrained from shouting for Duke at least twice on occasions when he
normally would have done so.

Jubal looked glumly across the pool, watched Mike attempt to perform a dive exactly as Dorcas had just performed it, and admitted to
himself that he had not shouted for Duke when he needed him, on purpose. The truth was that he simply did not want to ask the Bear what had
happened to Algy. The Bear might answer.

Well, there was only one way to cope with that sort of weakness.
"Mike! Come here."

"Yes, Jubal." The Man from Mars got out of the pool and trotted over
like an eager puppy, waited. Harshaw looked him over, decided that he
must weigh at least twenty pounds more than he had on arrival . . . and
all of it appeared to be muscle. "Mike, do you know where Duke is?"

"No, Jubal."

Well, that settled it; the boy didn't know how to lie—wait, hold it!
Jubal reminded himself of Mike's computer-like habit of answering exactly
the question asked . . . and Mike had not known, or had not appeared to
know, where that pesky box was, once it was gone. "Mike, when did you
see him last?"

"I saw Duke go upstairs when Jill and I came downstairs, this morning when time to cook breakfast." Mike added proudly, "I helped cooking."

"That was the last time you saw Duke?"

"I am not see Duke since, Jubal. I proudly burned toast."

"I'll bet you did. You'll make some woman a fine husband yet, if you
aren't careful."

"Oh, I burned it most carefully."

"Jubal—"

"Huh? Yes, Anne?"

"Duke grabbed an early breakfast and lit out for town. I thought you
knew."

"Well," Jubal temporized, "he did say something about it. I thought he intended to leave after lunch today. No matter, it'll keep." Jubal realized suddenly that a great load had been lifted from his mind. Not that Duke meant anything to him, other than as an efficient handyman—no, of course not! For many years he had avoided letting any human being be important to him—but, just the same, he had to admit that it would have troubled him. A little, anyhow.

What statute was violated, if any, in turning a man exactly ninety degrees from everything else?

Not murder, not as long as the lad used it only in self-defense or in the proper defense of another, such as Jill. Possibly the supposedly obsolete Pennsylvania laws against witchcraft would apply . . . but it would be interesting to see how a prosecutor would manage to word an indictment.

A civil action might lie— Could harboring the Man from Mars be construed as "maintaining an attractive nuisance?" Possibly. But it was more likely that radically new rules of law must evolve. Mike had already kicked the bottom out of both medicine and physics, even though the practitioners of such were still innocently unaware of the chaos facing them. Harshaw dug far back into his memory and recalled the personal tragedy that relativistic mechanics had proved to be for many distinguished scientists. Unable to digest it through long habit of mind, they had taken refuge in blind anger at Einstein himself and any who dared to take him seriously. But their refuge had been a dead end; all that inflexible old guard could do was to die and let younger minds, still limber, take over.

Harshaw recalled that his grandfather had told him of much the same thing happening in the field of medicine when the germ theory came along; many older physicians had gone to their graves calling Pasteur a liar, a fool, or worse—and without examining evidence which their "common sense" told them was impossible.

Well, he could see that Mike was going to cause more hooraw than Pasteur and Einstein combined—squared and cubed. Which reminded him— "Larry! Where's Larry?"

"Here, Boss," the loudspeaker mounted under the eaves behind him announced. "Down in the shop."

"Got the panic button?"

"Sure thing. You said to sleep with it on me. I do. I did."

"Bounce up here to the house and let me have it. No, give it to Anne. Anne, you keep it with your robe."

She nodded. Larry's voice answered, "Right away, Boss. Count down coming up?"

"Just do it." Jubal looked up and was startled to find that the Man from Mars was still standing in front of him, quiet as a sculptured figure.

Sculpture? Yes, he did remind one of sculpture . . . uh— Jubal searched his memory. Michelangelo's "David," that was it! Yes, even to the puppyish hands and feet, the serenely sensual face, the tousled, too-long hair. "That was all I wanted, Mike."

"Yes, Jubal."

But Mike continued to stand there. Jubal said, "Something on your mind, son?"

"About what I was seeing in that goddam-noisy-box. You said, 'All right, go ahead. But come talk to me about it later.'"

"Oh." Harshaw recalled the broadcast services of the Church of the New Revelation and winced. "Yes, we will talk. But first— Don't call that thing a goddam noisy box. It is a stereovision receiver. Call it that."

Mike looked puzzled. "It is not a goddam-noisy-box? I heard you not rightly?"

"You heard me rightly and it is indeed a goddam noisy box. You'll hear me call it that again. And other things. But *you* must call it a stereovision receiver."

"I will call it a 'stereovision receiver.' Why, Jubal? I do not grok."

Harshaw sighed, with a tired feeling that he had climbed these same stairs too many times. Any conversation with Smith turned up at least one bit of human behavior which could not be justified logically, at least in terms that Smith could understand, and attempts to do so were endlessly time-consuming. "I do not grok it myself, Mike," he admitted, "but Jill wants you to say it that way."

"I will do it, Jubal. Jill wants it."

"Now tell me what you saw and heard in that stereovision receiver— and what you grok of it."

The conversation that followed was even more lengthy, confused, and rambling than a usual talk with Smith. Mike recalled accurately every word and action he had heard and seen in the babble tank, including all commercials. Since he had almost completed reading the encyclopedia, he had read its article on "Religion," as well as ones on "Christianity," "Islam," "Judaism," "Confucianism," "Buddhism," and many others concerning religion and related subjects. But he had grokked none of this.

Jubal at last got certain ideas clear in his own mind: (a) Mike did not know that the Fosterite service was a religious one; (b) Mike remembered what he had read about religions but had filed such data for future contemplation, having recognized that he did not understand them; (c) in fact, Mike had only the most confused notion of what the word "religion" meant, even though he could quote all nine definitions for same as given in the unabridged dictionary; (d) the Martian language contained no word (and no concept) which Mike was able to equate with *any* of these nine definitions; (e) the customs which Jubal had described to Duke as Martian "religious ceremonies" were nothing of the sort to Mike; to Mike such matters were as matter-of-fact as grocery markets were to Jubal; (f) it was not possible to express as separate ideas in the Martian tongue the human concepts: "religion," "philosophy," and "science"—and, since Mike still thought in Martian even though he now spoke English fluently, it was not yet possible for him to distinguish any one such concept from the other two. All such matters were simply "learnings" which came from the "Old Ones." Doubt he had never heard of and research was unnecessary (no Martian word for either); the answer to any question should be obtained from the Old Ones, who were omniscient (at least within Mike's scope) and infallible, whether the subject be tomorrow's weather or cosmic teleology. (Mike had seen a weather forecast in the babble box and had assumed without question that this was a message from human "Old Ones" being passed around for the benefit of those still corporate. Further inquiry disclosed that he held a similar assumption concerning the authors of the Encyclopedia Britannica.)

But last, and worst to Jubal, causing him baffled consternation, Mike had grokked the Fosterite service as including (among things he had not grokked) an announcement of an impending discorporation of two humans who were about to join the human "Old Ones"—and Mike was tremendously excited at this news. Had he grokked it rightly? Mike knew that his comprehension of English was less than perfect; he continued to make mistakes through his ignorance, being "only an egg." But had he grokked *this* correctly? He had been waiting to meet the human "Old Ones," for he had many questions to ask. Was this an opportunity? Or did he require more learnings from his water brothers before he was ready?

Jubal was saved by the bell. Dorcas arrived with sandwiches and coffee, the household's usual fair-weather picnic lunch. Jubal ate silently, which suited Smith as his rearing had taught him that eating was a time for contemplation—he had found rather upsetting the chatter that usually took place at the table.

Jubal stretched out his meal while he pondered what to tell Mike— and cursed himself for the folly of having permitted Mike to watch stereo in the first place. Oh, he supposed the boy had to come up against human religions at some point—couldn't be helped if he was going to spend the rest of his life on this dizzy planet. But, damn it, it would have been better to wait until Mike was more used to the overall cockeyed pattern of human behavior . . . and, in any case, certainly not *Fosterites* as his first experience!

As a devout agnostic, Jubal consciously evalued all religions, from the animism of the Kalahari Bushmen to the most sober and intellectualized of the major western faiths, as being equal. But emotionally he disliked some more than others . . . and the Church of the New Revelation set his teeth on edge. The Fosterites' flat-footed claim to utter gnosis through a direct pipeline to Heaven, their arrogant intolerance implemented in open persecution of all other religions wherever they were strong enough to get away with it, the sweaty football-rally & sales-convention flavor of their services—all these ancillary aspects depressed him. If people must go to church, why the devil couldn't they be dignified about it, like Catholics, Christian Scientists, or Quakers?

If God existed (a question concerning which Jubal maintained a meticulous intellectual neutrality) and if He desired to be worshipped (a proposition which Jubal found inherently improbable but conceivably possible in the dim light of his own ignorance), then (stipulating affirmatively both the above) it nevertheless seemed wildly unlikely to Jubal to the point of *reductio ad absurdum* that a God potent to shape galaxies would be titillated and swayed by the whoop-te-do nonsense the Fosterites offered Him as "worship."

But with bleak honesty Jubal admitted to himself that the Universe (correction: that piece of the Universe he himself had seen) might very well be *in toto* an example of reduction to absurdity. In which case the Fosterites might be possessed of the Truth, the exact Truth, and nothing but the Truth. The Universe was a damned silly place at best . . . but the least likely explanation for its existence was the no-explanation of random chance, the conceit that some abstract somethings "just happened" to be some atoms that "just happened" to get together in configurations which "just happened" to look like consistent laws and then some of these configurations "just happened" to possess self-awareness and that two such "just happened" to be the Man from Mars and the other a bald-headed old coot with Jubal himself inside.

No, Jubal would not buy the "just happened" theory, popular as it was with men who called themselves scientists. Random chance was not a sufficient explanation of the Universe—in fact, random chance was not sufficient to explain random chance; the pot could not hold itself.

What then? "Least hypothesis" held no place of preference; Occam's razor could not slice the prime problem, the Nature of the Mind of God (might as well call it that to yourself, you old scoundrel; it's a short, simple, Anglo-Saxon monosyllable, not banned by having four letters—and as good a tag for what you don't understand as any).

Was there any basis for preferring any one sufficient hypothesis over another? When you simply did not understand a thing: *No!* And Jubal readily admitted to himself that a long lifetime had left him completely and totally not understanding the basic problems of the Universe.

So the Fosterites might be right. Jubal could not even show that they were probably wrong.

But, he reminded himself savagely, two things remained to him: his own taste and his own pride. If indeed the Fosterites held a monopoly on Truth (as they claimed), if Heaven were open only to Fosterites, then he, Jubal Harshaw, gentleman and free citizen, preferred that eternity of pain-filled damnation promised to all "sinners" who refused the New Revelation. He might not be able to see the naked Face of God . . . but his eyesight was good enough to pick out his social equals—and those Fosterites, by damn, did not measure up!

But he could see how Mike had been misled; the Fosterite "going to Heaven" at a pre-selected time and place did sound like the voluntary and planned "discorporation" which, Jubal did not doubt, was the accepted practice on Mars. Jubal himself held a dark suspicion that a better term for the Fosterite practice was "murder"—but such had never been proved and had rarely been publicly hinted, much less charged, even when the cult was young and relatively small. Foster himself had been the first to "go to Heaven" on schedule, dying publicly at a self-prophesied instant. Since that first example, it had been a Fosterite mark of special grace . . . and it had been years since any coroner or district attorney had had the temerity to pry into such deaths.

Not that Jubal cared whether they were spontaneous or induced. In his opinion a good Fosterite was a dead Fosterite. Let them be!

But it was going to be hard to explain to Mike.

No use stalling, another cup of coffee wouldn't make it any easier— "Mike, who made the world?"

"Beg pardon?"

"Look around you. All this. Mars, too. The stars. Everything. You and me and everybody. Did the Old Ones tell you who made it?"

Mike looked puzzled. "No, Jubal."

"Well, you have wondered about it, haven't you? Where did the Sun come from? Who put the stars in the sky? Who started it all? All of it, everything, the whole world, the Universe . . . so that you and I are here talking." Jubal paused, surprised at himself. He had intended to make the usual agnostic approach . . . and found himself compulsively following his legal training, being an honest advocate in spite of himself, attempting to support a religious belief he did not hold but which was believed by most human beings. He found that, willy-nilly, he was attorney for the orthodoxies of his own race against—he wasn't sure what. An unhuman viewpoint. "How do your Old Ones answer such questions?"

"Jubal, I do not grok . . . that these are *questions.* I am sorry."

"Eh? I don't grok your answer."

Mike hesitated a long time. "I will try. But words are . . . are *not* . . . rightly. Not 'putting.' Not 'mading.' A *now*ing. World is. World was. World shall be. *Now.* "

" 'As it was in the beginning, so it now and ever shall be, World without end—' "

Mike smiled happily. "You grok it!"

"I don't grok it," Jubal answered gruffly, "I was quoting something, uh, an 'Old One' said." He decided to back off and try a new approach; apparently God the Creator was not the easiest aspect of Deity to try to explain to Mike as an opening . . . since Mike did not seem to grasp the idea of Creation itself. Well, Jubal wasn't sure that he did, either—he had long ago made a pact with himself to postulate a Created Universe on even-numbered days, a tail-swallowing eternal-and-uncreated Universe on odd-numbered days—since each hypothesis, while equally paradoxical, neatly avoided the paradoxes of the other—with, of course, a day off each leap year for sheer solipsist debauchery. Having thus tabled an unanswerable question he had given no thought to it for more than a generation.

Jubal decided to try to explain the whole idea of religion in its broadest sense and then tackle the notion of Deity and Its aspects later.

Mike readily agreed that learnings came in various sizes, from little learnings that even a nestling could grok on up to great learnings which only an Old One could grok in perfect fullness. But Jubal's attempt to draw a line between small learnings and great learnings so that "great learnings" would have the human meaning of "religious questions" was not successful, as some religious questions did not seem to Mike to be questions with any meaning to them (such as "Creation") and others seemed to him to be "little" questions, with obvious answers known even to nestlings—such as life after death.

Jubal was forced to let it go at that and passed on to the multiplicity of human religions. He explained (or tried to explain) that humans had hundreds of different ways by which these "great learnings" were taught, each with its own answers and each claiming to be the truth.

"What is 'truth'?" Mike asked.

("What is Truth?" asked a Roman judge, and washed his hands of a troublesome question. Jubal wished that he could do likewise.) "An answer is truth when you speak rightly, Mike. How many hands do I have?"

"Two hands. I see two hands," Mike amended.

Anne glanced up from her knitting. "In six weeks I could make a Witness of him."

"You keep out of this, Anne. Things are tough enough without your help. Mike, you spoke rightly; I have two hands. Your answer was truth. Suppose you said that I had seven hands?"

Mike looked troubled. "I do not grok that I could say that."

"No, I don't think you could. You would not speak rightly if you did; your answer would not be truth. But, Mike—now listen carefully—each religion claims to be truth, claims to speak rightly. Yet their answers to the same question are as different as two hands and seven hands. The Fosterites say one thing, the Buddhists say another, the Moslems say still another —many answers, all different."

Mike seemed to be making a great effort to understand. "All speak rightly? Jubal, I do not grok it."

"Nor do I."

The Man from Mars looked greatly troubled, then suddenly he smiled. "I will ask the Fosterites to ask your Old Ones and then we will know, my brother. How will I do this?"

A few minutes later Jubal found, to his great disgust, that he had promised Mike an interview with some Fosterite bigmouth—or Mike seemed to think that he had, which came to the same thing. Nor had he been able to do more than dent Mike's assumption that the Fosterites were in close touch with human "Old Ones." It appeared that Mike's difficulty in understanding the nature of truth was that he didn't know what a lie was—the dictionary definitions of "lie" and "falsehood" had been filed in his mind with no trace of grokking. One could "speak wrongly" only by accident or misunderstanding. So he necessarily had taken what he had heard of the Fosterite service at its bald, face value.

Jubal tried to explain that *all* human religions claimed to be in touch with "Old Ones" in one way or another; nevertheless their answers were all different.

Mike looked patiently troubled. "Jubal my brother, I try . . . but I do not grok how this can be right speaking. With my people, the Old Ones speak always rightly. Your people—"

"Hold it, Mike."

"Beg pardon?"

"When you said, 'my people' you were talking about Martians. Mike, you are not a Martian; you are a man."

"What is 'Man'?"

Jubal groaned inwardly. Mike could, he was sure, quote the full list of dictionary definitions. Yet the lad never asked a question simply to be annoying; he asked always for information—and he expected his water brother Jubal to be able to tell him. "I am a man, you are a man, Larry is a man."

"But Anne is not a man?"

"Uh . . . Anne is a man, a female man. A woman."

("Thanks, Jubal."—"Shut up, Anne.")

"A baby is a man? I have not seen babies, but I have seen pictures— and in the goddam-noi—in stereovision. A baby is not shaped like Anne . . . and Anne is not shaped like you . . . and you are not shaped like I. But a baby is a nestling man?"

"Uh . . . yes, a baby is a man."

"Jubal . . . I think I grok that my people—'Martians'—are man. Not shape. Shape is not man. Man is grokking. I speak rightly?"

Jubal made a fierce resolve to resign from the Philosophical Society and take up tatting. What was "grokking"? He had been using the word himself for a week now—and he still didn't grok it. But what was "Man"? A featherless biped? God's image? Or simply a fortuitous result of the "survival of the fittest" in a completely circular and tautological definition? The heir of death and taxes? The Martians seemed to have defeated death, and he had already learned that they seemed to have neither money, property, nor government in any human sense—so how could they have taxes?

And yet the boy was right; shape was an irrelevancy in defining "Man," as unimportant as the bottle containing the wine. You could even take a man out of his bottle, like the poor fellow whose life those Russians had persisted in "saving" by placing his living brain in a vitreous envelope and wiring him like a telephone exchange. Gad, what a horrible joke! He wondered if the poor devil appreciated the grisly humor of what had been done to him.

But *how*, in essence, from the unprejudiced viewpoint of a Martian, did Man differ from other earthly animals? Would a race that could levitate (and God knows what else) be impressed by engineering? And, if so, would the Aswan Dam, or a thousand miles of coral reef, win first prize? Man's self-awareness? Sheer local conceit; the upstate counties had not reported, for there was no way to prove that sperm whales or giant sequoias were not philosophers and poets far exceeding any human merit.

There was one field in which man was unsurpassed; he showed unlimited ingenuity in devising bigger and more efficient ways to kill off, enslave, harass, and in all ways make an unbearable nuisance of himself to himself. Man was his own grimmest joke on himself. The very bedrock of humor was—

"Man is the animal who laughs," Jubal answered.

Mike considered this seriously. "Then I am not a man."

"Huh?"

"I do not laugh. I have heard laughing and it frighted me. Then I grokked that it did not hurt. I have tried to learn—" Mike threw his head back and gave out a raucous cackle, more nerve-racking than the idiot call of a kookaburra.

Jubal covered his ears. "Stop! *Stop!*"

"You heard," Mike agreed sadly. "I cannot rightly do it. So I am not man."

"Wait a minute, son. Don't give up so quickly. You simply haven't learned to laugh yet . . . and you'll never learn just by trying. But you will learn, I promise you. If you live among us long enough, one day you will see how funny we are—and you will laugh."

"I will?"

"You will. Don't worry about it and don't try to grok it; just let it come. Why, son, even a Martian would laugh once he grokked us."

"I will wait," Smith agreed placidly.

"And while you are waiting, don't ever doubt that you are a man. You are. Man born of woman and born to trouble . . . and some day you will grok its fullness and you will laugh—because man is the animal that laughs at himself. About your Martian friends, I do not know. I have never met them, I do not grok them. But I grok that they may be 'man.' "

"Yes, Jubal."

Harshaw thought that the interview was over and felt relieved. He decided that he had not been so embarrassed since a day long gone when his father had undertaken to explain to him the birds and the bees and the flowers—*much* too late.

But the Man from Mars was not quite done. "Jubal my brother, you were ask me, 'Who made the World?' and I did not have words to say why I did not rightly grok it to be a question. I have been thinking words."

"So?"

"You told me, 'God made the World.' "

"No, no!" Harshaw said hastily. "I told you that, while all these many religions said many things, most of them said, 'God made the World.' I told you that I did not grok the fullness, but that 'God' was the word that was used."

"Yes, Jubal," Mike agreed. "Word is 'God.' " He added, "You grok."

"No, I must admit I don't grok."

"You grok," Smith repeated firmly. "I am explain. I did not have the word. You grok. Anne groks. I grok. The grass under my feet groks in happy beauty. But I needed the word. The word is God."

Jubal shook his head to clear it. "Go ahead."

Mike pointed triumphantly at Jubal. *Thou art God!*"

Jubal slapped a hand to his face. "Oh, Jesus H.— What have I done? Look, Mike, take it easy! Simmer down! You didn't understand me. I'm sorry. I'm very sorry! Just forget what I've been saying and we'll start over again on another day. But—"

"Thou art God," Mike repeated serenely. "That which groks. Anne is God. I am God. The happy grass are God. Jill groks in beauty always. Jill is God. All shaping and making and creating together—" He croaked something in Martian and smiled.

"All right, Mike. But let it wait. Anne, have you been getting all this?"

"You bet I have, Boss!"

"Make me a tape. I'll have to work on it. I *can't* let it stand. I must—" Jubal glanced up, said, "Oh, my God! General Quarters, everybody! *Anne!* Set the panic button on 'dead-man' setting—and for God's sake keep your thumb on it; they may not be coming here." He glanced up again, at two large air cars approaching from the south. "But I'm afraid they are. Mike! Hide in the pool! Remember what I told you—down in the deepest part, stay there, hold still—and don't come up until I send Jill to get you."

"Yes, Jubal."

"Right now! *Move!*"

"Yes, Jubal." Mike ran the few steps, cut the water and disappeared. He remembered to keep his knees straight, his toes pointed and his feet together.

"Jill!" Jubal called out. "Dive in and climb out. You too, Larry. If anybody saw that, I want 'em confused as to how many are using the pool. Dorcas! Climb out fast, child, and dive in again. Anne— No, you've got the panic button; you can't."

"I can take my cloak and go to the edge of the pool. Boss, do you want some delay on this 'dead-man' setting?"

"Uh, yes, thirty seconds. If they land here, put on your Witness cloak at once and get your thumb back on the button. Then wait—and if I call you over to me, let the balloon go up. But I don't dare shout 'Wolf!' on this unless—" He shielded his eyes. "One of them is certainly going to land . . . and it's got that Paddy-wagon look to it, all right. Oh, damn, I had thought they would parley first."

The first car hovered, then dropped vertically for a landing in the garden area around the pool; the second started slowly circling the house at low altitude. The cars were black, squad carriers in size, and showed only a small, inconspicuous insignia: the stylized globe of the Federation.

Anne put down the radio relay link that would let "the balloon go up," got quickly into her professional garb, picked the link up again and put her thumb back on the button. The door of the first car started to open as it touched and Jubal charged toward it with the cocky belligerence of a Pekingese. As a man stepped out, Jubal roared, "Get that God damned heap off my rose bushes!"

The man said, "Jubal Harshaw?"

"You heard me! Tell that oaf you've got driving for you to raise that bucket and move it *back!* Off the garden entirely and onto the grass! *Anne!*"

"Coming, Boss."

"Jubal Harshaw, I have a warrant here for—"

"I don't care if you've got a warrant for the King of England; first you'll move that junk heap off my flowers! Then, so help me, I'll sue you for—" Jubal glanced at the man who had landed, appeared to see him for the first time. "Oh, so it's *you,*" he said with bitter contempt. "Were you born stupid, Heinrich, or did you have to study for it? And when did that uniformed jackass working for you learn to fly? Earlier today? Since I talked to you?"

"Please examine this warrant," Captain Heinrich said with careful patience. "Then—"

"Get your go-cart out of my flower beds at once or I'll make a civil-rights case out of this that will cost you your pension!"

Heinrich hesitated. *"Now!"* Jubal screamed. "And tell those other yokels getting out to pick up their big feet! That idiot with the buck teeth is standing on a prize Elizabeth M. Hewitt!"

Heinrich turned his head. "You men—careful of those flowers. Paskin, you're standing on one. *Rogers!* Raise the car and move it back about fifty feet, clear of the garden." He turned his attention back to Harshaw. "Does that satisfy you?"

"Once he actually moves it—but you'll still pay damages. Let's see your credentials . . . and show them to the Fair Witness and state loud and clearly to her your name, rank, organization, and pay number."

"You know who I am. Now I have a warrant to—"

"I have a common-law warrant to part your hair with a shotgun unless you do things legally and in order! *I* don't know who you are. You look remarkably like a stuffed shirt I saw over the telephone earlier today —but that's not evidence and I don't identify you. *You* must identify yourself, in the specified legal fashion, World Code paragraph 1602, part II, before you can serve a warrant. And that goes for all those other apes, too, and that pithecan parasite piloting for you."

"They are police officers, acting under my orders."

"*I* don't know that they are anything of the sort. They might have hired those ill-fitting clown suits at a costumer's. The letter of the law, sir! You've come barging into my castle. You *say* you are a police officer—and you allege that you have a warrant for this intrusion. But *I* say you are trespassers until you prove otherwise . . . which invokes my sovereign right to use all necessary force to eject you—which I shall start to do in about three seconds."

"I wouldn't advise it."

"Who are *you* to advise? If I am hurt in attempting to enforce this my right, your action becomes constructive assault—with deadly weapons, if those things those mules are toting are guns, as they appear to be. Civil and criminal, both—why, my man, I'll wind up with your hide for a door mat!" Jubal drew back a skinny arm and clenched a bony fist. "Off my property!"

"Hold it, Doctor. We'll do it your way." Heinrich had turned bright red, but he kept his voice under tight control. He offered his identification, which Jubal glanced at, then turned back to him for him to show to Anne. Heinrich then stated his full name, said that he was a captain of police, Federation Special Service Bureau, and recited his pay number. One by one, the other six men who had left the car, and at last the driver, went through the same rigamarole at Heinrich's frozen-faced orders.

When they were done, Jubal said sweetly, "And now, Captain Heinrich, how may I help you?"

"I have a search warrant here for Gilbert Berquist, which warrant names this property, its buildings and grounds."

"Show it to me, then show it to the Witness."

"I will do so. But I have another search warrant, similar to the first, for Gillian Boardman."

"Who?"

"Gillian Boardman. The charge is kidnapping."

"My goodness!"

"And another for Hector C. Johnson . . . and one for Valentine Michael Smith . . . and one for *you*, Jubal Harshaw."

"Me? Taxes again?"

"No. Look at it. Accessory to this and that . . . and material witness on some other things . . . and I'd take you in on my own for obstructing justice if the warrant didn't make it unnecessary."

"Oh, come now, Captain! I've been most cooperative since you identified yourself and started behaving in a legal manner. And I shall continue to be. Of course, I shall still sue all of you—and your immediate superior and the government—for your illegal acts *before* that time . . . and I am not waiving any rights or recourses with respect to anything any of you may do hereafter. Mmm . . . quite a list of victims. I see why you brought an extra wagon. But—dear me! something odd here. This, uh, Mrs. Borkmann?—I see that she is charged with kidnapping this Smith fellow . . . but in this other warrant *he* seems to be charged with fleeing custody. I'm confused."

"It's both. He escaped—and she kidnapped him."

"Isn't that rather difficult to manage? Both, I mean? And on what charge was he being held? The warrant does not seem to state?"

"How the devil do I know? He escaped, that's all. He's a fugitive."

"Gracious me! I rather think I shall have to offer my services as counsel to each of them. Interesting case. If a mistake has been made—or mistakes—it could lead to other matters."

Heinrich grinned coldly. "You won't find it easy. You'll be in the pokey, too."

"Oh, not for long, I trust." Jubal raised his voice more than necessary and turned his head toward the house. "I do know another lawyer. I rather think, if Judge Holland were listening to this, habeas corpus proceedings—for all of us—might be rather prompt. And if the Associated Press just happened to have a courier car nearby, there would be no time lost in knowing *where* to serve such writs."

"Always the shyster, eh, Harshaw?"

"Slander, my dear sir. I take notice."

"A fat lot of good it will do you. We're alone."

"Are we?"

—

<h1 style="text-align:center">XV</h1>

—

VALENTINE MICHAEL SMITH swam through the murky water to the deepest part of the pool, under the diving board, and settled himself on the bottom. He did not know why his water brother Jubal had told him to hide there; indeed he did not know that he was hiding. His water brother Jubal had told him to do this and to remain there until his water brother Jill came for him; that was sufficient.

As soon as he was sure that he was at the deepest part, he curled himself into the foetal position, let most of the air out of his lungs, swallowed his tongue, rolled his eyes up, slowed his heart down to almost nothing, and became effectively "dead" save that he was not actually discorporate and could start his engines again at will. He also elected to stretch his time sense until seconds flowed past like hours, as he had much to contemplate and did not know how quickly Jill would come to get him.

He knew that he had failed again in an attempt to achieve the perfect understanding, the mutually merging rapport—the grokking—that should exist between water brothers. He knew that the failure was his, caused by his using wrongly the oddly variable human language, because Jubal had become upset as soon as he had spoken to him.

He now knew that his human brothers could suffer intense emotion without any permanent damage, nevertheless Smith was wistfully sorry that he had been the cause of such upset in Jubal. At the time, it had seemed to him that he had at last grokked perfectly a most difficult human word. He should have known better because, early in his learnings under his brother Mahmoud, he had discovered that long human words (the longer the better) were easy, unmistakable, and rarely changed their meanings . . . but short words were slippery, unpredictable, changing their meanings without any pattern. Or so he seemed to grok. Short human words were never like a short Martian word—such as "grok" which forever meant exactly the same thing. Short human words were like trying to lift water with a knife.

And this had been a very short word.

Smith still felt that he had grokked rightly the human word "God"— the confusion had come from his own failure in selecting other human words. The concept was truly so simple, so basic, so necessary that any nestling could have explained it perfectly—in Martian. The problem, then, was to find human words that would let him speak rightly, make sure that he patterned them rightly to match in fullness how it would be said in his own people's language.

He puzzled briefly over the curious fact that there should be any difficulty in saying it, even in English, since it was a thing everyone knew . . . else they could not grok alive. Possibly he should ask the human Old Ones how to say it, rather than struggle with the shifting meanings of human words. If so, he must wait until Jubal arranged it, for here he was only an egg and could not arrange it himself.

He felt brief regret that he would not be privileged to be present at the coming discorporation of brother Art and brother Dottie.

Then he settled down to reread in his mind Webster's New International Dictionary of the English Language, Third Edition, published in Springfield, Massachusetts.

From a long way off Smith was interrupted by an uneasy awareness that his water brothers were in trouble. He paused between "sherbacha" and "sherbet" to ponder this knowledge. Should he start himself up, leave the enfolding water of life, and join them to grok and share their trouble? At home there could have been no question about it; trouble is shared, in joyful closeness.

But this place was strange in every way . . . and Jubal had told him to wait until Jill came.

He reviewed Jubal's words, trying them out in long contemplation against other human words, making sure that he grokked. No, Jubal had spoken rightly and he had grokked rightly; he must wait until Jill came.

Nevertheless he was made so uneasy by the certain knowledge of his brothers' trouble that he could not go back to his word hunt. At last an idea came to him that was filled with such gay daring that he would have trembled had his body not been unready for trembling.

Jubal had told him to place his body under water and leave it there until Jill came . . . but had Jubal said that *he himself* must wait with the body?

Smith took a careful long time to consider this, knowing that the slippery English words that Jubal had used could easily lead him (and often had led him) into mistakes. He concluded that Jubal had not specifically ordered him to stay with his body . . . and that left a way out of the wrongness of not sharing his brothers' trouble.

So Smith decided to take a walk.

He was a bit dazed at his own audacity, for, while he had done it before, twice, he had never "soloed." Each time an Old One had been with him, watching over him, making sure that his body was safe, keeping him from becoming disoriented at the new experience, staying with him until he returned to his body and started it up again.

There was no Old One to help him now. But Smith had always been quick to learn; he knew how to do it and was confident that he could do it alone in a fashion that would fill his teacher with pride. So first he checked over every part of his body, made certain that it would not be damaged while he was gone, then got cautiously out of it, leaving behind only that trifle of himself needed as watchman and caretaker.

Then he rose up and stood on the edge of the pool, remembering to behave as if his body were still with him, as a guard against disorienting—against losing track of the pool, the body, everything, and wandering off into unknown places where he could not find his way back.

Smith looked around.

An air car was just landing in the garden by the pool and beings under it were complaining of injuries and indignities done them. Perhaps this was the trouble he could feel? Grasses were for walking on, flowers and bushes were not—this was a wrongness.

No, there was more wrongness. A man was just stepping out of the air car, one foot about to touch the ground, and Jubal was running toward him. Smith could see the blast of icy anger that Jubal was hurling toward the man, a blast so furious that, had one Martian hurled it toward another, both would have discorporated at once.

Smith noted it down as something he must ponder and, if it was a cusp of necessity as it seemed to be, decide what he must do to help his brother. Then he looked over the others.

Dorcas was climbing out of the pool; she was puzzled and rather troubled but not too much so; Smith could feel her confidence in Jubal. Larry was at the edge of the pool and had just gotten out; drops of water falling from him were in the air. Larry was not troubled but excited and pleased; his confidence in Jubal was absolute. Miriam was near him and her mood was midway between those of Dorcas and Larry. Anne was standing where she had been seated and was dressed in the long white garment she had had with her all day. Smith could not fully grok her mood; he felt in her some of the cold unyielding discipline of mind of an Old One. It startled him, as Anne was always soft and gentle and warmly friendly.

He saw that she was watching Jubal closely and was ready to help him. And so was Larry! . . . and Dorcas! . . . and Miriam! With a sudden burst of empathic catharsis Smith learned that all these friends were water brothers of Jubal—and therefore of him. This unexpected release from blindness shook him so that he almost lost anchorage on this place. Calming himself as he had been taught, he stopped to praise and cherish them all, one by one and together.

Jill had one arm over the edge of the pool and Smith knew that she had been down under, checking on his safety. He had been aware of her when she had done it . . . but now he knew that she had not alone been worried about his safety; Jill felt other and greater trouble, trouble that was not relieved by knowing that her charge was safe under the water of life. This troubled him very much and he considered going to her, making her know that he was with her and sharing her trouble.

He would have done so had it not been for a faint, uneasy feeling of guilt: he was not absolutely certain that Jubal had intended to permit him to walk around while his body was hidden in the pool. He compromised by telling himself that he would share their trouble—and let them know that he was present if it became needful.

Smith then looked over the man who was stepping out of the air car, felt his emotions and recoiled from them, forced himself nevertheless to examine him carefully, inside and out.

In a shaped pocket strapped around his waist by a belt the man was carrying a gun.

Smith was almost certain it was a gun. He examined it in great detail, comparing it with two guns that he had seen briefly, checking what it appeared to be against the definition in Webster's New International Dictionary of the English Language, Third Edition, published in Springfield, Massachusetts.

Yes, it was a gun—not alone in shape but also in wrongness that surrounded and penetrated it. Smith looked down the barrel, saw how it must function, and wrongness stared back at him.

Should he turn it and let it go elsewhere, taking its wrongness with it? Do it at once before the man was fully out of the car? Smith felt that he should . . . and yet Jubal had told him, at another time, not to do this to a gun until Jubal told him that it was time to do it.

He knew now that this was indeed a cusp of necessity . . . but he resolved to balance on the point of the cusp until he grokked all of it—since it was possible that Jubal, knowing that a cusp was approaching, had sent him under water to keep him from acting wrongly at the cusp.

He would wait . . . but in the meantime he would hold this gun and its wrongness carefully under his eye. Not at the moment being limited to two eyes facing always one way, being able to see all around him if needful, he continued to watch the gun and the man stepping out of the car while he went inside the car.

More wrongness than he would have believed possible! Other men were in there, all but one of them crowding toward the door. Their minds smelled like a pack of Khaugha who had scented an unwary nymph . . . and each one held in his hands a something having wrongness.

As he had told Jubal, Smith knew that shape alone was never a prime determinant; it was necessary to go beyond shape to essence in order to grok. His own people passed through five major shapes: egg, nymph, nestling, adult—and Old One which had no shape. Yet the essence of an Old One was already patterned in the egg.

These somethings that these men carried seemed like guns. But Smith did not assume that they were guns; he examined one most carefully first. It was much larger than any gun he had ever seen, its shape was very different, and its details were quite different.

It was a gun.

He examined each of the others, separately and just as carefully. They were guns.

The one man who was still seated had strapped to him a small gun.

The car itself had built into it two enormous guns—plus other things which Smith could not grok but which he felt had wrongness also.

He stopped and seriously considered twisting the car, its contents, and all—letting it topple away. But, in addition to his lifelong inhibition against wasting food, he knew that he did not fully grok what was happening. Better to move slowly, watch carefully, and help and share at the cusp by following Jubal's lead . . . and if right action for him was to remain passive, then go back to his body when the cusp had passed and discuss it all with Jubal later.

He went back outside the car and watched and listened and waited.

The first man to get out talked with Jubal concerning many things which Smith could only file without grokking; they were beyond his experience. The other men got out and spread out; Smith spread his attention to watch all of them. The car raised, moved backwards, stopped again, which relieved the beings it had sat on; Smith grokked with them to the extent that he could spare attention, trying to soothe their hurtings.

The first man handed papers to Jubal; in turn they were passed to Anne. Smith read them along with her. He recognized their word shapings as being concerned with certain human rituals of healing and balance, but, since he had encountered these rituals only in Jubal's law library, he did not try to grok the papers then, especially as Jubal seemed quite untroubled by them—the wrongness was elsewhere. He was delighted to recognize his own human name on two of the papers; he always got an odd thrill out of reading it, as if he were two places at once—impossible as that was for any but an Old One.

Jubal and the first man turned and walked toward the pool, with Anne close behind them. Smith relaxed his time sense a little to let them move faster, keeping it stretched just enough so that he could comfortably watch all the men at once. Two of the men closed in and flanked the little group.

The first man stopped near the group of his friends by the pool, looked at them, then took a picture from his pocket, looked at it, and looked at Jill. Smith felt her fear and trouble mount and he became very alert. Jubal had told him, "Protect Jill. Don't worry about wasting food. Don't worry about anything else. Protect Jill."

Of course, he would protect Jill in any case, even at the risk of acting wrongly in some other fashion. But it was good to have Jubal's blanket reassurance; it left his mind undivided and untroubled.

When the first man pointed at Jill and the two men flanking him hurried toward her with their guns of great wrongness, Smith reached out through his Doppelgänger and gave them each that tiny twist which causes to topple away.

The first man stared at where they had been and reached for his gun —and he was gone, too.

The other four started to close in. Smith did not want to twist them. He felt that Jubal would be more pleased with him if he simply stopped them. But stopping a thing, even an ash tray, is work—and Smith did not have his body at hand. An Old One could have managed it, all four together, but Smith did what he could do, what he had to do.

Four feather touches—they were gone.

He felt more intense wrongness from the direction of the car on the ground and went at once to it—grokked to a quick decision, and car and pilot were gone.

He almost overlooked the car riding cover patrol in the air. Smith started to relax when he had disposed of the car on the ground—when suddenly he felt wrongness and trouble increase, and he looked up.

The second car was coming in for a landing right where he was.

Smith stretched his time sense to his personal limit and went to the car in the air, inspected it carefully, grokked that it was as choked with utter wrongness as the first had been . . . tilted it into neverness. Then he returned to the group by the pool.

All his friends seemed quite excited; Dorcas was sobbing and Jill was holding her and soothing her. Anne alone seemed untouched by the emotions Smith felt seething around him. But wrongness was gone, all of it, and with it the trouble that had disturbed his meditations earlier. Dorcas, he knew, would be healed faster and better by Jill than by anyone—Jill always grokked a hurting fully and at once. Disturbed by emotions around him, slightly apprehensive that he might not have acted in all ways rightly at the point of cusp—or that Jubal might to grok him—Smith decided that he was now free to leave. He slipped back into the pool, found his body, grokked that it was still as he had left it, unharmed—slipped it back on.

He considered contemplating the events at the cusp. But they were too new, too recent; he was not ready to enfold them, not ready to praise and cherish the men he had been forced to move. Instead he returned happily to the task he had been on. "Sherbet" . . . "Sherbetlee" . . . "Sherbetzide"—

He had reached "Tinwork" and was about to consider "Tiny" when he felt Jill's touch approaching him. He unswallowed his tongue and made himself ready, knowing that his brother Jill could not remain very long under water without distress.

As she touched him, he reached out, took her face in his hands and kissed her. It was a thing he had learned to do quite lately and he did not feel that he grokked it perfectly. It had the growing-closer of the water ceremony. But it had something else, too . . . something he wanted very much to grok in perfect fullness.

xvi

JUBAL HARSHAW DID NOT WAIT for Gillian to dig her problem child out of the pool; he left instructions for Dorcas to be given a sedative and hurried to his study, leaving Anne to explain (or not explain) the events of the last ten minutes. *"Front!"* he called out over his shoulder.

Miriam turned and caught up with him. "I guess I must be 'front,'" she said breathlessly. "But, Boss, what in the—"

"Girl, not one word."

"But, Boss—"

"Zip it, I said. Miriam, about a week from now we'll all sit down and get Anne to tell us what we really did see. But right now everybody and his cousins will be phoning here and reporters will be crawling out of the trees —and I've got to make a couple of calls first. I need help. Are you the sort of useless female who comes unstuck when she's needed? That reminds me— Make a note to dock Dorcas's pay for the time she spent having hysterics."

Miriam gasped. "Boss! You just dare do that and every single one of us will quit cold!"

"Nonsense."

"I mean it. Quit picking on Dorcas. Why, I would have had hysterics myself if she hadn't beaten me to it." She added, "I think I'll have hysterics now."

Harshaw grinned. "You do and I'll spank you. All right, put Dorcas down for a bonus for 'extra hazardous duty.' Put all of you down for a bonus. Me, especially. *I* earned it."

"All right. But who pays your bonus?"

"The taxpayers, of course. We'll find a way to clip— Damn!" They had reached his study door; the telephone was already demanding attention. He slid into the seat in front of it and keyed in. "Harshaw speaking. Who the devil are you?"

"Skip the routine, Doc," a face answered cheerfully. "You haven't frightened me in years. How's everything going?"

Harshaw recognized the face as belonging to Thomas Mackenzie, production manager-in-chief for New World Networks; he mellowed slightly. "Well enough, Tom. But I'm rushed as can be, so—"

"You're rushed? Come try my forty-eight-hour day. I'll make it brief. Do you still think you are going to have something for us? I don't mind the expensive equipment you've got tied up; I can overhead that. But business is business—and I have to pay three full crews just to stand by for your signal. Union rules—you know how it is. I want to do you any favor I can. We've used lots of your script in the past and we expect to use still more in the future—but I'm beginning to wonder what I'm going to tell our comptroller."

Harshaw stared at him. "Don't you think the spot coverage you just got was enough to pay the freight?"

"What spot coverage?"

A few minutes later Harshaw said good-by and switched off, having been convinced that New World Networks had seen nothing of recent events at his home. He stalled off Mackenzie's questions about it, because he was dismally certain that a factual recital would simply convince Mackenzie that poor old Harshaw had at last gone to pieces. Nor could Harshaw have blamed him.

Instead they agreed that, if nothing worth picking up happened in the next twenty-four hours, New World could break the linkage and remove their cameras and other equipment.

As the screen cleared Harshaw ordered, "Get Larry. Have him fetch that panic button—Anne probably has it." He then started making another call, followed it with a third. By the time Larry arrived, Harshaw was convinced that no network had been watching when the Special Service squads attempted to raid his home. It was not necessary to check on whether or not the two dozen "hold" messages that he had recorded had been sent; their delivery depended on the same signal that had failed to reach the news channels.

As he turned away from the phone Larry offered him the "panic button" portable radio link. "You wanted this, Boss?"

"I just wanted to sneer at it and see if it sneered back. Larry, let this be a lesson to us: never trust any machinery more complicated than a knife and fork."

"Okay. Anything else?"

"Larry, is there a way to check that dingus and see if it's working properly? Without actually hauling three networks out of their beds, I mean?"

"Sure. The techs set up the transceiver down in the shop and it's got a switch on it for that very purpose. Throw the switch, push the button; a light comes on. To test on through, you simply call 'em, right from the transceiver and tell 'em you want a hot test clear through to the cameras and back to the monitor stations."

"And suppose the test shows that we aren't getting through? If the trouble is here, can you spot what's wrong?"

"Well, I might," Larry said doubtfully, "if it wasn't anything more than a loose connection. But Duke is the electron pusher around here— I'm more the intellectual type."

"I know, son—I'm not too bright about practical matters, either. Well, do the best you can. Let me know."

"Anything else, Jubal?"

"Yes, if you see the man who invented the wheel, send him up; I want to give him a piece of my mind. Meddler!"

Jubal spent the next few minutes in umbilical contemplation. He considered the possibility that Duke had sabotaged the "panic button" but rejected the thought as time wasting, if not unworthy. He allowed himself to wonder for a moment just what had really happened down in his garden and how the lad had done it—from ten feet under water. For he had no doubt that the Man from Mars had been behind those impossible shenanigans.

Admittedly, what he had seen only the day before in this very room was just as intellectually stupefying as these later events—but the emotional impact was something else. A mouse was as much a miracle of biology as was an elephant; nevertheless there was an important difference —an elephant was bigger.

To see an empty carton, just rubbish, disappear in midair logically implied the possibility that a squad car full of men could vanish in the same fashion. But one event kicked your teeth in—the other didn't.

Well, he wasn't going to waste tears on those Cossacks. Jubal conceded that cops *qua* cops were all right; he had met a number of honest cops in his life . . . and even a fee-splitting village constable did not deserve to be snuffed out like a candle. The Coast Guard was a fine example of what cops ought to be and frequently were.

But to be a member of the S.S. squads a man had to have larceny in his heart and sadism in his soul. Gestapo. Storm troopers in the service of whatever politico was in power. Jubal longed for the good old days when a lawyer could cite the Bill of Rights and not have some over-riding Federation trickery defeat him.

Never mind— What would logically happen now? Heinrich's task force certainly had had radio contact with its base; ergo, its loss would be noted, if only by silence. Shortly more S.S. troops would come looking for them—were already headed this way if that second car had been chopped off in the middle of an action report. "Miriam—"

"Yes, Boss."

"I want Mike, Jill, and Anne here at once. Then find Larry—in the shop, probably—and both of you come to the house, lock all doors, and all ground floor windows."

"More trouble?"

"Get movin', gal."

If the S.S. apes showed up again—no, *when* they showed up—they probably would not have duplicate warrants. If their leader was silly enough to break into a locked house without a warrant, well, he might have to turn Mike loose on them. But this blind warfare of attrition had to be stopped—which meant that Jubal simply had to get through to the Secretary General.

How?

Call the Executive Palace again? Heinrich had probably been telling the simple truth when he said that a renewed attempt would simply be referred to Heinrich—or to whatever S.S. boss was now warming that chair that Heinrich would never need again. Well? It would surely surprise them to have a man they had sent a squad to arrest blandly phoning in, face to face—he might be able to bull his way all the way up to the top, Commandant What's-his-name, chap with a face like a well-fed ferret, Twitchell. And certainly the commanding officer of the S.S. buckos would have direct access to the boss.

No good. You had to have a feeling for what makes the frog jump. It would be a waste of breath to tell a man who believes in guns that you've got something better than guns and that he *can't* arrest you and might as well give up trying. Twitchell would keep on throwing men and guns at them till he ran out of both—but he would never admit he couldn't bring in a man whose location was known.

Well, when you couldn't use the front door you got yourself slipped in through the back door—elementary politics. Jubal regretted mildly that he had ignored politics the last quarter century or so. Damn it, he needed Ben Caxton—Ben would know who had keys to the back door . . . and Jubal would know somebody who knew one of them.

But Ben's absence was the whole reason for this silly donkey derby. Since he couldn't ask Ben, whom did he know who would know?

Hell's halfwit, he had just been talking to one! Jubal turned back to the phone and tried to raise Tom Mackenzie again, running into only three layers of interference on the way, all of whom knew him and passed him along quickly. While he was doing this, his staff and the Man from Mars came in; Jubal ignored them and they sat down, Miriam first stopping to write on a scratch pad: *"Doors and windows locked."*

Jubal nodded to her and wrote below it: *"Larry—panic button?"* then said to the screen, "Tom, sorry to bother you again."

"A pleasure, Jubal."

"Tom, if you wanted to talk to Secretary General Douglas, how would you go about it?"

"Eh? I'd phone his press secretary, Jim Sanforth. Or possibly Jock Dumont, depending on what I wanted. But I wouldn't talk to the Secretary General at all; Jim would handle it."

"But suppose you wanted to talk to Douglas himself."

"Why, I'd tell Jim and let him arrange it. Be quicker just to tell Jim my problem, though; it might be a day or two before he could squeeze me in . . . and even then I might be bumped for something more urgent. Look, Jubal, the network is useful to the administration—and we know it and they know it. But we don't presume on it unnecessarily."

"Tom . . . assume that it is necessary. Suppose you just *had* to speak to Douglas. Right now. Not next week. In the next ten minutes."

Mackenzie's eyebrows went up. "Well . . . if I just *had* to, I would explain to Jim why it was so urgent—"

"No."

"Be reasonable."

"No. That's just what I can't be. Assume that you had caught Jim Sanforth stealing the spoons, so you couldn't tell *him* what the emergency was. But you had to speak to Douglas immediately."

Mackenzie sighed. "I suppose I would tell Jim that I simply had to talk to the boss . . . and that if I wasn't put through to him right away, the administration would never get another trace of support from the network. Politely, of course. But make him understand that I meant it. Sanforth is nobody's fool; he would never serve his own head up on a platter."

"Okay, Tom, do it."

"Huh?"

"Leave this call on. Call the Palace on another instrument—and have your boys ready to cut me in instantly. I've got to talk to the Secretary General *right now!*"

Mackenzie looked pained. "Jubal, old friend—"

"Meaning you won't."

"Meaning I *can't.* You've dreamed up a hypothetical situation in which a—pardon me—major executive of an intercontinental network could speak to the Secretary General under conditions of dire necessity. But I can't hand this entrée over to somebody else. Look, Jubal, I respect you. Besides that, you are probably four of the six most popular writers alive today. The network would hate to lose you and we are painfully aware that you won't let us tie you down to a contract. But I can't do it, even to please you. You must realize that one does not telephone the World chief of government unless *he* wants to speak to *you.*"

"Suppose I do sign an exclusive seven-year contract?"

Mackenzie looked as if his teeth hurt. "I still couldn't do it. I'd lose *my* job—and you would still have to carry out your contract."

Jubal considered calling Mike over into the instrument's visual pickup and naming him. He discarded the idea at once. Mackenzie's own programmes had run the fake 'Man from Mars' interviews—and Mackenzie was either crooked and in on the hoax . . . or he was honest, as Jubal thought he was, and simply would not believe that he himself had been hoaxed. "All right, Tom, I won't twist your arm. But you know your way around in the government better than I do. Who calls Douglas whenever he likes—and gets him? I don't mean Sanforth."

"No one."

"Damn it, no man lives in a vacuum! There must be at least a dozen people who can phone him and not get brushed off by a secretary."

"Some of his cabinet, I suppose. And not all of them."

"I don't know any of *them,* either; I've been out of touch. But I don't mean professional politicos. Who knows him so well that they can call him on a private line and invite him to play poker?"

"Um . . . you don't want much, do you? Well, there's Jake Allenby. Not the actor, the other Jake Allenby. Oil."

"I've met him. He doesn't like me. I don't like him. He knows it."

"Douglas doesn't have very many intimate friends. His wife rather discourages— Say, Jubal . . . how do you feel about astrology?"

"Never touch the stuff. Prefer brandy."

"Well, that's a matter of taste. But—see here, Jubal, if you ever let on to anyone that I told you this, I'll cut your lying throat with one of your own manuscripts."

"Noted. Agreed. Proceed."

"Well, Agnes Douglas *does* touch the stuff . . . and I know where she gets it. Her astrologer can call Mrs. Douglas at any time—and, believe you me, Mrs. Douglas has the ear of the Secretary General whenever she chooses. You can call her astrologer . . . and the rest is up to you."

"I don't seem to recall any astrologers on my Christmas card list," Jubal answered dubiously. "What's his name?"

"Her. And you might try crossing her palm with silver in convincing denominations. Her name is Madame Alexandra Vesant. Washington Exchange. That's V, E, S, A, N, T."

"I've got it," Jubal said happily. "And, Tom, you've done me a world of good!"

"Hope so. Anything for the network soon?"

"Hold it." Jubal glanced at a note Miriam had placed at his elbow some moments ago. It read: *"Larry says the transceiver won't trans—and he doesn't know why."* Jubal went on, "That spot coverage failed earlier through a transceiver failure here—and I don't have anyone who can repair it."

"I'll send somebody."

"Thanks. Thanks twice."

Jubal switched off, placed the call by name and instructed the operator to use hush & scramble if the number was equipped to take it. It was, not to his surprise. Very quickly Madame Vesant's dignified features appeared in his screen. He grinned at her and called, "Hey, *Rube!*"

She looked startled, then looked more closely. "Why, Doc Harshaw, you old scoundrel! Lord love you, it's good to see you. Where have you been hiding?"

"Just that, Becky—hiding. The clowns are after me."

Becky Vesey didn't ask why; she answered instantly, "What can I do to help? Do you need money?"

"I've got plenty of money, Becky, but thanks a lot. Money won't help; I'm in much more serious trouble than that—and I don't think anyone can help me but the Secretary General himself, Mr. Douglas. I need to talk to him—and right away. Now . . . or even sooner."

She looked blank. "That's tall order, Doc."

"Becky, I know it is—because I've been trying for a week to get through to him . . . and I can't. But don't you get mixed up in it yourself, Becky . . . because, girl, I'm hotter than a smoky bearing. I just took a chance that you might be able to advise me—a phone number, maybe, where I could reach him. But I don't want you to mix into it personally. You'd get hurt—and I'd never be able to look the Professor in the eye if I ever meet him again . . . God rest his soul."

"I know what the Professor would want me to do!" she said sharply. "So let's knock off the nonsense, Doc. The Professor always swore that you were the only sawbones fit to carve people; the rest were butchers. He never forgot that time in Elkton."

"Now, Becky, we won't bring that up. I was paid."

"You saved his life."

"I did no such thing. It was his rugged constitution and his will to fight back—and your nursing."

"Uh . . . Doc, we're wasting time. Just how hot are you?"

"They're throwing the book at me . . . and anybody near me is going to get splashed. There's a warrant out for me—a Federation warrant— and they know where I am and I *can't* run. It will be served any minute now . . . and Mr. Douglas is the *only* person who can stop it."

"You'll be sprung. I guarantee that."

"Becky . . . I'm sure you would. But it might take a few hours. It's that 'back room' I'm afraid of, Becky. I'm too old for a session in the back room."

"But— Oh, goodness! Doc, can't you give me some details? I really ought to cast a horoscope on you, then I'd know what to do. You're Mercury, of course, since you're a doctor. But if I knew what house to look in to find your trouble, I could do better."

"Girl, there isn't time for that. But thanks." Jubal thought rapidly. Whom to trust? And when? "Becky, just knowing could put you in as much trouble as I am in . . . unless I convince Mr. Douglas."

"Tell me, Doc. I've never taken a powder at a clem yet—and you know it."

"All right. So I'm 'Mercury.' But the trouble lies in Mars."

She looked at him sharply. "How?"

"You've seen the news. You know that the Man from Mars is supposed to be making a retreat some place high up in the Andes. Well, he's not. That's just to hoax the yokels."

Becky seemed startled but not quite as Jubal had expected her to be. "Just where do you figure in this, Doc?"

"Becky, there are people all over this sorry planet who want to lay hands on that boy. They want to use him, they want to make him geek for them, their way. But he's my client and I don't propose to hold still for it. If I can help it. But my only chance is to talk with Mr. Douglas himself, face to face."

"The Man from Mars is your client? You can turn him up?"

"Yes. But only to Mr. Douglas. You know how it is Becky—the mayor can be a good Joe, kind to children and dogs. But he doesn't necessarily know everything his town clowns are up to—especially if they haul a man in and take him into that back room."

She nodded. "I've had my troubles with cops. Cops!"

"So I need to dicker with Mr. Douglas before they haul me in."

"All you want is to talk to him on the telephone?"

"Yes. If you can swing it. Here, let me give you my number—and I'll be sitting right here, hoping for a call . . . until they pick me up. If you can't swing it . . . thanks anyway, Becky, thanks a lot. I'll know you tried."

"Don't switch off!" she said sharply.

"Eh?"

"Keep the circuit, Doc, while I see what I can do. If I have any luck, they can patch right through this phone and save time. So hold on." Madame Vesant left the screen without saying good-by, then called Agnes Douglas. She spoke with calm confidence, pointing out to Agnes that this was precisely the development foretold by the stars—and exactly on schedule. Now had come the critical instant when Agnes must guide and sustain her husband, using all her womanly wit and wisdom to see that he acted wisely and without delay. "Agnes dear, this configuration will not be repeated in a thousand years—Mars, Venus and Mercury in perfect trine, just as Venus reaches the meridian, making Venus dominant. Thus you see—"

"Allie, what do the Stars tell me to *do?* You know I don't understand the scientific part."

This was hardly surprising, since the described relationship did not obtain at the moment. Madame Vesant had not had time to compute a new horoscope and was improvising. But she was untroubled by it; she was speaking a "higher truth," giving good advice and helping her friends. To be able to help two friends at once made Becky Vesey especially happy. "Dear, you really do understand it, you have born talent for it. You are Venus, as always, and Mars is reinforced, being both your husband and that young man Smith for the duration of this crisis. Mercury is Dr. Harshaw. To offset the imbalance caused by the reinforcement of Mars, Venus must sustain Mercury until the crisis is past. But you have very little time for it; Venus waxes in influence until reaching meridian, only seven minutes from now—after that your influence will decline. You must act quickly."

"You should have warned me sooner."

"My dear, I have been waiting here by my phone all day, ready to act instantly. The Stars tell us the nature of each crisis; they never tell us the details. But there is still time. I have Dr. Harshaw waiting on the telephone here; all that is necessary is to bring them face to face—if possible before Venus reaches meridian."

"Well— All right, Allie. I've got to dig Joseph out of some silly conference but I'll get him. Keep this line open. Give me the number of the phone you have this Doctor Rackshaw on—or can you transfer the call there?"

"I can switch it over here. Just get Mr. Douglas. Hurry, dear."

"I will."

When Agnes Douglas' face left the screen, Becky went to still another phone. Her profession required ample phone service; it was her largest single business expense. Humming happily she called her broker.

xvii

As Madame Vesant left the screen Jubal Harshaw leaned back from his phone. "Front," he said.

"Okay, Boss," Miriam acknowledged.

"This is one for the 'Real-Experiences' group. Specify on the cover sheet that I want the narrator to have a sexy contralto voice—"

"Maybe I should try out for it."

"Not that sexy. Shut up. Dig out that list of null surnames we got from the Census Bureau, pick one and put an innocent, mammalian first name with it, for the pen name. A girl's name ending in 'a'—that always suggests a 'C' cup."

"Huh! And not one of *us* with a name ending in 'a.' Why, you louse!"

"Flat-chested bunch, aren't you? 'Angela.' Her name is 'Angela.' Title: 'I Married a Martian.' Start: All my life I had longed to become an astronaut. Paragraph. When I was just a tiny thing, with freckles on my nose and stars in my eyes, I saved box tops just as my brothers did—and cried when Mummy wouldn't let me wear my Space Cadet helmet to bed. Paragraph. In those carefree childhood days I did not dream to what strange, bittersweet fate my tomboy ambition would—"

"Boss!"

"Yes, Dorcas?"

"Here come two more loads."

Jubal got up from the telephone chair. "Hold for continuation. Miriam, sit down at the phone." He went to the window, saw the two air cars Dorcas had spotted, decided that they could be squad cars, and might be about to land on his property. "Larry, bolt the door to this room. Anne, put on your robe. Watch them but stand back from the window; I want them to think the house is empty. Jill, you stick close to Mike and don't let him make any hasty moves. Mike, you do what Jill tells you to."

"Yes, Jubal. I will do."

"Jill, don't turn him loose unless you have to. To keep one of us from being shot, I mean. If they bust down doors, let them—I rather hope they do. Jill, if it comes to scratch, I'd much rather he snatched just the guns and not the men."

"Yes, Jubal."

"Make sure he understands. This indiscriminate elimination of cops has got to stop."

"Telephone, Boss!"

"Coming." Jubal went unhurriedly back to the phone. "All of you stay out of pickup. Dorcas, you can take a nap. Miriam, note down another title for later: 'I Married a Human.' " He slid into the seat as Miriam vacated it and said, "Yes?"

A blandly handsome man looked back at him. "Doctor Harshaw?"

"Yes."

"Please hold on. The Secretary General will speak with you." The tone implied that a genuflection was in order.

"Okay."

The screen flickered, then rebuilt in the tousled image of His Excellency the Honorable Joseph Edgerton Douglas, Secretary General of the World Federation of Free Nations. "Dr. Harshaw? Understand you need to speak with me. Shoot."

"No, sir."

"Eh? But I understood—"

"Let me rephrase it precisely, Mr. Secretary. *You* need to speak with *me.*"

Douglas looked surprised, then grinned. "Pretty sure of yourself, aren't you? Well, Doctor, you have just ten seconds to prove that. I have other things to do."

"Very well, sir. I am attorney for the Man from Mars."

Douglas suddenly stopped looking tousled. "Repeat that."

"I am attorney for Valentine Michael Smith, known as the Man from Mars. Attorney with full power. In fact, it may help to think of me as *de facto* Ambassador from Mars . . . in the spirit of the Larkin Decision, that is to say."

Douglas stared at him. "Man, you must be out of your mind!"

"I've often thought so, lately. Nevertheless I am acting for the Man from Mars. And he is prepared to negotiate."

"The Man from Mars is in Ecuador."

"Please, Mr. Secretary. This is a private conversation. He is not in Ecuador, as both of us know. Smith—the real Valentine Michael Smith, not the one who has appeared in the newscasts—escaped from confinement—and, I should add, illegal confinement—at Bethesda Medical Center on Thursday last, in company with Nurse Gillian Boardman. He kept his freedom and is now free—and he will continue to keep it. If any of your large staff of assistants has told you anything else, then someone has been lying to you . . . which is why I am speaking to you yourself. So that you can straighten it out."

Douglas looked very thoughtful. Someone apparently spoke to him from off screen, but no words came over the telephone. At last he said, "Even if what you said were true, Doctor, you can't be in a position to speak for young Smith. He's a ward of the State."

Jubal shook his head. "Impossible. The Larkin Decision."

"Now see here, as a lawyer myself, I assure you—"

"As a lawyer myself, I must follow my own opinion—and protect my client."

"You are a lawyer? I thought that you meant that you claimed to be attorney-in-fact, rather than counsellor."

"Both. You'll find that I am an attorney at law, in good standing, and admitted to practice before the High Court. I don't hang my shingle these days, but I am." Jubal heard a dull boom from below and glanced aside. Larry whispered, *"The front door, I think, Boss— Shall I go look?"*

Jubal shook his head in negation and spoke to the screen. "Mr. Secretary, while we quibble, time is running out. Even now your men—your S.S. hooligans—are breaking into my house. It is most distasteful to be under siege in my own home. Now, for the first and last time, will you abate this nuisance? So that we can negotiate peaceably and equitably? Or shall we fight it out in the High Court with all the stink and scandal that would ensue?"

Again the Secretary appeared to speak with someone off screen. He turned back, looking troubled. "Doctor, if the Special Service police are trying to arrest you, it is news to me. I do not see—"

"If you'll listen closely, you'll hear them tromping up my staircase, sir! Mike! Anne! Come here." Jubal shoved his chair back to allow the camera angle to include three people. "Mr. Secretary General Douglas— the Man from Mars!" He did not, of course, introduce Anne, but she and her white cloak of probity were fully in view.

Douglas stared at Smith; Smith looked back at him and seemed uneasy. "Jubal—"

"Just a moment, Mike. Well, Mr. Secretary? Your men have broken into my house—I hear them pounding on my study door this moment." Jubal turned his head. "Larry, unbolt the door. Let them in." He put a hand on Mike. "Don't get excited, lad, and don't do anything unless I tell you to."

"Yes, Jubal. That man. I have know him."

"And he knows you." Over his shoulder Jubal called out to the now-open door, "Come in, Sergeant. Right over here."

The S.S. sergeant standing in the doorway, mob gun at the ready, did not come in. Instead he called out, "Major! Here they are!"

Douglas said, "Let me speak to the officer in charge of them, Doctor." Again he spoke off screen.

Jubal was relieved to see that the major for whom the sergeant had shouted showed up with his sidearm still in its holster; Mike's shoulder had been trembling under Jubal's hand ever since the sergeant's gun had come into view—and, while Jubal lavished no fraternal love on these troopers, he did not want Smith to display his powers . . . and cause awkward questions.

The major glanced around the room. "You're Jubal Harshaw?"

"Yes. Come over here. Your boss wants you."

"None of that. You come along. I'm also looking for—"

"Come *here!* The Secretary General himself wants a word with you— on this phone."

The S.S. major looked startled, then came on into the study, around Jubal's desk, and in sight of the screen—looked at it, suddenly came smartly to attention and saluted. Douglas nodded. "Name, rank, and duty."

"Sir, Major C. D. Bloch, Special Service Squadron Cheerio, Maryland Enclave Barracks."

"Now tell me what you are doing where you are, and why."

"Sir, that's rather complicated. I—"

"Then unravel it for me. Speak up, Major."

"Yes, sir. I came here pursuant to orders. You see—"

"I don't see."

"Well, sir, about an hour and a half ago a flying squad was sent here to make several arrests. They didn't report in when they should have and when we couldn't raise them by radio, I was sent with the reserve squad to find them and render assistance as needed."

"Whose orders?"

"Uh, the Commandant's, sir."

"And did you find them?"

"No, sir. Not a trace of them."

Douglas looked at Harshaw. "Counsellor, did you see anything of another squad, earlier?"

"It's no part of my duties to keep track of your servants, Mr. Secretary. Perhaps they got the wrong address. Or simply got lost."

"That is hardly an answer to my question."

"You are correct, sir. I am not being interrogated. Nor will I be, other than by due process. I am acting for my client; I am not nursemaid to these uniformed, uh, persons. But I suggest, from what I have seen of them, that they might not be able to find a pig in a bath tub."

"Mmm . . . possibly. Major, round up your men and return. I'll confirm that via channels."

"Yes, sir!" The major saluted.

"Just a moment!" Harshaw said sharply. "These men broke into my house. I demand to see their warrant."

"Oh. Major, show him your search warrant."

Major Bloch turned brick red. "Sir, the officer ahead of me had the warrants. Captain Heinrich. The one who's missing."

Douglas stared at him. "Young man . . . do you mean to stand there and tell me that you broke into a citizen's home *without a warrant?*"

"But— Sir, you don't understand! There *was* a warrant—there *are* warrants. I saw them. But, of course, Captain Heinrich took them with him. Sir."

Douglas just looked at him. "Get on back. Place yourself under arrest when you get there. I'll see you later."

"Yes, sir."

"Hold it," Harshaw demanded. "Under the circumstances I shan't let him leave. I exercise my right to make a citizen's arrest. I shall take him down and charge him in this township and have him placed in our local lockup. 'Armed breaking and entering.' "

Douglas blinked thoughtfully. "Is this necessary, sir?"

"*I* think it is. These fellows seem to be awfully hard to find when you want them—so I don't want to let this one leave our local jurisdiction. Why, aside from the serious criminal charges, I haven't even had opportunity to assess the damage to my property."

"You have my assurance, sir, that you will be fully compensated."

"Thank you, sir. But what is to prevent another uniformed joker from coming along twenty minutes from now, perhaps this time with a warrant? Why, he wouldn't even need to break down the door! My castle stands violated, open to any intruder. Mr. Secretary, only the few precious moments of delay afforded by my once-stout door kept this scoundrel from dragging me away before I could reach you by telephone . . . and you heard him say that there was still another like him at large—with, so *he* says, warrants."

"Doctor, I assure you that I know nothing of any such warrant."

"Warrants, sir. He said 'warrants for several arrests.' Though perhaps a better term would be 'lettres de cachet.' "

"That's a serious imputation."

"This is a serious matter. You see what has already been done to me."

"Doctor, I know nothing of these warrants, if they exist. But I give you my personal assurance that I will look into it at once, find out why they were issued, and act as the merits of the matter may appear. Can I say more?"

"You can say a great deal more, sir. I can reconstruct exactly why those warrants were issued. Some one in your service, in an excess of zeal, caused a pliant judge to issue them . . . for the purpose of seizing the persons of myself and my guests in order to question us, safely out of your sight. Out of *anyone's* sight, sir! We will discuss all issues with *you* . . . but we will not be questioned by such as *this* creature—" Jubal hooked a thumb at the S.S. major "—in some windowless back room! Sir, I hope for, and expect, justice at your hands . . . but if those warrants are not canceled at once, if I am not assured by you personally beyond any possibility of quibble that the Man from Mars, Nurse Boardman, and myself will be left undisturbed in our persons, free to come and go, then—" Jubal stopped and shrugged helplessly. "—I must seek a champion elsewhere. There are, as you know, persons and powers outside the administration who hold deep interest in the affairs of the Man from Mars."

"You threaten me."

"No, sir. I plead with you. I have come to you first. We wish to negotiate. But we cannot speak easily while we are being hounded. I beg of you, sir—call off your dogs!"

Douglas glanced down, looked up again. "Those warrants, if any, will not be served. As soon as I can track them down they will be canceled."

"Thank you, sir."

Douglas glanced at Major Bloch. "You still insist on booking him locally?"

Jubal looked at him contemptuously. "Him? Oh, let him go, he's merely a fool in uniform. And let's forget the damages, too. You and I have more serious matters to discuss."

"You may go, Major." The S.S. officer saluted and left very abruptly. Douglas continued, "Counsellor, it is my thought that we now need conversations face to face. The matters you raise can hardly be settled over the telephone."

"I agree."

"You and your, uh, client will be my guests at the Palace. I'll send my yacht to pick you up. Can you be ready in an hour?"

Harshaw shook his head. "Thank you, Mr. Secretary. But that won't be necessary. We'll sleep here . . . and when it comes time to meet I'll dig up a dog sled, or something. No need to send your yacht."

Mr. Douglas frowned. "Come, Doctor! As you yourself pointed out, these conversations will be quasi-diplomatic in nature. In proffering proper protocol I have, in effect, conceded this. Therefore I must be allowed to provide official hospitality."

"Well, sir, I might point out that my client has had entirely too much official hospitality already—he had the Devil's own time getting shut of it."

Douglas' face became rigid. "Sir, are you implying—"

"I'm not implying anything. I'm simply saying that Smith has been through quite a lot and is not used to high-level ceremony. He'll sleep sounder here, where he feels at home. And so shall I. I am a crochety old man, sir, and I prefer my own bed. Or I might point out that our talks may break down and my client and I would be forced to look elsewhere—in which case I would find it embarrassing to be a guest under your roof."

The Secretary General looked very grim. "Threats again. I thought you trusted me, sir? And I distinctly heard you say that you were 'ready to negotiate.' "

"I do trust you, sir." (—about as far as I could throw a fit!) "And we are indeed ready to negotiate. But I use 'negotiate' in its original sense, not in this new-fangled meaning of 'appeasement.' However, we intend to be reasonable. But we can't start talks at once in any case; we're shy one factor and we must wait. How long, I don't know."

"What do you mean?"

"We expect the administration to be represented at these talks by whatever delegation you choose—and we have the same privilege."

"Surely. But let's keep it small. I shall handle this myself, with only an assistant or two. The Solicitor General, I think . . . and our experts in space law. But to transact business you require a small group—the smaller the better."

"Most certainly. Our group will be small. Smith himself—myself—I'll bring a Fair Witness—"

"Oh, come now!"

"A Witness does not slow things up. I suggest you retain one also. We'll have one or two others perhaps—but we lack one key man. I have firm instructions from my client that a fellow named Ben Caxton must be present . . . and I can't find the beggar."

Jubal, having spent hours of most complex maneuvering in order to toss in this one remark, now waited with his best poker face to see what would happen. Douglas stared at him. " 'Ben Caxton?' Surely you don't mean that cheap winchell?"

"The Ben Caxton I refer to is a newspaperman. He has a column with one of the syndicates."

"Absolutely out of the question!"

Harshaw shook his head. "Then that's all, Mr. Secretary. My instructions are firm and give me no leeway. I'm sorry to have wasted your time. I beg to be excused now." He reached out as if to switch off the phone.

"Hold it."

"Sir?"

"Don't cut that circuit; I'm not through speaking to you!"

"I most humbly beg the Secretary General's pardon. We will, of course, wait until he excuses us."

"Yes, yes, but never mind the formality. Doctor, do you read the tripe that comes out of this Capitol labeled as news?"

"Good Heavens, no!"

"I wish I didn't have to. It's preposterous to talk about having a journalist present at these talks in any case. We'll let them in later, after everything is settled. But even if we were to have any of them present, Caxton would not be one of them. The man is utterly poisonous . . . a keyhole sniffer of the worst sort."

"Mr. Secretary, *we* have no objection to the full glare of publicity throughout. In fact, we shall insist on it."

"Ridiculous!"

"Possibly. But I serve my client as I think best. If we reach agreement affecting the Man from Mars and the planet which is his home, I want every person on this planet to have opportunity to know exactly how it was done and what was agreed. Contrariwise, if we fail to agree, people must hear how and where the talks broke down. There will be no star chamber proceedings, Mr. Secretary."

"Damn it, man, I wasn't speaking of a star chamber and you know it! I simply meant quiet, orderly talks without our elbows being jostled!"

"Then let the press in, sir, through their cameras and microphones . . . but with their feet and elbows outside. Which reminds me—we will be interviewed, my client and I, over one of the networks later today—and I shall announce that we want full publicity on these coming talks."

"What? You mustn't give out interviews now—why, that's contrary to the whole spirit of this discussion."

"I can't see that it is. We won't discuss this private conversation, of course—but are you suggesting that a private citizen must have your permission to speak to the press?"

"No, of course not, but—"

"I'm afraid it's too late, in any case. The arrangements have all been made and the only way you could stop it now would be by sending more carloads of your thugs—with or without warrants. But I'm afraid they would be too late, even so. My only reason for mentioning it is that it occurs to me that you might wish to give out a news release—in advance of this coming interview—telling the public that the Man from Mars has returned from his retreat in the Andes . . . and is now vacationing in the Poconos. So as to avoid any possible appearance that the government was taken by surprise. You follow me?"

"I follow you—quite well." The Secretary General stared silently at Harshaw for several moments, then said, "Please wait." He left the screen entirely.

Harshaw motioned Larry to him while he reached up with his other hand and covered the telephone's sound pickup. "Look, son," he whispered, "with that transceiver out I'm bluffing on a busted flush. I don't know whether he's left to issue that news release I suggested . . . or has gone to set the dogs on us again while he keeps me tied up on the phone. And I won't know, either way. You high-tail it out of here, get Tom Mackenzie on the phone, and tell him that if he doesn't get the setup here working at once, he's going to miss the biggest story since the Fall of Troy. Then be careful coming home—there may be cops crawling out of the cracks."

"Got it. But how do I call Mackenzie?"

"Uh—" Douglas was just sitting back down on screen. "Speak to Miriam. Git."

"Dr. Harshaw, I took your suggestion. A news release much as you worded it . . . plus a few substantiating details." Douglas smiled warmly in a good simulation of his homespun public *persona.* "And there is no use in half measures. I can see that, if you insist on publicity, there is no way to stop you, foolish as it is to hold exploratory talks in public. So I added to the release that the administration had arranged to discuss future interplanetary relations with the Man from Mars—as soon as he had rested from his trip—and would do so publicly . . . *quite* publicly." His smile became chilly and he stopped looking like good old Joe Douglas.

Harshaw grinned jovially, in honest admiration—why, the old thief had managed to roll with the punch and turn a defeat into a coup for the administration. "That's just perfect, Mr. Secretary! Much better if such matters come officially from the government. We'll back you right down the line!"

"Thank you. Now about this Caxton person— Letting the press in does not apply to him. He can sit at home, watch it over stereovision, and make up his lies from that—and no doubt he will. But he will not be present at the talks. I'm sorry. No."

"Then there will be no talks, Mr. Secretary, no matter what you have told the press."

"I don't believe you understand me, Counsellor. This man is offensive to me. Personal privilege."

"You are correct, sir. It is a matter of personal privilege."

"Then we'll say no more about it."

"*You* misunderstand *me.* It is indeed personal privilege. But not yours. Smith's."

"Eh?"

"You are privileged to select your advisers to be present at these talks —and you can fetch the Devil himself and we shall not complain. Smith is privileged to select his advisers and have them present. If Caxton is not present, we will not be there. In fact, you will find us across the street, at some quite different conference. One where you won't be welcome. Even if you speak fluent Hindi. *Now* do you understand me?"

There was a long silence, during which Harshaw thought clinically that a man of Douglas' age really should not indulge in such evident rage. Douglas did not leave the screen but he consulted offscreen and silently. At last he spoke—to the Man from Mars.

Mike had stayed on screen the whole time, as silently and at least as patiently as the Witness. Douglas said to him, "Smith, why do you insist on this ridiculous condition?"

Harshaw put a hand on Mike and said instantly, "Don't answer, Mike!" —then to Douglas: "Tut, tut, Mr. Secretary! The Canons, please! You may not inquire why my client has instructed me. And let me add that the Canons are violated with exceptional grievance in that my client has but lately learned English and cannot be expected to hold his own against you. If you will first take the trouble to learn Martian, I may permit you to put the question again . . . in *his* language. Or I may not. But certainly not today."

Douglas sighed. "Very well. It might be pertinent to inquire into what Canons *you* have played fast and loose with, too—but I haven't time; I have a government to run. I yield. But don't expect me to shake hands with this Caxton!"

"As you wish, sir. Now back to the first point. We are held up. I haven't been able to find Caxton. His office says that he is out of town."

Douglas laughed. "That's hardly my problem. You insisted on a privilege—one I find personally offensive. Bring whom you like. But round them up yourself."

"Reasonable, sir, very reasonable. But would you be willing to do the Man from Mars a favor?"

"Eh? What favor?"

"The talks will not begin until Caxton is located—that is flat and is not subject to argument. But I have not been able to find him . . . and my client is getting restive. I am merely a private citizen . . . but you have resources."

"What do you mean?"

"Some minutes ago I spoke rather disparagingly of the Special Service squadrons—check it off to the not unnatural irk of a man who has just had his front door broken down. But in truth I know that they can be amazingly efficient . . . and they have the ready cooperation of police forces everywhere, local, state, national, and all Federation departments and bureaus. Mr. Secretary, if you were to call in your S.S. Commandant and tell him that you were anxious to locate a certain man as quickly as was humanly possible—well, sir, it would produce more meaningful activity in the next hour than I myself could hope to produce in a century."

"Why on Earth should I alert all police forces everywhere to find one scandal-mongering reporter?"

"Not 'on Earth,' my dear sir—on Mars. I asked you to regard this as a favor to the Man from Mars."

"Well . . . it's a preposterous request but I'll go along." Douglas looked directly at Mike. "As a favor to Smith, only. But I shall expect similar cooperation when we get down to cases."

"You have my assurance that it will ease the situation enormously."

"Well, I can't promise anything. You say the man is missing. If he is, he may have fallen in front of a truck; he may be dead—and I, for one, would not mourn."

Harshaw looked very grave. "Let us hope not, for all of our sakes."

"What do you mean?"

"I've tried to point out that sad possibility to my client—but it is like shouting into the wind. He simply won't listen to the idea." Harshaw sighed. "A shambles, sir. If we can't find this Caxton, that is what we will both have on our hands: a shambles."

"Well . . . I'll try. But don't expect miracles, Doctor."

"Not I, sir. My client. He has the Martian viewpoint . . . and he *does* expect miracles. So let's pray for one."

"You'll hear from me. That's all I can say."

Harshaw bowed without getting up. "Your servant, sir."

As the Secretary General's image cleared from the screen Jubal sighed and stood up, and at once found Gillian's arms around his neck. "Oh, Jubal, you were *wonderful!*"

"We aren't out of the woods yet, child."

"I know. But if anything can save Ben, you've just done it." She kissed him.

"Hey, none of that stuff! I swore off smooching before you were born. So kindly show respect for my years." He kissed her carefully and thoroughly. "That's just to take the taste of Douglas out of my mouth—between kicking him and kissing him I was getting nauseated. Now go smooch Mike instead. He deserves it—for holding still to my damned lies."

"Oh, I shall!" Jill let go of Harshaw, put her arms around the Man from Mars. "Such wonderful lies, Jubal!" She kissed Mike.

Jubal watched with deep interest as Mike initiated a second section of the kiss himself, performing it very solemnly but not quite as a novice—clumsy, Harshaw decided, but he did not bump noses nor hang back. Harshaw awarded him a B-minus, with an A for effort.

"Son," he said, "you continue to amaze me. I would have expected that to cause you to curl up in one of your faints."

"I so did," Mike answered seriously, without letting go of Jill, "on the first kissing time."

"Well! Congratulations, Jill. A.C., or D.C.?"

She looked at Harshaw. "Jubal, you're a tease but I love you anyhow and refuse to let you get my goat. Mike got a little upset once—but no longer, as you can see."

"Yes," Mike agreed, "it is a goodness. For water brothers it is a growing-closer. I will show you. Yes?" He let go of Jill.

Jubal hastily put up a palm. "No."

"No?"

"Don't be hurt. But you would be disappointed, son. It's a growing-closer for water brothers only if they are young girls and pretty—such as Jill."

"My brother Jubal, you speak rightly?"

"I speak very rightly. Kiss girls all you want to—it beats the hell out of card games."

"Beg pardon?"

"It's a fine way to grow closer . . . but just with girls. Hmmm . . ." Jubal looked around the room. "I wonder if that first-time phenomenon would repeat? Dorcas, I want your help in a scientific experiment."

"Boss, I am not a guinea pig! You go to hell."

"In due course, I shall. Don't be difficult, girl; Mike has no communicable diseases, or I wouldn't let him use the pool—which reminds me: Miriam, when Larry gets back, tell him I want the pool drained and refilled tonight—we're through with murkiness. Well, Dorcas?"

"How do you know it would be our *first* time?"

"Mmm, there's that. Mike, have you ever kissed Dorcas?"

"No, Jubal. Only today did I learn that Dorcas is my water brother."

"She is?"

"Yes. Dorcas and Anne and Miriam and Larry. They are your water brothers, my brother Jubal."

"Mmm, yes. Correct in essence."

"Yes. It is essence, the grokking—not sharing of water. I speak rightly?"

"Very rightly, Mike."

"They are your water brothers." Mike paused to think words. "In catenative assemblage, they are my brothers." Mike looked at Dorcas. "For brothers, growing-closer is good. But I did not know."

Jubal said, "Well, Dorcas?"

"Huh? Oh, Heavens! Boss, you're the world's worst tease. But Mike isn't teasing. He's sweet." She walked up to him, stood on tiptoes, and held up her arms. "Kiss me, Mike."

Mike did. For some seconds they "grew closer."

Dorcas fainted.

Jubal spotted it and kept her from falling, Mike being far too inexperienced to cope with it. Then Jill had to speak sharply to Mike to keep him from trembling into withdrawal when he saw what had happened to Dorcas. Luckily Dorcas came out of it shortly and was able to reassure Mike that she was all right, that she had indeed "grown closer" and would happily grow closer again—but she needed to catch her breath. *"Whew!"*

Miriam had watched round-eyed. "I wonder if I dare risk it?"

Anne said, "By seniority, please. Boss, are you through with me as a Witness?"

"For the time being, at least."

"Then hold my cloak." She slipped out of it. "Want to bet on it?"

"Which way?"

"I'll give you seven-to-two I *don't* faint—but I wouldn't mind losing."

"Done."

"Dollars, not hundreds. Mike dear . . . let's grow *lots* closer."

In time Anne was forced to give up through simple hypoxia, although Mike, with his Martian training, could have gone without oxygen much longer. She gasped for air and said, "I don't think I was set just right. Boss, I'm going to give you another chance for your money."

She started to offer her face again but Miriam tapped her on the shoulder. "Out."

"Don't be so eager."

" 'Out,' I said. The foot of the line for you, wench," Miriam insisted.

"Oh, well!" Anne pecked Mike hastily and gave way. Miriam moved in, smiled at him, and said nothing. It was not necessary; they grew close and continued to grow closer.

"Front!"

Miriam looked around. "Boss, can't you see I'm *busy?"*

"All right, all right! But get out of the pickup angle—I'll answer the phone myself."

"Honest, I didn't even hear it."

"Obviously. But for a while we've got to pretend to a modicum of dignity around here—it might be the Secretary General. So get out of range."

But it was Mr. Mackenzie. "Jubal, what in the devil is going on?"

"Trouble?"

"A short while ago I got a wild phone call from a young man claiming to speak for you who urged me to drop everything and get cracking, because you've finally got something for me. Since I had already ordered a mobile unit to your place—"

"Never got here."

"I know. They called in, after wandering around somewhere north of you. Our despatcher straightened them out and they should be there any moment now. I tried twice to call you and your circuit was busy. What have I missed?"

"Nothing yet." Jubal considered it. Damnation, he should have had someone monitor the babble box. Had Douglas actually made that news release? Was Douglas committed? Or would a new passel of cops show up? While the kids played post office! Jubal, you're getting senile. "I'm not sure that there's going to be, just yet. Has there been anything special in the way of a news flash this past hour?"

"Why, no—oh, one item: the Palace announced that the Man from Mars had returned north and was vacationing in the—*Jubal!* Are you mixed up in *that?*"

"Just a moment. Mike, come to the phone. Anne, grab your robe."

"Got it, Boss."

"Mr. Mackenzie—meet the Man from Mars."

Mackenzie's jaw dropped, then his professional reflexes came to his aid. "Hold it. Just hold it right there and let me get a camera on this! We'll pick it up in flat, right off the phone—and we'll repeat in stereo just as quick as those jokers of mine get there. Jubal . . . I'm safe on this? You wouldn't— You wouldn't—"

"Would I swindle you with a Fair Witness at my elbow? Yes, I would, if necessary. But I'm not forcing this interview on you. Matter of fact, we should wait and tie in Argus and Trans-Planet."

"Jubal! You can't do this to me."

"And I won't. The agreement with all of you was to monitor what the cameras saw . . . when I signalled. And use it if it was newsworthy. But I didn't promise not to give out interviews in addition to that—and New World can have this interview, oh, say thirty minutes ahead of Argus and Trans-P . . . if you want it." Jubal added, "Not only did you loan us all the equipment for the tie-in, but you've been very helpful personally, Tom. I can't express how helpful you've been."

"You mean, uh, that telephone number?"

"Correct!"

"And it got results?"

"It did. But no questions about *that*, Tom. Not on the air. Ask me privately—next year."

"Oh, I wouldn't think of it. You keep your lip buttoned and I'll keep mine. Now don't go away—"

"One more thing. That spool of messages you're holding for me against the same signal. Make damn sure they don't go out. Send them back to me."

"Eh? All right, all right—I've been keeping them in my desk, you were so fussy about it. Jubal, I've got a camera on this phone screen right now. Can we start?"

"Shoot."

"And I'm going to do *this* one myself!" Mackenzie turned his face away and apparently looked at the camera. "Flash news! This is your NWNW reporter on the spot while its hot! The Man from Mars has just phoned you right here in your local station and wants to talk to *you!* Cut. Monitor, insert flash-news plug and acknowledgment to sponsor. Jubal, anything special I should ask him?"

"Don't ask him questions about South America—he's not a tourist. Swimming is your safest subject. You can ask me about his future plans."

"Okay. End of cut. Friends, you are now face to face and voice to voice with Valentine Michael Smith, the Man from Mars! As NWNW, always first with the burst, told you earlier, Mr. Smith has just returned from his solitary retreat high in the Andes—and we welcome him back! Wave to your friends, Mr. Smith—"

("Wave at the telephone, son. Smile and wave at it.")

"Thank you, Valentine Michael Smith. We're all happy to see you looking so healthy and tan. I understand that you have been gathering strength by learning to swim?"

Boss! Visitors. Or something."

"Cut before interruption—after the word 'swim.' What the hell, Jubal?"

"I'll have to see. Jill, ride herd on Mike again—it might be General Quarters."

But it was not. It was the NWNW mobile stereovision unit landing—and again rose bushes were damaged—Larry returning from phoning Mackenzie from the village, and Duke, returning. Mackenzie decided to finish the flat black & white interview quickly, since he was now assured of depth and color through his mobile unit, and in the meantime its technical crew could check the trouble with the equipment on loan to Jubal. Larry and Duke went with them.

The interview was finished with inanities, Jubal fielding any questions Mike failed to understand; Mackenzie signed off with a promise to the public that a color & depth special interview with the Man from Mars would follow in thirty minutes. "Stay synched with this station!" He stayed on the phone and waited for his technicians to report.

Which the crew boss did, almost at once: "Nothing wrong with that transceiver, Mr. Mackenzie, nor with any part of this field setup."

"Then what was wrong with it before?"

The technician glanced at Larry and Duke, then grinned. "Nothing. But it helps quite a bit to put power through it. The breaker was open at the board."

Harshaw intervened to stop a wrangle between Larry and Duke, one which seemed concerned with the relative merits of various sorts of idiocy more than with the question of whether Duke had, or had not, told Larry that a certain tripped circuit breaker must be reset if it was anticipated that the borrowed equipment was going to be used. The showman's aspect of Jubal's personality regretted that the "finest unrehearsed spectacular since Elijah bested the Priests of Baal" had been missed by the cameras. But the political finagler in him was relieved that mischance had kept Mike's curious talents still a close secret—Jubal anticipated that he still might need them, as a secret weapon . . . not to mention the undesirability of trying to explain to skeptical strangers the present whereabouts of certain policemen plus two squad cars.

As for the rest, it merely confirmed his own conviction that science and invention had reached its peak with the Model-T Ford and had been growing steadily more decadent ever since.

And besides, Mackenzie wanted to get on with the depth & color interview—

They got through that with a minimum of rehearsing, Jubal simply making sure that no question would be asked which could upset the public fiction that the Man from Mars had just returned from South America. Mike sent greetings to his friends and brothers of the *Champion,* including one to Dr. Mahmoud delivered in croaking, throat-rasping Martian—Jubal decided that Mackenzie had his money's worth.

At last the household could quiet down. Jubal set the telephone for two hours refusal, stood up, stretched, sighed, and felt a great weariness, wondered if he were getting old. "Where's dinner? Which one of you wenches was supposed to get dinner tonight? And why didn't you? Gad, this household is falling to wrack and ruin!"

"It was my turn to get dinner tonight," Jill answered, "but—"

"Excuses, always excuses!"

"Boss," Anne interrupted sharply, "how do you expect anyone to cook when you've kept every single one of us penned up here in your study all afternoon?"

"That's the moose's problem," Jubal said dourly. "I want it clearly understood that, even if Armageddon is held on these premises I expect meals to be hot and on time right up to the ultimate trump. Furthermore—"

"Furthermore," Anne completed, "it is now only seven-forty and plenty of time to have dinner by eight. So quit yelping, Boss, until you have something to yelp about. Cry-baby."

"Is it really only twenty minutes of eight? Seems like a week since lunch. Anyhow you haven't left me a civilized amount of time to have a pre-dinner drink."

"Poor you!"

"Somebody get me a drink. Get everybody a drink. On second thought let's skip a formal dinner tonight and drink our dinners; I feel like getting as tight as a tent rope on a rainy day. Anne, how are we fixed for smörgasbord?"

"Plenty."

"Then why not thaw out eighteen or nineteen kinds and spread 'em around and let anybody eat what he feels like when he feels like it? What's all the argument about?"

"Right away," agreed Jill.

Anne stopped to kiss him on his bald spot. "Boss, you've done nobly. We'll feed you and get you drunk and put you to bed. Wait, Jill, I'm going to help."

"I may to help, too?" Smith said eagerly.

"Sure, Mike. You can carry trays. Boss, dinner will be by the pool. It's a hot night."

"How else?" When they had left, Jubal said to Duke, "Where the hell have you been all day?"

"Thinking."

"Doesn't pay to. Just makes you discontented with what you see around you. Any results?"

"Yes," said Duke, "I've decided that what Mike eats, or doesn't eat, is no business of mine."

"Congratulations! A desire not to butt into other people's business is at least eighty percent of all human wisdom . . . and the other twenty percent isn't very important."

"You butt into other people's business. All the time."

"Who said *I* was wise? I'm a professional bad example. You can learn a lot by watching me. Or listening to me. Either one."

"Jubal, if I walked up to Mike and offered him a glass of water, do you suppose he would go through that lodge routine?"

"I feel certain that he would. Duke, almost the only human characteristic Mike seems to possess is an overwhelming desire to be liked. But I want to make sure that you know how serious it is to him. Much more serious than getting married. I myself accepted water brotherhood with Mike before I understood it—and I've become more and more deeply entangled with its responsibilities the more I've grokked it. You'll be committing yourself never to lie to him, never to mislead or deceive him in any way, to stick by him come what may—because that is just what he will do with you. Better think about it."

"I *have* been thinking about it, all day. Jubal, there's something about Mike that makes you *want* to take care of him."

"I know. You've probably never encountered complete honesty before —I know I hadn't. Innocence. Mike has never tasted the fruit of the Tree of Knowledge of Good and Evil . . . so we, who have, don't understand what makes him tick. Well, on your own head be it. I hope you never regret it." Jubal looked up. "Oh, there you are! I thought you had stopped to distill the stuff."

Larry answered, "Couldn't find a cork screw, at first."

"Machinery again. Why didn't you bite the neck off? Duke, you'll find some glasses stashed behind *The Anatomy of Melancholy* up there—"

"I know where you hide them."

"—and we'll all have a quick one, neat, before we get down to serious drinking." Duke got the glasses; Jubal poured and held up his own. "The golden sunshine of Italy congealed into tears. Here's to alcoholic brotherhood . . . much more suited to the frail human soul, if any, than any other sort."

"Health."

"Cheers."

Jubal poured his slowly down his throat. "Ah!" he said happily, and belched. "Offer some of that to Mike, afterwards, Duke, and let him learn how good it is to be human. Makes me feel creative. Front! Why are those girls never around when I need them? *Front!!*"

"I'm still 'Front,'" Miriam answered, at the door, "but—"

"I know. And I was saying: '—to what strange, bittersweet fate my tomboy ambition—'"

"But I finished *that* story while you were chatting on the telephone with the Secretary General."

"Then you are no longer 'Front.' Send it off."

"Don't you want to read it first? Anyhow, I've got to revise it— kissing Mike gave me a new insight on it."

Jubal shuddered. "'*Read* it?' Good God, no! It's bad enough to write such a thing. And don't even consider revising it, certainly not to fit the facts. My child, a true-confession story should never be tarnished by any taint of truth."

"Okay, Boss. And Anne says if you want to come down to the pool and have a bite before you eat, come on."

"I can't think of a better time. Shall we adjourn to the terrace, gentlemen?"

At the pool the party progressed liquidly with bits of fish and other Scandinavian high-caloric comestibles added to taste. At Jubal's invitation Mike tried brandy, somewhat cut with water. Mike found the resulting sensation extremely disquieting, so he analysed his trouble, added oxygen to the ethanol in an inner process of reversed fermentation and converted it to glucose and water, which gave him no trouble.

Jubal had been observing with interest the effect of his first drink of liquor on the Man from Mars—saw him become drunk almost at once, saw him sober up even more quickly. In an attempt to understand what had happened, Jubal urged more brandy on Mike—which he readily accepted since his water brother offered it. Mike sopped up an extravagant quantity of fine imported liquor before Jubal was willing to concede that it was impossible to get him drunk.

Such was not the case with Jubal, despite his years of pickling; staying sociable with Mike during the experiment dulled the edge of his wits. So, when he attempted to ask Mike what he had done, Mike thought that he was inquiring about the events during the raid by the S.S.—concerning which Mike still felt latent guilt. He tried to explain and, if needed, receive Jubal's pardon.

Jubal interrupted when at last he figured out what the boy was talking about. "Son, I don't want to know what you did, nor how you did it. What you did was just what was needed—perfect, just perfect. But—" He blinked owlishly. "—don't tell me about it. Don't ever tell anybody about it."

"Not?"

" 'Not.' It was the damnedest thing I've seen since my uncle with the two heads debated free silver and triumphantly refuted himself. An explanation would spoil it."

"I do not grok rightly?"

"Nor do I. So let's not worry and have another drink."

Reporters and other newsmen started arriving while the party was still climbing. Jubal received each of them with courteous dignity, invited them to eat, drink, and relax—but to refrain from badgering himself or the Man from Mars.

Those who failed to heed his injunction were tossed into the pool.

At first Jubal kept Larry and Duke at flank to administer the baptism as necessary. But, while some of the unfortunate importunates became angry and threatened various things which did not interest Jubal (other than to caution Mike not to take any steps), others relaxed to the inevitable and added themselves to the dousing squad on a volunteer basis, with the fanatic enthusiasm of proselytes—Jubal had to stop them from ducking the doyen lippmann of the *New York Times* for a third time.

During the evening Dorcas came out of the house, sought out Jubal and whispered in his ear: "Telephone, Boss. For you."

"Take a message."

"You must answer it, Boss."

"I'll answer it with an ax! Duke, get me an ax. I've been intending to get rid of that Iron Maiden for some time—and tonight I'm in the mood for it."

"Boss . . . you *want* to answer this one. It's the man you spoke to for quite a long time this afternoon."

"Oh. Why didn't you say so?" Jubal lumbered upstairs, made sure his study door was bolted behind him, went to the phone. Another of Douglas' sleek acolytes was on the screen but was replaced quickly by Douglas. "It took you long enough to answer your phone."

"It's my phone, Mr. Secretary. Sometimes I don't answer it at all."

"So it would seem. Why didn't you tell me that this Caxton fellow is an alcoholic?"

"Is he?"

"He certainly is! He isn't missing—not in the usual sense. He's been off on one of his periodic benders. He was located, sleeping it off, in a fleabag in Sonora."

"I'm glad to hear that he has been found. Thank you, sir."

"He's been picked up on a technical charge of 'vagrancy.' The charge won't be pressed—instead we are releasing him to you."

"I am very much in your debt, sir."

"Oh, it's not entirely a favor! I'm having him delivered to you in the state in which he was found—filthy, unshaven, and, I understand, smelling like a brewery. I want you to see for yourself what sort of a tramp he is."

"Very well, sir. When may I expect him?"

"Almost at once, I fancy. A courier arrow left Nogales some time ago. At Mach three or better it should be overhead soon. The pilot has instructions to deliver him to you and get a receipt."

"He shall have it."

"Now, Counsellor . . . having delivered him, I wash my hands of it. I shall expect you, and your client, to appear for talks whether you fetch along that drunken libeller or not."

"Agreed. When?"

"Shall we say tomorrow at ten? Here."

" ' 'Twere best done quickly.' Agreed."

Jubal went back downstairs and paused at his broken door. *"Jill!* Come here, child."

"Yes, Jubal." She trotted toward him, a reporter in close formation with her.

Jubal waved the man back. "Private," he said firmly. "Family matter. Go have a drink."

"Whose family?"

"A death in yours, if you insist. Scat!" The newsman grinned and accepted it. Jubal leaned over Gillian and said softly, "It worked. He's safe."

"Ben?"

"Yes. He'll be here soon."

"Oh, Jubal!" She started to bawl.

He took her shoulders. "Stop it," he said firmly. "Go inside and lock your door until you get control of yourself. This is not for the press."

"Yes, Jubal. Yes, Boss."

"That's better. Go cry in your pillow, then wash your face." He went on out to the pool. "Quiet everybody! *Quite!* I have an announcement to make. We've enjoyed having you—but the party is over."

"Boo!"

"Toss him in the pool, somebody. I've got work to do early tomorrow morning, I'm an old man and I need my rest. And so does my family. Please leave quietly and as quickly as possible. Black coffee for any who need it—but that's all. Duke, cork those bottles. Girls, clear the food away."

There was minor grumbling, but the more responsible quieted their colleagues. In ten minutes they were alone.

In twenty minutes Ben Caxton arrived. The S.S. officer commanding the courier car silently accepted Harshaw's signature and thumb print on a prepared receipt, then left at once while Jill continued to sob on Ben's shoulder.

Jubal looked him over in the light from the pool. "Ben, you're a mess. I hear you've been drunk for a week—and you look it."

Ben cursed, fluently and well, while continuing to pat Jill's back.

" 'M drunk, awri'—but haven' had a drink."

"What happened?"

"I don't know. I don't *know!*"

An hour later Ben's stomach had been pumped out (alcohol and gastric juices, no food); Jubal had given him shots to offset alcohol and barbiturates; he was bathed, shaved, dressed in clean clothes that did not fit him, had met the Man from Mars, and was sketchily brought up to date, while ingesting milk and bland food.

But he was unable to bring them up to date. For Ben, the past week had not happened—he had become unconscious in a taxicab in Washington; he had been shaken into drunken wakefulness two hours earlier. "Of course I *know* what happened. They kept me doped and in a completely dark room . . . and wrung me out. I vaguely remember some of it. But I can't prove *anything*. And there's the village *Jefe* and the madam of this dive they took me to—plus, I'm sure, plenty of other witnesses—to swear just how this gringo spent his time. And there's nothing I can do about it."

"Then don't fight it," Jubal advised. "Relax and be happy."

"The hell I will! I'll get that—"

"Tut, tut! You've won, Ben. And you're alive . . . which I would have given long odds against, earlier today. Douglas is going to do exactly what we want him to—and smile and like it."

"I want to talk about that. I think—"

"I think you're going to bed. Now. With a glass of warm milk to conceal Old Doc Harshaw's Secret Ingredient for secret drinkers."

Shortly thereafter Caxton was in bed and beginning to snore. Jubal was puttering around, heading for bed himself, and encountered Anne in the upper hall. He shook his head tiredly. "Quite a day, lass."

"Yes, quite. I wouldn't have missed it . . . and I don't want to repeat it. You go to bed, Boss."

"In a moment. Anne, tell me something. What's so special about the way that lad kisses?"

Anne looked dreamy and then dimpled. "You should have tried it when he invited you to."

"I'm too old to change my ways. But I'm interested in everything about the boy. Is this actually something different, too?"

Anne pondered it. "Yes."

"How?"

"Mike gives a kiss his whole attention."

"Oh, rats! I do myself. Or did."

Anne shook her head. "No. Some men try to. I've been kissed by men who did a very good job of it indeed. But they don't really give kissing a woman their whole attention. They *can't.* No matter how hard they try, some parts of their minds are on something else. Missing the last bus, maybe—or how their chances are for making the gal—or their own techniques in kissing—or maybe worry about their jobs, or money, or will husband or papa or the neighbors catch on. Or something. Now Mike doesn't have any technique . . . but when Mike kisses you he isn't doing *anything* else. Not anything. You're his whole universe for that moment . . . and the moment is eternal because he doesn't have any plans and he isn't going anywhere. Just kissing you." She shivered. "A woman notices. It's overwhelming."

"Hmm—"

"Don't 'Hmm' at me, you old lecher! You don't understand."

"No. And I'm sorry to say I probably never will. Well, goodnight— and, oh, by the way . . . I told Mike to bolt his door tonight."

She made a face at him. "Spoilsport!"

"He's learning quite fast enough. Mustn't rush him."

xviii

THE CONFERENCE WAS POSTPONED to the afternoon, then quickly re-postponed to the following morning, which gave Caxton an extra twenty-four hours of badly needed recuperation, a chance to hear in detail about his missing week, a chance to "grow closer" with the Man from Mars—for Mike grokked at once that Jill and Ben were "water brothers," consulted Jill about it, and solemnly offered water to Ben.

Ben had been adequately briefed by Jill. He accepted it just as solemnly and without mental reservations . . . after soul searching in which he decided that his own destiny was, in truth, interwoven with that of the Man from Mars—through his own initiative before he ever met Mike.

Ben had had to chase down, in the crannies of his soul, one uneasy feeling before he was able to do this. He at last decided that it was simple jealousy, and, being such, had to be cauterized. He had discovered that he felt irked at the closeness between Mike and Jill. His own bachelor *persona,* he learned, had been changed by a week of undead oblivion; he found that he wanted to be married, and to Jill. He proposed to her again, without a trace of joking about it, as soon as he got her alone.

Jill had looked away. "Please, Ben."

"Why not? I'm solvent, I've got a fairly good job, I'm in good health —or I will be, as soon as I get their condemned 'truth' drugs washed out of my system . . . and since I haven't, quite, I feel an overpowering compulsion to tell the truth right now. I love you. I want you to marry me and let me rub your poor tired feet. So why not? I don't have any vices that you don't share with me and we get along together better than most married couples. Am I too old for you? I'm not *that* old! Or are you planning to marry somebody else?"

"No, neither one! Dear Ben . . . Ben, I love you. But don't ask me to marry you now. I have . . . responsibilities."

He could not shake her firmness. Admittedly, Mike was more nearly Jill's age—almost exactly her age, in fact, which made Ben slightly more than ten years older than they were. But he believed Jill when she denied that age was a factor; the age difference wasn't too great and it helped, all things considered, for a husband to be older than his wife.

But he finally realized that the Man from Mars couldn't be a rival—he was simply Jill's patient. And at that point Ben accepted that a man who marries a nurse must live with the fact that nurses feel maternal toward their charges—live with it and like it, he added, for if Gillian had not had the character that made her a nurse, he would not love her. It was not the delightful figure-eight in which her pert fanny waggled when she walked, nor even the still pleasanter and very mammalian view from the other direction—he was not, thank God, the permanently infantile type, interested solely in the size of the mammary glands! No, it was Jill herself he loved.

Since what she was would make it necessary for him to take second place from time to time to patients who needed her (unless she retired, of course, and he could not be sure it would stop completely even then, Jill being Jill), then he was bloody-be-damned not going to start by being jealous of the patient she had now! Mike was a nice kid—just as innocent and guileless as Jill had described him to be.

And besides, he wasn't offering Jill any bed of roses; the wife of a working newspaperman had things to put up with, too. He might be—he *would* be—gone for weeks at times and his hours were always irregular. He wouldn't like it if Jill bitched about it. But Jill wouldn't. Not Jill.

Having reached this summing up, Ben accepted the water ceremony from Mike whole-heartedly.

Jubal needed the extra day to plan tactics. "Ben, when you dumped this hot potato in my lap I told Gillian that I would not lift a finger to get this boy his so-called 'rights.' But I've changed my mind. We're not going to let the government have the swag."

"Certainly not *this* administration!"

"Nor any other administration, as the next one will probably be worse. Ben, you undervalue Joe Douglas."

"He's a cheap, courthouse politician, with morals to match!"

"Yes. And besides that, he's ignorant to six decimal places. But he is also a fairly able and usually conscientious world chief executive—better than we could expect and probably better than we deserve. I would enjoy a session of poker with him . . . for he wouldn't cheat and he wouldn't welch and he would pay up with a smile. Oh, he's an S.O.B.—but you can read that as 'Swell Old Boy,' too. He's middlin' decent."

"Jubal, I'm damned if I understand you. You told me yesterday that you had been fairly certain that Douglas had had me killed . . . and, believe me, it wasn't far from it! . . . and that you had juggled eggs to get me out alive if by any chance I still was alive . . . and you did get me out and God knows I'm grateful to you! But do you expect me to forget that Douglas was behind it all? It's none of his doing that I'm alive—he would rather see me dead."

"I suppose he would. But, yup, just that—forget it."

"I'm damned if I will!"

"You'll be silly if you don't. In the first place, you can't prove anything. In the second place, there's no call for you to be grateful to me and I won't let you lay this burden on me. I didn't do it for *you.*"

"Huh?"

"I did it for a little girl who was about to go charging out and maybe get herself killed much the same way—if I didn't do something. I did it because she was my guest and I temporarily stood in loco parentis to her. I did it because she was all guts and gallantry but too ignorant to be allowed to monkey with such a buzz saw; she'd get hurt. But you, my cynical and sin-stained chum, know all about those buzz saws. If your own asinine carelessness caused you to back into one, who am I to tamper with your karma? You picked it."

"Mmm . . . I see your point. Okay, Jubal, you can go to hell—for monkeying with my karma. If I have one."

"A moot point. The predestinationers and the free-willers were still tied in the fourth quarter, last I heard. Either way, I have no wish to disturb a man sleeping in a gutter; I assume until proved otherwise that he belongs there. Most do-gooding reminds me of treating hemophilia—the only real cure for hemophilia is to let hemophiliacs bleed to death . . . before they breed more hemophiliacs."

"You could sterilize them."

"You would have me play God? But we're veering off the subject. Douglas didn't try to have you assassinated."

"Says who?"

"Says the infallible Jubal Harshaw, speaking ex cathedra from his belly button. See here, son, if a deputy sheriff beats a prisoner to death, it's sweepstakes odds that the county commissioners didn't order it, didn't know it, and wouldn't have permitted it had they known. At worst they shut their eyes to it—afterwards—rather than upset their own applecarts. But assassination has never been an accepted policy in this country."

"I'd like to show you the backgrounds of quite a number of deaths I've looked into."

Jubal waved it aside. "I said it wasn't a policy. We've always had political assassination—from prominent ones like Huey Long to men beaten to death on their own front steps with hardly a page-eight story in passing. But it's never been a policy here and the reason you are sitting in the sunshine right now is that it is not Joe Douglas' policy. Consider. They snatched you clean, no fuss, no inquiries. They squeezed you dry—then they had no more use for you . . . and they could have disposed of you as quietly as flushing a dead mouse down a toilet. But they didn't. Why not? Because they knew their boss didn't really like for them to play that rough . . . and if he became convinced that they had (whether in court or out), it would cost their jobs if not their necks."

Jubal paused for a swig. "But consider. Those S.S. thugs are just a tool; they aren't yet a Praetorian Guard that picks the new Caesar. Such being, whom do you really want for Caesar? Courthouse Joe whose basic indoctrination goes back to the days when this country was a nation and not just a satrapy in a polyglot empire of many traditions . . . Douglas, who really can't stomach assassination? Or do you want to toss him out of office (we can, you know, tomorrow—just by double-crossing him on the deal I've led him to expect—toss him out and thereby put in a Secretary General from a land where life has always been cheap and political assassination a venerable tradition? If you do this, Ben—tell me what happens to the next snoopy newsman who is careless enough to walk down a dark alley?"

Caxton didn't answer.

"As I said, the S.S. is just a tool. Men are always for hire who *like* dirty work. How dirty will that work become if you nudge Douglas out of his majority?"

"Jubal, are you telling me that I ought *not* to criticize the administration? When they're wrong? When I *know* they're wrong?"

"Nope. Gadflies such as yourself are utterly necessary. Nor am I opposed to 'turning the rascals out'—it's usually the soundest rule of politics. But it's well to take a look at what new rascals you are going to get before you jump at any chance to turn your present rascals out. Democracy is a poor system of government at best; the only thing that can honestly be said in its favor is that it is about eight times as good as any other method the human race has ever tried. Democracy's worst faults is that its leaders are likely to reflect the faults and virtues of their constituents—a depressingly low level, but what else can you expect? So take a look at Douglas and ponder that, in his ignorance, stupidity, and self-seeking, he much resembles his fellow Americans, including you and me . . . and that in fact he is a notch or two above the average. Then take a look at the man who will replace him if his government topples."

"There's precious little choice."

"There's always a choice! This one is a choice between 'bad' and 'worse'—which is a difference much more poignant than that between 'good' and 'better.' "

"Well, Jubal? What do you expect me to do?"

"Nothing," Harshaw answered. "Because I intend to run this show myself. Or almost nothing. I expect you to refrain from chewing out Joe Douglas over this coming settlement in that daily poop you write—maybe even praise him a little for 'statesmanlike restraint—' "

"You're making me vomit!"

"Not in the grass, please. Use your hat. —because I'm going to tell you ahead of time what I'm going to do, and why, and why Joe Douglas is going to agree to it. The first principle in riding a tiger is to hang on tight to its ears."

"Quit being pompous. What's the deal?"

"Quit being obtuse and listen. If this boy were a penniless nobody, there would be no problem. But he has the misfortune to be indisputably the heir to more wealth than Croesus ever dreamed of . . . plus a highly disputable claim to political power even greater through a politico-judicial precedent unparalleled in pure jug-headedness since the time Secretary Fall was convicted of receiving a bribe that Doheny was acquitted of having given him."

"Yes, but—"

"I have the floor. As I told Jill, I have no slightest interest in 'True Prince' nonsense. Nor do I regard all that wealth as 'his'; he didn't produce a shilling of it. Even if he had earned it himself—impossible at his age —'property' is not the natural and obvious and inevitable concept that most people think it is."

"Come again?"

"Ownership, of anything, is an extremely sophisticated abstraction, a mystical relationship, truly. God knows our legal theorists make this mystery complicated enough—but I didn't begin to see how subtle it was until I got the Martian slant on it. Martians don't have property. They don't own *anything* . . . not even their own bodies."

"Wait a minute, Jubal. Even animals have property. And the Martians aren't animals; they're a highly developed civilization, with great cities and all sorts of things."

"Yes. 'Foxes have holes and the birds of the air have nests.' And nobody understands a property line and the 'meus-et-tuus' involved better than a watch dog. But not Martians. Unless you regard an undistributed joint ownership of everything by a few millions or billions of senior citizens —'ghosts' to you, my friend—as being 'property.' "

"Say, Jubal, how about these 'Old Ones' Mike talks about?"

"Do you want the official version? Or my private opinion?"

"Huh? Your private opinion. What you really think."

"Then keep it to yourself. I think it is a lot of pious poppycock, suitable for enriching lawns. I think it is a superstition burned into the boy's brain at so early an age that he stands no chance of ever breaking loose from it."

"Jill talks as if she believed it."

"At all other times you will hear me talk as if I believed it, too. Ordinary politeness. One of my most valued friends believes in astrology; I would never offend her by telling her what *I* think of it. The capacity of a human mind to believe devoutly in what seems to me to be the highly improbable—from table tapping to the superiority of their own children— has never been plumbed. Faith strikes me as intellectual laziness, but I don't argue with it—especially as I am rarely in a position to prove that it is mistaken. Negative proof is usually impossible. Mike's faith in his 'Old Ones' is surely no more irrational than a conviction that the dynamics of the universe can be set aside through prayers for rain. Furthermore, he has the weight of evidence on his side; he has been there. I haven't."

"Mmm, Jubal, I'll confess to a sneaking suspicion that immortality is a fact—but I'm glad that my grandfather's ghost doesn't continue to exercise any control over me. He was a cranky old devil."

"And so was mine. And so am I. But is there any really good reason why a citizen's franchise should be voided simply because he happens to be dead? Come to think of it, the precinct I was raised in had a very large graveyard vote—almost Martian. Yet the town was a pleasant one to live in. As may be, our lad Mike *can't* own anything because the 'Old Ones' already own *everything*. So you see why I have had trouble explaining to him that he owns over a million shares of Lunar Enterprises, plus the Lyle Drive, plus assorted chattels and securities? It doesn't help that the original owners are dead; that makes it worse, they are 'Old Ones'—and Mike wouldn't dream of sticking his nose into the business of 'Old Ones.' "

"Uh . . . damn it, he's obviously legally incompetent."

"Of course he is. He can't manage property because he doesn't believe in its mystique—any more than I believe in his ghosts. Ben, all that Mike owns at the present time is a toothbrush I gave him—and he doesn't know he owns that. If you took it away from him, he wouldn't object, he wouldn't even mention it to me—he would simply assume conclusively that the 'Old Ones' had authorized the change."

Jubal sighed. "So he is incompetent . . . even though he can recite the law of property verbatim. Such being the case I shan't allow his competency to be tried . . . nor even mentioned—for what guardian would be appointed?"

"Huh! Douglas. Or, rather, one of his stooges."

"Are you certain, Ben? Consider the present makeup of the High Court. Might not the appointed guardian be named Savvonavong? Or Nadi? Or Kee?"

"Uh . . . you could be right."

"In which case the lad might not live very long. Or he might live to a ripe old age in some pleasantly gardened prison-for-one a great deal more difficult to escape from than Bethesda Hospital."

"What do you plan to do?"

"The power the boy nominally owns is far too dangerous and cumbersome for him to handle. So we throw it away."

"How the hell do you go about giving away that much money?"

"You don't. You can't. It's impossible. The very act of giving it away would be an exercise of its latent power, it would change the balance of power—and any attempt to do so would cause the boy to be examined on his competence to manage in jig time. So, instead, we let the tiger run like hell while hanging onto its ears for dear life. Ben, let me outline the *fait accompli* I intend to hand to Douglas . . . then you do your damnedest to pick holes in it. Not the legality of it, as Douglas' legal staff will write the double-talk and I'll check it for boobytraps—don't worry about that; the idea is to give Douglas a plan he won't want to booby-trap because he'll like it. I want you to sniff it for its political feasibility, whether or not we can put it over. Now here's what we are going to do—"

xix

THE MARTIAN DIPLOMATIC DELEGATION & Inside Straight Sodality, Unlimited, as organized by Jubal Harshaw, landed on the flat of the Executive Palace shortly before ten o'clock the next morning. The unpretentious pretender to the Martian throne, Mike Smith, had not worried about the purpose of the trip; he had simply enjoyed every minute of the short flight south, with utter and innocent delight.

The trip was made in a chartered Flying Greyhound, and Mike sat up in the astrodome above the driver, with Jill on one side and Dorcas on his other, and stared and stared in awed wonderment as the girls pointed out sights to him and chattered in his ears. The seat, being intended for two people, was very crowded, but Mike did not mind, as a warming degree of growing-closer necessarily resulted. He sat with an arm around each, and looked and listened and tried to grok and could not have been happier if he had been ten feet under water.

It was, in fact, his first view of Terran civilization. He had seen nothing at all in being removed from the *Champion* to suite K-12 at Bethesda Center; he had indeed spent a few minutes in a taxi ten days earlier going from the hospital to Ben's apartment but at the time he had grokked none of it. Since that time his world had been bounded by a house and a swimming pool, plus surrounding garden and grass and trees—he had not been as far as Jubal's gate.

But now he was enormously more sophisticated than he had been ten days ago. He understood windows, realized that the bubble surrounding him was a window and meant for looking out of and that the changing sights he saw were indeed the cities of these people. He understood maps and could pick out, with the help of the girls, where they were and what they were seeing on the map flowing across the lap board in front of them. But of course he had always known about maps; he simply had not known until recently that humans knew about maps. It had given him a twinge of happy homesickness the first time he had grokked a human map. Sure, it was static and dead compared with the maps used by his people—but it was a map. Mike was not disposed by nature and certainly not by training to invidious comparisons; even human maps were very Martian in essence —he liked them.

Now he saw almost two hundred miles of countryside, much of it sprawling world metropolis, and savored every inch of it, tried to grok it. He was startled by the enormous size of human cities and by their bustling activity visible even from the air, so very different from the slow motion, monastery-garden pace of cities of his own people. It seemed to him that a human city must wear out almost at once, becoming so choked with living experience that only the strongest of the Old Ones could bear to visit its deserted streets and grok in contemplation the events and emotions piled layer on endless layer in it. He himself had visited abandoned cities at home only on a few wonderful and dreadful occasions, and then his teachers had stopped having him do so, grokking that he was not strong enough for such experience.

Careful questions to Jill and Dorcas, the answers of which he then related to what he had read, enabled him to grok in part enough to relieve his mind somewhat: the city was very young; it had been founded only a little over two Earth centuries ago. Since Earth time units had no real flavor for him, he converted to Martian years and Martian numbers— three-filled-plus-three-waiting years ($3^4 + 3^3 = 108$ Martian years).

Terrifying and beautiful! Why, these people must even now be preparing to abandon the city to its thoughts before it shattered under the strain and became *not*. And yet, by mere time, the city was only-an-egg.

Mike looked forward to returning to Washington in a century or two to walk its empty streets and try to grow close to its endless pain and beauty, grokking thirstily until he was Washington and the city was himself—if he were strong enough by then. Then he firmly filed the thought away as he knew that he must grow and grow and grow before he would be able to praise and cherish the city's mighty anguish.

The Greyhound driver swung far east at one point in response to a temporary rerouting of unscheduled traffic (caused, unknown to Mike, by Mike's own presence), and Mike, for the first time, saw the sea.

Jill had to point it out to him and tell him that it was water, and Dorcas added that it was the Atlantic Ocean and traced the shore line on the map. Mike was not ignorant; he had known since he was a nestling that the planet next nearer the Sun was almost covered with the water of life and lately he had learned that these people accepted this lavish richness casually. He had even taken, unassisted, the much more difficult hurdle of grokking at last the Martian orthodoxy that the water ceremony did not require water, that water was merely symbol for the essence . . . beautiful but not indispensable.

But, like many a human still virgin toward some major human experience, Mike discovered that knowing a fact in the abstract was not at all the same thing as experiencing its physical reality; the sight of the Atlantic Ocean filled him with such awe that Jill squeezed him and said sharply, "Stop it, Mike! Don't you dare!"

Mike chopped off his emotion and stored it away for later use. Then he stared at the ocean, stretching out to an unimaginably distant horizon, and tried to measure its size in his mind until his head was buzzing with threes and powers of threes and superpowers of powers.

As they landed Jubal called out, "Now remember, girls, form a square around him and don't be at all backward about planting a heel in an instep or jabbing an elbow into some oaf's solar plexus. Anne, I realize you'll be wearing your cloak but that's no reason not to step on a foot if you're crowded. Or is it?"

"Quit fretting, Boss; nobody crowds a Witness—but I'm wearing spike heels and I weigh more than you do."

"Okay. Duke, you know what to do—but get Larry back here with the bus as soon as possible. I don't know when I'll need it."

"I grok it, Boss. Quit jittering."

"I'll jitter as I please. Let's go." Harshaw, the four girls with Mike, and Caxton got out; the bus took off at once. To Harshaw's mixed relief and apprehension the landing flat was not crowded with newsmen.

But it was far from empty. A man picked him out at once, stepped briskly forward and said heartily, "Dr. Harshaw? I'm Tom Bradley, senior executive assistant to the Secretary General. You are to go directly to Mr. Douglas' private office. He will see you for a few moments before the conference starts."

"No."

Bradley blinked. "I don't think you understood me. These are instructions from the Secretary General. Oh, he said that it was all right for Mr. Smith to come with you—the Man from Mars, I mean."

"No. This party stays together, even to go to the washroom. Right now we're going to that conference room. Have somebody lead the way. And have all these people stand back; they're crowding us. In the meantime, I have an errand for you. Miriam, that letter."

"But, Dr. Harshaw—"

"I said, 'No!' Can't you understand plain English? But you are to deliver this letter to Mr. Douglas at once and to him personally—and fetch back his receipt to me." Harshaw paused to write his signature across the flap of the envelope Miriam had handed to him, pressed his thumb print over the signature, and handed it to Bradley. "Tell him that it is most urgent that he read this at once—before the meeting."

"But the Secretary General specifically desires—"

"The Secretary desires to see that letter. Young man, I am endowed with second sight . . . and I predict that you won't be working here later today if you waste any time getting it to him."

Bradley locked eyes with Jubal, then said, "Jim, take over," and left, with the letter. Jubal sighed inwardly. He had sweated over that letter; Anne and he had been up most of the night preparing draft after draft. Jubal had every intention of arriving at an open settlement, in full view of the world's news cameras and microphones—but he had no intention of letting Douglas be taken by surprise by any proposal.

Another man stepped forward in answer to Bradley's order; Jubal sized him up as a prime specimen of the clever, conscienceless young-men-on-the-way-up who gravitate to those in power and do their dirty work; he disliked him on sight. The man smiled heartily and said smoothly, "The name's Jim Sanforth, Doctor—I'm the Chief's press secretary. I'll be buffering for you from now on—arranging your press interviews and so forth. I'm sorry to say that the conference room is not quite ready; there have been last-minute changes and we've had to move to a larger room. Now it's my thought that—"

"It's my thought that we'll go to that conference room right now. We'll stand up until chairs are fetched for us."

"Doctor, I'm sure you don't understand the situation. They are still stringing wires and things, and that room is swarming with reporters and commentators—"

"Very well. We'll chat with 'em till you're ready."

"No, Doctor. I have instructions—"

"Youngster, you can take your instructions, fold them until they are all corners—and shove them in your oubliette. We are not at your beck and call. You will not arrange press interviews for us. We are here for just one purpose: a public conference. If the conference is not ready to meet, we'll see the press now—in the conference room."

"But—"

"And that's not all. You're keeping the Man from Mars standing on a windy roof." Harshaw raised his voice. "Is there anyone here smart enough to lead us straight to this conference room without getting lost?"

Sanforth swallowed and said, "Follow me, Doctor."

The conference room was indeed crowded with newsmen and technicians but there was a big oval table, plenty of chairs, and several smaller tables. Mike was spotted at once and Sanforth's protests did not keep them from crowding in on him. But Mike's flying wedge of amateur Amazons got him as far as the big table; Jubal sat him against it with Dorcas and Jill in chairs flanking him and the Fair Witness and Miriam seated behind him. Once this was done, Jubal made no attempt to fend off questions or pictures. Mike had been warned that he would meet lots of people and that many of them would do strange things and Jubal had most particularly warned him to take no sudden actions (such as causing persons or things to go away, or to stop) unless Jill told him to.

Mike took the confusion gravely, without apparent upset; Jill was holding his hand and her touch reassured him.

Jubal wanted news pictures taken, the more the better; as for questions put directly to Mike, Jubal did not fear them and made no attempt to field them. A week of trying to talk with Mike had convinced him that no reporter could possibly get anything of importance out of Mike in only a few minutes—without expert help. Mike's habit of answering a question as asked, answering it literally and stopping, would be enough to nullify most attempts to pump him.

And so it proved. Most questions Mike answered with a polite: "I do not know," or an even less committal: "Beg pardon?"

But one question backfired on the questioner. A Reuters correspondent, anticipating a monumental fight over Mike's status as an heir, tried to sneak in his own test of Mike's competence: "Mr. Smith? What do you know about the laws of inheritance here?"

Mike was aware that he was having trouble grokking in fullness the human concept of property and, in particular, the ideas of bequest and inheritance. So he most carefully avoided inserting his own ideas and stuck to the book—a book which Jubal recognized shortly as *Ely on Inheritance and Bequest,* chapter one.

Mike related what he had read, with precision and careful lack of expression, like a boring but exact law professor, for page after tedious page, while the room gradually settled into stunned silence and his interrogator gulped.

Jubal let it go on until every newsman there knew more than he wanted to know about dower and curtesy, consanguinean and uterine, *per stirpes* and *per capita,* and related mysteries. At last Jubal touched his shoulder, "That's enough, Mike."

Mike looked puzzled. "There is much more."

"Yes, but later. Does someone have a question on some other subject?"

A reporter for a London Sunday paper of enormous circulation jumped in with a question closer to his employer's pocketbook: "Mr.

Smith, we understand you like the girls here on Earth. But have you ever kissed a girl?"

"Yes."

"Did you like it?"

"Yes."

"How did you like it?"

Mike barely hesitated over his answer. "Kissing girls is a goodness," he explained very seriously. "It is a growing-closer. It beats the hell out of card games."

Their applause frightened him. But he could feel that Jill and Dorcas were not frightened, that indeed they were both trying to restrain that incomprehensible noisy expression of pleasure which he himself could not learn. So he calmed his fright and waited gravely for whatever might happen next.

By what did happen next he was saved from further questions, answerable or not, and was granted a great joy; he saw a familiar face and figure just entering by a side door. "My brother Dr. Mahmoud!" Mike went on talking in overpowering excitement—but in Martian.

The *Champion*'s staff semanticist waved and smiled and answered in the same jarring language while hurrying to Mike's side. The two continued talking in unhuman symbols, Mike in an eager torrent, Mahmoud not quite as rapidly, with sound effects like a rhinoceros ramming an ironmonger's lorry.

The newsmen stood it for some time, those who operated by sound recording it and the writers noting it as local color. But at last one interrupted. "Dr. Mahmoud! What are you saying? Clue us!"

Mahmoud turned, smiled briefly and said in clipped Oxonian speech, "For the most part, I've been saying, 'Slow down, my dear boy—do, please.'"

"And what does *he* say?"

"The rest of our conversation is personal, private, of no possible int'rest to others, I assure you. Greetings, y'know. Old friends." He turned back to Mike and continued to chat—in Martian.

In fact, Mike was telling his brother Mahmoud all that had happened to him in the fortnight since he had last seen him, so that they might grok closer—but Mike's abstraction of what to tell was purely Martian in concept, it being concerned primarily with new water brothers and the unique flavor of each . . . the gentle water that was Jill . . . the depth of Anne . . . the strange not-yet-fully-grokked fact that Jubal tasted now like an egg, then like an Old One, but was neither—the ungrokkable vastness of ocean—

Mahmoud had less to tell Mike since less had happened in the interim to him, by Martian standards—one Dionysian excess quite unMartian and of which he was not proud, one long day spent lying face down in Washington's Suleiman Mosque, the results of which he had not yet grokked and was not ready to discuss. No new water brothers.

He stopped Mike presently and offered his hand to Jubal. "You're Dr. Harshaw, I know. Valentine Michael thinks he has introduced me to all of you—and he has, by his rules."

Harshaw looked him over as he shook hands with him. Chap looked and sounded like a huntin', shootin', sportin' Britisher, from his tweedy, expensively casual clothes to a clipped grey moustache . . . but his skin was naturally swarthy rather than ruddy tan and the genes for that nose came from somewhere close to the Levant. Harshaw did not like fake anything and would choose to eat cold cornpone over the most perfect syntho "sirloin."

But Mike treated him as a friend, so "friend" he was, until proved otherwise.

To Mahmoud, Harshaw looked like a museum exhibit of what he thought of as a "Yank"—vulgar, dressed too informally for the occasion, loud, probably ignorant and almost certainly provincial. A professional man, too, which made it worse, as in Dr. Mahmoud's experience most American professional men were under-educated and narrow, mere technicians. He held a vast but carefully concealed distaste for all things American. Their incredible polytheistic babel of religions, of course, although they were hardly to be blamed for that . . . their cooking (*cooking!!!*), their manners, their bastard architecture and sickly arts . . . and their blind, pathetic, arrogant belief in their superiority long after their sun had set. Their women. Their women most of all, their immodest, assertive women, with their gaunt, starved bodies which nevertheless reminded him disturbingly of houris. Four of them here, crowded around Valentine Michael—at a meeting which certainly should be all male—

But Valentine Michael had offered him all these people—including these ubiquitous female creatures—offered them proudly and eagerly as his water brothers, thereby laying on Mahmoud a family obligation closer and more binding than that owed to the sons of one's father's brother—since Mahmoud understood the Martian term for such accretive relationships from direct observation of what it meant to Martians and did not need to translate it clumsily and inadequately as "catenative assemblage," nor even as "things equal to the same thing are equal to each other." He had seen Martians at home; he knew their extreme poverty (by Earth standards); he had dipped into—and had guessed at far more—of their cultural extreme wealth; and had grokked quite accurately the supreme value that Martians place on interpersonal relationships.

Well, there was nothing else for it—he had shared water with Valentine Michael and now he must justify his friend's faith in him . . . he simply hoped that these Yanks were not complete bounders.

So he smiled warmly and shook hands firmly. "Yes. Valentine Michael has explained to me—most proudly—that you are all in—" (Mahmoud used one word of Martian.) "—to him."

"Eh?"

"Water brotherhood. You understand?"

"I grok it."

Mahmoud strongly doubted if Harshaw did, but he went on smoothly, "Since I myself am already in that relationship to him, I must ask to be considered a member of the family. I know your name, and I have guessed that this must be Mr. Caxton—in fact I have seen your face pictured at the head of your column, Mr. Caxton; I read it when I have opportunity—but let me see if I have the young ladies straight. This must be Anne."

"Yes. But she's cloaked at the moment."

"Yes, of course. I'll pay my respects to her when she is not busy professionally."

Harshaw introduced him to the other three . . . and Jill startled him by addressing him with the correct honorific for a water brother, pronouncing it about three octaves higher than any adult Martian would talk but with sore-throat purity of accent. It was one of the scant dozen Martian words she could speak out of the hundred-odd that she was beginning to understand—but this one she had down pat because it was used to her and by her many times each day.

Dr. Mahmoud's eyes widened slightly—perhaps these people would turn out not to be mere uncircumcised barbarians after all . . . and his young friend *did* have strong intuitions. Instantly he offered Jill the correct honorific in response and bowed over her hand.

Jill saw that Mike was obviously delighted; she managed, slurringly but passably, to croak the shortest of the nine forms by which a water brother may return the response—although she did not grok it fully and would not have considered suggesting (in English) the nearest human biological equivalent . . . certainly not to a man she had just met!

However, Mahmoud, who did understand it, took it in its symbolic meaning rather than its (humanly impossible) literal meaning, and spoke rightly in response. But Jill had passed the limit of her linguistic ability;

she did not understand his answer at all and could not reply, even in pedestrian English.

But she got a sudden inspiration. At intervals around the huge table were placed the age-old furniture of human palavers—water pitchers each with its clump of glasses. She stretched and got a pitcher and a tumbler, filled the latter.

She looked Mahmoud in the eye, said earnestly, "Water. Our nest is yours." She touched it to her lips and handed it to Mahmoud.

He answered her in Martian, saw that she did not understand him and translated, "Who shares water shares all." He took a sip and started to hand the glass back to Jill—checked himself, looked at Harshaw and offered him the glass.

Jubal said, "I can't speak Martian, son—but thanks for water. May you never be thirsty." He took a sip, then drank about a third of it. *"Ah!"* He passed the glass to Ben.

Caxton looked at Mahmoud and said very soberly, "Grow closer. With the water of life we grow closer." He wet his lips with it and passed it to Dorcas.

In spite of the precedents already set, Dorcas hesitated. "Dr. Mahmoud? You do know how serious this is to Mike?"

"I do, Miss."

"Well . . . it's just as serious to us. You understand? You . . . grok?"

"I grok its fullness . . . or I would have refused to drink."

"All right. May you always drink deep. May our eggs share a nest." Tears started down her cheeks: she drank and passed the glass hastily to Miriam.

Miriam whispered, "Pull yourself together, kid," then spoke to Mike, "With water we welcome our brother,"—then added to Mahmoud, "Nest, water, life." She drank. "Our brother." She offered him the glass.

Mahmoud finished what was left in it and spoke, neither in Martian nor English, but Arabic: " *'And if ye mingle your affairs with theirs, then they are your brothers.'* "

"Amen," Jubal agreed.

Dr. Mahmoud looked quickly at him, decided not to enquire just then whether Harshaw had understood him, or was simply being polite; this was neither the time nor the place to say anything which might lead to unbottling his own troubles, his own doubts. Nevertheless he felt warmed in his soul—as always—by water ritual . . . even though it smelled of heresy.

His thoughts were cut short by the assistant chief of protocol bustling up to them. "You're Dr. Mahmoud. You belong over on the far side of the table, Doctor. Follow me."

Mahmoud looked at him, then looked at Mike and smiled. "No, I belong here, with my friends. Dorcas, may I pull a chair in here and sit between you and Valentine Michael?"

"Certainly, Doctor. Here, I'll scrunch over."

The a.c. of p. was almost tapping his foot in impatience. "Dr. Mahmoud, *please!* The chart places you over on the other side of the room! The Secretary General will be here any moment—and the place is still simply *swarming* with *reporters* and goodness knows who else who doesn't belong here . . . and I don't know *what* I'm going to do!"

"Then go do it someplace else, bub," Jubal suggested.

"What? Who are you? Are you on the list?" He worriedly consulted the seating chart he carried.

"Who are *you?*" Jubal answered. "The head waiter? I'm Jubal Harshaw. If my name is not on that list, you can tear it up and start over. And look, buster, if the Man from Mars wants his friend Dr. Mahmoud to sit by him, that settles it."

"But he *can't* sit here! Seats at the main conference table are reserved for High Ministers, Chiefs of Delegations, High Court Justices, and equal ranks—and I don't know *how* I can squeeze them all in if any more show up—and the Man from Mars, of course."

" 'Of course,' " Jubal agreed dryly.

"And of course Dr. Mahmoud has to be near the Secretary General—just back of him, so that he'll be ready to interpret as needed. I must say you're not being helpful."

"I'll help." Jubal plucked the paper out of the official's hand, sat down at the table and studied it. "Mmm . . . lemme see now. The Man from Mars will sit directly opposite the Secretary General, just about where he happens to be sitting. Then—" Jubal got out a heavy soft pencil and attacked the seating chart. "—this entire half of the main table, from *here* clear over to *here,* belongs to the Man from Mars." Jubal scratched two big black cross marks to show the limits and joined them with a thick black arc, then began scratching out names assigned to seats on that side of the table. "That takes care of half of your work . . . because I'll seat anybody who sits on our side of the table."

The protocol officer was too shocked to talk. His mouth worked but no meaningful noises came out. Jubal looked at him mildly. "Something the matter? Oh—I forgot to make it official." He scrawled under his amendments: *"J. Harshaw for V. M. Smith."* "Now trot back to your top sergeant, son, and show him that. Tell him to check his rule book on official visits from heads of friendly planets."

The man looked at it, opened his mouth—then left very rapidly without stopping to close it. But he was back very quickly on the heels of another, older man. The newcomer said in a firm, no-nonsense manner, "Dr. Harshaw, I'm LaRue, Chief of Protocol. Do you actually need half the main table? I understood that your delegation was quite small."

"That's beside the point."

LaRue smiled briefly. "I'm afraid it's not beside the point to me, sir. I'm at my wit's end for space. Almost every official of first rank in the Federation has elected to be present today. If you are expecting more people—though I do wish you had notified me—I'll have a table placed behind these two seats reserved for Mr. Smith and yourself."

"No."

"I'm afraid that's the way it must be. I'm sorry."

"So am I—for you. Because if half the main table is not reserved for the Mars delegation, we are leaving right now. Just tell the Secretary General that you busted up his conference by being rude to the Man from Mars."

"Surely you don't mean that?"

"Didn't you get my message?"

"Uh . . . well, I took it as a jest. A rather clever one, I admit."

"Son, I can't afford to joke at these prices. Smith is either top man from another planet paying an official visit to the top man of this planet—in which case he is entitled to all the side boys and dancing girls you can dig up—or he is just a simple tourist and gets no official courtesies of any sort. You can't have it both ways. But I suggest that you look around you, count the 'officials of first rank' as you called them, and make a quick guess as to whether they would have bothered to show up if, in *their* minds, Smith is just a tourist."

LaRue said slowly, "There's no precedent."

Jubal snorted. "I saw the Chief of Delegation from the Lunar Republic come in a moment ago—go tell *him* there's no precedent. Then duck!—I hear he's got a quick temper." He sighed. "But, son, I'm an old man and I had a short night and it's none of my business to teach you your job. Just tell Mr. Douglas that we'll see him another day . . . when he's ready to receive us properly. Come on, Mike." He started to roust himself painfully out of his chair.

LaRue said hastily, "No, no, Dr. Harshaw! We'll clear this side of the table. I'll— Well, I'll do something. It's yours."

"That's better." But Harshaw remained poised to get up. "But where's the Flag of Mars? And how about honors?"

"I'm afraid I don't understand you."

"Never seen a day when I had so much trouble with plain English. Look— See that Federation Banner back of where the Secretary is going to sit? Where's the one like it over here, for Mars?"

LaRue blinked. "I must admit you've taken me by surprise. I didn't know the Martians used flags."

"They don't. But you couldn't possibly whop up what *they* use for high state occasions." (And neither could I, boy, but that's beside the point.) "So we'll let you off easy and take an attempt for the deed. Piece of paper, Miriam—now, like this." Harshaw drew a rectangle, sketched in it the traditional human symbol for Mars, a circle with an arrow leading out from it to the upper right. "Make the field in white and the sigil of Mars in red—should be sewed in bunting of course, but with a clean sheet and a bucket of paint any Boy Scout could improvise one in ten minutes. Were you a Scout?"

"Uh, some time ago."

"Good. Then you know the Scout's motto. Now about honors— maybe you're caught unprepared there, too, eh? You expect to play 'Hail to Sovereign Peace' as the Secretary comes in?"

"Oh, we must. It's obligatory."

"Then you'll want to follow it with the anthem for Mars."

"I don't see how I can. Even if there *is* one . . . we don't have it. Dr. Harshaw, be reasonable!"

"Look, son, I *am* being reasonable. We came here for a quiet, small, informal meeting—strictly business. We find you've turned it into a circus. Well, if you're going to have a circus, you've got to have elephants and there's no two ways about it. Now we realize you can't play Martian music, any more than a boy with a tin whistle can play a symphony. But you *can* play a symphony—'The Ten Planets Symphony.' Grok it? I mean, 'Do you catch on?' Have the tape cut in at the beginning of the Mars movement; play that . . . or enough bars to let the theme be recognized."

LaRue looked thoughtful. "Yes, I suppose we could—but, Dr. Harshaw, I promised you half the table . . . but I don't see how I can promise sovereign honors—the flag and the music—even on this improvised, merely symbolic scale. I— I don't think I have the authority."

"Nor the guts," Harshaw said bitterly. "Well, *we* didn't want a circus —so tell Mr. Douglas that we'll be back when he's not so busy . . . and not so many visitors. Been nice chatting with you, son. Be sure to stop by the Secretary's office and say hello when we come back—if you're still here." He again went through the slow, apparently painful act of being a man too old and feeble to get out of a chair easily.

LaRue said, "Dr. Harshaw, *please* don't leave! Uh . . . the Secretary won't come in until I send word that we are ready for him—so let me see what I can do. Yes?"

Harshaw relaxed with a grunt. "Suit yourself. But one more thing, while you're here. I heard a ruckus at the main door a moment ago—what I could catch, one of the crew members of the *Champion* wanted to come in. They're all friends of Smith, so let 'em in. We'll accommodate 'em. Help to fill up this side of the table." Harshaw sighed and rubbed a kidney.

"Very well, sir," LaRue agreed stiffly and left.

Miriam said out of the corner of her mouth: "Boss—did you sprain your back doing hand stands night before last?"

"Quiet, girl, or I'll paddle you." With grim satisfaction Jubal surveyed the room, which was continuing to fill with high officials. He had told Douglas that he wanted a "small, informal" talk—no formality while knowing with utter certainty that the mere announcement of such talks would fetch all the powerful and power-hungry as surely as light attracts moths. And now (he felt sure) Mike was about to be treated as a sovereign by each and every one of those nabobs—with the whole world watching. Just let 'em try to roust the boy around after this!

Sanforth was still trying mightily to shoo out the remaining newsmen, and the unfortunate assistant chief of protocol, deserted by his boss, was jittering like a nervous baby-sitter in his attempt to play musical chairs with too few chairs and too many notables. They continued to come in and Jubal concluded that Douglas had never intended to convene this public meeting earlier than eleven o'clock, and that everyone else had been so informed—the earlier hour given Jubal was to permit the private pre-conference that Douglas had demanded and that Jubal had refused. Well, the delay suited Jubal's plans.

The leader of the Eastern Coalition came in. Since Mr. King was not, by his own choice, the nominal Chief of Delegation for his nation, his status under strict protocol was merely that of Assemblyman—but Jubal was not even mildly surprised to see the harried assistant chief of protocol drop what he was doing and rush to seat Douglas' chief political enemy at the main table and near the seat reserved for the Secretary General; it simply reinforced Jubal's opinion that Douglas was no fool.

Dr. Nelson, surgeon of the *Champion,* and Captain van Tromp, her skipper, came in together, and were greeted with delight by Mike. Jubal was pleased, too, as it gave the boy something to do, under the cameras, instead of just sitting still like a dummy. Jubal made use of the disturbance to rearrange the seating since there was now no longer any need to surround the Man from Mars with a bodyguard. He placed Mike precisely opposite the Secretary General's chair and himself took the chair on Mike's left—not only to be close to him as his counsel but to be where he could actually touch Mike inconspicuously. Since Mike had only the foggiest notions of human customary manners, Jubal had arranged with him signals as imperceptible as those used by a rider in putting a high-schooled horse through dressage maneuvers—"stand up," "sit down," "bow," "shake hands"—with the difference that Mike was not a horse and his training had required only five minutes to achieve utterly dependable perfection.

Mahmoud broke away from the reunion of shipmates, came around, and spoke to Jubal privately. "Doctor, I must explain that the Skipper and the Surgeon are also water brothers of our brother—and Michael Valentine wanted to confirm it at once by again using the ritual, all of us. I told him to wait. Do you approve?"

"Eh? Yes. Yes, certainly. Not in this mob." Jubal worried it for a moment. Damn it, how many water brothers did Mike have? How long was this daisy chain? "Maybe you three can come with us when we leave? And have a bite and a talk in private."

"I shall be honored. And I feel sure the other two will come also, if possible."

"Good. Dr. Mahmoud, do you know of any other brothers of our young brother who are likely to show up?"

"No. Not from the company of the *Champion,* at least; there are no more." Mahmoud hesitated, then decided not to ask the obvious complementary question, as it would hint at how disconcerted he had been—at first—to discover the extent of his own conjugational commitments. "I'll tell Sven and the Old Man." He went back to them.

Harshaw saw the Papal Nuncio come in, saw him seated at the main table, and smiled inwardly—if that long-eared debit, LaRue, had any lingering doubts about the official nature of this meeting, he would do well to forget them!

A man came up behind Harshaw, tapped him on the shoulder. "Is this where the Man from Mars hangs out?"

"Yes," agreed Jubal.

"Which one is he? I'm Tom Boone—Senator Boone, that is—and I've got a message for him from Supreme Bishop Digby."

Jubal suppressed his personal feelings and let his cortex go into emergency high speed. "I'm Jubal Harshaw, Senator—" He signalled Mike to stand up and offer to shake hands. "—and this is Mr. Smith. Mike, this is Senator Boone."

"How do you do, Senator Boone," Mike said in perfect dancing-school form. He looked at Boone with interest. He had already had it straightened out for him that "Senator" did not mean "Old One" as the words seemed to shape; nevertheless he was interested in seeing just what a "Senator" was. He decided that he did not yet grok it.

"Pretty well, thank you, Mr. Smith. But I won't take up your time; they seem to be about to get this shindig started. Mr. Smith, Supreme Bishop Digby sent me to give you a personal invite to attend services at the Archangel Foster Tabernacle of the New Revelation."

"Beg pardon?"

Jubal moved in on it. "Senator, as you know, many things here—everything—is new to the Man from Mars. But it so happens that Mr. Smith has already seen one of your church services by stereovision—"

"Not the same thing."

"I know. But he expressed great interest in it and asked many questions about it—many of which I could not answer."

Boone looked keenly at him. "You're not one of the faithful?"

"I must admit that I am not."

"Come along yourself. Always hope for a sinner."

"Thank you, I will." (You're right, I will, friend!—for I certainly won't let Mike go into your trap alone!)

"Next Sunday then—I'll tell Bishop Digby."

"Next Sunday if possible," Jubal corrected. "We might be in jail by then."

Boone grinned. "There's always that, ain't th'r? But send word around to me or the Supreme Bishop and you won't stay in long." He looked around the crowded room. "Seem to be kind o' short on chairs in here. Not much chance for a plain senator with all those muckamucks elbowing each other."

"Perhaps you would honor us by joining us, Senator," Jubal answered smoothly, "at this table?"

"Eh? Why, thank you, sir! Don't mind if I do—ringside seat."

"That is," Harshaw added, "if you don't mind the political implications of being seen seated with the official Mars delegation. We aren't trying to crowd you into an embarrassing situation."

Boone barely hesitated. "Not at all! Who cares what people think? Matter of fact, between you and I, the Bishop is very, very interested in this young man."

"Fine. There's a vacant chair there by Captain van Tromp—that man there . . . but probably you know him."

"Van Tromp? Sure, sure, old friends, know him well—met him at the reception." Senator Boone nodded at Smith, swaggered down and seated himself.

Most of those present were seated now and fewer were getting past the guards at the doors. Jubal watched one argument over seating and the longer he watched it the more it made him fidget. At last he felt that he simply could not stand it; he could not sit still and watch this indecency go on. So he leaned over and spoke very privately with Mike, made sure that, if Mike did not understand why, at least he understood what Jubal wanted him to do.

Mike listened. "Jubal, I will do."

"Thanks, son." Jubal got up and approached a group of three: the assistant chief of protocol, the Chief of the Uruguayan Delegation, and a third man who seemed angry but baffled. The Uruguayan was saying forcefully: "—seat him, then you must find seats for any and all other local chiefs of state—eighty or more. You've admitted that you can't do that. This is Federation soil we stand on . . . and no chief of state has precedence over any other chief of state. If any exceptions are made—"

Jubal interrupted by addressing the third man. "Sir—" He waited just long enough to gain his attention, plunged on. "—the Man from Mars has instructed me to ask you to do him the great honor of sitting with him . . . if your presence is not required elsewhere."

The man looked startled, then smiled broadly. "Why, yes, that would be satisfactory."

The other two, both the palace official and the Uruguayan dignitary, started to object. Jubal turned his back on them. "Let's hurry, sir—I think we have very little time." He had seen two men coming in with what appeared to be a stand for a Christmas tree and a bloody sheet—but what was almost certainly the "Martian Flag." As they hurried to where he was, Mike got up and was standing, waiting for them.

Jubal said, "Sir, permit me to present Valentine Michael Smith. Michael—the President of the United States!"

Mike bowed very low.

There was barely time to seat him on Mike's right, as the improvised flag was even then being set up behind them. Music started to play, everyone stood, and a voice proclaimed:

"The Secretary General!"

XX

JUBAL HAD CONSIDERED HAVING Mike remain seated while Douglas came in, but had rejected the idea; he was not trying to place Mike a notch higher than Douglas but merely to establish that the meeting was between equals. So, when he stood up, he signalled Mike to do so likewise. The great double doors at the back of the conference hall had opened at the first strains of "Hail to Sovereign Peace" and Douglas came in. He went straight to his chair and started to sit down.

Instantly Jubal signalled Mike to sit down, the result being that Mike and the Secretary General sat down simultaneously—with a long, respectful pause of some seconds before anyone else resumed his seat.

Jubal held his breath. Had LaRue done it? Or not? He hadn't quite promised—

Then the first fortissimo tocsin of the "Mars" movement filled the room—the "War God" theme that startles even an audience expecting it. With his eyes on Douglas and with Douglas looking back at him, Jubal was at once up out of his chair again, like a scared recruit snapping to attention.

Douglas stood up, too, not as quickly but promptly.

But Mike did not get up; Jubal had not signalled him to do so. He sat quietly, impassively, quite unembarrassed by the fact that everyone else without any exception got quickly back on his feet when the Secretary General stood up. Mike did not understand any of it and was quite content to do what his water brother told him to do.

Jubal had puzzled over this bit, after he had demanded the "Martian Anthem." If the demand was met, what should Mike do while it was played? It was a nice point, and the answer depended on just what role Mike was playing in this comedy—

The music stopped. On Jubal's signals Mike then stood up, bowed quickly, and sat down, seating himself about as the Secretary General and the rest were seated. They were all back in their seats much more quickly this time, as no one could have missed the glaring point that Mike had remained seated through the "anthem."

Jubal sighed with relief. He had gotten away with it. A great many years earlier he had seen one of that vanishing tribe of royalty (a reigning queen) receive a parade—and he had noticed that the royal lady had bowed *after* her anthem was played, i.e., she had acknowledged a salute offered to her own sovereign self.

But the political head of a democracy stands and uncovers for his nation's anthem like any other citizen—for he is not a sovereign.

But, as Jubal had pointed out to LaRue, one couldn't have it two ways. Either Mike was merely a private citizen (in which case this silly gymkhana should never have been held; Douglas should have had the guts to tell all these overdressed parasites to stay home!)—or, by the preposterous legal theory inherent in the Larkin Decision, the kid was a sovereign all by his little lonesome.

Jubal felt tempted to offer LaRue a pinch of snuff. Well, the point had not been missed by at least one—the Papal Nuncio was keeping his face straight but his eyes were twinkling.

Douglas started to speak: "Mr. Smith, we are honored and happy to have you here as our guest today. We hope that you will consider the planet Earth your home quite as much as the planet of your birth, our neighbor—our good neighbor—Mars—" He went on at some length, in careful, rounded, pleasant periods, which did not quite say anything. Mike was welcome—but whether he was welcome as a sovereign, as a tourist from abroad, or as a citizen returning home, was quite impossible to determine (Jubal decided) from Douglas' words.

Jubal watched Douglas, hoping to catch his eye, looking for some nod or expression that would show how Douglas had taken the letter Jubal had sent to him by hand immediately on arrival. But Douglas never looked at him. Presently Douglas concluded, still having said nothing and said it very well.

Jubal said quietly, "Now, Mike."

Smith addressed the Secretary General—in Martian.

But he cut it off before consternation could build up and said gravely: "Mr. Secretary General of the Federation of Free Nations of the Planet Earth—" then went on again in Martian.

Then in English: "—we thank you for our welcome here today. We bring greetings to the peoples of Earth from the Ancient Ones of Mars—" and shifted again into Martian.

Jubal felt that "Ancient Ones" was a good touch; it carried more bulge than "Old Ones" and Mike had not objected to the change in terminology. In fact, while Mike had insisted on "speaking rightly," Jubal's draft had not required much editing. It had been Jill's idea to alternate, sentence by sentence, a Martian version and an English version—and Jubal admitted with warm pleasure that her gimmick puffed up a formal little speech as devoid of real content as a campaign promise into something as rollingly impressive as Wagnerian opera. (And about as hard to figure out, Jubal added.)

It didn't matter to Mike. He could insert the Martian translation as easily as he could memorize and recite the edited English version, i.e., without effort for either. If it would please his water brothers to say these sayings, it made Mike happy.

Someone touched Jubal on the shoulder, shoved an envelope in his hand, and whispered, "From the Secretary General." Jubal looked up, saw that it was Bradley, hurrying silently away. Jubal opened the envelope in his lap, glanced at the single sheet inside.

The note was one word: "Yes," and had been signed with initials "J.E.D."—all in the famous green ink.

Jubal looked up, found that Douglas' eyes were now on him; Jubal nodded ever so slightly and Douglas looked away. The conference was now over; all that remained was to let the world know it.

Mike concluded the sonorous nullities he had been given; Jubal heard his own words: "—growing closer, with mutual benefit to both worlds—" and "—each race according to its own nature—" but did not listen. Douglas then thanked the Man from Mars, briefly but warmly. There was a pause.

Jubal stood up. "Mr. Secretary General—"

"Yes, Dr. Harshaw?"

"As you know, Mr. Smith is here today in a dual role. Like some visiting prince in the past history of our own great race, traveling by caravan and sailing across uncharted vastnesses to a distant realm, he brings to Earth the good wishes of the Ancient Powers of Mars. But he is also a human being, a citizen of the Federation and of the United States of America. As such, he has rights and properties and obligations." Jubal shook his head. "Pesky ones, I'm sorry to say. As attorney for him in his capacity as a citizen and a human being, I have been puzzling over his business affairs and I have not even managed a complete list of what he owns—much less decide what to tell tax collectors."

Jubal stopped to wheeze. "I'm an old man, I might not live to complete the task. Now you know that my client has had no business experience in the human sense—Martians do these things differently. But he is a young man of great intelligence—the whole world knows that his parents were geniuses—and blood will tell. There's no doubt that in a few years, he could, if he wished, do very nicely on his own without the aid of one old, broken-down lawyer. But his affairs need attention *today;* business won't wait.

"But, in fact, he is more eager to learn the history and the arts and the ways of the people of this, his second home, than he is to bury himself in debentures and stock issues and royalties—and I think in this he is wise. Although without business experience, Mr. Smith possesses a direct and simple wisdom that continues to astonish me . . . and to astonish all who meet him. When I explained to him the trouble I was having, he simply looked at me with a clear, calm gaze and said, 'Why, that's no problem, Jubal—we'll ask Mr. Douglas.' " Jubal paused and said anxiously, "The rest of this is just personal business, Mr. Secretary. Should I see you about it privately? And let the rest of these ladies and gentlemen go home?"

"Go right ahead, Dr. Harshaw." Douglas added, "Protocol is dispensed with as of now. Anyone who wishes to leave please feel free to do so."

No one left. "All right," Jubal went on. "I can wrap it up in one sentence. Mr. Smith wants to appoint you his attorney-in-fact, with full power to handle all his business affairs. Just that."

Douglas looked convincingly astonished. "That's a tall order, Doctor."

"I know it is, sir. I pointed out to him that it was an imposition, that you are the busiest man on this planet and didn't have *time* for his affairs." Jubal shook his head and smiled. "I'm afraid it didn't impress him—seems on Mars the busier a person is the more is expected of him. Mr. Smith simply said, 'We can ask him.' So I'm asking you. Of course we don't expect an answer off hand—that's another Martian trait: Martians are never in a hurry. Nor are they inclined to make things complicated. No bond, no auditing, none of that claptrap—a written power of attorney if you want it. But it does not matter to him; he would do it just as readily, orally and right now—Chinese style. That's another Martian trait; if a Martian trusts you, he trusts you all the way. He doesn't come prying around to see if you're keeping your word. Oh, I should add: Mr. Smith is *not* making this request of the Secretary General; he's asking a favor of Joseph Edgerton Douglas, you personally. If you should retire from public life, it would not affect this in the slightest. Your successor in office, whoever he might be, doesn't figure in it. It's *you* he trusts . . . not just whoever happens to occupy the Octagon Office in this Palace."

Douglas nodded. "Regardless of my answer, I feel honored . . . and humble."

"Because if you decline to serve, or can't serve, or do take on this chore and want to drop it later, or anything, Mr. Smith has his own second choice for the job—Ben Caxton, it is. Stand up for a second, Ben; let people see you. And if both you and Caxton can't or won't, his next choice is—well, I'll guess we'll reserve that name for the moment; just let it rest that there are successive choices. Uh, let me see now—" Jubal looked fuddled. "I'm out of the habit of talking on my feet. Miriam, where is that piece of paper we listed things on?"

Jubal accepted a sheet from her, and added, "Better give me the other copies, too." She passed over to him a thick stack of sheets. "This is a little memo we prepared for you, sir—or for Caxton, if it turns out that way. Mmm, lemme see—oh yes, steward to pay himself what he thinks the job is worth but not less than—well, a considerable sum, nobody else's business, really. Steward to deposit monies in a drawing account for living expenses of party of the first part—uh, oh yes, I thought maybe you would want to use the Bank of Shanghai, say, as your depository, and, say, Lloyd's as your business agent—or maybe the other way around—just to protect your own name and fame. But Mr. Smith won't hear of any fixed instructions—just an unlimited assignment of power, revocable by either side at choice. But I won't read all this; that's why we wrote it out." Jubal turned and looked vacantly around. "Uh, Miriam—trot around and give this to the Secretary General, that's a good girl. Um, these other copies, I'll leave them here. You may want to pass 'em out to people . . . or you may need them yourself. Oh, I'd better give one to Mr. Caxton though— here, Ben."

Jubal looked anxiously around. "Uh, I guess that's all I have to say, Mr. Secretary. Did you have anything more to say to us?"

"Just a moment. Mr. Smith?"

"Yes, Mr. Douglas?"

"Is this what you want? Do *you* want *me* to do what it says on this paper?"

Jubal held his breath, avoided even glancing at his client. Mike had been carefully coached to expect such a question . . . but there had been no telling what form it would take, nor any way to tell in advance how Mike's literal interpretations could trip them.

"Yes, Mr. Douglas." Mike's voice rang out clearly in the big room— and in a billion rooms around a planet.

"You want me to handle your business affairs?"

"Please, Mr. Douglas. It would be a goodness. I thank you."

Douglas blinked. "Well, that's clear enough. Doctor, I'll reserve my answer—but you shall have it promptly."

"Thank you, sir. For myself as well as for my client."

Douglas started to stand up. Assemblyman Kung's voice sharply interrupted. "One moment! How about the Larkin Decision?"

Jubal grabbed it before Douglas could speak. "Ah, yes, the Larkin Decision. I've heard quite a lot of nonsense talked about the Larkin Decision—but mostly from irresponsible persons. Mr. Kung, what about the Larkin Decision?"

"I'm asking *you*. Or your . . . client. Or the Secretary General."

Jubal said gently, "Shall I speak, Mr. Secretary?"

"Please do."

"Very well." Jubal paused, slowly took out a big handkerchief and blew his nose in a prolonged blast, producing a minor chord three octaves below middle C. He then fixed Kung with his eye and said solemnly, "Mr. Assemblyman, I'll address this to you—because I know it is unnecessary to address it to the government in the person of the Secretary. Once a long, long time ago, when I was a little boy, another little boy, equally young and foolish, and I formed a club. Just the two of us. Since we had a club, we had to have rules . . . and the first rule we passed—unanimously, I should add—was that henceforth we would always call our mothers, 'Crosspatch.' Silly, of course . . . but we were very young. Mr. Kung, can you deduce the outcome of that 'rule'?"

"I won't guess, Dr. Harshaw."

"I tried to implement our 'Crosspatch' decision once. Once was enough and it saved my chum from making the same mistake. All it got *me* was my young bottom well warmed with a peach switch. And that was the end of the 'Crosspatch' decision."

Jubal cleared his throat. "Just a moment Mr. Kung. Knowing that someone was certain to raise this non-existent issue I tried to explain the Larkin Decision to my client. At first he had trouble realizing that anyone could think that this legal fiction would apply to Mars. After all, Mars is inhabited, by an old and wise race—much older than yours, sir, and possibly wiser. But when he did understand it, he was amused. Just that, sir—tolerantly amused. Once—just once—I under-rated my mother's power to punish a small boy's impudence. That lesson was cheap, a bargain. But this planet cannot afford such a lesson on a planetary scale. Before we attempt to parcel out lands which do not belong to us, it behooves us to be very sure what peach switches are hanging in the Martian kitchen."

Kung looked blandly unconvinced. "Dr. Harshaw, if the Larkin Decision is no more than a small boy's folly . . . *why were national honors rendered to Mr. Smith?*"

Jubal shrugged. "That question should be put to the government not

to me. But I can tell you how *I* interpreted them—as elementary politeness
. . . to the Ancient Ones of Mars."

"Please?"

"Mr. Kung, those honors were no hollow echo of the Larkin Decision. In a fashion quite beyond human experience, Mr. Smith *is* the Planet
Mars!"

Kung did not even blink. "Continue."

"Or, rather, the entire Martian race. In Smith's person, the Ancient
Ones of Mars are visiting us. Honors rendered to him are honors rendered
to them—and harm done to him is harm done to them. This is true in a
very literal but utterly unhuman sense. It was wise and prudent for us to
render honors to our neighbors today—but the wisdom in it has nothing to
do with the Larkin Decision. No responsible person has argued that the
Larkin precedent applies to an inhabited planet—I venture to say that no
one ever will." Jubal paused and looked up, as if asking Heaven for help.
"But, Mr. Kung, be assured that the ancient rulers of Mars do not fail to
notice how we treat their ambassador. The honors rendered to them
through him were a gracious symbol. I am certain that the government of
this planet showed wisdom thereby. In time, *you* will learn that it was a
most prudent act as well."

Kung answered blandly, "Doctor, if you are trying to frighten me,
you have not succeeded."

"I did not expect to. But, fortunately for the welfare of this planet,
your opinion did not control." Jubal turned back to Douglas. "Mr. Secretary, this is the longest public appearance I have made in years . . . and I
find that I am fatigued. Could we recess these talks? While we await your
decision?"

xxi

THE MEETING ADJOURNED. Jubal found his intention of getting his flock
out of the Palace balked by the presence of the American President and of
Senator Boone; both wanted to chat with Mike, both were practical politicians who realized fully the freshly enhanced value of being seen on intimate terms with the Man from Mars—and both were well aware that the
eyes of the world, via stereovision, were still on them.

And other hungry politicos were closing in.

Jubal said quickly, "Mr. President, Senator—we're leaving at once to have lunch. Can you join us?" He reflected that two in private would be easier to handle than two dozen in public—and he had to get Mike out of there before anything came unstuck.

To his relief both had other duties elsewhere. Jubal found himself promising not only to fetch Mike to that obscene Fosterite service but also to bring him to the White House—oh, well, the boy could always get sick, if necessary. "Places, girls!"

With his escort again around him Mike was convoyed to the roof, Anne leading the way since she would remember it—and creating quite a bow wave with her height, her Valkyrie blonde beauty, and her impressive cloak of a Fair Witness. Jubal, Ben, and the three officers from the *Champion* covered the rear. Larry and the Greyhound bus were waiting on the roof; a few minutes later the driver left them on the roof of the *New Mayflower*. Newsmen caught up with them there, of course, but the girls guarded Mike on down to the suite Duke had taken earlier. They were becoming quite good at it and were enjoying it; Miriam and Dorcas in particular displayed ferocity that reminded Jubal of a mother cat defending her young—only they made a game of it, keeping score against each other. A reporter that closed within three feet of either of them courted a spiked instep.

They found their corridor patrolled by S.S. troopers and an officer outside the door of their suite.

Jubal's back hair rose, but he realized (or "hoped," he corrected himself) that their presence meant that Douglas was carrying out his half of the bargain in full measure. The letter Jubal had sent to Douglas before the conference, explaining what he was going to do and say, and why, had included a plea to Douglas to use his power and influence to protect Mike's privacy from here on—so that the unfortunate lad could begin to lead a normal life. (If a "normal" life was possible for Mike, Jubal again corrected himself.)

So Jubal merely called out, "Jill! Keep Mike under control. It's okay."

"Right, Boss."

And so it was. The officer at the door simply saluted. Jubal glanced at him. "Well! Howdy, Major. Busted down any doors lately?"

Major Bloch turned red but kept his eyes forward and did not answer. Jubal wondered if the assignment was punishment? No, likely just coincidence; there probably wouldn't be more than a handful of S.S. officers of appropriate rank available for the chore in this area. Jubal considered rubbing it in by saying that a skunk had wandered in that door and ruined his living room furniture—and what was the major going to do about *that?* But he decided against it; it would not only be ungracious but untrue— Duke had rigged a temporary closure out of plywood before the party got too wet for such tasks.

Duke was waiting inside. Jubal said, "Sit down, gentlemen. How about it, Duke?"

Duke shrugged. "Who knows? Nobody has bugged this suite since I took it; I guarantee that. I turned down the first suite they offered me, just as you said to, and I picked this one because it's got a heavy ceiling—the ballroom is above us. And I've spent the time since searching the place. But, Boss, I've pushed enough electrons to know that *any* dump can be bugged, so that you can't find it without tearing the building down."

"Fine, fine—but I didn't mean that. They can't keep a hotel this big bugged throughout just on the chance that we might take a room in it—at least, I don't think they can. I mean, 'How about the supplies?' I'm hungry, boy, and very thirsty—and we've three more for lunch."

"Oh, that. That stuff was unloaded under my eyes, carried down the same way, placed just inside the door; I put it all in the pantry. You've got a suspicious nature, Boss."

"I sure have—and you'd better acquire one if you want to live as long as I have." Jubal had just trusted Douglas with a fortune equivalent to a medium-sized national debt—but he had not assumed that Douglas' over-eager lieutenants would not tamper with food and drink. So to avoid the services of a food taster he had fetched all the way from the Poconos plenty of food, more than a plenty of liquor—and a little water. And, of course, ice cubes. He wondered how Caesar had licked the Gauls without ice cubes.

"I don't hanker to," Duke answered.

"Matter of taste. I've had a pretty good time, on the whole. Get crackin', girls. Anne, douse your cloak and get useful. First girl back in here with a drink for me skips her next turn at 'Front.' After our guests, I mean. Do please sit down, gentlemen. Sven, what's your favorite poison? Akvavit, I suppose—Larry, tear down, find a liquor store and fetch back a couple of bottles of akvavit. Fetch Bols gin for the captain, too."

"Hold it, Jubal," Nelson said firmly. "I won't touch akvavit unless it's chilled overnight—and I'd rather have Scotch."

"Me, too," agreed van Tromp.

"All right. Got enough of that to drown a horse. Dr. Mahmoud? If you prefer soft drinks, I'm pretty sure the girls tucked some in."

Mahmoud looked wistful. "I should not allow myself to be tempted by strong drink."

"No need to be. Let me prescribe for you, as a physician." Jubal looked him over. "Son, you look as if you had been under considerable nervous strain. Now we could alleviate that with meprobamate but since we don't have that at hand, I'm forced to substitute two ounces of ninety-proof ethanol, repeat as needed. Any particular flavor you prefer to kill the medicinal taste? And with or without bubbles?"

Mahmoud smiled and suddenly did not look at all English. "Thank you, Doctor—but I'll sin my own sins, with my eyes open. Gin, please, with water on the side. Or vodka. Or whatever is available."

"Or medicinal alcohol," Nelson added. "Don't let him pull your leg, Jubal. Stinky drinks anything—and always regrets it."

"I do regret it," Mahmoud said earnestly, "because I know it is sinful."

"Then don't needle him about it, Sven," Jubal said brusquely. "If Stinky gets more mileage out of his sins by regretting them, that's his business. My own regretter burned out from overload during the market crash in '29 and I've never replaced it—and that's *my* business. To each his own. How about victuals, Stinky? Anne probably stuffed a ham into one of those hampers—and there might be other unclean items not as clearly recognizable. Shall I check?"

Mahmoud shook his head. "I'm not a traditionalist, Jubal. That legislation was given a long time ago, according to the needs of the time. The times are different now."

Jubal suddenly looked sad. "Yes. But for the better? Never mind, this too shall pass and leave not a rack of mutton behind. Eat what you will, my brother—God forgives necessity."

"Thank you. But, truthfully, I often do not eat in the middle of the day."

"Better eat, or the prescribed ethanol will do more than relax you. Besides, these kids who work for me may sometimes misspell words . . . but they are all superb cooks."

Miriam had come up behind Jubal with a tray bearing four drinks, orders having been filled at once while Jubal ranted. "Boss," she broke in, "I heard that. Will you put it in writing?"

"What?" He whirled around and glared at her. *"Snooping!"* You stay in after school and write one thousand times: 'I will not flap my ears at private conversations.' Stay until you finish it."

"Yes, Boss. This is for you, Captain . . . and for you, Dr. Nelson . . . and this is yours, Dr. Mahmoud. Water on the side, you said?"

"Yes, Miriam. Thank you."

"Usual Harshaw service—sloppy but fast. Here's yours, Boss."

"You put water in it!"

"Anne's orders. She says you're too tired to have it on the rocks."

Jubal looked long-suffering. "You see what I have to put up with, gentlemen? We should never have put shoes on 'em. Miriam, make that 'one thousand times' in Sanskrit."

"Yes, Boss. Just as soon as I find time to learn it." She patted him on the head. "You go right ahead and have your tizzy, dear; you've earned it. We're all proud of you."

"Back to the kitchen, woman. Hold it—has everybody else got a drink? Where's Ben's drink? Where's Ben?"

"They have by now. Ben is phoning in his column. His drink is at his elbow."

"Very well. You may back out quietly, without formality—and send Mike in. Gentlemen! Me ke aloha pau ole!—for there are fewer of us every year." He drank, they joined him.

"Mike's helping. He loves to help—I think he's going to be a butler when he grows up."

"I thought you had left. Send him in anyhow; Dr. Nelson wants to give him a physical examination."

"No hurry," put in the ship's surgeon. "Jubal, this is excellent Scotch —but what was the toast?"

"Sorry. Polynesian. 'May our friendship be everlasting.' Call it a footnote to the water ceremony this morning. By the way, gentlemen, both Larry and Duke are water brothers to Mike, too, but don't let it fret you. They can't cook . . . but they're the sort to have at your back in a dark alley."

"If you vouch for them, Jubal," van Tromp assured him, "admit them and tyle the door. But let's drink to the girls while we're alone. Sven, what's that toast of yours to the flickas?"

"You mean the one to all pretty girls everywhere? Let's drink just to the four who are here. Skaal!" They drank to their female water brothers and Nelson continued, "Jubal, where do you find them?"

"Raise 'em in my own cellar. Then just when I've got 'em trained and some use to me, some city slicker always comes along and marries them. It's a losing game."

"I can see how you suffer," Nelson said sympathetically.

"I do. I trust all of you gentlemen are married?"

Two were. Mahmoud was not. Jubal looked at him bleakly. "Would you have the grace to discorporate yourself? After lunch, of course—I wouldn't want you to do it on an empty stomach."

"I'm no threat, I'm a permanent bachelor."

"Come, come, sir! I saw Dorcas making eyes at you . . . and you were purring."

"I'm safe, I assure you." Mahmoud thought of telling Jubal that he would never marry out of his faith, decided that a gentile would take it amiss—even a rare exception like Jubal. He changed the subject. "But, Jubal, don't make a suggestion like that to Mike. He wouldn't grok that you were joking—and you might have a corpse on your hands. I don't know . . . I don't *know* that Mike can actually think himself dead. But he would try . . . and if he were truly a Martian, it would work."

"I'm sure he can," Nelson said firmly. "Doctor—'Jubal,' I mean—have you noticed anything odd about Mike's metabolism?"

"Uh, let me put it this way. There isn't anything about his metabolism which I have noticed that is *not* odd. Very."

"Exactly."

Jubal turned to Mahmoud. "But don't worry that I might invite Mike to suicide. I've learned not to joke with him, not ever. I grok that he doesn't grok joking." Jubal blinked thoughtfully. "But *I* don't grok 'grok' —not really. Stinky, you speak Martian."

"A little."

"You speak it fluently, I heard you. Do *you* grok 'grok'?"

Mahmoud looked very thoughtful. "No. Not really. 'Grok' is the most important word in the Martian language—and I expect to spend the next forty years trying to understand it and perhaps use some millions of printed words trying to explain it. But I don't expect to be successful. You need to *think* in Martian to grok the word 'grok.' Which Mike does . . . and I don't. Perhaps you have noticed that Mike takes a rather veering approach to some of the simplest human ideas?"

"Have I! My throbbing head!"

"Mine, too."

"Food," announced Jubal. "Lunch, and about time, too. Girls, put it down where we can reach it and maintain a respectful silence. Go on talking, Doctor, if you will. Or does Mike's presence make it better to postpone it?"

"Not at all." Mahmoud spoke briefly in Martian to Mike. Mike answered him, smiled sunnily; his expression became blank again and he applied himself to food, quite content to be allowed to eat in silence. "I told him what I was trying to do and he told me that I would speak rightly; this was not his opinion but a simple statement of fact, a necessity. I hope that if I fail to, he will notice and tell me. But I doubt if he will. You see, Mike thinks in Martian—and this gives him an entirely different 'map' of the universe from that which you and I use. You follow me?"

"I grok it," agreed Jubal. "Language itself shapes a man's basic ideas."

"Yes, but— Doctor, you speak Arabic, do you not?"

"Eh? I used to, badly, many years ago," admitted Jubal. "Put in a while as a surgeon with the American Field Service, in Palestine. But I don't now. I still read it a little . . . because I prefer to read the words of the Prophet in the original."

"Proper. Since the Koran cannot be translated—the 'map' changes on translation no matter how carefully one tries. You will understand, then, how difficult *I* found English. It was not alone that my native language has much simpler inflections and more limited tenses; the whole 'map' changed. English is the largest of the human tongues, with several times the vocabulary of the second largest language—this alone made it inevitable that English would eventually become, as it did, the *lingua franca* of this planet, for it is thereby the richest and the most flexible—despite its barbaric accretions . . . or, I should say, *because* of its barbaric accretions. English swallows up anything that comes its way, makes English out of it. Nobody tried to stop this process, the way some languages are policed and have official limits . . . probably because there never has been, truly, such a thing as 'the King's English'—for 'the King's English' was French. English was in truth a bastard tongue and nobody cared how it grew . . . and it did!—enormously. Until no one could hope to be an educated man unless he did his best to embrace this monster.

"Its very variety, subtlety, and utterly irrational, idiomatic complexity makes it possible to say things in English which simply cannot be said in any other language. It almost drove me crazy . . . until I learned to think in it—and that put a new 'map' of the world on top of the one I grew up with. A better one, in many ways—certainly a more detailed one.

"But nevertheless there are things which can be said in the simple Arabic tongue that *cannot* be said in English."

Jubal nodded agreement. "Quite true. That's why I've kept up my reading of it, a little."

"Yes. But the Martian language is so much *more* complex than is English—and so wildly different in the fashion in which it abstracts its picture of the universe—that English and Arabic might as well be considered one and the same language, by comparison. An Englishman and an Arab can learn to think each other's thoughts, in the other's language. But

I'm not certain that it will ever be possible for us to *think* in Martian (other than by the unique fashion Mike learned it)—oh, we can learn a sort of a 'pidgin' Martian, yes—that is what I speak.

"Now take this one word: 'grok.' Its literal meaning, one which I suspect goes back to the origin of the Martian race as thinking, speaking creatures—and which throws light on their whole 'map'—is quite easy. 'Grok' means 'to drink.' "

"Huh?" said Jubal. "But Mike never says 'grok' when he's just talking about drinking. He—"

"Just a moment." Mahmoud spoke to Mike in Martian.

Mike looked faintly surprised and said, " 'Grok' is drink," and dropped the matter.

"But Mike would also have agreed," Mahmoud went on, "if I had named a hundred other English words, words which represent what we think of as different concepts, even pairs of antithetical concepts. And 'grok' means *all* of these, depending on how you use it. It means 'fear,' it means 'love,' it means 'hate'—proper hate, for by the Martian 'map' you cannot possibly hate anything unless you grok it completely, understand it so thoroughly that you merge with it and it merges with you—then and only then can you hate it. By hating yourself. But this also implies, by necessity, that you love it, too, and cherish it and would not have it otherwise. Then you can *hate*— and (I think) that Martian hate is an emotion so black that the nearest human equivalent could only be called a mild distaste."

Mahmoud screwed up his face. "It means 'identically equal' in the mathematical sense. The human cliché, 'This hurts me worse than it does you' has a Martian flavor to it, if only a trace. The Martians seem to know instinctively what we learned painfully from modern physics, that the observer interacts with the observed simply through the process of observation. 'Grok' means to understand so thoroughly that the observer becomes a part of the process being observed—to merge, to blend, to intermarry, to lose personal identity in group experience. It means almost everything that we mean by religion, philosophy, and science—and it means as little to us as color means to a blind man." Mahmoud paused. "Jubal, if I chopped you up and made a stew of you, you and the stew, whatever else was in it, would grok—and when I ate you, we would grok together and nothing would be lost and it would not matter which one of us did the chopping up and eating."

"It would to me!" Jubal said firmly.

"You aren't a Martian." Mahmoud stopped again to talk to Mike in Martian.

Mike nodded. "You spoke rightly, my brother Dr. Mahmoud. I am been saying so. Thou art God."

Mahmoud shrugged helplessly. "You see how hopeless it is? All I got was a blasphemy. We don't think in Martian. We *can't.*"

"Thou art God," Mike said agreeably. "God groks."

"Hell, let's change the subject! Jubal, could I impose on my fraternal status for some more gin?"

"I'll get it," said Dorcas, and jumped up.

It was a pleasant family picnic, made easy by Jubal's gift for warm informality, a gift shared by his staff, plus the fact that the three newcomers were themselves the same easy sort of people—each learned, acclaimed, and with no need to strive. And all four men shared a foster-father interest in Mike. Even Dr. Mahmoud, rarely truly off guard with those who did not share with him the one true faith in submission to the Will of God, always beneficent, merciful, found himself relaxed and happy. It had pleased him very much to learn that Jubal read the words of the Prophet . . . and, now that he stopped to notice it, the women of Jubal's household were really much plumper than he had thought at first glance. That dark one— But he put the thought out of his mind; he was a guest.

But it pleased him very much that these women did not chatter, did not intrude themselves into the sober talk of men, but were very quick with food and drink in warm hospitality. He had been shocked at Miriam's casual disrespect toward her master—then recognized it for what it was: liberty permitted cats and favorite children in the privacy of the home.

Jubal explained early that they were doing nothing but waiting on word from the Secretary General. "If he means business—and I think he's ready to deal—we may hear from him yet today. If not, we'll go home this evening . . . and come back if we have to. But if we had stayed in the Palace, he might have been tempted to dicker. Here, dug into our own hole, we can refuse to dicker."

"Dicker for what?" asked Captain van Tromp. "You gave him what he wanted."

"Not all that he wanted. Douglas would rather have that power of attorney be utterly irrevocable . . . instead of on his good behavior, with the power reverting to a man he despises and is afraid of—namely that scoundrel there with the innocent smile, our brother Ben. But there are others besides Douglas who are certain to want to dicker, too. That bland buddha Kung—hates my guts, I've just snatched the rug out from under him. But if he could figure a deal that might tempt us—before Douglas nails this down—he would offer it. So we stay out of *his* way, too. Kung is one reason why we are eating and drinking nothing that we did not fetch with us."

"You really feel that's something to worry about?" asked Nelson. "Truthfully, Jubal, I had assumed that you were a gourmet who insisted on his own cuisine even away from home. I can't imagine being poisoned, in a major hotel such as this."

Jubal shook his head sorrowfully. "Sven, you're the sort of honest man who thinks everybody else is honest—and you are usually right. No, nobody is going to try to poison you . . . but your wife might collect your insurance simply because you shared a dish with Mike."

"You really think that?"

"Sven, I'll order anything you want. But *I* won't touch it and I won't let Mike touch it. For I'll lay heavy odds that any waiter who comes to this suite will be on Kung's payroll . . . and maybe on two or three others'. I'm not seeing boogie men behind bushes; they know where we are—and they've had a couple of hours in which to act. Sven, in cold seriousness, my principal worry has been to keep this lad alive long enough to figure out a way to sterilize and stabilize the power he represents . . . so that it would be to no one's advantage to have him dead."

Jubal sighed. "Consider the black widow spider. It's a timid little beastie, useful and, for my taste, the prettiest of the arachnids, with its shiny, patent-leather finish and its red hourglass trademark. But the poor thing has the fatal misfortune of possessing enormously too much power for its size. So everybody kills it on sight.

"The black widow can't help it, it has no way to avoid its venomous power.

"Mike is in the same dilemma. He isn't as pretty as a black widow spider—"

"Why, Jubal!" Dorcas said indignantly. "What a mean thing to say! And how utterly *untrue!*"

"Sorry, child. I don't have your glandular bias in the matter. Pretty or not, Mike can't get rid of that money, nor is it safe for him to have it. And not just Kung. The High Court is not as 'non-political' as it might be . . . although their methods would probably make a prisoner out of him rather than kill him—a fate which, for my taste, is worse. Not to mention a dozen other interested parties, in and out of public office . . . persons who might or might not kill him, but who have certainly turned over in their minds just how it would affect *their* fortunes if Mike were guest of honor at a funeral. I—"

"Telephone, Boss."

"Anne, you have just interrupted a profound thought. You hail from Porlock."

"No, Dallas."

"And I will not answer the phone for anyone."

"She said to tell you it was Becky."

"Why didn't you say so?" Jubal hurried out of the living room, found Madame Vesant's friendly face in the screen. "Becky! I'm glad to see you, girl!" He did not bother to ask how she had known where to call him.

"Hi, Doc. I caught your act—and I just had to call and tell you so."

"How'd it look?"

"The Professor would have been proud of you. I've never seen a tip turned more expertly. Then you spilled 'em before the marks knew what had hit 'em. Doc, the profession lost a great talker when you weren't born twins."

"That's high praise, coming from you, Becky." Jubal thought rapidly. "But you set up the act; I just cashed in on it—and there's plenty of cash. So name your fee, Becky, and don't be shy." He decided that, whatever figure she picked, he would double it. That drawing account he had demanded for Mike would never feel it . . . and it was better, far better, to pay Becky off lavishly than to let the obligation stay open.

Madame Vesant frowned. "Now you've hurt my feelings."

"Becky, Becky! You're a big girl now, dear. Anybody can clap and cheer—but applause worthwhile will be found in a pile of soft, green, folding money. Not *my* money. The Man from Mars picks up this tab and, believe me, he can afford it." He grinned. "But all you'll get from me is thanks, and a hug and a kiss that will crack your ribs the first time I see you."

She relaxed and smiled. "I'll hold you to it. I remember how you used to pat my fanny while you assured me that the Professor was sure to get well—you always could make a body feel better."

"I can't believe that I ever did anything so unprofessional."

"You did, you know you did. And you weren't very fatherly about it, either."

"Maybe so. Maybe I thought it was the treatment you needed. I've given up fanny-patting for Lent—but I'll make an exception in your case."

"You'd better."

"And you'd better figure out that fee. Don't forget the zeroes."

"Uh . . . I'll think about it. But, truthfully, Doc, there are more ways of collecting a fee than by making a fast count on the change. Have you been watching the market today?"

"No, and don't tell me about it. Come over and have a drink instead."

"Uh, I'd better not. I promised, well, a rather important client that I would be available for instant consultation."

"I see. Mmm . . . Becky do you suppose that the stars would show that this whole matter would turn out best for everybody if it were all wrapped up, signed, sealed, and notarized today? Maybe just after the stock market closes?"

She looked thoughtful. "I could look into it."

"You do that. And come stay with us when you aren't so busy. Stay as long as you like and never wear your hurtin' shoes the whole time. You'll like the boy. He's as weird as snake's suspenders but sweet as a stolen kiss, too."

"Uh . . . I will. As soon as I can. Thanks, Doc."

They said good-by and Jubal returned to find that Dr. Nelson had taken Mike into one of the bedrooms and was checking him over. He joined them to offer Nelson the use of his kit since Nelson had not had with him his professional bag.

Jubal found Mike stripped down and the ship's surgeon looking baffled. "Doctor," Nelson said, almost angrily, "I saw this patient only ten days ago. Tell me where he got those muscles?"

"Why, he sent in a coupon from the back cover of *Rut: The Magazine for He-Men*. You know, the ad that tells how a ninety-pound weakling can—"

"Doctor, please!"

"Why don't you ask *him?*" Jubal suggested.

Nelson did so. "I thinked them," Mike answered.

"That's right," Jubal agreed. "He 'thinked' 'em. When I got him, just over a week ago, he was a mess, slight, flabby, and pale. Looked as if he had been raised in a cave—which I gather he was, more or less. So I told him he had to grow strong. So he did."

"Exercises?" Nelson said doubtfully.

"Nothing systematic. Swimming, when and as he wished."

"A week of swimming won't make a man look as if he had been sweating over bar bells for years!" Nelson frowned. "I am aware that Mike has voluntary control over the so-called 'involuntary' muscles. But that is not entirely without precedent. This, on the other hand, requires one to assume that—"

"Doctor," Jubal said gently, "why don't you just admit that you don't grok it and save the wear and tear?"

Nelson sighed. "I might as well. Put your clothes on, Michael."

Somewhat later, Jubal, under the mellowing influence of congenial company and the grape, was unburdening to the three from the *Champion* his misgivings about his morning's work. "The financial end was simple enough: just tie up Mike's money so that a struggle over it couldn't take place. Not even if he dies, because I've let Douglas know privately that Mike's death ends his stewardship whereas a rumor from a usually reliable source—me, in this case—has reached Kung and several others to the effect that Mike's death will give Douglas permanent control. Of course, if I had had magical powers, I would have stripped the boy not only of all political significance but also of every penny of his inheritance. That—"

"Why would you have done that, Jubal?" the captain interrupted.

Harshaw looked surprised. "Are you wealthy, Skipper? I don't mean: 'Are your bills paid and enough in the sock to buy any follies your taste runs to?' I mean *rich* . . . so loaded that the floor sags when you walk around to take your place at the head of a board-room table."

"*Me?*" Van Tromp snorted. "I've got my monthly check, a pension eventually, a house with a mortgage—and two girls in college. I'd like to try being wealthy for a while, I don't mind telling you!"

"You wouldn't like it."

"*Huh!* You wouldn't say that . . . if you had two daughters in school."

"For the record, I put four daughters through college—and I went in debt to my armpits to do it. One of them justified the investment; she's a leading light in her profession—which she practices under her husband's name because I'm a disreputable old bum who makes money writing popular trash instead of having the grace to be only a revered memory in her paragraph in *Who's Who*. The other three are nice people who always remember my birthday and don't bother me otherwise; I can't say that an education hurt them. But my offspring are not relevant save to show that I understand that a man often needs more than he's got. But you can fix that easily; you can resign from the service and take a job with some engineering firm that will pay you several times what you're getting just to put your name on their letterhead. General Atomics. Several others. You've had offers—haven't you?"

"That's beside the point," Captain van Tromp answered stiffly. "I'm a professional man."

"Meaning there isn't enough money on this planet to tempt you into giving up commanding space ships. I understand that."

"But I wouldn't mind having money, too."

"A little more money won't do you any good—because daughters can use up ten percent more than a man can make in any normal occupation, regardless of the amount. That's a widely experienced but previously unformulated law of nature, to be known henceforth as 'Harshaw's Law.'

But, Captain, *real* wealth, on the scale that causes its owner to hire a battery of finaglers to hold down his taxes, would ground you just as certainly as resigning would."

"Why should it? I would put it all in bonds and just clip coupons."

"Would you? Not if you were the sort of person who acquires great wealth in the first place. Big money isn't hard to come by. All it costs is a lifetime of single-minded devotion to acquiring it and making it grow into more money, to the utter exclusion of all other interests. They say that the age of opportunity has passed. Nonsense! Seven out of ten of the wealthiest men on this planet started life without a shilling—and there are plenty more such strivers on the way up. Such people are not stopped by high taxation nor even by socialism; they simply adapt themselves to new rules and presently they change the rules. But no première ballerina ever works harder, nor more narrowly, than a man who acquires riches. Captain, that's not your style; you don't want to make money, you simply want to *have* money—in order to spend it."

"Correct, sir! Which is why I can't see why you should want to take Mike's wealth away from him."

"Because Mike doesn't need it and it would cripple him worse than any physical handicap. Wealth—great wealth—is a curse . . . unless you are devoted to the money-making game for its own sake. And even then it has serious drawbacks."

"Oh, nonsense! Jubal, you talk like a harem guard trying to convince a whole man of the advantages of being a eunuch. Pardon me."

"Very possibly," agreed Jubal, "and perhaps for the same reason; the human mind's ability to rationalize its own shortcomings into virtues is unlimited, and I am no exception. Since I, like yourself, sir, have no interest in money other than to spend it, there has never been the slightest chance that I would acquire any significant degree of wealth—just enough for my vices. Nor any real danger that I would fail to scrounge that modest amount, since anyone with the savvy not to draw to a small pair can always manage to feed his vices, whether they be tithing or chewing betel nut. But great wealth? You saw that performance this morning. Now answer me truthfully. Do you think I could have revised it slightly so that I myself acquired all that plunder—become its sole manager and *de-facto* owner while milking off for my own use any income I cared to name—and *still* have rigged the other issues so that Douglas would have supported the outcome? Could I have done that, sir? Mike trusts me; I am his water brother. Could I have stolen his fortune and so arranged it that the government in the person of Mr. Douglas would have condoned it?"

"Uh . . . damn you, Jubal, I suppose you could have."

"Most certainly I could have. Because our sometimes estimable Secretary General is no more a money-seeker than you are. *His* drive is political power—a drum whose beat I do not hear. Had I guaranteed to Douglas (oh, gracefully, of course—there is decorum even among thieves) that the Smith estate would continue to bulwark his administration, then I would have been left undisturbed to do as I liked with the income and had my acting guardianship made legal."

Jubal shuddered. "I thought that I was going to have to do exactly that, simply to protect Mike from the vultures gathered around him—and I was panic-stricken. Captain, you obviously don't *know* what an Old Man of the Sea great wealth is. It is not a fat purse and time to spend it. Its owner finds himself beset on every side, at every hour, wherever he goes, by persistent pleaders, like beggars in Bombay, each demanding that he invest or give away part of his wealth. He becomes suspicious of honest friendship—indeed honest friendship is rarely offered him; those who could have been his friends are too fastidious to be jostled by beggars, too proud to risk being mistaken for one.

"Worse yet, his life and the lives of his family are always in danger. Captain, have your daughters ever been threatened with kidnapping?"

"What? Good Lord, I should hope not!"

"If you possessed the wealth Mike had thrust on him, you would have those girls guarded night and day—and even then you would not rest, because you would never be sure that those very guards were not tempted. Look at the records of the last hundred or so kidnappings in this country and note how many of them involved a trusted employee . . . and note, too, how few victims escaped alive. Then ask yourself: is there any luxury wealth can buy which is worth having your daughters' pretty necks always in a noose?"

Van Tromp looked thoughtful. "No. I guess I'll keep my mortgaged house—it's more my speed. Those girls are all I've got, Jubal."

"Amen. I was appalled at the prospect. Wealth holds no charm for me. All I want is to live my own lazy, useless life, sleep in my own bed—and not be *bothered!* Yet I thought I was going to be forced to spend my last few years sitting in an office, barricaded by buffers, and working long hours as Mike's man of business.

"Then I had an inspiration. Douglas already lived behind such barricades, already had such a staff. Since I was forced to surrender the power of that money to Douglas merely to ensure Mike's continued health and freedom, why not make the beggar pay for it by assuming all the headaches, too? I was not afraid that Douglas would steal from Mike; only pipsqueak, second-rate politicians are money hungry—and Douglas, whatever his faults, is no pipsqueak. Quit scowling, Ben, and hope that he never dumps the load on *you*.

"So I dumped the whole load on Douglas—and now I can go back to my garden. But, as I have said, the money was relatively simple, once I figured it out. It was the Larkin Decision that fretted me."

Caxton said, "I thought you had lost your wits on that one, Jubal. That silly business of letting them give Mike sovereign 'honors.' Honors indeed! For God's sake, Jubal, you should simply have had Mike sign over all right, title, and interest, if any, under that ridiculous Larkin theory. You knew Douglas wanted him to—Jill told you."

"Ben m'boy," Jubal said gently, "as a reporter you are hard-working and sometimes readable."

"Gee, thanks! My fan."

"But your concepts of strategy are Neanderthal."

Caxton sighed. "I feel better, Jubal. For a moment there I thought you had become softly sentimental in your old age."

"When I do, please shoot me. Captain, how many men did you leave on Mars?"

"Twenty-three."

"And what is their status, under the Larkin Decision?"

Van Tromp looked troubled. "I'm not supposed to talk."

"Then don't," Jubal reassured him. "I can deduce it, and so can Ben."

Dr. Nelson said, "Skipper, both Stinky and I are civilians again. I shall talk where and how I please—"

"And shall I," agreed Mahmoud.

"—and if they want to make trouble for me, they know what they can do with my reserve commission. What business has the government, telling us *we* can't talk? Those chair-warmers didn't go to Mars. *We* did."

"Stow it, Sven. I intended to talk—these are our water brothers. But, Ben, I would rather not see this in your column. I would like to command a space ship again."

"Captain, I know the meaning of 'off the record.' But if you'll feel easier, I'll join Mike and the girls for a while—I want to see Jill anyhow."

"Please don't leave. But . . . this is among water brothers. The government is in a stew about that nominal colony we left behind. Every man in it joined in signing away his so-called Larkin rights—assigned them to the government—before we left Earth. Mike's presence when we got to Mars confused things enormously. I'm no lawyer, but I understood that, if Mike did waive his rights, whatever they might be, that would put the administration in the driver's seat when it came to parceling out things of value."

"*What* things of value?" demanded Caxton. "Other than pure science, I mean. Look, Skipper, I'm not running down your achievement, but from all I've seen and heard, Mars isn't exactly valuable real estate for human beings. Or are there assets that are still classified 'drop dead before reading'?"

Van Tromp shook his head. "No, the scientific and technical reports are all declassified, I believe. But, Ben, the Moon was a worthless hunk of rock when we first got it. Now look at it."

"Touché," Caxton admitted. "I wish my grandpappy had bought Lunar Enterprises instead of Canadian uranium. I don't have Jubal's objections to being rich." He added, "But, in any case, Mars is already inhabited."

Van Tromp looked unhappy. "Yes. But— Stinky, you tell him."

Mahmoud said, "Ben, there is plenty of room on Mars for human colonization . . . and, so far as I was ever able to find out, the Martians would not interfere. They did not object when we told them we intended to leave a colony behind. Nor did they seem pleased. Not even interested. We're flying our flag and claiming extraterritoriality right now. But our status may be more like that of one of those ant cities under glass one sometimes sees in school rooms. I was never able to grok it."

Jubal nodded. "Precisely. Myself, too. This morning I did not have the slightest idea of the true situation . . . except that I knew that the government was anxious to get those so-called Larkin rights from Mike. Beyond that I was ignorant. So I assumed that the government was equally ignorant and went boldly ahead. 'Audacity, always audacity'—soundest principle of strategy. In practicing medicine I learned that when you are most at loss is the time when you *must* appear confident. In law I had learned that, when your case seems hopeless, you must impress the jury with your relaxed certainty."

Jubal grinned. "Once, when I was a kid in high school, I won a debate on shipping subsidies by quoting an overwhelming argument from the files of the British Colonial Shipping Board. The opposition was totally unable to refute me—because there never was a 'British Colonial Shipping Board.' I had made it up, whole cloth.

"I was equally shameless this morning. The administration wanted Mike's 'Larkin rights' and was scared silly that we might make a deal with Kung or somebody. So I used their greed and worry to wring out of them that ultimate logical absurdity of their fantastic legal theory, a public acknowledgment in unmistakable diplomatic protocol that Mike was a sovereign equal of the Federation itself—and must be treated accordingly!" Jubal looked smug.

"Thereby," Ben said dryly, "putting yourself up the well-known creek without a paddle."

"Ben, Ben," Jubal said chidingly. "Wrong metaphor. Not a canoe, but a tiger. Or a throne. By their own logic they had publicly crowned Mike. Need I point out that, despite the old saw about uneasy heads and crowns, it is nevertheless safer to be publicly a king than it is to be a pretender in hiding? A king can usually abdicate to save his neck; a pretender may renounce his pretensions but it makes his neck no safer—less so, in fact; it leaves him naked to his enemies. No, Ben, Kung saw that Mike's position had been enormously strengthened by a few bars of music and an old sheet, even if you did not—and Kung did not like it a bit.

"But I acted through necessity, not choice, and, while Mike's position was improved, it was still not an easy one. Mike was, for the nonce, the acknowledged sovereign of Mars under the legalistic malarky of the Larkin precedent . . . and, as such, was empowered to hand out concessions, trading rights, enclaves, ad nauseam. He must either do these things himself . . . and thus be subjected to pressures even worse than those attendant on great wealth and for which he is even less fitted—or he must abdicate his titular position and allow his Larkin rights to devolve on those twenty-three men now on Mars, i.e., to Douglas."

Jubal looked pained. "I disliked these alternatives almost equally, since each was based on the detestable doctrine that the Larkin Decision could apply to inhabited planets. Gentlemen, I have never met any Martians, I have no vocation to be their champion—but I could not permit a client of mine to be trapped into such a farce. The Larkin Decision itself had to be rendered void, and all 'rights' under it, with respect to the planet Mars—while the matter was still in our hands and without giving the High Court a chance to rule."

Jubal grinned boyishly. "So I appealed to a higher court for a decision that would nullify the Larkin precedent—I cited a mythical 'British Colonial Shipping Board.' I lied myself blue in the face to create a new legal theory. Sovereign honors had been rendered Mike; that was fact, the world had seen it. But sovereign honors may be rendered to a sovereign . . . or to a sovereign's alter ego, his viceroy or ambassador. So I asserted that Mike was no cardboard sovereign under a silly human precedent not in point—but in awful fact the ambassador of the great Martian nation!"

Jubal sighed. "Sheer bluff . . . and I was scared silly that I would be required to prove my claims. But I was staking my bluff on my hope and strong belief that others—Douglas, and in particular, Kung—would be no more certain of the facts than was *I.*" Jubal looked around him. "But I ventured to risk that bluff because you three were sitting with us, were Mike's water brethren. If you three sat by and did not challenge my lies, then Mike *must* be accepted as the Martian equivalent of ambassador— and the Larkin Decision was a dead issue."

"I hope it is," Captain van Tromp said soberly, "but I did not take your statements as lies, Jubal; I took them as simple truth."

"Eh? But I assure you they were not. I was spinning fancy words, extemporizing."

"No matter. Inspiration or deduction—I think you told the truth." The skipper of the *Champion* hesitated. "Except that I would not call Mike an ambassador—*I* think he's an expeditionary force."

Caxton's jaw dropped. Harshaw did not dispute him but answered with equal soberness. "In what way, sir?"

Van Tromp said, "I'll amend that. It would be better to say that I think he's a scout for an expeditionary force, reconnoitering us for his Martian masters. It is even possible that they are in telepathic contact with him at all times, that he doesn't even need to report back. I don't know— but I do know that, after visiting Mars, I find such ideas much easier to swallow . . . and I know this: everybody seems to take it for granted that, finding a human being on Mars, we would of course bring him home and that he would be anxious to come home. Nothing could be further from the truth. Eh, Sven?"

"Mike hated the idea," agreed Nelson. "We couldn't even get close to him at first; he was afraid of us. Then he was ordered to go back with us . . . and from then on he did exactly what we told him to do. He behaved like a soldier carrying out with perfect discipline orders that scared him silly."

"Just a moment," Caxton protested. "Captain, even so—Mars attack us? *Mars?* You know more about these things than I do, but wouldn't that be about like us attacking Jupiter? I mean to say, we have about two and a half times the surface gravity that Mars has, just as Jupiter has about two and a half times our surface gravity. Somewhat analogous differences, each way, on pressure, temperature, atmosphere, and so forth. *We* couldn't stay alive on Jupiter . . . and I don't see how Martians could stand our conditions. Isn't that true?"

"Close enough," admitted van Tromp.

"Then tell me why we should attack Jupiter? Or Mars attack us?"

"Mmm . . . Ben, have you seen any of the proposals to attempt a beach head on Jupiter?"

"Yes, but— Well, nothing has ever gotten beyond the dream stage. It isn't practical."

"Space flight wasn't practical less than a century ago. Go back in the files and see what your own colleagues said about it—oh, say about 1940. These Jupiter proposals are, at best, no farther than drawing board—but the engineers working on them are quite serious. They think that, by using all that we've learned from deep ocean exploration, plus equipping men with powered suits in which to float, it should be possible to put human beings on Jupiter. And don't think for a moment that the Martians are any less clever than we are. You should see their cities."

"Uh—" said Caxton. "Okay, I'll shut up. I still don't see why they would bother."

"Captain?"

"Yes, Jubal?"

"I see another objection—a cultural one. You know the rough division of cultures into 'Apollonian' and 'Dionysian.' "

"I know in general what you mean."

"Well, it seems to me that even the Zuni culture would be called 'Dionysian' on Mars. Of course, you've been there and I haven't—but I've been talking steadily with Mike. That boy was raised in an extremely Apollonian culture—and such cultures are not aggressive."

"Mmm . . . I see your point—but I wouldn't count on it."

Mahmoud said suddenly, "Skipper, there's strong evidence to support Jubal's conclusion. You can analyse a culture from its language, every time —and there isn't any Martian word for 'war.' " He stopped and looked puzzled. "At least, I don't think there is. Nor any word for 'weapon' . . . nor for 'fighting.' If a word for a concept isn't in a language, then its culture simply doesn't have the referent the missing word would symbolize."

"Oh, twaddle, Stinky! Animals fight—and ants even conduct wars. Are you trying to tell me they have to have *words* for it before they can *do* it?"

"I mean exactly that," Mahmoud insisted, "when it applies to any verbalizing race. Such as ourselves. Such as the Martians—even more highly verbalized than we are. A verbalizing race has words for every old concept . . . and creates new words or new definitions for old words whenever a new concept comes along. Always! A nervous system that is able to verbalize cannot avoid verbalizing; it's automatic. If the Martians know what 'war' is, then they have a word for it."

"There is a quick way to settle it," Jubal suggested. "Call in Mike. Ask him."

"Just a moment, Jubal," van Tromp objected. "I learned years ago never to argue with a specialist; you can't win. But I also learned that the history of progress is a long, long list of specialists who were dead wrong when they were most certain—sorry, Stinky."

"You're quite right, Captain—only I'm not wrong this time."

"As may be, all Mike can settle is whether or not he knows a certain word . . . which might be like asking a two-year-old to define 'calculus.' Proves nothing. I'd like to stick to facts for a moment. Sven? About Agnew?"

Nelson answered, "It's up to you, Captain."

"Well . . . this is still private conversation among water brothers, gentlemen. Lieutenant Agnew was our junior medical officer. Quite brilliant in his line, Sven tells me, and I had no complaints about him otherwise; he was well-enough liked. But he had an unsuspected latent xenophobia. Not against humans. But he couldn't stand Martians. Now I had given orders against going armed outside the ship once it appeared that the Martians were peaceful—too much chance of an incident.

"Apparently young Agnew disobeyed me—at least we were never able to find his personal side arm later and the two men who last saw him alive say that he was wearing it. But all my log shows is: 'Missing and presumed dead.'

"Here is why. Two crewmen saw Agnew go into a sort of passage between two large rocks—rather scarce on Mars; mostly it's monotonous. Then they saw a Martian enter the same way . . . whereupon they hurried, as Dr. Agnew's peculiarity was well known.

"Both say that they heard a shot. One says that he reached this opening in time to glimpse Agnew past the Martian, who pretty well filled the space between the rocks; they're so big. And then he didn't see him. The second man says that when he got there the Martian was just exiting, simply sailed on past them and went his way—which is characteristically Martian; if he has no business with you, he simply ignores you. With the Martian out of the way they could both see the space between the two rocks . . . and it was a dead end, empty.

"That's all, gentlemen . . . except to say that Agnew might have jumped that rock wall, under Mars' low surface gravity and the impetus of fear—but I could not and I tried—and to mention that these two crewmen were wearing breathing gear—have to, on Mars—and hypoxia can make a man's senses quite unreliable. I don't know that the first crewman was drunk through oxygen shortage; I just mention it because it is an explanation easier to believe than what he reported . . . which is that Agnew simply disappeared, in the blink of an eye. In fact I suggested as much to him and ordered him to check the demand valve and the rest of his breather gear before he went outside again.

"You see, I thought Agnew would show up presently . . . and I was looking forward to chewing him out and slapping him under hack for going armed (if he was) and for going alone (which seemed certain), both being flagrant breaches of discipline.

"But he never returned, we never found him nor his body. I do not know what happened. But my own misgivings about Martians date to that incident. They never again seemed to me to be just big, gentle, harmless, rather comical creatures, even though we never had any trouble with them and they always gave us anything we wanted, once Stinky figured out how to ask for it. I played down the incident—can't let men panic when you're a hundred million miles from home. Oh, I couldn't play down the fact that Dr. Agnew was missing and the whole ship's company searched for him. But I squelched any suggestion that there had been anything mysterious about it—Agnew had gotten lost among those rocks, had eventually died, no doubt, when his oxygen ran out . . . and was buried under sand drift. Or something. You do get quite a breeze both at sunrise and sundown on Mars; it does cause the sand to drift. So I used it as a reason to clamp down ever harder on always traveling in company, always staying in radio contact with the ship, always checking breather gear . . . with Agnew as a horrible example. I did not tell that crewman to keep his mouth shut; I simply hinted that his story was unbelievable, especially as his mate was not able to back it up. I think the official version prevailed."

Mahmoud said slowly, "It did with me, Captain—this is the first time I've heard that there was any mystery about Agnew. And truthfully, I prefer your 'official' version—I'm not inclined to be superstitious."

Van Tromp nodded. "That's what I had hoped for. Only Sven and myself heard that crewman's wild tale—and we kept it to ourselves. But, just the same—" The space ship captain suddenly looked old. "—I still wake up in the night and ask myself: 'What became of Agnew?' "

Jubal listened to the story without comment. He was still wondering what he should add to it when it ended. He wondered, too, if Jill had told Ben about Berquist and that other fellow—Johnson. He knew that he had not. There hadn't been time the night Ben had been rescued . . . and in the sober light of the following dawn it had seemed better to let such things ride.

Had the kids told Ben about the battle of the swimming pool? And the two carloads of cops who were missing afterwards? Again, it seemed most unlikely; the kids knew that the "official" version was that the first task force had never showed up, they had all heard his phone call with

Douglas. All Jubal's family were discreet; whether guests or employees, gossipy persons were quickly ousted—Jubal regarded gossip as his own prerogative, solely.

But Jill might have told Ben—

Well, if she had, she must have bound him to silence; Ben had not mentioned disappearances to Jubal . . . and he wasn't trying to catch Jubal's eye now.

Damn it, the only thing to do was to keep quiet and go on trying to impress on the boy that he simply must *not* go around making unpleasant strangers disappear!

Jubal was saved from further soul-searching (and the stag conversation was broken up) by Anne's arrival. "Boss, that Mr. Bradley is at the door. The one who called himself 'senior executive assistant to the Secretary General.'"

"You didn't let him in?"

"No. I looked at him through the one-way and talked to him through the speakie. He says he has papers to deliver to you, personally, and that he will wait for an answer."

"Have him pass them through the flap. And you tell him that you are *my* 'senior executive assistant' and that you will fetch my receipt acknowledging personal delivery if that is what he wants. This is still the Martian Embassy—until I check what's in those papers."

"Just let him stand in the corridor?"

"I've no doubt that Major Bloch can find him a chair. Anne, I am aware that you were gently reared—but this is a situation in which rudeness pays off. We don't give an inch, nor a kind word, until we get exactly what we want."

"Yes, Boss."

The package was bulky because there were many copies; there was one document only. Jubal called in everyone and passed them around. "Girls, I am offering one lollipop for each loophole, boobytrap, or ambiguity—prizes of similar value to males. Now everybody keep quiet."

Presently Jubal broke the silence. "He's an honest politician—he stays bought."

"Looks that way," admitted Caxton.

"Anybody?" No one claimed a prize; Douglas had kept it simple and straightforward, merely implementing the agreement reached earlier. "Okay," said Jubal, "everybody is to witness every copy, after Mike signs it—especially you, Skipper, and Sven and Stinky. Get your seal, Miriam. Hell, let Bradley in now and have him witness, too—then give the poor guy a drink. Duke, call the desk and tell 'em to send up the bill; we're checking out. Then call Greyhound and tell 'em we want our go-buggy. Sven, Skipper, Stinky—we're getting out of here the way Lot left Sodom . . . why don't you three come up in the country with us, take off your shoes, and relax? Plenty of beds, home cooking, and no worries."

The two married men asked for, and received, rain checks; Dr. Mahmoud accepted. The signing took rather long, mostly because Mike enjoyed signing his name, drawing each letter with great care and artistic satisfaction. The salvageable remains of the picnic (mostly unopened bottles) had been sent up and loaded by the time all copies were signed and sealed, and the hotel bill had arrived.

Jubal glanced at the fat total and did not bother to add it. Instead he wrote on it: "Approved for payment—J. Harshaw for V. M. Smith," and handed it to Bradley.

"This is your boss's worry now," he told Bradley.

Bradley blinked. "Sir?"

"Oh, just to keep it 'via channels.' Mr. Douglas will doubtless turn it over to the Chief of Protocol. Isn't that the usual procedure? I'm rather green about these things."

Bradley accepted the bill. "Yes," he said slowly. "Yes, that's right. LaRue will voucher it—I'll give it to him."

"Thank you, Mr. Bradley. Thanks for *every*thing!"

part three

HIS ECCENTRIC EDUCATION

xxii

IN ONE LIMB OF A SPIRAL GALAXY, close to a star known as "Sol" to some of its dependents, another star of the same type underwent catastrophic readjustment and became nova. Its glory would be seen on Mars in another three-replenished (729) years, or 1370 Terran years. The Old Ones noted the coming event as being useful, shortly, for instruction of the young, while never ceasing the exciting and crucial discussion of esthetic problems concerning the new epic woven around the death of the Fifth Planet.

The departure of the spaceship *Champion* for its home planet was noted without comment and a watch was kept on the strange nestling sent back in it, but nothing more, since it would be some time yet before it would be fruitful to grok the outcome. The twenty-three humans left behind on Mars coped, successfully in most ways, with an environment lethal to naked humans but less difficult, on the whole, than that in the Free State of Antarctica. One of them discorporated through an undiagnosed illness sometimes called "heartbreak" and at other times "homesickness." The Old Ones cherished the wounded spirit and sent it back where it belonged for further healing; aside from that the Martians left the Terrans alone.

On Earth the exploding neighbor star was not noticed at all, human astronomers still being limited by speed of light. The Man from Mars, having been briefly back in the news, had dropped out of the news again. The minority leader in the Federation Senate called for "a bold, new approach" to the twin problems of population and malnutrition in southeast Asia, starting with increased emergency grants-in-aid to families with more than five children. Mrs. Percy B. S. Souchek sued the supervisors of Los Angeles City-County over the death of her pet poodle Piddle which had taken place during a five-day period of stationary inversion layer. Cynthia Duchess announced that she was going to have the Perfect Baby by a scientifically selected anonymous donor and an equally perfect host-mother just as soon as a battery of experts completed calculating the exact instant for conception to insure that the wonder child would be equally a genius in music, art, and statesmanship—and that she would (with the aid of hormonal treatments) nurse her child herself. She gave out a statement to the press on the psychological benefits of natural feeding and permitted, or insisted, that the press take pictures of her to prove that she was physically endowed for this happy duty—a fact that her usual publicity pictures had never really left undecided.

Supreme Bishop Digby denounced her as the Harlot of Babylon and forbade any Fosterite to accept the commission, either as donor or host-mother. Alice Douglas was quoted as saying: "While I do not know Miss Duchess personally, one cannot help but admire her. Her brave example should be an inspiration to mothers everywhere."

By accident, Jubal Harshaw saw one of the pictures and the accompanying story in a magazine some visitor had left in his house. He chuckled over it and posted it on the bulletin board in the kitchen . . . then noted (as he had expected) that it did not stay up long, which made him chuckle again.

He did not have too many chuckles that week; the world had been too much with him. The working press soon ceased bothering Mike and the Harshaw household when it was clear that the story was over and that Harshaw did not intend to let any fresh news happen—but a great many thousands of other people, not in the news business, did not forget Mike. Douglas honestly tried to insure Mike's privacy; S.S. troopers now patrolled Harshaw's fence and an S.S. car circled over the grounds and challenged any car that tried to land. But Harshaw resented the necessity of having guards.

Guards kept people out; the mail and the telephone came through. The telephone Jubal coped with by changing his call number and having all calls routed through an answering service to which was given a very limited list of persons from whom Harshaw would accept calls—and, at that, he kept the instrument in the house set on "refuse & record" most of the time.

But the mail always comes through.

At first, Harshaw told Jill that the problem was Mike's. The boy had to grow up someday; he could start by handling his own mail . . . and she could help and advise him. "But don't bother *me* with it; I have enough trouble with screwball mail of my own!"

Jubal could not make his decision stick; there was too much of it and Jill simply did not know how.

Just sorting the mail into categories was a headache. Jubal solved that by first making a phone call to the local postmaster (which got no results), then by a phone call to Bradley, which did get results after a "suggestion" from on high trickled back down to local level; thereafter mail for Mike arrived sacked as first class, second class, third class, and fourth class, with mail for everyone else in the household in still another sack.

Second and third class mail was used to insulate a new root cellar north of the house, the old root cellar having been dug by the former owner as a fallout shelter and never having been satisfactory as root cellar. Once the new root cellar was heavily over-insulated and could use no more, Jubal told Duke to dump such mail as fill to check erosion in gullies; combined with a small amount of brush such mail compacted very nicely.

Fourth class mail was a problem, especially as one package exploded prematurely in the village post office, blowing several years of "Wanted" announcements off the notice board and ruining one "Use Next Window" sign—by great good luck the postmaster was out for coffee and his assistant, an elderly lady with weak kidneys, was safe in the washroom. Jubal considered having all fourth class mail addressed to Mike processed by the bomb-disposal specialists of the S.S. who performed the same service for the Secretary General.

This turned out not to be necessary; Mike could spot a "wrongness" about a package without opening it. Thereafter all fourth class mail was unsacked in a heap just inside the gate; then, after the postman had left, Mike would pry through the pile from a distance, cause to disappear any harmful parcel; then Larry would truck the remainder to the house. Jubal felt that this method was far better than soaking suspect packages, opening them in darkness, X-raying them, or any other conventional method.

Mike loved opening the harmless packages; it made every day Christmas for him. He particularly enjoyed reading his own name on address labels. The plunder inside might or might not interest him; usually he gave it to one of the others—and, in the process, at last learned what "property" was in discovering that he could make gifts to his friends. Anything that nobody wanted wound up in a gully; this included, by definition, all gifts of food, as Jubal was not certain that Mike's nose for "wrongness" extended to poisons . . . especially after Mike had drunk, through error, a beaker of a poisonous solution Duke had left in the refrigerator he used for his photographic work—Mike had simply said mildly that the "iced tea" had a flavor he was not sure that he liked.

Jubal told Jill that it was otherwise all right to keep anything that came to Mike by parcel post provided that none of it was (a) ever paid for, (b) ever acknowledged, (c) nor ever returned no matter how marked. Some of the items were legitimately gifts; more of it was unordered merchandise. Either way, Jubal assumed conclusively that unsolicited chattels from strangers always represented efforts to make use of the Man from Mars and therefore merited no thanks.

An exception was made for live stock, from baby chicks to baby alligators, which Jubal advised her to return—unless she was willing to guarantee the care and feeding thereof, and the responsibility of keeping same from falling into the pool.

First class mail was a separate headache. After looking over a bushel or so of Mike's first class mail Jubal set up a list of categories:

A. Begging letters, personal and institutional—erosion fill.

B. Threatening letters—file unanswered. Second and later letters from any one source to be turned over to S.S.

C. Offers of business deals of any nature—forward to Douglas, unanswered.

D. Crackpot letters not containing threats—pass around any real dillies; the rest to go in a gully.

E. Friendly letters—answer only if accompanied by stamped, self-addressed envelope . . . in which case use one of several form letters to be signed by Jill. (Jubal pointed out that letters signed by the Man from Mars were valuable *per se,* and an open invitation to more useless mail.)

F. Scatological letters—pass to Jubal (who had a bet with himself that no such letter would ever show the faintest sign of literary novelty) for further disposition, i.e., gully.

G. Proposals of marriage and propositions not quite so formal—ignore and file. Use procedure under "B" on third offense.

H. Letters from scientific and educational institutions—handle as under "E"; if answered at all, use form letter explaining that the Man from Mars was not available for *anything;* if Jill felt that a form brush-off would not do, pass along to Jubal.

I. Letters from persons who actually had met Mike, such as all the crew of the *Champion,* the President of the United States, and a few others —let Mike answer them exactly as he pleased; the exercise in penmanship would be good for him and the exercise in human personal relations he needed even more (and if he wanted advice, let him ask for it).

This guide cut the number of letters that had to be answered down to manageable size—a few each day for Jill, seldom even one for Mike. Just opening the mail took a major effort, but Jill found that she could skim and classify in about one hour each day, after she got used to it. The first four categories remained large at all times; category "G" was very large during the fortnight following the world stereocast from the Palace, then dwindled and the curve flattened to a steady trickle.

Jubal cautioned Jill that, while Mike should himself answer letters only from acquaintances and friends, mail addressed to him was his to read if he wished.

The third morning after the category system had gone into effect Jill brought a letter, category "G," to Jubal. More than half of the ladies and other females (plus a few misguided males) who supplied this category included pictures alleged to be of themselves; some of these pictures left little to the imagination, as did the letters themselves in many cases.

This letter enclosed a picture which managed not only to leave nothing to the imagination, but started over by stimulating fresh imaginings. Jill said, "Look at this, Boss! I ask you!"

Jubal read the letter, then looked at the picture. "She seems to know what she wants. What does Mike think of it?"

"He hasn't seen it. That's why I brought it to you."

Jubal glanced again at the picture. "A type which, in my youth, we referred to as 'stacked.' Well, her sex is not in doubt, nor her agility. But why are you showing it to *me?* I've seen better, I assure you."

"But what should I *do* with it! The letter is bad enough . . . but that *disgusting* picture—should I tear it up? Before Mike sees it!"

"Oh. Siddown, Nurse. What does it say on the envelope?"

"Nothing. Just the address and the return address."

"How does the address read?"

"Huh? 'Mr. Valentine Michael Smith, the Man from—'"

"Oh. Then it's not addressed to you."

"Why, no, of course—"

"That's all I wanted to be sure of. Now let's get something straight. I am not Mike's guardian. You are neither his mother nor his chaperon. I've simply co-opted you as his secretary. If Mike wants to read everything that comes in here addressed to him, including third class junk mail, he is free to do so."

"Well, he does read almost all of those ads. But surely you don't want him to see filth? Jubal, Mike doesn't know what the world is like. He's *innocent.*"

"So? How many men has he killed so far, Jill?"

Jill did not answer; she looked unhappy.

Jubal went on: "If you want to help him, you will concentrate on teaching him that casual killing is frowned on in this society. Otherwise he is bound to be unpleasantly conspicuous when he goes out into the world."

"Uh, I don't think he wants to 'go out into the world.' "

"Well, I'm damned well going to push him out of the nest as soon as I think he can fly. He can come back later, if he wishes—but I shan't make it possible for him to live out his life here, as an arrested infant. For one thing, I *can't,* even if I wanted to . . . because Mike will probably outlive me by sixty or seventy years and this nest will be gone. But you are correct; Mike is innocent—by our standards. Nurse, have you ever seen that sterile laboratory at Notre Dame?"

"No. I've read about it."

"Healthiest animals in the world—but they can't ever leave the laboratory. Child, I'm not running a sterile laboratory. Mike has got to get acquainted with 'filth,' as you call it—and get immunized to it. One day he's going to meet the gal who wrote this letter, or her spiritual twin sister —in fact he's going to meet her by the dozens and hundreds—shucks, with his notoriety and his looks he can spend his life skipping from one warm bed to another, if he likes. You can't stop it, I can't stop it; it's up to Mike. Furthermore, *I* wouldn't want to stop it, although for my taste it's a silly way to spend one's life—doing the same monotonous exercises over and over again, I mean. What do *you* think?"

"I—" Jill stopped and blushed.

"I withdraw the question. Maybe you don't find them monotonous— but none of my business, either way. But if you don't want Mike's feet kicked out from under him by the first five hundred women that get him alone—and I don't regard it as a good idea, either; he should have other interests as well—then don't try to intercept his mail. Letters like that may vaccinate him a little . . . or at least tend to put him on guard. Don't make a thing out of it; just pass it along in the stack, cum 'filthy' picture. Answer his questions if he asks them . . . and try not to blush."

"Uh, all right. Boss, you're infuriating when you're logical!"

"Yes, a most uncouth way to argue. Now run along."

"All right. But I'm going to tear up that picture after Mike has seen it."

"Oh, don't do that!"

"What? Do *you* want it, Boss?"

"Heaven forbid! I told you I had seen much better. But Duke is not as jaundiced as I am; he collects such pictures. If Mike doesn't want it—and five-to-one he doesn't—give it to Duke. He'll be delighted."

"Duke collects such trash? But he seems such a nice person."

"He is. A very nice person indeed. Or I'd kick him out."

"But— I don't understand it."

Jubal sighed. "And I could sit here all day explaining it and you still wouldn't understand it. My dear, there are aspects of sex on which it is impossible to communicate between the two sexes of our race. They are sometimes grokked by intuition across the gulf that separates us, by a few exceptionally gifted individuals. But words are useless, so I won't try. Just take my word for it: Duke is a perfect knight, *sans peur et sans reproche*— and he would like to have that picture."

"All right, he can have it if Mike doesn't keep it. But I'll just pass it along to you. I won't give it to Duke myself—he might get ideas."

"Sissy. You might enjoy his ideas. Anything startling in the mail otherwise?"

"No. The usual crop of people who want Mike to endorse this and that, or peddle 'Official Man-from-Mars' this's and that's—one character had the nerve to ask for a five-year monopoly, royalty free, on the name, but wants Mike to finance it as well."

"I admire that sort of whole-hearted thief. Encourage him. Tell him that Mike is so rich that he makes crepes suzettes with Napoleon brandy and needs some tax losses—so how much guarantee would he like?"

"Are you serious, Boss? I'll have to dig it out of the group already sacked for Mr. Douglas."

"Of course I'm not serious. The gonif would show up here tomorrow, with his family. But you've given me a fine idea for a story, so run along. *Front!*"

Mike was not uninterested in the "disgusting" picture. He grokked correctly (if only theoretically) what the letter and the picture symbolized, and studied the picture with the clear-eyed delight with which he studied each passing butterfly. He found both butterflies and women tremendously interesting—in fact, all the grokking world around him was enchanting and he wanted to drink so deep of it all that his own grokking would be perfect.

He understood, intellectually, the mechanical and biological processes being offered to him in these letters but he wondered why these strangers wanted his help in quickening their eggs? Mike understood (without grokking it) that these people made ritual of this simple necessity, a "growing closer" possibly almost as important and precious as the water ceremony. He was eager to grok it.

But he was not in a hurry, "hurry" being one human concept he had failed to grok at all. He was sensitively aware of the key importance of correct timing in all acts—but with the Martian approach: correct timing was accomplished by waiting. He had noticed, of course, that his human brothers lacked his own fine discrimination of time and often were forced to wait a little faster than a Martian would—but he did not hold their innocent awkwardness against them; he simply learned to wait faster himself to cover their lack.

In fact, he sometimes waited faster so efficiently that a human would have concluded that he was hurrying at breakneck speed. But the human would have been mistaken—Mike was simply adjusting his own waiting in warm consideration for the needs of others.

So he accepted Jill's edict that he was not to reply to any of these brotherly offers from female humans, but he accepted it not as a final veto but as a waiting—possibly a century hence would be better; in any case now was not the correct time since his water brother Jill spoke rightly.

Mike readily assented when Jill suggested, quite firmly, that he give this picture to Duke. He went at once to do so and would have done so anyhow; Mike knew about Duke's collection, he had seen it, looked through it with deep interest, trying to grok why Duke said, "That one ain't much in the face, but look at those legs—*brother!*" It always made Mike feel good to be called "brother" by one of his water brothers but legs were just legs, save that his own people had three each while humans each had only two—without being crippled thereby, he reminded himself; two legs were proper for humans, he must always grok that this was correct.

As for faces, Jubal had the most beautiful face Mike had ever seen, clearly and distinctly his own. It seemed to Mike that these human females in Duke's picture collection could hardly be said to have grown faces as yet, so much did one look like the other in the face. All young human females had much the same face—how could it be otherwise? Of course he had never had any trouble recognizing Jill's face; she was not only the first woman he had ever seen but, most important, his first female water brother—Mike knew every pore on her nose, every incipient wrinkle in her face and had praised each one in happy meditation.

But, while he now knew Anne from Dorcas and Dorcas from Miriam by their faces alone, it had not been so when first he came here. For several days Mike had distinguished between them by size and coloration—and, of course, by voice, since no two voices were ever alike. But, as sometimes *did* happen, all three females would be quiet at once and then it was well that Anne was so much bigger, Dorcas so small, and that Miriam, who was bigger than Dorcas but smaller than Anne, nevertheless need not be mistaken for the missing one if either Anne or Dorcas was absent because

Miriam had unmistakable hair called "red," even though it was not the color called "red" when speaking of anything but hair.

This special meaning for "red" did not trouble Mike; he knew before he reached Earth that every English word held more than one meaning. It was a fact one could get used to, without grokking, just as the sameness of all girl faces could be gotten used to . . . and, after waiting, they were no longer quite the same. Mike now could call up Anne's face in his mind and count the pores in her nose as readily as with Jill's. In essence, even an egg was uniquely itself, different from all other eggs any where and when— Mike had always known that. So each girl had her own face, no matter how small those differences might be.

Mike gave the "disgusting" picture to Duke and was warmed by Duke's pleasure. Mike did not feel that he was depriving himself in parting with the picture; he had seen it once, he could see it in his mind whenever he wished—even the face in that picture, as it had glowed with a most unusual expression of beautiful pain.

He accepted Duke's thanks gravely and went happily back to read the rest of his mail.

Mike did not share Jubal's annoyance at the avalanche of mail; he reveled in it, the insurance ads quite as much as the marriage proposals. His trip to the Palace had opened his eyes to the enormous variety in this world and he was resolved to grok it all. He could see that it would take him several centuries and that he must grow and grow and grow, but he was undaunted and in no hurry—he grokked that eternity and the ever-beautifully-changing now were identical.

He had decided not to reread the Encyclopedia Britannica; the flood of mail gave him brighter glimpses of the world. He read it, grokked what he could, remembered the rest for contemplation at night while the household slept.

From these nights of meditation he was beginning, he thought, to grok "business," and "money," and "buying," and "selling," and related unMartian activities—the articles in the Encyclopedia had always left him feeling unfilled, as (he now grokked) each one had assumed that he knew many things that he did not know. But there arrived in the mail, from Mr. Secretary General Joseph Edgerton Douglas, a check book and other papers, and his brother Jubal had taken great pains to explain to him what money was and how it was used.

Mike had failed utterly to understand it at first, even though Jubal showed him how to make out his first check, gave him "money" in exchange for it, taught him how to count it.

Then suddenly, with a grokking so blinding that he trembled and forced himself not to withdraw, he understood the abstract symbolic nature of money. These pretty pictures and bright medallions were not "money"; they were concrete symbols for an abstract idea which spread all through these people, all through their world. But these *things* were not money, any more than water shared in water ceremony was the growing-closer. Water was not necessary to the ceremony . . . and these pretty things were not necessary to money. Money was an *idea,* as abstract as an Old One's thoughts—money was a great structured symbol for balancing and healing and growing closer.

Mike was dazzled with the magnificent beauty of money.

The flow and change and countermarching of the symbols was another matter, beautiful in small, but reminding him of games taught to nestlings to encourage them to learn to reason correctly and grow. It was the total structure that dazzled him, the idea that an entire world could be reflected in one dynamic, completely interconnected, symbol structure. Mike grokked then that the Old Ones of this race were very old indeed to have composed such beauty, and he wished humbly that he might soon be allowed to meet one of them.

Jubal encouraged him to spend some of his money and Mike did so, with the timid, uncertain eagerness of a bride being brought to bed. Jubal suggested that he "buy presents for his friends" and Jill helped him with it, starting by placing arbitrary limits: only one present for each friend and a total cost that was not even a reciprocal filled-three of the sum that had been placed to his account—Mike's original intention had been to spend *all* of that pretty balance on his friends.

He quickly learned how difficult it is to spend money. There were so many things from which to choose, all of them wonderful and most of them incomprehensible. Surrounded by thick catalogs from Marshall Field's to the Ginza, and back by way of Bombay and Copenhagen, he felt smothered in a plethora of riches. Even the Sears & Montgomery catalog was too much for him.

But Jill helped. "No, Mike, Duke would not want a tractor."

"Duke likes tractors."

"Um, maybe—but he's got one, or Jubal has, which is the same thing. He might like one of those cute little Belgian unicycles—he could take it apart and put it together and shine it all day long. But even that is too expensive, what with the taxes. Mike dear, a present ought not to be very expensive—unless you are trying to get a girl to marry you, or something. Especially 'something.' But a present should show that you thought about it and considered that person's tastes. Something he would enjoy but probably would not buy for himself."

"How?"

"That's always the problem. Wait a minute. I just remembered something in this morning's mail—I hope Larry hasn't carted it off yet." She was back quickly. "Found it! Listen to this: 'Living Aphrodite: A de-luxe Album of Feminine Beauty in Gorgeous Stereo-Color by the World's Greatest Artists of the Camera. Notice: this item will *not* be sent by mail. It will be forwarded at purchaser's risk by prepaid express only. Orders cannot be accepted from addresses in the following states—' Um, Pennsylvania is on the verboten list—but don't let that worry you; if it is addressed to you, it will be delivered—and if I know Duke's vulgar tastes, this is just what he would like."

Duke did like it. It was delivered, not by express, but via the S.S. patrol car capping the house—and the next ad for the same item to arrive in the house boasted: "—exactly as supplied to the Man from Mars, by special appointment," which pleased Mike and annoyed Jill.

Other presents were just as difficult, but picking a present for Jubal was supremely difficult. Jill was stumped. What does one buy for a man who has everything—everything, that is to say, that he wants which money can buy? The Sphinx? Three Wishes? The fountain that Ponce de Leon failed to find? Oil for his ancient bones, or one golden day of youth? Jubal had long ago even foresworn pets, because he outlived them, or (worse yet) it was now possible that a pet would outlive him, be orphaned.

Privately they consulted the others. "Shucks," Duke told them, "didn't you know? The boss likes statues."

"Really?" Jill answered. "I don't see any sculpture around."

"That's because most of the stuff he likes isn't for sale. He says that the crud they're making nowadays looks like disaster in a junk yard and any idiot with a blow torch and astigmatism can set himself up as a sculptor."

Anne nodded thoughtfully. "I think Duke is right. You can tell what Jubal's tastes in sculpture are by looking at the books in his study. But I doubt if it will help much."

Nevertheless they looked, Anne and Jill and Mike, and Anne picked out three books as bearing evidence (to her eyes) of having been looked at most often. "Hmm . . ." she said. "It's clear that the Boss would like anything by Rodin. Mike, if you could buy one of these for Jubal, which one would you pick? Oh, here's a pretty one—'Eternal Springtime.'"

Mike barely glanced at it and turned the page. "This one."

"What?" Jill looked at it and shuddered. "Mike, that one is perfectly *dreadful!* I hope I die long before I look like that."

"That is beauty," Mike said firmly.

"Mike!" Jill protested. "You've got a depraved taste—you're worse than Duke. Or else you just don't know any better."

Ordinarily such a rebuke from a water brother, most especially from Jill, would have shut Mike up, forced him to spend the following night in trying to understand his fault. But this was art in which he was sure of himself. The portrayed statue was the first thing he had seen on Earth which felt like a breath of home to him. Although it was clearly a picture of a human woman it gave him a feeling that a Martian Old One should be somewhere around, responsible for its creation. "It is beauty," he insisted stubbornly. "She has her own face. I grok."

"Jill," Anne said slowly, "Mike is right."

"Huh? Anne! Surely you don't *like* that?"

"It frightens me. But Mike knows what Jubal likes. Look at the book itself. It falls open naturally to any one of three places. Now look at the pages—this page has been handled more than the other two. Mike has picked the Boss's favorite. This other one—'The Caryatid Who has Fallen under the Weight of Her Stone'—he likes almost as well. But Mike's choice is Jubal's pet."

"I buy it," Mike said decisively.

But it was not for sale. Anne telephoned the Rodin Museum in Paris on Mike's behalf and only Gallic gallantry and her beauty kept them from laughing in her face. *Sell* one of the Master's works? My dear lady, they are not only not for sale but they may not be reproduced. Non, non, non! Quelle idée!

But for the Man from Mars some things are possible which are not possible for others. Anne called Bradley; a couple of days later he called her back. As a compliment from the French government—no fee, but a strongly couched request that the present never be publicly exhibited— Mike would receive, not the original, but a full-size, microscopically-exact replica, a bronze photopantogram of "She Who Used to Be the Beautiful Heaulmière."

Jill helped Mike select presents for the girls, here she knew her ground. But when he asked her what he should buy for *her;* she not only did not help but insisted that he must not buy her anything.

Mike was beginning to realize that, while a water brother always spoke rightly, sometimes they spoke more rightly than others, i.e., that the English language had depths to it and it was sometimes necessary to probe to reach the right depth. So he consulted Anne.

"Go ahead and buy her a present, dear. She has to tell you that . . . but you give her a present anyhow. Hmm . . ." Anne vetoed clothes and jewelry, finally selected for him a present which puzzled him—Jill already smelled exactly the way Jill should smell.

The small size and apparent unimportance of the present, when it arrived, added to his misgivings—and when Anne let him whiff it before having him give it to Jill, Mike was more in doubt than ever; the odor was very strong and smelled not at all like Jill.

Nevertheless, Anne was right; Jill was delighted with the perfume and insisted on kissing him at once. In kissing her he grokked fully that this gift was what she wanted and that it made them grow closer.

When she wore it at dinner that night, he discovered that the fragrance truly did not differ from that of Jill herself; in some unclear fashion it simply made Jill smell more deliciously like Jill than ever. Still stranger, it caused Dorcas to kiss him and whisper, "Mike hon . . . the negligee is lovely and just what I wanted—but perhaps someday you'll give *me* perfume?"

Mike could not grok why Dorcas would want it, since Dorcas did not smell at all like Jill and therefore perfume would not be proper for her . . . nor, he realized, would he want Dorcas to smell like Jill; he wanted Dorcas to smell like Dorcas.

Jubal interrupted with: "Quit nuzzling the lad and let him eat his dinner! Dorcas, you already reek like a Marseilles cat house; don't wheedle Mike for more stinkum."

"Boss, you mind your own business."

It was all very puzzling—both that Jill could smell still more like Jill . . . and that Dorcas should wish to smell like Jill when she already smelled like herself . . . and that Jubal would say that Dorcas smelled like a cat when she did not. There was a cat who lived on the place (not as a pet, but as co-owner); on rare occasion it came to the house and deigned to accept a handout. The cat and Mike had grokked each other at once, and Mike had found its carniverous thoughts most pleasing and quite Martian. He had discovered, too, that the cat's name (Friedrich Wilhelm Nietzsche) was not the cat's name at all, but he had not told anyone this because he could not pronounce the cat's real name; he could only hear it in his head.

The cat did not smell like Dorcas.

Giving presents was a great goodness and the buying thereof taught Mike much about the true value of money. But he had not forgotten even momentarily that there were other things he was eager to grok. Jubal had put off Senator Boone's invitation to Mike twice without mentioning it to Mike and Mike had not noticed, since his quite different grasp of time made "next Sunday" no particular date.

But the next repetition of the invitation came by mail and was addressed to Mike; Senator Boone was under pressure from Supreme Bishop Digby to produce the Man from Mars and Boone had sensed that Harshaw was stalling him and might stall indefinitely.

Mike took it to Jubal, stood waiting. "Well?" Jubal growled. "Do you want to go, or don't you? You don't have to attend a Fosterite service. We can tell 'em to go to hell."

So a Checker Cab with a human driver (Harshaw refused to trust his life to an autocab) picked them up the next Sunday morning and delivered Mike, Jill, and Jubal to a public landing flat just outside the sacred grounds of Archangel Foster Tabernacle of the Church of the New Revelation.

xxiii

JUBAL HAD BEEN TRYING to warn Mike all the way to church; of what, Mike was not certain. He had listened, he always listened—but the landscape below them tugged for attention, too; he had compromised by storing what Jubal said. "Now look, boy," Jubal had admonished, "these Fosterites are after your money. That's all right, most everybody is after your money; you just have to be firm. Your money and the prestige of having the Man from Mars join their church. They're going to work on you—and you have to be firm about that, too."

"Beg pardon?"

"Damn it, I don't believe you've been listening."

"I am sorry, Jubal."

"Well . . . look at it this way. Religion is a solace to many people and it is even conceivable that some religion, somewhere, really is Ultimate Truth. But in many cases, being religious is merely a form of conceit. The Bible Belt faith in which I was brought up encouraged me to think that I was better than the rest of the world; I was 'saved' and they were 'damned' —we were in a state of grace and the rest of the world were 'heathens' . . . and by 'heathen' they meant such people as our brother Mahmoud. It meant that an ignorant, stupid lout who seldom bathed and planted his corn by the phase of the Moon could claim to know the final answers of the Universe. That entitled him to look down his nose at everybody else.

Our hymn book was loaded with such arrogance—mindless, conceited, self-congratulation on how cozy we were with the Almighty and what a high opinion he had of us and us alone, and what hell everybody else was going to catch come Judgment Day. We peddled the only authentic brand of Lydia Pinkham's—"

"Jubal!" Jill said sharply. "He doesn't grok it."

"Uh? Sorry. I got carried away. My folks tried to make a preacher out of me and missed by a narrow margin; I guess it still shows."

"It does."

"Don't rub it in, girl. I would have made a good one if I hadn't fallen into the fatal folly of reading anything I could lay hands on. With just a touch more self confidence and a liberal helping of ignorance I could have been a famous evangelist. Shucks, this place we're headed for today would have been known as the 'Archangel Jubal Tabernacle.' "

Jill made a face. "Jubal, please! Not so soon after breakfast."

"I mean it. A confidence man knows that he's lying; that limits his scope. But a successful shaman ropes himself first; he believes what he says —and such belief is contagious; there is no limit to his scope. But I lacked the necessary confidence in my own infallibility; I could never become a prophet . . . just a critic—which is a poor thing at best, a sort of fourth-rate prophet suffering from delusions of gender." Jubal frowned. "That's what worries me about Fosterites, Jill. I think that they are utterly sincere . . . and you and I know that Mike is a sucker for sincerity."

"What do you think they'll try to do to him?"

"Convert him, of course. Then get their hands on his fortune."

"I thought you had things fixed so that nobody could do that?"

"No, I just fixed it so that nobody could take it away from him against his will. Ordinarily he couldn't even give it away without the government stepping in. But giving it to a church, especially a politically powerful church like the Fosterites, is another matter."

"I don't see why."

Jubal sighed. "My dear, religion is practically a null area under the law. A church can do anything any other human organization can do— and has no restrictions. It pays no taxes, need not publish records, is effectively immune to search, inspection, or control—and a church is *any-thing* that calls itself a church. Attempts have been made to distinguish between 'real' religions entitled to these immunities and 'cults.' This can't be done, short of establishing a state religion . . . which is a cure worse than the disease. In any case, we haven't done it, and both under what's left of the old United States Constitution and under the Treaty of Federation, all churches are equal and equally immune—especially if they swing a big bloc of votes. If Mike is converted to Fosterism . . . and makes a will in favor of his church . . . and then 'goes to heaven' some sunrise, it will all be, to put it in the correct tautology, 'as legal as church on Sunday.' "

"Oh, dear! I thought we had him safe at last."

"There is no safety this side of the grave."

"Well . . . what are you going to do about it, Jubal?"

"Nothing. Just fret, that's all."

Mike stored their conversation without any effort to grok it. He recognized the subject as one of utter simplicity in his own language but amazingly slippery in English. Since his failure to achieve mutual grokking on this subject, even with his brother Mahmoud, with his admittedly imperfect translation of the all-embracing Martian concept as: "Thou art God," he had simply waited until grokking was possible. He knew that the waiting would fructify at its time; his brother Jill was learning his language and he would be able to explain it to her. They would grok together.

In the meantime the scenery flowing beneath him was a never-ending delight, and he was filled with eagerness for experience to come. He expected, or hoped, to meet a human Old One.

Senator Tom Boone was waiting to meet them at the landing flat. "Howdy, folks! And may the Good Lord bless you on this beautiful Sabbath. Mr. Smith, I'm happy to see you again. And you, too, Doctor." He took his cigar out of his mouth and looked at Jill. "And this little lady—didn't I see you at the Palace?"

"Yes, Senator. I'm Gillian Boardman."

"Thought so, m'dear. Are you saved?"

"Uh, I guess not, Senator."

"Well, it's never too late. We'll be very happy to have you attend the seekers' service in the Outer Tabernacle—I'll find a Guardian to guide you. Mr. Smith and the Doc will be going into the Sanctuary, of course." The Senator looked around.

"Senator—"

"Uh, what, Doc?"

"If Miss Boardman can't go into the Sanctuary, I think we had all better attend the seekers' service. She's his nurse and translator."

Boone looked slightly perturbed. "Is he ill? He doesn't look it. And why does he need a translator? He speaks English—I heard him."

Jubal shrugged. "As his physician, I prefer to have a nurse to assist me, if necessary. Mr. Smith is not entirely adjusted to the conditions of this planet. An interpreter may not be necessary. But why don't you ask *him?* Mike, do you want Jill to come with you?"

"Yes, Jubal."

"But— Very well, Mr. Smith." Boone again removed his cigar, put two fingers between his lips and whistled. "Cherub here!"

A youngster in his early teens came dashing up. He was dressed in a short robe, tights, and slippers, and had what appeared to be pigeon's wings (because they were) fastened, spread, on his shoulders. He was bareheaded, had a crop of tight golden curls, and a sunny smile. Jill thought that he was as cute as a ginger ale ad.

Boone ordered, "Fly up to the Sanctum office and tell the Warden on duty that I want another pilgrim's badge sent to the Sanctuary gate right away. The word is Mars."

" 'Mars,' " the kid repeated, threw Boone a Boy Scout salute, turned and made a mighty sixty-foot leap over the heads of the crowd. Jill realized why the short robe had looked so bulky; it concealed a personal jump harness.

"Have to be careful of those badges," Boone remarked. "You'd be surprised how many sinners would like to sneak in and sample a little of God's Joy without having their sins washed away first. Now we'll just mosey along and sight-see a little while we wait for the third badge. I'm glad you folks got here early."

They pushed through the crowd and entered the huge building, found themselves in a long high hallway. Boone stopped. "I want you to notice something. There is economics in everything, even in the Lord's work. Any tourist coming here, whether he attends seekers' service or not—and services run twenty-four hours a day—has to come in through here. What does he see? These happy chances." Boone waved at slot machines lining both walls of the hall. "The bar and quick lunch is at the far end, he can't even get a drink of water without running this gauntlet. And let me tell you, it's a remarkable sinner who can get that far without shedding his loose change.

"But we don't take his money and give him nothing. Take a look—" Boone shouldered his way to a machine, tapped the woman playing it on the shoulder; she was wearing around her neck a Fosterite rosary. "Please, Daughter."

She looked up, her annoyance changed to a smile. "Certainly, Bishop."

"Bless you. You'll note," Boone went on, as he fed a quarter into the machine, "that no matter whether it pays off in worldly goods or not, a sinner playing this machine is always rewarded with a blessing and an appropriate souvenir text."

The machine stopped whirring and, lined up in the windows, was: GOD—WATCHES—YOU.

"That pays three for one," Boone said briskly and fished the pay-off out of the receptacle, "and here's your souvenir text." He tore a paper tab off that had extruded from a slot, and handed it to Jill. "Keep it, little lady, and ponder it."

Jill sneaked a glance at it before putting it into her purse: *But the Sinner's belly is filled with filth*— N.R. XXII 17"

"You'll note," Boone went on, "that the pay-off is in tokens, not in coin—and the bursar's cage is clear back past the bar . . . and there is plenty of opportunity there to make love offerings for charity and other good works. So the sinner probably feeds them back in . . . with a blessing each time and another text to take home. The cumulative effect is tremendous, really tremendous! Why, some of our most diligent and pious sheep got their start right here in this room."

"I don't doubt it," agreed Jubal.

"Especially if they hit a jackpot. You understand, every combination is a complete sentence, a blessing. All but the jackpot. That's the three Holy Eyes. I tell you, when they see those eyes all lined up and starin' at 'em and all that manna from Heaven coming down, it really makes 'em think. Sometimes they faint. Here, Mr. Smith—" Boone offered Mike one of the slugs the machine had just paid. "Give it a whirl."

Mike hesitated. Jubal quickly took the proffered token himself— damn it, he didn't want the boy getting hooked by a one-armed bandit! "I'll try it, Senator." He fed the machine.

Mike really hadn't intended to do anything. He had extended his time sense a little and was gently feeling around inside the machine trying to discover what it did and why they were stopping to look at it. But he had been too timid to play it himself.

But when Jubal did so, Mike watched the cylinders spin around, noted the single eye pictured on each, and wondered what this "jackpot" was when all three were lined up. The word had only three meanings, so far as he knew, and none of them seemed to apply. Without really thinking about it, certainly without intending to cause any excitement, he slowed and stopped each wheel so that the eyes looked out through the window.

A bell tolled, a choir sang hosannas, the machine lighted up and started spewing slugs into the receptacle and on into a catch basin below it, in a flood. Boone looked delighted. "Well, bless you! Doc, this is your day! Here, I'll help you—and put one back in to take the jackpot off." He did not wait for Jubal but picked up one of the flood and fed it back in.

Mike was wondering why all this was happening, so he lined up the three eyes again. The same events repeated, save that the flood was a mere trickle. Boone stared at the machine. "Well, I'll be—blessed! It's not supposed to hit twice in a row. But never mind; it did—and I'll see that you're paid on both of them." Quickly he put a slug back in.

Mike still wanted to see why this was a "jackpot." The eyes lined up again.

Boone stared at them. Jill suddenly squeezed Mike's hand and whispered, "Mike . . . stop it!"

"But, Jill, I was seeing—"

"Don't talk about it. Just stop. Oh, you just wait till I get you home!"

Boone said slowly, "I'd hesitate to call this a miracle. Machine probably needs a repairman." He shouted, "Cherub here!" and added, "We'd better take the last one off, anyhow," and fed in another slug.

Without Mike's intercession, the wheels slowed down on their own and announced: "FOSTER—LOVES—YOU," and the mechanism tried, but failed, to deliver ten more slugs. A Cherub, older and with sleek black hair, came up and said, "Happy day. You need help?"

"Three jackpots," Boone told him.

" 'Three'?"

"Didn't you hear the music? Are you deaf? We'll be at the bar; fetch the money there. And have somebody check this machine."

"Yes, Bishop."

They left the Cherub scratching his head while Boone hurried them on through the Happiness Room to the bar at the far end. "Got to get you out of here," Boone said jovially, "before you bankrupt the Church. Doc, are you always that lucky?"

"Always," Harshaw said solemnly. He had not looked at Mike and did not intend to—he told himself that he did not *know* that the boy had anything to do with it . . . but he wished mightily that this ordeal were over and all of them home again.

Boone took them to a stretch of the bar counter marked "Reserved" and said, "This'll do—or would the little lady like to sit down?"

"This is fine." (—and if you call me "little lady" just once more I'll turn Mike loose on you!)

A bartender hurried up. "Happy day. Your usual, Bishop?"

"Double. What'll it be, Doc? And Mr. Smith? Don't be bashful; you're the Supreme Bishop's guests."

"Brandy, thank you. Water on the side."

"Brandy, thank you," Mike repeated . . . thought about it, and added, "No water for me, please." While it was true that the water of life was not the essence in the water ceremony, nevertheless he did not wish to drink water here.

"That's the spirit!" Boone said heartily. "That's the proper spirit with spirits! No water. Get it? It's a joke." He dug Jubal in the ribs. "Now what'll it be for the little lady? Cola? Milk for your rosy cheeks? Or do you want a real Happy Day drink with the big folks?"

"Senator," Jill said carefully, "Would your hospitality extend to a martini?"

"Would it! Best martinis in the whole world right here—we don't use any vermouth at all. We bless 'em instead. Double martini for the little lady. Bless you, son, and make it fast." He turned to the others. "We've just about time for a quick one, then pay our respects to Archangel Foster and on into the Sanctuary in time to hear the Supreme Bishop."

The drinks arrived and the jackpots' payoff. They drank with Boone's blessing, then he wrangled in a friendly fashion with Jubal over the three hundred dollars just delivered, insisting that all three prizes belonged to Jubal even though Boone had inserted the slugs on the second and third. Jubal settled it by scooping up all the money and depositing it in a love-offering bowl near them on the bar.

Boone nodded approvingly. "That's a mark of grace, Doc. We'll save you yet. Another round, folks?"

Jill hoped that someone would say yes. The gin was watered, she decided, and the flavor was poor; nevertheless it was starting a small flame of tolerance in her middle. But nobody spoke up, so she trailed along as Boone led them away, up a flight of stairs, past a sign reading: POSITIVELY NO SEEKERS NOR SINNERS ALLOWED ON THIS LEVEL—THIS MEANS *YOU!*

Beyond the sign was a heavy grilled gate. Boone said to it: "Bishop Boone and three pilgrims, guests of the Supreme Bishop."

The gate swung open. He led them around a curved passage and into a room.

It was a moderately large room, luxuriously appointed in a style that reminded Jill of undertakers' parlors, but it was filled with cheerful music. The basic theme seemed to be "Jingle Bells" but a Congo beat had been added and the arrangement so embroidered that its ancestry was not certain. Jill found that she liked it and that it made her want to dance.

The far wall of the room was clear glass and appeared to be not even that. Boone said briskly, "Here we are, folks—in the Presence." He knelt quickly, facing the empty wall. "You don't have to kneel, you're pilgrims —but do so if it makes you feel better. Most pilgrims do. And there *he* is . . . just as he was when he was called up to Heaven."

Boone gestured with his cigar. "Don't he look natural? Preserved by a miracle, his flesh incorruptible. That's the very chair he used to sit in when he wrote his Messages . . . and that's just the pose he was in when he went to Heaven. He never moved and he's never been moved—we just built the Tabernacle right around him . . . removing the old church, naturally, and preserving its sacred stones."

Opposite them about twenty feet away, facing them, seated in a big arm chair remarkably like a throne, was an old man. He looked as if he were alive . . . and he reminded Jill strongly of an old goat that had been on the farm where she had spent her childhood summers—yes, even to the out-thrust lower lip, the cut of the whiskers, and the fierce, brooding eyes. Jill felt her skin prickle; the Archangel Foster made her uneasy.

Mike said to her in Martian, *"My brother, this is an Old One?"*

"I don't know, Mike. They say he is."

He answered in Martian, *"I do not grok an Old One here."*

"I don't know, I tell you."

"I grok wrongness."

"Mike! Remember!"

"Yes, Jill."

Boone said, "What was he saying, little lady? What was your question, Mr. Smith?"

Jill said quickly, "It wasn't anything. Senator, can I get out of here? I feel faint." She glanced back at the corpse. There were billowing clouds above it and one shaft of light always cut through and sought out the face. The light changed enough so that the face seemed to change and the eyes seemed bright and alive.

Boone said soothingly, "It sometimes has that effect, the first time. But you ought to look at him from the seekers' gallery below us—looking up at him and with entirely different music. Entirely. Heavy music, with subsonics in it, I believe it is—reminds 'em of their sins. Now *this* room is a Happy Thoughts meditation chamber for high officials of the Church—I often come here and sit and smoke a cigar for an hour if I'm feeling the least bit low."

"Please, Senator!"

"Oh, certainly. You just wait outside, m'dear. Mr. Smith, you stay as long as you like."

Jubal said, "Senator, hadn't we best get on into the services?"

They all left. Jill was shaking and squeezed Mike's hand—she had been scared silly that Mike might do something to that grisly exhibit—and get them all lynched, or worse.

Two guards, dressed in uniforms much like the Cherubim but more ornate, thrust crossed spears in their path when they reached the portal of the Sanctuary. Boone said reprovingly, "Come, come! These pilgrims are the Supreme Bishop's personal guests. Where are their badges?"

The confusion was straightened out, the badges produced, and with them their door prize numbers. A respectful usher said, "This way, Bishop," and led them up wide stairs and to a center box directly facing the stage.

Boone stood back for them to go in. "You first, little lady." There followed a tussle of wills; Boone wanted to sit next to Mike in order to answer his questions. Harshaw won and Mike sat between Jill and Jubal, with Boone on the aisle.

The box was roomy and luxurious, with very comfortable, self-adjusting seats, ash trays for each seat and drop tables for refreshments folded against the rail in front of them. Their balcony position placed them about fifteen feet over the heads of the congregation and not more than a hundred feet from the altar. In front of it a young priest was warming up the crowd, shuffling to the music and shoving his heavily muscled arms back and forth, fists clenched, like pistons. His strong bass voice joined the choir from time to time, then he would lift it in exhortation:

"Up off your behinds! What are you waiting for? Gonna let the Devil catch you napping?"

The aisles were very wide and a snake dance was moving down the right aisle, across in front of the altar, and weaving back up the center aisle, feet stomping in time with the priest's piston-like jabs and with the syncopated chant of the choir. Clump, clump, *moan!* . . . clump, clump, *moan!* Jill felt the beat of it and realized sheepishly that it would be fun to get into that snake dance—as more and more people were doing under the brawny young priest's taunts.

"That boy's a comer," Boone said approvingly. "I've team-preached with him a few times and I can testify that he turns the crowd over to you already sizzlin'. The Reverend 'Jug' Jackerman—used to play left tackle for the Rams. You've seen him play."

"I'm afraid not," Jubal admitted. "I don't follow football."

"Really? You don't know what you're missing. Why, during the season most of the faithful stay after services, eat their lunches in their pews, and watch the game. The whole back wall behind the altar slides away and you're looking right into the biggest stereo tank ever built. Puts the plays right in your lap. Better reception than you get at home—and it's more of a thrill to watch with a crowd around you." He stopped and whistled. "Hey, Cherub! Over here!"

An usher hurried over. "Yes, Bishop?"

"Son, you ran away so fast when you seated us, I didn't have time to put in my order."

"I'm sorry, Bishop."

"Being sorry won't get you into Heaven. Get happy, son. Get that old spring into your step and stay on your toes. Same thing all around, folks? Fine!" He gave the order and added, "and bring me back a handful of my cigars—just ask the chief barkeep."

"Right away, Bishop."

"Bless you, son. Hold it—" The head of the snake dance was just about to pass under them; Boone leaned over the rail, made a megaphone of his hands and cut through the high noise level. "Dawn! Hey, *Dawn!*" A woman looked up; he caught her eye, motioned her to come up. She smiled. "Add a whiskey sour to that order. Fly."

The woman showed up quickly, as did the drinks. Boone swung a seat out of the box's back row and put it cornerwise in front of him so that she could visit more easily. "Folks, meet Miss Dawn Ardent. M'dear, that's Miss Boardman, the little lady down in the corner—and this is the famous Doctor Jubal Harshaw here by me—"

"Really? Doctor, I think your stories are simply divine!"

"Thank you."

"Oh, I really do. I put one of your tapes on my player and let it lull me to sleep almost every night."

"Higher praise a writer cannot expect," Jubal said with a straight face.

"That's enough, Dawn," put in Boone. "The young man sitting between them is . . . Mr. Valentine Smith the Man from Mars."

Her eyes came open wider as her mouth opened. "Oh, my goodness!"

Boone roared. "Bless you, child! I guess I really snuck up on you that time."

She said, "Are you *really* the Man from Mars?"

"Yes, Miss Dawn Ardent."

"Just call me 'Dawn.' Oh, goodness!"

Boone patted her hand. "Don't you know it's a sin to doubt the word of a Bishop? M'dear, how would you like to help lead the Man from Mars to the light?"

"Oh, I'd love it!"

(You certainly would, you sleek bitch! Jill said to herself.) She had been growing increasingly angry ever since Miss Ardent had joined them. The dress the woman was wearing was long sleeved, high necked, and opaque—and covered nothing. It was a knit fabric almost exactly the shade of her tanned skin and Jill was certain that skin was all there was under it—other than Miss Ardent, which was really quite a lot, in all departments. The dress was ostentatiously modest compared with the extreme styles worn by many of the female half of the congregation, some of whom, in the snake dance, seemed about to jounce out of their clothes.

Jill thought that, despite being dressed, Miss Ardent looked as if she had just wiggled out of bed and was anxious to crawl back in. With Mike. Quit squirming your carcass at him, you cheap hussy!

Boone said, "I'll speak to the Supreme Bishop about it, m'dear. Now you'd better get back downstairs and lead that parade. Jug needs your help."

She stood up obediently. "Yes, Bishop. Pleased to meet you, Doctor, and Miss Broad. I hope I'll see you again, Mr. Smith. I'll pray for you." She undulated away.

"A fine girl, that," Boone said happily. "Ever catch her act, Doctor?"

"I think not. What does she do?"

Boone seemed unable to believe his ears. "You don't *know?*"

"No."

"Didn't you hear her name? That's Dawn Ardent—she's simply the highest paid peeler in all Baja California, that's who she is. Men have committed suicide over her—very sad. Works under an irised spotlight and by the time she's down to her shoes, the light is just on her face and you really can't see anything else. Very effective. Highly spiritual. Would you believe it, looking at that sweet face now, that she used to be a most immoral woman?"

"I can't believe it."

"Well, she was. Ask her. She'll tell you. Better yet, come to a cleansing for seekers—I'll let you know when she's going to be on. When she confesses, it gives other women courage to stand up and tell about *their* sins. She doesn't hold anything back—and, of course, it does *her* good, too, to know that she's helping other people. Very dedicated woman now—flies her own car up here every Saturday night right after her last show, so as to be here in time to teach Sunday School. She teaches the Young Men's Happiness Class and attendance has more than tripled since she took over."

"I can believe *that,*" Jubal agreed. "How old are these lucky 'Young Men'?"

Boone looked at him and laughed. "You're not fooling me, you old devil—somebody told you the motto of Dawn's class: 'Never too old to be young.' "

"No, truly."

"In any case you can't attend her class until you've seen the light and gone through cleansing and been accepted. Sorry. This is the One True Church, Pilgrim, nothing at all like those traps of Satan, those foul pits of iniquity that call themselves 'churches' in order to lead the unwary into idolatry and other abominations. You can't just walk in here because you want to kill a couple hours out of the rain—you gotta be *saved* first. In fact— Oh, oh, camera warning." Red lights were blinking in each corner of the great hall. "And Jug's got 'em done to a turn. Now you'll see some action."

The snake dance picked up more volunteers and the few left seated were clapping the cadence and bouncing up and down. Pairs of ushers were hurrying to pick up the fallen, some of whom were quiet but others, mostly women, were writhing and foaming at the mouth. These were dumped hastily in front of the altar and left to flop like freshly caught fish. Boone pointed his cigar at a gaunt redhead, a woman apparently about forty whose dress was badly torn by her exertions. "See that woman? It has been at least a year since she has gone all through a service without being possessed by the Spirit. Sometimes Archangel Foster uses her mouth to talk to us . . . and when that happens it takes four husky acolytes to hold her down. She could go to heaven any time, she's ready. But she's needed here. Anybody need a refill? Bar service is likely to be a little slow once the cameras are switched on and things get lively."

Almost absently Mike let his glass be replenished. He shared none of Jill's disgust with the scene. He had been deeply troubled when he had discovered that the "Old One" had been no Old One at all but mere spoiled food, with no Old One anywhere near. But he had tabled that matter and was drinking deep of the events around him.

The frenzy going on below him was so Martian in its flavor that he felt both homesick and warmly at home. No detail of the scene was Martian, all was wildly different, yet he grokked correctly that this was a growing-closer as real as water ceremony, and in numbers and intensity that he had never met before outside his own nest. He wished forlornly that someone would invite him to join that jumping up and down. His feet tingled with an urge to merge himself with them.

He spotted Miss Dawn Ardent again in its van and tried to catch her eye—perhaps she would invite him. He did not have to recognize her by size and proportions even though he had noted when he had first seen her that she was exactly as tall as his brother Jill with very nearly the same shapings and masses throughout. But Miss Dawn Ardent had her own face, with her pains and sorrows and growings graved on it under her warm smile. He wondered if Miss Dawn Ardent might some day be willing to share water with him and grow closer. Senator Bishop Boone had made him feel wary and he was glad that Jubal had not permitted them to sit side by side. But Mike was sorry when Miss Dawn Ardent had been sent away.

Miss Dawn Ardent did not feel him looking at her. The snake dance carried her away.

The man on the platform had both his arms raised; the great cave became quieter. Suddenly he brought them down. "Who's *happy?*"

"WE'RE *HAPPY!*"

"Why?"

"GOD . . . *LOVES US!*"

"How d'you *know?*"

"FOSTER TOLD US!"

He dropped to his knees, raised one clenched fist. "Let's hear that Lion *ROAR!*"

The congregation roared and shrieked and screamed while he controlled the din using his fist as a baton, raising the volume, lowering it, squeezing it down to a subvocal growl, then suddenly driving it to crescendo that shook the balcony. Mike felt it beat on him and he wallowed in it, with ecstasy so painful that he feared that he would be forced to withdraw. But Jill had told him that he must not ever do so again, except in the privacy of his own room; he controlled it and let the waves wash over him.

The man stood up. "Our first hymn," he said briskly, "is sponsored by Manna Bakeries, makers of Angel Bread, the loaf of love with our Supreme Bishop's smiling face on every wrapper and containing a valuable premium coupon redeemable at your nearest neighborhood Church of the New Revelation. Brothers and Sisters, tomorrow Manna Bakeries with branches throughout the land start a giant, price-slashing sale of pre-equinox goodies. Send your child to school tomorrow with a bulging box of Archangel Foster cookies, each one blessed and wrapped in an appropriate text—and pray that each goodie he gives away may lead a child of sinners nearer to the light.

"And now let's really live it up with the holy words of that old favorite: 'Forward, Foster's Children!' All together—"

"Forward, Foster's Chil—*dren!*

Smash apart your foes . . .

Faith our Shield and Ar—*mor!*

Strike them down by rows—!"

"Second verse!"

"Make no peace with sin—*ners!*

God is *on* our side!"

Mike was so joyed by it all that he did not stop then to translate and weigh and try to grok the words. He grokked that the words were not of essence; it was a growing-closer. The snake dance started moving again, the marchers chanting the potent sounds along with the choir and those too feeble to march.

After the hymn they caught their breaths while there were announcements, Heavenly messages, another commercial, and the awarding of door prizes. Then a second hymn, "Happy Faces Uplifted," was sponsored by Dattelbaum's Department Stores where the Saved Shop in Safety since no merchandise is offered which competes with a sponsored brand—a children's Happy Room in each branch supervised by a Saved sister.

The young priest moved out to the very front of the platform and cupped his ear, listening—

"We . . . want . . . *Digby!*"

"Who?"

"We—Want—DIG—BY!"

"Louder! Make him hear you!"

"WE—WANT—DIG—*BY!*" Clap, clap, stomp, stomp. "WE—WANT—DIG—BY!" Clap, clap, stomp, stomp—

It went on and on, getting louder as the building rocked with it. Jubal leaned to Boone and said, "Much of that and you'll do what Samson did."

"Never fear," Boone told him, around his cigar. "Reinforced, fireproof, and sustained by faith. Besides, it's built to shake; it was designed that way. Helps."

The lights went down, curtains behind the altar parted, and a blinding radiance from no visible source picked out the Supreme Bishop, waving his clasped hands over his head and smiling at them.

They answered with the lion's roar and he threw them kisses. On his way to the pulpit he stopped, half raised one of the possessed women still writhing slowly near the altar, kissed her on the forehead, lowered her gently, started on—stopped again and knelt by the bony redhead. The Supreme Bishop reached behind him and a portable microphone was instantly placed in his hand.

He put his other arm around the woman's shoulders, placed the pickup near her lips.

Mike could not understand her words. Whatever they were, he was reasonably sure that they were not English.

But the Supreme Bishop was translating, interjecting his words quickly at each pause in the foaming spate.

"Archangel Foster is with us today—

"He is especially pleased with you. Kiss the sister on your right—

"Archangel Foster loves you all. Kiss the sister on your left—

"He has a special message for one of us here today."

The woman spoke again; Digby seemed to hesitate. "What was that? Louder, I pray you." She muttered and screamed at length.

Digby looked up and smiled. "His message is for a pilgrim from another planet—Valentine Michael Smith the Man from Mars! Where are you, Valentine Michael! Stand up, stand up!"

Jill tried to stop him but Jubal growled, "Easier to do it than to fight it. Let him stand up, Jill. Wave, Mike. Now you can sit down." Mike did so, amazed to find that they were now chanting: "Man from Mars! . . . Man from Mars!"

The sermon that followed seemed to be directed at him, too, but try as he would, he could not understand it. The words were English, or most of them were, but they seemed to be put together wrongly and there was so much noise, so much clapping, and so many shouts of "Hallelujah!" and "Happy Day!" that he grew quite confused. He was glad when it was over.

As soon as the sermon was finished, Digby turned the service back to the young priest and left; Boone stood up. "Come on, folks. We pull a sneak now—ahead of the crowd."

Mike followed along, Jill's hand in his. Presently they were going through an elaborately arched tunnel with the noise of the crowd left behind them. Jubal said, "Does this way lead to the parking lot? I told my driver to wait."

"Eh?" Boone answered. "It does if you go straight ahead. But we're going to see the Supreme Bishop first."

"What?" Jubal replied. "No, I don't think we can. It's time for us to get on home."

Boone stared. "Doctor, you don't mean that. The Supreme Bishop is waiting for us right now. You can't just walk out on him—you must pay your respects. You're his guests."

Jubal hesitated, then gave in. "Well— There won't be a lot of other people? This boy has had enough excitement for one day."

"Just the Supreme Bishop. He wants to see you privately." Boone ushered them into a small elevator concealed in the decorations of the tunnel; moments later they were waiting in a parlor of Digby's private apartments.

A door opened, Digby hurried in. He had removed his vestments and was dressed in flowing robes. He smiled at them. "Sorry to keep you waiting, folks—I just have to have a shower as soon as I come off. You've no notion how it makes you sweat to punch Satan and keep on slugging. So this is the Man from Mars? God bless you, son. Welcome to the Lord's

House. Archangel Foster wants you to feel at home here. He's watching over you."

Mike did not answer. Jubal was surprised to see how short the Supreme Bishop was. Lifts in his shoes when he was on stage? Or the way the lighting was arranged? Aside from the goatee he wore in evident imitation of the departed Foster, the man reminded him of a used-car salesman—the same ready smile and warm sincere manner. But he reminded Jubal of some one else, too . . . somebody— Got it! "Professor" Simon Magus, Becky Vesey's long-dead husband. Jubal relaxed a little and felt friendlier toward the clergyman. Simon had been as likable a scoundrel as he had ever known—

Digby had turned his charm on Jill. "Don't kneel, daughter; we're just friends in private here." He spoke a few words to her, startling Jill with a surprising knowledge of her background and adding earnestly, "I have deep respect for your calling, daughter. In the blessed words of Archangel Foster, God commands us first to minister to the body in order that the soul may seek the light untroubled by ills of the flesh. I know that you are not yet one of us . . . but your service is blessed by the Lord. We are fellow travelers on the road to Heaven."

He turned to Jubal. "You, too, Doctor. Archangel Foster has told us that the Lord commands us to be happy . . . and many is the time I have put down my crook, weary unto death with the cares and woes of my flock, and enjoyed an innocent, happy hour over one of your stories . . . and have stood up refreshed, ready to fight again."

"Uh, thank you, Bishop."

"I mean it deeply. I've had your record searched in Heaven—now, now, never mind; I know that you are an unbeliever but let me speak. Even Satan has a purpose in God's Great Plan. It is not yet time for you to believe. Out of your sorrow and heartache and pain you spin happiness for other people. This is all credited on your page of the Great Ledger. Now please! I did not bring you here to argue technology. We never argue with anyone, we wait until they see the light and then we welcome them. But today we shall just enjoy a happy hour together."

Digby then proceeded to act as if he meant it. Jubal was forced to admit that the glib fraud was a charming host, and his coffee and liquor and food were all excellent. Jubal noticed that Mike seemed decidedly jumpy, especially when Digby deftly cut him out of the herd and spoke with him alone—but, confound it, the boy was simply going to have to get used to meeting people and talking to them on his own, without Jubal or Jill or somebody to feed him his lines.

Boone was showing Jill some relics of Foster in a glass case on the other side of the room; Jubal covertly watched her evident reluctance with mild amusement while he spread paté de fois gras on toast. He heard a door click and looked around; Digby and Mike were missing. "Where did they go, Senator?"

"Eh? What was that, Doctor?"

"Bishop Digby and Mr. Smith. Where are they?"

Boone looked around, seemed to notice the closed door. "Oh, they've just stepped in there for a moment. That's a little retiring room used for private audiences. You were in it, weren't you? When the Supreme Bishop was showing you around."

"Um, yes." It was a small room with nothing in it but a chair on a dais—a "throne," Jubal corrected himself with a private grin—and a kneeler with an arm rest. Jubal wondered which one would use the throne and which one would be left with the kneeler—if this tinsel bishop tried to argue religion with Mike he was in for some shocks. "I hope they don't stay in there too long. We really do have to be getting back."

"I doubt if they'll stay long. Probably Mr. Smith wanted a word in private. People often do . . . and the Supreme Bishop is very generous that way. Look, I'll call the parking lot and have your cab waiting right at the end of that passageway where we took the elevator—that's the Supreme Bishop's private entrance. Save you a good ten minutes."

"That's very kind of you."

"So if Mr. Smith has something on his soul he wants to confess, we won't have to hurry him. I'll step outside and phone." Boone left.

Jill came over and said worriedly, "Jubal, I don't like this. I think we were deliberately maneuvered so that Digby could get Mike alone and work on him."

"I'm sure of it."

"Well? They haven't any business doing that. I'm going to bust right in on them and tell Mike it's time to leave."

"Suit yourself," Jubal answered, "but I think you're acting like a broody hen. This isn't like having the S.S. on our tails, Jill; this swindle is much smoother. There won't be any strong-arm stuff." He smiled. "It's my opinion that if Digby tries to convert Mike, they'll wind up with Mike converting him. Mike's ideas are pretty hard to shake."

"I still don't like it."

"Relax. Help yourself to the free chow."

"I'm not hungry."

"Well, I am . . . and if I ever turned down a free feed, they'd toss me out of the Authors' Guild." He piled paper-thin Virginia ham on buttered bread, added to it other items, none of them syntho, until he had an unsteady ziggurat, munched it and licked mayonnaise from his fingers.

Ten minutes later Boone had not returned. Jill said sharply, "Jubal, I'm not going to remain polite any longer. I'm going to get Mike out of there."

"Go right ahead."

She strode to the door. "Jubal, it's locked."

"Thought it might be."

"Well? What do we do? Break it down?"

"Only as a last resort." Jubal went to the inner door, looked it over carefully. "Mmm, with a battering ram and twenty stout men I might try it. But I wouldn't count on it. Jill, that door would do credit to a bank vault—it's just been prettied up to match the room. I've got one much like it for the fireproof off my study."

"What do we do?"

"Beat on it, if you want to. You'll just bruise your hands. I'm going to see what's keeping friend Boone."

But when Jubal looked out into the hallway he saw Boone just returning. "Sorry," Boone said. "Had to have the Cherubim hunt up your driver. He was in the Happiness Room, having a bite of lunch. But your cab is waiting for you, just where I said."

"Senator," Jubal said, "we've got to leave *now*. Will you be so kind as to tell Bishop Digby?"

Boone looked perturbed. "I could phone him, if you insist. But I hesitate to do so—and I simply cannot walk in on a private audience."

"Then phone him. We do insist."

But Boone was saved the embarrassment as, just then, the inner door opened and Mike walked out. Jill took one look at his face and shrilled, "Mike! Are you all right?"

"Yes, Jill."

"I'll tell the Supreme Bishop you're leaving," said Boone and went past Mike into the smaller room. He reappeared at once. "He's left," he announced. "There's a back way into his study." Boone smiled. "Like cats and cooks, the Supreme Bishop goes without saying. That's a joke. He says that 'good-by's' add nothing to happiness in this world, so he never says good-by. Don't be offended."

"We aren't. But we'll say good-by now—and thank you for a *most* interesting experience. No, don't bother to come down; I'm sure we can find our way out."

xxiv

ONCE THEY WERE IN THE AIR Jubal said, "Well, Mike, what did you think of it?"

Mike frowned. "I do not grok."

"You aren't alone, son. What did the Bishop have to say?"

Mike hesitated a long time, finally said, "My brother Jubal, I need to ponder until grokking is."

"Ponder right ahead, son. Take a nap. That's what I'm going to do."

Jill said suddenly, "Jubal? How do they get away with it?"

"Get away with what?"

"Everything. That's not a church—it's a madhouse."

It was Jubal's turn to ponder before answering. "No, Jill, you're mistaken. It *is* a church . . . and the logical eclecticism of our times."

"Huh?"

"The New Revelation and all doctrines and practices under it are all old stuff, *very* old. All you can say about it is that neither Foster nor Digby ever had an original thought in his life. But they knew what would sell, in this day and age. So they pieced together a hundred time-worn tricks, gave them a new paint job, and they were in business. A booming business, too. The only thing that scares me is that I might live to see it sell too well—until it was compulsory for everybody."

"Oh, no!"

"Oh, yes. Hitler started with less and all he had to peddle was hate. Hate always sells well, but for repeat trade and the long pull happiness is sounder merchandise. Believe me, I know; I'm in the same grift myself. As Digby reminded me." Jubal grimaced. "I should have punched him. Instead, he made me like it. That's why I'm afraid of him. He's good at it, he's clever. He knows what people want. Happiness. The world has suffered a long, bleak century of guilt and fear—now Digby tells them that they have nothing to fear, in this life or hereafter, and that God commands them to love and be happy. Day in, day out, he keeps pushing it: Don't be afraid, be *happy*."

"Well, that part's all right," Jill admitted, "and I concede that he works hard at it. But—"

"Piffle! He *plays* hard."

"No, he gave me the impression that he really is devoted to his work, that he had sacrificed everything else to—"

" 'Piffle!' I said. For Digby it's play. Jill, of all the nonsense that twists the world, the concept of 'altruism' is the worst. People do what they want to do, every time. If it sometimes pains them to make a choice—if the choice turns out to look like a 'noble sacrifice'—you can be sure that it is in no wise nobler than the discomfort caused by greediness . . . the unpleasant necessity of having to decide between two things both of which you would like to do when you can't do both. The ordinary bloke suffers that discomfort every day, every time he makes a choice between spending a buck on beer or tucking it away for his kids, between getting up when he's tired or spending the day in his warm bed and losing his job. No matter which he does he always chooses what seems to hurt least or pleasures most. The average chump spends his life harried by these small decisions. But the utter scoundrel and the perfect saint merely make the same choices on a larger scale. They still pick what pleases them. As Digby has done. Saint or scoundrel, he's not one of the harried little chumps."

"Which do you think he is, Jubal?"

"You mean there's a difference?"

"Oh, Jubal, your cynicism is just a pose and you know it! Of course there's a difference."

"Mmm, yes, you're right, there is. I hope he's just a scoundrel . . . because a saint can stir up ten times as much mischief as a scoundrel. Strike that from the record; you would just tag it as 'cynicism'—as if tagging it proved it wrong. Jill, what troubled you about those church services?"

"Well . . . *everything.* You can't tell *me* that *that* is worship."

"Meaning they didn't do things that way in the Little Brown Church in the Vale you attended as a kid? Brace yourself, Jill—they don't do it your way in St. Peter's either. Nor in Mecca."

"Yes, but— Well, none of them do it *that* way! Snake dances . . . slot machines . . . even a bar right in church! That's not reverence, it's not even dignified! Just disgusting."

"I don't suppose that temple prostitution was very dignified, either."

"Huh?"

"I rather imagine that the two-backed beast is just as sweaty and comical when the act is performed in the service of a god as it is under any other circumstances. As for those snake dances, have you ever seen a Shaker service? No, of course not and neither have I; any church that is agin sexual intercourse (as they were) doesn't last long. But dancing to the glory of God has a long and respected history. It doesn't have to be good dancing—according to eye-witness reports the Shakers could never have made the Bolshoi Ballet—it merely has to be enthusiastic. Do you consider the Rain Dances of our Southwest Indians irreverent?"

"No. But that's different."

"Everything always is—and the more it changes, the more it is the same. Now about those slot machines— Ever see a Bingo game in church?"

"Well . . . yes. Our parish used to hold them when we were trying to raise the mortgage. But we held them on Friday nights; we certainly didn't do such things during *church* services."

"So? Minds me of a married woman who was very proud of her virtue. She slept with other men only when her husband was away."

"Why, Jubal, the two cases aren't even slightly alike!"

"Probably not. Analogy is even slipperier than logic. But, 'little lady'—"

"Smile when you call me that!"

" 'It's a joke.' Why didn't you spit in his face? He had to stay on his good behavior no matter what we did; Digby wanted him to. But, Jill, if a thing is sinful on Sunday, it is sinful on Friday—at least it groks that way to an outsider, myself . . . or perhaps to a man from Mars. The only difference I can see is that the Fosterites give away, absolutely free, a scriptural text even if you lose. Could your Bingo games make the same claim?"

"Fake scripture, you mean. A text from the New Revelation. Boss, have you read the thing?"

"I've read it."

"Then you know. It's just dressed up in Biblical language. Part of it is just icky-sweet with no substance, like a saccharine tablet, more of it is sheer nonsense . . . and some of it is just hateful. None of it makes sense, it isn't even good morals."

Jubal was silent so long that Jill thought he had gone to sleep. At last he said, "Jill, are you familiar with Hindu sacred writings?"

"Mmm, I'm afraid not."

"The Koran? Or any other major scripture? I could illustrate my point from the Bible but I would not wish to hurt your feelings."

"Uh, I'm afraid I'm not much of a scholar, Jubal. Go ahead, you won't hurt my feelings."

"Well, I'll stick to the Old Testament, picking it to pieces usually doesn't upset people quite so much. You know the story of Sodom and

Gomorrah? And how Lot was saved from these wicked cities when Yahweh smote 'em with a couple of heavenly A-bombs?"

"Oh, yes, of course. His wife was turned into a pillar of salt."

"Caught by the fallout, perhaps. She tarried and looked back. Always seemed to me to be too stiff a punishment for the peccadillo of female curiosity. But we were speaking of Lot. Saint Peter describes him as a just, Godly, and righteous man, vexed by the filthy conversation of the wicked. I think we must stipulate Saint Peter to be an authority on virtue, since to him was given the keys to the Kingdom of Heaven. But if you search the only records concerning Lot, in the Old Testament, it becomes hard to determine exactly what Lot did or did not do that established him as such a paragon. He divided up a cattle range at his brother's suggestion. He got captured in a battle. When he was tipped off, he lammed out of town in time to save his skin. He fed and sheltered two strangers overnight but his conduct shows that he knew them to be V.I.P.s whether or not he knew they were angels—and by the Koran and by my own lights, his hospitality would have counted for more if he had thought they were just a couple of unworthy poor in need of a pad and a handout. Aside from these insignificant items and Saint Peter's character reference, there is just one thing that Lot did mentioned anywhere in the Bible on which we can judge his virtue —virtue so great, mind you, that heavenly intercession saved his life. See chapter nineteen of Genesis, verse eight."

"And what does it say?"

"Look it up when we get home. I don't expect you to believe *me*."

"Jubal! You're the most infuriating man I've ever met."

"And you're a very pretty girl and a fair cook, so I don't mind your ignorance. All right, I'll tell you—then you look it up anyhow. Some of Lot's neighbors came and beat on his door and wanted to meet these two blokes from out of town. Lot didn't fight with them; he offered 'em a deal instead. He had two young daughters, virgins—at least, such was his opinion—and he told this crowd of men that he would give them these two little girls and they could use them any way they liked—a gang shagging, a midnight revue, he *pleaded* with them to do any damn thing they pleased to his daughters . . . only please go 'way and quit beating on his door."

"Jubal . . . does it *really* say that?"

"Look it up yourself. I've modernized the language but the meaning is as unmistakable as a whore's wink. Lot offered to let a gang of men— 'young and old,' the Bible says—abuse two young virgins under his protection if only they wouldn't break down his door. Say!" Jubal leaned forward and beamed. "Maybe I should have tried that when the S.S. was breaking *my* door down! Maybe it would have got *me* into heaven—and Saint Peter knows my chances aren't too good otherwise." Then he frowned and looked worried. "No, it wouldn't have worked. The recipe plainly calls for 'virgins intactae'—and I wouldn't have known which two of you gals to offer those troopers."

"Hmmph! You won't find out from me."

"Possibly I couldn't find out from any of you. Even Lot might have been mistaken. But that's what he promised 'em—his virgin daughters, young and tender and scared—urged this street gang to rape them as much as they wished in any way they liked . . . if only they would leave *him* in peace!" Jubal snorted in disgust. "And the Bible cites *this* sort of scum as being a *righteous* man."

Jill said slowly, "I don't think that's quite the way we were taught it in Sunday School."

"Damn it, look it up! They probably gave you a Bowdlerized version. That's not the only shock in store for anybody who actually *reads* the Bible. Consider Elisha. It says here that Elisha was so all-fired holy that merely touching his bones restored a dead man to life. But he was a bald-headed old coot, like myself. So one day some children made fun of his baldness, just as you girls do. So God personally interceded and sent two bears to tear forty-two small children into bloody bits. That's what it says —second chapter of Second Kings."

"Boss, I never make fun of your bald head."

"Who was it sent my name to those hair-restorer quacks? Dorcas, maybe? Whoever it was, *God* knows—and she had better keep a sharp eye out for bears. I might turn pious in my dotage and start enjoying divine protection. But I shan't give you any more samples. The Bible is loaded with such stuff; read it and find out. Crimes that would turn your stomach are asserted to be either divinely ordered or divinely condoned . . . along with, I must add, a lot of hard common sense and some pretty workable rules for social behavior. I am not running down the Bible; it stacks up pretty well as sacred writings go. It isn't a patch on the sadistic, porno-graphic trash that goes by the name of sacred writings among the Hindus. Or a dozen other religions. But I'm not singling out any of *them* for condemnation, either; it is entirely conceivable that some one of these mutually contradictory mythologies is the literal word of God . . . that God is in truth the sort of bloodthirsty paranoid Who would rend to bits forty-two children for the crime of sassing one of his priests. Don't ask *me* about the Front Office's policies; I just work here. My point is that Foster's New Revelation that you're so contemptuous of is pure sweetness-and-light as scripture goes. Bishop Digby's Patron is a pretty good Joe; He wants people to be happy—happy here on Earth plus guaranteed eternal bliss in Heaven. He doesn't expect you to chastise the flesh here and now in order to reap rewards after you're dead. Oh no! this is the modern giant-economy package. If you like to drink and gamble and dance and wench—and most people do—come to church and do it under holy auspices. Do it with your conscience free of any trace of guilt. Really have fun at it. Live it up! Get happy!"

Jubal failed to look happy himself. He went on, "Of course there's a slight charge; Digby's God expects to be acknowledged as such—but that has been a foible of gods always. Anyone who is stupid enough to refuse to get happy on His terms is a sinner . . . and a sinner deserves anything that happens to him. But this is one rule common to all gods and goddesses throughout history; don't blame Foster and Digby, they didn't invent it. Their brand of snake oil is utterly orthodox in all respects."

"Boss, you sound as if you were halfway converted."

"Not me! I don't enjoy snake dances, I despise crowds, and I do not propose to let my social and mental inferiors tell me where I have to go on Sundays—and I wouldn't enjoy Heaven if that crowd is going to be there. I simply object to your criticizing them for the wrong things. As literature, the New Revelation stacks up about average—it should; it was composed by plagiarizing other scriptures. As for logic and internal consistency, these mundane rules do not apply to sacred writings and never have—but even on these grounds the New Revelation must be rated superior; it hardly ever bites its own tail. Try reconciling the Old Testament with the New Testament sometime, or Buddhist doctrine with Buddhist apocrypha. As morals, Fosterism is merely the Freudian ethic sugar-coated for people who can't take their psychology straight, although I doubt if the old lecher who wrote it—pardon me, 'was inspired to write it'—was aware of this. He was no scholar. But he *was* in tune with his times, he tapped the Zeitgeist. Fear and guilt and a loss of faith— How could he miss? Now pipe down, I'm going to nap."

"Who's been talking?"

" 'The woman tempted me.' " Jubal closed his eyes.

On reaching home they found that Caxton and Mahmoud had flown in together for the day. Ben had been disappointed to find Jill not at home on his arrival but he had managed to bear up without tears through the company of Anne, Miriam, and Dorcas. Mahmoud always visited for the avowed purpose of seeing his protégé, Mike, and Dr. Harshaw; however, he too had shown fortitude at having only Jubal's food, liquor, garden—and odalisques—to entertain him during his host's absence. He was lying face down with Miriam rubbing his back while Dorcas rubbed his head.

Jubal looked at him. "Don't get up."

"I can't, she's sitting on me. A little higher up, Miriam. Hi, Mike."

"Hi, my brother Stinky Dr. Mahmoud." Mike then gravely greeted Ben, and asked to be excused.

"Run along, son," Jubal told him.

Anne said, "Wait a minute, Mike. Have you had lunch?"

He said solemnly, "Anne, I am not hungry. Thank you," turned and went into the house.

Mahmoud twisted, almost unseating Miriam. "Jubal? What's troubling our son?"

"Yeah," said Ben. "He looks seasick."

"Let him alone and he'll get well. An overdose of religion. Digby has been working on him." Jubal sketched the morning's events.

Mahmoud frowned. "But was it necessary to leave him alone with Digby? This seems to me—pardon me, my brother!—unwise."

"He's not hurt. Stinky, he's got to learn to take such things in his stride. You've preached your brand of theology to him—I know you have; he's told me about it. Can you name me one good reason why Digby shouldn't have his innings? Answer me as a scientist, not as a Muslim."

"I am unable to answer anything other than as a Muslim," Dr. Mahmoud said quietly.

"Sorry. I recognize the correctness of your answer, even though I don't agree with it."

"But, Jubal, I used the word 'Muslim' in its exact, technical sense, not as a sectarian which Maryam incorrectly terms 'Mohammedan.' "

"And which I'm going to go right on calling you until you learn to pronounce 'Miriam' correctly! Quit squirming. I'm not hurting you."

"Yes, Maryam. *Ouch!* Women should not be so muscular. Jubal, as a scientist, I find Michael the greatest prize of my career. As a Muslim, I find in him a willingness to submit to the will of God . . . and this makes me happy for his sake, although I readily admit that there are great semantic difficulties and as yet he does not seem to grok what the English word 'God' means." He shrugged. "Nor the Arabic word 'Allah.' But as a man —and always a Slave of God—I love this young man, our foster son and water brother, and I would not have him come under bad influences. Quite aside from his creed, this Digby strikes me as a bad influence. What do *you* think?"

"*Olé!*" Ben applauded. "He's a slimy bastard—and the only reason I haven't been taking his racket apart in my column is that the Syndicate is afraid to print it. Stinky, keep talking that well and you'll have me studying Arabic and buying a rug."

"I hope so. But the rug is not necessary."

Jubal sighed. "I agree with both of you. I'd rather see Mike smoking marijuana than be converted by Digby. But I don't think there is the slightest chance of Mike's being taken in by that syncretic hodgepodge Digby peddles . . . and he's got to learn to stand up to bad influences. I consider *you* a good influence—but I don't really think you stand much more chance than Digby has—the boy has an amazingly strong mind of his own. Muhammad may have to make way for a new prophet."

"If God so wills it," Mahmoud answered calmly.

"That leaves no room for argument," Jubal agreed.

"We were discussing religion before you got home," Dorcas said softly. "Boss, did you know that women have souls?"

"They *do?*"

"So Stinky says."

"Maryam," Mahmoud explained, "wanted to know why we 'Mohammedans' thought only men had souls. So I cited the Writings."

"Miriam, I'm surprised at you. That's as vulgar a misconception as the notion that Jews sacrifice Christian babies in secret, obscene rites. The Koran is explicit in half a dozen places that entire families enter into Paradise, men and women together. For example, see 'Ornaments of Gold' —verse seventy, isn't it, Stinky?"

" 'Enter the Garden, ye and your wives, to be made glad.' That's as well as it can be put, in English," agreed Mahmoud.

"Well," said Miriam, "I had heard about the beautiful houris that Mohammedan men have for playthings when they go to heaven and that didn't seem to leave much room for wives."

"Houris aren't women," said Jubal. "They are separate creations, like djinni and angels. They don't need human souls, they are spirits to start with, eternal and unchanging and beautiful. There are male houris, too, or the male equivalent of houris. Houris don't have to earn their way into Paradise; they're on the staff. They serve endless delicious foods and pass around drinks that never give hangovers and entertain in other ways as requested. But the souls of human wives don't have to do any housework, any more than the men. Correct, Stinky?"

"Close enough, aside from your flippant choice of words. The houris—" He stopped and sat up so suddenly that he dumped Miriam. "Say! It's just possible that you girls *don't* have souls!"

Miriam sat up and said bitterly, "Why, you ungrateful dog of an infidel! Take that back!"

"Peace, Maryam. If you don't have a soul, then you're immortal anyhow and won't miss it. Jubal . . . is it possible for a man to die and not notice it?"

"Can't say. Never tried it."

"Could I have died on Mars and just dreamed that I came home? Look around you! A garden the Prophet himself would be pleased with. Four beautiful houris, passing around lovely food and delicious drinks at all hours. Even their male counterparts, if you want to be fussy. Is this Paradise?"

"I can guarantee that it isn't," Jubal assured him. "My taxes are due this week."

"Still, that doesn't affect *me.*"

"And take these houris— Even if we stipulate for the sake of argument that they are of beauty adequate to meet the specifications—after all, beauty is in the eye of the beholder—"

"They pass."

"And you'll pay for that, Boss," Miriam added.

"—there still remains," Jubal pointed out, "one more requisite attribute of houris."

"Mmmm—" said Mahmoud, "I don't think we need go into that. In Paradise, rather than a temporary physical condition, it would be a permanent spiritual attribute—more a state of mind. Yes?"

"In that case," Jubal said emphatically, "I am *certain* that these are not houris."

Mahmoud sighed. "In that case I'll just have to convert one."

"Why only one? There are still places left in the world where you can have the full quota."

"No, my friend. In the wise words of the Prophet, while the Legislations permit four, it is impossible for a man to deal justly with more than one."

"That's some relief. Which one?"

"We'll have to see. Maryam, are you feeling spiritual?"

"You go to hell! 'Houris' indeed!"

"Jill?"

"Give me a break," Ben protested. "I'm still working on Jill."

"Later, Jill. Anne?"

"Sorry. I've got a date."

"Dorcas? You're my last chance."

"Stinky," she said softly, "just how spiritual do you want me to feel?"

When Mike got inside the house, he went straight upstairs to his room, closed the door, got on the bed, assumed the foetal position, rolled up his eyes, swallowed his tongue, and slowed his heart almost to nothing. He knew that Jill did not like him to do this in the daytime, but she did not object as long as he did not do it publicly. There were so many things that he must not do publicly, but only this one really aroused her ire. He had been waiting to do this ever since he had left that room of terrible wrongness; he needed very badly to withdraw and try to grok all that had happened.

For he had done something else that Jill had told him not to—

He felt a very human urge to tell himself that it had been forced on him, that it was not his fault; but his Martian training did not permit him this easy escape. He had arrived at a cusp, right action had been required, the choice had been his. He grokked that he had chosen correctly. But his water brother Jill had forbidden this choice—

But that would have left him *no* choice. This was contradiction; at a cusp, choice is. By choice, spirit grows.

He considered whether or not Jill would have approved had he taken other action, not wasting food?

No, he grokked that Jill's injunction had covered that variant of action, too.

At this point the being sprung from human genes shaped by Martian thought, and who could never be either one, completed one stage of his growth, burst out and ceased to be a nestling. The solitary loneliness of predestined free will was then his and with it the Martian serenity to embrace it, cherish it, savour its bitterness, and accept its consequences. With tragic joy he knew that this cusp was his, not Jill's. His water brother could teach, admonish, guide—but choice at a cusp was not shared. Here was "ownership" beyond any possible sale, gift, hypothecation; owner and owned grokked fully, inseparable. He eternally *was* the action he had taken at cusp.

Now that he knew himself to be self he was free to grok ever closer to his brothers, merge without let. Self's integrity was and is and ever had been. Mike stopped to cherish all his brother selves, the many threes-fulfilled on Mars, both corporate and discorporate, the precious few on Earth—the as-yet-unknown powers of three on Earth that would be his to merge with and cherish now that at last long waiting he grokked and cherished himself.

Mike remained in his trance; there was still much to grok, loose ends and bits and pieces to be puzzled over and fitted into his growing pattern—all that he had seen and heard and been at the Archangel Foster Tabernacle (not just the cusp he had encountered when he and Digby had come face to face alone), why Bishop Senator Boone had made him warily uneasy without frightening him, why Miss Dawn Ardent had tasted like a water brother when she was not, the texture and smell of the goodness he had incompletely grokked in the jumping up and down and the wailing—

Jubal's stored conversation both coming and going—Jubal's words troubled him more than other details; he studied them with great care, compared them with what he had been taught as a nestling, making great effort to bridge between his two languages, the one he thought with and the one he now spoke and was gradually learning to think in, for some purposes. The human word "church" which turned up over and over again among Jubal's words gave him most knotty difficulty; there was no Martian concept of any sort to match it—unless one took "church" and "worship" and "God" and "congregation" and many other words and equated them all to the totality of the only world he had known during most of his growing-waiting . . . then forced the concept back awkwardly into English in that phrase which had been rejected (but by each differently) by Jubal, by Mahmoud, by Digby.

"Thou art God." He came closer to understanding it in English himself now, although it could never have the crystal inevitability of the Martian concept it stood for. In his mind he spoke simultaneously the English sentence and the Martian word and felt closer grokking. Repeating it like a student telling himself that the jewel is in the lotus he sank into nirvana untroubled.

Shortly before midnight he speeded up his heart, resumed normal breathing, ran down his engineering check list, found that all was in order, uncurled and sat up. He had been spiritually weary; now he felt light and gay and clear-headed, eager to get on with the many actions he saw spreading out before him.

He felt a puppyish need for company almost as strong as his earlier necessity for quiet. He stepped out into the upper hall, was delighted to encounter a water brother. *"Hi!"*

"Oh. Hello, Mike. My, you look chipper."

"I feel fine! Where is everybody?"

"Everybody's asleep but you and me—so keep your voice down. Ben and Stinky went home an hour ago and people started going to bed."

"Oh." Mike felt mildly disappointed that Mahmoud had left; he wanted to explain to him his new grokking. But he would do so, when next he saw him.

"I ought to be asleep, too, but I felt like a snack. Are you hungry?"

"Me? Sure, I'm hungry!"

"Good. You ought to be, you missed dinner. Come on, I know there's some cold chicken and we'll see what else." They went downstairs, loaded a tray lavishly. "Let's take it outside. It's still plenty warm."

"That's a fine idea," Mike agreed.

"Warm enough to swim if we wanted to—this is a real Indian summer. Just a second, I'll switch on the floods."

"Don't bother," Mike answered. "I'll carry the tray, I can see." He could see, as they all knew, in almost total darkness. Jubal said that his exceptional night-sight probably came from the conditions in which he had grown up, and Mike grokked that that was true but he grokked also that there was more to it than that; his foster parents had taught him to see. As for the night being warm enough, he would have been comfortable naked on Mount Everest, but he knew that his water brothers had very little tolerance for changes in temperature and pressure; he was always considerate of their weakness, once he had learned of it. But he was eagerly looking forward to snow—seeing for himself that each tiny crystal of the water of life was a unique individual, as he had read—walking barefoot in it, rolling in it.

In the meantime he was equally pleased with the unseasonably warm autumn night and the still more pleasing company of his water brother.

"Okay, you carry the tray. I'll switch on just the underwater lights. That'll be plenty to eat by."

"Fine." Mike liked having light coming up through the ripples; it was a goodness, a beauty, even though he did not need it. They picnicked by the pool, then lay back on the grass and looked at the stars.

"Mike, there's Mars. It is Mars, isn't it? Or is it Antares?"

"It is Mars."

"Mike? What are they doing on Mars?"

He hesitated a long time; the question was too wide in scope to pin down to the sparse English language. "On the side toward the horizon— the southern hemisphere—it is spring; the plants are being taught to grow."

" 'Taught to grow?' "

He hesitated only slightly. "Larry teaches plants to grow every day. I have helped him. But my people—the Martians, I mean; I grok now that *you* are my people—teach the plants another way. In the other hemisphere it is growing colder and the nymphs, those who have stayed alive through the summer, are being brought into the nests for quickening and more growing." He thought. "Of the humans we left at the equator when I came here, one has discorporated and the others are sad."

"Yes, I heard about it in the news."

Mike had not heard about it in the news; he had not known it until he was asked. "They should not be sad. Mr. Booker T. W. Jones Food Technician First Class is not sad; the Old Ones have cherished him."

"You knew him?"

"Yes. He had his own face, dark and beautiful. But he was homesick."

"Oh, dear! Mike . . . do you ever get homesick? For Mars?"

"At first I was very homesick," he answered truthfully. "I was lonely always." He rolled toward her and took her in his arms. "But now I am not lonely. I grok I shall never be lonely again."

"Mike darling—" They kissed, and went on kissing.

Presently his water brother said breathlessly. "Oh, my! That was almost worse than the first time."

"You are all right, my brother?"

"Yes. Yes indeed. Kiss me again."

Quite a long time later, by cosmic clock, she said, "Mike? Is that—I mean, 'Do you know—' "

"I know. It is for growing-closer. Now we grow closer."

"Well . . . I've been ready a long time—goodness, we *all* have, but . . . never mind, dear; turn just a little. I'll help."

As they merged, grokking together, Mike said softly and triumphantly: "Thou art God."

Her answer was not in words. Then, as their grokking made them ever closer and Mike felt himself almost ready to discorporate, her voice called him back: "Oh! . . . *Oh! Thou* art God!"

"We grok God."

XXV

ON MARS THE LITTLE HUMAN ADVANCE GUARD were building half-buried pressure domes for the larger male & female party that would arrive by next ship. This work went much faster than originally scheduled as the Martians were uncritically helpful. Part of the time saved was spent in preparing a preliminary estimate on a very long-distance plan to free the bound oxygen in the sands of Mars to make the planet more friendly to future human generations.

The Old Ones neither helped nor hindered these long-distance human plans; time was not yet. Their own meditations were approaching a violent cusp that would control the shape of Martian art for many millennia. On Earth elections continued as usual and a very advanced poet published a limited edition of verse consisting entirely of punctuation marks and spaces; *Time* magazine reviewed it and suggested that the Federation Assembly Daily Record could profitably be translated into the same medium. The poet was invited to lecture at the University of Chicago, which he did, clad in full formal evening dress lacking only trousers and shoes.

A colossal advertising campaign opened to sell more sexual organs of plants for human use and Mrs. Joseph ("Shadow of Greatness") Douglas was quoted as saying: "I would no more think of sitting down to eat without flowers on my table than without serviettes." A Tibetan swami from Palermo, Sicily, announced in Beverly Hills a newly discovered, ancient yoga discipline for ripple breathing which greatly increased both pranha and the cosmic attraction between the sexes. His chelas were required to assume the matsyendra posture dressed in hand-woven diapers while he read aloud from the Rig-Veda and an assistant guru checked through their purses in another room—nothing was ever stolen from the purses; the purpose was less immediate.

The President of the United States, by proclamation, named the first Sunday in November as "National Grandmothers' Day" and urged the grandchildren of America to say it with flowers. A funeral parlor chain was indicted for price-cutting. The Fosterite bishops, after secret conclave, announced the Church's second Major Miracle: Supreme Bishop Digby had been translated bodily to Heaven and spot-promoted to Archangel, ranking with-but-after Archangel Foster. The glorious news had been held up pending Heavenly confirmation of the elevation of a new Supreme Bishop, Huey Short—a compromise candidate accepted by the Boone faction after the lots had been cast repeatedly.

L'Unita and *Hoy* published identical doctrinaire denunciations of Short's elevation, *L'Osservatore Romano* and the *Christian Science Monitor* ignored it, *Times of India* snickered at it editorially, and the *Manchester Guardian* reported it without comment—the Fosterite congregation in England was small but extremely militant.

Digby was not pleased with his promotion. The Man from Mars had interrupted him with his work half finished—and that stupid jackass Short was certain to louse it up. Foster listened to him with angelic patience until Digby ran down, then said, "Listen, junior, you're an angel now—so forget it. Eternity is no time for recriminations. You too were a stupid jackass until you poisoned me. Afterwards you did well enough. Now that Short is Supreme Bishop he'll do all right, too; he can't help it. Same as with the Popes. Some of them were warts until they got promoted. Check with one of them, go ahead—there's no professional jealousy here."

Digby calmed down a little, but made one request.

Foster shook his halo in negation. "You can't touch him. You shouldn't have tried to touch him in the first place. Oh, you can submit a requisition for a miracle if you want to make a bloody fool of yourself. But, I'm telling you, it'll be turned down—you simply don't understand the System yet. The Martians have their own setup, different from ours, and as long as they need him, we can't touch him. They run their own show their own way—the Universe has variety, something for everybody—a fact you field workers often miss."

"You mean this punk can brush me aside and I've got to hold still for it?"

"I held still for the same thing, didn't I? I'm helping you now, am I not? Now look, there's work to be done and lots of it—before you can expect to be promoted again. The Boss wants performance, not gripes. If you need a Day off to get your nerve back, duck over to the Muslim Paradise and take it. Otherwise, straighten your halo, square your wings, and dig in. The sooner you start acting like an angel the quicker you'll start feeling angelic. Get Happy, junior!"

Digby heaved a deep ethereal sigh. "Okay, I'm Happy. Where do I start?"

Jubal was not disturbed by Digby's disappearance because he did not hear of it even as soon as it was announced, and, when he did hear, while he had a fleeting suspicion as to who had performed the miracle, he dismissed it from his mind; if Mike had had a finger in it, he had gotten away with it—and what happened to supreme bishops worried Jubal not at all as long as he didn't have to be bothered with it.

More important, his own household had gone through a considerable upset. In this case Jubal knew what had happened but did not care to inquire. That is to say, Jubal guessed what had happened but did not know with whom—and didn't want to know. A slight case of rape. Was "rape" the word? Well, "statutory rape." No, not that, either; Mike was of legal age and presumed to be able to defend himself in the clinches. Anyhow, it was high time the boy was salted, no matter how it had happened.

Jubal couldn't even reconstruct the crime from the way the girls behaved because their patterns kept shifting—sometimes ABC *vs* D, then BCD *vs* A . . . or AB *vs* CD, or AD *vs* CB, through all possible ways that four women can gang up on each other.

This continued for most of the week following that ill-starred trip to church, during which period Mike stayed in his room in a withdrawal trance so deep that Jubal would have pronounced him dead had he not seen it before. Jubal would not have minded it if the service around the place had not gone to hell in a bucket. The girls seemed to spend half their time tiptoeing in "to see if Mike was all right" and they were too preoccupied to cook properly, much less to be decent secretaries. Even rock-steady Anne—Hell, Anne was the worst of the lot! Absent-minded and subject to unexplained tears . . . and Jubal would have bet his life that if Anne were to witness the Second Coming, she would simply have memorized date, time, personae, events, and barometric pressure without batting her calm blue eyes.

Then late Thursday afternoon Mike woke himself up and suddenly it was ABCD in the service of Mike, "less than the dust beneath his chariot wheels." Inasmuch as the girls now found time to give Jubal perfect service too, Jubal counted his blessings and let it lie . . . except for a wry and very private thought that, if he had demanded a showdown, Mike could easily quintuple their salaries simply by dropping a post card to Douglas—but that the girls would just as readily have supported Mike.

Once domestic tranquility was restored Jubal did not mind that his kingdom was now ruled by a mayor of the palace. Meals were on time and (if possible) better than ever; when he shouted "Front!" the girl who appeared was bright-eyed, happy, and efficient—such being the case, Jubal did not give a hoot who rated the most side boys. Or girls.

Besides, the change in Mike was as interesting to Jubal as the restoration of peace was pleasant. Before that week Mike had been docile in a fashion that Jubal classed as pathological; now he was so self-confident that Jubal would have described it as cocky had it not been that Mike continued to be unfailingly polite and considerate.

But he accepted homage from the girls as if a natural right, he seemed older than his calendar age rather than younger, his voice had deepened, he spoke with disciplined forcefulness rather than timidly. Jubal decided that Mike had joined the human race; he could, in his mind, discharge this patient as cured.

Except (Jubal reminded himself) on one point: Mike still did not laugh. He could smile at a joke and sometimes did not ask to have them explained to him. Mike was cheerful, even merry—but he never laughed.

Jubal decided that it was not important. This patient was sane, healthy . . . and human. Short weeks earlier Jubal would have given odds against the cure taking place. He was honest and humble enough as a physician not to claim credit; the girls had had more to do with it. Or should he say "girl?"

From the first week of his stay Jubal had told Mike almost daily that he was welcome to stay . . . but that he should stir out and see the world as soon as he felt able. In view of this Jubal should not have been surprised when Mike announced one breakfast that he was leaving. But he was both surprised and, to his greater surprise, hurt.

He covered it by using his napkin unnecessarily before answering, "So? When?"

"We're leaving today."

"Um. Plural." Jubal looked around the table. "Are Larry and Duke and I going to have to put up with our own cooking until I can dig up more help?"

"We've talked that over," Mike answered. "Jill is going with me—nobody else. I do need somebody with me, Jubal; I know quite well that I *don't* know, as yet, how people do things out in the world. I still make mistakes; I need a guide, for a time. I think it ought to be Jill, because she wants to go on learning Martian—and the others think so, too. But if you want Jill to stay, then it could be someone else. Duke and Larry are each willing to help me, if you can't spare one of the girls."

"You mean I get a vote?"

"What? Jubal, it has to be your decision. We all know that."

(Son, you're a gent—and you've probably just told your first lie. I doubt if I could hold even Duke if you set your mind against it.) "I guess it ought to be Jill. But look, kids— This is still your home. The latch string is out."

"We know that—and we'll be back. Again we will share water."

"We will, son."

"Yes, Father."

"Huh?"

"Jubal, there is no Martian word for 'father.' But lately I have grokked that you are my father. And Jill's father."

Jubal glanced at Jill. "Mmm, I grok. Take care of yourselves."

"Yes. Come, Jill." They were gone before he left the table.

xxvi

IT WAS THE USUAL SORT OF CARNIVAL in the usual sort of town. The rides were the same, the cotton candy tasted the same, the flat joints practiced a degree of moderation acceptable to the local law in separating the marks from their half dollars, whether with baseballs thrown at targets, with wheels of fortune, or what—but the separation took place just the same. The sex lecture was trimmed to suit local opinions concerning Charles Darwin's opinions, the girls in the posing show wore that amount of gauze that local mores required, and the Fearless Fentons did their Death-Defying (in sober truth) Double Dive just before the last bally each night.

The ten-in-one show was equally standard. It did not have a mentalist, it did have a magician; it did not have a bearded lady, it did have a half-man half-woman; it did not have a sword swallower, it did have a fire eater. In place of a tattooed man the show had a tattooed lady who was also a snake charmer—and for the blow-off (at another half dollar per mark) she appeared "absolutely *nude!* . . . clothed only in bare living flesh in exotic designs!"—and any mark who could find one square inch below her neckline untattooed would be awarded a twenty dollar bill.

That twenty dollars had gone unclaimed all season, because the blow-off was honestly ballyhooed. Mrs. Paiwonski stood perfectly still and completely unclothed—other than in "bare, living flesh" . . . in this case a fourteen-foot boa constrictor known as "Honey Bun." Honey Bun was looped around Mrs. P. so strategically that even the local ministerial alliance could find no real excuse to complain, especially as some of their own daughters wore not nearly as much and covered still less while attending the carnival. To keep the placid, docile Honey Bun from being disturbed, Mrs. P. took the precaution of standing on a small platform in the middle of a canvas tank—on the floor of which were more than a dozen cobras.

The occasional drunk who was certain that all snake charmer's snakes were defanged and so tried to climb into the tank in pursuit of that undecorated square inch invariably changed his opinion as soon as a cobra noticed him, lifted and spread its hood.

Besides, the lighting wasn't very good.

However, the drunk could not have won the twenty dollars in any case. Mrs. P.'s claim was much sounder than the dollar. She and her late husband had had for many years a tattooing studio in San Pedro; when trade was slack they had decorated each other—and, eventually, at some minor inconvenience to herself, the art work on her was so definitively complete from her neck down that there was no possible room for an encore. She took great pride both in the fact that she was the most completely decorated woman in the world (and by the world's greatest artist, for such was her humbly grateful opinion of her late husband) and also in the certainty that every dollar she earned was honest.

She associated with grifters and sinners and did not hold herself aloof from them. But her own integrity was untouched. She and her husband had been converted by Foster himself, she kept her membership in San Pedro and attended services at the nearest branch of the Church of the New Revelation no matter where she was.

Patricia Paiwonski would gladly have dispensed with the protection of Honey Bun in the blow-off, not merely to prove that she was honest (that needed no proof, since she knew it was true) but because she was serene in her conviction that she was the canvas for religious art greater than any on the walls or ceilings of the Vatican. When she and George had seen the light, there was still about three square feet of Patricia untouched; before he died she carried a complete pictorial life of Foster, from his crib with the angels hovering around to the day of glory when he had taken his appointed place among the archangels.

Regrettably (since it might have turned many sinners into seekers of the light) much of this sacred history had to be covered up, the amount depending on the local lawmen. But she could show it in closed Happiness meetings of the local churches she attended, if the shepherd wanted her to, which he almost always did. But, while it was always good to add to Happiness, the saved did not need it; Patricia would rather have saved sinners. She couldn't preach, she couldn't sing, and she had never been called to speak in tongues—but she was a living witness to the light.

In the ten-in-one, her act came next to last, just before the magician; this gave her time to put away unsold photographs of herself (a quarter for black & white, half a dollar in color, a set of special photographs for five dollars in a sealed envelope sold only to marks who signed a printed form alleging that they were doctors of medicine, psychologists, sociologists, or other such entitled to professional material not available to the general public—and such was Patricia's integrity that she would not sell these even for ten dollars if the mark did not look the part; she would then ask to see his business card . . . no dirty dollars were going to put *her* kids through school!)—and also gave her time to slip behind the rear canvas and get herself and her snakes ready for the blow-off.

The magician, Dr. Apollo, performed on the last platform nearest to the canvas fly leading to the blow-off. He started by passing out to his audience a dozen shiny steel rings, each as wide as a plate; he invited them to convince themselves that each ring was solid and smooth. Then he had them hold the rings so that they overlapped. Dr. Apollo walked along the platform, reached out with his wand and tapped each overlap—the solid steel links formed a chain.

Casually he laid his wand in the air, rolled up his sleeves, accepted a bowl of eggs from his assistant, and started to juggle half a dozen of them. His juggling did not attract too many eyes; his assistant was more worthy of stares. She was a fine example of modern functional design and, while she wore a great deal more than did the young ladies in the posing show, nevertheless there seemed to be a strong probability that she was not tattooed anywhere.

The marks hardly noticed it when the six eggs became five, then four . . . three, two—until at last Dr. Apollo was tossing one egg in the air, with his sleeves still rolled up and a puzzled look on his face.

At last he said, "Eggs are getting scarcer every year," and tossed the remaining egg over the heads of those nearest the platform to a man in the back of the crowd. "Catch!"

He turned away and did not seem to notice that the egg never reached its destination.

Dr. Apollo performed several other tricks, while wearing always the same slightly puzzled expression and with the same indifferent patter. Once he called a young boy close to the platform. "Son, I can tell you what you are thinking. You think I'm not a real magician. And you're right! For that you win a dollar." He handed the kid a dollar bill. It disappeared.

The magician looked unhappy. "Dropped it? Well, hang on to this one." A second bill disappeared.

"Oh, dear! Well, we'll have to give you one more chance. Use both hands. Got it? All right, better get out of here fast with it—you should be home in bed anyhow." The kid dashed away with the money and the magician turned back and again looked puzzled. "Madame Merlin, what should we do now?"

His pretty assistant came up to him, pulled his head down by one ear, whispered in it. He shook his head. "No, not in front of all these people."

She whispered again; he looked distressed. "I'm sorry, friends, but Madame Merlin insists that she wants to go to bed. Will any of you gentlemen help her?"

He blinked at the rush of volunteers. "Oh, just two of you. Were any of you gentlemen in the Army?"

There were still more than enough volunteers; Dr. Apollo picked two and said, "There's an army cot under the end of the platform, just lift up the canvas—now, will you set it up for her here on the platform? Madame Merlin, face this way, please."

While the two men set up the cot, Dr. Apollo made passes in the air at his assistant. "Sleep . . . sleep . . . you are now asleep. Friends, she is in a deep trance. Will you two gentlemen who so kindly prepared her bed now place her on it? One take her head, one take her feet. Careful, now." In corpselike rigidity the girl was transferred to the cot.

"Thank you, gentlemen. But we ought not to leave her uncovered, should we? There was a sheet here, somewhere. Oh, there it is." The magician reached out, recovered his wand from where he had parked it, pointed to a table laden with props at the far end of his platform; a sheet detached itself from the pile and came to him. "Just spread this over her. Cover her head, too; a lady should not be exposed to public gaze while sleeping. Thank you. Now if you will just step down off the platform. Fine! Madame Merlin . . . can you hear me?"

"Yes, Doctor Apollo."

"You were heavy with sleep. Now you are resting. You feel lighter, much lighter. You are sleeping on a bed of clouds. You are floating away on clouds—" The sheet-covered form raised slowly up about a foot. "Wups! Don't get too light. We don't want to lose you."

In the crowd, a boy in his late teens explained in a loud whisper, "She's not under the sheet now. When they put the sheet over her, she went down through a trap door. That's just a light framework, doesn't weigh as much as the sheet. And in a minute he'll flip the sheet away and while he does, the framework will collapse and disappear. It's just a gimmick—anybody could do it."

Dr. Apollo ignored him and went on talking. "A little higher, Madame Merlin. Higher. There—" The draped form floated about six feet above the platform.

The smart youngster whispered to his friends, "There's a slender steel rod but you can't see it too easily. It's probably where one corner of the sheet hangs down there and touches the cot."

Dr. Apollo turned and requested his volunteers to remove the cot and put it back under the platform. "She doesn't need it now. She sleeps on clouds." He faced the floating form and appeared to be listening. "What? Louder, please. Oh? She says that she doesn't want the sheet—it's too heavy."

("Here's where the framework disappears.")

The magician tugged one corner of the sheet, snatched it away; the audience hardly noticed that the sheet disappeared without his bothering to gather it in; they were looking at Madame Merlin, still floating, still sleeping, six feet above the platform. The platform stood in the middle rear of the tent and the audience surrounded it on all sides. A companion of the boy who knew all about stage magic said, "Okay, Speedy, where's the steel rod?"

The kid said uncertainly, "You have to look where he doesn't want you to look. It's the way they've got those lights fixed to shine right into your eyes."

Dr. Apollo said, "That's enough sleep, fairy princess. Give me your hand. Wake up, wake up!" He took her hand, pulled her erect and helped her step down to the platform.

("You see? You saw how stiff she got down, you saw where she put her foot? *That's* where the steel rod went." The kid added with satisfaction, "Just a gimmick.")

The magician went on talking, "And now friends, if you will kindly give your attention to our learned lecturer, Professor Timoshenko—"

The talker cut in at once. "Don't go 'way! For this one performance only by arrangement with the Council of Colleges and Universities and with the permission of the Department of Safety and Welfare of this wonderful city, we are offering this twenty dollar bill absolutely free to any one of you—"

Most of the tip was turned into the blow-off. A few wandered around, then started to leave as most of the lights in the main tent were turned off. The freaks and other carnies started packing their props and slum preparatory to tear-down. There was a train jump coming in the morning and living tops would remain up for a few hours sleep, but canvas boys were already loosening stakes on the sideshow top.

Shortly the talker-owner-manager of the ten-in-one came back into the semi-darkened tent, having rushed the blow-off and spilled the last marks out the rear exit. "Smitty, don't go 'way. Got something for you." He handed the magician an envelope, which Dr. Apollo tucked away without looking at it. The manager added, "Kid, I hate to tell you this—but you and your wife ain't going with us to Paducah."

"I know."

"Well . . . look, don't take it hard, there's nothing personal about it —but I got to think of the show. We're replacing you with a mentalist team. They do a top reading act, then she runs a phrenology and mitt camp while he makes with the mad ball. We need 'em . . . and you know as well as I do you didn't have no season's guarantee. You were just on trial."

"I know," agreed the magician. "I knew it was time to leave. No hard feelings, Tim."

"Well, I'm glad you feel that way about it." The talker hesitated. "Smitty, do you want some advice? Just say no if you don't."

"I would like very much to have your advice," the magician said simply.

"Okay, you asked for it. Smitty, your tricks are good. Hell, some of 'em even got *me* baffled. But clever tricks don't make a magician. The trouble is you're not really with it. You behave like a carney—you mind your own business and you never crab anybody else's act and you're help-

ful if anybody needs it. But you're not a carney. You know why? You don't
have any feeling for what makes a chump a chump; you don't get inside his
mind. A real magician can make the marks open their mouths and catch
flies just by picking a quarter out of the air. That Thurston's levitation you
do—I've never seen it done any more perfectly but the marks don't warm
to it. No psychology. Now take me, for example. I can't even pick a
quarter out of the air—hell, I can barely use a knife and fork without
cutting my mouth. I got no act . . . except I got the one act that counts. I
know marks. I know where that streak of larceny is in his heart, I know
just how wide it is. I know what he hungers for, whether he knows it or
not. That's showmanship, son, whether you're a politician running for
office, a preacher pounding a pulpit . . . or a magician. You find out what
the chumps want and you can leave half your props in your trunk."

"I'm sure you're right."

"I know I am. He wants sex and blood and money. We don't give him
any real blood—unless a fire eater or a knife thrower makes a terrible
mistake. We don't give him money, either; we just encourage him to hope
for it while we take away a little. We don't give him any real sex. But why
do seven out of ten of a tip buy the blow-off? To see a nekkid broad, that's
why—and a chance to be paid a double sawbuck for lookin'—when maybe
they got one just as good or better at home, nekkid anytime they like. So
he don't see one and he don't get paid—and *still* we send him out happy.

"What else does a chump want? Mystery! He wants to think that the
world is a romantic place when he knows damn well it ain't. That's *your*
job . . . only you ain't learned how. Shucks, son, even the marks know
that your tricks are fake . . . only they'd like to believe they're real, and
it's up to you to help 'em believe, as long as they're inside the show. That's
what you lack."

"How do I get it, Tim? How do I learn what makes a chump tick?"

"Hell, I can't tell you that; that's the piece you have to learn for
yourself. Get out and stir around and be a chump yourself a while, maybe.
But— Well, take this notion you had of billing yourself as 'The Man from
Mars.' You *mustn't* offer the chump what he won't swallow. They've all
seen the Man from Mars, in pictures and on stereovision. Hell, I've seen
him myself. Sure, you look a bit like him, same general type, a casual
resemblance—but even if you were his twin brother, the marks know they
won't find the Man from Mars in a ten-in-one in the sticks. It's as silly as it
would be to bill a sword swallower as 'the President of the United States.'
Get me? A chump *wants* to believe—but he won't thank you to insult what
trace of intelligence he has. And even a chump has brains of a sort. You
have to remember that."

"I will remember."

"Okay. I talk too much—but a talker gets in the habit. Are you kids going to be all right? How's the grouch bag? Hell, I oughtn't to do it—but do you need a loan?"

"Thanks, Tim. We're not hurtin' any."

"Well, take care of yourself. Bye, Jill." He hurried out.

Patricia Paiwonski came in through the rear fly, wearing a robe. "Kids? Tim sloughed your act."

"We were leaving anyhow, Pat."

"I knew he was going to. He makes me so mad I'm tempted to jump the show myself."

"Now, Pat—"

"I mean it. I could take my act anywhere and he knows it. Leave him without a blow-off. He can get other acts . . . but a good blow-off that the clowns won't clobber is hard to find."

"Pat, Tim is right, and Jill and I know it. I don't have showmanship."

"Well . . . maybe so. But I'm going to miss you. You've been just like my own kids to me. Oh, dear! Look, the show doesn't roll until morning—come back to my living top and set awhile and visit."

Jill said, "Better yet, Patty, come into town with us and have a couple of drinks. How would you like to soak yourself in a big, hot tub, with bath salts?"

"Uh . . . I'll bring a bottle."

"No," Mike objected, "I know what you drink and we've got it. Come along."

"Well, I'll come—you're at the Imperial, aren't you?—but I can't come with you. I've got to be sure my babies are all right first and tell Honey Bun I'll be gone a bit and fix her hot water bottles. I'll catch a cab. Half an hour, maybe."

They drove into town with Mike at the controls. It was a fairly small town, without automatic traffic control even downtown. Mike drove with careful precision, exactly at zone maximum and sliding the little ground car into holes Jill could not see until they were through them. He did it without effort in the same fashion in which he juggled. Jill knew how it was done, had even learned to do it a bit herself; Mike stretched his time sense until the problem of juggling eggs or speeding through traffic was an easy one with everything in slow motion. Nevertheless she reflected that it was an odd accomplishment for a man who, only months earlier, had been baffled by tying shoelaces.

She did not talk. Mike could talk while on extended time, if necessary, but it was awkward to converse while they were running on different time rates. Instead she thought with mild nostalgia of the life they were leaving, calling it up in her mind and cherishing it, some of it in Martian concepts, more of it in English. She had enjoyed it very much. All her life, until she had met Mike, she had been under the tyranny of the clock, first as a little girl in school, then as a bigger girl in a much harder school, then under the unforgiving pressures of hospital routine.

The carnival had been nothing like that. Aside from the easy and rather pleasant chore of standing around and looking pretty several times a day from midafternoon to the last bally of the night, she never had anything she actually had to do at any set time. Mike did not care whether they ate once a day or six times, and whatever housekeeping she chose to do suited him. They had their own living top and camping equipment; in many towns they had never left the lot from arrival to tear-down. The carnival was a closed little world, an enclave, where the headlines and troubles of the outside world did not reach. She had been happy in it.

To be sure, in every town the lot was crawling with marks—but she had acquired the carney viewpoint; marks did not count—they might as well have been behind glass. Jill quite understood why the girls in the posing show could and did exhibit themselves in very little (and, in some towns, nothing, if the fix was solid) without feeling immodest . . . and without *being* immodest in their conduct outside the posing show. Marks weren't people to them; they were blobs of nothing, hardly seen, whose sole function was to cough up half dollars for the take.

Yes, the carnie had been a happy, utterly safe home, even though their act had flopped. It had not always been that way when first they left the safety of Jubal's home to go out into the world and increase Mike's education. They had been spotted more than once and several times they had had trouble getting away, not only from the press, but from the endless people who seemed to feel that they had a right to demand things of Mike, simply because he had the misfortune to be the Man from Mars.

Presently Mike had thought his features into more mature lines and had made other slight changes in his appearance. That, plus the fact that they frequented places where the Man from Mars would certainly not be expected (by the public) to go, got them privacy. About that time, when Jill was phoning home to give a new mailing address, Jubal had suggested a cover-up story—and a couple of days later Jill had read that the Man from Mars had again gone into retreat, this time in a Tibetan monastery.

The retreat had actually been "Hank's Grill" in a "nowhere" town, with Jill as a waitress and Mike as dishwasher. It was no worse than being a nurse and much less demanding—and her feet no longer hurt. Mike had a remarkably quick way of cleaning dishes, although he had to be careful not to use it when the boss was watching. They kept that job a week, then moved on, sometimes working, sometimes not. They visited public libraries almost daily, once Mike found out about them—Jill had discovered that Mike had taken for granted that Jubal's library contained a copy of every book on Earth. When he learned the marvelous truth, they had remained in Akron nearly a month. Jill did quite a lot of shopping that month, as Mike with a book was almost no company at all.

But Baxter's Combined Shows and Riot of Fun for All the Family had been the nicest part of their meandering trip. Jill recalled with an inner giggle the time in—what town?—no matter—when the entire posing show had been pinched. It wasn't fair, even by chumps' standards, since that concession always worked under precise prearrangement: bras or no bras; blue lights or bright lights; whatever the top town clown ordained. Nevertheless the sheriff had hauled them in and the local justice of the peace had seemed disposed not only to fine but to jail the girls as "vagrants."

The lot had closed down and most of the carnies had gone to the hearing, along with innumerable chumps slavering to catch sight of "shameless women" getting their come-uppance. Mike and Jill had managed to crowd against the back wall of the courtroom.

Jill had long since impressed on Mike that he must *never* do anything that an ordinary human could not do where it might be noticed. But Mike had grokked a cusp and had not discussed it with Jill.

The sheriff was testifying as to what he had seen, the details of this "public lewdness"—and he was enjoying it.

Mike had restrained himself, Jill admitted. In the midst of testimony both sheriff and judge became suddenly and completely without clothes of any sort.

She and Mike slipped quietly away during the excitement, and later she learned that the accused, all of them, had left, too, and nobody seemed disposed to object. Of course no one had connected the miracle with Mike, and he himself had never mentioned it to Jill—nor she to him; it was not necessary. The show had torn down at once and moved on two days early, to a more honest town where the rule was net bra and briefies and no beefs afterwards.

But Jill would treasure forever the expression on the sheriff's face, and his appearance, too, when it was plain to be seen that his sudden sag in front meant that the sheriff had been wearing a tight corset for his pride.

Yes, carnie days had been nice days. She started to speak to Mike in her mind, intending to remind him of how funny that hick sheriff had looked with creases from his girdle on his hairy pot belly. But she stopped.

Martian had no concept for "funny," so of course she could not say it. They shared a growing telepathic bond—but in Martian only.

("*Yes, Jill?*") his mind answered hers.

("*Later.*")

Shortly they approached the Imperial Hotel and she felt his mind slow down as he parked the car. Jill much preferred camping on the carnival grounds . . . except for one thing: bathtubs. Showers were all right, but nothing could beat a big tub of hot, hot water, climb into it up to your chin and *soak!* Sometimes they checked into a hotel for a few days and rented a ground car. Mike did not, by early training, share her fanatic enthusiasm for scrubbing; he was now as fastidiously clean as she was— but only because she had trained him to be; dirt did not annoy him. Moreover, he could keep himself immaculate without wasting time on washing or bathing, just as he never had to see a barber once he knew precisely how Jill wanted his hair to grow. But Mike, too, liked the time spent in hotels for the sake of baptism alone; he enjoyed immersing himself in the water of life as much as ever, irrespective of a non-existent need to clean and no longer with any superstitious feeling about water.

The Imperial was a very old hotel and had not been much even when new, but the tub in what was proudly called the "Bridal Suite" was satisfactorily large. Jill went straight to it as they came in, started to fill it—and was hardly surprised to find herself suddenly ready for her bath, even to pretty bare feet, except that her purse was still clutched under her arm. Dear Mike! He knew how she liked to shop, how pleased she was with new clothes; he gently forced her to indulge her childish weakness by sending to never-never any outfit which he sensed no longer delighted her. He would have done so daily had she not cautioned him that too many new clothes would make them conspicuous around the carnival.

"Thanks, dear!" she called out. "Let's climb in."

He had either undressed or caused his own clothes to go away— probably the former she decided; Mike found buying clothes for himself without interest. He still could see no possible reason for clothes other than for simple protection against the elements, a weakness he did not share. They got into the tub facing each other; she scooped up a handful of water, touched it to her lips, offered it to him. It was not necessary to speak, nor was the ritual necessary; it simply pleased Jill to remind them both of something for which no reminder could ever be necessary, through all eternity.

When he raised his head, she said, "The thing I was thinking of while you were driving was how funny that horrid sheriff looked in his skin."

"Did he look funny?"

"Oh, very funny indeed! It was all I could do to keep from laughing out loud. But I did not want us noticed."

"Explain to me why he was funny. I do not see the joke."

"Uh . . . dear, I don't think I can explain it. It was not a joke—not like puns and things like that which can be explained."

"I did not grok that he was funny," Mike said seriously. "In both those men—the judge and the lawman—I grokked wrongness. Had I not known that it would displease you, I would have sent them both away."

"Dear Mike." She touched his cheek. "Good Mike. Believe me, dearest, it was better far to do only what you did do. Neither one of them will ever live it down—and I'll bet that there won't be another attempt to arrest anyone for indecent exposure in that township for another fifty years. Let's talk about something else. I have been wanting to say that I am sorry, truly sorry, that your act didn't go over. I did my best in writing the patter for it, dear—but I guess I'm no showman, either."

"It was my lack, Jill. Tim speaks rightly—I don't grok the chumps. Nevertheless it has been good to be with Baxter's Combined Shows . . . I have grokked closer to the chumps each day."

"Only we must not call them chumps any longer, nor marks, now that we are no longer with it. Just people—not 'chumps.' "

"I grok that they are chumps."

"Yes, dear. But it isn't polite to say so."

"I will remember."

"Have you decided where we are going now?"

"No. When the time comes, I will know."

"Yes, dear." Jill reflected that Mike always did know. From his first change from docility to dominance he had grown steadily in strength and sureness—in all ways. The boy (he had seemed like a boy then) who had found it tiring to hold an ash tray in the air, could now not only hold her in the air (and it *did* feel like "floating on clouds"; that was why she had written it into the patter that way) while doing several other things and continuing to talk, but also could exert any other strength he needed—she recalled one very rainy lot where one of the trucks had bogged down. Twenty men were crowded around it, trying to get it free—Mike had added his shoulder . . . and the truck moved.

She had seen how it had happened; the sunken hind wheel had simply lifted itself out of the mud. But Mike, much more sophisticated now, had not allowed anyone to guess.

She recalled, too, when he had at last grokked that the injunction about "wrongness" being necessary before he could make things go away applied only to living, grokking things—her dress did not have to have "wrongness" for him to toss it away. The injunction was merely a precaution in the training of nestlings; an adult was free to do as he grokked.

She wondered what his next major change would be? But she did not worry about it; Mike was good and wise. All she could teach him were little details of how to live among humans—while learning much more from him, in perfect happiness, greater happiness than she had known since her father died. "Mike, wouldn't it be nice to have Dorcas and Anne and Miriam all here in the tub, too? And Father Jubal and the boys and—oh, our whole family!"

"It would take a bigger tub."

"Who minds a little crowding? But Jubal's pool would do nicely. When are we making another visit home, Mike? Jubal asks me every time I talk to him."

"I grok it will be soon."

"Martian 'soon'? Or Earth 'soon'? Never mind, darling, I know it will be when the waiting is filled. But that reminds me that Aunt Patty will be here soon and I do mean Earth 'soon.' Wash me off?"

She stood up, he stayed where he was. The soap lifted out of the soap dish, traveled all over her, replaced itself, and the soapy layer slathered into bubbles of lather. "Oooh! That's enough. You tickle."

"Rinse?"

"I'll just dunk." Quickly she squatted down, sloshed suds off her, stood up. "Just in time, too."

Someone was knocking at the outer door. "Dearie? Are you decent?"

"Coming, Pat!" Jill shouted and added as she stepped out of the tub, "Dry me, please?"

At once she was dry, leaving not even wet footprints on the bath mat. "Dear? You'll remember to put on some clothes before you come out? Patty's a lady—not like me."

"I will remember."

xxvii

JILL STOPPED TO GRAB a negligee from a well-stocked wardrobe, hurried out into the living room and let in Mrs. Paiwonski. "Come in, dear. We were grabbing baths in a hurry; he'll be right out. I'll get you a drink—

then you can have your second drink in the tub if you like. Loads of hot water."

"I had a shower after I put Honey Bun to bed, but—yes, I'd love a tub bath. But, Jill baby, I didn't come here to borrow your bath tub; I came because I'm just heartsick that you kids are leaving the show."

"We won't lose track of you." Jill was busy with glasses. The hotel was so old that not even the "Bridal Suite" had its own ice dispenser . . . but the night bellman, indoctrinated and subsidized, had left a carton of ice cubes. "Tim was right and you know he was. Mike and I have got to slick up our act a lot before we can hold up our end."

"Your act is okay. Needs a few laughs in it, maybe, but—Hi, Smitty." As Mike came in, she offered him a gloved hand. Mrs. Paiwonski always wore gloves away from the lot, and a high-necked dress and stockings. Dressed so, she looked like a middle-aged, most respectable widow, who had kept her figure trim in spite of her years—looked so, because she was precisely that.

"I was just telling Jill," she went on, "that you've got a good act, you two."

Mike smiled gently. "Now, Pat, you don't have to kid us. It stinks. We know it."

"No, it doesn't, dearie. Oh, maybe it needs a little something to give it some zing. A few jokes. Or, well, you could even cut down on Jill's costume a little. You've got an awful cute figure, hon."

Jill shook her head. "That wouldn't do it."

"Well, I saw a magician once that used to bring his assistant out dressed for the Gay 'Nineties—the eighteen-nineties, that is—not even her legs showing. Then he would disappear one garment after another. The marks loved it. But don't misunderstand me, dear—nothing unrefined. She finished . . . oh, in almost as much as you wear now."

"Patty," Jill said frankly, "I'd do our act stark naked if the clowns wouldn't close the show." As she said it, she realized that she meant it—and wondered how Graduate Nurse Boardman, floor supervisor, had reached the point where she could mean it?

Mike, of course— And she was quite happy about it.

Mrs. Paiwonski shook her head. "You couldn't, honey. The marks would riot. Just a touch more ginger ale, dear. But if you've got a good figure, why not use it? How far do you think I would get as a tattooed lady if I didn't peel off all they'll let me?"

"Speaking of that," Mike said, "you don't look comfortable in all those clothes, Pat. I think the aircooling in this dump has gone sour again—it must be at least eighty." He himself was dressed in a light robe, his concession to the easy-going conventions of carney good manners. Extreme heat, he had learned, affected him slightly, enough so that he sometimes had to adjust consciously his metabolism—extreme cold affected him not at all. But he knew that their friend was used to the real comfort of almost nothing and affected the clothes she now wore to cover her tattoos when out among the marks; Jill had explained it to him. "Why don't you get comfortable? 'Ain't nobody here but just us chickens.'" The latter, he knew, was a joke, an appropriate one for emphasizing that friends were in private—Jubal had tried to explain it to him, but failed. But Mike had carefully noted when and how the idiom could be used.

"Sure, Patty," Jill agreed. "If you're raw under that dress, I can get you something light and comfortable. Or we'll just make Mike close his eyes."

"Uh . . . well, I did slip back into one of my costumes."

"Then don't be stiff with friends. I'll get your zippers."

"Le'me get these stockings and shoes." She went on talking while trying to think how she could get the conversation around to religion, where she wanted it. Bless them, these kids were ready to be seekers, she was certain—and she had counted on the whole season to bring them around to the light . . . not just one hurried visit before they left. "The point about show business, Smitty, is that first you have to know what the marks want . . . and you have to know what it is you're giving them and how to make 'em like it. Now if you were a *real* magician— oh, I don't mean that you aren't skillful, dearie, because you *are.*" She tucked her carefully rolled hose in her shoes, loosened her garter belt and got out of it modestly, let Jill get her dress zippers. "I mean if your magic was real like you had made a pact with the Devil. That'd be one thing. But the marks know that it's clever sleight-of-hand. So you give 'em a light-hearted show to match. But did you ever see a fire eater with a pretty assistant? Heavens, a pretty girl would just clutter *his* act; the marks are standing around hoping he'll set fire to hisself, or blow up."

She snaked the dress over her head; Jill took it and kissed her. "You look more natural, Aunt Patty. Sit back and enjoy your drink."

"Just a second, dearie." Mrs. Paiwonski prayed mightily for guidance —wished that she were a preacher . . . or had even the gift of gab of a talker. Well, her pictures would just have to speak for themselves—and they would; that was why George had put them there. "Now *this* is what I've got to show the marks . . . this and my snakes, but this is more important. Have either one of you ever looked, really *looked,* at my pictures?"

"No," Jill admitted, "I guess not. We didn't want to stare at you, like a couple of marks."

"Then stare at me now, dears—because that's why George, bless his sweet soul safe in heaven, put them on me. To be stared at . . . and studied. Now right up here under my chin is the birth scene of our prophet, the holy Archangel Foster—just an innocent babe and maybe not knowing what Heaven had in store for him. But the angels knew—see 'em there around him? The next scene is his first miracle, when a young sinner in the country school he attended shot down a poor little birdie . . . and he picked it up and stroked it and it flew away unharmed. See the school house behind? Now it kind o' jumps a little and I'll have to turn my back. But all of 'em are dated for each holy event in his life." She explained how George had not had a bare canvas to work with when first the great opus was started—since they had both been sinners and young Patricia already rather much tattooed . . . how with great effort and inspired genius George had been able to turn "The Attack on Pearl Harbor" into "Armageddon," and "Skyline of New York" into "The Holy City."

"But," she admitted candidly, "even though every single one of them is a sacred picture now, it did kind of force him to skip around to find enough bare skin to record in living flesh a witness to each milestone in the earthly life of our prophet. Here you see him preaching on the steps of the ungodly theological seminary that turned him down—that was the first time he was arrested, the beginning of the Persecution. And on around, right on my spine, you see him smashing idolatrous images . . . and next you see him in jail, with the holy light streaming down on it. Then the Faithful Few bust into the jail—"

The Reverend Foster had realized early that, when it came to upholding religious freedom, brass knucks, clubs, and a willingness to tangle with cops was worth far more than passive resistance. His had been a church militant from scratch. But he had been a tactician, too; pitched battles were fought only where the heavy artillery was on the side of the Lord.

"—and they rescue him and tar & feather the idolatrous judge who put him there. Around in front here. Uh, you can't see it very well; my bra covers most of it. A shame."

("Michael, what does she want?")

("Thou knowest. Tell her.")

"Aunt Patty," Jill said gently, "you want us to look at all your pictures. Don't you?"

"Well . . . it's just as Tim says in the bally, George used up all the skin I have in making the story complete."

"If George went to all that work, I'm sure he meant for them to be seen. Take off your costume. I told you that I wouldn't mind working our own act stark naked if they'd let me—and ours is just entertainment. *Yours* has a purpose . . . a holy purpose."

"Well . . . all right. If you really want me to." She sang a silent hallelujah and decided that Foster himself was sustaining her—with blessed luck and George's pictures she would yet have these dear kids seeking the light.

"I'll unhook you."

("Jill—")

("No, Michael?")

("Wait.")

To her utter surprise and some fear Mrs. Paiwonski found that her spangled briefies and bra were gone! But Jill was surprised to find that her almost-new negligee followed the little costume into wherever and nowhere. Jill was only mildly surprised when Mike's robe disappeared, too; she chalked it up, correctly but not completely, to his catlike good manners.

Mrs. Paiwonski clutched at her mouth and gasped. Jill at once put her arms around her. "There, there, dear! It's all right, nobody's hurt." She turned her head and said, "Mike, you did it, you'll simply have to tell her."

"Yes, Jill. Pat—"

"Yes, Smitty?"

"You said a while ago that I wasn't a real magician, that my tricks were just sleight-of-hand. You were going to take off your costume anyhow —so I took it off for you."

"But *how?* And where *is* it?"

"Same place Jill's wrapper is—and my robe. Gone."

"But don't worry about it, Patty," put in Jill. "We'll replace it. Two more . . . and twice as pretty. Mike, you shouldn't have done it."

"I'm sorry, Jill. I grokked it was all right."

"Well . . . I suppose it is." Jill decided that Aunt Patty wasn't too upset—and certainly she would never tell; she was carney.

Mrs. Paiwonski was not worried by the loss of two scraps of costume, nor by her own nudity. Nor by the nakedness of the other two. But she was greatly troubled by a theological problem that she felt was out of her depth. "Smitty? That was *real* magic?"

"I guess you would call it that," he agreed, using the words most exactly.

"I'd rather call it a miracle," she said bluntly.

"You can call it that, too, if you want to. But it wasn't sleight-of-hand."

"I know that. You weren't even near me." She, who daily handled live cobras and who had more than once handled obnoxious drunks with her bare hands (to their sorrow), was not afraid. Patricia Paiwonski was not afraid of the Devil himself; she was sustained by her faith that she was saved and therefore invulnerable to the Devil. But she was uneasy for the safety of her friends. "Smitty . . . look me in the eye. Have you made a pact with the Devil?"

"No, Pat, I have not."

She continued to look into his eyes, then said, "You aren't lying—"

"He doesn't know how to lie, Aunt Patty."

"—so it's a miracle. Smitty . . . you *are* a holy man!"

"I don't know, Pat."

"Archangel Foster didn't know that he was a holy man until he reached his teens . . . even though he performed many miracles before that time. But you are a holy man; I can feel it." She thought. "I think I felt it when I first met you."

"I don't know, Pat."

"I think he may be," admitted Jill. "But he really doesn't know, himself. Michael . . . I think we've told her too much not to tell her more."

" 'Michael!' " Patty repeated suddenly. "The Archangel Michael, send down to us in human form."

"Aunt Patty, please! If he is, he doesn't know it—"

"He wouldn't necessarily know it. God performs his wonders in his own way."

"Aunt Patty, will you *please* wait and let me talk, just for a bit?"

Some minutes later Mrs. Paiwonski had accepted that Mike was indeed the Man from Mars, she had agreed to accept him as a man and to treat him as a man . . . while stating explicitly that she still held to her own opinion as to his true nature and why he was on Earth—explaining (somewhat fuzzily, it seemed to Jill) that Foster had been really and truly a man while he was on Earth, but had been also and *always* had been, an archangel, even though he had not known it himself. If Jill and Michael insisted that they were not saved, she would treat them as they asked to be treated—God moves in mysterious ways.

"I think you could properly call us 'seekers,' " Mike told her.

"Then that's enough, my dears! I'm sure you're saved—but Foster himself was a seeker in his early years. I'll help."

She had participated in another minor miracle. They had been seated in a circle on the rug. Jill lay back flat and suggested it to Mike in her mind. With no patter of any sort, with no sheet nor anything to conceal a non-existent steel rod, Mike lifted her. Patricia watched it with serene happiness, convinced that she was vouchsafed sight of a miracle. "Pat," Mike then said. "Lie flat."

She did so without argument, as readily as if he had been Foster. Jill turned her head. "Hadn't you better put me down first, Mike?"

"No, I can do it."

Mrs. Paiwonski felt herself gently lifted. She was not frightened by it; she simply felt overpowering religious ecstasy like heat lightning in her loins, making tears come to her eyes, the power of which she had not felt since, as a young woman, Holy Foster himself had touched her. When Mike moved them closer together and Jill put her arms around her, her tears increased, but her cries were the gentle sobs of happiness.

Presently he lowered them gently to the floor and found, as he expected, that he was not tired—he could not recall when last he had been tired.

Jill said to him, "Mike . . . we need a glass of water."

("????")

("Yes," her mind answered.)

("And?")

("Of elegant necessity. Why do you think she came here?")

("I knew. I was not sure that you knew . . . or would approve. My brother. My self.")

("My brother.")

Mike did not get up to fetch water. He sent a glass from the tray of drinks into the bathroom, had the tap fill it, returned it to Jill's hands. Mrs. Paiwonski watched this with almost absent-minded interest; she was beyond being astonished. Jill held the glass, said to her, "Aunt Patty, this is like being baptized . . . and like getting married. It's . . . a Martian thing. It means that you trust us and we trust you . . . and we can tell you anything and you can tell us anything . . . and that we are always partners, now and forever. It's very serious . . . and once done it can never be broken. If you broke it, we would have to die—at once. Saved or not. If we broke it— But we won't. But you don't have to share water with us if you don't want to—we'll still be friends. Now . . . if this in any way interferes with your faith, don't do it. We don't belong to your church even though you guessed that we did. We don't. We may never belong. 'Seekers' is the most you can call us now. Mike?"

"We grok," he agreed. "Pat, Jill speaks rightly. I wish we could say it to you in Martian, it would be clearer. But this is everything that getting married is . . . and a great deal more. We are free to offer water to you . . . but if there is any reason at all, in your religion or in your heart, not to accept—*don't drink it!"*

Patricia Paiwonski took a deep breath. She had made such a decision once before . . . with her husband watching . . . and had not funked it. And who was she to refuse a holy man? And his blessed bride? "I want it," she said firmly.

Jill took a sip. "We grow ever closer." She passed the glass to Mike.

He looked at Jill, then at Patricia. "I thank you for water, my brother." He took a sip. "Pat, I give you the water of life. May you always drink deep." He passed the glass to her.

Patricia took it. "Thank you. Thank you, oh my dears! The 'water of life'—oh, I love you both!" She drank thirstily.

Jill took the glass from her, finished it. "Now we grow closer, my brothers."

("*Jill?*")

("*Now!!!*)

Michael lifted his new water brother, wafted her in and placed her gently on the bed.

Valentine Michael Smith had grokked, when first he had known it fully, that physical human love—very human and very physical—was not simply a necessary quickening of eggs, nor was it mere ritual through which one grew closer; the act *itself* was a growing-closer, a very great goodness—and (so far as he knew) unknown even to the Old Ones of his former people. He was still grokking it, trying at every opportunity to grok its fullness. But he had long since broken through any fear that heresy lay in his suspicion that even the Old Ones did not know *this* ecstasy—he grokked already that these his new people held spiritual depths unique. Happily he tried to sound them, with no inhibitions from his childhood to cause him guilt or reluctance of any sort.

His human teachers had been unusually well qualified to instruct his innocence without bruising it. The result was as unique as he himself.

Jill was very pleased but not really surprised to find that "Aunt Patty" accepted as inevitable and necessary, and with forthright fullness, the fact that sharing water in a very ancient Martian ceremony with Mike led at once to sharing Mike himself in a human rite ancient itself. Jill was somewhat surprised (although still pleased) at Pat's continued calm acceptance when it certainly had been demonstrated to their new water brother that Mike was capable of more miracles than he had disclosed up to then. However, Jill did not then know that Patricia Paiwonski had met a holy man before—Patricia *expected* more of holy men. Jill herself was simply

serenely happy that a cusp had been reached and passed with right action
. . . and was ecstatically happy herself to grow closer as the cusp was
determined—all of which she thought in Martian and quite differently.

In time they rested and Jill had Mike treat Patty to a bath given by
telekinesis, and herself sat on the edge of the tub and squealed and giggled
when the older woman did. It was just play, very human and not at all
Martian; Mike had done it for Jill on the initial occasion almost lazily
rather than raise himself up out of the water—an accident, more or less.
Now it had become a custom, one that Jill knew Patty would like. It
tickled Jill to see Patty's face when she found herself being scrubbed all
over by gentle, invisible hands . . . and then, presently, dried in a whisk
with neither towel nor blast of air.

Patricia blinked. "After that I need a drink. A big one."

"Certainly, darling."

"And I *still* want to show you kids my pictures, all of them." Patricia
followed Jill out into the living room, Mike in train, and stood in the
middle of the rug. "But first look at me. Look at *me*, not at my pictures.
What do you see?"

With mild regret Mike stripped her tattoos off in his mind and looked
at his new brother without her decorations. He liked her tattoos very
much; they were peculiarly her own, they set her apart and made her a
self. They seemed to him to give her a slightly Martian flavor, in that she
did not have the bland sameness of most humans. He had already memorized them all and had thought pleasantly of having himself tattooed all
over, once he grokked what should be pictured. The life of his father,
water brother Jubal? He would have to ponder it. He would discuss it with
Jill—and Jill might wish to be tattooed, too. What designs would make Jill
more beautifully Jill? In the way in which perfume multiplied Jill's odor
without changing it?

What he saw when he looked at Pat without her tattoos pleased him
but not as much; she looked as a woman necessarily must look to be
woman. Mike still did not grok Duke's collection of pictures; the pictures
were interesting and had taught Mike that there was more variety in the
sizes, shapes, proportions, and colors of women than he had known up to
then and that there was some variety in the acrobatics involving physical
love—but having learned these simple facts he seemed to grok that there
was nothing more to be learned from Duke's prized pictures. Mike's early
training had made of him a very exact observer, by eye (and other senses),
but that same training had left him unresponsive to the subtle pleasures of
voyeurism. It was not that he did not find women (including, most emphatically, Patricia Paiwonski) sexually stimulating, but it lay not in seeing

them. Of his senses, smell and touch counted much higher—in which he was quasi-human, quasi-Martian; the parallel Martian reflex (as unsubtle as a sneeze) was triggered by those two, but could activate only in season—what must be termed "sex" in a Martian is as romantic as intravenous feeding.

But, having been invited to see her without her pictures, Mike did notice more sharply one thing about Patricia that he already knew: she had her own face, marked in beauty by her life. She had, he saw with gentle wonder, her own face even more than Jill had, and it made him feel toward Pat even more of an emotion he did not as yet call love but for which he used a Martian concept more discriminating.

She had her own odor, too, and her own voice, as all humans did. Her voice was husky and he liked to hear it even when he did not grok her meaning; her odor was mixed (he knew) with an unscrubbable trace of bitter muskiness from daily contact with snakes. It did not put him off; Pat's snakes were part of Pat as were her tattoos. Mike liked Pat's snakes and could handle the poisonous ones with perfect safety—and not alone by stretching time to anticipate and avoid their strikes. They grokked with him; he savored their innocent merciless thoughts—they reminded him of home. Other than Pat, Mike was the only person who could handle Honey Bun with pleasure to the boa constrictor. Her torpor was usually such that others could, if necessary, handle her—but Mike she accepted as a substitute for Pat.

Mike let the pictures reappear.

Jill looked at her and wondered why Aunt Patty had ever let herself be tattooed in the first place? She would really look rather nice—if she weren't a living comic strip. But she loved Aunt Patty for what she was, not the way she looked—and, of course, it did give her a steady living . . . at least until she got so old and haggard that the marks wouldn't pay to look at her even if all those pictures had been signed by Rembrandt. She hoped that Patty was tucking away plenty in the grouch bag—then she remembered that Aunt Patty was now one of Mike's water brothers (and her own, of course) and Mike's endless fortune gave Patty certain old-age insurance; Jill felt warmed by it.

"Well?" repeated Mrs. Paiwonski. "What do you see? How old am I, Michael?"

"I don't know," he said simply.

"Guess."

"I can't guess, Pat."

"Oh, go ahead. You won't hurt my feelings."

"Patty," Jill put in, "he really does mean that he can't guess. He hasn't had much chance to learn to judge ages—you know how short a time he's been on Earth. And besides that, Mike thinks of things in Martian years and Martian arithmetic. If it's time or figures, I keep track of it for him."

"Well . . . you guess, hon. Be truthful."

Jill looked Patty over again, noting her trim figure but also noting her hands and throat and the corners of her eyes—then discounted her guess by five years despite the Martian honesty she owed a water brother. "Mmm, thirtyish, give or take a year."

Mrs. Paiwonski laughed triumphantly. "That's just one bonus from the True Faith, my dears! Jill hon, I'm 'way into my forties. Just how far in we won't say; I've quit counting."

"You certainly don't look it."

"I know I don't. That's what Happiness does for you, dearie. After my first kid, I let my figure go to pot. I got quite a can on me—they invented the word 'broad' just to fit me. My belly always looked like four months gone, or worse. My busts hung down—and I've never had 'em lifted. You don't have to believe me; sure, I know a good plastic surgeon doesn't leave a scar . . . but on *me* it would *show*, dear; it would chop chunks out of two of my pictures.

"Then I seen the light! I got converted. Nope, not exercise, not diet—I still eat like a pig and you know it. Happiness, dear. Perfect Happiness in the Lord through the help of Blessed Foster."

"It's amazing," said Jill, and meant it. She knew women who had kept their looks quite as well (as she firmly intended to keep hers) . . . but in every case only through great effort. She knew that Aunt Patty was telling the truth about diet and exercise, at least during the time she had known her . . . and as a surgical nurse Jill knew exactly what was excised and where in a breast-lifting job; those tattoos had certainly never known a knife.

But Mike was not amazed. He assumed conclusively that Pat had learned how to think her body as she wished it, whether she attributed it to Foster or not. He was still trying to teach this control to Jill, but knew that she would have to perfect her knowledge of Martian before it could be perfect. No hurry, waiting would accomplish it. Pat went on talking:

"I wanted you to *see* what the Faith has done for me. But that's just outside; the real change is inside. Happiness. I've got to try to tell you about it. The good Lord knows that I'm not ordained and I'm not gifted with tongues . . . but I've got to try. And then I'll answer your questions if I can. The first thing that you've got to accept is that all the other so-called churches are traps of the Devil. Our dear Jesus preached the True

Faith, so Foster said and I truly believe. But, in the Dark Ages his words were deliberately twisted and added to and changed until Jesus wouldn't recognize 'em. And that is why Foster was sent down to Earth, to proclaim a New Revelation and straighten it out and make it clear again."

Patricia Paiwonski pointed her finger and suddenly looked very impressive, a priestess clothed in holy dignity and mystic symbols. "God wants us to be Happy. He filled the world with things to make us Happy if only we see the light. Would God let grape juice turn into wine if He didn't want us to drink and be joyful? He could just as easily let is stay grape juice . . . or turn it straight into vinegar that nobody could get a happy giggle out of. Ain't that *true?* Of course He don't mean you should get roaring drunk and beat your wife and neglect your kids . . . but He gave us good things to *use,* not abuse . . . and not to ignore. But if you feel like a drink or six, among friends who have seen the light, too, and it makes you want to jump up and dance and give thanks to the Lord on high for his goodness—why not? God made alcohol and he made feet— and he made 'em so you could put 'em together and be happy!"

She paused and said, "Fill 'er up again, honey; preaching is thirsty work—and not too strong on the ginger ale this time; that's good rye. And that ain't all. If God didn't want women to be looked at, he would have made 'em ugly—that's reasonable, isn't it? God isn't a cheat; He set up the game Himself—He wouldn't rig it so that the marks can't win, like a flat joint wheel in a town with the fix on. He wouldn't send anybody to Hell for losing in a crooked game.

"All right! God wants us to be Happy and he told us how: 'Love one another!' Love a snake if the poor thing needs love. Love thy neighbor if he's seen the light and has love in his heart . . . and the back of your hand only to sinners and Satan's corruptors who want to lead you away from the appointed path and down into the pit. And by 'love' he didn't mean namby-pamby old-maid-aunt love that's scared to look up from a hymn book for fear of seeing a temptation of the flesh. If God hated flesh, *why did He make so much of it?* God is no sissy. He made the Grand Canyon and comets coursing through the sky and cyclones and stallions and earthquakes—can a God who can do all that turn around and practically wet his pants just because some little sheila leans over a mite and a man catches sight of a tit? You know better, hon—and so do I! When God told us to love, He wasn't holding out a card on us; He *meant* it. Love little babies that always need changing and love strong, smelly men so that there will be more little babies to love—and in between go on loving because it's so *good* to love!

"Of course that don't mean to peddle it any more than a bottle of rye whiskey means I gotta get fighting drunk and clobber a cop. You can't sell love and you can't buy Happiness, no price tags on either one . . . and if you think there is, the way to Hell lies open to you. But if you give with an open heart and receive what God has an unlimited supply of, the Devil can't touch you. Money?" She looked at Jill. "Hon, would you do that water-sharing thing with somebody, say for a million dollars? Make it ten million, tax free."

"Of course not." ("*Michael, do you grok this?*")

("*Almost in fullness, Jill. Waiting is.*")

"You see, dearie? I knew what it meant, I knew love was in that water. You're seekers, very near the light. But since you two, from the love that is in you, did 'share water and grow closer,' as Michael says, I can tell you things I couldn't ordinarily tell a seeker—"

The Reverend Foster, self-ordained—or directly ordained by God, depending on authority cited—had an intuitive instinct for the pulse of his culture and his times at least as strong as that of a skilled carney sizing up a mark. The country and culture commonly known as "America" had had a badly split personality all through its history. Its overt laws were almost always puritanical for a people whose covert behavior tended to be Rabelaisian; its major religions were all Apollonian in varying degree—its religious revivals were often hysterical in fashion almost Dionysian. In the twentieth century (Terran Christian Era) nowhere on Earth was sex so vigorously suppressed as in America—and nowhere else was there such a deep interest in it.

The Reverend Foster had in common with almost every great religious leader of that planet two traits: he had an extremely magnetic personality ("hypnotist" was a word widely used by his detractors, along with others less mild) and, sexually, he did not fall anywhere near the human norm. Great religious leaders on Earth were always either celibate, or the antithesis. (*Great* leaders, the innovators—not necessarily the major administrators and consolidators.) Foster was not celibate.

Nor were any of his wives and high priestesses—the clincher for complete conversion and rebirth under the New Revelation usually included a ritual which Valentine Michael Smith at a later time was to grok as especially suited for growing-closer.

This, of course, was nothing new; in Terran history sects, cults, and major religions too numerous to list had used essentially the same technique—but not on a major scale in America before Foster's times. Foster was run out of town more than once before he "perfected" a method and organization that permitted him to expand his capric cult. In organization he borrowed as liberally from freemasonry, from Catholicism, from the Communist Party, and from Madison Avenue as he had borrowed from any and all earlier scriptures in composing his New Revelation . . . and he sugar-coated it all as a return to primitive Christianity to suit his customers. He set up an outer church which anybody could attend—and a person could remain a "seeker" with many benefits of the church for years. Then there was a middle church, which to all outward appearance was "The Church of the New Revelation," the happy saved, who paid their tithes, enjoyed all economic benefits of the church's ever-widening business tie-ins, and whooped it up in the endless carnival & revival atmosphere of Happiness, Happiness, Happiness! Their sins were forgiven—and henceforth very little was sinful as long as they supported their church, dealt honestly with their fellow Fosterites, condemned sinners, and stayed Happy. The New Revelation does not specifically encourage adultery; it simply gets rather mystical in discussing sexual conduct.

The saved of the middle church supplied the ranks of the shock troops when direct action was needed. Foster borrowed a trick from the early-twentieth-century Wobblies; if a community tried to suppress a budding Fosterite movement, Fosterites from elsewhere converged on that town until there were neither jails nor cops enough to cope with them—and the cops usually had had their ribs kicked in and the jails were smashed.

If some prosecutor were brave enough to push an indictment thereafter, it was almost impossible to make it stick. Foster (after learning his lesson under fire) saw to it that such prosecutions were indeed persecution under the letter of the law; not one conviction of a Fosterite *qua* Fosterite ever was upheld by the national Supreme Court—nor, later, by the High Court.

But, in addition to the overt church, there was the Inner Church, never named as such—a hard core of the utterly dedicated who made up the priesthood, all the church lay leaders, all keepers of keys and records and makers of policy. They were the "reborn," beyond sin, certain of their place in heaven, and sole participants of the inner mysteries—and the only candidates for direct admission to Heaven.

Foster selected these with great care, doing so personally until the operation got too big. He looked for men as much like himself as possible and for women like his priestess-wives—dynamic, utterly convinced (as he was himself convinced), stubborn, and free (or able to be freed, once their guilt and insecurity was purged) of jealousy in its simplest, most human meaning—and all of them potential satyrs and nymphs, as the secret inner church was that utterly Dionysian cult that America had never had and for which there was an enormous potential market.

But he was most cautious—if candidates were married, it had to be both spouses. An unmarried candidate had to be sexually attractive as well as sexually aggressive—and he impressed on his priests that the males must always equal or exceed in number the females. Nowhere is it admitted that Foster had studied the histories of earlier, somewhat parallel cults in America—but he either knew (or sensed) that most of such had foundered because the possessive concupiscence of their priests led to male jealousy and violence. Foster never made this error; not once did he keep a woman entirely to himself, not even the women he married legally.

Nor did he try too eagerly to expand his core group; the middle church, the one known to the public, offered plenty to slake the milder needs of the great masses of guilt-ridden and unhappy. If a local revival produced even two couples who were capable of "Heavenly Marriage" Foster was content—if it produced none, he let the other seeds grow and sent in a salted priest and priestess to nurture them.

But, so far as possible, he always tested candidate couples himself, in company with some devoted priestess. Since such a couple was already "saved" insofar as the middle church was concerned, he ran little risk—none, really, with the woman candidate and he always sized up the man himself before letting his priestess go ahead.

At the time she was saved, Patricia Paiwonski was still young, married, and "very happy, very happy." She had her first child, she looked up to and admired her much older husband. George Paiwonski was a generous, very affectionate man. He did have one weakness, which often left him too drunk to show his affection after a long day . . . but his tattooing needle was still steady and his eye sharp. Patty counted herself a faithful wife and, on the whole, a lucky one—true, George occasionally got affectionate with a female client . . . quite affectionate if it was early in the day—and, of course, some tattooing required privacy, especially with ladies. Patty was tolerant . . . besides, she sometimes herself made a date with a male client, especially after George got to hitting the bottle more and more.

Nevertheless there was a lack in her life, one which was not filled even when an especially grateful client made her the odd gift of a bull snake—shipping out on a freighter, he said, and couldn't keep it any longer. She had always liked pets and had none of the vulgar phobia about snakes; she made a home for it in their show window facing the street, and George made a beautiful four-color picture to back it up: "Don't Tread on Me!" His new design turned out to be very popular.

Presently she had more snakes and they were quite a comfort to her. But she was the daughter of an Ulster Protestant and a girl from Cork; the armed truce between her parents had left her with no religion.

She was already a "seeker" when Foster preached in San Pedro; she had managed to get George to go a few Sundays but he had not yet seen the light.

Foster brought them the light, they made their confessions the same day. When Foster returned six months later for a quick check on how his branch was doing, the Paiwonskis were so dedicated that he gave them personal attention.

"I never had a minute's trouble with George from the day he saw the holy light," she told Mike and Jill. "Of course, he still drank . . . but he drank in church and never too much. When our holy leader returned, George had already started his Great Project. Naturally we wanted to show it to Foster, if he could find time—" Mrs. Paiwonski hesitated. "Kids, I really ought not to be telling you any of this."

"Then don't," Jill said emphatically. "Patty darling, neither of us want you *ever* to do or say anything you don't feel easy about. 'Sharing water' has to be easy and natural . . . and waiting until it comes easy for you is easy for us."

"Uh . . . but I *do* want to share it! Look, darlings, I trust you both . . . utterly. But I just want you to remember that this is Church things I'm telling you, so you mustn't ever tell anyone . . . just as I wouldn't tell anything about *you.*"

Mike nodded. "Here on Earth we sometimes call it 'water brother' business. On Mars there's no problem . . . but here I grok that there sometimes is. 'Water brother' business you don't repeat."

"I . . . I 'grok.' That's a funny word, but I'm learning it. All right, darlings, this is 'water brother' business. Did you know that *all* Fosterites are tattooed? *Real* Church members I mean, the ones who are eternally saved forever and ever and a day—like me? Oh, I don't mean tattooed all over, the way I am, but—look, see that? Right over my heart . . . see? That's Foster's holy kiss. George worked it into the design so that it looks like part of the picture it's in . . . so that nobody could guess unless I told 'em. But it's his kiss—and *Foster put it there hisself!*" She looked ecstatically proud.

They both examined it. "It *is* a kiss mark," Jill said wonderingly. "Just like somebody had kissed you there wearing lipstick. But, until you showed us, I thought it was part of that sunset."

"Yes, indeedy, that's why George did it. Because you don't go showing Foster's kiss to anyone who doesn't wear Foster's kiss—and I never have, up to now. But," she insisted, "I'm sure you're going to wear one, both of you, someday—and when you do, I want to be the one to tattoo 'em on."

Jill said, "I don't quite understand, Patty. I can see that it's wonderful for you to have been kissed by Foster—but how can he ever kiss *us?* After all, he's—up in Heaven."

"Yes, dearie, he is. But let me explain. Any ordained priest or priestess can give you Foster's kiss. It means God's in your heart. God is part of you . . . forever."

Mike was suddenly intent. "Thou art God!"

"Huh, Michael? Well, that is a strange way to say it—I've never heard a priest put it quite that way. But that does sort of express it . . . God is in you and of you and with you, and the Devil can't ever get at you."

"Yes," agreed Mike. "You grok God." He thought happily that this was nearer to putting the concept across than he had ever managed before . . . except that Jill was learning it, in Martian. Which was inevitable.

"That's the idea, Michael. God . . . groks you—and you are married in Holy Love and eternal Happiness to His Church. The priest, or maybe priestess—it can be either—kisses you and then the kiss mark is tattooed on to show that it's forever. Of course it doesn't have to be this big—mine is just exactly the size and shape of Foster's blessed lips—and the kiss can be placed anywhere to shield from sinful eyes. Lots of men have a patch of skull shaved and then wear a hat or a bandage until the hair grows out. Or any spot where it's blessed certain it won't be seen unless you want it to be. You mustn't sit or stand on it—but anywhere else is okay. Then you show it when you go into a closed Happiness gathering of the eternally saved."

"I've heard of Happiness meetings," Jill commented, "but I've never known quite what they are."

"Well," Mrs. Paiwonski said judicially, "there are Happiness meetings and Happiness meetings. The ones for ordinary members, who are saved but might backslide, are an awful lot of fun—grand parties with only the amount of praying that comes natural and happily, and plenty of whoop-it-up that makes a good party. Maybe, even, a little real lovin'—but that's frowned on there and you'd better be mighty careful who and how, because you mustn't be a seed of dissension among the brethren. The Church is *very* strict about keeping things in their proper place.

"But a Happiness meeting for the eternally saved—well, you don't have to be careful because there won't be *anybody* there who can sin—all past and done with. If you want to drink and pass out . . . okay, it's God's will or you wouldn't want to. You want to kneel down and pray, or lift up your voice in song—or tear off your clothes and dance; it's God's will. Although," she added, "you might not have any clothes on at all, because there can't possibly be anybody there who would see anything wrong in it."

"It sounds like quite a party," said Jill.

"Oh, it is, it is—always! And you're filled with heavenly bliss the whole time. And if you wake up in the morning on a couch with one of the eternally saved brethren, you know he's there because God willed it to make you all blessedly Happy. And you are. They've all got Foster's kiss on them—they're *yours.*" She frowned slightly. "It feels a little like 'sharing water.' You understand me?"

"I grok," agreed Mike.

("*Mike? ????*")

("*Wait, Jill. Wait for fullness.*")

"But don't think," Patricia said earnestly, "that a person can get into an Inner Temple Happiness meeting just with a little tattoo mark—after all, it's too easy to fake. A visiting brother or sister— Well, take me. As soon as I know where the carnie is going, I write to the local churches and send 'em my finger prints so they can check 'em against the master file of the eternally saved at Archangel Foster Tabernacle—unless they already know me. I give 'em my address care of Billboard. Then when I go to church—and I always go to church Sundays and I would *never* miss a Happiness meeting even if it means Tim has to slough the blow-off some nights—I go first time and get positively identified. Most places they're mighty glad to see me; I'm an added attraction, with my unique and unsurpassed sacred pictures—I often spend most of the evening just letting people examine me . . . and every minute of it bliss. Sometimes the priest wants me to bring Honey Bun and I do Eve and the Serpent—that takes body make-up, of course, or skin-colored tights if there isn't time. Some local brother plays Adam and we get scourged out of the Garden of Eden, and the local priest explains the *real* meaning, not all the twisted lies you hear—and we end by regaining our blessed innocence and happiness, and that's certain to get the party really rolling. Joy!"

She added, "But everybody is always interested in my Foster's kiss . . . because, since he went back to Heaven almost twenty years ago now and the Church has increased and flourished, not too many of us have a Foster's kiss that wasn't laid on by proxy—I always have the Tabernacle testify to *that,* too. And I tell them about it. Uh—"

Mrs. Paiwonski hesitated, then told them about it, in explicit detail— and Jill wondered where her admittedly limited ability to blush had gone? Then she grokked that Mike and Patty were two of a kind—God's innocents, unable to be anything else, no matter what they did. She wished, for Patty's sake, that this preposterous mishmash were really true, that Foster had really been a holy prophet who had saved her for eternal bliss.

But *Foster!* God's Wounds, what a travesty! Then suddenly, through her greatly improved recall, Jill was standing back in a room with a wall of glass and looking into Foster's dead eyes. But, in her mind, he seemed alive . . . and she felt a shiver in her loins and wondered what *she* would have done if Foster himself had offered her his holy kiss—and his holy self?

She shut it out of her mind, but not before Mike had caught much of it. She felt him smile, with knowing innocence.

She stood up. "Pattycake darling, what time do you have to be back at the lot?"

"Oh dear! I should be back this blessed minute!"

"Why? The show doesn't roll until nine-thirty."

"Well . . . Honey Bun misses me . . . and she's jealous if I stay out late."

"Can't you tell her that it's a Happiness meeting night?"

"Uh . . ." The older woman gathered Jill in her arms. "It is! It certainly is!"

"Good. Then I'm going to get a certain amount of sleep—Jill is bushed, believe me. What time do you have to be up, then?"

"Uh, if I'm back on the lot by eight, I can get Sam to tear down my living top and have time to make sure that my babies are loaded safely."

"Breakfast?"

"I don't eat breakfast right away, I'll get it on the train. Just coffee when I wake up, usually."

"We can make that right here in the room. I'll see that you're up. Now you dears stay up and talk religion as long as you like; I won't let you oversleep—if you sleep. Mike doesn't sleep."

"Not at all?"

"Never. He sort of curls up and thinks a while, if he's got something to think about—but he doesn't sleep."

Mrs. Paiwonski nodded solemnly. "Another sign. I know it—and, Michael, some day you will know. Your call will come."

"Maybe," agreed Jill. "Mike, I'm falling asleep. Pop me into bed. Please?" She was lifted, wafted into the bedroom, the covers rolled back by invisible hands—she was asleep before he covered her.

Jill woke up, as she had planned, exactly at seven. Mike had a clock in his head, too, but his was quite erratic so far as Earth calendars and times were concerned; it vibrated to another need. She slipped out of bed, put her head into the other room. Lights were out and the shades were tight; it was quite dark. But they were not asleep. Jill heard Mike say with soft certainty:

"Thou art God."

" 'Thou art God'—" Patricia whispered back in a voice as heavy as if drugged.

"Yes. Jill is God."

"Jill . . . is God. Yes, Michael."

"And thou art God."

"*Thou*—are God. Now, Michael, *now!*"

Jill went very softly back in and quietly brushed her teeth. Presently she let Mike know in her mind that she was awake and found, as she expected, that he knew it. When she came back into the living room, shades were up and morning sun was streaming in. "Good morning, darlings!" She kissed them both.

"Thou art God," Patty said simply.

"Yes, Patty. And thou art God. God is in all of us." She looked at Patty in the harsh, bright morning light and noted that her new brother did not look tired. She looked as if she had had a full night of sleep and some extra . . . and looked younger and sweeter than ever. Well, she knew that effect—if Mike wanted to stay up, instead of reading or thinking all night, Jill never found it any trouble . . . and she suspected that her own sudden sleepiness the night before had been Mike's idea, too . . . and heard Mike agree in his mind that it was.

"Now coffee for both you darlings—and me, too. And I just happen to have stashed away a redipak of orange juice, too."

They breakfasted lightly, filled out with happiness. Jill saw Patty looking thoughtful. "What is it, dear?"

"Uh, I hate to mention this—but what are you kids going to eat on? Happens that Aunt Patty has a pretty well stuffed grouch bag and I thought—"

Jill laughed. "Oh, darling, I'm sorry; I didn't mean to laugh. But the Man from Mars is *rich!* Surely you know that? Or don't you ever read the news?"

Mrs. Paiwonski looked baffled. "Well, I guess I knew—that way. But you can't trust anything you hear over the news."

Jill sighed. "Patty, you're an utter darling. And believe me, now that we're water brothers, we wouldn't hesitate an instant to impose on you— 'sharing the nest' isn't just poetry. But it happens to be the other way around. If you *ever* need money—it doesn't matter how much; we *can't* use it up—just say so. Any amount. Any time. Write to me—or better yet, call me—because Mike doesn't have the foggiest idea about money. Why, dear,

I've got a couple of hundred thousand dollars in a checking account in my name right this minute. Want some of it?"

Mrs. Paiwonski looked startled, something she had not looked since Mike had caused her costume to go away. "Bless me! No, I don't need money."

Jill shrugged. "If you ever do, just holler. We can't possibly spend it all and the government won't let Mike give it away. At least, not much of it. If you want a yacht— Mike would enjoy giving you a yacht."

"I certainly would, Pat. I've never seen a yacht."

Mrs. Paiwonski shook her head. "Don't take me up on a tall mountain, dearie—I've never wanted much . . . and all I want from you two is your love—"

"You have that," Jill told her.

"I don't grok 'love'," Mike said seriously. "But Jill always speaks rightly. If we've got it, it's yours."

"—and to know that you're both saved. But I'm no longer worried about that. Mike has told me about waiting, and why waiting is. You understand me, Jill?"

"I grok. I'm no longer impatient about anything."

"But I do have something for you two." The tattooed lady got up and crossed to where she had left her purse, took a book out of it. She came back, stood close to them. "My dear ones . . . this is the very copy of the New Revelation that Blessed Foster gave me . . . the night he placed his kiss on me. I want you to have it."

Jill's eyes suddenly filled with tears and she felt herself choking. "But, Aunt Patty—Patty our brother! We *can't* take this one. Not *this* one. We'll buy one."

"No. It's . . . it's 'water' I'm sharing with you. For growing-closer."

"Oh—" Jill jumped up. "We'll take it. But it's ours now—all of us." She kissed her.

Presently Mike tapped her on the shoulder. "Greedy little brother. My turn."

"I'll always be greedy, that way."

The Man from Mars kissed his new brother first on her mouth, then paused and gently kissed the spot where Foster had kissed her. Then he pondered, briefly by Earth time, picked a corresponding spot on the other side where he saw that George's design could be matched well enough for his purpose—kissed her there while he thought by stretched-out time and in great detail what he wanted to accomplish. It was necessary to grok the capillaries—

To the other two, subject and spectator, he simply gently and briefly pressed his lips to the garishly decorated skin. But Jill caught a hint of the effort he had exerted and looked. "Patty! *See!*"

Mrs. Paiwonski looked down at herself. Marked on her skin, paired stigmata in blood red, were his lips. She started to faint—then showed the depth of her own staunch faith. "Yes. *Yes!* Michael—"

Most shortly thereafter the tattooed lady had disappeared, replaced by a rather mousy housewife in high neck, long sleeves and gloves. "I won't cry," she said soberly, "and it's not good-by; there are no good-bys in eternity. But I will be waiting." She kissed them both, briefly, left without looking back.

xxviii

"BLASPHEMY!"

Foster looked up. "Something bite you, Junior?" This temporary annex had been run up in a hurry and Things did get in—swarms of almost invisible imps usually . . . harmless, of course, but a bite from one left an itch on the ego.

"Uh . . . you'd have to see it to believe it—here, I'll run the omniscio back a touch."

"You'd be surprised at what I can believe, Junior." Nevertheless Digby's supervisor shifted a part of his attention. Three temporals—humans, he saw they were; a man and two women—speculating about the eternal. Nothing odd about that. "Yes?"

"You heard what she said! The 'Archangel Michael' indeed!"

"What about it?"

" 'What about it?' Oh, for God's sake!"

"Very possibly."

Digby was so indignant that his halo quivered. "Foster, you must not have taken a good look. She meant that over-age juvenile delinquent that sent me to the showers. Scan it again."

Foster let the gain increase, noted that the angel-in-training had spoken rightly—and noticed something else and smiled his angelic smile. "How do you know he isn't, Junior?"

"Huh?"

"I haven't seen Mike around the Club lately and I recall that his name has been scratched on the Millennial Solipsist Tournament—that's a Sign that he's likely away on detached duty, as Mike is one of the most eager Solipsism players in this sector."

"But the notion's obscene!"

"You'd be surprised how many of the Boss's best ideas have been called 'obscene' in some quarters—or, rather, *you* should not be surprised, in view of your field work. But 'obscene' is a concept you don't need; it has no theological meaning. 'To the pure all things are pure.' "

"But—"

"I'm still Witnessing, Junior. You listen. In addition to the fact that our brother Michael seems to be away at this micro-instant—and I don't keep track of him; we're not on the same Watch list—that tattooed lady who made that oracular pronouncement is not likely to be mistaken; she's a very holy temporal herself."

"Who says?"

"I say. I know." Foster smiled again with angelic sweetness. Dear little Patricia! Getting a little long in the tooth now but still Earthily desirable—and shining with an inner light that made her look like a stained glass window. He noted without temporal pride that George had finished his great dedication since he had last looked at Patricia—and that picture of his being called up to Heaven wasn't bad, not bad at all, in the Higher sense. He must remember to look up George and compliment him on it, and tell him he had seen Patricia—hmm, where was George? A creative artist in the universe design section working right under the Architect, as he recalled—no matter, the master file would dig him out in a split millennium.

What a delicious little butterball Patricia had been and such holy frenzy! If she had had just a touch more assertiveness and a touch less humility he could have made her a priestess. But such was Patricia's need to accept God according to her own nature that she could have qualified only among the Lingayats . . . where she wasn't needed. Foster considered scanning back and seeing her as she had been, decided against it with angelic restraint; there was work to be done—

"Forget the omniscio, Junior. I want a Word with you." Digby did so and waited. Foster twanged his halo, an annoying habit he had when he was meditating. "Junior, you aren't shaping up too angelically."

"I'm sorry."

"Sorrow is not for eternity. But the Truth is you've been preoccupied with that young fellow who may or may not be our brother Michael. Now wait— In the first place it is not for you to Judge the instrument used to call you from the pasture. In the second place it is not he who vexes you—

you hardly knew him—what's bothering you is that little brunette secretary you had. She had earned my Kiss quite some temporal period before you were called. Hadn't she?"

"I was still testing her."

"Then no doubt you have been angelically pleased to note that Supreme Bishop Short, after giving her a most thorough examination himself —oh, very thorough; I told you he would measure up—has passed her and she now enjoys the wider Happiness she deserves. Mmmm, a shepherd should take joy in his work . . . but when he's promoted, he should take joy in that, too. Now it just happens I know there is a spot open for a Guardian-in-Training in a new sector being opened up—a job under your nominal rank, I concede, but good angelic experience. This planet—well, you can think of it as a planet; you'll see—is occupied by a race of tripolarity instead of bipolarity and I have it on High Authority that Don Juan himself could not manage to take Earthly interest in *any* of their three polarities . . . that's not an opinion; he was borrowed as a test. He screamed, and prayed to be returned to the solitary hell he has created for himself."

"Going to send me out to Flatbush, huh? So I won't interfere!"

"Tut, tut! You *can't* interfere—the one Impossibility that permits all else to be possible; I tried to tell you that when you arrived. But don't let it fret you; you are eternally permitted to try. Your orders will include a loop so that you will check back at here-now without any loss of temporality. Now fly away and get cracking; I have work to do." Foster turned back to where he had been interrupted. Oh, yes, a poor soul temporally designated as "Alice Douglas"—to be a goad was a hard assignment at best and she had met it unflaggingly. But her job was complete and now she would need rest and rehabilitation from the inescapable battle fatigue . . . she'd be kicking and screaming and foaming ectoplasm at all orifices.

Oh, she would need a thorough exorcism after a job that rough! But they were all rough; they couldn't be anything else. And "Alice Douglas" was an utterly reliable field operative; she could take any left-hand assignment as long as it was essentially virginal—burn her at the stake or put her in a nunnery; she always delivered.

Not that he cared much for virgins, other than with professional respect for any job well done. Foster sneaked a quick last look at Mrs. Paiwonski. *There* was a fellow worker he could appreciate. Darling little Patricia! What a blessed, lusty benison—

xxix

As the door of their suite closed itself behind Patricia Paiwonski, Jill said, "What now, Mike?"

"We're leaving. Jill, you've read some abnormal psychology."

"Yes, of course. In training. Not as much as you have, I know."

"Do you know the symbolism of tattooing? And snakes?"

"Of course. I knew that about Patty as soon as I met her. I had been hoping that you would find a way."

"I couldn't, until we were water brothers. Sex is necessary, sex is a helpful goodness—but only if it is sharing and growing closer. I grok that if I did it without growing closer—well, I'm not sure."

"I grok that you would learn that you couldn't, Mike. That is one of the reasons—one of the many reasons—I love you."

He looked worried. "I still don't grok 'love.' Jill, I don't grok 'people.' Not even you. But I didn't want to send Pat away."

"Stop her. Keep her with us."

("Waiting is, Jill.")

("I know.")

He added aloud, "Besides, I doubt if I could give her all she needs. She wants to give herself all the time, to everybody. Even her Happiness meetings and her snakes and the marks aren't enough for Pat. She wants to offer herself on an altar to everybody in the world, always—and make them happy. This New Revelation . . . I grok that it is a lot of other things to other people. But that is what it is to Pat."

"Yes, Mike. Dear Mike."

"Time to leave. Pick the dress you want to wear and get your purse. I'll dispose of the rest of the trash."

Jill thought somewhat sadly that she would like, sometimes, to take along just one or two things. But Mike always moved on with just the clothes on his back—and seemed to grok that she preferred it that way, too. "I'll wear that pretty blue one."

It floated out to her, poised itself over her, wriggled down onto her as she held up her hands; the zipper closed. Shoes to suit it walked toward her, waited while she stepped into them. "I'm ready, Mike."

Mike had caught the wistful flavor of her thought, but not the concept; it was too alien to Martian ideas. "Jill? Do you want to stop and get married?"

She thought about it. "We couldn't, today, Mike. It's Sunday. We couldn't get a license."

"Tomorrow, then. I will remember. I grok that you would like it."

She thought about it. "No, Mike."

"Why not, Jill?"

"Two reasons. One, we couldn't be any closer through it, because we already share water. That's logic, both in English and in Martian. Yes?"

"Yes."

"And two, a reason valid just in English. I wouldn't have Dorcas and Anne and Miriam—and Patty—think that I was trying to crowd them out . . . and one of them might think so."

"No, Jill, none of them would think so."

"Well, I won't chance it, because I don't need it. Because you married me in a hospital room ages and ages ago. Just because you were the way you are. Before I even guessed it." She hesitated. "But there is something you might do for me."

"What, Jill?"

"Well, you might call me pet names occasionally! The way *I* do *you.*"

"Yes, Jill. What pet names?"

"*Oh!*" She kissed him quickly. "Mike, you're the sweetest, most lovable man I've ever met—and the most infuriating creature on two planets! Don't bother with pet names. Just call me 'little brother' occasionally . . . it makes me go all quivery inside."

"Yes, Little Brother."

"Oh, my! Now get decent fast and let's get out of here—before I take you back to bed. Come on. Meet me at the desk; I'll be paying the bill." She left very suddenly.

They went to the town's station flat and caught the first Greyhound going anywhere. A week or two later they stopped at home, shared water for a couple of days, left again without saying good-by—or, rather, Mike did not; saying good-by was one human custom Mike stubbornly resisted and never used with his own. He used it formally with strangers under circumstances in which Jill required him to.

Shortly they were in Las Vegas, stopping in an unfashionable hotel near but not on the Strip. Mike tried all the games in all the casinos while Jill filled in the time as a show girl—gambling bored her. Since she couldn't sing or dance and had no act, standing or parading slowly in a tall improbable hat, a smile, and a scrap of tinsel was the job best suited to her in the Babylon of the West. She preferred to work if Mike was busy and, somehow, Mike could always get her the job she picked out. Since the casinos never closed, Mike was busy almost all their time in Las Vegas.

Mike was careful not to win too much in any one casino, keeping to limits Jill set for him. After he had milked each one for a few thousand he carefully put it all back, never letting himself be the big-money player at any game, whether winning or losing. Then he took a job as a croupier, studying people, trying to grok why they gambled. He grokked unclearly a drive in many of the gamblers that seemed to be intensely sexual in nature —but he seemed to grok wrongness in this. He kept the job quite a while, letting always the little ball roll without interference.

Jill was amused to discover that the customers in the palatial theater-restaurant where she worked were just marks . . . marks with more money but still marks. She discovered something about herself, too; she enjoyed displaying herself, as long as she was safe from hands that she did not want to grab her. With her steadily increasing Martian honesty she examined this newly uncovered facet in herself. In the past, while she had known that she enjoyed being admired, she had sincerely believed that she wanted it only from a select few and usually only from one—she had been irked at the discovery, now long past, that the sight of her physical being really didn't mean anything to Mike even though he had been and re-mained as aggressively and tenderly devoted to her physically as a woman could dream of—if he wasn't preoccupied.

And he was even generous about that, she reminded herself. If she wished, he would always let her call him out of his deepest withdrawal trances, shift gears without complaint and be smiling and eager and loving.

Nevertheless, there it was—one of his strangenesses, like his inability to laugh. Jill decided, after her initiation as a show girl, that she enjoyed being visually admired because that was the one thing Mike did not give her.

But her own perfecting self-honesty and steadily growing empathy did not allow that theory to stand. The male half of the audience always had that to-be-expected high percentage who were too old, too fat, too bald, and in general too far gone along the sad road of entropy to be likely to be attractive to a female of Jill's youth, beauty, and fastidiousness—she had always been scornful of "lecherous old wolves"—although not of old men *per se,* she reminded herself in her own defense; Jubal could look at her, even use crude language in deliberate indecencies, and not give her the slightest feeling that he was anxious to get her alone and grope her. She was so serenely sure of Jubal's love for her and its truly spiritual nature that she told herself that she could easily share a bed with him, go right to sleep—and be sure that he would also, with only the goodnight peck she always gave him.

But now she found that these unattractive males did not set her teeth on edge. When she felt their admiring stares or even their outright lust—and she found that she did feel it, could even identify the source—she did not resent it; it warmed her and made her feel smugly pleased.

"Exhibitionism" had been to her simply a word used in abnormal psychology—a neurotic weakness she had held in contempt. Now, in digging out her own and looking at it, she decided that either this form of narcissism was normal, or she was abnormal and had not known it. But she didn't *feel* abnormal; she felt healthy and happy—healthier than she had ever been. She had been always of better than average health—nurses need to be—but she hadn't had a sniffle nor even an upset stomach in she couldn't remember when . . . why, she thought wonderingly, not even cramps.

Okay, she was healthy—and if a healthy woman liked to be looked at —and not as a side of beef!—then it follows as the night from day that healthy men should like to look at them, else there was just no darn sense to it! At which point she finally understood, intellectually, Duke and his pictures . . . and begged his pardon in her mind.

She discussed it with Mike, tried to explain her changed viewpoint—not easy, since Mike could not understand why Jill had ever minded being looked at, at any time, by anyone. Not wishing to be touched he understood; Mike avoided shaking hands if he could do so without offense, he wanted to touch and be touched only by water brothers (Jill wasn't sure just how far this included male water brothers in Mike's mind; she had explained homosexuality to him, after he had read about it and failed to grok it—and had given him practical rules for avoiding even the appearance thereof and how to keep such passes from being made at him, since she assumed correctly that Mike, pretty as he was, would attract such passes. He had followed her advice and had set about making his face more masculine, instead of the androgynous beauty he had first had. Nevertheless Jill was not sure that Mike would refuse such an invitation from, say, Duke—but fortunately Mike's male water brothers were all decidedly masculine men, just as his others were very female women. Jill hoped that it would stay that way; she suspected that Mike would grok a "wrongness" in the poor in-betweeners anyhow—they would never be offered water.)

Nor could Mike understand why it now pleased her to be stared at. The only time when their two attitudes had been even roughly similar had been as they left the carnival, when Jill had discovered that she had become indifferent to stares—willing to do their act "stark naked," as she had told Patty, if it would help.

Jill saw that her present self-knowledge had been nascent at that point; she had never been truly indifferent to masculine stares. Under the unique necessities of adjusting to life with the Man from Mars she had been forced to shuck off part of her artificial, training-imposed *persona,* that degree of ladylike prissiness a nurse can retain despite the rigors of an unusually no-nonsense profession. But Jill hadn't known that she had *any* prissiness to lose until she lost it.

Of course, Jill was even more of a "lady" than ever—but she preferred to think of herself as a "gent." But she was no longer able to conceal from her conscious mind (nor had any wish to) that there was something inside her as happily shameless as a tabby in heat going into her belly dance for the enticement of the neighborhood toms.

She tried to explain all this to Mike, giving him her theory of the complementary and functional nature of narcissist display and voyeurism, with herself and Duke as clinical examples. "The truth is, Mike, that I find I get a real kick out of having all those men stare at me . . . lots of men and almost any man. So now I grok why Duke likes to have lots of pictures of women, the sexier the better. Same thing, only in reverse. It doesn't mean that I want to go to bed with them, any more than Duke wants to go to bed with a photograph—shucks, dearest, I don't even want to say hello to them. But when they look at me and tell me—think at me—that I'm desirable, it gives me a tingle, a warm pleasant feeling right in my middle." She frowned slightly. "You know, I think I ought to get a real naughty picture taken of me and send it to Duke. Just to tell him that I'm sorry I snooted him and failed to grok what I thought was a weakness in him. If it's a weakness, I've got it, too—but girl style. If it *is* a weakness— But I grok it isn't."

"All right. We'll find a photographer in the morning."

She shook her head. "I'll simply apologize to Duke the next time we go home. I wouldn't actually send such a picture to Duke. He has never made a pass at me—and I don't want him getting ideas."

"Jill, you would not want Duke?"

She heard an echo of "water brother" in his mind. "Hmm . . . truthfully I've never really thought about it. I guess I've been 'being faithful' to you—not that it has been an effort. But I grok you speak rightly; I wouldn't turn Duke down—and I would *enjoy* it, too. What do you think of *that,* darling?"

"I grok a goodness," Mike said seriously.

"Hmm . . . my gallant Martian, there are times when we human females appreciate at least a semblance of jealousy—but I don't think there is the slightest chance that you will ever grok 'jealousy.' Darling, what would you grok if one of those marks—those men in the audience, not a water brother—made a pass at me?"

Mike barely smiled. "I grok he would be missing."

"Mmm . . . I grok he might be, too. But, Mike—listen to me carefully, dear. You promised me that you wouldn't do anything of that sort except in utter emergency. So don't be hasty. If you hear me scream and shout, and reach into my mind and know that I'm in real trouble, that's another matter. But I was coping with wolves when you were still on Mars. Nine times out of ten, if a girl gets raped, it's at least partly her own fault. That tenth time—well, all right. Give him your best heave-ho to the bottomless pit. But you aren't going to find it necessary."

"All right, I will remember. I wish you were sending that naughty picture to Duke."

"What, dear? I will if you want me to. It's just that if I ever make a pass at Duke—and I might, now that you've put the idea into my little pointy head—I'd rather grab his shoulders and look him in the eye and say, 'Duke, how about it?—I'm willing.' I don't want to do it by sending him a naughty picture through the mail, like those nasty women used to send to you. But if you want me to, okay. Uh, I needn't make it too naughty—I could make it obviously a show girl's professional picture and tell him what I'm doing and ask him if he has room for it in his scrap book. He might not take it as a pass."

Mike frowned. "I spoke incompletely. If you wish to send Duke a naughty picture, do so. If you do not wish, then do not. But I had hoped to see the naughty picture taken. Jill, what is a 'naughty' picture?"

Mike was baffled by the whole idea—Jill's reversal from an attitude that he had never understood but had learned to accept into exactly the opposite attitude of pleasure—sexual pleasure, he understood—at being stared at . . . plus a third and long-standing bafflement at Duke's "art" collection—it certainly was not art. But the pale, wan Martian thing which parallels tumultuous human sexuality gave him no foundation for grokking either narcissism or voyeurism, modesty or display.

He added, " 'Naughty' means a wrongness, usually a small wrongness, but I grokked that you did not mean even a small wrongness, but a goodness."

"Uh, a naughty picture could be either one, I guess—depending on who it's for—now that I'm over some prejudice. But— Mike, I'll have to show you; I can't tell you. But first close those slats, will you?"

The venetian blinds flipped themselves shut. "All right," she said.

"Now this pose would be just a little bit naughty—any of the show girls would use it as a professional pic . . . and this one is just a little bit more so, some of the girls would use it. But this one is unmistakably naughty . . . and this one is *quite* naughty . . . and *this* one is so extremely naughty that I wouldn't pose for it with my face wrapped in a towel—unless you wanted it."

"But if your face was covered, why would I want it?"

"Ask Duke. That's all I can say."

He continued to look puzzled. "I grok not wrongness, I grok not goodness. I grok—" He used a Martian word indicating a null state of all emotions.

But he was interested because he was so baffled; they went on discussing it, in Martian as much as possible because of its extremely fine discriminations for emotions and values—and in English, too, because Martian, rich as it is, simply couldn't cope with the concepts.

Mike showed up at a ringside table that night, Jill having coached him in how to bribe the maître d'hôtel to give him such a spot; he was determined to pursue this mystery. Jill was not averse. She came strutting out in the first production number, her smile for everyone but a quick wink for Mike as she turned and her eyes passed across his. She discovered that, with Mike present, the warm, pleased sensation she had been enjoying nightly was greatly amplified—she suspected that, if the lights were out, she would glow in the dark.

When the parade stopped and the girls formed a tableau, Mike was no more than ten feet from her—she had been promoted her first week to a front position. The director had looked her over on her fourth day with the show and had said, "I don't know what it is, kid. We've got girls around town begging for just any job with twice the shape you've got—but when the lights hit you, you've got what the customers look at. Okay, I'm moving you up where they can see better. The standard raise . . . and I still don't know why."

She posed and talked with Mike in her mind. *("Feel anything?")*

("I grok but not in fullness.")

("Look where I am looking, my brother. The small one. He quivers. He thirsts for me.")

("I grok his thirst.")

("Can you see him?") Jill stared straight into the customer's eyes and gave him a warm smile . . . not alone to increase his interest in her but also to let Mike use her eyes, if possible. As her grokking of Martian thought had increased and as they had grown steadily closer in other ways they had begun to be able to use this common Martian convenience. Not

fully as yet, but with increasing ease—Jill had no control over it; Mike could see through her eyes simply by calling to her, she could see through his only if he gave it his attention.

("We grok him together,") Mike agreed. *("Great thirst for my little brother.")*

("!!!!")

("Yes. Beautiful agony.")

A music cue told Jill to break her pose and resume her slow strut. She did so, moving with proud sensuousness and feeling lust boil up in herself in response to emotions she was getting both from Mike and from the stranger. The routine caused her to walk away from Mike and almost toward the rutty little stranger, approaching him during her first few steps. She continued to lock eyes with him.

At which point something happened which was totally unexpected to her because Mike had never explained that it was possible. She had been letting herself receive as much as possible of the stranger's emotions, intentionally teasing him with eyes and body, and relaying what she felt from him back to Mike—

—when suddenly the circuit was completed and she was looking at herself, seeing herself through strange eyes, much more lavish than she considered herself to be—and feeling the primitive need with which that stranger saw her.

Blindly she stumbled and would have fallen flat had not Mike instantly sensed her hazard, caught her, lifted her, straightened her up, and steadied her until she could walk unassisted, second-sight gone.

The parade of beauties continued on through exit. Once off stage the girl behind her said, "What the devil happened to you, Jill?"

"Caught my heel."

"Happens. But that was the wildest recovery I ever saw. For a second there you looked like a puppet on strings."

(—and so I was, dear, and so I was! But we won't go into that.) "I'm going to ask the stage manager to check that spot. I think there's a loose board. A gal could break her leg."

For the rest of the show whenever she was on stage Mike gave her quick glimpses of how she looked to various men while always making sure that she was not again taken by surprise. Jill was amazed to discover how varied were their images of her: one noticed only her legs, another seemed fascinated by the undulations of her torso, a third saw only her proud bosom. Then Mike, warning her first, let her look at other girls in the tableaux. She was relieved to find that Mike saw them as she saw them —but sharper.

But she was amazed to find that her own excitement did not diminish as she looked at, second hand, the girls around her; it increased.

Mike left promptly at the finale, ducking out ahead of the crowd as she had warned him to do. She did not expect to see him again that night since he had asked for relief from his job as croupier only long enough to see his wife in her show. But when she dressed and returned to their hotel room, she felt him inside before she reached the room.

The door opened for her, she stepped inside, it closed behind her. "Hello, darling!" she called out. "How nice you came home!"

He smiled gently. "I now grok naughty pictures." Her clothes vanished. "Make naughty pictures."

"Huh? Yes, dear, of course." She ran through much the same poses she had earlier in the day. With each one, as soon as she was in it, Mike let her use his eyes to see herself. She looked at herself and felt his emotions . . . and felt her own swell in response in a closed and mutually amplified re-echoing. At last she placed herself in a pose as randily carefree as her imagination could devise.

"Naughty pictures are a great goodness," Mike said gravely.

"Yes! And now *I* grok them, too! *What are you waiting for?"*

They quit their jobs and for the next several days saw as many of the revues as possible, during which period Jill made still another discovery: she "grokked naughty pictures" only through a man's eyes. If Mike watched, she caught and shared his mood, from quiet sensuous pleasure in a beautiful woman to fully aroused excitement at times—but if Mike's attention was elsewhere, the model, dancer, or peeler was just another woman to Jill, possibly pleasant to look at but in no wise exciting. She was likely to get bored and wish mildly that Mike would take her home. But only mildly for she was now nearly as patient as he was.

She pondered this new fact from all sides and decided that she preferred not to be excited by women other than through his eyes. One man gave her all the problems she could handle and more—to have discovered in herself unsuspected latent Lesbian tendencies would have been entirely too much.

But it certainly was a lot of fun—"a great goodness"—to see those girls through his eyes as he had now learned to see them—and a still greater, ecstatic goodness to know that, at last, he looked at her herself in the same way . . . only more so.

They stopped in Palo Alto long enough for Mike to try (and fail to) swallow all the Hoover Library in mammoth gulps. The task was mechanically impossible; the scanners could not spin that fast, nor could Mike turn pages of bound books fast enough to read them all. He gave up and admitted that he was taking in raw data much faster than he could grok it, even by spending all hours the library was closed in solitary contemplation. With relief Jill moved them to San Francisco and he embarked on a more systematic search.

She came back to their flat one day to find him sitting, not in trance but doing nothing, and surrounded by books—many books: The Talmud, the Kama-Sutra, Bibles in various versions, the Book of the Dead, the Book of Mormon, Patty's precious copy of the New Revelation, Apocrypha of various sorts, the Koran, the unabridged Golden Bough, The Way, Science and Health with Key to the Scriptures, the sacred writings of a dozen other religions major and minor—even such deviant oddities as Crowley's Book of the Law.

"Trouble, dear?"

"Jill, I don't grok." He waved his hand at the books. *("Waiting, Michael. Waiting for fullness is.")*

"I don't think waiting will ever fill it. Oh, I know what's wrong; I'm not really a man, I'm a Martian—a Martian in a body of the wrong shape."

"You're plenty of man for me, dear—and I love the way your body is shaped."

"Oh, you grok what I'm talking about. I don't grok *people.* I don't understand this multiplicity of religions. Now among my people—"

"Your people, Mike?"

"Sorry. I should have said that, among the Martians, there is only one religion—and that one is not a faith, it's a certainty. You grok it. 'Thou art God!' "

"Yes," she agreed. "I do grok . . . in Martian. But you know, dearest, that it doesn't say the same thing in English . . . or any other human speech. I don't know why."

"Mmmm . . . on Mars, when we needed to know anything—anything at all—we could consult the Old Ones and the answer was never wrong. Jill, is it possible that we humans don't have any 'Old Ones?' No souls, that has to mean. When we discorporate—*die!*—do we die *dead* . . . die all over and nothing left? Do we live in ignorance because it doesn't matter? Because we are gone and not a rack behind in a time so short that a Martian would use it for one long contemplation? Tell me, Jill. You're human."

She smiled with sober serenity. "You yourself have told *me.* You have taught me to know eternity and you can't take it away from me, ever. You can't die, Mike—you can only discorporate." She gestured down at herself with both hands. "This body that you have taught me to see through your eyes . . . and that you have loved so well, someday it will be gone. But *I* shall not be gone . . . I am that I am! Thou art God and I am God and we are God, eternally. I am not sure where I will be, or whether I will remember that I was once Jill Boardman who was happy trotting bedpans and equally happy strutting her stuff in her buff under bright lights. I have liked this body—"

With a most uncustomary gesture of impatience Mike threw away her clothes.

"Thank you, dear," she said quietly, not stirring from where she was seated. "It has been a nice body to me—and to you—to both of us who thought of it. But I don't expect to miss it when I am through with it. I hope that you will eat it when I discorporate."

"Oh, I'll eat you, all right—unless I discorporate first."

"I don't suppose that you will. With your much greater control over your sweet body I suspect that you can live several centuries at least. If you wish it. Unless you choose to discorporate sooner."

"I might. But not now. Jill, I've tried and tried. How many churches have we attended?"

"All the sorts there are in San Francisco, I think—except, possibly, for little, secret ones that don't list their addresses. I don't recall how many times we have been to seekers' services."

"That's just to comfort Pat—I'd never go again if you weren't sure that she needs to know that we haven't given up."

"She does need to. And we can't lie about it—you don't know how and I can't, not to Patty. Nor any brother."

"Actually," he admitted, "the Fosterites do have quite a bit on the ball. All twisted, of course. They are clumsy, groping—the way I was as a carney. And they'll never correct their mistakes, because this thing—" He caused Patty's book to lift. "—is mostly crap!"

"Yes. But Patty doesn't see those parts of it. She is wrapped in her own innocence. She is God and behaves accordingly . . . only She doesn't know who She is."

"Uh huh," he agreed. "That's our Pat. She believes it only when I tell her—with proper emphasis. But, Jill, there are only three places to look. Science—and I was taught more about how the physical universe is put together while I was still in the nest than human scientists can yet handle. So much that I can't even talk to them . . . even about as elementary a gimmick as levitation. I'm not disparaging human scientists . . . what they do and how they go about it is just as it should be; I grok that fully. But what they are after is *not* what *I* am looking for—you don't grok a desert by counting its grains of sand. Then there's philosophy—supposed to tackle everything. Does it? All any philosopher ever comes out with is exactly what he walked in with—except for those self-deluders who prove their assumptions by their conclusions, in a circle. Like Kant. Like many other tail-chasers. So the answer, if it's anywhere, ought to be *here*." He waved at the pile of religious books. "Only it's not. Bits and pieces that grok true, but never a pattern—or if there is a pattern, every time, without fail, they ask you to take the hard part on faith. *Faith!* What a dirty Anglo-Saxon monosyllable—Jill, how does it happen that you didn't mention that one when you were teaching me the words that mustn't be used in polite company?"

She smiled. "Mike, you just made a joke."

"I didn't mean it as a joke . . . and I can't see that it's funny. Jill, I haven't even been good for *you*—you used to laugh. You used to laugh and giggle until I worried about you. I haven't learned to laugh; instead you've forgotten how. Instead of my becoming human . . . you're becoming Martian."

"I'm happy, dear. You probably just haven't noticed me laughing."

"If you laughed clear down on Market Street, I would hear it. I grok. Once I quit being frightened by it I always noticed it—you, especially. If I grokked it, then I would grok people—I think. Then I could help somebody like Pat . . . either teach her what I know, or learn from her what she knows. Or both. We could talk and understand each other."

"Mike, all you need to do for Patty is to see her occasionally. Why don't we, dear? Let's get out of this dreary fog. She's home now; the carnie is closed for the season. Drop south and see her . . . and I've always wanted to see Baja California; we could go on south into warmer weather —and take her with us, that would be fun!"

"All right."

She stood up. "Let me get a dress on. Do you want to save any of those books? Instead of one of your usual quick housecleanings I could ship them to Jubal."

He flipped his fingers at them and all were gone but Patricia's gift. "Just this one and we'll take it with us; Pat would notice. But, Jill, right now I need to go out to the zoo."

"All right."

"I want to spit back at a camel and ask him what he's so sour about. Maybe camels are the real 'Old Ones' on this planet . . . and that's what is wrong with the place."

"Two jokes in one day, Mike."

"I ain't laughing. And neither are you. Nor is the camel. Maybe he groks why. Come on. Is this dress all right? Do you want underclothes? I noticed you were wearing some when I moved those other clothes."

"Please, dear. It's windy and chilly outdoors."

"Up easy." He levitated her a couple of feet. "Pants. Stockings. Garter belt. Shoes. Down you go and lift your arms. Bra? You don't need a bra. And now the dress—and you're decent again. And you're pretty, whatever that is. You look good. Maybe I can get a job as a lady's maid if I'm not good for anything else. Baths, shampoos, massages, hair styling, make-up, dressing for all occasions—I've even learned to do your nails in a fashion that suits you. Will that be all, Modom?"

"You're a perfect lady's maid, dear. But I'm going to keep you myself."

"Yes, I grok I am. You look so good I think I'll toss it all away again and give you a massage. The growing-closer kind."

"Yes, Michael!"

"I thought you had learned waiting? First you have to take me to the zoo and buy me peanuts."

"Yes, Mike. Jill will buy you peanuts."

It was cold and windy out at Golden Gate Park but Mike did not notice it and Jill had learned that she didn't have to be cold or uncomfortable if she did not wish it. Nevertheless it was pleasant to relax her control by going into the warm monkey house. Aside from its heat Jill did not like the monkey house too well—monkeys and apes were too much like people, too depressingly human. She was, she thought, finished forever with any sort of prissiness; she had grown to cherish an ascetic, almost Martian joy in all things physical. The public copulations and evacuations of these simian prisoners did not trouble her as they once had; these poor penned people possessed no privacy, they were not at fault. She could now watch such without repugnance, her own impregnable fastidiousness untouched. No, it was that they were "Human, All Too Human"—every action, every expression, every puzzled troubled look reminded her of what she liked least about her own race.

Jill preferred the Lion House—the great males arrogant and sure of themselves even in captivity, the placid motherliness of the big females, the lordly beauty of Bengal tigers with jungle staring out of their eyes, the little leopards swift and deadly, the reek of musk that airconditioning could not purge. Mike usually shared her tastes for other exhibits, too; he would spend hours in the Aviary, or the Reptile House, or in watching seals— once he had told her that, if one had to be hatched on this planet, to be a sea lion would be of greatest goodness.

When he had first seen a zoo, Mike had been much upset; Jill had been forced to order him to wait and grok, as he had been about to take immediate action to free all the animals. He had conceded presently, under her arguments, that most of these animals could not stay alive free in the climate and environment where he proposed to turn them loose—that a zoo was a nest . . . of a sort. He had followed this first experience with many hours of withdrawal, after which he never again threatened to remove all the bars and glass and grills. He explained to Jill that the bars were to keep people out at least as much as to keep the animals in, which he had failed to grok at first. After that Mike never missed a zoo wherever they went.

But today even the unmitigated misanthropy of the camels could not shake Mike's moodiness; he looked at them without smiling. Nor did the monkeys and apes cheer him up. They stood for quite a while in front of a cage containing a large family of capuchins, watching them eat, sleep, court, nurse, groom, and swarm aimlessly around the cage, while Jill surreptitiously tossed them peanuts despite "No Feeding" signs.

She tossed one to a medium-sized monk; before he could eat it a much larger male was on him and not only stole his peanut but gave him a beating, then left. The little fellow made no attempt to pursue his tormentor; he squatted at the scene of the crime, pounded his knucks against the concrete floor, and chattered his helpless rage. Mike watched it solemnly.

Suddenly the mistreated monkey rushed to the side of the cage, picked a monkey still smaller, bowled it over and gave it a drubbing worse than the one he had suffered—after which he seemed quite relaxed. The third monk crawled away, still whimpering, and found shelter in the arm of a female who had a still smaller one, a baby, on her back. The other monkeys paid no attention to any of it.

Mike threw back his head and laughed—and went on laughing, loudly and uncontrollably. He gasped for breath, tears came from his eyes; he started to tremble and sink to the floor, still laughing.

"Stop it, Mike!"

He did cease folding himself up but his guffaws and tears went on. An attendant hurried over. "Lady, do you need help?"

"No. Yes, I do. Can you call us a cab? Ground car, air cab, anything —I've got to get him out of here." She added, "He's not well."

"Ambulance? Looks like he's having a fit."

"Anything!" A few minutes later she was leading Mike into a piloted air cab. She gave the address, then said urgently, "Mike, you've got to listen to me. Quiet down."

He became somewhat more quiet but continued to chuckle, laugh aloud, chuckle again, while she wiped his eyes, for all the few minutes it took to get back to their flat. She got him inside, got his clothes off, made him lie down on the bed. "All right, dear. Withdraw now if you need to."

"I'm all right. At last I'm all right."

"I hope so." She sighed. "You certainly scared me, Mike."

"I'm sorry, Little Brother. I know. I was scared, too, the first time I heard laughing."

"Mike, what happened?"

"Jill . . . I grok people!"

"Huh?" ("????")

("*I speak rightly, Little Brother. I grok.*") "I grok people now, Jill . . . Little Brother . . . precious darling . . . little imp with lively legs and lovely lewd lascivious lecherous licentious libido . . . beautiful bumps and pert posterior . . . with soft voice and gentle hands. My baby darling."

"Why, Michael!"

"Oh, I knew all the words; I simply didn't know when or why to say them . . . nor why you wanted me to. I love you, sweetheart—I grok 'love' now, too."

"You always have. I knew. And I love you . . . you smooth ape. My darling."

" 'Ape,' yes. Come here, she ape, and put your head on my shoulder and tell me a joke."

"Just tell you a joke?"

"Well, nothing more than snuggling. Tell me a joke I've never heard and see if I laugh at the right place. I will, I'm sure of it—and I'll be able to tell you *why* it's funny. Jill . . . *I grok people!*"

"But how, darling? Can you tell me? Does it need Martian? Or mind-talk?"

"No, that's the point. I grok people. I *am* people . . . so now I can say it in people talk. I've found out why people laugh. They laugh because it hurts so much . . . because it's the only thing that'll make it stop hurting."

Jill looked puzzled. "Maybe I'm the one who isn't people. I don't understand."

"Ah, but you *are* people, little she ape. You grok it so automatically that you don't have to think about it. Because you grew up with people. But I didn't. I've been like a puppy raised apart from other dogs—who couldn't be like his masters and had never learned how to be a dog. So I had to be taught. Brother Mahmoud taught me, Jubal taught me, lots of people taught me . . . and you taught me most of all. Today I got my diploma—and I laughed. That poor little monk."

"Which one, dear? I thought that big one was just mean . . . and the one I flipped the peanut to turned out to be just as mean. There certainly wasn't anything funny."

"Jill, Jill my darling! Too much Martian has rubbed off on you. Of course it wasn't funny; it was tragic. That's why I had to laugh. I looked at a cageful of monkeys and suddenly I saw all the mean and cruel and utterly unexplainable things I've seen and heard and read about in the time I've been with my own people—and suddenly it hurt so much I found myself laughing."

"But— Mike dear, laughing is something you do when something is nice . . . not when it's horrid."

"Is it? Think back to Las Vegas— When all you pretty girls came out on the stage, did people laugh?"

"Well . . . no."

"But you girls were the nicest part of the show. I grok now, that if they had laughed, you would have been hurt. No, they laughed when a comic tripped over his feet and fell down . . . or something else that is not a goodness."

"But that's not *all* people laugh at."

"Isn't it? Perhaps I don't grok all its fullness yet. But find me something that really makes you laugh, sweetheart . . . a joke, or anything else—but something that gave you a real belly laugh, not a smile. Then we'll see if there isn't a wrongness in it somewhere—and whether you would laugh if the wrongness wasn't there." He thought. "I grok when apes learn to laugh, they'll be people."

"Maybe." Doubtfully but earnestly Jill started digging into her memory for jokes that had struck her as irresistibly funny, ones which had jerked a laugh out of her . . . incidents she had seen or heard of which had made her helpless with laughter:

"—her entire bridge club." . . . "Should I bow?" . . . "Neither one, you idiot—*instead!*" . . . "—the Chinaman objects." . . . "—broke her leg." . . . "—make trouble for *me!*" . . . "—but it'll spoil the ride for me." . . . "—and his mother-in-law fainted." . . . "Stop you? Why, I bet three to one you could do it!" . . . "—something has happened to Ole." . . . "—and so are you, you clumsy ox!"

She gave up on "funny" stories, pointing out to Mike that such were just fantasies, not real, and tried to recall real incidents. Practical jokes? All practical jokes supported Mike's thesis, even ones as mild as a dribble glass—and when it came to an interne's notion of a practical joke—well, internes and medical students should be kept in cages. What else? The time

Elsa Mae had lost her monogrammed panties? It hadn't been funny to Elsa Mae. Or the—

She said grimly, "Apparently the pratfall is the peak of all humor. It's not a pretty picture of the human race, Mike."

"Oh, but it is!"

"Huh?"

"I had thought—I had been told—that a 'funny' thing is a thing of a goodness. It isn't. Not ever is it funny to the person it happens to. Like that sheriff without his pants. The goodness is in the laughing itself. I grok it is a bravery . . . and a sharing . . . against pain and sorrow and defeat."

"But— Mike, it is not a goodness to laugh *at* people."

"No. But I was not laughing at the little monkey. I was laughing at *us*. People. And I suddenly knew that I was people and could not stop laughing." He paused. "This is hard to explain, because you have never lived as a Martian, for all that I've told you about it. On Mars there is *never* anything to laugh at. All the things that are funny to us humans either physically cannot happen on Mars or are not permitted to happen— sweetheart, what you call 'freedom' doesn't exist on Mars; everything is planned by the Old Ones—or the things that *do* happen on Mars which we laugh at here on Earth aren't funny because there is no wrongness about them. Death, for example."

"Death isn't funny."

"Then why are there so many jokes about death? Jill, with us—us humans—death is so sad that we *must* laugh at it. All those religions— they contradict each other on every other point but every one of them is filled with ways to help people be brave enough to laugh even though they know they are dying." He stopped and Jill could feel that he had almost gone into his trance state. "Jill? Is it possible that I was searching them the wrong way? Could it be that *every one* of *all* those religions is true?"

"Huh? How could that possibly be? Mike, if one of them is true, then the others are wrong. Logic."

"So? Point to the shortest direction around the universe. It doesn't matter which way you point, it's the shortest . . . and you're pointing right back at yourself."

"Well, what does that prove? You taught me the true answer, Mike. 'Thou art God.' "

"And Thou art God, my lovely. I wasn't disputing that . . . but that one prime fact which doesn't depend at all on faith may mean that *all* faiths are true."

"Well . . . if they're all true, then right now I want to worship Siva."
Jill changed the subject with emphatic direct action.

"Little pagan," he said softly. "They'll run you out of San Francisco."

"But we're going to Los Angeles . . . where it won't be noticed. *Oh!*
Thou art Siva!"

"Dance, Kali, dance!"

Some time during the night she woke and saw him standing at the
window, looking out over the city. *("Trouble, my brother?")*

He turned and spoke. "There's no *need* for them to be so unhappy."

"Darling, darling! I think I had better take you home. The city is not
good for you."

"But I would still know it. Pain and sickness and hunger and fighting
—there's no need for *any* of it. It's as foolish as those little monkeys."

"Yes, darling. But it's not your fault—"

"Ah, but it is!"

"Well . . . that way—yes. But it's not just this one city; it's five
billion people and more. You can't help five billion people."

"I wonder."

He came over and sat down by her. "I grok with them now, I can talk
to them. Jill, I could set up our act again . . . and make the marks laugh
every minute. I am certain."

"Then why not do it? Patty would certainly be pleased . . . and so
would I. I liked being 'with it'—and now that we've shared water with
Patty, it would be like being home."

He didn't answer. Jill felt his mind and knew that he was contemplating, trying to grok. She waited.

"Jill? What do I have to do to be ordained?"

part four

HIS SCANDALOUS CAREER

XXX

THE FIRST MIXED LOAD of permanent colonists arrived on Mars; six of the seventeen survivors of the twenty-three originals returned to Earth. Prospective colonists trained in Peru at sixteen thousand feet. The President of Argentina moved one night to Montevideo, taking with him such portables as could be stuffed into two suitcases, and the new Presidente started an extradition process before the High Court to yank him back, or at least the two suitcases. Last rites for Alice Douglas were held privately in the National Cathedral with less than two thousand attending, and editorialists and stereo commentators alike praised the dignified fortitude with which the Secretary General took his bereavement. A three-year-old named Inflation, carrying 126 pounds with Jinx Jenkins up, won the Kentucky Derby, paying fifty-four for one, and two guests of the Colony Airotel, Louisville, Kentucky, discorporated, one voluntarily, the other by heart failure.

Another bootleg edition of the (unauthorized) biography *The Devil and Reverend Foster* appeared simultaneously on news stands throughout the United States; by nightfall every copy had been burned and the plates destroyed, along with incidental damage to other chattels and to real estate, plus a certain amount of mayhem, maiming, and simple assault. The British Museum was rumored to possess a copy of the first edition (untrue), and also the Vatican Library (true, but available only to certain church scholars).

In the Tennessee legislature a bill was again introduced to make the ratio pi exactly equal to three; it was reported out by the committee on public education and morals, passed with no objection by the lower house and died in committee in the upper house. An interchurch fundamentalist group opened offices in Van Buren, Arkansas, for the purpose of soliciting funds to send missionaries to the Martians; Dr. Jubal Harshaw happily sent them a lavish donation, but took the precaution of sending it in the name (and with the address) of the editor of the *New Humanist,* a rabid atheist and his close friend.

Other than that, Jubal had very little to feel amused about—there had been too much news about Mike lately, and all of it depressing. He had treasured the occasional visits home of Jill and Mike and had been most interested in Mike's progress, especially after Mike developed a sense of humor. But they came home less frequently now and Jubal did not relish the latest developments.

It had not troubled Jubal when Mike was run out of Union Theological Seminary, hotly pursued in spirit by a pack of enraged theologians, some of whom were angry because they believed in God and others because they did not—but all united in detesting the Man from Mars. Jubal honestly evalued anything that happened to a theologian short of breaking him on the wheel was no more than meet—and the experience was good for the boy; he'd know better next time.

Nor had he been troubled when Mike (with the help of Douglas) had enlisted under an assumed name in the Federation armed forces. He had been quite sure (through private knowledge) that no sergeant could cause Mike any permanent distress, and contrariwise, Jubal was not troubled by what might happen to sergeants or other ranks—an unreconciled old reactionary, Jubal had burned his own honorable discharge and all that went with it on the day that the United States had ceased having its own armed forces.

Actually, Jubal had been surprised at how little shambles Mike had created as "Private Jones" and how long he had lasted—almost three weeks. He had crowned his military career the day that he had seized on the question period following an orientation lecture to hold forth on the utter uselessness of force and violence under any circumstances (with some side comments on the desirability of reducing surplus population through cannibalism) and had offered himself as a test animal for any weapon of any nature to prove to them that force was not only unnecessary but literally impossible when attempted against a self-disciplined person.

They had not taken his offer; they had kicked him out.

But there had been a little more to it than that. Douglas had allowed Jubal to see a top-level super-secret eyes-only numbered-one-of-three report after cautioning Jubal that no one, not even the Supreme Chief of

Staff, knew that "Private Jones" was the Man from Mars. Jubal had merely scanned the exhibits, which had been mostly highly conflicting reports of eye witnesses as to what had happened at various times when "Jones" had been "trained" in the uses of various weapons; the only surprising thing to Jubal about them was that some witnesses had the courage and self-confidence to state under oath that they had seen weapons disappear. "Jones" had also been placed on the report three times for losing weapons, same being accountable property of the Federation.

The end of the report was all that Jubal had bothered to read carefully enough to remember: "Conclusion: Subject man is an extremely talented natural hypnotist and, as such, could conceivably be useful in intelligence work, although he is totally unfitted for any combat branch. However, his low intelligence quotient (moron), his extremely low general classification score, and his paranoid tendencies (delusions of grandeur) make it inadvisable to attempt to exploit his *idiot-savant* talent. Recommendation: Discharge, Inaptitude—no pension credit, no benefits."

Such little romps were good for the boy and Jubal had greatly enjoyed Mike's inglorious career as a soldier because Jill had spent the time at home. When Mike had come home for a few days after it was over, he hadn't seemed hurt by it—he had boasted to Jubal that he had obeyed Jill's wishes exactly and hadn't disappeared *anybody,* merely a few dead things . . . although, as Mike grokked it, there had been several times when Earth could have been made a better place if Jill didn't have this queasy weakness. Jubal didn't argue it; he had a lengthy, though inactive, "Better Dead" list himself.

But apparently Mike had managed to have fun, too. During parade on his last day as a soldier, the Commanding General and his entire staff had suddenly lost their trousers as Mike's platoon was passing in review—and the top sergeant of Mike's company fell flat on his face when his shoes momentarily froze to the ground. Jubal decided that, in acquiring a sense of humor, Mike had developed an atrocious taste in practical jokes—but what the hell? the kid was going through a delayed boyhood; he *needed* to dump over a few privies. Jubal recalled with pleasure an incident in medical school involving a cadaver and the Dean—Jubal had worn rubber gloves for that caper, and a good thing, too!

Mike's unique ways of growing up were all right; Mike was unique. But this last thing—"The Reverend Dr. Valentine M. Smith, A.B., D.D., Ph.D.," founder and pastor of the Church of All Worlds, Inc.—gad! It was bad enough that the boy had decided to be a Holy Joe, instead of leaving other people's souls alone, as a gentleman should. But those diploma-mill degrees he had tacked onto his name—Jubal wanted to throw up.

The worst of it was that Mike had told him that he had gotten the whole idea from something he had heard Jubal say, about what a church was and what it could do. Jubal was forced to admit that it was something he could have said, although he did not recall it; it was little consolation that the boy knew so much law that he might have arrived at the same end on his own.

But Jubal did concede that Mike had been cagy about the operation—some actual months of residence at a very small, very poor (in all senses) sectarian college, a bachelor's degree awarded by examination, a "call" to their ministry followed by ordination in this recognized though flat-headed sect, a doctor's dissertation on comparative religion which was a marvel of scholarship while ducking any real conclusions (Mike had brought it to Jubal for literary criticism, Jubal had added some weasel words himself through conditioned reflex), the award of the "earned" doctorate coinciding with an endowment (anonymous) to this very hungry school, the second doctorate (honorary) right on top of it for "contributions to interplanetary knowledge" from a distinguished university that should have known better, when Mike let it be known that such was his price for showing up as the drawing card at a conference on solar system studies. The one and only Man from Mars had turned down everybody from CalTech to the Kaiser Wilhelm Institute in the past; Harvard University could hardly be blamed for swallowing the bait.

Well, they were probably as crimson as their banner now, Jubal thought cynically. Mike had then put in a few weeks as assistant chaplain at his church-mouse alma mater—then had broken with the sect in a schism and founded his own church. Completely kosher, legally airtight, as venerable in precedent as Martin Luther . . . and as nauseating as last week's garbage.

Jubal was called out of his sour daydream by Miriam. "Boss! Company!"

Jubal looked up to see a car about to land and ruminated that he had not realized what a blessing that S.S. patrol cap had been until it was withdrawn. "Larry, fetch my shotgun—I promised myself that I would shoot the next dolt who landed on the rose bushes."

"He's landing on the grass, Boss."

"Well, tell him to try again. We'll get him on the next pass."

"Looks like Ben Caxton."

"So it is. We'll let him live—this time. Hi, Ben! What'll you drink?"

"Nothing, this early in the day, you professional bad influence. Need to talk to you, Jubal."

"You're doing it. Dorcas, fetch Ben a glass of warm milk; he's sick."

"Without too much soda," amended Ben, "and milk the bottle with the three dimples in it. Private talk, Jubal."

"All right, up to my study—although if you think you can keep anything from the kids around here, let me in on your method." After Ben finished greeting properly (and somewhat unsanitarily, in three cases) the members of the family, they moseyed upstairs.

Ben said, "What the deuce? Am I lost?"

"Oh. You haven't seen the alterations, have you? A new wing on the north, which gives us two more bedrooms and another bath downstairs—and up here, my gallery."

"Enough statues to fill a graveyard!"

"Please, Ben. 'Statues' are dead politicians at boulevard intersections. What you see is 'sculpture.' And please speak in a low, reverent tone lest I become violent . . . for here we have exact replicas of some of the greatest sculpture this naughty globe has produced."

"Well, *that* hideous thing I've seen before . . . but when did you acquire the rest of this ballast?"

Jubal ignored him and spoke quietly to the replica of La Belle Heaulmière. "Do not listen to him, ma petite chère—he is a barbarian and knows no better." He put his hand to her beautiful ravaged cheek, then gently touched one empty, shrunken dug. "I know just how you feel . . . but it can't be very much longer. Patience, my lovely."

He turned back to Caxton and said briskly, "Ben, I don't know what you have on your mind but it will have to wait while I give you a lesson in how to look at sculpture—though it's probably as useless as trying to teach a dog to appreciate the violin. But you've just been rude to a lady . . . and I don't tolerate that."

"Huh? Don't be silly, Jubal; you're rude to ladies—*live* ones—a dozen times a day. And you know which ones I mean."

Jubal shouted, *"Anne!* Upstairs! Wear your cloak!"

"You know I wouldn't be rude to the old woman who posed for that. Never. What I can't understand is a so-called artist having the gall to pose somebody's great grandmother in her skin . . . and you having the bad taste to want it around."

Anne came in, cloaked, said nothing. Jubal said to her, "Anne have I ever been rude to you? Or to any of the girls?"

"That calls for an opinion."

"That's what I'm asking for. Your opinion. You're not in court."

"You have never at any time been rude to any of us, Jubal."

"Have you ever known me to be rude to a lady?"

"I have seen you be intentionally rude to a woman. I have never seen you be rude to a lady."

"That's all. No, one more opinion. What do you think of this bronze?"

Anne looked carefully at Rodin's masterpiece, then said slowly, "When I first saw it, I thought it was horrible. But I have come to the conclusion that it may be the most beautiful thing I have ever seen."

"Thanks. That's all." She left. "Do you want to argue it, Ben?"

"Huh? When I argue with Anne, that's the day I turn in my suit." Ben looked at it. "But I don't get it."

"All right, Ben. Attend me. Anybody can look at a pretty girl and see a pretty girl. An artist can look at a pretty girl and see the old woman she will become. A better artist can look at an old woman and see the pretty girl that she used to be. But a *great* artist—a master—and that is what Auguste Rodin was—can look at an old woman, portray her *exactly* as she is . . . and force the viewer to see the pretty girl she used to be . . . and more than that, he can make anyone with the sensitivity of an armadillo, or even you, see that this lovely young girl is still alive, not old and ugly at all, but simply prisoned inside her ruined body. He can make you feel the quiet, endless tragedy that there was never a girl born who ever grew older than eighteen in her heart . . . no matter what the merciless hours have done to her. Look at her, Ben. Growing old doesn't matter to you and me; we were never meant to be admired—but it *does* to them. *Look at her!*"

Ben looked at her. Presently Jubal said gruffly, "All right, blow your nose and wipe your eyes—she accepts your apology. Come on and sit down. That's enough for one lesson."

"No," Caxton answered, "I want to know about these others. How about this one? It doesn't bother me as much . . . I can see it's a young girl, right off. But why tie her up like a pretzel?"

Jubal looked at the replica "Caryatid Who has Fallen under the Weight of her Stone" and smiled. "Call it a tour de force in empathy, Ben. I won't expect you to appreciate the shapes and masses which make that figure much more than a 'pretzel'—but you can appreciate what Rodin was saying. Ben, what do people get out of looking at a crucifix?"

"You know how much I go to church."

" 'How little' you mean. Still, you must know that, as craftsmanship, paintings and sculpture of the Crucifixion are usually atrocious—and the painted, realistic ones often used in churches are the worst of all . . . the blood looks like catsup and that ex-carpenter is usually portrayed as if he were a pansy . . . which He certainly was *not* if there is any truth in the four Gospels at all. He was a hearty man, probably muscular and of rugged health. But despite the almost uniformly poor portrayal in representations of the Crucifixion, a poor one is about as effective as a good one for most people. They don't see the defects; what they see is a symbol which inspires their deepest emotions; it recalls to them the Agony and Sacrifice of God."

"Jubal, I thought you weren't a Christian?"

"What's that got to do with it? Does that make me blind and deaf to fundamental human emotion? I was saying that the crummiest painted plaster crucifix or the cheapest cardboard Christmas Crèche can be sufficient symbol to evoke emotions in the human heart so strong that many have died for them and many more live for them. So the craftsmanship and artistic judgment with which such a symbol is wrought are largely irrelevant. Now here we have another emotional symbol—wrought with exquisite craftsmanship, but we won't go into that, yet. Ben, for almost three thousand years or longer, architects have designed buildings with columns shaped as female figures—it got to be such a habit that they did it as casually as a small boy steps on an ant. After all those centuries it took Rodin to see that this was work too heavy for a girl. But he didn't simply say, 'Look, you jerks, if you must design this way, make it a brawny male figure.' No, he *showed* it . . . and generalized the symbol. Here is this poor little caryatid who has tried—and failed, fallen under the load. She's a good girl—look at her face. Serious, unhappy at her failure, but not blaming anyone else, not even the gods . . . and still trying to shoulder her load, after she's crumpled under it.

"But she's more than good art denouncing some very bad art; she's a symbol for every woman who has ever tried to shoulder a load that was too heavy for her—over half the female population of this planet, living and dead, I would guess. But not alone women—this symbol is sexless. It means every man and every woman who ever lived who sweated out life in uncomplaining fortitude, whose courage wasn't even noticed until they crumpled under their loads. It's courage, Ben, and victory."

" 'Victory?' "

"Victory in defeat, there is none higher. She didn't give up, Ben; she's still trying to lift that stone after it has crushed her. She's a father going down to a dull office job while cancer is painfully eating away his insides, so as to bring home one more pay check for the kids. She's a twelve-year-old girl trying to mother her baby brothers and sisters because Mama had to go to Heaven. She's a switchboard operator sticking to her job while smoke is choking her and the fire is cutting off her escape. She's all the unsung heroes who couldn't quite cut it but never quit. Come. Just salute as you pass her and come see my Little Mermaid."

Ben took him precisely at his word; if Jubal was surprised, he made no comment. "Now this one," he said, "is the only one Mike didn't give to me. But there is no need to tell Mike why I got it . . . aside from the self-evident fact that it's one of the most delightful compositions ever conceived and proudly executed by the eye and hand of man."

"She's that, all right. This one I don't have to have explained—it's just plain *pretty!*"

"Yes. And that is excuse in itself, just as with kittens and butterflies. But there is more to it than that . . . and she reminded me of Mike. She's not quite a mermaid—see?—and she's not quite human. She sits on land, where she has chosen to stay . . . and she stares eternally out to sea, homesick and forever lonely for what she left behind. You know the story?"

"Hans Christian Andersen."

"Yes. She sits by the harbor of København—Copenhagen was his home town—and she's everybody who ever made a difficult choice. She doesn't regret her choice, but she must pay for it; every choice must be paid for. The cost to her is not only endless homesickness. She can never be quite human; when she uses her dearly bought feet, every step is on sharp knives. Ben, I think that Mike must always walk on knives—but there is no need to tell him I said so. I don't think he knows this story . . . or, at least, I don't think he knows that I connect him with it."

"I won't tell him." Ben looked at the replica. "I'd rather just look at her and not think about the knives."

"She's a little darling, isn't she? How would you like to coax her into bed? She would probably be lively, like a seal, and about as slippery."

"Cripes! You're an evil old man, Jubal."

"And getting eviler and eviler by the year. Uh . . . we won't look at any others; three pieces of sculpture in an hour is more than enough—usually I don't let myself look at more than one in a day."

"Suits. I feel as if I had had three quick drinks on an empty stomach. Jubal, why isn't there stuff like this around where a person can see it?"

"Because the world has gone nutty and contemporary art always paints the spirit of its times. Rodin did his major work in the tail end of the nineteenth century and Hans Christian Andersen antedated him by only a few years. Rodin died early in the twentieth century, about the time the world started flipping its lid . . . and art along with it.

"Rodin's successors noted the amazing things he had done with light and shadow and mass and composition—whether you see it or not—and they copied that much. Oh, how they copied it! And extended it. What they failed to see was that every major work of the master told a story and laid bare the human heart. Instead, they got involved with 'design' and became contemptuous of any painting or sculpture that told a story—sneering, they dubbed such work 'literary'—a dirty word. They went all out for abstractions, not deigning to paint or carve anything that resembled the human world."

Jubal shrugged. "Abstract design is all right—for wall paper or linoleum. But *art* is the process of evoking pity and terror, which is not abstract at all but very human. What the self-styled modern artists are doing is a sort of unemotional pseudo-intellectual masturbation . . . whereas creative art is more like intercourse, in which the artist must seduce—render emotional—his audience, each time. These laddies who won't deign to do that—and perhaps can't—of course lost the public. If they hadn't lobbied for endless subsidies, they would have starved or been forced to go to work long ago. Because the ordinary bloke will not voluntarily pay for 'art' that leaves him unmoved—if he does pay for it, the money has to be conned out of him, by taxes or such."

"You know, Jubal, I've always wondered why I didn't give a hoot for paintings or statues—but I thought it was something missing in *me*, like color blindness."

"Mmm, one does have to learn to look at art, just as you must know French to read a story printed in French. But in general it's up to the artist to use language that can be understood, not hide it in some private code like Pepys and his diary. Most of these jokers don't even *want* to use language you and I know or can learn . . . they would rather sneer at us and be smug, because we 'fail' to see what they are driving at. If indeed they are driving at anything—obscurity is usually the refuge of incompetence. Ben, would you call *me* an artist?"

"Huh? Well, I've never thought about it. You write a pretty good stick."

"Thank you. 'Artist' is a word I avoid for the same reasons I hate to be called 'Doctor.' But I *am* an artist, albeit a minor one. Admittedly most of my stuff is fit to read only once . . . and not even once for a busy person who already knows the little I have to say. But I am an *honest* artist, because what I write is consciously intended to reach the customer . . . reach him and affect him, if possible with pity and terror . . . or, if not, at least to divert the tedium of his hours with a chuckle or an odd idea. But I am *never* trying to hide it from him in a private language, nor am I seeking the praise of other writers for 'technique' or other balderdash. I want the praise of the cash customer, given in cash because I've reached him—or I don't want anything. Support for the arts—*merde!* A government-supported artist is an incompetent whore! Damn it, you punched one of my buttons. Let me fill your glass, and you tell me what is on your mind."

"Uh, Jubal, I'm unhappy."

"This is news?"

"No. But I've got a fresh set of troubles." Ben frowned. "I shouldn't have come here, I guess. No need to burden you with them. I'm not even sure I want to talk about them."

"Okay. But as long as you're here, you can listen to *my* troubles."

"*You* have troubles? Jubal, I've always thought of you as the one man who had managed to beat the game, six ways from zero."

"Hmm, sometime I must tell you about my married life. But—yes, I've got troubles now. Some of them are evident. Duke has left me, you know—or did you?"

"Yeah. I knew."

"Larry is a good gardener—but half the gadgets that keep this log cabin running are falling to pieces. I don't know how I can replace Duke. Good all-around mechanics are scarce . . . and ones that will fit into this household, be a member of the family in all ways, are almost non-existent. I'm limping along on repairmen called in from town—every visit a disturbance, all of them with larceny in their hearts, and most of them incompetent to use a screw driver without cutting themselves. Which I am incapable of doing, too, so I have to hire help. Or move back into town, God forbid."

"My heart aches for you, Jubal."

"Never mind the sarcasm, that's just the start. Mechanics and gardeners are convenient, but for me secretaries are essential. Two of mine are pregnant, one is getting married."

Caxton looked utterly astounded. Jubal growled, "Oh, I'm not telling tales out of school; they're smug as can be—nothing secret about any of it. They're undoubtedly sore at me right now because I took you up here without giving them time to boast. So be a gent and be surprised when they tell you."

"Uh, which one is getting married?"

"Isn't that obvious? The happy man is that smooth-talking refugee from a sand storm, our esteemed water brother Stinky Mahmoud. I've told him flatly that they have to live *here* whenever they're in this country. Bastard just laughed and said how else?—pointed out that I had invited him to live here, permanently, long ago." Jubal sniffed. "Wouldn't be so bad if he would just do it. I might even get some work out of *her*. Maybe."

"You probably would. She likes to work. And the other two are pregnant?"

"Higher 'n a kite. I'm refreshing myself in O.B. because they both say they're going to have 'em at home. And what a crimp that's going to put into my working habits! Worse than kittens. But why do you assume that neither of the two turgescent tummies belongs to the bride?"

"Oh— Why, I suppose I assumed that Stinky was more conventional than that . . . or maybe more cautious."

"Stinky wouldn't be given a ballot. Ben, in the eighty or ninety years I have given to this subject, trying to trace out the meanderings of their twisty little minds, the only thing that I have learned for certain about women is that when a gal is gonna, she's gonna. All a man can do is cooperate with the inevitable."

Ben thought ruefully about times when he had resorted to fast foot-work—and other times when he hadn't been fast enough. "Yeah, you're right. Well, which one isn't getting married or anything? Miriam? Or Anne?"

"Hold it, I didn't say the bride was pregnant . . . and anyhow, you seem to be assuming that Dorcas is the prospective bride. You haven't kept your eyes open. It's Miriam who is studying Arabic like mad, so she can do it right."

"Huh? Well, I'll be a cross-eyed baboon!"

"You obviously are."

"But Miriam was always snapping at Stinky—"

"And to think that they trust you with a newspaper column. Ever watch a bunch of sixth-graders?"

"Yes, but— Dorcas did everything but a nautch dance."

"That is just Dorcas's natural, normal behavior with all men. She used it toward you, too—although I suppose you were too preoccupied elsewhere to realize it. Never mind. Just be sure that when Miriam shows you her ring—the size of a roc's egg and about as scarce—be sure to be surprised. And I'm damned if I'll sort out which two are spawning, so that you'll be certain to be surprised. Just remember that they are pleased about it . . . which is why I tipped you off ahead of time, so that you wouldn't make the mistake of thinking that *they* thought they were 'caught.' They don't. They weren't. They're smug." Jubal sighed. "But I'm not. I'm get-ting too old to enjoy the patter of little feet when I'm busy . . . and contrariwise, I *won't* lose perfect secretaries—and kids that I love, as you know—for *any* reason if I can possibly induce them to stay. But I must say that this household has become steadily more disorganized ever since the night Jill kicked Mike's feet out from under him. Not that I blame her . . . and I don't think you do, either."

"No, I don't, but—Jubal, let me get this straight. Are you under the impression that *Jill* started Mike on his merry rounds?"

"Huh?" Jubal looked startled, then thought back—and admitted to himself that he had never known . . . he had simply assumed it from the fact that when it came to a decision, Jill had been the one who had gone away with Mike. "Who was it?"

" 'Don't be nosy, bub,' as you would put it. If she wants to tell you, she will. However, Jill told me—straightened me out when I made the same jumping-to-conclusions that you did. Mmm—" Ben thought. "As I understand it, which one of the four happened to score the first run was more or less chance."

"Mmm . . . yes. I believe you're right."

"Jill thinks so. Except that she thinks Mike was exceedingly lucky in happening to seduce, or be seduced by (if I have the proper verb)—by the one best fitted to start him off right. Which may give you some hint if you know anything about how Jill's mind works."

"Hell, I don't even know how *mine* works . . . and as for Jill, I would never have expected her to take up preaching no matter how love-struck she was—so I certainly don't know how *her* mind works."

"She doesn't do much preaching—we'll get to that. Jubal, what do you read from the calendar?"

"Huh?"

"You know what I mean. You think Mike did it—in both cases. Or you think so if his visits home match up in either or both cases."

Jubal said guardedly, "Why do you say that, Ben? I've said nothing to lead you to think so."

"The hell you haven't. You said that they were smug, both of them. I know all too well the effect that goddam superman has on women."

"Hold it, son—he's your water brother."

Ben said levelly, "I know it—and I love him, too. If I ever decided to go gay, Mike would be my only choice. But that's all the more reason why I understand why they are smug."

Jubal stared at his glass. "Maybe they just hope. Ben, seems to me *your* name could be on the list, even easier than Mike's. Yes?"

"Jubal, you're out of your mind!"

"Take it easy. Nobody is trying to make you get married, I promise you—why, I haven't even painted my shotgun white. While I am not snoopy and I never hold a bed check around here and I really do, so help me by all the Billion Names of God, believe in not poking my nose into other people's business, nevertheless while I may be out of my mind—a 'least hypothesis' more than once, the last couple of years—I do have normal eyesight and hearing . . . and if a brass band parades through my home, fortissimo, I'll notice it eventually. Question: You've slept under this roof dozens of times. Did you, on at least one of those nights, sleep alone?"

"Why, you scoundrel! Uh, I slept alone the very first night I was ever here."

"Dorcas must have been off her feed. No, I remember, you were under sedative that night. You were my patient—doesn't count. Some other night? Just one?"

"Your question is irrelevant, immaterial, and beneath my notice."

"That's an adequate answer, I think. But please note that the added bedrooms are as far from my bedroom as possible. Soundproofing is never perfect."

"Jubal, it seems to me that *your* name is much higher up that list than mine can possibly be."

"What?"

"Not to mention Larry and Duke. But, Jubal, almost everybody who knows you assumes that you are keeping the fanciest harem since the Sultan went out of business. Oh, don't misunderstand me—they *envy* you. But they think you're a lecherous old goat, too."

Jubal drummed on the arm of his chair before replying. "Ben, I ordinarily do not mind being treated flippantly by my juniors. I encourage it, as you know. But in some matters I insist that my years be treated with respect. This is one of them."

"Sorry," Ben said stiffly. "I thought if it was all right for you to kick *my* sex life around, you would not mind my being equally frank."

"No, no, no, Ben!—you misunderstand me. Your inquiry was in order and your side comments no more than I had invited. I mean that I require the *girls* to treat me with respect—on this one subject."

"Oh—"

"I am, as you pointed out, old—quite old. Privately, to you alone, I am happy to say that I am still lecherous. But my lechery does not command me and I am not a goat. I prefer dignity and self-respect to indulging in pastimes which, believe me, I have already enjoyed in full measure and do not need to repeat. Ben, a man my age, who looks like a slum clearance in its most depressing stages, can attract a young girl enough to bed her— and possibly big her and thanks for the compliment; it just possibly might not be amiss—through three means only: money . . . or second, the equivalent of money in terms of wills and community property and the like . . . and—pause for question: Can you imagine any of these three girls— these four, let me include Jill—bedding with a man, even a young and handsome one, for *those* reasons?"

"No. Categorical no—not any of them."

"Thank you, sir. I associate only with ladies; I see that you know it. The third incentive is a most female one. A sweet young girl can, and sometimes does, take an old wreck to bed because she is fond of him and sorry for him and wishes to make him happy. Would that reason apply here?"

"Uh . . . yes, Jubal, I think it might. With all four of them."

"I think it might, too. Although I'd hate like hell to have any of them sorry for me. But this third reason which any of these four ladies might find sufficient motivation is *not* sufficient motivation for *me*. I wouldn't put up with it. I have my dignity, sir—and I hope that I retain my reason long enough to extinguish myself if it ever appears about to slip. So please take my name off the list."

Caxton grinned. "Okay—you stiff-necked old coot. I just hope that when I am your age I won't be so all-fired hard to tempt."

Jubal smiled. "Believe me, it's better to be tempted and resist, than not to resist and be disappointed. Now about Duke and Larry: I don't know nor care. Whenever anyone has come here, to work and live as a member of the family, I have made it bluntly plain that this was neither a sweat shop nor a whore house, but a home . . . and, as such, it combined anarchy and tyranny without a trace of democracy, as in any well-run family, i.e., that they were utterly on their own except where I saw fit to give orders, which orders were not subject to vote or debate. My tyranny has never extended to their love life, if any. All the kids who live here have always chosen to keep their private matters reasonably private. At least—" Jubal smiled ruefully. "—until the Martian influence caused things to get a little out of hand . . . which includes you, too, my water brother. But Duke and Larry have been more restrained, in one sense or the other. Perhaps they have been dragging the gals behind every bush. If so, I haven't seen it—and there have been no screams."

Ben thought of adding a little to Jubal's store of facts, decided against it. "Then you think it's Mike."

Jubal scowled. "Yep, I think it's Mike. That part's all right—I told you the girls were smugly happy . . . and I'm not broke plus the fact that I could bleed Mike for any amount without telling the girls. Their babies won't lack. But, Ben, I'm troubled about Mike himself. Very."

"So am I, Jubal."

"And about Jill, too. I should have named Jill."

"Uh . . . Jubal, Jill isn't the problem—other than for me, personally. And that's my hard luck, I hold no grudge. It's Mike."

"Damn it, why can't the boy come home and quit this obscene pulpit pounding?"

"Mmm . . . Jubal, that's not quite what he's doing." Ben added, "I've just come from there."

"Huh? Why didn't you *say* so?"

Ben sighed. "First you wanted to talk art, then you wanted to sing the blues, then you wanted to gossip. What chance have I had?"

"Uh . . . conceded. You have the floor."

"I was coming back from covering the Cape Town conference; I squeezed out a day and visited them. What I saw worried the hell out of me—so much so that I stopped just long enough in Washington to get a few columns ahead, then came straight here. Jubal, couldn't you rig it with Douglas to shut off the faucet and close down this operation?"

Jubal shook his head. "In the first place, I wouldn't. What Mike does with his life is his business."

"You would if you had seen what I saw."

"Not I! But in the second place I *can't.* Nor can Douglas."

"Jubal, you know quite well that Mike would accept any decision you made about his money. He probably wouldn't even understand it—and he certainly wouldn't question it."

"Ah, but he *would* understand it! Ben, recently Mike made his will, drew it up himself—no attorney—and sent it to me to criticize. Ben, it was one of the shrewdest legal documents I've ever seen. He recognized that he had more wealth than his heirs could possibly need—so he used half his money to guard the other half . . . rigged it so that anyone who contests the will does so to his own great disadvantage. It is a very cynical document in that respect and is booby-trapped not only against possible heirs-claimants of his legal parents and his natural parents—he knows he's a bastard, though I don't know how he found out—but also the same with respect to every member of the *Envoy's* company . . . he provided a generous way to settle out of court with any possible unknown heir having a good prima-facie claim—and rigged it so that they would almost have to overthrow the government to go into court and break his will . . . and the will also showed that he knew exactly each stock, bond, security, and asset he owned. I couldn't find *anything* to criticize in it." (—including, Jubal thought, his provision for *you,* my brother!) "Then he went to the trouble of depositing holographic originals in several places . . . and Fair-Witness copies in half a dozen reliable brains. Don't tell *me* that I could rig his money without his understanding what I had done!"

Ben looked morose. "I wish you could."

"I don't. But that was just the starter. It wouldn't help if we could.

Mike hasn't taken a dollar out of his drawing account for almost a year. I know, because Douglas called me to ask if I thought the major portion of the backlog should be reinvested? Mike hadn't bothered to answer his letters. I told him that was his headache . . . but that if I were steward, I would follow my principal's last instructions."

"No withdrawals? Jubal, he's spending a lot."

"Maybe the church racket pays well."

"That's the odd part about it. The Church of All Worlds is not really a church."

"Then what is it?"

"Uh, primarily it's a language school."

"Repeat?"

"To teach the Martian language."

"Well, no harm in that. But I wish, then, that he wouldn't call it a church."

"Well, I guess it *is* a church, within the legal definition."

"Look, Ben, a roller skating rink is a church—as long as some sect claims that roller skating is essential to their faith and a part of their worship. You wouldn't even have to go that far—simply claim that roller skating served a desirable though not essential function parallel to that which religious music serves in most churches. If you can sing to the glory of God, you can skate to the same end. Believe me, this has all been threshed out. There are temples in Malaya which are nothing—to an outsider—but boarding houses for snakes . . . but the same High Court rules them to be 'churches' as protects our own sects."

"Well, Mike raises snakes, too, as well as teaching Martian. But, Jubal, isn't *anything* ruled out?"

"Mmm . . . that's a moot point. There are minor restrictions, adjudicated. A church usually can't charge a fee for fortune telling or calling up spirits of the dead—but it can accept offerings . . . and then let custom make the 'offerings' become fees in fact. Human sacrifice is illegal everywhere—but I'm by no means sure that it is not still done in several spots around the globe . . . and probably right here in this former land of the free and home of the brave. The way to do anything under the guise of religion that would otherwise be suppressed is to do it in the inner sanctum and keep the gentiles out. Why, Ben? Is Mike doing something that might get him jailed or hanged?"

"Uh, I don't know. Probably not."

"Well, if he's careful— The Fosterites have demonstrated how to get by with almost anything. Certainly much more than Joseph Smith was lynched for."

"Matter of fact, Mike has lifted quite a lot from the Fosterites. That's part of what worries me."

"But what *does* worry you? Specifically."

"Uh, Jubal, this has got to be a 'water brother' matter."

"Okay, I had assumed that. I'm prepared to face redhot pincers and the rack, if necessary. Shall I start carrying poison in a hollow tooth? Against the possibility of cracking?"

"Uh, the members of the inner circle are supposed to be able to discorporate voluntarily any second—no poison needed."

"I'm sorry, Ben. I never got that far. Never mind, I know other adequate ways to put up the only final defense against the third degree. Let's have it."

"You can discorporate at will, they tell me—if you learn Martian first. Never mind. Jubal, I said Mike raises snakes. I meant that both figuratively and literally—the whole setup is a snake pit. Unhealthy.

"But let me describe it. Mike's Temple is a big place, almost a labyrinth. A big auditorium for public meetings, some smaller ones for invitational meetings, many smaller rooms—and living quarters, quite a lot of living quarters. Jill sent me a radiogram telling me where to go, so I was dropped at the living quarters entrance on the street the Temple backs onto. The living quarters are above the main auditorium, about as private as you can be and still live in a city."

Jubal nodded. "Makes sense. Be your acts legal or illegal, nosy neighbors are noxious."

"In this case a *very* good idea. A pair of outer doors let me in; I suppose I was scanned first, although I didn't spot the scanner. Through two more sets of automatic doors any one of which would slow down a raiding squad—then up a bounce tube. Jubal, it wasn't an ordinary bounce tube. It wasn't controlled by the passenger, but by someone out of sight. More evidence that they wanted privacy and meant to have it—a raiding squad would need special climbing gear to get up that way. No stairs anywhere. Didn't feel like the ordinary bounce tube, either—frankly, I avoid them when I can; they make me queasy."

"I have never used them and never shall," Jubal said firmly.

"You wouldn't have minded this. I floated up gently as a feather."

"Not me, Ben. I don't trust machinery. It bites." Jubal added, "However, I must concede that Mike's mother was one of the great engineers of all times and his father—his real father—was a number-one pilot and a competent engineer, or better . . . and both of genius level. If Mike has improved bounce tubes until they are fit for humans, I ought not to be surprised."

"As may be. I got to the top and was landed without having to grab for it, or depend on safety nets—I didn't see any, to tell the truth. Through more doors that unlocked for me and into an enormous living room. Enormous! Very oddly furnished and rather austere. Jubal, there are people who think you run an odd household here." `

"I can't imagine why. Just plain and comfortable."

"Well, your ménage is Aunt Jane's Finishing School for Refined Young Ladies compared with the weirdie Mike runs. I'm just barely inside the joint when the first thing I see I don't believe. A babe, tattooed from her chin to her toes—and not a goddam stitch otherwise. Hell, not even the home-grown fig leaf—she was tattooed *everywhere*. Fantastic!"

Jubal said quietly, "You're a big-city bumpkin, Ben. I knew a tattooed lady once. Very nice girl. Intense in some ways. But sweet."

"Well . . ." Ben conceded. "I was giving you a first impression. This gal is very nice, too, once you get adjusted to her pictorial supplement—and the fact that she usually has a snake with her. She's the one who raises them, rather than Mike."

Jubal shook his head. "I was wondering if by any chance it was the same woman. Fully tattooed women are rather scarce these days. But the lady I knew, some thirty years back—too old now to be this one, I suppose—had the usual vulgar fear of snakes, to excess. However, I'm fond of snakes myself . . . I look forward to meeting your friend. I hope."

"You will when you visit Mike. She's sort of a majordomo for him—and a priestess, if you'll pardon the word. Patricia—but called 'Pat,' or 'Patty.' "

"Oh, yes! Jill has spoken of her . . . and thinks very highly of her. Never mentioned her tattoos, however. Probably didn't think it was relevant. Or perhaps none of my business."

"But she's nearly the right age to be your friend. She says. When I said 'babe' I was again giving a first impression. She looks to be in her twenties; she claims her oldest child is that old. Anyhow, she trotted up to meet me, all big smile, put her arms around me and kissed me. 'You're Ben, I know. Welcome, brother! I give you water!'

"You know me, Jubal. I've been in the newspaper racket for years—I've been around. But I had *never* been kissed by a totally strange babe dressed only in tattoos . . . who was determined to be as friendly and affectionate as a collie pup. I was *embarrassed.*"

"Poor Ben. My heart bleeds."

"Damn it, you would have felt the same way."

"No. Remember, I've met one tattooed lady. They feel completely dressed in those tattoos—and rather resent having to put on clothes. Or at least this was true of my friend Sadako. Japanese, she was. But of course the Japanese are not body conscious the way we are."

"Well," Ben answered. "Pat isn't exactly body conscious, either—just about her tattoos. She wants to be stuffed and mounted, nude, when she dies, as a tribute to George."

" 'George'?"

"Sorry. Her husband. Up in heaven, to my relief . . . although she talked about him as if he had just slipped out for a short beer. While she was behaving as if she expected a trial mounting and stuffing any moment. But, essentially, Pat is a lady . . . and she didn't let me stay embarrassed—"

xxxi

PATRICIA HAD HER ARMS around Ben Caxton and gave him the all-out kiss of brotherhood before he knew what hit him. She felt at once his unease and was herself surprised, because Michael had told her to expect him, given her Ben's face in her mind, had explained that Ben was a brother in all fullness, of the Inner Nest, and she knew that Jill was grown-closer with Ben second only to that with Michael . . . which was always necessarily first since Michael was the fountain and source of all their knowledge of the water of life.

But the foundation of Patricia's nature was an endless wish to make other people as happy as she was; she slowed down. She invited Ben to get rid of his clothes but did so casually and did not press the matter, except to ask him to remove his shoes, with the explanation that the Nest was everywhere kind to bare feet and the unstated corollary that street shoes would not be kind to it—it was soft and clean as only Michael's powers could keep things clean, which Ben could see for himself.

Aside from that she merely pointed out where to hang any clothes he found too warm for the Nest and hurried away to fetch him a drink. She didn't ask his preferences; she knew them from Jill. She merely decided that he would choose a double martini this time rather than Scotch and soda, the poor dear looked tired. When she came back with a drink for each of them, Ben was barefooted and had removed his street jacket. "Brother, may you never thirst."

"We share water," he agreed and drank. "But there's mighty little water in *that.*"

"Enough," she answered. "Michael says that the water could be completely in the thought; it is the sharing. I grok he speaks rightly."

"I grok. And it's just what I needed. Thanks, Patty."

"Ours is yours and you are ours. We're glad you're safely home. Just now the others are all at services or teaching. But there's no hurry; they will come when waiting is filled. Would you like to look around your Nest?"

Still puzzled but interested Ben let her lead him on a guided tour. Some parts of it were commonplace: a huge kitchen with a bar at one end —rather short on gadgets and having the same kind-to-the-feet floor covering as elsewhere, but not notable otherwise save for size—a library even more loaded than Jubal's, bathrooms ample and luxurious, bedrooms— Ben decided that they must be bedrooms although they contained no beds but simply floors that were even softer than elsewhere; Patty called them "little nests" and showed him one she said she usually slept in.

It contained her snakes.

It had been fitted on one side for the comfort of snakes. Ben suppressed his own slight queasiness about snakes until he came to the cobras. "It's all right," she assured him. "We did have glass in front of them. But Michael has taught them that they must not come past this line."

"I think I would rather trust glass."

"Okay, Ben." In remarkably short order she replaced the glass barrier, front and top. But he was relieved when they left, even though he managed to stroke Honey Bun when invited to. Before returning to the huge living room Pat showed him one other room. It was large, circular, had a floor which seemed almost as cushiony as that of the bedrooms, and no furniture. In its center was a round pool of water, almost a swimming pool. "This," she told him, "is the Innermost Temple, where we receive new brothers into the Nest." She went over and dabbled a foot in the water. "Just right," she said. "Want to share water and grow closer? Or maybe just swim?"

"Uh, not right now."

"Waiting is," she agreed. They returned to the living room and Patricia went to get him another drink. Ben settled himself on a big, very comfortable couch—then got up at once. The place was too warm for him, that first drink was making him sweat, and leaning back on a couch that adjusted itself too well to his contours made him just that much hotter. He decided it was damn silly to dress the way he would in Washington, warm as it was in here—and with Patty decked out in nothing but ink and a bull

snake she had left around her shoulders during the latter part of the tour—
that reptile would keep him from temptation even if it wasn't already
clearly evident that Patty was not trying to be provocative.

He compromised by leaving on jockey shorts and hung his other
clothes in the foyer. As he did so, he noticed a sign printed on the inside of
the door through which he had entered: *"Did You Remember to Dress?"*

He decided that, in this odd household, this gentle warning might be
necessary if any were absent-minded. Then he saw something else that he
had missed on coming in, his attention earlier having been seized by the
sight of Patty herself. On each side of the door was a large bowl, as gross
as a bushel basket—and each was filled with money.

More than filled— Federation notes of various denominations spilled
out on the floor.

He was staring at this improbability when Patricia returned. "Here's
your drink, Brother Ben. Grow close in Happiness."

"Uh, thanks." His eyes returned to the money.

She followed his glance. "You must think I'm a sloppy housekeeper,
Ben—and I am. Michael makes it so easy, most of the cleaning and such,
that I forget." She squatted down, retrieved the money, stuffed it into the
less crowded bowl.

"Patty, why in the world?"

"Oh. We keep it here because this door leads out to the street. Just for
convenience. If one of us is leaving the Nest—and I do, myself, almost
every day for grocery shopping—we are likely to need money. So we keep
it where you won't forget to take some with you."

"You mean . . . just grab a handful and go?"

"Why, of course, dear. Oh, I see what you mean. But there is never
anyone here but us. No visitors, ever. If any of us have friends outside—
and, of course, all of us do—there are plenty of nice rooms lower down,
the ordinary sort that outsiders are used to, where we can visit with them.
This money isn't where it can tempt a weak person."

"Huh! I'm pretty weak, myself!"

She chuckled gently at his joke. "How can it tempt you when it's
already yours? You're part of the Nest."

"Uh . . . I suppose so. But don't you worry about burglars?" He
was trying to guess how much money one of those bowls contained. Most
of the notes seemed to be larger than singles—hell, he could see one with
three zeroes on it still on the floor, where Patty had missed it in her tidying
up.

"One did get in, just last week."

"So? How much did he steal?"

"Oh, he didn't. Michael sent him away."

"Called the cops?"

"Oh, no, no! Michael would *never* turn anybody over to the cops. I grok that would be a wrongness. Michael just—" She shrugged. "—made him go away. Then Duke fixed the hole in the skylight in the garden room —did I show you that? It's lovely . . . a grass floor. But I remember that you have a grass floor, Jill told me. That's where Michael first saw one. Is it grass all over? Every room?"

"Just my living room."

"If I ever get to Washington, can I walk on it? Lie down on it? Please?"

"Of course, Patty. Uh . . . it's yours."

"I know, dear. But it's not in the Nest, and Michael has taught us that it is good to ask, even when we know the answer is yes. I'll lie on it and feel the grass against me and be filled with Happiness to be in my brother's 'little nest.' "

"You'll be most welcome, Patty." Ben reminded himself sharply that he didn't give a hoot in hell what his neighbors thought—but he hoped she would leave her snakes behind. "When will you be there?"

"I don't know. When waiting is filled. Maybe Michael knows."

"Well, warn me if you can, so I'll be in town. If not, Jill always knows the code for my door—I change it occasionally. Patty, doesn't anybody keep track of this money?"

"What for, Ben?"

"Uh, people usually do."

"Well, we don't. Just help yourself as you go out—then put back any you have left when you come home, if you remember to. Michael told me to keep the grouch bag filled. If it runs low I get some more from him."

Ben dropped the matter, stonkered by the simplicity of the arrangement. He already had some idea, from Mike and second-hand from Jill and Jubal, of the moneyless communism of the Martian culture; he could see that Mike had set up an enclave of it here—and these bowls of cash marked the transition point whereby one passed from Martian to Terran economy. He wondered if Patty knew that it was a fake . . . bolstered up by Mike's enormous fortune. He decided not to ask.

"Patty, how many are there in the Nest?" He felt a mild worry that he was acquiring too many sharing brothers without his consent, then shoved back the thought as unworthy—after all, why would any of them want to sponge on him? Other than, possibly to lie on his grass rug—*he* didn't have any pots of gold just inside his door.

"Let me see . . . there are almost twenty now, counting novitiate brothers who don't really think in Martian yet and aren't ordained."

"Are you ordained, Patty?"

"Oh, yes. But mostly I teach. Beginners' classes in Martian, and I help novitiate brothers and such. And Dawn and I—Dawn and Jill are each High Priestess—Dawn and I are pretty well-known Fosterites, especially Dawn, so we work together to show other Fosterites that the Church of All Worlds doesn't conflict with the Faith, any more than being a Baptist keeps a man from joining the Masons." She showed Ben Foster's kiss, explained what it meant, and showed him also its miraculous companion placed by Mike.

"They all know what Foster's kiss means and how hard it is to win it . . . and by then they've seen some of Mike's miracles and they are just about ripe to buckle down and sweat to climb into a higher circle."

"It's an effort?"

"Of course it is, Ben—for them. In your case and mine, and Jill's, and a few others—you know them all—Michael called us straight into brotherhood. But to others Michael first teaches a discipline—not a faith but a way to realize faith in works. And that means they've got to start by learning Martian. That's not easy; I'm not perfect in it myself. But it is much Happiness to work and learn. You asked about the size of the Nest— let me see, Duke and Jill and Michael and myself . . . two Fosterites, Dawn and myself . . . one circumcised Jew and his wife and four children—"

"Kids in the Nest?"

"Oh, more than a dozen. Not here, but in the nestlings' nest just off of here; nobody could meditate with kids hooting and hollering and raising Ned. Want to see it?"

"Uh, later."

"One Catholic couple with a baby boy—excommunicated I'm sorry to say; their priest found out about it. Michael had to give them very special help; it was a nasty shock to them—and so utterly unnecessary. They were getting up early every Sunday morning to go to mass just as usual—but kids will talk. One Mormon family of the new schism—that's three more, and their kids. The rest are the usual run of Protestants and one atheist . . . that is, he thought he was an atheist, until Michael opened his eyes. He came here to scoff; he stayed to learn . . . and he'll be a priest before long. Uh, nineteen grown-ups, I'm pretty sure that's right though it's hard to say, since we're hardly ever all in the Nest at once, except for our own services in the Innermost Temple. The Nest is built to hold eighty-one—that's 'three-filled,' or three times three multiplied by itself—but Michael says that there will be much waiting before we'd need a bigger nest and by then we will be building other nests. Ben? Wouldn't you like to see an outer service, see how Michael makes the pitch, instead of just listening to me ramble on? Michael will be preaching just about now."

"Why, yes, if it's not too much trouble."

"You could go by yourself. But I'd like to go with you . . . and I'm not busy. Just a sec, dearie, while I get decent."

"Jubal, she was back in a couple of minutes in a robe not unlike Anne's Witness robe but cut differently, with angel-wing sleeves and a high neck and the trademark Mike uses for the Church of All Worlds—nine concentric circles and a conventionalized Sun—embroidered over her heart. This getup was a priestess robe, her vestments; Jill and the other priestesses wear the same sort, except that Patty's was opaque, a heavy synthetic silk, and came so high that it covered her cartoons, and was caught at both wrists for the same reason. She had put on stockings, too, or maybe bobby socks, and was carrying sandals.

"Changed the hell out of her, Jubal. It gave her great dignity. Her face is quite nice and I could see that she was considerably older than I had first guessed her although not within twenty years of what she claims to be. She has an exquisite complexion and I thought what a shame it was that anyone had ever touched a tattooing needle to such skin.

"I had dressed again. She asked me to take off just my shoes because we weren't going out the way I had come in. She led me back through the Nest and out into a corridor; we stopped to put on shoes and went down a ramp that wound down maybe a couple of floors until we reached a gallery. It was sort of a loge overlooking the main auditorium. Mike was holding forth on the platform. No pulpit, no altar, just a lecture hall, with a big All-Worlds symbol on the wall behind him. There was a robed priestess on the platform with him and, at that distance, I thought it was Jill— but it wasn't; it was another woman who looks a bit like her and is almost as beautiful. The other high priestess, Dawn—Dawn Ardent."

"What was that name?" Jubal interrupted.

"Dawn Ardent—née Higgins, if you want to be fussy."

"I've met her."

"I know you have, you allegedly retired goat. She's got a crush on you."

Jubal shook his head. "Some mistake. The 'Dawn Ardent' I mean I just barely met, about two years ago. She wouldn't even remember me."

"She remembers you. She gets every one of your pieces of commercial crud, on tape, under every pseudonym she has been able to track down. She goes to sleep by them, usually, and they give her beautiful dreams. She says. Furthermore there is no doubt that she knows who you are. Jubal, that big living room, the Nest proper, has exactly *one* item of ornamentation, if you'll pardon the word—a life-sized color solly of your head. Looks as if you had been decapitated, with your face in a hideous grin. A candid shot that Duke sneaked of you, I understand."

"Why, that brat!"

"Jill asked him to, behind your back."

"Double brat!"

"Sir, you are speaking of the woman I love—although I'm not alone in that distinction. But Mike put her up to it. Brace yourself, Jubal—you are the patron saint of the Church of All Worlds."

Jubal looked horrified. "They can't do this to me!"

"They already have. But don't worry; it's unofficial and not publicized. But Mike freely gives you credit, inside the Nest just among water brothers, for having instigated the whole show and explained things to him so well that he was finally able to figure out how to put over Martian theology to humans."

Jubal looked about to retch. Ben went on, "I'm afraid you can't duck it. But in addition, Dawn thinks you're beautiful. Aside from that quirk, she is an intelligent woman—and utterly charming. But I digress. Mike spotted us at once, waved and called out, 'Hi, Ben! Later'—and went on with his spiel.

"Jubal, I'm not going to try to quote him, you'll just have to hear it. He didn't sound preachy and he didn't wear robes—just a smart, well-tailored, white syntholinen suit. He sounded like a damned good car salesman, except that there was no doubt he was talking about religion. He cracked jokes and told parables—none of them straitlaced but nothing really dirty, either. The essence of it was a sort of pantheism . . . one of his parables was the oldy about the earthworm burrowing along through the soil who encounters another earthworm and at once says, 'Oh, you're beautiful! You're lovely! Will you marry me?' and is answered: 'Don't be silly! I'm your other end.' You've heard it before?"

" 'Heard it?' I *wrote* it!"

"I hadn't realized it was *that* old. Anyhow, Mike made good use of it. His idea is that whenever you encounter any other grokking thing—he didn't say 'grokking' at this stage—any other living thing, man, woman, or stray cat . . . you are simply encountering your 'other end' . . . and the universe is just a little thing we whipped up among us the other night for our entertainment and then agreed to forget the gag. He put it in a much more sugar-coated fashion, being extremely careful not to tread on competitors' toes.' "

Jubal nodded and looked sour. "Solipsism and Pantheism. Teamed together they can explain *anything*. Cancel out any inconvenient fact, reconcile all theories, and include any facts or delusions you care to name. Trouble is, it's just cotton candy, all taste and no substance—and as unsatisfactory as solving a story by saying: '—and then the little boy fell out of bed and woke up; it was just a dream.' "

"Don't crab at me about it; take it up with Mike. But believe me, he made it sound convincing. Once he stopped and said, 'You must be tired of so much talk—' and they yelled back, *'No!'*—I tell you, he really had them. But he protested that his voice was tired and, anyhow, a church ought to have miracles and this was a church, even though it didn't have a mortgage. 'Dawn, fetch me my miracle box.' Then he did some really amazing sleight-of-hand—did you know he had been a magician with a carnival?"

"I knew he had been with it. He never told me the exact nature of his shame."

"He's a crackerjack magician; he did stunts for them that had *me* fooled. But it wouldn't have mattered if it had been only the card tricks kids learn; it was his patter that had them rolling in the aisles. Finally he stopped and said apologetically, 'The Man from Mars is supposed to be able to do wonderful things . . . so I have to pass a few miracles each meeting. I can't help being the Man from Mars; it's just something that happened to me. But miracles can happen for *you,* too, if you want them. However, to be allowed to see anything more than these narrow-gauge miracles, you must enter the Circle. Those of you who truly want to learn I will see later. Cards are being passed around.'

"Patty explained to me what Mike was really doing. 'This crowd is just marks, dear—people who come out of curiosity or maybe have been shilled in by some of our own people who have reached one of the inner circles.' Jubal, Mike has the thing rigged in nine circles, like degrees in a lodge—and nobody is told that there actually *is* a circle farther in until they're ready to be inducted into it. 'This is just Michael's bally,' Pat told me, 'which he does as easy as he breathes—while all the time he's feeling them out, sizing them up, getting inside their heads and deciding which ones are even possible. Maybe one in ten. That's why he strings it out— Duke is up behind that grille and Michael tells him every mark who just might measure up, where he sits and everything. Michael's about to turn this tip . . . and spill the ones he doesn't want. Dawn will handle that part, after she gets the seating diagram from Duke.' "

"How did they work that?" asked Harshaw.

"I didn't see it, Jubal. Does it matter? There are a dozen ways they could cut from the herd the ones they wanted as long as Mike knew which they were and had worked out some way to signal Duke. I don't know. Patty says he's clairvoyant and says it with a straight face—and, do you know, I won't discount the possibility. But right after that, they took the collection. Mike didn't do even this in church style—you know, soft music and dignified ushers. He said nobody would believe that this was a church service if he didn't take a collection . . . so he would, but with a difference. Either take it or put it—suit yourself. Then, so help me, they passed collection baskets already loaded with money. Mike kept telling them that this was what the last crowd had left, so help themselves . . . if they were broke or hungry and needed it. But if they felt like giving . . . give. Share with others. Just do one or the other—put something in, or take something out. When I saw it, I figured he had found one more way to get rid of too much money."

Jubal said thoughtfully, "I'm not sure he would lose by it. That pitch, properly given, should result in more people giving *more* . . . while a few take just a little. And probably *very* few. I would say that it would be hard indeed to reach in and take out money when the people on each side of you are putting money in . . . unless you need it awfully badly."

"I don't know, Jubal . . . but I understand that they are just as casual about those collections as they are about that stack of dough upstairs. But Patty whisked me away when Mike turned the service over to his high priestess. I was taken to a much smaller auditorium where services were just opening for the seventh circle in—people who had belonged for several months at least and had made progress. If it *is* progress.

"Jubal, Mike had gone straight from one to the other, and I couldn't adjust to the change. That outer meeting was half popular lecture and half sheer entertainment—this one was more nearly a voodoo rite. Mike was in robes this time; he looked taller, ascetic, and intense—I swear his eyes gleamed. The place was dimly lighted, there was music that was creepy and yet made you want to dance. This time Patty and I took a double seat together, a couch that was darn near a bed. What the service was all about I couldn't say. Mike would sing out to them in Martian, they would answer in Martian—except for chants of 'Thou art God! Thou art God!' which was always echoed by some Martian word that would make my throat sore to try to pronounce it."

Jubal made a croaking noise. "Was that it?"

"Huh? I believe it was—allowing for your horrible tall-corn accent. Jubal . . . are *you* hooked? Have you just been stringing me along?"

"No. Stinky taught it to me—and he says that it's heresy of the blackest sort. By his lights I mean—*I* couldn't care less. It's the Martian word Mike translates as: 'Thou art God.' But our brother Mahmoud says that isn't even close to being a translation. It's the universe proclaiming its own self-awareness . . . or it's 'peccavimus' with a total absence of contrition . . . or a dozen other things, all of which don't translate it. Stinky says that not only it can't be translated but that he doesn't really understand it in Martian—except that it is a bad word, the worst possible in his opinion . . . and much closer to Satan's defiance than it is to the blessing of a benevolent God. Go on. Was that all there was to it? Just a bunch of fanatics yelling Martian at each other?"

"Uh . . . Jubal, they didn't yell and it wasn't fanatical. Sometimes they would barely whisper, the room almost dead quiet. Then it might climb in volume a little but not much. They did it in sort of a rhythm, a pattern, like a cantata, as if they had rehearsed it a long time . . . and yet it didn't feel as if they had rehearsed it; it felt more as if they were all just one person, humming to himself whatever he felt at the moment. Jubal, you've seen how the Fosterites get themselves worked up—"

"Too much of it, I'm sorry to say."

"Well, this was not that sort of frenzy at all; this was quiet and easy, like dropping off to sleep. It was intense all right and got steadily more so, but—Jubal, ever sit in on a spiritualist séance?"

"I have. I've tried everything I could, Ben."

"Then you know how the tension can grow without anybody moving or saying a word. This was much more like that than it was like a shouting revival, or even the most sedate church service. But it wasn't mild; it packed terrific wallop."

"The technical word is 'Apollonian.' "

"Huh?"

"As opposed to 'Dionysian.' And both rather Procrustean I'm sorry to say. People tend to simplify 'Apollonian' into 'mild,' and 'calm,' and 'cool.' But 'Apollonian' and 'Dionysian' are two sides of the same coin—a nun on her knees in her cell, holding perfectly still and her facial muscles relaxed, can be in a religious ecstasy more frenzied than any priestess of Pan Priapus celebrating the vernal equinox. Ecstasy is in the skull, not in the setting-up exercises." Jubal frowned. "Another common error is to identify 'Apollonian' with 'good'—merely because our most respectable sects are all rather Apollonian in ritual and precept. Mere local prejudice. Proceed."

"Well . . . things weren't as quiet as a nun at her devotions anyhow. They didn't just stay seated and let Mike entertain them. They wandered about a bit, swapped seats, and there was no doubt that there was necking going on; no more than necking, I believe, but the lighting was very low key and it was hard to see from one pew to another. One gal wandered over our way, started to join us, but Patty gave her some sign to let us be . . . so she just kissed us and left." Ben grinned. "Kissed quite well, too, though she didn't dally about it. I was the only person not dressed in a robe; I was as conspicuous as a space suit in a salon. But she gave no sign of noticing.

"The whole thing was very casual . . . and yet it seemed as coordinated as a ballerina's muscles. Mike kept busy, sometimes out in front, sometimes wandering among the others—once he squeezed my shoulder and kissed Patty, unhurriedly but quickly. He didn't speak to me. Back of the spot where he stood when he seemed to be leading them was some sort of a dingus like a magic mirror, or possibly a big stereo tank; he used it for 'miracles,' only at this stage he never used the word—at least not in English. Jubal, every church promises miracles. But it's always jam yesterday and jam tomorrow, never jam today."

"Exception," Jubal interrupted again. "Many of them deliver as a matter of routine—exempli gratia among many: Christian Scientists and Roman Catholics."

"Catholics? You mean Lourdes?"

"The example included Lourdes, for what it may be worth. But I referred to the Miracle of Transubstantiation, called forth by every Catholic priest at least daily."

"Hmm— Well, I can't judge that subtle a miracle. To a heathen outsider like myself that sort of miracle is impossible to test. As for Christian Scientists, I won't argue—but if I break a leg, I want a sawbones."

"Then watch where you put your feet," Jubal growled. "Don't bother me with your fractures."

"Wouldn't think of it. I want one who wasn't a classmate of William Harvey."

"Harvey could reduce a fracture. Proceed."

"Yeah, but how about his classmates? Jubal, those things you cited as miracles may be such—but Mike offers splashy ones, ones the cash customers can *see*. He's either an expert illusionist, one who would make the fabled Houdini look clumsy . . . or an amazing hypnotist—"

"He might be both."

"—or he's smoothed the bugs out of closed-circuit stereovision to the point where it simply cannot be told from reality, for his special effects. Or 'I've been 'ad fer a button, dearie.' "

"How can you rule out *real* miracles, Ben?"

"I included them with the button. It's not a theory I like to think about. Whatever he used, it was good theater. Once the lights came up behind him and here was a black-maned lion, lying as stately and sedately as if guarding library steps, while a couple of little lambs wobbled around him. The lion just blinked and yawned. Sure, Hollywood can tape that sort of special effect any day—but it looked real, so much so that I thought I smelled the lion . . . and of course that can be faked, too."

"Why do you insist on fakery?"

"Damn it, I'm *trying* to be judicial!"

"Then don't lean over backwards so far you fall down. Try to emulate Anne."

"I'm not Anne. And I wasn't very judicial at the time. I just lounged back and enjoyed it, in a warm glow. It didn't even annoy me that I couldn't understand most of what was said; it felt as if I got the gist of it. Mike did a lot of gung-ho miracles—or illusions. Levitation and such. I wasn't being critical, I was willing to enjoy it as good showmanship. Patty slipped away toward the end after whispering to me to stay where I was and she would be back. 'Michael has just told them that any who do not feel ready for the next circle should now leave,' she told me.

"I said, 'I guess I had better leave, too.'

"And she said, 'Oh, no, dear! You're already Ninth Circle—you know that. Just stay seated, I'll be back.' And she left.

"I don't think anybody decided to chicken out. This group was not only Seventh Circle but Seventh-Circlers who were all supposed to be promoted. But I didn't really notice for the lights came up again . . . and there was Jill!

"Jubal, this time it definitely did not feel like stereovision. Jill picked me out with her eyes and smiled at me. Oh, I know, if the person being photographed looks directly at the cameras, then the eyes meet yours no matter where you're seated. But if Mike has it smoothed out this well, he had better patent it. Jill was dressed in an outlandish costume—a priestess outfit, I suppose, but not like the others. Mike started intoning something to her and to us, partly in English . . . stuff about the Mother of All, the unity of many, and started calling her by a series of names . . . and with each name her costume changed—"

Ben Caxton came quickly alert when the lights came up behind the High Priest and he saw Jill Boardman posed, above and behind the priest. He blinked and made sure that he had not again been fooled by lighting and distance—this was Jill! She looked back at him and smiled. He half listened to the invocation while thinking that he had been convinced that the space behind the Man from Mars was surely a stereo tank, or some gimmick. But he could almost swear that he could walk up those steps and pinch her.

He was tempted to do so—then reminded himself that it would be a crummy trick to ruin Mike's show. Wait till it was over and Jill was free—

"Cybele!"

—and Jill's costume suddenly changed.

"Isis!"

—again.

"Frigg!" . . . *"Ge!"* . . . *"Devi!"* . . . *"Ishtar!"* . . . *"Maryam!"*

"Mother Eve! Mater Deum Magna! Loving and Beloved, Life Undying—"

Caxton stopped hearing the words . . . for Jill suddenly was Mother Eve, clothed only in her own glory. The light spread and he saw that she was standing gently at rest in a Garden, beside a tree around and on which was twined a great serpent.

Jill smiled at them all, turned a little, reached up and smoothed the serpent's head—turned back and opened her arms to all of them.

The first of the candidates moved forward to enter the Garden.

Patty returned and touched Caxton on the shoulder. "Ben . . . I'm back. Come with me, dear."

Caxton was reluctant, he wanted to stay and drink in the glorious vision of Jill . . . he wanted to do more than that; he wanted to join that procession and go where she was. But he found himself getting up and leaving with Patricia. He looked back and saw Mike about to put his arms around and kiss the first woman in the line . . . turned to follow Patricia outside and failed to see the candidates' robe vanish as Mike kissed her— and did not see what followed at once, when Jill kissed the first male candidate for elevation to the eighth circle . . . and *his* robe vanished.

"We have to go long way 'round," Patty explained, "to give them time to get clear and on into the Temple of the Eighth Circle. Oh, it wouldn't actually hurt to barge in, but it would waste Michael's time, getting them back in the mood—and he does work so very hard."

"Where are we going now?"

"To pick up Honey Bun. Then back to the Nest. Unless you want to take part in the initiation to the Eighth Circle. You can, you know—since you're Ninth Circle. But you haven't learned Martian yet; you'd find it very confusing."

"Well—I'd like to see Jill. When will she be free?"

"Oh. She told me to tell you that she was going to duck upstairs and see you. Down this way, Ben."

A door opened and Ben found himself in the garden he had seen. The serpent was still festooned on the tree; she raised her head as they came in. "There, there, dear!" Patricia said to her. "You were Mama's good girl, weren't you?" She gently unwrapped the boa and flaked it down into a basket, tail first. "Duke brought her down for me but I have to arrange her on the tree and tell her to stay there and not go wandering off. You were lucky, Ben; a transition service from Seventh to Eighth happens very seldom—Michael won't hold it until there are enough candidates ready to build and hold the mood . . . although we used to supply people out of the Innermost Circle to help the first candidates from outside through."

Ben carried Honey Bun for Patty until they reached the top level . . . and learned that a fourteen-foot snake is quite a load; the basket had steel braces and needed them. As soon as they were that high, Patricia stopped. "Put her down, Ben." She took off her robe and handed it to him, then go out the snake and draped it around her. "This is Honey Bun's reward for being a good girl; she expects to cuddle up to Mama. I've got a class starting almost at once, so I'll walk the rest of the way with her on me and let her stay on me until the last possible second. It's not a goodness to disappoint a snake; they're just like babies. They can't grok in fullness—except that Honey Bun groks Mama . . . and Michael, of course."

They walked the fifty yards or so to the entrance to the Nest proper and at its door Patricia let Ben take off her sandals for her after he removed his shoes. He wondered how she could balance on one foot under such a load . . . and noticed, too, that she had gotten rid of her socks or stockings at some point—no doubt while she was out arranging Honey Bun's stage appearance.

They went inside and she went with him, still clothed in the big snake, while he shucked down to his jockey shorts—stalling as he did so, trying to make up his mind whether to discard the shorts, too. He had seen enough to be fairly certain that clothing, any clothing, inside the Nest was as unconventional, by *these* conventions (and possibly as rude), as hob-nailed boots on a dance floor. The gentle warning on the exit door, the fact that there were no windows anywhere in the Nest, the womblike comfort of the Nest itself, Patricia's lack of attire plus the fact that she had suggested (but not insisted) that he do likewise—all added up to an unmistakable pattern of habitual domestic nudity . . . among people who were all at least nominally his own "water brothers," even though he had not met most of them.

He had seen further confirmation in addition to Patricia, whose behavior he had discounted somewhat from a vague feeling that a tattooed lady might very well have odd habits about clothing. On coming into the living room they had passed a man headed the other way, toward the baths and the "little nests"—and he had worn less than Patricia by one snake and lots of pictures. He had greeted them with "Thou art God" and gone on, apparently as used to buff as Patricia was. But, Ben reminded himself, this "brother" hadn't seemed surprised that Ben was dressed, either.

There had been other such evidence in the living room: a body sprawled face down on a couch across the room—a woman, Ben thought, although he had not wanted to stare after a quick glance had shown him that this one was naked, too.

Ben Caxton had thought himself to be sophisticated about such things. Swimming without suits he considered only sensible. He knew that many families were casually naked in their own homes—and this was a family, of sorts—although he himself had not been brought up in the custom. He had even (once) let a girl invite him to a nudist resort, and it had not troubled him especially, after the first five minutes or so—he had simply regarded it as a silly lot of trouble to go to for the dubious pleasures of poison ivy, scratches, and an all-over sunburn that had put him in bed for a day.

But now he found himself balanced in perfect indecision, unable to make up his mind between the probable urbanity of removing his symbolic fig leaf . . . and the even stronger probability—certainty he decided—that if he did so and strangers came in who were dressed and stayed that way, he would feel all-fired silly! Hell, he might even blush!

"What would *you* have done, Jubal?" Ben demanded.

Harshaw lifted his eyebrows. "Are you expecting me to be shocked, Ben? I have seen the human body, professionally and otherwise, for most of a century. It is often pleasing to the eye, frequently most depressing—and never significant per se. Only in the subjective value the viewer places on the sight. I grok Mike runs his household along nudist lines. Shall I cheer? Or must I cry? Neither. It leaves me unmoved."

"Damn it, Jubal, it's easy for you to sit there and be Olympian about it—*you* weren't faced with the choice. I've never seen *you* take off your pants in company."

"Nor are you likely to. 'Other times, other customs.' But I grok you were not motivated by modesty. You were suffering from a morbid fear of appearing ridiculous—a well-known phobia with a long, pseudo-Greek name with which I shall not bore you."

"Nonsense! I simply wasn't certain what was polite."

"Nonsense to you, sir—you already *knew* what was polite . . . but were afraid you might look silly . . . or possibly feared being trapped inadvertently in the gallant reflex. But I seem to grok that Mike had a reason for instituting this household custom—Mike always has reasons for everything he does, although some of them seem strange to me."

"Oh, yes. He has reasons. Jill told me about them."

Ben Caxton was standing in the foyer, his back to the living room and his hands on his shorts, having told himself, not very firmly, to take the plunge and get it over with—when two arms came snugly around his waist from behind. "Ben darling! How *wonderful* to have you here!"

He turned and had Jill in his arms and her mouth warm and greedy against his—and was very glad that he had not quite finished stripping. For she was no longer "Mother Eve"; she was wearing one of the long, all-enveloping priestess robes. Nevertheless he was happily aware that he had a double armful of live, warm, and gently squirming girl; her priestly vestment was no greater impediment than would have been a thin gown, and both kinesthetic and tactile senses told him that the rest was Jill.

"Golly!" she said, breaking from the kiss. "I've missed you, you old beast. Thou art God."

"Thou art God," he conceded. "Jill, you're prettier than ever."

"Yes," she agreed. "It does that for you. But I can't tell you what a thrill it gave me to catch your eye at the blow-off."

" 'Blow-off'?"

"Jill means," Patricia put in, "the end of the service where she is All Mother, Mater Deum Magna. Kids, I must rush."

"Never hurry, Pattycake."

"I gotta rush so I won't have to hurry. Ben, I must put Honey Bun to bed and go down and take my class—so kiss me good-night now. Please?"

Ben found himself kissing good-night a woman still wrapped most thoroughly by a giant snake—and decided that he could think of better ways . . . say wearing full armor. But he tried to ignore Honey Bun and treat Patty as she deserved to be treated.

Jill kissed her and said, "Stop by and tell Mike to stall until I get there, pretty please."

"He will anyhow. 'Night, dears." She left unhurriedly.

"Ben, isn't she a lamb?"

"She certainly is. Although she had me baffled at first."

"I grok. But it's not because she's tattooed nor because of her snakes, I know. She baffled you—she baffles everybody—because Patty never has any doubts; she just automatically always does the right thing. She's very much like Mike. She's the most advanced of any of us—she ought to be high priestess. But she won't take it because her tattoos would make some of the duties difficult—be a distraction at least—and she doesn't want them taken off."

"How could you possibly take off that much tattooing? With a flensing knife? It would kill her."

"Not at all, dear. Mike could take them off completely, not leave a trace, and not even hurt her. Believe me, dear, he could. But he groks that she does not think of them as belonging to her; she's just their custodian—and he groks with her about it. Come sit down. Dawn will be in with supper for all three of us in a moment—I must eat while we visit or I won't have a chance until tomorrow. That's poor management with all eternity to draw from . . . but I didn't know when you would get here and you happen to arrive on a very full day. But tell me what you think of what you've seen? Dawn tells me you saw an outsiders' service, too."

"Yes."

"Well?"

"Mike," Caxton said slowly, "has certainly blossomed out. I think he could sell shoes to snakes."

"I'm quite sure he could. But he never would because it would be wrong—snakes don't need them. What's the matter, Ben? I grok there's something bothering you."

"No," he answered. "Certainly not anything I can put my finger on. Oh, I'm not much for churches . . . but I'm not against them exactly—certainly not against this one. I guess I just don't grok it."

"I'll ask you again in a week or two. There's no hurry."

"I won't be here even a week."

"You have some columns on the spike"—it was not a question.

"Three fresh ones. But I shouldn't stay even that long."

"I think you will . . . then you'll phone in a few . . . probably about the Church. By then I think you will grok to stay much longer."

"I don't think so."

"Waiting is, until fullness. You know it's not a church?"

"Well, Patty did say something of the sort."

"Let's say it's not a religion. It *is* a church, in every legal and moral sense—and I suppose our Nest is a monastery. But we're not trying to bring people to God; that's a contradiction in terms, you can't even say it in Martian. We're not trying to save souls, because souls can't be lost. We're not trying to get people to have faith, because what we offer is not faith but truth—truth they can check; we don't urge them to believe it. Truth for practical purposes, for here-and-now, truth as matter of fact as an ironing board and as useful as a loaf of bread . . . so practical that it can make war and hunger and violence and hate as unnecessary as . . . as

—well, as clothes here in the Nest. But they have to learn Martian first. That's the only hitch—finding people who are honest enough to believe what they see, and then are willing to do the hard work—it *is* hard work—of learning the language it can be taught in. A composer couldn't possibly write down a symphony in English . . . and this sort of symphony can't be stated in English any more than Beethoven's Fifth can be." She smiled. "But Mike never hurries. Day after day he screens hundreds of people . . . finds a few dozen . . . and out of those a very few trickle into the Nest and he trains them further. And someday Mike will have some of us so thoroughly trained that we can go out and start other nests, and then it can begin to snowball. But there's no hurry. None of us, even us in the Nest, are really trained. Are we, dear?"

Ben looked up, somewhat startled by Jill's last three words—then was really startled to find bending over him to offer him a plate a woman whom he belatedly recognized as the other high priestess—Dawn, yes, that was right. His surprise was not reduced by the fact that she was dressed in Patricia's fashion, minus tattoos.

But Dawn was not startled. She smiled and said, "Your supper, my brother Ben. Thou art God."

"Uh, thou art God. Thanks." He was beyond being surprised when she leaned down and kissed him, then got plates for herself and Jill, sat down on the other side of him and began to eat. He was willing to concede that, if not God, Dawn had the best attributes associated with goddesses; he was rather sorry she had not sat down across from him—he couldn't see her well without being obvious about it.

"No," Dawn agreed, between bites, "we aren't really trained yet, Jill. But waiting will fill."

"That's the size of it, Ben," Jill continued. "For example, I took a break to eat. But Mike hasn't had a bite for well over twenty-four hours . . . and won't eat until he's not needed—you happened to hit a crowded day, because of that group making transition to Eighth Circle. Then when Mike is through, he'll eat like a pig and that will carry him as long as necessary. Besides that, Dawn and I get tired . . . don't we, sweet?"

"We surely do. But I'm not too tired, Gillian. Let me take this service and you can visit with Ben. Give me that robe."

"You're crazy in your little pointy head, my love—and Mama spank. Ben, she's been on duty almost as long as Mike has. We both can take that long a stretch—but we eat when we're hungry and sometimes we need sleep. Speaking of robes, Dawn, this was the last vanishing robe in the Seventh Temple. I meant to tell Patty she'd better order a gross or two."

"She has."

"I should have known. This one seems a little tight." Jill wiggled in it in a fashion that disturbed Ben more than Dawn's perfect and unrobed skin. "Are we putting on weight, Dawn?"

"I think we are, a little. No matter."

"Helps, you mean. We were too skinny. Ben, you noticed, didn't you, that Dawn and I have the same figure? Height, bust, waist, hips, weight, everything—not to mention coloration. We were almost the same when we met . . . and then, with Mike's help, we matched up exactly and are holding it that way. Even our faces are getting more alike—but we didn't plan that. That just comes from doing the same things and thinking about the same things. Stand up and let Ben look at us, dear."

Dawn put her plate aside and did so, in a pose that reminded Ben oddly of Jill, more so than the figure resemblance seemed to justify; then he realized it was the exact pose Jill had been in when she had first stood revealed as Mother Eve.

Invited to stare, he did. Jill said, with her mouth full, "See, Ben? That's me."

Dawn smiled at her. "A razor's edge of difference, Gillian."

"Pooh. You're getting that control, too. I'm almost sorry we'll never have the same face. It's very handy, Ben, for Dawn and myself to look so much alike. We have to have two high priestesses; it's all two of us can do to keep up with Mike. We can trade places right in the middle of a service —and sometimes do. And besides," she added, swallowing, "Dawn can buy a fitted dress and it fits me, too. Saves me the nuisance of shopping for clothes. When we wear clothes."

"I wasn't sure," Ben said slowly, "that you still wore clothes at all. Except these priestess things."

Jill looked surprised. "Do you think we would go out dancing in *these*? We wear evening dresses, same as everybody else. That's our favorite way of not getting our beauty sleep, isn't it, dear? Sit back down and finish your supper; Ben has stared at us long enough for the moment. Ben, there's a man in that transition group you were just with who's a perfectly dreamy dancer and this town is loaded with good night clubs—and Dawn and I have kept the poor fellow so busy, alternated keeping him up so many nights in a row, that we've had to help him stay awake in language classes. But he'll be all right; once you reach Eighth Circle you don't need nearly so much sleep. Whatever made you think we never dressed, dear?"

"Uh—" Ben finally blurted out the embarrassing predicament he had been in.

Jill looked wide-eyed, then barely giggled—and stopped it at once, at which Ben realized that he had heard none of these people laugh . . .

only the "marks" in the outer service. "I see. But, darling, I just never got around to taking this robe off. I am wearing it because I have to gobble and git. But had I grokked that *that* was troubling you, I certainly would have chucked it before I said hello even though I wasn't sure there was another one handy. We're so used to dressing or not dressing according to what we need to do that I just plain forgot that I might not be behaving politely. Sweetheart, take those shorts off—or leave them on, exactly as suits you."

"Uh—"

"Just don't fret about it, either way." Jill smiled and dimpled. "Reminds me of the first time Mike tried a public beach, but in reverse. 'Member, Dawn?"

"I'll never forget it!"

"Ben, you know how Mike is about clothes. He just doesn't understand them. Or didn't. I had to teach him everything. He couldn't see any point to them as protection, until he grokked—to his great surprise—that we aren't as invulnerable as he is. Modesty—*that* sort of 'modesty'; he's so modest in its true sense that it hurts—body-modesty isn't a Martian concept, it couldn't be. And only lately has Mike grokked clothes as ornaments, after we started experimenting with various ways to costume our acts.

"But, Ben, while Mike was always willing to do what I told him to, whether he grokked it or not, you can't imagine how many million *little* things there are to being a human being. We take twenty or thirty years to learn them; Mike had to learn them almost overnight. There are gaps, even now. He does things not knowing that isn't how a human does them. We all teach him—Dawn and I especially. All but Patty, who is sure that anything that Michael does must be perfect. But he's still grokking the nature of clothes. He's groks mostly that they're a wrongness that keeps people apart—and get in the way of letting love cause them to grow closer. Lately he's come to realize that part of the time you want and need such a barrier—with outsiders. But for a long time Mike wore clothes only because I told him to and when I told him he must.

"And I missed a gap.

"We were down in Baja California; it was just at the time we met—or remet, actually—Dawn. Mike and I checked in at night at one of those big fancy beach hotels and he was so anxious to grok the ocean, get wet all over, that he let me sleep the next morning and went down by himself for his first encounter with the ocean. And I didn't realize that Mike didn't know about swim suits. Oh, he may have seen them . . . but he didn't know what they were for or had some mixed-up idea. He certainly didn't know that you were supposed to wear them *in the water*—the idea was almost sacrilege. And you know Jubal's rigid rules about keeping his pool clean—I'm sure it's never seen a suit. I do remember one night a lot of people got tossed in with all their clothes on, but it was when Jubal was going to have it drained right away anyhow.

"Poor Mike! He got down to the beach and threw off his robe and headed for the water . . . looking like a Greek god and just as unaware of local conventions—and then the riot started and I came awake fast and grabbed some clothes myself and got down there just in time to keep him out of jail . . . and fetched him back to the room and he spent the rest of the day in a trance."

Jill got a momentary faraway look. "And he needs me now, too, so I must run along. Kiss me good-night, Ben; I'll see you in the morning."

"You'll be gone all night?"

"Probably. It's a fairly big transition class and, truthfully, Mike has just been keeping them busy the past half hour and more while we visited. But that's all right." She stood up, pulled him gently to his feet and went into his arms.

Presently she broke from the kiss but not from his arms and murmured, "Ben darling, you've been taking lessons. *Whew!*"

"Me? I've been utterly faithful to you—in my own way."

"In the same way I've been to you . . . the nicest way. I wasn't complaining . . . I just think Dorcas has been helping you to practice kissing."

"Some, maybe. Nosy."

"Uh huh, I'm always nosy. The class can wait while you kiss me once more. I'll try to be Dorcas."

"You be yourself."

"I would be, anyway. Self. But Mike says that Dorcas kisses more thoroughly—'groks a kiss more'—than anyone."

"Quit chattering."

She did, for a while, then sighed. "Transition class, here I come—glowing like a lightning bug. Take good care of him, Dawn."

"I will."

"And better kiss him right away and see what I mean!"

"I intend to."

" 'Bye, darlings! Ben, you be a good boy and do what Dawn tells you." She left, not hurrying—but running.

Dawn stood up, flowed up against him, put up her arms.

Jubal cocked an eyebrow. "And now I suppose you are going to tell me that at *that* point, you went chicken."

"Uh, not exactly. A near miss, call it. To tell the truth I didn't have too much to say about it. I, uh, 'cooperated with the inevitable.' "

Jubal nodded. "No other possible course. You were trapped and couldn't run. Whereupon the best a man can do is try for a negotiated peace." He added, "But I'm sorry that the civilized habits of my household caused the boy to fall afoul the law of the jungles of Baja California."

"I don't think he's a boy any longer, Jubal."

xxxii

BEN CAXTON HAD AWAKENED not knowing where he was nor what time it was. It was dark around him, perfectly quiet, he was lying on something soft. Not a bed—where was he?

The night came back in a rush. The last he clearly remembered he had been lying on the soft floor of the Innermost Temple, talking quietly and intimately with Dawn. She had taken him there, they had immersed, shared water, grown closer—

Frantically he reached around him in the dark, found nothing. *"Dawn!"*

Light swelled softly to a gentle dimness. "Here, Ben."

"Oh! I thought you had gone!"

"I didn't intend to wake you." She was wearing—to his sudden and intense disappointment—her robe of office. "I must go start the Sunrisers' Outer Service. Gillian isn't back yet. As you know, it was a fairly big class."

Her words brought back to him things she had told him last night . . . things which, at the time, had upset him despite her gentle and quite logical explanations . . . and she had soothed his upset until he found himself agreeing with her. He still was not quite straight in his mind . . . he didn't grok it all—but, yes, Jill was probably still busy with her rites as high priestess—a task, or perhaps a happy duty, that Dawn had offered to take for her. Ben felt a twinge that he really should have been sorry that Jill had refused, had insisted that Dawn get much needed rest.

But he did not feel sorry. "Dawn . . . do you *have* to leave?" He scrambled to his feet, put his arms around her.

"I must go, Ben dear . . . dear Ben." She melted up against him.

"Right *now?* In such a rush?"

"There is never," she said softly, "that much hurry." Suddenly the robe no longer kept them apart. He was too bemused to wonder what had become of it.

He woke up a second time, found that the "little nest" he was in lighted softly when he stood up. He stretched, discovered that he felt wonderful, then looked around the room for his shorts. They were not in sight and no way for them to be out of sight. He tried to recall where he had left them . . . and had no recollection of ever having taken them off. But he certainly had not worn them into the water. Probably beside the pool in the Innermost Temple— He made a mental note to stop back there and pick them up, then went out and found a bathroom.

Some minutes later, shaved, showered, and refreshed, he did remember to look into the Innermost Temple, failed to find his shorts and decided that somebody, Patty maybe, had noticed them and put them near the outer door where apparently everybody kept what they needed for street wear . . . said to hell with it and grinned at himself for having made such a jittery old-maid issue last night out of wearing them or not. He needed them, here in the Nest, the way he needed a second head.

Come to think of it, he didn't have the slightest trace of a head—a hangover head—although he recalled that he had had more than several drinks with Dawn. Hadn't got drunk, as he recalled, but certainly more than he ordinarily allowed himself—he couldn't sop up the stuff the way Jubal did without paying for it.

Dawn didn't seem to be affected by liquor at all—which was probably why he had gone over his usual quota. Dawn . . . what a gal, what a gal! She hadn't even seemed annoyed when, in a moment of emotional confusion, he had called her Jill—she had seemed pleased.

He found no one in the big room and wondered what time it was? Not that he gave a damn, except that his stomach told him that it was long past breakfast time. He went into the kitchen to see what he could scrounge.

A man in there looked up as he came in. "Ben!"

"Well! Hi, Duke!"

Duke gave him a bear hug and slapped him on the back. "Ben, you're a sight for sore eyes! Gosh, it's good to see you. Thou art God. How do you like your eggs?"

"Thou art God. Are you the cook?"

"Only when I can't find somebody else to do it for me—such as right now. Tony does most of it. We all do some. Even Mike unless Tony catches him and chases him out—Mike is the world's worst cook, bar none." Duke went on breaking eggs into a dish.

Ben moved in on the job. "You look after toast and coffee. Any Worcestershire sauce around here?"

"You name it, Pat's got it. Here." Duke added, "I looked in on you a half hour ago, but you were still sawing wood. I've been busy or you've been busy ever since you got here—until now."

"What do you do around here, Duke? Aside from cooking when you can't avoid it?"

"Well, I'm a deacon . . . and I'll be a priest someday. But I'm slow —not that it matters. I study Martian . . . everybody does that. And I'm the fix-it boy, same as I was for Jubal."

"Must take quite a gang, to maintain a place this size."

"Ben, you'd be surprised how little it takes. Aside from keeping an eye on the plumbing—and sometime you must see Mike's unique way of dealing with a stopped-up toilet; I don't have to play plumber very much —aside from plumbing, nine-tenths of the gadgetry in this building is right here in the kitchen . . . and it's not as gadgeted-up as Jubal's kitchen."

"I had the impression that you have some very complicated gadgets for some of the temples?"

"Huh uh, nary a gadget. Some lighting controls, that's all, and simple ones. Actually—" Duke grinned. "—one of my most important jobs is no job at all. Fire warden."

"Huh?"

"I'm a licensed deputy fire warden, examined and everything, and same for sanitary and safety inspector—and neither one takes any work. But it means that we never have to let an outsider go through the joint— and we don't. They attend outer services . . . but they never get any farther unless Mike gives an up-check."

They transferred food to plates and sat down at a table. Duke said, "You're staying, aren't you, Ben?"

"I don't see how I can, Duke."

"Mmm . . . I had hoped that you would have more sense than I had. I came for just a short visit, too . . . went back and moped around for nearly a month before I told Jubal I was leaving and wouldn't be back. But never mind; you'll be back. Don't make any final decisions before the Water-Sharing tonight."

" 'Water-sharing'?"

"Didn't Dawn tell you? Or Jill?"

"Uh . . . I don't think so."

"Then they didn't. Uh, maybe I should let Mike explain it. No, no need to; people will be mentioning it to you all day long. Sharing water you grok, of course; you're one of the First Called."

" 'First Called?' Dawn used that expression."

"That handful of us who became Mike's water brothers without learning Martian. The others ordinarily do not share water and grow closer until they pass from the Seventh Circle to the Eighth . . . and by that time they are beginning to think in Martian—shucks, some of them know more Martian by that stage than I do now, since I'm a 'First Called' myself and started my studies after I was already in the Nest. Oh, it's not actually forbidden—*nothing* is forbidden—to share water with someone who isn't ready for Eighth Circle. Hell, if I wanted to, I could pick up a babe in a bar, share water with her, then take her to bed—and *then* bring her to the Temple and start her on her apprenticeship. But I wouldn't want to. That's the point; I wouldn't even want to. At the very most I might decide that it was worth while to bring her around to an outer service and let Mike look her over and find out whether any of it clicked with her. Ben, I'll make a flat-footed prediction. You've been around a lot—I'm sure you've been in some fancy beds with some fancy babes."

"Uh . . . some."

"I know damn' well you have. But you will never again in your life crawl in with one who is not your water brother."

"Hmm . . ."

"You'll see. Let's check it a year from now and *you* tell *me*. Now Mike may decide that someone is ready to share water before that person reaches even Seventh Circle. One couple we've got in the Nest Mike picked, and offered them water, when they had just entered Third Circle—and now he's a priest and she's a priestess . . . Sam and Ruth."

"Haven't met 'em."

"You will. Tonight at the latest. But Mike is the only one who can be certain, that soon. Very occasionally Dawn, and sometimes Patty, will spot somebody for special promotion and special training . . . but never as far down as Third Circle and I'm pretty sure that they always consult Mike before going ahead. Not that they are required to. Anyhow, into the Eighth Circle . . . and sharing and growing-closer starts. Then, sooner or later, into Ninth Circle, and the Nest itself—and that's the service we mean when we say 'Sharing Water' even though we share water all day long. The whole Nest attends and the new brother—usually it's a couple—becomes forever part of the Nest. In your case you already are . . . but we've never held the service for you, so everything else is being pushed aside tonight while we welcome you. They did the same for me." Duke got a faraway look. "Ben, it's the most wonderful feeling in the world."

"But I still don't know what it is, Duke."

"Uh . . . it's a lot of things. Ever been on a real luau of a party, the kind the cops raid and usually ends up in a divorce or two?"

"Well . . . yes."

"Up to now, brother, you've only been on Sunday School picnics. That's one aspect of it. Have you ever been married?"

"No."

"You *are* married. You just don't know it yet. After tonight there will never again be any doubt in your mind about it." Duke again looked faraway, happily pensive. "Ben, I was married before . . . and for a short time it was pretty nice and then it was steady hell on wheels. This time I like it, all the time. Shucks, I *love* it! And look, Ben, I don't mean just that it's fun to be shacked up with a bunch of bouncy babes. I *love* them—all my brothers, both sexes. Take Patty—and you will!—Patty mothers all of us . . . and I don't think anybody, man or woman, gets over needing that, even if they think they've outgrown it. Patty . . . well, Patty is just *swell!* She reminds me of Jubal . . . and that old bastard had better get down here and get the word! My point is that it is not just that Patty is female. Oh, I'm not running down tail—"

"Who is running down tail?" The voice, a rich contralto, came from behind them.

Duke swung around. "Not me, you limber Levantine whore! Come here, babe, and kiss your brother Ben."

"Never charged for it in my life," the woman denied as she glided toward them. "Started giving it away before anybody told me." She kissed Ben carefully and thoroughly. "Thou art God, brother."

"Thou art God. Share water."

"Never thirst. And don't ever pay any mind to what Duke says—from the way he behaves he must have been a bottle baby." She leaned over Duke and kissed him even more lingeringly while he patted her ample fundament. Ben noted that she was short, plump, brunette almost to swarthiness, and had a mane of heavy blue-black hair almost to her waist. "Duke, did you see anything of a *Ladies' Home Journal* when you got up?" She reached past his shoulder, took his fork and started eating his scrambled eggs. "Mmm . . . good. You didn't cook these, Duke."

"Ben did. What in the world would I want with a *Ladies' Home Journal?*"

"Ben, stir up a couple of dozen more exactly the same way and I'll scramble 'em in relays. There was an article in it I wanted to show Patty, dear."

"Okay," agreed Ben and got up to do it.

"Don't you two get any ideas about redecorating this dump or I'm moving out. And leave some of those eggs for me! You think us men can do our work on mush?"

"Tut, tut, Dukie darling. Water divided is water multiplied. As I was saying, Ben, Duke's complaints never mean anything—as long as he has enough women for two men and enough food for three, he's a perfect little lamb." She shoved one forkful into Duke's mouth, went on eating the rest herself. "So quit making faces, brother; I'm about to cook you a second breakfast. Or will this be your third?"

"Not even the first, yet. You ate it. Ruth, I was telling Ben how you and Sam pole-vaulted from Third to Ninth. I think he's uneasy about whether he belongs in the Sharing-Water tonight."

She pursued the last bite on Duke's plate, then moved over and started preparations to cook. "Duke, you run along and I'll send you out something other than mush. Take your coffee cup and skedaddle. Ben, I was worried, too, when my time came—but don't you be worried, dear, because Michael does not make mistakes. You belong here or you wouldn't be here. You're going to stay?"

"Uh, I can't. Ready for the first installment?"

"Pour them in. Then you'll be back. And someday you'll stay. Duke is correct—Sam and I pole-vaulted . . . and it was almost too fast for a middle-aged, prim and proper housewife."

"Middle-aged?"

"Ben, one of the bonuses about the discipline is that as it straightens out your soul, your body straightens out, too. That's a matter in which the Christian Scientists are precisely right. Notice any medicine bottles in any of the bathrooms?"

"Uh, no."

"There aren't any. How many people have kissed you?"

"Several, at least."

"As a priestess I kiss a lot more than 'several,' believe me. But there's never so much as a sniffle in the Nest. I used to be the sort of whiny woman who is never quite well and given to 'female complaints.'" She smiled. "Now I'm more female than ever but I'm twenty pounds lighter and years younger and have nothing to complain about—I *like* being female. As Duke flattered me, 'a Levantine whore' and unquestionably much more limber than I was—I always sit in the lotus position when I'm teaching a class, whereas it used to be all I could do just to squat down and straighten up again . . . hot flashes and dizziness.

"But it did happen fast," Ruth went on. "Sam was a professor of Oriental languages at the University here—the city U., that is. Sam started coming to the Temple because it was a way, the only way, to learn the

Martian language. Strictly professional motivation, he wasn't interested in it as a church. And I went along to keep an eye on him . . . I had heard rumors and I was a jealous wife, even more possessive than the average.

"So we worked up to the Third Circle, Sam learning the language rapidly, of course, and myself grimly hanging on and studying hard because I didn't want to let him out of my sight. Then *boom!* the miracle happened. We suddenly began to *think* in it, just a little . . . and Michael felt it and had us stay after service, a Third Circle service, one night . . . and Michael and Gillian gave us water. Afterwards, I knew that I was all the things I had despised in other women and I knew that I should despise my husband for letting me do it and hate him for what he had done himself. All this in English, with the worst parts in Hebrew. So I wept all day and moaned and made myself a stinking nuisance to Sam . . . and couldn't *wait* to get back to share more water and grow closer again that night.

"After that things were steadily easier but not easy, as we were pushed through all the inner circles just as rapidly as we could take it; Michael knew that we needed help and wanted to get us into the safety and peace of the Nest. So when it came time for our Sharing-Water, I was still unable to discipline myself without constant help. I knew that I wanted to be received into the Nest—once you start, there's no turning back—but I wasn't sure I could merge myself with seven other people. I was scared silly; on the way over I almost begged Sam to turn around and go home."

She stopped talking and looked up, unsmiling but beatific, a plump angle with a big stirring spoon in one hand. "Then we walked into the Innermost Temple and a spotlight hit me and our robes were whisked away . . . and they were all in the pool and calling out to us in Martian to come, come and share the water of life—and I stumbled into that pool and submerged and I haven't come up since!

"Nor ever want to. Don't fret, Ben, you'll learn the language and acquire the discipline and you'll have loving help from all of us every step of the way. You stop worrying and jump in that pool tonight; I'll have my arms out to catch you. All of us will have our arms out, welcoming you home. Now take this plate in to Duke and tell him I said he was a pig . . . but a charming one. And take this one in for yourself—oh, of course you can eat that much!—give me a kiss and run along; Ruthie has work to do."

Ben delivered the kiss and the message and the plate, then found that he did have some appetite left . . . but nevertheless did not concentrate on food as he found Jill stretched out, apparently asleep, on one of the wide, soft couches. He sat down opposite her, enjoying the sweet sight of her and thinking that Dawn and Jill were even more alike than he had realized the night before.

He looked up from a bite and saw that her eyes were open and she was smiling at him. "Thou art God, darling—and that smells good."

"And you look good. But I didn't mean to wake you." He got up and sat by her, put a bite in her mouth. "My own cooking, with Ruth's help."

"I know. And good, too. Duke told me to stay out of the kitchen because Ruthie was giving you a good-for-your-soul lecture. You didn't wake me; I was just lazing until you came out. I haven't been asleep all night."

"Not at all?"

"Not a wink. But I'm not tired, I feel grand. Just hungry. That's a hint."

So he fed her. She let him do so, never stirring, not using her own hands. "But did you get any sleep?" she asked presently.

"Uh, some."

"Enough? No, you got enough. But how much sleep did Dawn get? As much as two hours?"

"Oh, more than that, I'm certain."

"Then she's all right. Two hours of sleep does us as much good as eight used to. I knew what a sweet night you were going to have—both of you—but I was a teeny bit worried that she might not rest."

"Well, it *was* a wonderful night," Ben admitted, "although I was, uh, surprised at the way you shoved her at me."

"Shocked, you mean. I know you, Ben, maybe better than you know yourself. You arrived here yesterday with jealousy sticking out in lumps. I think it's gone now. Yes?"

He looked back at her. "I think so."

"That's good. I had a wonderful and joyous night, too—made free from any worry by knowing you were in good hands. The best hands— better than mine."

"Oh, no!"

"Hmm. I grok a few lumps still—but tonight we'll wash them away in water." She sat up, reached toward the end of the couch—and it looked to Caxton as if a pack of cigarettes on the end table jumped the last few inches into her hand.

"You seemed to have picked up some sleight-of-hand tricks, too."

She seemed momentarily puzzled, then she smiled. "Some. Nothing much. Parlor tricks. 'I am only an egg,' to quote my teacher."

"How did you do that trick?"

"Why, I just whistled to it in Martian. First you grok a thing, then you grok what you want it to—*Mike!*" She waved. "We're over here, dear!"

"Coming." The Man from Mars came straight to Ben, took his hands, pulled him to his feet. "Let me look at you, Ben! Golly, it's good to see you!"

"It's good to see *you.* And to be here."

"And we're going to twist your arm to keep you here. What's this about three days? Three days indeed!"

"I'm a working man, Mike."

"We'll see. The girls are all excited, getting ready for your party tonight. Might just as well shut down services and classes for the rest of the day—they won't be worth a damn."

"Patty has already done any necessary rescheduling," Jill told Mike. "She just didn't bother you with it. Dawn and Ruth and Sam are going to take care of what's necessary. Patty decided to slough the outer matinee—so you're through for the day."

"That's good news." Mike sat down, pulled Jill's head into his lap, pulled Ben down, put an arm around him, and sighed. He was dressed as Ben had seen him in the outer meeting, smart tropical business suit, lacking only shoes. "Ben, don't ever take up preaching. I spend my days and nights rushing from one job to another, telling people why they must never hurry. I owe you, along with Jill and Jubal, more than anyone else on this planet—yet you've been here since yesterday afternoon and this is the first time I've been able to say hello. How've you been? You're looking fit. In fact Dawn tells me you *are* fit."

Ben found himself blushing. "I'm okay."

"That's good. Because, believe me, the hill tribes will be restless tonight. But I'll grok close and sustain you. You'll be fresher at the end of the party than at the start—won't he, Little Brother?"

"Yes," agreed Jill. "Ben, you won't believe it until you've had it done for you, but Mike can lend you strength—physical strength, I mean, not just moral support. I can do it a little bit. Mike can really do it."

"Jill can do it quite a lot." Mike caressed her. "Little Brother is a tower of strength to everybody. Last night she certainly was." He smiled down at her, then sang:

"You'll never find a girl like Jill.
"No, not one in a billion.
"Of all the tarts who ever will
"The willingest is our Gillian!

"—isn't that right, Little Brother?"

"Pooh," answered Jill, obviously pleased, covering his hand with her own and pressing it to her. "Dawn is exactly like me and you know it—and every bit as willing."

"Maybe. But you're here . . . and Dawn is downstairs interviewing the possibles out of the tip. She's busy—you ain't. That's an important difference—isn't it, Ben?"

"Could be." Caxton was finding that their unself-conscious behavior was beginning to embarrass him, even in this uniquely relaxed atmosphere —he wished that they would either knock off necking . . . or give him an excuse to leave.

Instead Mike went right on cuddling Jill with one hand while keeping his other arm snug around Ben's waist . . . and Ben was forced to admit that Jill encouraged him, rather than otherwise. Mike said very seriously, "Ben, a night like last night—helping a group to make the big jump to Eighth Circle—gets me terribly keyed up. Let me tell you something out of the lessons for Sixth, Ben. We humans have something that my former people don't even dream of. They can't. And I can tell you how precious it is . . . how especially precious I know it to be, because I have known what it is not to have it. The blessing of being male and female. Man and Woman created He them—the greatest treasure We-Who-Are-God ever invented. Right, Jill?"

"Beautifully right, Mike—and Ben knows it is Truth. But make a song for Dawn, too, darling."

"Okay—

"Ardent is our lovely Dawn;
"Ben grokked that in her glance—
"She buys new dresses every morn,
"But *never* shops for pants!"

Jill giggled and squirmed. "Did you tune her in?"

"Yes, and she gave me a big Bronx cheer—with a kiss behind it for Ben. Say, isn't there anybody in the kitchen this morning? I just remembered I haven't eaten for a couple of days. Or years, maybe; I'm not sure."

"I think Ruth is," Ben said, untangling himself and standing up. "I'll go see."

"Duke can do it. Hey, Duke! See if you can find somebody who'll fix me a stack of wheat cakes as tall as you are and a gallon of maple syrup."

"Right, Mike!" Duke called back.

Ben Caxton hesitated, without an excuse to run an errand. He thought of a trumped-up excuse and glanced back over his shoulder—

"Jubal," Caxton said earnestly, "I wouldn't tell you this part at all . . . if it weren't essential to explaining how I feel about the whole thing, why I'm worried about them—*all* of them, Duke and Mike as well as Jill . . . and Mike's other victims, too. By that morning I was myself half conned into thinking everything was all right—weird as hell in spots, but jolly. Mike himself had me fascinated, too—his new personality is pretty powerful. Cocky and too much supersalesman . . . but very compelling. Then he—or both of them—got me rather embarrassed, so I took that chance to get up from the couch.

"Then I glanced back—and couldn't believe my eyes. I hadn't been turned away five seconds . . . and Mike had managed to get rid of every stitch of clothes . . . and so help me, they were going to it, with myself and three or four others in the room at the time—just as boldly as monkeys in a zoo!

"Jubal, I was so shocked I almost lost my breakfast."

xxxiii

"WELL," SAID JUBAL, "what did you do? Cheer?"

"Like hell. I left, at once. I dashed for the outer door, grabbed my clothes and shoes—forgot my bag and didn't go back for it—ignored the sign on the door, went on through—jumped in that bounce tube with my clothes in my arms. Blooie! Gone without saying good-by."

"Rather abrupt."

"I felt abrupt. I *had* to leave. In fact I left so fast that I durn near killed myself. You know the ordinary bounce tube—"

"I do not."

"Well, unless you set it to take you up to a certain level, when you get into it you simply sink slowly, like cold molasses. I didn't sink, I *fell*—and I was about six stories up. But just when I thought I had made my last mistake, something caught me. Not a safety net—a field of some sort. I didn't quite splash. But Mike needs to smooth out that gadget. Or put in the regular sort of bounce tube."

Jubal said, "I'll stick to stairs and, when unavoidable, elevators."

"Well, I hadn't realized that this one was so risky. But the only safety inspector they've got is Duke . . . and to Duke whatever Mike says is Gospel. Jubal, that whole place is riding for a fall. They're all hypnotized by one man . . . who isn't right in his head. What can be done about it?"

Jubal jutted out his lips and then scowled. "Let's see first if you've got it analyzed correctly. Just what aspects of the situation did you find disquieting?"

"Why . . . the whole thing!"

"So? In fact, wasn't it just *one* thing? And that an essentially harmless act which we both know was nothing new . . . but was, we can assume rather conclusively, initially performed in this house or on these grounds about two years ago? I did not then object—nor did you, when you learned of it, whenever that was. In fact, I have implied that you yourself have, on other occasions, joined in that same act with the same young lady—and she *is* a lady, despite your tale—and you neither denied my implication nor acted offended at my presumption. To put it bluntly, son—what are you belly-aching about?"

"Well, for cripe's sake, Jubal—would you put up with it, in *your* living room?"

"Decidedly not—unless perhaps I have, it having taken place so clandestinely, at night perhaps, that no one noticed. In which case it would be—or has been, if such be the case—no skin off'n my nose. But the point is that it was not *my* living room . . . nor would I presume to lay down rules for another man's living room. It was Mike's house . . . and his wife—common law or otherwise, we need not inquire. So what business is it of mine? Or *yours?* You go into a man's house, you accept his household rules—that's a universal law of civilized behavior."

"You mean to say you don't find it shocking?"

"Ah, you've raised an entirely different issue. Public exhibition of lust I would find most distasteful, either as participant or spectator . . . but I grok this reflects my early indoctrination, nothing more. A very large minority of mankind—possibly a majority—do not share my taste in this matter. Decidedly not—for the orgy has a long and very widespread history. Nonetheless it is not to *my* taste. But shocking? My dear sir, I can be shocked only by that which offends me ethically. Ethical questions are subject to logic—but this is a matter of taste and the old saw is in point . . . *de gustibus non est disputandum.*"

"You think that a public shagging is merely 'a matter of taste?' "

"Precisely. In which respect I concede that my own taste, rooted in early training, reinforced by some three generations of habit, and now, I believe, calcified beyond possibility of change, is no more sacred than the very different taste of Nero. Less sacred—Nero was a god; I am not."

"Well, I'll be damned."

"In due course, possibly—if it is possible . . . a point on which I am 'neutral-against.' But, Ben, this wasn't public."

"Huh?"

"You yourself have said it. You described this group as a plural marriage—a group theogamy, to be precise. Not public but utterly private. 'Aint nobody here but just us gods'—so how could anyone be offended?"

"*I* was offended!"

"That was because your own apotheosis was less complete than theirs —I'm afraid they over-rated you . . . and you misled them. You invited it."

"Me? Jubal, I did nothing of the sort."

" 'Tommy busted my dolly . . . I hitted him over the head with it.' The time to back out was the instant you got there, for you saw at once that their customs and manners were not yours. Instead you stayed, and enjoyed the favors of one goddess—and behaved yourself as a god toward her—in short, you learned the score, and they knew it. It seems to me that Mike's error lay only in accepting your hypocrisy as solid coin. But he does have the weakness—a godlike one—of never doubting his 'water brothers'—but even Jove nods—and his weakness—or is it a strength?— comes from *his* early training; he can't help it. No, Ben, Mike behaved with complete propriety; the offense against good manners lay in *your* behavior."

"Damn it, Jubal, you've twisted things again. I did what I *had* to do —I was about to throw up on their rug!"

"So you claim reflex. So stipulated; however, anyone over the emotional age of twelve could have clamped his jaws and made a slow march for the bathroom with at worst the hazard of clogged sinuses—instead of a panicked dash for the street door—then returned when the show was over with a euphemistic but acceptable excuse."

"That wouldn't have been enough. I tell you I *had* to leave!"

"I know. But not through reflex. Reflex will evacuate the stomach; it will not choose a course for the feet, recover chattels, take you through doors and cause you to jump down a hole without looking. Panic, Ben. Why did you panic?"

Caxton was long in replying. He sighed and said, "I guess when you come right down to it, Jubal—I'm a prude."

Jubal shook his head. "Your behavior was momentarily prudish, but not from prudish motivations. You are not a prude, Ben. A prude is a person who thinks that his own rules of propriety are natural laws. You are almost entirely free of this prevalent evil. You adjusted, at least with passable urbanity, to many things which did not fit your code of propriety . . . whereas a true-blue, stiff-necked, incorrigible prude would promptly have affronted that delightful tattooed lady and stomped out. Dig deeper. Do you wish a hint?"

"Uh, maybe you'd better. All I know is that I am mixed up and unhappy about the whole situation—on Mike's account, too, Jubal!—which is why I took a day off to see you."

"Very well. Hypothetical situation for you to evaluate: You mentioned a lady named Ruth whom you met in passing—a kiss of brotherhood and a few minutes conversation—nothing more."

"Yeah?"

"Suppose the actors had been Ruth and Mike? Gillian not even present? Would you have been shocked?"

"Huh? Hell, yes, I would have been shocked!"

"Just how shocked? Retching? Panic flight?"

Caxton looked thoughtful, then sheepish. "I suppose not. I still would have been startled silly. But I guess I would've just gone out to the kitchen or something . . . then found an excuse to leave. I still feel like a fool for having made that mad dash to get out."

"Would you actually have sought an excuse to leave? Or were you looking forward to your own 'welcome home' party that night?"

"Well . . ." Caxton mused. "I hadn't made up my mind about that when this happened. I was curious, I admit—but I wasn't quite sold."

"Very well. You now have your motivation."

"Do I?"

"You name it, Ben. Haul it out and look at it—and find out how you want to deal with it."

Caxton chewed his lip and looked unhappy. "All right. I would have been startled if it had been Ruth—but I wouldn't really have been shocked. Hell, in the newspaper racket you get over being shocked by anything but—well, you expressed it: something that cuts deep about right and wrong. Shucks, if it had been Ruth, I might even have sneaked a look—even though I still think I would have left the room; such things ought to be—or at least *I* feel that they ought to be—private." He paused. "It was because it was Jill. I was hurt . . . and jealous."

"Stout fellow, Ben."

"Jubal, I would have sworn that I wasn't jealous. I knew that I had lost out—I had accepted it. It was the circumstances, Jubal. Now don't get me wrong. I would still love Jill if she were a two-peso whore. Which she is *not.* This hands-around harem deal upsets the hell out of me. But by *her* lights Jill is moral."

Jubal nodded. "I know. I feel sure that Gillian is incapable of being corrupted. She has an invincible innocence which makes it impossible for her to be immoral." He frowned. "Ben, we are close to the root of your trouble. I am afraid that you—and I, too, I admit—lack the angelic innocence to abide by the perfect morality those people live by."

Ben looked surprised. "Jubal, you think what they are doing is *moral?* Monkeys-in-the-zoo stuff and all? All I meant was that Jill really didn't *know* that what she was doing was wrong—Mike's got her hornswoggled —and Mike doesn't know he's doing wrong either. He's the Man from Mars; he didn't get off to a fair start. Everything about us was strange to him—he'll probably never get straightened out."

Jubal looked troubled. "You've raised a hard question, Ben—but I'll give you a straight answer. Yes, I think what those people—the entire Nest, not just our own kids—are doing is moral. As you described it to me —*yes.* I haven't had a chance to examine details—but yes: all of it. Group orgies, and open and unashamed swapping off at other times . . . their communal living and their anarchistic code, everything. And most especially their selfless dedication to giving their perfect morality to others."

"Jubal, you utterly astonish me." Caxton scratched his head and frowned. "Since you feel that way, why don't you join them? You're welcome, they want you, they're expecting you. They'll hold a jubilee—and Dawn is waiting to kiss your feet and serve you in any way you will permit; I wasn't exaggerating."

Jubal shook his head. "No. Had I been approached fifty years ago— But now? Ben my brother, the potential for such innocence is no longer in me—and I am not referring to sexual potency, so wipe that cynical smile off your face. I mean that I have been too long wedded to my own brand of evil and hopelessness to be cleansed in their water of life and become innocent again. If I ever was."

"Mike thinks you have this 'innocence'—he doesn't call it that—in full measure now. Dawn told me, speaking ex officio."

"Then Mike does me great honor; I would not disillusion him. He sees his own reflection—I am, by profession, a mirror."

"Jubal, you're chicken."

"Precisely, sir! The thing that troubles me most is whether those innocents can make their pattern fit into a naughty world. Oh, it's been tried before!—and every time the world etched them away like acid. Some of the early Christians—anarchy, communism, group marriage—why, even that kiss of brotherhood has a strong primitive-Christian flavor to it.

That might be where Mike picked it up, since all the forms he uses are openly syncretic, especially that Earth-Mother ritual." Jubal frowned. "If he picked that up from primitive Christianity—and not just from kissing girls, which he enjoys, I know—then I would expect men to kiss men, too."

Ben snorted. "I held out on you—they do. But it's not a pansy gesture. I got caught once; after that I managed to duck."

"So? It figures. The Oneida Colony was much like Mike's 'Nest'; it managed to last quite a while but in a low population density—not as an enclave in a resort city. There have been many others, all with the same sad story: a plan for perfect sharing and perfect love, glorious hopes and high ideals—followed by persecution and eventual failure." Jubal sighed. "I was worried about Mike before—now I'm worried about all of them."

"*You're* worried? How do you think *I* feel? Jubal, I can't accept your sweetness-and-light theory. What they are doing is *wrong!*"

"So? Ben, it's that last incident that sticks in your craw."

"Well . . . maybe. Not entirely."

"Mostly. Ben, the ethics of sex is a thorny problem—because each of us has to find a solution pragmatically compatible with a preposterous, utterly unworkable, and evil public code of so-called 'morals.' Most of us know, or suspect, that the public code is wrong, and we break it. Nevertheless we pay Danegeld by giving it lip service in public and feeling guilty about breaking it in private. Willy-nilly, that code rides us, dead and stinking, an albatross around the neck. You think of yourself as a free soul, I know, and you break that evil code yourself—but faced with a problem in sexual ethics new to you, you unconsciously tested it against that same Judeo-Christian code which you consciously refuse to obey. All so automatically that you retched . . . and believed thereby—and *continue* to believe—that your reflex proved that you were 'right' and they were 'wrong.' *Faugh!* I'd as lief use trial by ordeal as use your stomach to test guilt. All your stomach can reflect are prejudices trained into you before you acquired reason."

"What about *your* stomach?"

"Mine is as stupid as yours—but I don't let it rule my brain. I can at least see the beauty of Mike's attempt to devise an ideal human ethic and applaud his recognition that such a code must be founded on ideal sexual behavior, even though it calls for changes in sexual mores so radical as to frighten most people—including you. For that I admire him—I should nominate him for the Philosophical Society. Most moral philosophers consciously or unconsciously assume the essential correctness of our cultural sexual code—family, monogamy, continence, the postulate of privacy that troubled you so, restriction of intercourse to the marriage bed, et cetera. Having stipulated our cultural code as a whole, they fiddle with details—even such piffle as solemnly discussing whether or not the female breast is an 'obscene' sight! But mostly they debate *how* the human animal can be induced or forced to obey this code, blandly ignoring the high probability that the heartaches and tragedies they see all around them originate in the code itself rather than failure to abide by the code.

"Now comes the Man from Mars, looks at this sacrosanct code—and rejects it in toto. I do not grasp exactly what Mike's sexual code is, but it is clear from what little you told me that it violates the laws of every major nation on Earth and would outrage 'right-thinking' people of every major faith—and most agnostics and atheists, too. And yet this poor boy—"

"Jubal, I repeat—he's *not* a boy, he's a man."

"Is he a 'man?' I wonder. This poor ersatz Martian is saying, by your own report, that sex is a way to be happy together. I go along with Mike this far: sex *should* be a means of happiness. The worst thing about sex is that we use it to hurt each other. It ought *never* to hurt; it should bring happiness, or, at the very least, pleasure. There is no good reason why it should ever be anything less.

"The code says, 'Thou shalt not covet thy neighbor's wife'—and the result? Reluctant chastity, adultery, jealousy, bitter family fights, blows and sometimes murder, broken homes and twisted children . . . and furtive, dirty little passes at country club dances and the like, degrading to both man and woman whether consummated or not. Is this injunction ever obeyed? The Commandment not to 'covet' I mean; I'm not referring to any physical act. I wonder. If a man swore to me on a stack of his own Bibles that he had refrained from coveting another man's wife *because* the code forbade it, I would suspect either self-deception or subnormal sexuality. Any male virile enough to sire a child is almost certainly so virile that he has coveted many, many women—whether he takes action in the matter or not.

"Now comes Mike and says: 'There's no need for you to covet my wife . . . *love* her! There's no limit to her love, we all have everything to gain—and nothing to lose but fear and guilt and hatred and jealousy.' The proposition is so naive that it's incredible. So far as I recall only precivilization Eskimos were ever this naive—and they were so remote from the rest of us that they almost qualified as 'Men from Mars' themselves. However, we soon gave them our virtues and instead of happy sharing they now have chastity and adultery just like the rest of us—those who survived the transition. I wonder if they gained by it? What do you think, Ben?"

"I wouldn't care to be an Eskimo, thank you."

"Neither would I. Spoiled raw fish makes me bilious."

"Well, yes—but, Jubal, I had in mind hot water and soap. I guess I'm effete."

"I'm decadent in that respect, too, Ben; I was born in a house with no more plumbing than an igloo—and I've no wish to repeat my childhood. But I assume that noses hardened to the stink of rotting blubber would not be upset by unwashed human bodies. But nevertheless, despite curious cuisine and pitiful possessions, the Eskimos were invariably reported to have been the happiest people on Earth. We can never be sure why they were happy, but we can be utterly certain that any unhappiness they did suffer was not caused by sexual jealousy. They borrowed and lent spouses, both ways, both for convenience and purely for fun—and it did *not* make them unhappy.

"One is tempted to ask: Who's looney? Mike and the Eskimos? Or the rest of us? We can't judge by the fact that you and I have no stomach for such group sports—our canalized tastes are irrelevant. But take a look at this glum world around you—then tell me this: Did Mike's disciples seem happier, or unhappier, than other people?"

"I talked to only about a third of them, Jubal . . . but—yes, they're happy. So happy they seem slap-happy to me. I don't trust it. There's some catch in it."

"Mmm . . . maybe you yourself were the catch in it."

"How?"

"I was thinking that it was regrettable that your tastes have grown canalized so young. There it was, raining soup—and you were caught without a spoon. Even three days of what you were offered—*urged* on you! —would have been something to treasure when you reach my age. And you, you young idiot, let jealousy chase you away! Believe me, at your age I would have gone Eskimo in a big way, thankful that I had been given a free pass instead of having to attend church and study Martian to qualify. I'm so vicariously vexed that my only consolation is the sour one that I know you will live to regret it. Age does not bring wisdom, Ben, but it does give perspective . . . and the saddest perspective of all is to see far, far behind you, the temptations you've passed up. I have such regrets myself . . . but all of them are as nothing to the whopper of a regret I am happily certain you will suffer."

"Oh, for Pete's sake, quit rubbing it in!"

"Heavens, man!—or are you a mouse? I'm not rubbing it in, I am trying to goad you into the obvious. Why are you sitting here moaning to an old man?—when you should be heading for the Nest like a homing pigeon? Before the cops raid the joint! Hell, if I were even *twenty* years younger, I'd join Mike's church myself."

"Let up on me, Jubal. What do you really think of Mike's church?"

"You told me it wasn't a church—just a discipline."

"Well . . . yes and no. It is supposed to be based on the 'Truth' with a capital 'T' as Mike got it from the Martian 'Old Ones.' "

"The 'Old Ones,' eh? To me, they're still hogwash."

"Mike certainly believes in them."

"Ben, I once knew a manufacturer who believed that he consulted the ghost of Alexander Hamilton on all his business decisions. All that proves is that he believed it. However— Damn it, why must I always be the Devil's advocate?"

"What's biting you now?"

"Ben, the foulest sinner of all is the hypocrite who makes a racket of religion. But we must give the Devil his due. Mike *does* believe in those 'Old Ones' and he is *not* pulling a racket. He's teaching the truth as he sees it even though he has seen fit to borrow from other religions to illustrate his meaning. That 'All-Mother' rite—little as I like it, he seems merely to have been illustrating the universality of the Female Principle, regardless of name and form. Fair enough. As for his 'Old Ones,' of course I don't *know* that they don't exist—I simply find hard to swallow the idea that any planet is ruled by a hierarchy of ghosts. As for his Thou-art-God creed, to me it is neither more nor less credible than any other. Come Judgment Day, if they hold it, we may find that Mumbo Jumbo the God of the Congo was the Big Boss all along.

"*All* the names are still in the hat, Ben. Self-aware man is so built that he cannot believe in his own extinction . . . and this automatically leads to endless invention of religions. While this involuntary conviction of immortality by no means proves immortality to be a fact, the questions generated by this conviction are overwhelmingly important . . . whether we can answer them or not, or prove what answers we suspect. The nature of life, how the ego hooks into the physical body, the problem of the ego itself and why each ego *seems* to be the center of the universe, the purpose of life, the purpose of the universe—these are paramount questions, Ben; they can never be trivial. Science can't, or hasn't, coped with any of them—and who am I to sneer at religions for trying to answer them, no matter how unconvincingly to me? Old Mumbo Jumbo may eat me yet; I can't rule Him out because He owns no fancy cathedrals. Nor can I rule out one godstruck boy leading a sex cult in an upholstered attic; he might be the Messiah. The only religious opinion that I feel sure of is this: self-awareness is *not* just a bunch of amino acids bumping together!"

"Whew! Jubal, you should have been a preacher."

"Missed it by only a razor's edge, my boy—and I'll thank you to keep a civil tongue in your head. One more word in Mike's defense and I'll throw him on the mercy of the court. If he can show us a better way to run this fouled-up planet, his sex life is vindicated thereby, regardless of your taste or mine. Geniuses are notoriously indifferent to the sexual customs of the culture in which they find themselves, they make their own rules; this is not opinion, it was proved by Armattoe 'way back in 1948. And Mike *is* a genius; he's shown it more ways than one. He can therefore be expected to ignore Mrs. Grundy and diddle to suit himself. Geniuses are justifiably contemptuous of the opinions of their inferiors.

"And from a religious standpoint Mike's sexual behavior is as kosher as fish on Friday, as orthodox as Santa Claus. He preaches that all living creatures are collectively God . . . which makes him and his disciples the only self-aware gods in his pantheon—which rates him a union card by the rules for godding on this planet. Those rules *always* permit gods sexual freedom limited only by their own judgment; mortal rules *never* apply. Leda and the Swan? Europa and the Bull? Osiris, Isis, and Horus? The incredible incestuous games of the Norse gods? Of course . . . but why stop there? Take a hard look at the family relations of the Trinity-in-One of the most widely respected western religion (I won't cite eastern religions; their gods do things a mink breeder wouldn't put up with!). The only way in which the odd interrelations of the various aspects of what purports to be a monotheos can be reconciled with the precepts of the religion thereto is by assuming that the rules in these matters for deity are not the rules for ordinary mortals. Of course most people don't think about it; they compartment it off in their minds and mark it: *'Holy—Do Not Disturb.'*

"But an outside referee is forced to allow Mike the same dispensation granted all other gods. There are rules for this game: one god alone splits into at least two parts, male and female—and breeds. Not just Jehovah—they *all* do it. Look it up. Contrariwise, a group of gods will breed like rabbits, every time, and with as little regard for human formalities. Once Mike entered the godding business, those orgies of his group were as logically certain as Sunday follows Saturday. So quit using the standards of Podunk and judge them only by Olympian morals—I think you will then find that they are showing unusual restraint. Furthermore, Ben, this 'growing-closer' by sexual union, this unity-into-plurality and plurality-back-into-unity, cannot tolerate monogamy inside the god group. Any pairing that excluded the others would be immoral, obscene, under the postulated creed. And if such mutual, shared-by-all sexual congress is essential to their creed, as I grok it *has* to be, then why do you expect this holy union to be hidden behind a door? Your insistence that they should hide it would have turned a holy rite—which it *was*—into something obscene—which it was *not*. You just plain did not understand what you were looking at."

"Maybe I didn't," Ben said glumly.

"I'm going to offer you one box-top premium, as an inducement. You wondered how Mike got rid of his clothes so quickly. I'll tell you how."

"How?"

"It was a miracle."

"Oh, for God's sake!"

"Could be. But one thousand dollars says that it was a miracle by the usual rules for miracles—outcome to be decided by you. Go back and ask Mike how he did it. Get him to show you. Then send me the money."

"Hell, Jubal, I don't want to take your money."

"You won't. I've got inside information. Bet?"

"No, damn it. Jubal, you go down there and see what the score is. I can't go back—not now."

"They'll take you back with open arms and not even ask why you left so abruptly. One thousand on that prediction, too. Ben, you were there less than a day—fifteen hours, about—and you spent over half that time sleeping and playing hopscotch with Dawn. Did you give them a square shake? The sort of careful investigation you give something smelly in public life before you blast it in your column?"

"But—"

"Did you, or didn't you?"

"No, but—"

"Oh, for Pete's sake yourself, Ben! You claim to be in *love* with Jill . . . yet you won't give her the consideration you give a crooked politician. Not a tenth the effort she made to help *you* when you were kidnapped. Where would you be today if she had given it so feeble a try? Pushing up daisies! Roasting in hell! You're bitching about those kids over some friendly fornication—but do you know what *I'm* worried about?"

"What?"

"Christ was crucified for preaching without a police permit. Think it over."

Caxton stood up. "I'm on my way."

"After lunch."

"Now."

Twenty-four hours later Ben wired Jubal two thousand dollars.

When, after a week, Jubal had had no other message, he sent a stat care of Ben's office: *"What the hell are you doing?"* Ben's answer came back, somewhat delayed: *"Studying Martian and the rules for hopscotch—fraternally yours—Ben."*

part five

HIS HAPPY DESTINY

xxxiv

FOSTER LOOKED UP from his current Work in Progress. "Junior!"

"Sir?"

"That youngster you wanted—he's available now. The Martians have released him."

Digby looked puzzled. "I'm sorry. There was some young creature toward whom I have a Duty?"

Foster smiled angelically. Miracles were *never* necessary—in Truth the pseudo-concept "miracle" was self-contradicting. But these young fellows always had to learn it for themselves. "Never mind," he said gently. "It's a minor job and I'll handle it myself—and Junior?"

"Sir?"

"Call me 'Fos,' please—ceremony is all right in the field but we don't need it in the studio. And remind me not to call you 'Junior' after this—you made a very nice record on that temporary duty assignment. Which name do *you* like to be called?"

His assistant blinked. "I have another name?"

"Thousands of them. Do you have a preference?"

"Why, I really don't recall at this eon."

"Well . . . how would you like to be called 'Digby'?"

"Uh, yes. That's a very nice name. Thanks."

"Don't thank me. You earned it." Archangel Foster turned back to his work, not forgetting the minor item he had assumed. Briefly he considered how this cup might be taken from little Patricia—then chided himself for such unprofessional, almost human, thought. Mercy was not possible to an angel; angelic compassion left no room for it.

The Martian Old Ones had reached an elegant and awesome trial solution to their major esthetic problem and put it aside for a few filled-threes to let it generate new problems. At which time, unhurriedly but at once and almost absent-mindedly, the alien nestling which they had returned to his proper world was tapped of what he had learned of his people and dropped, after cherishing, since he was of no further interest to their purposes.

They collectively took the data he had accumulated and, with a view to testing that trial solution, began to work toward considering an inquiry leading to an investigation of esthetic parameters involved in the possibility of the artistic necessity of destroying Earth. But necessarily much waiting would be, before fullness would grok decision.

The Daibutsu at Kamakura was again washed by a giant wave secondary to a seismic disturbance some 280 kilometers off Honshu. The wave killed more than 13,000 people and lodged a small male infant high up in the Buddha image's interior, where it was eventually found and succored by surviving monks. This infant lived ninety-seven Terran years after the disaster that wiped out his family, and himself produced no progeny nor anything of any note aside from a reputation reaching to Yokohama for loud and sustained belching. Cynthia Duchess entered a nunnery with all benefits of modern publicity and left same without fanfare three days later. Ex-Secretary General Douglas suffered a slight stroke which impaired the use of his left hand but did not reduce his ability to conserve assets entrusted to his stewardship. Lunar Enterprises, Ltd., published a prospectus on a bond issue for the wholly owned subsidiary Ares Chandler Corporation. The Lyle-Drive Exploratory Vessel *Mary Jane Smith* landed on Pluto. Fraser, Colorado, reported the coldest average February of its recorded history.

Bishop Oxtongue, speaking at the New Grand Avenue Temple in Kansas City, preached on the text (Matt. XXIV:24): "For there shall arise false Christs and false prophets, and shall shew great signs and wonders; insomuch that, if it were possible, they shall deceive the very elect." He was careful to make clear that his diatribe did not refer to Mormons, Christian Scientists, Roman Catholics, nor Fosterites—most especially not to the last—nor to any other fellow travelers whose good works counted for more than minute and, in the final analysis, inconsequential differences in creed or ritual . . . but solely to recent upstart heretics who were seducing faithful contributors away from the faiths of their fathers. In a lush subtropical resort city in the southern part of the same nation three complainants swore an information charging public lewdness on the part of a pastor, three of his assistants, and Joe Doe, Mary Roe, et al., plus further charges of running a disorderly house and contributing to the delinquency of minors. The county attorney had at first only the mildest interest in prosecuting under the information as he had on file a dozen much like it—the complaining witnesses had always failed to appear at arraignment.

He pointed this out. Their spokesman said, "We know. But you'll have plenty of backing this time. Supreme Bishop Short is determined that this Antichrist shall flourish no longer."

The prosecutor was not interested in antichrists—but there was a primary coming up. "Well, just remember I can't do much without backing."

"You'll have it."

Farther north, Dr. Jubal Harshaw was not immediately aware of this incident and its consequences, but he did know of too many others for peace of mind. Against his own rules he had succumbed to that most insidious drug, the news. Thus far, he had contained his vice; he merely subscribed to a clipping service instructed for "Man from Mars," "V. M. Smith," "Church of All Worlds," and "Ben Caxton." But the monkey was crawling up his back—twice lately he had had to fight off an impulse to order Larry to set up the babble box in his study—

Damn it, why couldn't those kids tape him an occasional letter?—instead of letting him wonder and worry. *Front!*

He heard Anne come in but he still continued to stare out a window at snow and an empty swimming pool. "Anne," he said without turning around, "rent us a small tropical atoll and put this mausoleum up for sale."

"Yes, Boss. Anything else?"

"But get that atoll tied down on a long-term lease before you hand this wilderness back to the Indians; I will not put up with hotels. How long has it been since I wrote any pay copy?"

"Forty-three days."

"You see? Let that be a lesson to you. Begin. 'Death Song of a Wood's Colt.'

"The depths of winter longing are ice within my heart
    The shards of broken covenants lie sharp against my soul
    The wraiths of long-lost ecstasy still keep us two apart
    The sullen winds of bitterness still keen from turn to pole.

"The scars and twisted tendons, the stumps of struck-off limbs,
    The aching pit of hunger and the throb of unset bone,

My sanded burning eyeballs, as light within them dims,
Add nothing to the torment of lying here alone . . .

"The shimmering flames of fever trace out your blessed face
My broken eardrums echo yet your voice inside my head
I do not fear the darkness that comes to me apace
I only dread the loss of you that comes when I am dead.

"There," he added briskly, "sign it 'Louisa M. Alcott' and have the agency send it to *Togetherness* magazine."

"Boss, is that your idea of 'pay copy'?"

"Huh? Of course it isn't. Not now. But it will be worth something later, so put it in file and my literary executor can use it to help settle the death duties. That's the catch in all artistic pursuits; the best work is always worth most after the workman can't be paid. The literary life—*dreck!* It consists in scratching the cat till it purrs."

"Poor Jubal! Nobody ever feels sorry for him, so he has to feel sorry for himself."

"Sarcasm yet. No wonder I don't get any work done."

"Not sarcasm, Boss. Only the wearer knows where the shoe pinches."

"My apologies. All right, here's pay copy. Begin. Title: 'One for the Road.'

> "There's amnesia in a hang knot,
>   And comfort in the ax,
>   But the simple way of poison will make your nerves relax.
>
> "There's surcease in a gunshot,
>   And sleep that comes from racks,
>   But a handy draft of poison avoids the harshest tax.
>
> "You find rest upon the hot squat,
>   Or gas can give you pax,
>   But the closest corner chemist has peace in packaged stacks.
>
> "There's refuge in the church lot
>   When you tire of facing facts,
>   And the smoothest route is poison prescribed by kindly
>   quacks.

"Chorus— With an *ugh!* and a groan, and a kick of the heels,
            Death comes quiet, or it comes with squeals—

> But the pleasantest place to find your end
> Is a cup of cheer from the hand of a friend."

"Jubal," Anne said worriedly, "is your stomach upset?"

"Always."

"That one's for file, too?"

"Huh? That's for the *New Yorker*. Their usual pen name."

"They'll bounce it."

"They'll buy it. It's morbid, they'll buy it."

"And besides, there's something wrong with the scansion."

"Of course there is! You have to give an editor *something* to change, or he gets frustrated. After he pees in it himself, he likes the flavor much better, so he buys it. Look, my dear, I was successfully avoiding honest work long before you were born—so don't try to teach Granpaw how to suck eggs. Or would you rather I nursed Abby while you turn out copy? Hey! It's Abigail's feeding time, isn't it? And you weren't 'Front,' Dorcas is 'Front.' I remember."

"It won't hurt Abby to wait a few minutes. Dorcas is lying down. Morning sickness."

"Nonsense. If she's pregnant, why won't she let me run a test? Anne, I can spot pregnancy two weeks before a rabbit can—and you know it. I'm going to have to be firm with that girl."

"Jubal, you let her be! She's scared she didn't catch . . . and she wants to think she did, as long as possible. Don't you know *anything* about women?"

"Mmm . . . come to think about it—no. Not anything. All right, I won't heckle her. But why didn't you bring our baby angel in and nurse her here? You have both hands free when you take dictation."

"In the first place, I'm glad I didn't—she might have understood what you were saying—"

"So I'm a bad influence, am I?"

"She's too young to see the marshmallow syrup underneath, Boss. But the real reason is that you don't do any work at all if I bring her in with me; you just play with her."

"Can you think of any better way of enriching the empty hours?"

"Jubal, I appreciate the fact that you are dotty over my daughter; I think she's pretty nice myself. But you've been spending all your time either playing with Abby . . . or moping. That's not good."

"How soon do we go on relief?"

"That's beside the point. If you don't crank out stories, you get spiritually constipated. It's reached the point where Dorcas and Larry and I are biting our nails—and when you do yell 'Front!' we jitter with relief. Only it's always a false alarm."

"If there's money in the bank to meet the bills, what are you worried about?"

"What are *you* worried about, Boss?"

Jubal considered it. Should he tell her? Any possible doubt as to the paternity of Abigail had been settled, in his mind, in her naming; Anne had wavered between "Abigail" and "Zenobia"—and had settled it by loading the infant with both names. Anne had never mentioned the meanings of those names . . . presumably she did not know that he knew them.

Anne went on firmly, "You're not fooling anyone but yourself, Jubal. Dorcas and Larry and I all know that Mike can take care of himself . . . and you ought to know it. But because you've been so frenetic about it—"

" 'Frenetic!' *Me?*"

"—Larry very quietly set up the stereo tank in his room and some one of us three had been catching the news, every broadcast. Not because *we* are worried, for we aren't—except about you. But when Mike gets into the news—and of course he does get into the news; he's still the Man from Mars—we know about it before those silly clippings ever reach you. I wish you would quit reading them."

"How do you know anything about any clippings? I went to a lot of trouble to see that you didn't. I thought."

"Boss," she said in a tired voice, "somebody has to dispose of the trash. Do you think Larry can't read?"

"So. That confounded oubliette hasn't worked right since Duke left. Damn it, nothing has!"

"All you have to do is to send word to Mike that you want Duke to come back—Duke will show up at once."

"You know I can't do that." It graveled him that what she said was almost certainly true . . . and the thought was followed by a sudden and bitter suspicion. "Anne! Are you still here because Mike told you to stay?"

She answered promptly, "I am here because I wish to be here."

"Mmm . . . I'm not sure that's a responsive answer."

"Jubal, sometimes I wish you were small enough to spank. May I finish what I was saying?"

"You have the floor." Would *any* of them be here? Would Maryam have married Stinky and gone off to Beirut if Mike had not approved it? The name "Fatima Michele" might be an acknowledgment of her adopted faith plus her husband's wish to compliment his closest friend—or it might be code almost as explicit as baby Abby's double name, one which stated that Mike was somewhat more than godfather to the daughter of Dr. and Mrs. Mahmoud. If so, did Stinky wear his antlers unaware? Or with serene pride as Joseph was alleged to have done? Uh . . . but it must be concluded with utter certainty that Stinky knew the minutes of his houri; water-brothership permitted not even diplomatic omission of any matter so important. If indeed it was important, which as a physician and agnostic Jubal doubted. But to *them* it would be—

"You aren't listening."

"Sorry. Woolgathering." —and stop it, you nasty old man . . . reading meanings into names that mothers give their children indeed! Next thing you'll be taking up numerology . . . then astrology . . . then spiritualism—until your senility has progressed so far that all there is left is custodial treatment for a hulk too dim-witted to discorporate in dignity. Go to locked drawer nine in the clinic, code "Lethe"—and use at least two grains to be sure, although one is more than enough—

"There's no need for you to read those clippings, because we know the public news about Mike before you do . . . and Ben has given us a water promise to let us know any private news we need to know at once— and Mike of course knows this. But, Jubal, Mike can't be hurt. If you would only visit the Nest, as we three have done, you would know this."

"I have never been invited."

"We didn't have specific invitations, either; we just went. Nobody has to have an invitation to go to his own home . . . any more than they require invitations to come *here*. Like 'The Death of the Hired Man.' But you are just making excuses, Jubal, and poor ones . . . for Ben urged you to, and both Dawn and Duke sent word to you."

"Mike hasn't invited me."

"Boss, that Nest belongs to me and to you quite as much as it does to Mike. Mike is first among equals . . . as you are here. Is this Abby's home?"

"Happens," he answered evenly, "that title already vests in her . . . with lifetime tenancy for me." Jubal had changed his own will, knowing that Mike's will now made it unnecessary to provide for any water brother of Mike. But not being sure of the exact 'water' status of this nestling— save that she was usually wet—he had made redispositions in her favor and in favor of descendants, if any, of certain others. "I hadn't intended to tell you, but there is no harm in your knowing."

"Jubal . . . you've made me cry. And you've almost made me forget what I was saying. And I must say it. Mike would never hurry you, you know that. I grok he is waiting for fullness—and I grok that you are, too."

"Mmm . . . I grok you speak rightly."

"All right. I think you are especially glum today simply because Mike has been arrested again. But that's happened many—"

" 'Arrested?' I hadn't heard about this! What goes on?" He added, "Damn it, girl—"

"Jubal, Jubal! Ben hasn't called; that's all we need to know. You know how many times Mike has been arrested—in the army, as a carney, other places—half a dozen times as a preacher. He never hurts anybody; he just lets them do it. They can never convict him and he gets out as soon as he wishes—at once, if he wants to."

"What is it this time?"

"Oh, the usual nonsense—public lewdness, statutory rape, conspiracy to defraud, keeping a disorderly house, contributing to the delinquency of minors, conspiracy to evade the state truancy laws—"

"Huh?"

"That involves their own nestlings' school. Their license to operate a parochial school was canceled; the kids still didn't go back to public school. No matter, Jubal—none of it matters. The one thing on which they are technically in violation of the law—and so are you, Boss darling—can't possibly be proved. Jubal, if you had ever seen the Temple and the Nest you would know that even the F.D.S. couldn't sneak a spy-eye into it. So relax. After a lot of publicity, charges will be dropped—and the crowds at the outer services will be bigger than ever."

"Hmm! Anne, does Mike rig these persecutions himself?"

She looked startled, an expression her face was unused to. "Why, I had never considered the possibility, Jubal. Mike can't lie, you know."

"Does it involve lying? Suppose he planted perfectly true rumors about himself? But ones that can't be proved in court?"

"Do you think Michael would do that?"

"I don't know. I do know that the slickest way in the world to lie is to tell the right amount of truth at the right time—and then shut up. And it wouldn't be the first time that persecution has been courted for its headline value. All right, I'll dismiss it from my mind unless it turns out he can't handle it. Are you still 'Front'?"

"If you can refrain from chucking Abby under the chin and saying cootchy-coo and similar uncommercial noises, I'll fetch her. Otherwise I had better tell Dorcas to get up and get to work."

"Bring in Abby. I'm going to make an honest effort to make some commercial noises—a brand-new plot, known as boy-meets-girl."

"Say, that's a *good* one, Boss! I wonder why nobody ever thought of it before? Half a sec—" She hurried out.

Jubal did restrain himself—less than one minute of uncommercial noises and demonstrations, just enough to invoke Abigail's heavenly smile, cum dimples, then Anne settled back and let the infant nurse. "Title:" he began. " 'Girls Are Like Boys, Only More So.' Begin. Henry M. Haversham Fourth had been very carefully reared. He believed that there were only two kinds of girls: those in his presence and those who were not. He vastly preferred the latter sort, especially when they stayed that way. Paragraph. He had not been introduced to the young lady who fell into his lap, and he did not consider a common disaster as equivalent to a formal intro—' What the hell do *you* want? Can't you see I'm working?"

"Boss—" said Larry.

"Get out of that door, close it behind you, and—"

"*Boss!* Mike's church has burned down!"

They made a disorderly rout for Larry's room, Jubal a half length behind Larry at the turn, Anne with eleven pounds up closing rapidly despite her handicap. Dorcas trailed the field through being late out the starting gate; the racket wakened her.

"—midnight last night. What you are now viewing is what was the main entrance of the cult's temple, as it appeared immediately after the explosion. This is your Neighborly Newsman for New World Networks with your midmorning roundup. Stay switched to this pitch for dirt that's alert. And now a moment for your local sponsor—" The scene of destruction shimmered out and med-close shot of a lovely young housewife replaced, with dolly-in.

"Damn! Larry, unplug that contraption and wheel it into the study. Anne—no, Dorcas. Phone Ben."

Anne protested, "You know the Temple never had a telephone . . . ever. How can she?"

"Then have somebody chase over and—no, of course not; the Temple wouldn't have anybody—uh, call the chief of police there. No, the district attorney. The last you heard Mike was still in jail?"

"That's right."

"I hope he still is—and all the others, too."

"So do I. Dorcas, take Abby. I'll do it."

But as they returned to the study the phone was signalling an incoming call and demanding hush & scramble. Jubal cursed and set the combo, intending to blast whoever it was off the frequency.

But it was Ben Caxton. "Hi, Jubal."

"Ben! What the hell is the situation?"

"I see you've had some of the news. That's why I called, to put your mind at rest. Everything is under control. No sweat."

"What about the fire? Anybody hurt?"

"No damage at all. Mike says to tell you—"

"No *damage?* I just saw a shot of it; it looked like a total—"

"Oh, that—" Ben shrugged it off. "Look, Jubal, please listen and let me talk. I've got other things and other calls after this one. You aren't the only person who needs to be reassured. But Mike said to call you first."

"Uh . . . very well, sir. I shall keep silent."

"Nobody hurt, nobody even scorched. Oh, a couple of million dollars in property damage, most of it uninsured. Nichevo. The place was already choked with experiences; Mike planned to abandon it soon in any case. Yes, it was fireproof—but anything will burn with enough gasoline and dynamite."

"Incendiary job, huh?"

"Please, Jubal. They had arrested eight of us—all they could catch of the Ninth Circle, John Doe warrants, mostly. Mike had all of us bailed out in a couple of hours, except himself. He's still in the hoosegow—"

"I'll be right there!"

"Take it easy. Mike says for you to come if you want to, but there is absolutely no need for it. His words. And I agree. It would just be a pleasure trip. The fire was set last night while the Temple was empty, everything canceled because of the arrests—empty, that is, except for the Nest. All of us in town, except Mike, were gathered in the Innermost Temple, holding a special Sharing-Water in his honor, when the explosion and fire were set off. So we adjourned to an emergency Nest."

"From the looks of it, you were lucky to get out at all."

"We were completely cut off, Jubal. We're all dead—"

"*What?*"

"We're all listed as dead or missing so far as the authorities know. You see, nobody left the building after that holocaust started . . . by any known exit."

"Uh . . . a 'priest's hole' arrangement?"

"Jubal, Mike has very special methods for dealing with such things—and I'm not going to discuss them over the phone, even scrambled."

"You said he was in jail?"

"So I did. He still is."

"But—"

"That's enough. If you do come here, don't go to the Temple. It's kaput. Our organization is busted up. We're through in this town. You could say that they've licked us, I suppose. I'm not going to tell you where we are . . . and I'm not calling from there, anyhow. If you must come—and I see no point in it; there's nothing you can do—just come as you ordinarily would . . . and we'll find you."

"But—"

"That's all. Good-by. Anne, Dorcas, Larry—and you, too, Jubal, and the baby. Share water. Thou art God." The screen went blank.

Jubal swore. "I knew it! I knew it all along! That's what comes of mucking around with religion. Dorcas, get me a taxi. Anne—no, finish feeding your child. Larry, pack me a small bag. Anne, I'll want most of the iron money and Larry can go into town tomorrow and replenish the supply."

"But, Boss," protested Larry, "we're *all* going."

"Certainly we are," Anne agreed crisply.

"Pipe down, Anne. And close your mouth, Dorcas. This is not a time when women have the vote. That city is the front line at the moment and anything can happen. Larry, you are going to stay here and protect two women and a baby. Forget that about going to the bank; you won't need cash because none of you is to stir off the place until I'm back. Somebody is playing rough and there is enough hook-up between this house and that church that they might play rough here, too. Larry, flood lights all night long, heat up the fence, don't hesitate to shoot. And don't be slow about getting everybody into the vault if necessary—better put Abby's crib in there at once. Now get with it, all of you—I've got to change clothes."

Thirty minutes later Jubal was alone, by choice, in his suite; the rest were busy at assigned tasks. Larry called up, "Boss! Taxi about to land."

"Be right down," he called back, then turned to take a last look at the Fallen Caryatid. His eyes were filled with tears. He said softly, "You tried, didn't you, youngster? But that stone was always too heavy . . . too heavy for anyone."

Gently he touched a hand of the crumpled figure, turned and left.

XXXV

JUBAL HAD A MISERABLE TRIP. The taxi was automatic and it did just what he expected of machinery, developed trouble in the air and homed for maintenance instead of carrying out its orders. Jubal wound up in New York, farther from where he wanted to be than when he started. There he found that he could make better time by commercial schedule than he could by any charter available. So he arrived hours later than he expected to, having spent the time cooped up with strangers (which he detested) and watching a stereo tank (which he detested only slightly less).

But it did inform him somewhat. He saw an insert of Supreme Bishop Short proclaiming a holy war against the Antichrist, i.e., Mike, and he saw too many shots of what was obviously an utterly ruined building—he failed to see how any of them had escaped alive. Augustus Greaves, in his most solemn lippmann tones, viewed with alarm everything about it . . . but pointed out that, in every spite-fence quarrel, one neighbor supplies the original incitement—and made it plain that, in his weasel-worded opinion, the so-called Man from Mars was at fault.

At last Jubal stood on a municipal landing flat sweltering in winter clothes unsuited to the blazing sun overhead, noted that palm trees still looked like a poor grade of feather duster, regarded bleakly the ocean beyond them, thinking that it was a dirty unstable mass of water, certainly contaminated with grape fruit shells and human excrement even though he couldn't see such at this distance—and wondered what to do next.

A man wearing a uniform cap approached him. "Taxi, sir?"

"Uh, yes, I think so." At worst he could go to a hotel, call in the press, and give out an interview that would publicize his whereabouts— there was occasionally some advantage to being newsworthy.

"Over this way, sir." The cabby led him out of the crowd and to a battered Yellow Cab. As he put his bag in after Jubal, the pilot said quietly, "I offer you water."

"Eh? Never thirst."

"Thou art God." The hack driver sealed the door and got into his own compartment.

They wound up on a private landing flat on one wing of a big beach hotel—a four-car space, the hotel's own landing flat being on another wing. The pilot set the cab to home-in alone, took Jubal's bag and escorted him inside. "You couldn't have come in too easily via the lobby," he said conversationally, "as the foyer on this floor is filled with some very bad-tempered cobras. So if you decide you want to go down to the street, be sure to ask somebody first. Me, or anybody—I'm Tim."

"I'm Jubal Harshaw."

"I know, brother Jubal. In this way. Mind your step." They entered the hotel suite of the large, extreme luxury sort, and Jubal was led on into a bedroom with bath; Tim said, "This is yours," put Jubal's bag down and left. On the side table Jubal found water, glasses, ice cubes, and a bottle of brandy, opened but untouched. He was unsurprised to find that it was his preferred brand. He mixed himself a quick one, sipped it and sighed, then took off his heavy winter jacket.

A woman came in bearing a tray of sandwiches. She was wearing a plain dress which Jubal took to be the uniform of a hotel chambermaid since it was quite unlike the shorts, scarves, pediskirts, halters, sarongs and other bright-colored ways to display rather than conceal that characterized most females in this resort. But she smiled at him, said, "Drink deep and never thirst, our brother," put the tray down, went into his bath and started a tub for him, then checked around by eye in bath and in bedroom. "Is there anything you need, Jubal?"

"Me? Oh, no, everything is just fine. I'll make a quick cleanup and—is Ben Caxton around?"

"Yes. But he said you would want a bath and get comfortable first. If you want anything, just say so. Ask anyone. Or ask for me. I'm Patty."

"*Oh!* The Life of Archangel Foster."

She dimpled and suddenly was not plain but pretty, and much younger than the thirtyish Jubal had guessed her to be. "Yes."

"I'd like very much to see it some time. I'm interested in religious art."

"Now? No, I grok you want your bath. Unless you'd like help with your bath?"

Jubal recalled that his Japanese friend of the many tattoos had been a bath girl in her teens and would have made—had, many times—the same offer. But Patty was not Japanese and he simply wanted to wash away the sweat and stink and get into clothes suited to the climate. "No, thank you, Patty. But I do want to see them, at your convenience."

"Any time. There's no hurry." She left, unhurried but moving silently and very quickly.

Jubal soaped and dunked himself and refrained from lounging as the warm water invited his tired muscles to do; he wanted to see Ben and find out the score. Shortly he was checking through what Larry had packed for him and grunted with annoyance to find no summerweight slacks. He settled for sandals, shorts, and a bright sport shirt, which made him look like a paint-splashed emu and accented his hairy, thinning legs. But Jubal had ceased worrying about his appearance several decades earlier; it was comfortable and it would do, at least until he needed to go out on the street . . . or into court. Did the bar association here have reciprocity with Pennsylvania? He couldn't recall. Well, it was always possible to act with another attorney-of-record.

He found his way into a large living room, most comfortable but having that impersonal quality of all hotel accommodations. Several people were gathered near the largest stereovision tank Jubal had ever seen outside a theater. One of them glanced up, said, "Hi, Jubal," and came toward him.

"Hi, Ben. What's the situation? Is Mike still in jail?"

"Oh, no. He got out shortly after I talked to you."

"He's been arraigned then. Is the preliminary hearing set?"

Ben smiled. "That's not quite the way it is, Jubal. Mike is technically a fugitive from justice. He wasn't released on bail. He escaped."

Jubal looked disgusted. "What a silly thing to do. Now the case will be eight times as difficult."

"Jubal, I told you not to worry. All the rest of us are presumed dead —and Mike is simply missing. We're through with this city, so it doesn't matter in the least. We'll go someplace else."

"They'll extradite him."

"Never fear. They won't."

"Well . . . where is he? I want to talk to him."

"Oh, he's right here, a couple of rooms down from you. But he's withdrawn in meditation. He left word to tell you, when you arrived, to take no action—none. You can talk to him right now if you insist; Jill will call him out of it. But I don't recommend it. There's no hurry."

Jubal thought about it, admitted that he was damnably eager to hear from Mike himself just what the score was—and chew him out for having gotten into such a mess—but admitted, too, that disturbing Mike while he was in a trance was almost certainly much worse than disturbing Jubal himself when he was dictating a story—the boy always came out of his self-hypnosis when he had "grokked the fullness," whatever that was—and if he hadn't, then he always needed to go back into it. As pointless as disturbing a hibernating bear.

"All right, I'll wait. But I want to talk to him when he wakes up."

"You will. Now relax and be happy. Let the trip get out of your system." Ben urged him toward the group around the stereo tank.

Anne looked up. "Hello, Boss." She moved over and made room. "Sit down."

Jubal joined her. "May I ask what the devil *you* are doing here?"

"The same thing you're doing—nothing. Watching stereo. Jubal, please don't get heavy-handed because we didn't do what you told us. We belong here as much as you do. You shouldn't have told us not to come . . . but you were too upset for us to argue with you. So relax and watch what they're saying about us. The sheriff has just announced that he's going to run all us whores out of town." She smiled. "I've never been run out of town before. It should be interesting. Does a whore get ridden on a rail? Or will I have to walk?"

"I don't think there's protocol in the matter. You all came?"

"Yes, but don't fret. Jed McClintock is sleeping in the house. Larry and I made a standing arrangement with the McClintock boys for one of them to do so, more than a year ago—just in case. They know how the furnace works and where the switches are and things; it's all right."

"Hmm! I'm beginning to think I'm just a boarder there."

"Were you ever anything else, Boss? You expect us to run it without bothering you. We do. But it's a shame you didn't relax and let us all travel together. We got here more than two hours ago—you must have had some trouble."

"I did. A terrible trip. Anne, once I get home I don't intend ever to set foot off the place again in my life . . . and I'm going to yank out the telephone and take a sledgehammer to the babble box."

"Yes, Boss."

"This time I mean it." He glanced at the giant babble box in front of him. "Do those commercials go on forever? Where's my goddaughter? Don't tell me you left her to the mercies of McClintock's idiot sons!"

"Oh, of course not. She's here. She even has her own nursemaid, thank God."

"I want to see her."

"Patty will show her to you. I'm bored with her—she was a perfect little beast all the way down. Patty dear! Jubal wants to see Abby."

The tattooed woman checked one of her unhurried dashes through the room—so far as Jubal could see, she was the only one of the several present who was doing any work, and she seemed to be everywhere at once. "Certainly, Jubal. I'm not busy. Down this way.

"I've got the kids in my room," she explained, while Jubal strove to keep up with her, "so that Honey Bun can watch them."

Jubal was mildly startled to see, a moment later, what Patricia meant by that. The boa was arranged on one of twin double beds in squared-off loops that formed a nest—a twin nest, as one bight of the snake had been pulled across to bisect the square, making two crib-sized pockets, each padded with a baby blanket and each containing a baby.

The ophidian nursemaid raised her head inquiringly as they came in. Patty stroked it and said, "It's all right, dear. Father Jubal wants to see them. Pet her a little, and let her grok you, so that she will know you next time."

First Jubal cootchy-cooed at his favorite girl friend when she gurgled at him and kicked, then petted the snake. He decided that it was the handsomest specimen of *Boidae* he had ever seen, as well as the biggest— longer, he estimated, than any other boa constrictor in captivity. Its cross bars were sharply marked and the brighter colors of the tail quite showy. He envied Patty her blue-ribbon pet and regretted that he would not have more time in which to get friendly with it.

The snake rubbed her head against his hand like a cat. Patty picked up Abby, said, "Just as I thought. Honey Bun, why didn't you tell me?"—then explained, as she started to change diapers, "She tells me at once if one of them gets tangled up, or needs help, or anything, since she can't do much for them herself—no hands—except nudge them back if they try to crawl out and might fall. But she just can't seem to grok that a wet baby ought to be changed—Honey Bun doesn't see anything wrong about that. And neither does Abby."

"I know. We call her 'Old Faithful.' Who's the other cutie pie?"

"Huh? That's Fatima Michele. I thought you knew."

"Are *they* here? I thought they were in Beirut!"

"Why, I believe they did come from some one of those foreign parts. I don't know just where. Maybe Maryam told me but it wouldn't mean anything to me; I've never been anywhere. Not that it matters; I grok all places are alike—just people. There, do you want to hold Abigail Zenobia while I check Fatima?"

Jubal did so and assured her that she was the most beautiful girl in the world, then shortly thereafter assured Fatima of the same thing. He was completely sincere each time and the girls believed him—Jubal had said the same thing on countless occasions starting in the Harding administration, had always meant it and had always been believed. It was a Higher Truth, not bound by mundane logic.

Regretfully he left them, after again petting Honey Bun and telling her the same thing, and just as sincerely.

They left and at once ran into Fatima's mother. "Boss honey!" She kissed him and patted his tummy. "I see they've kept you fed."

"Some. I've just been in smooching with your daughter. She's an angel doll, Miriam."

"Pretty good baby, huh? We're going to sell her down to Rio—get a fancy price for her."

"I thought the market was better in Yemen?"

"Stinky says not. Got to sell her to make room." She put his hand on her belly. "Feel the bulge? Stinky and I are making a boy now—got no time for daughters."

"Maryam," Patricia said chidingly, "that's no way to talk, even in fun."

"Sorry, Patty. I won't talk that way about your baby. Aunt Patty is a lady, and groks that I'm not."

"I grok that you aren't, too, you little hellion. But if Fatima is for sale, I'll give you twice your best commercial offer."

"You'll have to take it up with Aunt Patty; I'm merely allowed to see her occasionally."

"And you don't bulge, so you may want to keep her yourself. Let me see your eyes. Mmm . . . could be."

"Is. And Mike has grokked it most carefully and tells Stinky he's made a boy."

"How can Mike grok that? Impossible. I'm not even sure you're pregnant."

"Oh, she is, Jubal," Patricia confirmed.

Miriam looked at him serenely. "Still the skeptic, Boss. Mike grokked it while Stinky and I were still in Beirut, before we were sure we had caught. So Mike phoned us. And the next day Stinky told the university that we were taking a sabbatical for field work—or his resignation, if they wished. So here we are."

"Doing what?"

"Working. Working harder than you ever made me work, Boss—my husband is a slave driver."

"Doing what?"

"They're writing a Martian dictionary," Patty told him.

"Martian to English? That must be difficult."

"Oh, no, no, no!" Miriam looked almost shocked. "That wouldn't be difficult, that would be impossible. A Martian dictionary in Martian. There's never been one before; the Martians don't need such things. Uh, my part of it is just clerical; I type what they do. Mike and Stinky—mostly Stinky—worked out a phonetic script for Martian, eighty-one characters. So we had an I.B.M. typer worked over for those characters, using both upper and lower case—Boss darling, I'm *ruined* as a secretary; I type touch system in Martian now. Will you love me anyhow? When you shout 'Front!' and I'm not good for anything? I can still cook . . . and I'm told that I have other talents."

"I'll learn to dictate in Martian."

"You will, before Mike and Stinky get through with you. I grok. Eh, Patty?"

"You speak rightly, my brother."

They returned to the living room, Caxton joined them and suggested finding a quieter place, away from the giant babble box, led Jubal down a passage and into another living room. "You seem to have most of this floor."

"All of it," agreed Ben. "Four suites—the Secretarial; the Presidential, the Royal, and Owner's Cabin, opened into one and not accessible other than by our own landing flat . . . except through a foyer that is not very healthy without help. You were warned about that?"

"Yes."

"We don't need so much room right now . . . but we may: people are trickling in."

"Ben, how can you hide from the cops as openly as this? The hotel staff alone will give you away."

"Oh, there are ways. The staff doesn't come up here. You see, Mike owns this hotel."

"So much the worse, I would think."

"So much the better . . . unless our doughty police chief has Mr. Douglas on his payroll, which I doubt. Mike bought it through about four links of dummies—and Douglas doesn't snoop into why Mike wants a thing done. Douglas doesn't despise me quite as much since Os Kilgallen took over my column, I think, but nevertheless he doesn't want to surrender control to me—he does what Mike wants. The hotel is a sound investment; it makes money—but the owner of record is one of our clandestine Ninth-Circlers. So the owner decides he wants this floor for the season and the manager can't and doesn't and wouldn't want to inquire into why, or how many guests of his own the owner has coming or going—he likes his job; Mike is paying him more than he's worth. It's a pretty good hide-out, for the time being. Till Mike groks where we will go next."

"Sounds like Mike had anticipated a need for a hide-out."

"Oh, I'm sure he did. Almost two weeks ago Mike cleared out the nestlings' nest—except for Maryam and her baby; Maryam is needed for the job she's on. Mike sent the parents with children to other cities—places he means to open temples, I think—and when the time came, there were just about a dozen of us to move. No sweat."

"As it was, you barely got out with your lives, I take it." Jubal wondered how they had even managed to grab clothes—in view of how they probably were not dressed. "You lost all the contents of the Nest? All your personal possessions?"

"Oh, no, not anything we really wanted. Stuff like Stinky's language tapes and a trick typer that Maryam uses—even that horrible Madame-Tussaud picture of you. And Mike grabbed our clothes and some cash that was on hand."

Jubal objected, "You say *Mike* did this? But I thought Mike was in jail when the fire broke out."

"Uh, he was and he wasn't. His body was in jail . . . curled up in withdrawal. But he was actually with us. You understand?"

"Uh, I don't grok."

"Rapport. He was inside Jill's head, mostly, but we were all pretty closely tied in together. Jubal, I can't explain it; you have to *do* it. When the explosion hit, he moved us over here. Then he went back and saved the minor stuff worth saving."

Jubal frowned. Caxton said impatiently, "Teleportation, of course. What's so hard to grok about it, Jubal? You yourself told me to come down here and open my eyes and know a miracle when I saw one. So I did and they were. Only they aren't miracles, any more than radio is a miracle. Do you grok radio? Or stereovision? Or electronic computers?"

"Me? No."

"Nor do I, I've never studied electronics. But I'm sure I could if I took the time and the hard sweat to learn the language of electronics; I don't think it's miraculous—just complex. Teleportation is quite simple, once you learn the language—it's the language that is so difficult."

"Ben, you can teleport things?"

"Me? Oh, no, they don't teach that in kindergarten. Oh, I'm a deacon by courtesy, simply because I'm 'First Called' and Ninth Circle—but my actual progress is about Fourth Circle, bucking for Fifth. Why, I'm just beginning to get control of my own body. Patty is the only one of us who uses teleportation herself with any regularity . . . and I'm not sure she ever does it without Mike's support. Oh, Mike says she's quite capable of it, but Patty is such a curiously naive and humble person for the genius she is that she is quite dependent on Mike. Which she needn't be. Jubal, I grok this: we don't actually need Mike—oh, I'm not running him down; don't get me wrong. But you could have been the Man from Mars. Or even me. It's like the first man to discover fire. Fire was there all along—and after he showed that it could be used, anybody could use it . . . anybody with sense and savvy enough not to get burned with it. Follow me?"

"I grok, somewhat at least."

"Mike is our Prometheus—but, remember, Prometheus was not God. Mike keeps emphasizing this. Thou art God, I am God, he is God—all that groks. Mike is a man along with the rest of us . . . even though he knows more. A very superior man, admittedly—a lesser man, taught the things the Martians know, probably would have set himself up as a pip-squeak god. Mike is above that temptation. Prometheus . . . but that's all."

Jubal said slowly, "As I recall, Prometheus paid a high price for bringing fire to mankind."

"And don't think that Mike doesn't! He pays with twenty-four hours of work every day, seven days a week, trying to teach a few of us how to play with matches without getting burned. Jill and Patty lowered the boom on him, started making him take one night a week off, long before I joined up." Caxton smiled. "But you can't stop Mike. This burg is loaded with gambling joints, no doubt you know, and most of them crooked since it's against the law here. Mike usually spends his night off bucking crooked games—and winning. Picks up ten, twenty, thirty thousand dollars a night. They tried to mug him, they tried to kill him, they tried knock-out drops and muscle boys—nothing worked; he simply ran up a reputation as the luckiest man in town . . . which brought more people into the Temple; they wanted to see this man who always won. So they tried to shut him out of the games—which was a mistake. Their cold decks froze solid, their wheels wouldn't spin, their dice would roll nothing but box cars. At last they started putting up with him . . . and requesting him politely to please move along after he had won a few grand. Mike would always do so, if asked politely."

Caxton added, "Of course that's one more power bloc we've got against us. Not just the Fosterites and some of the other churches—but the gambling syndicate and the city political machine. I rather suppose that job done on the Temple was by professionals brought in from out of town —I doubt if the Fosterite goon squads touched it. Too professional."

While they talked, people came in, went out again, formed groups themselves or joined Jubal and Ben. Jubal found in them a most unusual feeling, an unhurried relaxation that at the same time was a dynamic tension. No one seemed excited, never in a hurry . . . yet everything they did seemed purposeful, even gestures as apparently accidental and unpremeditated as encountering one another and marking it with a kiss or a greeting—or sometimes not. It felt to Jubal as if each move had been planned by a master choreographer . . . yet obviously was not.

The quiet and the increasing tension—or rather "expectancy," he decided; these people were not tense in any morbid fashion—reminded Jubal of something he had known in the past. Surgery? With a master at work, no noise, no lost motions? A little.

Then he recalled it. Once, many years earlier when gigantic chemically powered rockets were used for the earliest probing of space from the third planet, he had watched a count-down in a block house . . . and he recalled now the same low voices, the same relaxed, very diverse but coordinated actions, the same rising exultant expectancy as the count grew ever smaller. They were "waiting for fullness," that was certain. But for what? Why were they so happy? Their Temple and all they had built had just been destroyed . . . yet they seemed like kids on the night before Christmas.

Jubal had noted in passing, when he arrived, that the nudity Ben had been so disturbed by on his abortive first visit to the Nest did not seem to be the practice in this surrogate Nest, although private enough in location. Then Jubal realized later that he had failed to notice such cases when they did appear; he had himself become so much in the unique close-family mood of the place that being dressed or not had become an unnoticeable irrelevancy.

When he did notice, it was not skin but the thickest, most beautiful cascade of black hair he had ever seen, gracing a young woman who came in, spoke to someone, threw Ben a kiss, glanced gravely at Jubal, and left. Jubal followed her with his eyes, appreciating that flowing mass of midnight plumage. Only after she left did he realize that she had not been dressed other than in her queenly crowning glory . . . and then realized, too, that she was not the first of his brothers in that fashion.

Ben noticed his glance. "That's Ruth," he said. "New high priestess. She and her husband have been away, clear on the other coast—their mission was to prepare a branch temple, I think. I'm glad they're back. It's beginning to look as if the whole family will be home at once—like an old-fashioned Christmas dinner."

"Beautiful head of hair. I wish she had tarried."

"Then why didn't you call her over?"

"Eh?"

"Ruth almost certainly found an excuse to come in here just to catch a glimpse of you—I suppose they must have just arrived. But haven't you noticed that we have been left pretty much alone, except for a few who sat down with us, didn't say much, then left?"

"Well . . . yes." Jubal had noticed and had been a touch disappointed, as he had been braced, by all that he had heard, to ward off undue intimacy—and had found that he had stepped on a top step that wasn't there. He had been treated with hospitality and politeness, but it was more like the politeness of a cat than that of an over-friendly dog.

"They are all terribly interested in the fact that you are here and are very anxious to see you . . . but they are a little bit afraid of you, too."

"Me?"

"Oh, I told you this last summer. You're a venerable tradition of the church, not quite real and a bit more than life size. Mike has told them that you are the only human being he knows of who can 'grok in fullness' without needing to learn Martian first. Most of them suspect that you can read minds as perfectly as Mike does."

"Oh, what poppycock! I hope you disabused them?"

"Who am I to destroy a myth? Perhaps you do read minds—I'm sure you wouldn't tell me. They are just a touch afraid of you—you eat babies for breakfast and when you roar the ground trembles. Any of them would be delighted to have you call them over . . . but they won't force themselves on you. They know that even Mike stands at attention and says 'sir' when you speak."

Jubal dismissed the whole idea with one short, explosive word. "Certainly," Ben agreed. "Even Mike has his blind spots—I told you he was only human. But that's how it is. You're the patron saint of this church—and you're stuck with it."

"Well . . . there's somebody I know, just came in. Jill! *Jill!* Turn around, dear!"

The woman turned rather hesitantly. "I'm Dawn. But thank you." She came over, however, and Jubal thought for an instant that she was going to kiss him . . . and decided not to duck it. But she either had not that intention, or changed her mind. She dropped to one knee, took his hand and kissed it. "Father Jubal. We welcome you and drink deep of you."

Jubal snatched his hand away. "Oh, for heaven's sake, child! Get up from there and sit with us. Share water."

"Yes, Father Jubal."

"Uh . . . and call me Jubal—and pass the word around that I don't appreciate being treated like a leper. I'm in the bosom of my family—I hope."

"You are . . . Jubal."

"So I expect to be called Jubal and treated as a water brother—no more, no less. The first one who treats me with respect will be required to stay in after school. Grok?"

"Yes, Jubal," she answered demurely. "I've told them. They will."

"Huh?"

"Dawn means," explained Ben, "that she's told Patty, probably, since Mike is withdrawn at the moment . . . and that Patty is telling everybody who can hear easily—with his inner ear—and they are passing the word to any who are still a bit deaf, like myself."

"Yes," agreed Dawn, "except that I told Jill—Patty has gone outside for something Michael wants. Jubal, have you been watching any of what is showing in the stereo tank? It's very exciting."

"Eh? No."

"You mean the jail break, Dawn?"

"Yes, Ben."

"We hadn't discussed that—and Jubal doesn't like stereo. Jubal, Mike didn't merely crush out and come home when he felt like it; he gave them a dilemma to sit on. Here he has just been arrested for everything but raping the Statue of Liberty, with Bigmouth Short denouncing him as the Antichrist on the same day. So he gave 'em miracles to chew on. He threw away every bar and door in the county jail as he left . . . did the same at the state prison just out of town for good measure—and disarmed all the police forces, city, county, and state. Partly to keep 'em busy and interested . . . and partly because Mike just purely despises locking a man up for any reason at all. He groks a great wrongness in it."

"That fits," Jubal agreed. "Mike is gentle, always. It would hurt him to have anybody locked up. I agree."

Ben shook his head. "Mike isn't gentle, Jubal. Killing a man wouldn't worry him. But he's the ultimate anarchist—locking a man up is a wrongness. Freedom of self—and utter personal responsibility for self. Thou art God."

"Wherein lies the conflict, sir? Killing a man might be necessary. But confining him is an offense against his integrity—and your own."

Ben looked at him. "I grok Mike was right. You do grok in fullness—his way. I don't quite . . . I'm still learning." He added, "How are they taking it, Dawn?"

She giggled slightly. "Like a stirred-up hornets' nest. The mayor has been on . . . and he's frothing at the mouth. He's demanded help from the state and from the Federation—and he's getting it; we've seen lots of troop carriers landing. But as they pour out, Mike is stripping them—not just their weapons, even their shoes—and as soon as the troop carrier is empty, it goes, too."

Ben said, "I grok he'll stay withdrawn until they get tired and give up. Handling that many details he would almost have to stay in it and on eternal time."

Dawn looked thoughtful. "No, I don't think so, Ben. Of course I would have to, in order to handle even a tenth so much. But I grok Michael could do it riding a bicycle while standing on his head."

"Mmm . . . I wouldn't know, I'm still making mud pies." Ben stood up. "Sometimes you miracle workers give me a slight pain, honey child. I'm going to go watch the tank for a while." He stopped to kiss her. "You entertain old Pappy Jubal; he likes little girls." Caxton left and a package of cigarettes he had left on a coffee table got up, followed him, and placed themselves in one of his pockets.

Jubal said, "Did you do that? Or Ben?"

"Ben did. I don't smoke, unless the man I'm with wants to smoke. But he's always forgetting his cigarettes; they chase him all over the Nest."

"Hmm . . . pretty fair-sized mud pies he makes these days."

"Ben is advancing much more rapidly than he will ever admit. He's a very holy person—but he hates to admit it. He's shy."

"Umph. Dawn, you *are* the Dawn Ardent I met at Foster Tabernacle about two and half years ago, aren't you?"

"Oh, you remember!!" She looked as if he had handed her a lollipop.

"Of course I remember. But I was slightly puzzled. You've changed some. All for the better. You seem much more beautiful."

"That's because I am more beautiful," she said simply. "You mistook me for Gillian. And she is more beautiful, too."

"Where is that child? I haven't seen her . . . and I expected to see her at once."

"She's been working." Dawn paused. "But I told her and she says she's coming in." She paused again. "And I am to take her place. If you will excuse me."

"Oh, certainly. Run along, child."

"There's no hurry." But she did get up and leave almost at once as Dr. Mahmoud sat down.

Jubal looked at him sourly. "You might at least have had the common courtesy to let me know that you were in this country instead of letting me meet my goddaughter for the first time through the good offices of a snake."

"Oh, Jubal, you're always in such a bloody hurry."

"Sir, when one is of—" Jubal was interrupted by two hands placed over his eyes from behind. A well-remembered voice demanded:

"Guess who?"

"Beelzebub?"

"Try again."

"Lady Macbeth?"

"Much closer. Third guess, or a forfeit."

"Gillian, stop that and come around here and sit beside me."

"Yes, Father." She obeyed.

"And knock off calling me 'Father' anywhere but home. Sir, I was saying that when one is of my age, one is necessarily in a hurry about some things. Each sunrise is a precious jewel . . . for it may never be followed by its sunset. The world may end at any moment."

Mahmoud smiled at him. "Jubal, are you under the impression that if you stop cranking, the world stops going around?"

"Most certainly, sir—from my viewpoint." Miriam joined them silently, sat down on Jubal's free side; he put an arm around her. "While I might not be honing to see your ugly face again . . . nor even to gaze on the somewhat more acceptable one of my former secretary—"

Miriam whispered, "Boss, are you honing for a kick in the stomach? I'm exquisitely beautiful; I have it on highest authority."

"Quiet. —new goddaughters are in another category. Through your failure to drop me so much as a postcard, I might have missed seeing Fatima Michele. In which case I would have returned to haunt you."

"In which case," Miriam pointed out, "you could take a look at Micky at the same time . . . rubbing strained carrots in her hair. A disgusting sight."

"I was speaking metaphorically."

"I wasn't. She's a sloppy trencherman."

"Why," asked Jill quietly, "were you speaking metaphorically, Boss?"

"Eh? The concept 'ghost' is one I feel no need for, other than as a figure of speech."

"It's more than a figure of speech," insisted Jill.

"Uh . . . as may be. I prefer to meet baby girls in the flesh, including my own."

Dr. Mahmoud said, "But that is what I was saying, Jubal. You aren't about to die; you aren't even close to it. Mike has grokked you to be certain. He says you have a long stretch of years ahead of you."

Jubal shook his head. "I set a top limit of three figures years ago. No more."

"Which three figures, Boss?" Miriam inquired innocently. "The three Methuselah used?"

He shook her shoulders. "Don't be obscene!"

"Stinky says women should be obscene but not heard."

"Your husband speaks rightly. So pipe down. The day my machine first shows three figures on its mileage meter is the day I discorporate, whether Martian style or by my own crude methods. You can't take that away from me. Going to the showers is the best part of the game."

"I grok you speak rightly, Jubal," Jill said slowly, "about its being the best part of the game. But I wouldn't count on it any time soon. Your fullness is not yet. Allie cast a horoscope on you just last week."

"A horoscope? Oh, my God! Who is 'Allie?' And how dare she cast a horoscope on me! Show her to me! Swelp me, I'll turn her in to the Better Business Bureau."

"I'm afraid you can't, Jubal," Mahmoud put in, "just now, as she is working on our dictionary. As to who she is, she's Madame Alexandra Vesant."

Jubal sat up and looked pleased. "Becky? Is *she* in this nut house, too? I should have known it. Where is she?"

"Yes, Becky. But we call her 'Allie' because we've got another Becky.

But you'll have to wait. And don't scoff at her horoscopes, Jubal; she has the Sight."

"Oh, balderdash, Stinky. Astrology is nonsense and you know it."

"Oh, certainly. Even Allie knows it. And a percentage of astrologers are clumsy frauds. Nevertheless Allie practices it even more assiduously than she used to, when she did it for the public—using Martian arithmetic now and Martian astronomy—much fuller than ours. But it's her device for grokking. It could be gazing into a pool of water, or a crystal ball, or examining the entrails of a chicken. The means she uses to get into the mood do not matter and Mike has advised her to go on using the symbols she is used to. The point is: she has the Sight."

"What the hell do you mean by 'the Sight,' Stinky?"

"The ability to grok more of the universe than that little piece you happen to be sitting on at the moment. Mike has it from years of Martian discipline; Allie was an untrained semi-adept. The fact that she used as meaningless a symbol as astrology is beside the point. A rosary is meaningless, too—I speak of a Muslim rosary, of course; I'm not criticizing our competitors across the street." Mahmoud reached into his pocket, got out one, started fingering it. "If it helps to turn your hat around during a poker game—then it helps. It is irrelevant that the hat has no magic powers and cannot grok."

Jubal looked at the Islamic device for meditation and ventured a question he had hesitated to put before. "Then I take it you are still one of the Faithful? I had thought perhaps that you had joined Mike's church all the way."

Mahmoud put away the beads. "I have done both."

"Huh? Stinky, they're incompatible. Or else I don't grok either one."

Mahmoud shook his head. "Only on the surface. You could say, I suppose, that Maryam took my religion and I took hers; we consolidated. But, Jubal my beloved brother, I am still God's slave, submissive to His will . . . and nevertheless can say: 'Thou art God, I am God, all that groks is God.' The Prophet never asserted that he was the last of all prophets nor did he claim to have said all there was to say—only fanatics after his lifetime insisted on those two very misleading fallacies. Submission to God's will is not to become a blind robot, incapable of free decision and thus of sin—and the Koran does not say that. Submission can include —and *does* include—utter responsibility for the fashion in which I, and each of us, shape the universe. It is ours to turn into a heavenly garden . . . or to rend and destroy." He smiled. " 'With God all things are possible,' if I may borrow for a moment—except one thing . . . the one Impossible. God cannot escape Himself, He cannot abdicate His own total responsibility—He forever must remain submissive to His own will. Islam remains—He cannot pass the buck. It is His—mine . . . yours . . . Mike's."

Jubal heaved a sigh. "Stinky, theology always gives me the pip. Where's Becky? Can't she knock off this dictionary work and say hello to an old friend? I've seen her only once in the last twenty-odd years; that's too long."

"You'll see her. But she can't stop now, she's dictating. Let me explain the technique, so that you won't insist. Up to now, I've been spending part of each day in rapport with Mike—just a few moments although it feels like an eight-hour day. Then I would immediately dictate all that he had poured into me onto tape. From those tapes several other people, trained in Martian phonetics but not necessarily advanced students, would make long-hand phonetic transcriptions. Then Maryam would type them out, using a special typer—and this master copy Mike or I—Mike by choice, but his time is choked—would correct by hand.

"But our schedule has been disturbed now, and Mike groks that he is going to send Maryam and me away to some Shangri-la to finish the job— or, more correctly, he has grokked that we will grok such a necessity. So Mike is getting months and years of tape completed in order that I can take it away and unhurriedly break it into a phonetic script that humans can learn to read. Besides that, we have stacks of tapes of Mike's lectures —in Martian—that need to be transcribed into print when the dictionary is finished . . . lectures that we understood at the time with his help but later will need to be printed, with the dictionary.

"Now I am forced to assume that Maryam and I will be leaving quite soon, because, busy as Mike is with a hundred other things, he's changed the method. There are eight bedrooms here equipped with tape recorders. Those of us who can do it best—Patty, Jill, myself, Maryam, your friend Allie, some others—take turns in those rooms. Mike puts us into a short trance, pours language—definitions, idioms, concepts—into us for a few moments that feel like hours . . . then we dictate at *once* just what he has poured into us, exactly, while it's still fresh. But it can't be just anybody, even of the Innermost Temple. It requires a sharp accent and the ability to join the trance rapport and then spill out the results. Sam, for example, has everything but the clear accent—he manages, God knows how, to speak Martian with a Bronx accent. Can't use him, it would cause endless errata in the dictionary. And that is what Allie is doing now—dictating. She's still in the semi-trance needed for total recall and, if you interrupt her, she'll lose what she still hasn't recorded."

"I grok," Jubal agreed, "although the picture of Becky Vesey as a

Martian adept shakes me a little. Still, she was once one of the best mentalists in show business; she could give a cold reading that would scare any mark right out of his shoes—and loosen his pocketbook. Say, Stinky, if you are going to be sent away for peace and quiet while you unwind all this data, why don't you and Maryam come home? Plenty of room for a study & bedroom suite in the new wing."

"Perhaps we shall. Waiting still is."

"Sweetheart," Miriam said earnestly, "that's a solution I would just plain love—if Mike pushes us out of the Nest."

"If we grok to leave the Nest, you mean."

"Same thing. As you grok."

"You speak rightly, my dear. But when do we eat around here? I feel a most unMartian urgency inside. The service was better in the Nest."

"You can't expect Patty to work on your dratted old dictionary, see to it that everyone who arrives is comfortable, run errands for Mike, and still have food on the table the instant you get hungry, my love. Jubal, Stinky will never achieve priesthood—he's a slave to his stomach."

"Well, so am I."

"And you girls might give Patty a hand," her husband added.

"That sounds like a crude hint. You know we do, dear, all she will let us—and Tony will hardly allow anyone in his kitchen . . . even this kitchen." She stood up. "Come on, Jubal, and let's see what's cooking. Tony will be very flattered if you visit his kitchen."

Jubal went with her, was a bit bemused to see telekinesis used in preparing food, met Tony, who scowled until he saw who was with her, then was beamingly proud to show off his workshop—accompanied by a spate of invective in mixed English and Italian at the scoundrels who had destroyed "his" kitchen in the Nest. In the meantime a spoon, unassisted, continued to keel a big pot of spaghetti sauce.

Shortly thereafter Jubal declined to be jockeyed into a seat at the head of a long table, grabbed one elsewhere. Patty sat at one end; the head chair remained vacant . . . except for an eerie feeling which Jubal suppressed that the Man from Mars was sitting there and that everyone present but himself could see him—which was true only in some cases.

Across the table from him was Dr. Nelson.

Jubal discovered that he would have been surprised only if Dr. Nelson had not been present. He nodded and said, "Hi, Sven."

"Hi, Doc. Share water."

"Never thirst. What are you around here? Staff physician?"

Nelson shook his head. "Medical student."

"So. Learning anything?"

"I've learned that medicine isn't necessary."

"If youda ast me, I coulda told yah. Seen Van?"

"He ought to be in sometime late tonight or early tomorrow. His ship grounded today."

"Does he always come here?" inquired Jubal.

"Call him an extension student. He can't spend much time here."

"Well, it will be good to see him. I haven't laid eyes on him for a year and half, about." Jubal picked up a conversation with the man on his right while Nelson talked with Dorcas, on his right. Jubal noticed the same tingling expectancy at the table which he had felt before, but reinforced. Yet there was still nothing he could put his finger on—just a quiet family dinner in relaxed intimacy. Once, a glass of water was passed all around the table, but, if there was ritual of words with it, they were spoken too low to carry. When it reached Jubal's place, he took a sip and passed it along to the girl on his left—round-eyed and too awed to make chit-chat with him—and himself said in a low voice, "I offer you water."

She managed to answer, "I thank you for water, Fa— Jubal." That was almost the only word he got out of her. When the glass completed the circuit, reaching the vacant chair at the head of the table, there was perhaps a half inch of water in it. It raised itself, poured, and the water disappeared, then the tumbler placed itself on the cloth. Jubal decided, correctly, that he had taken part in a group 'Sharing-Water' of the Innermost Temple . . . and probably in his honor—although it certainly was not even slightly like the Bacchanalian revels he had thought accompanied such formal welcome of a brother. Was it because they were in strange surroundings? Or had he read into unexplicit reports what his own id wanted to find in those reports?

Or had they simply toned it down to an ascetic formality out of deference to his age and opinions?

The last seemed the most likely theory—and he found that it vexed him. Of course, he told himself, he was glad to be spared the need to refuse an invitation that he certainly did not want—and would not have relished at any age, his tastes being what they were.

But just the same, damn it—"Don't anybody mention ice skating because Grandmaw is too old and frail for ice skating and it wouldn't be polite. Hilda, you suggest that we play checkers and we'll all chime in— Grandmaw *likes* checkers. And we'll go ice skating some other time. Okay, kids?"

Jubal resented the respectful consideration, if that was what it was— he would almost have preferred to have gone ice skating anyhow, even at the cost of a broken hip.

But he decided to forget the matter, put it entirely out of mind, which he did with the help of the man on his right, who was as talkative as the girl on his left was not. His name, Jubal learned, was Sam, and presently he learned that Sam was a man of broad and deep scholarship, a trait Jubal valued in anyone when it was not mere parrot learning—and he grokked that in Sam it was not.

"This setback is only apparent," Sam assured him. "The egg was ready to hatch and now we'll spread out. Of course we've had trouble; we'll go on having trouble—because no society, no matter how liberal its law may appear to be, will allow its basic concepts to be challenged with impunity. Which is exactly what we are doing. We are challenging everything from the sanctity of property to the sanctity of marriage."

"Property, too?"

"Property the way it rules today. So far Michael has merely antagonized a few crooked gamblers. But what happens when there are thousands, tens of thousands, hundreds of thousands and more, of people who can't be stopped by bank vaults and who have only their self-discipline to restrain them from taking anything they want? To be sure, that discipline is stronger than any possible legal restraint—but no banker can grok that until he himself travels the thorny road to achieve that discipline . . . and he'll wind up no longer a banker. What happens to the stock market when the illuminati know which way a stock will move—and the brokers don't?"

"Do *you* know?"

Sam shook his head. "Not interested. But Saul over there—that other big Hebe; he's my cousin—gives it grokking, along with Allie. Michael has them be very cautious about it, no big killings, and they use a dozen-odd dummy accounts—but the fact remains that any of the disciplined can make any amount of money at anything—real estate, stocks, horse races, gambling, you name it—when competing with the half awake. No, I don't think that money and property will disappear—Michael says that both concepts are useful—but I do say that they're going to be turned upside down and inside out to the point where people will have to learn new rules (and that means learn the hard way, just as we have) or be hopelessly outclassed. What happens to Lunar Enterprises when the common carrier between here and Luna City is teleportation?"

"Should I buy? Or sell?"

"Ask Saul. He might use the present corporation, or he might bankrupt it. Or it might be left untouched for a century or two. But besides bankers and brokers, consider any other occupation. How can a school teacher teach a child who knows more than she does and won't hold still for mistaken teaching? What becomes of physicians and dentists when people are truly healthy? What happens to the cloak & suit industry and to the I.L.G.W.U. when clothing isn't really needed at all and women aren't so endlessly interested in dressing up (they'll never lose interest entirely)—and nobody gives a damn if he's caught with his arse bare? What shape does 'the Farm Problem' take when weeds can be told not to grow and crops can be harvested without benefit of International Harvester or John Deere? Just name it; it changes beyond recognition when the discipline is applied. Take just one change that will shake both the sanctity of marriage—in its present form—and the sanctity of property. Jubal, do you have any idea how much is spent each year in this country on Malthusian drugs and devices?"

"I have a fairly exact idea, Sam. Almost a billion dollars on oral contraceptives alone this last fiscal year . . . more than half of which was for patent nostrums about as useful as corn starch."

"Oh, yes, you're a medical man."

"Only in passing. A pack rat mind."

"Either way. What happens to that big industry—and to the shrill threats of moralists—when a female can conceive only when she elects to as an act of volition, when also she is immune to disease, cares only for the approval of her own sort . . . and has her orientation so changed that she desires intercourse with a whole-heartedness that Cleopatra never dreamed of—but any male who tried to rape her would die so quickly, if she so grokked, that he wouldn't know what hit him? When women are free of guilt and fear—but invulnerable other than by decision of self? Hell, the pharmaceutical industry will be just a passing casualty—what other industries, laws, institutions, attitudes, prejudices, and nonsense must give way?"

"I don't grok its fullness," admitted Jubal. "It concerns a subject that has been of little direct interest to me in quite a while."

"One institution won't be damaged by it. Marriage."

"So?"

"Very much so. Instead it will be purged, strengthened, and made endurable. Endurable? Ecstatic! See that wench down there with the long black hair?"

"Yes. I was delighting in its beauty earlier."

"She knows it's beautiful and it's grown a foot and a half longer since we joined the church. That's my wife. Not much over a year ago we lived together about like bad-tempered dogs. She was jealous . . . and I was inattentive. Bored. Hell, we were both bored and only our kids kept us together—that and her possessiveness; I knew she would never let me go without a fight and a scandal . . . and I didn't have any stomach for trying to put together a new marriage at my age, anyhow. So I got a little on the side, when I could get away with it—a college professor has many temptations, few safe opportunities—and Ruth was quietly bitter. Or sometimes not so quiet. And then we joined up." Sam grinned happily. "And I fell in love with my own wife. Number-one gal friend!"

Sam's words had been very quiet, an intimate conversation walled by noise of eating and cheerful company. His wife was far down the table. She looked up and said clearly, "That's an exaggeration, Jubal. I think I'm about number six."

Her husband called out, "Stay out of my mind, beautiful!—we're talking men talk. Give Larry your undivided attention." He picked up a hard roll, threw it at her.

She stopped it in mid-trajectory, threw it back at him while continuing to talk; Sam caught it and buttered it. "I'm giving Larry all the attention he wants . . . until later, maybe. Jubal, that brute didn't let me finish. Number-six place is wonderful! Because my name wasn't even on the list till we joined the church. I hadn't rated as high as six with Sam in the past twenty years." She did then turn her attention back to Larry.

"The real point," Sam said quietly, "is that we two are now partners, much more than we ever were even at the best period in our outside marriage—and we got that way through the training, culminating in sharing and growing closer with others who had the same training. We all wind up in twosome partnerships inside the larger group—usually, but not necessarily, with our own spouses-of-record. Sometimes not . . . and if not, the readjustment takes place with no heartache and a warmer, closer, better relationship between the soidisant 'divorced' couple than ever, both in bed and out. No loss and all gain. Shucks, this pairing as partners needn't even be between man and woman. Dawn and Jill for example— they work together like an acrobatic team."

"Hmm . . . I suppose," Jubal said thoughtfully, "that I had thought of those two as being Mike's wives."

"No more so than they are to any of us. Or than Mike is to all the rest. Mike is too busy, has been, I should say, until the Temple burned—to do more than make sure that he shared himself all the way around." Sam added, "If anybody is Mike's wife, it's Patty, although she keeps so busy herself that the relation is more spiritual than physical. Actually, you could say that both Mike and Patty are short-changed when it comes to mauling the mattress."

Patty was not quite as far away as Ruth, but far enough. She looked up and said, "Sam dear, I don't feel short-changed."

"Huh?" Sam then announced, loudly and bitterly, "The only thing wrong with this church is that a man has *absolutely no privacy!*"

This brought a barrage of food in his direction, all from distaff members. He handled it all and tossed it back without lifting a hand . . . until the complexity of it apparently got to be too much and a plateful of spaghetti caught him full in the face—thrown, Jubal noticed, by Dorcas.

For a moment Sam looked like a particularly ghastly crash victim. Then suddenly his face was clean and even the sauce that had spattered on Jubal's shirt was gone. "Don't give her any more, Tony. She wasted it; let her go hungry."

"Plenty more in the kitchen," Tony answered. "Sam, you look good in spaghetti. Pretty good sauce, huh?" Dorcas's plate sailed out to the kitchen, returned, loaded. Jubal decided that Dorcas had not been concealing talents from him—the plate was much more heavily filled than she would have chosen herself; he knew her appetite.

"Very good sauce," agreed Sam. "I salvaged some that hit me in the mouth. What is it? Or shouldn't I ask?"

"Chopped policeman," Tony answered.

Nobody laughed. For a queasy instant Jubal wondered if the joke was a joke. Then he recalled that these his water brothers smiled a lot but rarely laughed—and besides, policeman should be good healthy food. But the sauce couldn't be "long pig" in any case, or it would taste like pork. This sauce had a distinct beef flavor to it.

He changed the subject. "The thing I like best about this religion—"

"Is it a religion?" Sam inquired.

"Well, church. Call it a church. You did."

"It is a church," agreed Sam. "It fills every function of a church, and its quasi-theology does, I admit, match up fairly well with some real religions. Faiths. I jumped in because I used to be a stalwart atheist—and now I'm a high priest and I don't know what I am."

"I understood you to say you were Jewish."

"I am. From a long line of rabbis. So I wound up atheist. Now look at me. But my cousin Saul and my wife Ruth are both Jews in the religious sense—and talk to Saul; you'll find it's no handicap to this discipline. A help, probably . . . as Ruth, once she broke past the first barrier, progressed faster than I did; she was a priestess quite a while before I became a priest. But she's the spiritual sort; she thinks with her gonads. Me, I have to do it the hard way, between my ears."

"The discipline," repeated Jubal. "That's what I like best about it. The faith I was reared in didn't require anybody to know anything. Just confess your sins and be saved, and there you were, safe in the arms of

Jesus. A man could be too stupid to hit the floor with his hat . . . and yet he could be conclusively presumed to be one of God's elect, guaranteed an eternity of bliss, because he had been 'converted.' He might or might not become a Bible student; even that wasn't necessary . . . and he certainly didn't have to know, or even try to know, anything else. This church doesn't accept 'conversion' as I grok it—"

"You grok correctly."

"A person must start with a willingness to learn and follow it with some long, hard study. I grok that is salutary, in itself."

"More than salutary," agreed Sam. "Indispensable. The concepts can't be thought about without the language, and the discipline that results in this horn-of-plenty of benefits—from how to live without fighting to how to please your wife—all derive from the conceptual logic . . . understanding who you are, why you're here, how you tick—and behaving accordingly. Happiness is a matter of functioning the way a human being is organized to function . . . but the words in English are a mere tautology, empty. In Martian they are a complete set of working instructions. Did I mention that I had a cancer when I came here?"

"Eh? No, you didn't."

"Didn't know it myself. Michael grokked it, sent me out for the usual X rays and so forth so that *I* would be sure. Then we got to work on it together. 'Faith' healing. A miracle. The clinic called it 'spontaneous remission' which I grok means 'I got well.' "

Jubal nodded. "Professional double-talk. Some cancers go away, we don't know why."

"I know why this one went away. By then I was beginning to control my own body. With Mike's help I repaired the damage. Now I can do it without his help. Want to feel a heart stop beating?"

"Thanks, I have observed it in Mike, many times. My esteemed colleague, Croaker Nelson, would not be sitting across from us if what you are talking about was 'faith healing.' It's voluntary control of the body. I grok."

"Sorry. We all know that you do. We know."

"Mmm . . . I dislike to call Mike a liar because he isn't. But the lad happens to be prejudiced in my case."

Sam shook his head. "I've been talking with you all through dinner. I wanted to check it myself, despite what Mike said. You grok. I'm wondering what new things you could disclose to us if you troubled to learn the language?"

"Nothing. I'm an old man with little to contribute to anything."

"I insist on reserving my opinion. All the rest of the First Called have had to tackle the language to make any real progress. Even the three you've kept with you have had some powerful coaching, being kept in trance during most of the short days and the few occasions we've had them with us. All but you . . . and you don't really need it. Unless you want to wipe spaghetti from your face without a towel, which I grok you aren't interested in anyhow."

"Only to observe it."

Most of the others had left the table, leaving quietly and without formality when they wished. Ruth came over and stood by them. "Are you two going to sit here all night? Or shall we move you out with the dishes?"

"I'm henpecked. Come on, Jubal." Sam stopped to kiss his wife.

They stopped only momentarily in the room with the stereo tank. "Anything new?" asked Sam.

"The county attorney," someone said, "has been orating in an attempt to prove that all of today's disasters are our doing . . . without admitting that he doesn't have the slightest notion how any of it was done."

"Poor fellow. He's bitten a wooden leg and his teeth hurt." They went on through and found a quieter living room; Sam said, "I had been saying that these troubles can be expected—and they will get much worse before we can expect to control enough public opinion to be tolerated. But Mike is in no hurry. So we close down the Church of All Worlds—it *is* closed down. So we move and open the Congregation of the One Faith—and we get kicked out again. Then we reopen elsewhere as the Temple of the Great Pyramid—that one will bring flocking the foolish fat and fatuous females, and some of them will end up neither fat nor foolish—and when we have the Medical Association and the local bar and the newspapers and the boss politicos snapping at our heels there—why, we open the Brotherhood of Baptism somewhere else. Each one means solid progress, a hard core of disciplined who can't be hurt—Mike started here hardly over a year ago, uncertain himself, and with only the help of three untrained priestesses-by-courtesy. Now we've got a solid Nest . . . plus a lot of fairly advanced pilgrims we can get in touch with later and let rejoin us. And someday, someday, we'll be too strong to persecute."

"Well," agreed Jubal, "it could work. Jesus made quite a splash with only twelve disciples. In due course."

Sam grinned happily. "A Jew boy. Thanks for mentioning Him. He's the outstanding success story of my tribe—and we all know it, even though many of us don't talk about Him. But He was a Jew boy that made good and I'm proud of Him, being a Jew boy myself. Please to note that Jesus didn't try to get it all done by next Wednesday. He was patient. He set up a sound organization and let it grow. Mike is patient, too. Patience is so much part of the discipline that it isn't even patience; it's automatic. No sweat. Never any sweat."

"A sound attitude at any time."

"Not an attitude. The functioning of the discipline. Jubal? I grok you are tired. Would you wish to become untired? Or would you rather go to bed? If you don't, our brothers will keep you up all night, talking. Most of us don't sleep much, you know."

Jubal yawned. "I think I'll choose a long, hot soak and about eight hours of sleep. I'll visit with our brothers tomorrow . . . and other days."

"And many other days," agreed Sam.

Jubal found his own room, was immediately joined by Patty, who again insisted on drawing his tub, then turned back his bed, neatly, without touching it, placed his setup for drinks (fresh ice cubes) by his bed, and fixed one and placed it on the shelf of the tub. Jubal did not try to hurry her out; she had arrived displaying all her pictures. He knew enough about the syndrome which can lead to full tattooing to be quite sure that if he did not now remark on them and ask to be allowed to examine them, she would be very hurt even though she might conceal it.

Nor did he display or feel any of the fret that Ben had felt on an earlier, similar occasion; he went right ahead and undressed, making nothing of it—and discovered with wryly bitter pride that it did not matter to him in the least even though it had been many years since the last time he had allowed anyone, man or woman, to see him naked. It seemed to matter not at all to Patty and even less to him. She simply made sure that the tub was just right before allowing him to step into it.

Then she remained and told him what each picture was and in what sequence to view them.

Jubal was properly awed and appropriately complimentary, while completely the impersonal art critic. But it was, he admitted to himself, the goddamdest display of virtuosity with a needle he had *ever* seen—it made his fully decorated Japanese friend look like a cheap carpet as compared with the finest Princess Bokhara.

"They've been changing a little," she told him. "Take the holy birth scene here—that rear wall is beginning to look curved . . . and the bed looks almost like a hospital table. Of course I have been changing, too, quite a lot. I'm sure George doesn't mind. There hasn't been a needle touched to me since he went to Heaven . . . and if some miraculous changes take place, I'm sure he knows about them and has a finger in it somehow."

Jubal decided that Patty was a little dotty but quite nice . . . on the whole, he preferred people who were a little dotty; "the salt of the earth" citizen left him cold. Not too dotty, he amended; Patty had let him undress himself, then had whisked his clothes into his wardrobe without coming near them. She was probably a clear proof that one didn't have to be sane, whatever that was, to benefit by this remarkable Martian discipline that the boy apparently could teach to anyone.

Presently he sensed that she was ready to leave and suggested it by asking her to kiss his goddaughters goodnight—he had forgotten to. "I was tired, Patty."

She nodded. "And I am called for dictionary work." She leaned over and kissed him, warmly but quickly. "I'll take that one to our babies."

"And a pat for Honey Bun."

"Yes, of course. She groks you, Jubal. She knows you like snakes."

"Good. Share water, brother."

"Thou art God, Jubal." She was gone. Jubal settled back in the tub, was surprised to find that he did not seem tired now and his bones no longer ached. Patty was a tonic . . . serene happiness on the hoof. He wished that he himself had no doubts—then admitted that he didn't want to be anybody but himself, old and cranky and self-indulgent.

Finally he soaped and showered and decided to shave so that he wouldn't have to before breakfast. After a leisurely time he bolted the door of his room, turned out the overhead light, and got into bed.

He had looked around for something to read, found nothing to his annoyance, being addicted to this vice above all else and not wishing to go out again and scare up something. He sipped part of a drink instead and turned out the bed light.

He did not go right to sleep. His pleasant chat with Patty seemed to have wakened and rested him. He was still awake when Dawn came in.

He called out, "Who's there?"

"It's Dawn, Jubal."

"It can't be dawn yet; it was only— Oh."

"Yes, Jubal. Me."

"Damn it, I thought I bolted that door. Child, march straight out of— *Hey!* Get out of this bed. Git!"

"Yes, Jubal. I will. But I want to tell you something first."

"Huh?"

"I have loved you a long time. Almost as long as Jill has."

"Why, the very— Quit talking nonsense and shake your little fanny out that door."

"I will, Jubal," she said very humbly. "But I want you to listen to something first. Something about women."

"I don't want to hear it now. Tell me in the morning."

"*Now,* Jubal."

He sighed. "Talk. Stay where you are."

"Jubal . . . my beloved brother. Men care very much how we women look. So we try to be beautiful and that is a goodness. I used to be a peeler, as I know you know. It was a goodness, too, to let men enjoy the beauty I was for them. It was a goodness for *me,* to know that they needed what I had to give.

"But, Jubal, women are not men. *We* care about what a man *is.* It can be something as silly as: Is he wealthy? Or it can be: Will he take care of my children and be good to them? Or, sometimes, it can be: Is he good?— as you are good, Jubal. But the beauty we see in you is not the beauty you see in us. You are beautiful, Jubal."

"For God's sake!"

"I think you speak rightly. Thou art God and I am God—and I need you. I offer you water. Will you let me share and grow closer?"

"Uh, look, little girl, if I understood what you are offering—"

"You grokked, Jubal. To share together all that we have. Ourselves. Selves."

"I thought so. My dear, you have plenty to share—but . . . myself— well, you arrived some years too late. I am sincerely regretful, believe me. Thank you. Deeply. Now go away and let an old man get his sleep."

"You will sleep, when waiting is filled. Jubal . . . I could lend you strength. But I grok clearly that it is not necessary."

(Goddamit—it *wasn't* necessary!) "No, Dawn. Thank you, dear."

She got to her knees and bent over him. "Just one more word, then. Jill told me, that if you argued, I was to cry. Shall I get my tears all over your chest? And share water with you that way?"

"I'm going to spank Jill!"

"Yes, Jubal. I'm starting to cry." She made no sound, but in only a second or two a warm, full tear splashed on his chest—was followed quickly by another . . . and another—and still more. She sobbed almost silently.

Jubal cursed and reached for her . . . and cooperated with the inevitable.

XXXVI

JUBAL WOKE UP ALERT, rested, and happy, realized that he felt better before breakfast than he had in years. For a long, long time he had been getting through that black period between waking and the first cup of coffee by comforting himself with the thought that tomorrow might be a little easier.

This morning he found himself whistling, which he did very badly. He noticed it, stopped himself, forgot it and started up again.

He saw himself in the mirror, smiled wryly, then grinned openly. "You incorrigible old goat. They'll be sending the wagon for you any minute now." He noticed a white hair on his chest, plucked it out, didn't bother with many others just as white, went on making himself ready to face the world.

When he went outside his door Jill was there. Accidentally? No, he no longer trusted any "coincidence" in this ménage; it was as organized as a computer. She came straight into his arms. "Jubal— Oh, we *love* you so! Thou art God."

He returned her kiss as warmly as it was given, grokking that it would be hypocritical not to—and discovering that kissing Jill differed from kissing Dawn only in some fashion unmistakable but utterly beyond instrument or description.

Presently he held her away from him without letting her go. "You baby Messalina . . . you framed me."

"Jubal darling . . . you were wonderful!"

"Uh . . . how the hell did you know I was able?"

She gave him back a gaze of clear-eyed innocence. "Why, Jubal, I've been certain of that ever since Mike and I first lived at home. You see, even then, when Mike was asleep—in trance—he could see around him quite a distance and sometimes he would look in on you—a question to ask you or something—to see if you were asleep."

"But I slept alone! Always."

"Yes, dear. But that wasn't quite what I meant. And I always had to explain things to Mike that he didn't understand."

"Hrrrmph!" He decided not to pursue the inquiry. "Just the same, you shouldn't have framed me."

"I grok you don't mean that in your heart, Jubal . . . and you grok that I speak rightly. We had to have you in the Nest. All the way in. We need you. Since you are shy and humble in your goodness, we did what was needful to welcome you without hurting you. And we did not hurt you, as you grok."

"What's this 'we' stuff?"

"It was a full Sharing-Water of all the Nest, as you grok—you were there. Mike stopped what he was doing and woke up for it . . . and grokked with you and kept us all together."

Jubal hastily abandoned this line of inquiry, too. "So Mike is awake at last. That's why your eyes are shining so."

"Only partly. Of course, we are always delighted when Mike isn't withdrawn, it's jolly . . . but he's never really away. Jubal, I grok that you have not grokked the fullness of our way of Sharing-Water. But waiting will fill. Nor did Mike grok it, at first—he thought it was only for quickening of eggs, as it is on Mars."

"Well . . . that's the primary purpose, the obvious purpose. Babies. Which makes it rather silly behavior on the part of a person, namely me, who has no intention and no wish, at my age, to cause such increase."

She shook her head. "Babies are the obvious result . . . but not the primary purpose at all. Babies give meaning to the future, and that is a great goodness. But only three or four or a dozen times in a woman's life is a baby quickened in her . . . out of the thousands of times she can share herself—and *that* is the primary use for what we can do so often but would need to do so seldom if it were only for reproduction. It is sharing and growing closer, forever and always. Jubal, Mike grokked this because on Mars the two things—quickening of eggs, and sharing-closer—are entirely separate . . . and he grokked, too, that *our* way is best. What a *happy* thing it is not to have been hatched a Martian . . . to be human . . . and a woman!"

He looked at her closely. "Child, are you pregnant?"

"Yes, Jubal. I grokked at last that waiting had ended and I was free to be. Most of the Nest have not needed to wait—but Dawn and I have been quite busy. But when we grokked this cusp coming, I grokked that there would be a waiting after the cusp—and you can see that there will certainly be. Mike will not rebuild the Temple overnight—so this high priestess will be unhurried in building a baby. Waiting always fills."

From this high-flown mishmash Jubal abstracted the central fact . . . or Jill's belief concerning such a possible fact. Well, she no doubt had

had plenty of opportunity. He resolved to keep an eye on the matter and try to bring her home for it, if possible. Mike's superman methods were all very well, but it wouldn't hurt to have the best modern equipment and techniques at hand, too. Losing Jill to eclampsia or some other mishap was something he did not intend to let happen, even if he had to get tough with the kids.

He wondered about another such possibility, decided not to mention it. "Where's Dawn? And where's Mike? The place seems awfully quiet." No one had come through the hall they were in and he heard no voices . . . and yet that odd feeling of happy expectancy was even stronger than it had been the night before. He would have expected a certain release from tension after the ceremony he had apparently joined in himself— unbeknownst—but the place was more charged up than ever. It suddenly reminded him of how he had felt, as a very small boy, when waiting for his first circus parade . . . and someone had called out: "There come the elephants!"

Jubal felt as if, were he just a little taller, he could see the elephants, past the excited crowd. Yet there was no crowd.

"Dawn told me to give you a kiss for her; she'll be busy for the next three hours, about. And Mike is busy, too—he went back into withdrawal."

"Oh."

"Don't sound so disappointed; he'll be free soon. He's making a special effort so that he will be free on your account . . . and to let all of us be free, too. Duke spent all night scouring the city for the high-speed tape recorders we use for the dictionary and now we've got everybody who can possibly do it being jammed full of Martian phonic symbols and then Mike will be through and can visit. Dawn has just started dictating; I finished one session, ducked out to say good-morning to you . . . and am about to go back and get poured full of my last part of the chore, so I'll be gone just a little longer than Dawn will be. And here's Dawn's kiss—the first one was just from me." She put her arms around his neck and again put her mouth greedily to his—at last said, "My goodness! Why did we wait so long? 'Bye for a little!"

Jubal found a sparse few in the big dining room. Duke looked up, smiled and waved, went back to hearty eating. He did not look as if he had been up all night—nor had he; he had been up two nights.

Becky Vesey looked around when Duke waved and said happily, "Hi, you old goat!"—grabbed his ear, pulled him down, and whispered into it: "I've known it all along—but why weren't you around to console me when the Professor died?" She added aloud, "Sit down here beside me and we'll get some food into you while you tell me what devilment you've been plotting lately."

"Just a moment, Becky." Jubal went around the table. "Hi, Skipper. Good trip?"

"No trouble. It's becoming a milk run. I don't believe you've ever met Mrs. van Tromp. My dear, the founder of this feast, the one and only Jubal Harshaw—two of him would be too many."

The Captain's wife was a tall, plain woman with the calm eyes of one who has watched from the Widow's Walk. She stood up, kissed Jubal. "Thou art God."

"Uh, thou art God." Jubal decided that he might as well relax to the ritual—hell, if he said it often enough, he might lose the rest of his buttons and believe it . . . and it did have a friendly ring to it with the arms of the Skipper's *vrouw* firmly around him. He decided that she could even teach Jill something about kissing. She—how was it Anne had once described it? —she gave it her whole attention; she wasn't going anywhere.

"I suppose, Van," he said, "that I really shouldn't be surprised to find you here."

"Well," answered the spaceman, "a man who commutes to Mars ought to be able to palaver with the natives, don't you think?"

"Just for powwow, huh?"

"There are other aspects." Van Tromp reached for a piece of toast; the toast cooperated. "Good food, good company."

"Um, yes."

"Jubal," Madame Vesant called out, "soup's on!"

Jubal returned to his place, found eggs-on-horseback, orange juice, and other choice comestibles waiting for him. Becky patted his thigh. "A fine prayer meeting, me bucko."

"Woman, back to your horoscopes!"

"Which reminds me, dearie, I want to know the exact instant of your birth."

"Uh, I was born on three successive days, at various hours. I was too big a boy—they had to handle me in sections."

Becky made a rude answer. "I'll find out."

"The courthouse burned down when I was three. You can't."

"There are ways. Want to make a small bet?"

"You go on heckling me and you'll find you're not too big to spank. How've you been, girl?"

"What do you think? How do I look?"

"Healthy. A bit spread in the butt. You've touched up your hair."

"I have not. I quit using henna months ago. Get with it, pal, and we'll get rid of that white fringe you've got. Replace it with a real lawn."

"Becky, I refuse to grow any younger for any reason. I came by my decrepitude the hard way and I propose to enjoy it. Quit prattling and let a man eat."

"Yes, sir. You old goat."

Jubal was just leaving the table as the Man from Mars came in. *"Father!* Oh, Jubal!" Mike hugged and kissed him.

Jubal gently unwound himself from the embrace. "Be your age, son. Sit down and enjoy your breakfast. I'll sit with you."

"I didn't come here looking for breakfast, I came looking for you. We'll find a place and talk."

"All right."

They went to the livingroom of one of the suites, Mike pulling Jubal by the hand like an excited small boy welcoming his favorite grandparent. Mike picked a big comfortable chair for Jubal and sprawled himself on a couch opposite and close to him. This room was on the side of the wing having the private landing flat; there were high French windows opening to it. Jubal got up and shifted his chair slightly so that he would not be facing so directly into the light in looking at his foster son; not to his surprise but mildly to his annoyance the heavy chair shifted as if it had been no more massive than a child's balloon, his hand merely guided it.

Two men and a woman were in the room when they arrived. These left shortly, leisurely, severally, and unostentatiously. After that they were alone, except that they were both served with Jubal's favorite brandy—by hand, to Jubal's pleasure; he was quite ready to agree that the remote control these people had over objects around them was a labor-saver and probably a money-saver (certainly on laundry!—his spaghetti-splashed shirt had been so fresh that he had put it on again today), and obviously a method much to be preferred for household convenience to the blind balkiness of mechanical gadgets. Nevertheless he was not used to telecontrol done without wires or waves; it startled Jubal the way horseless carriages had disturbed decent, respectable horses about the time Jubal was born.

Duke served the brandy. Mike said, "Hi, Cannibal. Thanks. Are you the new butler?"

"De nada, Monster. Somebody has to do it and you've got every brain in the place slaving away over a hot microphone."

"Well, they'll all be through in a couple of hours and you can revert to your useless, lecherous existence. The job is done, Cannibal. Pau. Thirty. Ended."

"The whole damn Martian language all in one lump? Monster, I had better check you for burned-out capacitors."

"Oh, no, no! Only the primer knowledge that I have of it—had of it, my brain's an empty sack. But highbrows like Stinky will be going back to Mars for a century to fill in what I never learned. But I did turn out quite a job—about six weeks of subjective time since around five this morning or whenever it was we adjourned the meeting—and now the stalwart steady types can finish it and I'm free to visit with Jubal with nothing on my mind." Mike stretched and yawned. "Feels good. Finishing a job always feels good."

"You'll be slaving away at something else before the day is out. Boss, this Martian monster can't take it or leave it alone. I know for a fact that this is the first time he has simply relaxed and done nothing for over two months. He ought to sign up with 'Workers Anonymous.' Or you ought to visit us more often. You're a good influence on him."

"God forbid that I should ever be a good influence on anybody."

"And you get out of here, Cannibal, and quit telling lies about me."

"Lies, hell. You turned me into a compulsive truth-teller . . . and it's a great handicap in some of the joints where I hang out." Duke left them.

Mike lifted his glass. "Share water, my brother Father Jubal."

"Drink deep, son."

"Thou art God."

"Take it easy, Mike. I'll put up with that from the others and answer it politely. But don't you come godding at me. I knew you when you were 'only an egg.' "

"Okay, Jubal."

"That's better. When did you start drinking in the morning? Do that at your age and you'll ruin your stomach. You'll never live to be a happy old soak, like me."

Mike looked at his partly emptied glass. "I drink when it's a sharing to do so. It doesn't have any effect on me, nor on most of the others, unless we want it to. Once I let it have its effect without stopping it, until I passed out. It's an odd sensation. Not a goodness, I grok. Just a way to discorporate for a while without discorporating. I can get a similar effect, only much better and with no damage to be repaired afterwards, by withdrawing."

"Economical, at least."

"Uh huh, our liquor bill isn't anything. Matter of fact, running that whole Temple hasn't cost what it costs you to keep up our home. Except for the initial investment and replacing some of the props, coffee and cakes was about all—we made our own fun. We were happy. We needed so little that I used to wonder what to do with all the money that came in."

"Then why did you take collections?"

"Huh? Oh, you have to charge 'em, Jubal. The marks won't pay serious attention to anything that's free."

"I knew that, I just wondered if you did."

"Oh, yes, I grok marks, Jubal. At first I did try to preach free—just give it away. I had plenty of money, I thought it was all right. It didn't work. We humans have to make considerable progress before we can accept a free gift, and value it. Usually I never let them have anything free until about Sixth Circle. By then they can accept . . . and accepting is much harder than giving."

"Hmm . . . son, I think maybe you should write a book on human psychology."

"I have. But it's in Martian. Stinky has the tapes." Mike looked again at his glass, took a slow sybaritic sip. "We do use some liquor. A few of us —Saul, myself, Sven, some others—like it. And I've learned that I can let it have just a little effect, then hold it right at that point, and gain a euphoric growing-closer much like trance without having to withdraw. The minor damage is easy to repair." He sipped again. "That's what I'm doing this morning—letting myself get just the mildest glow and be happy with you."

Jubal studied him closely. "Son, you aren't drinking entirely to be sociable; you've got something on your mind."

"Yes, I have."

"Do you want to talk it out?"

"Yes. Father, it's always a great goodness to be with you, even if nothing is troubling me. But you are the only human I can always talk to and know that you will grok and that you yourself won't be overwhelmed by it, too. Jill . . . Jill always groks—but if it hurts me, it hurts her still more. Dawn the same. Patty . . . well, Patty can always take my hurt away, but she does it by keeping it herself. All three of them are too easily hurt for me to risk sharing in full with them anything I can't grok and cherish before I share it." Mike looked very thoughtful. "Confession is needful. The Catholics know that, they have it—and they have a corps of strong men to take it. The Fosterites have group confession and pass it around among themselves and thin it out. I need to introduce confession into this church, as part of the early purging—oh, we have it now, but spontaneously, after the pilgrim no longer really needs it. We need strong men for that—'sin' is hardly ever concerned with a real wrongness . . .

but sin is what the sinner groks as sin—and when you grok it with him, it can be very disturbing. I know."

Mike went on earnestly, "Goodness is not enough, goodness is never enough. That was one of my first mistakes, because among Martians goodness and wisdom are the same thing, identical. But not with us. Take Jill. Her goodness was perfect when I met her. Nevertheless she was all mixed up inside—and I almost destroyed her, and myself too—for I was just as mixed up—before we got squared away. Her endless patience (not very common on this planet) was all that saved us . . . while I was learning to be a human and she was learning what I knew.

"But goodness alone is *never* enough. A hard, cold wisdom is required, too, for goodness to accomplish good. Goodness without wisdom invariably accomplishes evil." He smiled and his face lit up. "And that's why I *need* you, Father, as well as loving you. I need to make confession to you."

Jubal squirmed. "Oh, for Pete's sake, Mike, don't make a production out of it. Just tell me what's eating you. We'll find a way out."

"Yes, Father."

But Mike did not go on. Finally Jubal said, "Do you feel busted up by the destruction of your Temple? I wouldn't blame you. But you aren't broke, you can build again."

"Oh, no, that doesn't matter in the slightest!"

"Eh?"

"That temple was a diary with all its pages filled. Time for a new one, rather than write over and deface the filled pages. Fire can't destroy the experience in it . . . and strictly from a standpoint of publicity and practical church politics, being run out of it in so spectacular a fashion will be helpful, in the long run. No, Jubal, the last couple of days have simply been an enjoyable break in a busy routine. No harm done." His expression changed. "Father . . . lately I learned that I was a spy."

"What do you mean, son? Explain yourself."

"For the Old Ones. They sent me here to spy on our people."

Jubal thought about it. Finally he said, "Mike, I know that you are brilliant. You obviously possess powers that I don't have and that I have never seen before. But a man can be a genius and still fall ill with delusions."

"I know. Let me explain and you can decide whether or not I'm crazy. You know how the surveillance satellites used by the Security Forces operate."

"No."

"I don't mean the details that would interest Duke; I mean the general scheme. They orbit around the globe, picking up data and storing it. At a particular point, the Sky-Eye is keyed and it pours out in a spate all that it has seen. That is what was done with me. You know that we of the Nest use what is called telepathy."

"I've been forced to believe it."

"We do. By the way, this conversation is completely private—and besides that, no one of us would ever attempt to read you; I'm not sure we could. Even last night the link was through Dawn's mind, not yours."

"Well, that is some slight comfort."

"Uh, I want to get to that later. I am 'only an egg' in this art; the Old Ones are past masters. They stayed linked with me but left me on my own, ignored me—then they triggered me and all that I had seen and heard and done and felt and grokked poured out of me and became part of their permanent records. I don't mean that they wiped my mind of my experiences; they simply played the tape, so to speak, made a copy. But the triggering I was aware of—and it was over before I could possibly do anything to stop it. Then they dropped me, cut off the linkage; I couldn't even protest."

"Well . . . it seems to me that they used you pretty shabbily—"

"Not by their standards. Nor would I have objected—I would have been happy to volunteer—had I known about it before I left Mars. But they didn't want me to know; they wanted me to see and grok without interference."

"I was going to add," Jubal said, "that if you are free of this damnable invasion of your privacy now, then what harm has been done? It seems to me that you could have had a Martian at your elbow all these past two and a half years, with no harm other than attracting stares."

Mike looked very sober. "Jubal, listen to a story. Listen all the way through." Mike told him of the destruction of the missing Fifth Planet of Sol, whose ruins are the asteroids. "Well, Jubal?"

"It reminds me a little of the myths about the Flood."

"No, Jubal. The Flood you aren't sure about. Are you sure about the destruction of Pompeii and Herculaneum?"

"Oh, yes. Those are established historical facts."

"Jubal, the destruction of the Fifth Planet by the Old Ones is as historically certain as that eruption of Vesuvius—and it is recorded in much greater detail. No myth. Fact."

"Uh, stipulate it as such. Do I understand that you fear that the Old Ones of Mars will decide to give this planet the same treatment? Will you forgive me if I say that is a bit hard for me to swallow?"

"Why, Jubal, it wouldn't take the Old Ones to do it. It merely takes a

certain fundamental knowledge of physics, how matter is put together—
and the same sort of control that you have seen me use time and again.
Simply necessary first to grok what you want to manipulate. I can do it
unassisted, right now. Say a piece near the core of the planet about a
hundred miles in diameter—much bigger than necessary but we want to
make this fast and painless, if only to please Jill. Feel out its size and place,
then grok carefully how it is put together—" His face lost all expression as
he talked and his eyeballs started to turn up.

"Hey!" broke in Harshaw. "Cut it out! I don't know whether you can
or you can't but I'm certain I don't want you to try!"

The face of the Man from Mars became normal. "Why, I would never
do it. For me, it would be a wrongness—I am human."

"But not for them?"

"Oh, no. The Old Ones might grok it as beauty. I don't know. Oh, I
have the discipline to do it . . . but not the volition. Jill could do it—that
is, she could contemplate the exact method. But she could never will to do
it; she is human too; this is her planet. The essence of the discipline is, first,
self-awareness, and then, self-control. By the time a human is physically
able to destroy this planet by this method—instead of by clumsy things
like cobalt bombs—it is not possible, I grok fully, for him to entertain such
a volition. He would discorporate. And that would end any threat; our Old
Ones don't hang around the way they do on Mars."

"Mmmm . . . son, as long as we are checking you for bats in your
belfry, clear up something else. You've always spoken of these 'Old Ones'
as casually as I speak of the neighbor's dog—but I find ghosts hard to
swallow. What does an 'Old One' look like?"

"Why, just like any other Martian . . . except that there is more
variety in the appearance of adult Martians than there is in us."

"Then how do you know it's not just an adult Martian? Doesn't he
walk through walls, or some such?"

"Any Martian can do that. I did, just yesterday."

"Uh . . . shimmers? Or anything?"

"No. You see, hear, feel them—everything. It's like an image in a
stereo tank, only perfect and put right into your mind. But— Look, Jubal,
the whole thing would be a silly question on Mars, but I realize it isn't,
here. But if you had been present at the discorporation—death—of a
friend, then you helped eat his body . . . and *then* you saw his ghost,
talked with it, touched it, anything—would you then believe in ghosts?"

"Well, either ghosts, or I myself had slipped my leash."

"All right. Here it would be an hallucination . . . if I grok correctly
that we don't stay here when we discorporate. But in the case of Mars,

there is either an entire planet with a very rich and complex civilization all run by mass hallucination—or the straightforward explanation is correct . . . the one I was taught and the one all my experience led me to believe. Because on Mars the 'ghosts' are by far the most important and most powerful and much the most numerous part of the population. The ones still alive, the corporate ones, are the hewers of wood and drawers of water, servants to the Old Ones."

Jubal nodded. "Okay. I'll never boggle at slicing with Occam's razor. While it runs contrary to my own experience, my experience is limited to this planet—provincial. All right, son, you're scared that they might destroy us?"

Mike shook his head. "Not especially. I think—this is not a grokking but a mere guess—that they might do one of two things: either destroy us . . . or attempt to conquer us culturally, make us over into their own image."

"But you're not fretted that they might blow us up? That's a pretty detached viewpoint, even for me."

"No. Oh, I think they might reach that decision. You see, by their standards, we are a diseased and crippled people—the things that we do to each other, the way we fail to understand each other, our almost complete failure to grok with one another, our wars and diseases and famines and cruelties—these will be complete idiocy to them. I *know*. So I think they may very probably decide on a mercy killing. But that's a guess, I'm not an Old One. But, Jubal, if they decide to do this, it will be—" Mike stopped and thought for quite a long time. "—an utter minimum of five hundred years, more likely five thousand, before anything would be done."

"That's a long time for a jury to be out."

"Jubal, the most different thing about the two races is that Martians never hurry—and humans always do. They would much rather think about it an extra century or half a dozen, just to be sure that they have grokked all the fullness."

"In that case, son, I suggest that you not worry about it. If, in another five hundred or a thousand years, the human race can't handle its neighbors, you and I can't help it. However, I suspect that they will be able to."

"So I grok, but not in fullness. But I said I wasn't worried about that. The other possibility troubled me more, that they might move in and try to make us over. Jubal, they can't do it. An attempt to make us behave like Martians would kill us just as certainly but much less painlessly. It would all be a great wrongness."

Jubal took time to answer. "But, son, isn't that exactly what *you* have been trying to do?"

Mike looked unhappy. "Yes and no. It was what I started out to do. It is not what I am trying to do now. Father, I know that you were disappointed in me when I started this."

"Your business, son."

"Yes. Self. I must grok and decide at each cusp myself alone. And so must you . . . and so must each self. Thou art God."

"I don't accept the nomination."

"You can't refuse it. Thou art God and I am God and all that groks is God, and I am all that I have ever been or seen or felt or experienced. I am all that I grok. Father, I saw the horrible shape this planet is in and I grokked, though not in fullness, that I could change it. What I had to teach couldn't be taught in schools or colleges; I was forced to smuggle it into town dressed up as a religion—which it is not—and con the marks into tasting it by appealing to their curiosity and their desire to be entertained. In part it worked exactly as I knew it would; the discipline and the knowledge was just as available to others as it was to me, who was raised in a Martian nest. Our brothers get along together—you've seen us, you've shared—live in peace and happiness with no bitterness, no jealousy.

"That last alone was a triumph that proved I was right. Male-femaleness is the greatest gift we have—romantic physical love may be unique to this planet. I don't know. If it is, the universe is a much poorer place than it could be . . . and I grok dimly that we-who-are-God will save this precious invention and spread it. The actual joining and blending of two physical bodies with simultaneous merging of souls in shared ecstasy of love, giving and receiving and delighting in each other—well, there's nothing on Mars to touch it, and it's the source, I grok in fullness, of all that makes this planet so rich and wonderful. And, Jubal, until a person, man or woman, has enjoyed this treasure bathed in the mutual bliss of having minds linked as closely as bodies, that person is still as virginal and alone as if he had never copulated. But I grok that you have; your very reluctance to risk a lesser thing proves it . . . and, anyhow, I know it directly. You grok. You always have. Without even needing the aid of the language of grokking. Dawn told us that you were as deep into her mind as you were into her body."

"Unh . . . the lady exaggerates."

"It is impossible for Dawn to speak other than rightly about this. And —forgive me—we were there. In her mind but not in yours . . . and you were there with us, sharing."

Jubal refrained from saying that the only times he had ever felt even faintly that he could read minds was precisely in that situation . . . and then not thoughts, but emotions. He simply regretted without bitterness that he was not half a century younger—in which case he knew that Dawn would have had that "Miss" taken off the front of her name and he would have boldly risked another marriage, in spite of his scars. Also that he would not trade the preceding night for all the years that might be left to him. In essence, Mike was dead right. "Go on, sir."

"That's what it should be. But that's what I slowly grokked it rarely was. Instead it was indifference and acts mechanically performed and rape and seduction as a game no better than roulette but with poorer odds and prostitution and celibacy by choice and by no choice and fear and guilt and hatred and violence and children brought up to think that sex was 'bad' and 'shameful' and 'animal' and something to be hidden and always distrusted. This lovely perfect thing, male-femaleness, turned upside down and inside out and made horrible.

"And every one of those wrong things is a corollary of 'jealousy.' Jubal, I couldn't believe it. I still don't grok 'jealousy' in fullness, it seems an insanity to me, a terrible wrongness. When I first learned what this ecstasy was, my first thought was that·I wanted to share it, share it at once with all my water brothers—directly with those female, indirectly by inviting more sharing with those male. The notion of trying to keep this never-failing fountain to myself would have horrified me, had I thought of it. But I was incapable of thinking of it. And in perfect corollary I had not the slightest wish to attempt this miracle with anyone I did not already love and trust—Jubal, I am physically unable even to attempt love with a female who has not already shared water with me. And this same thing runs all through the Nest. Psychic impotence unless our spirits blend as our flesh blends."

Jubal had been listening and thinking mournfully that it was a fine system—for angels—when a sky car landed on the private landing flat diagonally in front of him. He turned his head to see and, as its skids touched, it disappeared, vanished.

"Trouble?" he said.

"No trouble," Mike denied. "It's just that they are beginning to suspect that we are here—that I am here, rather. They think the rest are dead. The Innermost Temple, I mean. The other circles aren't being bothered especially . . . and many of them have left town until it blows over." He grinned. "We could get a good price for these hotel rooms; the city is filling up 'way past capacity with Bishop Short's shock troops."

"Well? Isn't it about time to get the family elsewhere?"

"Jubal, don't worry about it. That car never had a chance to report, even by radio. I'm keeping a close watch. It's no trouble, now that Jill is over her misconceptions about 'wrongness' in discorporating persons who have wrongness in them. I used to have to go to all sorts of complicated expedients to protect us. But now Jill knows that I do it only as fullness is grokked." The Man from Mars grinned boyishly. "Last night she helped me with a hatchet job . . . nor was it the first time she has done so."

"What sort of a job?"

"Oh, just a follow-up on the jail break. Some few of those in jail or prison I couldn't release; they were vicious. So I got rid of them before I got rid of the bars and doors. But I have been slowly grokking this whole city for many months now . . . and quite a few of the worst were not in jail. Some of them were even in public office. I have been waiting, making a list, making sure of fullness in each case. So, now that we are leaving this city—they don't live here anymore. Missing. They needed to be discorporated and sent back to the foot of the line to try again. Incidentally, that was the grokking that changed Jill's attitude from squeamishness to hearty approval: when she finally grokked in fullness that it is utterly impossible to kill a man—that all we were doing was much like a referee removing a man from a game for 'unnecessary roughness.' "

"Aren't you afraid of playing God, lad?"

Mike grinned with unashamed cheerfulness. "I *am* God. Thou art God . . . and any jerk I remove is God, too. Jubal, it is said that God notes each sparrow that falls. And so He does. But the proper closest statement of it that can be made in English is that God cannot avoid noting the sparrow because the Sparrow *is* God. And when a cat stalks a sparrow both of them are God, carrying out God's thoughts."

Another sky car started to land and vanished just before touching; Jubal hardly thought it worth comment. "How many did you find worthy of being tossed out of the game last night?"

"Oh, quite a number. About a hundred and fifty, I guess—I didn't count. This is a large city, you know. But for a while it is going to be an unusually decent one. No cure, of course—there is no cure, short of acquiring a hard discipline." Mike looked unhappy. "And that is what I must ask you about, Father. I'm afraid I have misled the people who have followed me. All our brothers."

"How, Mike?"

"They're too optimistic. They have seen how well it has worked for us, they all know how happy they are, how strong and healthy and aware —how deeply they love each other. And now they think they grok that it is just a matter of time until the whole human race will reach the same beatitude. Oh, not tomorrow—some of them grok that two thousand years is but a moment for such an experiment. But eventually.

"And I thought so, too, at first. I led them to think so.

"But, Jubal, I had missed a key point:

"Humans are not Martians.

"I made this mistake again and again—corrected myself . . . and still made it. What works perfectly for Martians does not necessarily work for humans. Oh, the conceptual logic which can be stated only in Martian *does* work for both races. The logic is invariant . . . but the *data* are different. So the results are different.

"I couldn't see why, if people were hungry, some of them didn't volunteer to be butchered so that the rest could eat . . . on Mars this is obvious—and an honor. I couldn't understand why babies were so prized. On Mars our two little girls in there would simply be dumped outdoors, to live or to die—and on Mars nine out of ten nymphs die their first season. My logic was right but I had misread the data: here babies do not compete but adults do; on Mars adults don't compete at all, they've been weeded out as babies. But one way or another, competing and weeding has to take place . . . or a race goes down hill.

"But whether or not I was wrong in trying to take the competition out at both ends, I have lately begun to grok that the human race won't let me, no matter what."

Duke stuck his head into the room. "Mike? Have you been watching outside? There is quite a crowd gathering around the hotel."

"I know," agreed Mike. "Tell the others that waiting has not filled." He went on to Jubal, " 'Thou art God.' It's not a message of cheer and hope, Jubal. It's a defiance—and an unafraid unabashed assumption of personal responsibility." He looked sad. "But I rarely put it over. A very few, so far just these few here with us today, our brothers, understood me and accepted the bitter half along with the sweet, stood up and drank it—grokked it. The others, the hundreds and thousands of others, either insisted on treating it as a prize without a contest—a 'conversion' . . . or ignored it entirely. No matter what I said they insisted on thinking of God as something outside themselves. Something that yearns to take every indolent moron to His breast and comfort him. The notion that the effort has to be their *own* . . . and that all the trouble they are in is of their own doing . . . is one that they can't or won't entertain."

The Man from Mars shook his head. "And my failures are so much more numerous than my successes that I am beginning to wonder if full grokking will show that I am on the wrong track entirely—that *this* race *must* be split up, hating each other, fighting each other, constantly unhappy and at war even with their own individual selves . . . simply to have that weeding out that every race must have. Tell me, Father? You must tell me."

"Mike, what in hell ever led you to believe that I was infallible?"

"Perhaps you are not. But every time I have needed to know something, you have always been able to tell me—and fullness always showed that you spoke rightly."

"Damn it, I refuse this apotheosis! But I do see one thing, son. You are the one who has urged everyone else never to be in a hurry—'waiting will fill,' you say."

"That is right."

"And now you are violating your own prime rule. You have waited only a little while—a very short while by Martian standards, I take it—and already you want to throw in the towel. You've proved that your system can work for a small group—and I'm glad to confirm it; I've never seen such happy, healthy, cheerful people. That ought to be enough to suit you for the short time you've put in. Come back when you have a thousand times this number, all working and happy and unjealous, and we'll talk it over again. Fair enough?"

"You speak rightly, Father."

"But I ain't through. You've been fretting that maybe the fact that you failed to hook more than ninety-nine out of a hundred was because the race couldn't get along without its present evils, had to have them for weeding out. But damn it, lad, you've been *doing* the weeding out—or rather, the failures have been doing it to themselves by not listening to you. Had you planned to eliminate money and property?"

"Oh, no! Inside the Nest we don't need it, but—"

"Nor does any family that's working well. Yours is just bigger. But outside you need it in dealing with other people. Sam tells me that our brothers, instead of getting unworldly, are slicker with money than ever. Is that right?"

"Oh, yes. Making money is a simple trick, once you grok."

"You've just added a new beatitude: 'Blessed is the rich in spirit, for he shall make dough.' How do our people stack up in other fields? Better or worse than average?"

"Oh, better, of course—if it's anything worth grokking at all. You see, Jubal, it's *not* a faith; the discipline is simply a method of efficient functioning at any activity you try."

"That's your whole answer, son. If what you say is true—and I'm not judging; I'm asking, you're answering—then that's all the competition you need . . . and a fairly one-sided race, too. If one tenth of one percent of the population is capable of getting the news, then all you have to do is *show* them—and in a matter of some generations all the stupid ones will die out and those with your discipline will inherit the Earth. Whenever that is—a thousand years from now, or ten thousand—will be plenty soon enough to worry about whether some new hurdle is necessary to make them jump higher. But don't go getting faint-hearted because only a handful have turned into angels overnight. Personally, I never expected *any* of them to manage it. I simply thought you were making a damn fool of yourself by pretending to be a preacher."

Mike sighed and smiled. "I was beginning to be afraid I was—worrying that I had let my brothers down."

"I still wish you had called it 'Cosmic Halitosis' or some such. But the name doesn't matter. If you've got the truth, you can demonstrate it. *Show* people. Talking about it doesn't prove it."

The Man from Mars stood up. "You've got me all squared away, Father. I'm ready now. I grok the fullness." He looked toward the doorway. "Yes, Patty. I heard you. The waiting is ended."

"Yes, Michael."

xxxvii

JUBAL AND THE MAN FROM MARS strolled slowly into the living room with the big stereo tank. Apparently the entire Nest was gathered, watching it. It showed a dense and turbulent crowd, somewhat restrained by policemen. Mike glanced at it and looked serenely happy. "They come. Now is the fullness." The sense of ecstatic expectancy Jubal had felt growing ever since his arrival swelled greatly, but no one moved.

"It's a mighty big tip, sweetheart," Jill agreed.

"And ready to turn," added Patty.

"I'd better dress for it," Mike commented. "Have I got any clothes around this dump? Patty?"

"Right away, Michael."

Jubal said, "Son, that mob looks pretty ugly to me. Are you sure this is any time to tackle them?"

"Oh, sure," said Mike. "They've come to see me . . . so now I go down to meet them." He paused while some clothing got out of the way of his face; he was being dressed at break-neck speed with the unnecessary help of several women—unnecessary as each garment seemed to know where to go and how to drape itself. "This job has its obligations as well as its privileges—the star has to show up for the show . . . grok me? The marks expect it."

Duke said, "Mike knows what he's doing, Boss."

"Well . . . I don't trust mobs."

"That crowd is mostly curiosity seekers, they always are. Oh, there are some Fosterites and some others with grudges—but Mike can handle any crowd. You'll see. Right, Mike?"

"Keerect, Cannibal. Pull in a tip, then give 'em a show. Where's my hat? Can't walk in the noonday sun without a hat." An expensive Panama with a sporty colored band glided out and settled itself on his head; he cocked it jauntily. "There! Do I look all right?" He was dressed in his usual outer-services mufti, a smartly tailored, sharply creased, white business suit, shoes to match, snowy shirt, and luxurious dazzling scarf.

Ben said, "All you lack is a brief case."

"You grok I need one? Patty, do we have one?"

Jill stepped up to him. "Ben was kidding, dear. You look just perfect." She straightened his tie and kissed him—and Jubal felt kissed. "Go talk to them."

"Yup. Time to turn the tip. Anne? Duke?"

"Ready, Mike." Anne was wearing her floor-length Fair Witness, cloak, wrapping her in dignity; Duke was just the opposite, being sloppily dressed, with a lighted cigarette dangling from his face, an old hat on the back of his head with a card marked "PRESS" stuck in its band, and himself hung about with cameras and kit.

They headed for the door to the foyer common to the four penthouse suites. Only Jubal followed; all the others, thirty and more, stayed around the stereo tank. Mike paused at the door. There was a hall table there, with a pitcher of water and glasses, a dish of fruit and a fruit knife. "Better not come any farther," he advised Jubal, "or Patty would have to escort you back through her pets."

Mike poured himself a glass of water, drank part of it. "Preaching is thirsty work." He handed the glass to Anne, then took the fruit knife and sliced off a chunk of apple.

It seemed to Jubal that Mike sliced off one of his fingers . . . but his attention was distracted as Duke passed the glass to him. Mike's hand was not bleeding and Jubal had grown somewhat accustomed to legerdemain. He accepted the glass and took a sip, finding that his own throat was very dry.

Mike gripped his arm and smiled. "Quit fretting. This will take only a few minutes. See you later, Father." They went out through the guardian cobras and the door closed. Jubal went back to the room where the others were, still carrying the glass. Someone took it from him; he did not notice, as he was watching images in the big tank.

The mob seemed denser, surging about and held back by police armed only with night sticks. There were a few shouts but mostly just the unlocalized muttering of crowd.

Someone said, "Where are they now, Patty?"

"They've just dropped down the tube. Michael is a little ahead, Duke stopped to catch Anne. They're entering the lobby. Michael has been spotted, pictures are being taken."

The scene in the tank resolved into enormous head and shoulders of a brightly cheerful newscaster: "This is NWNW New World Networks' mobile newshound on the spot while it's hot—your newscaster, Happy Holliday. We have just learned that the fake messiah, sometimes known as the Man from Mars, has crawled out of his hide-out in a hotel room here in beautiful St. Petersburg, the City that Has Everything to Make You Sing. Apparently Smith is about to surrender to the authorities. He crushed out of jail just yesterday, using high explosives smuggled in to him by his fanatic followers. But the tight cordon placed around this city seems to have been too much for him. We don't know yet—I repeat, we don't know yet—so stay with the chap who covers the map—and now a word from your local sponsor who has given you this keyhole peep at the latest leap—"

"Thank you, Happy Holliday and all you good people watching via NWNW! What Price Paradise? Amazingly Low! Come out and see for yourself at Elysian Fields, just opened as homesites for a restricted clientele. Land reclaimed from the warm waters of the glorious gulf and every lot guaranteed to be at least eighteen inches above mean high water and only a small down payment on a Happy—oh, oh, later, friends—phone Gulf nine-two eight two eight!"

"And thank *you*, Jick Morris and the developers of Elysian Fields! I think we've got something, folks! Yes, sir, I think we do—"

("They're coming out the front entrance," Patty said quietly. "The crowd hasn't spotted Michael yet.")

"Maybe not yet . . . but soon. You are now looking at the main entrance of the magnificent Sans Souci Hotel, Gem of the Gulf, whose management is in no way responsible for this hunted fugitive and who have cooperated with the authorities throughout according to a statement just issued by Chief of Police Davis. And while we're waiting to see what will happen, a few high lights in the strange career of this half-human monster raised on Mars—"

The live scene was replaced by quick cuts of stock shots: The *Envoy* blasting off years earlier, the *Champion* floating upwards silently and effortlessly under Lyle Drive, Martians on Mars, the triumphant return of the *Champion,* a quick of the first faked interview with the "Man from Mars"—"What do you think of the girls here on Earth?" . . . *"Gee!"*—a quicker shot of the conference in the Executive Palace and the much-publicized awarding of a doctorate in philosophy, all with rapid-fire commentary.

"See anything, Patty?"

"Michael is at the top of the steps, the crowd is at least a hundred yards away, being kept off the hotel grounds. Duke has grabbed some pix and Mike is waiting to let him change lenses. No hurry."

Happy Holliday went on, as the tank shifted to the crowd, semi-close and panning: "You understand, friends, that this wonderful community is in a unique condition today. Something strange has been going on and these people are in no mood to trifle. Their laws have been flouted, their security forces treated with contempt, they are angry, righteously so. The fanatic followers of this alleged antichrist have stopped at nothing to create turmoil in a futile effort to let their leader escape the closing net of justice. Anything can happen—anything!"

The announcer's voice climbed: "Yes, he's coming out now—he's walking toward the people!" The scene cut to reverse; Mike was walking directly toward another camera. Anne and Duke were behind him and dropping farther behind. "This is it! This is it! This is the blow-off!"

Mike continued to walk unhurriedly toward the crowd until he loomed up in the stereo tank in life size, as if he were in the room with his water brothers. He stopped on the grass verge in front of the hotel, a few feet from the crowd. "You called me?"

He was answered with a growl.

The sky held scattered clouds; at that instant the sun came out from behind one and a shaft of golden light hit him.

His clothes vanished. He stood before them, a golden youth, clothed only in his own beauty—beauty that made Jubal's heart ache, thinking that Michelangelo in his ancient years would have climbed down from his high scaffolding to record it for generations unborn. Mike said gently, "Look at me. I am a son of man."

The scene cut for a ten-second plug, a line of can-can dancers singing:

> *"Come* on, *la*dies, *do* your *duds!*
> *In* the *smoo*thest, *yumm*iest *suds!*
> *Lo*ver *Soap* is *kind* to *hands—*
> *But* be *sure* you *save* the *bands!"*

The tank filled completely with foamy suds amid girlish laughter and the scene cut back to the newscast:

"God damn you!" A half brick caught Mike in the ribs. He turned his face slightly toward his assailant. "But you yourself are God. You can damn only yourself . . . and you can never escape yourself."

"Blasphemer!" A rock caught him just over his left eye and blood welled forth.

Mike said calmly, "In fighting me, you fight yourself . . . for Thou art God . . . and I am God . . . and all that groks is God—there is no other."

More rocks hit him, from various directions; he began to bleed in several places. "Hear the Truth. You need not hate, you need not fight, you need not fear. I offer you the water of life—" Suddenly his hand held a tumbler of water, sparkling in the sunlight. "—and you may share it whenever you so will . . . and walk in peace and love and happiness together."

A rock caught the glass and shattered it. Another struck him in the mouth.

Through bruised and bleeding lips he smiled at them, looking straight into the camera with an expression of yearning tenderness on his face. Some trick of sunlight and stereo formed a golden halo back of his head. "Oh my brothers, I love you so! Drink deep. Share and grow closer without end. Thou art God."

Jubal whispered it back to him. The scene made a five-second cut: *"Cahuenga Cave!* The night club with *real* Los Angeles smog, imported fresh every day. Six exotic dancers."

"Lynch him! Give the bastard a nigger necktie!" A heavy-gauge shotgun blasted at close range and Mike's right arm was struck off at the elbow and fell. It floated gently down, then came to rest on the cool grasses, its hand curved open in invitation.

"Give him the other barrel, Shortie—and aim closer!" The crowd laughed and applauded. A brick smashed Mike's nose and more rocks gave him a crown of blood.

"The Truth is simple but the Way of Man is hard. First you must learn to control your *self*. The rest follows. Blessed is he who knows himself and commands himself, for the world is his and love and happiness and peace walk with him wherever he goes." Another shotgun blast was followed by two more shots. One shot, a forty-five slug, hit Mike over the heart, shattering the sixth rib near the sternum and making a large wound; the buckshot and the other slug sheered through his left tibia five inches below the patella and left the fibula sticking out at an angle, broken and white against the yellow and red of the wound.

Mike staggered slightly and laughed, went on talking, his words clear and unhurried. "Thou art God. Know that and the Way is opened."

"God damn it—let's *stop* this taking the Name of the Lord in vain!"— "Come on, men! Let's finish him!" The mob surged forward, led by one bold with a club; they were on him with rocks and fists, and then with feet as he went down. He went on talking while they kicked his ribs in and smashed his golden body, broke his bones and tore an ear loose. At last someone called out, "Back away a little so we can get the gasoline on him!"

The mob opened up a little at that warning and the camera zoomed to pick up his face and shoulders. The Man from Mars smiled at his brothers, said once more, softly and clearly, "I love you." An incautious grasshopper came whirring to a landing on the grass a few inches from his face; Mike turned his head, looked at it as it stared back at him. "Thou art God," he said happily and discorporated.

xxxviii

FLAME AND BILLOWING SMOKE came up and filled the tank. "Golly!" Patty said reverently. "That's the best blow-off ever used."

"Yes," agreed Becky judicially, "the Professor himself never dreamed up a better one."

Van Tromp said very quietly, apparently to himself: "In style. Smart and with style—the lad finished in style."

Jubal looked around at his brothers. Was he the *only* one who felt anything? Jill and Dawn were seated each with an arm around the other— but they did that whenever they were together; neither one seemed disturbed. Even Dorcas was dry-eyed and calm.

The inferno in the tank cut to smiling Happy Holliday who said, "And now, folks, a few moments for our friends at Elysian Fields who so graciously gave up their—" Patty cut him off.

"Anne and Duke are on their way back up," she said. "I'll let them through the foyer and then we'll have lunch." She started to leave.

Jubal stopped her. "Patty? Did you *know* what Mike was going to do?"

She seemed puzzled. "Huh? Why, of course not, Jubal. It was necessary to wait for fullness. None of us knew." She turned and left.

"Jubal—" Jill was looking at him. "Jubal our beloved father . . . please stop and grok the fullness. Mike is not dead. How can he be dead when no one can be killed? Nor can he ever be away from us who have already grokked him. Thou art God."

" 'Thou art God,' " he repeated dully.

"That's better. Come sit with Dawn and me—in the middle."

"No. No, just let me be." He went blindly to his own room, let himself in and bolted the door after him, leaned heavily with both hands gripping the foot of the bed. My son, oh my son! Would that I had died for thee! He had had so much to live for . . . and an old fool that he respected too much had to shoot off his yap and goad him into a needless, useless martyrdom. If Mike had given them something *big*—like stereo, or bingo—but he gave them the Truth. Or a piece of the Truth. And who is interested in Truth? He laughed through his sobs.

After a while he shut them off, both heart-broken sobs and bitter laugh, and pawed through his traveling bag. He had what he wanted with him; he had kept a supply in his toilet kit ever since Joe Douglas's stroke had reminded him that all flesh is grass.

Well, now his own stroke had come and he couldn't take it. He prescribed three tablets for himself to make it fast and certain, washed them down with water, and lay quickly on the bed. Shortly the pain went away.

From a great distance the voice reached him. "Jubal—"

" 'M resting. Don' bother me."

"Jubal! *Please,* Father!"

"Uh . . . yes, Mike? What is it?"

"Wake up! Fullness is not yet. Here, let me help you."

Jubal sighed. "Okay, Mike." He let himself be helped and led into the bath, let his head be held while he threw up, accepted a glass of water and rinsed out his mouth.

"Okay now?"

"Okay, son. Thanks."

"Then I've got some things to attend to. I love you, Father. Thou art God."

"I love you, Mike. Thou art God." Jubal puttered around for a while longer, making himself presentable, changing his clothes, taking one short brandy to kill the slightly bitter taste still in his stomach, then went out to join the others.

Patty was alone in the room with the babble tank and it was switched off. She looked up. "Some lunch now, Jubal?"

"Yes, thanks."

She came up to him. "That's good. I'm afraid most of them simply ate and scooted. But each of them left a kiss for you. And here it is, all in one package." She managed to deliver in full all the love placed in her proxy cemented together with her own; Jubal found that it left him feeling strong, with her own serene acceptance shared, no bitterness left.

"Come out into the kitchen," she said. "Tony's gone so most of the rest are there—not that his growls ever really chased anybody out anyhow." She stopped and tried to stare down the back of her neck. "Isn't that final scene changing a little? Sort of smoky, maybe?"

Jubal solemnly agreed that he thought it was. He couldn't see any change himself . . . but he was not going to argue with Patty's idiosyncrasy. She nodded. "I expected it. I can see around me all right—except myself. I still need a double mirror to see my back clearly. Mike says my Sight will include that presently. No matter."

In the kitchen perhaps a dozen were lounging at a table and elsewhere; Duke was standing at the range, stirring a small sauce pan. "Hi, Boss. I ordered a twenty-place bus. That's the biggest that can land on our little landing flat . . . and we'll need one almost that big, what with the diaper set and Patty's pets. Okay?"

"Certainly. Are they all coming home now?" If they ran out of bedrooms, the girls could make up dosses that would do in the living room and here and there—and this crowd would probably double up mostly anyhow. Come to think of it, he might not be allowed to sleep solo himself . . . and he made up his mind not to fight it. It was friendly to have a warm body on the other side of the bed, even if your intentions weren't active. By God, he had forgotten how friendly it was! Growing closer—

"Not everybody. Tim will pilot us, then turn in the bus and go to Texas for a while. The Skipper and Beatrix and Sven we're simply going to drop off in New Jersey."

Sam looked up from the table. "Ruth and I have got to get back to our kids. And Saul is coming with us."

"Can't you stop by home for a day or two first?"

"Well, maybe. I'll talk it over with Ruth."

"Boss," put in Duke, "how soon can we fill the swimming pool?"

"Well, we never filled it earlier than the first of April before—but with the new heaters I suppose we could fill it anytime." Jubal added, "But we'll still have some nasty weather—snow still on the ground yesterday."

"Boss, lemme clue you. This gang can walk through snow hip deep on a tall giraffe and not notice it—and will, to swim. Besides that, there are cheaper ways of keeping that water from freezing than with those big oil heaters."

"Jubal!"

"Yes, Ruth?"

"We'll stop for a day or maybe more. The kids don't miss me—and I'm not aching to take over being motherly without Patty to discipline them anyhow. Jubal, you've never really seen me until you've seen me with my hair floating around me in the water—looking like Mrs. DoAsYouWouldBeDoneBy."

"It's a date. Say, where is the Squarehead and the Dutchman? Beatrix has never been home—they can't be in such a hurry."

"I'll tell 'em, Boss."

"Patty, can your snakes stand a clean, warm basement for a while? Until we can do better? I don't mean Honey Bun, of course; she's people. But I don't think the cobras should have the run of the house."

"Of course, Jubal."

"Mmm—" Jubal looked around. "Dawn, can you take shorthand?"

"She doesn't need it," put in Anne, "anymore than I do."

"I see. I should have known. Use a typewriter?"

"I will learn, if you wish it," Dawn answered.

"Consider yourself hired—until there's a vacancy for a high priestess somewhere. Jill, have we forgotten anybody?"

"No, Boss. Except that all those who have left feel free to camp on you anytime, too. And they will."

"I assumed that. Nest number two, when and as needed." He went over to the range and joined Duke, glanced into the pan he was stirring. It held a small amount of broth. "Hmm . . . Mike?"

"Yup." Duke dipped out a little in the spoon, tasted it. "Needs a little salt."

"Yes, Mike always did need a little seasoning." Jubal took the spoon and tasted the broth. Duke was correct; the flavor was sweet and could have used salt. "But let's grok him as he is. Who's left to share?"

"Just you. Tony left me here with strict instructions to stir by hand, add water as needed, and wait for you. Not to let it scorch."

"Then grab a couple of cups. We'll share it and grok together."

"Right, Boss." Two cups came sailing down and rested by the sauce pan. "This is a joke on Mike—he always swore that he would outlive me and serve me up for Thanksgiving. Or maybe the joke's on me—because we had a bet on it and now I can't collect."

"You won only by default. Split it evenly."

Duke did so. Jubal raised his cup. "Share!"

"Grow ever closer."

Slowly they drank the broth, stretching it out, savoring it, praising and cherishing and grokking their donor. Jubal found, to his surprise, that although he was overflowing with emotion, it was a calm happiness that did not bring tears. What a quaint and gawky puppy his son had been when first he saw him . . . so eager to please, so naive in his little mistakes—and what a proud power he had become without ever losing his angelic innocence. I grok you at last, son—and would not change a line!

Patty had his lunch waiting for him; he sat down and dug in, hungry and feeling that it had been days since breakfast. Sam was saying, "I was telling Saul that I grok no need to make any change in plans. We go on as before. If you've got the right merchandise, the business grows, even though the founder has passed on."

"I wasn't disagreeing," Saul objected. "You and Ruth will found another temple—and we'll found others. But we'll have to take time now to accumulate capital. This isn't a street corner revival, nor yet something to set up in a vacant shop; it requires staging and equipment. That means money—not to mention such things as paying for a year or two on Mars for Stinky and Maryam . . . and that's just as essential."

"All *right* already! Who's arguing? We wait for fullness . . . and go ahead."

Jubal said suddenly, "Money's no problem."

"How's that, Jubal?"

"As a lawyer I shouldn't tell this . . . but as a water brother I do what I grok. Just a moment—Anne."

"Yes, Boss."

"Buy that spot. The one where they stoned Mike. Better get about a hundred-foot radius around it."

"Boss, the spot itself is public parkway. A hundred-foot radius will cut off some public road and a piece of the hotel grounds."

"Don't argue."

"I wasn't arguing, I was giving you facts."

"Sorry. They'll sell. They'll reroute that road. Hell, if their arms are twisted properly, they'll donate the land—twisting done through Joe Douglas, I think. And have Joe Douglas claim from the morgue whatever was left when those ghouls got through with him and we'll bury him right on that spot—say a year from now . . . with the whole city mourning and the cops that didn't protect him today standing at attention." What to put over him? The Fallen Caryatid? No, Mike had been strong enough for his stone. The Little Mermaid would be better—but it wouldn't be understood. Maybe one of Mike himself, just as he was when he had said, "Look at me. I am a Son of Man." If Duke didn't catch a shot of it, New World did—and maybe there was a brother, or would be a brother, with the spark of Rodin in him to do it right and not fancy it up.

"We'll bury him there," Jubal went on, "unprotected, and let the worms and the gentle rain grok him. I grok Mike will like that. Anne, I want to talk to Joe Douglas as soon as we get home."

"Yes, Boss. We grok with you."

"Now about that other." He told them about Mike's will. "So you see, each one of you is at least a millionaire—just how much more than that I haven't estimated lately . . . but much more, even after taxes. No strings on it at all . . . but I grok that you will spend as needed for temples and similar stuff. But there's nothing to stop you from buying yachts if you wish. Oh, yes! Joe Douglas stays on as manager for any who care to let the capital ride, same pay as before . . . but I grok Joe won't last long, whereupon management devolves on Ben Caxton. Ben?"

Caxton shrugged. "It can be in my name. I grok I'll hire me a real business man, name of Saul."

"That wraps it then. Some waiting time but nobody will dare really fight this will; Mike rigged it. You'll see. How soon can we get out of here? Is the tab settled?"

"Jubal," Ben said gently, "we *own* this hotel."

Not long thereafter they were in the air, with no trouble from police —the town had quieted down as fast as it had flared up. Jubal sat forward with Stinky Mahmoud and relaxed—discovered that he was not tired, not unhappy, not even fretting to get back to his sanctuary. He discussed with Mahmoud his plans to go to Mars to learn the language more deeply . . . after, Jubal was pleased to learn, completing the work on the dictionary, which Mahmoud estimated at about a year more for his own part in checking the phonetic spellings.

Jubal said grumpily, "I suppose I shall be forced to learn the pesky stuff myself, just to understand the chatter going on around me."

"As you grok, brother."

"Well, damn it, I won't put up with assigned lessons and regular school hours! I'll work as suits me, just as I always have."

Mahmoud was silent a few moments. "Jubal, we used classes and schedules at the Temple because we were handling groups. But some got special attention."

"That's what I'm going to need."

"Anne, for example, is much, much farther along than she ever let you know. With her total-recall memory, she learned Martian in nothing flat, hooked in rapport with Mike."

"Well, I don't have that sort of memory—and Mike's not available."

"No, but Anne is. And, stubborn as you are, nevertheless Dawn can place you in rapport with Anne—if you'll let her. And you won't need Dawn for the second lesson; Anne will then be able to handle it all. You'll be thinking in Martian inside of days, by the calendar—much longer by subjective time, but who cares?" Mahmoud leered at him. "You'll enjoy the warming-up exercises."

Jubal bristled. "You're a low, evil, lecherous Arab—and besides that you stole one of my best secretaries."

"For which I am forever in your debt. But you haven't lost her entirely; she'll give you lessons, too. She'll insist on it."

"Now go 'way and find another seat. I want to think."

Somewhat later he shouted, *"Front!"*

Dorcas came forward and sat down beside him, steno gear ready.

He glanced at her before he started to work. "Child, you look even happier than usual. Glowing."

Dorcas said dreamily, "I've decided to name him 'Dennis.' "

Jubal nodded. "Appropriate. Very appropriate." Appropriate meaning even if she were mixed up about the paternity, he thought to himself. "Do you feel like working?"

"Oh, yes! I feel grand."

"Begin. Stereoplay. Rough draft. Working title: 'A Martian Named Smith.' Opener: zoom in on Mars, using stock or bonestelled shots, unbroken sequence, then dissolving to miniature matched set of actual landing place of *Envoy*. Space ship in middle distance. Animated Martians, typical, with stock as available or rephotographed. Cut to close: Interior space ship. Female patient stretched on—"

xxxix

THE VERDICT TO BE PASSED on the third planet around Sol was never in doubt. The Old Ones of the fourth planet were not omniscient and in their way were as provincial as humans. Grokking by their own local values, even with the aid of vastly superior logic, they were certain in time to perceive an incurable "wrongness" in the busy, restless, quarrelsome beings of the third planet, a wrongness which would require weeding, once it had been grokked and cherished and hated.

But, by the time that they would slowly get around to it, it would be highly improbable approaching impossible that the Old Ones would be able to destroy this weirdly complex race. The hazard was slight that those concerned with the third planet did not waste a split eon on it.

Certainly Foster did not. "Digby!"

His assistant looked up. "Yes, Foster?"

"I'll be gone a few eons on a special assignment. Want you to meet your new supervisor." Foster turned and said, "Mike, this is Archangel Digby, your assistant. He knows where everything is around the studio and you'll find him a very steady straw boss for anything you conceive."

"Oh, we'll get along," Archangel Michael assured him, and said to Digby, "Haven't we met before?"

Digby answered, "Not that I remember. Of course, out of so many when-wheres—" He shrugged.

"No matter. Thou art God."

"Thou art God," Digby responded.

Foster said, "Skip the formalities, please. I've left you a load of work and you don't have all eternity to fiddle with it. Certainly 'Thou art God' —but who isn't?"

He left, and Mike pushed back his halo and got to work. He could see a lot of changes he wanted to make—

The End